NIGHT WITHOUT STARS

Peter F. Hamilton

NIGHT WITHOUT STARS

CHRONICLE OF THE FALLERS

MACMILLAN

First published 2016 by Macmillan
an imprint of Pan Macmillan
20 New Wharf Road, London N1 9RR
Associated companies throughout the world
www.panmacmillan.com

ISBN 978–0–230–76949–6

Typeset by Palimpsest Book Production Limited, Falkirk, Stirlingshire
Printed and bound by CPI Group (UK) Ltd, Croydon, CR0 4YY

Visit www.panmacmillan.com to read more about all our books
and to buy them. You will also find features, author interviews and
news of any author events, and you can sign up for e-newsletters
so that you're always first to hear about our new releases.

To Marcus and Rebecca Lewis

For all their friendship and laughter
during an amazingly long summer

Music as background for reading *Night Without Stars* has been created by film and TV composer Steve Buick. His long, evocative soundscapes work as the perfect atmospheric accompaniment to any part of the book. Search 'Peter F. Hamilton's Night Without Stars: Atmospheres and Soundscapes' on Amazon, iTunes or any digital music store worldwide. You can find out more at www.evokescape.com.

Commonwealth Timeline

1,000,000 BC (approx.)

    Raiel armada invades the Void. Never returns.

AD

1200   Prime species' home star system and renegade Prime colony star (Dyson pair) quarantined behind force fields by the Anomine.

1900   Starflyer crash-lands on Far Away, 400 light years from Earth.

2037   First attempted human rejuvenation, Jeff Baker.

2050   Nigel Sheldon and Ozzie Isaacs open a wormhole to surface of Mars.

2057   Wormhole opened to Proxima Centuri. Start of interstellar colonization.

2100   Eight new worlds settled. Official formation of Intersolar Commonwealth Council, the 'Parliament of Worlds'.

2100 onward   Massive expansion of human settlements across H-congruous planets. Rise of the Big15 industrial worlds.

2102   Huxley's Haven founded, genetic conformist constitution.

2150   Prime star disappears from Earth's sky – unnoticed.

2163   *High Angel* discovered orbiting Icalanise.

2222   Paula Myo born on Huxley's Haven.

2270   Prime star pair identified as Dyson Emission Spectrum twins.

2380   Dudley Bose observes Dyson Alpha vanish.

2381   Starship *Second Chance* flies to Dyson Alpha.

2381–2383 Starflyer War.

2384   First colony fleet (Brandt Dynasty) leaves to found human colony outside Commonwealth.

2545 onward   Use of large starships to establish Commonwealth 'External' worlds.

2550   Commonwealth Navy Exploration fleet founded to explore the galaxy beyond the External worlds.

2560   Commonwealth Navy ship *Endeavour* circumnavigates galaxy, captained by Wilson Kime; discovery of the Void.

2603   Navy discovers seventh *High Angel*-type ship.

2620   Raiel confirm their status as ancient galactic race who lost a war against the Void.

2833   Completion of ANA (Advanced Neural Activity) first stage on Earth. Grand Family members begin memory download into ANA.

2867   Sheldon Dynasty gigalife project partially successful, first human body biononic supplements for regeneration and general iatrics.

2872   Start of Higher human culture, biononic enrichment allowing a society of slow-paced long life, rejection of commercial economics and old political ideologies.

2913   Earth begins absorption of 'mature' humans into ANA; the inward migration begins.

2984   Formation of radical Highers who wish to convert the human race to Higher culture.

3000   Sheldon Dynasty colony fleet (thirty starships) leaves

Commonwealth, believed to possess long-range trans-galactic flight capability.

3001   Ozzie produces uniform neural entanglement effect, known as the gaiafield.

3040   Commonwealth invited to join Centurion Station, the Void observation project supervised by Raiel, a joint enterprise between alien species.

3120   ANA officially becomes Earth's government; total planetary population fifty million (activated bodies) and falling.

3126   Brandt Dynasty trans-galactic colony fleet launched.

3150   External world Ellezelin settled.

3255   Kerry, a radical Higher Angel, arrives on Anagaska, Inigo's conception.

This Era (time uncertain)   Edeard born in the Void.

3320   Inigo begins duty tour at Centurion star system, his first dream.

3324   Inigo settles on Ellezelin, founds Living Dream movement, begins construction of Makkathran2.

3326   Nigel Sheldon's mission into the Void.

3328   The Void expels Bienvenido into intergalactic space.

3331   Sheldon Dynasty leaves the Commonwealth.

3336   Laura Brandt opens exploratory wormhole to Ursell.

3407   Ozzie departs Commonwealth for the Spike to build a 'galactic dream'.

3589   Ethan elected as Cleric Conservator of Living Dream; announces Pilgrimage into the Void.

3590   The Void transcends.

3593   Ry Evine's Liberty mission.

List of Characters

Bienvenido

Laura Brandt *Molecular physicist*

Joey Stein *Hyperspace theorist*

Kysandra *The Warrior Angel*

Demitri *ANAdroid*

Marek *ANAdroid*

Valeri *ANAdroid*

Fergus *ANAdroid*

Florian *Forest warden*

Ry Evine *Pilot Major, People's Astronaut Regiment*

Anala Em Yulei *Pilot Major Astronaut Regiment*

Chaing *Captain, People's Security Regiment*

Jenifa *Corporal, People's Security Regiment*

Lurvri *Lieutenant, People's Security Regiment*

Corilla *Student, Chaing's informant*

Stonal *Director, Section Seven*

Yaki *Director, PSR Opole office*

Ashya Kukaida *Colonel, PSR Opole office, records division*

Castillito *Florian's mother, civil rights lawyer*

Terannia *Florian's aunt, music club manager*

Matthieu *Terannia's partner, musician*

Joffler *Drug dealer*

Rohanna *Joffler's girlfriend*

Hokianga *Colonel, Opole Regiment*

Lukan *Underworld driver*

Roxwolf *Opole's top underworld boss*

Billop *Opole underworld boss*

Faustina *Chief Scientist, Section Seven*

Adolphus *Prime Minister*

Terese *Deputy Prime Minister*

Commonwealth

Paula Myo *Senior Investigator, Serious Crimes Bureau*

Andromeda Galaxy Settlement

Nigel Sheldon *Inventor of Wormhole Technology*

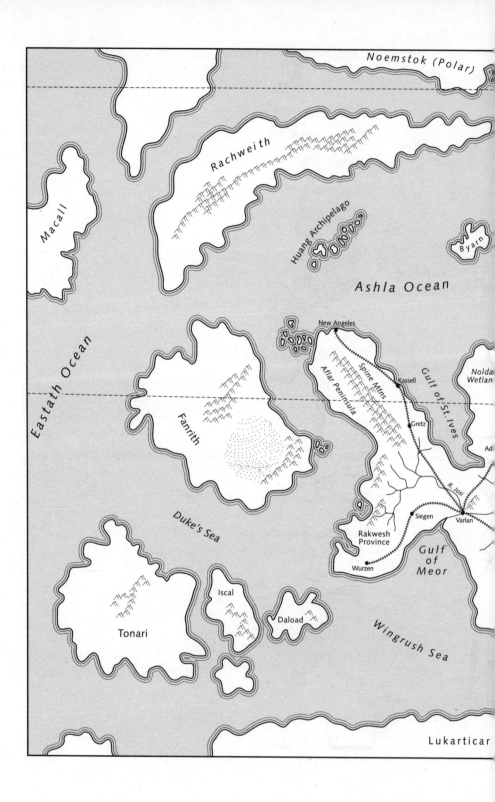

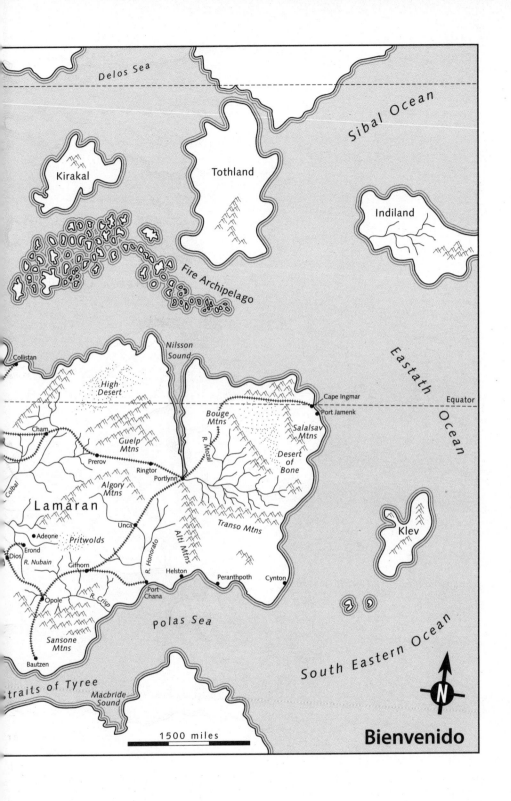

Delos Sea

Sibal Ocean

Kirakal

Tothland

Indiland

Fire Archipelago

Nilsson Sound

Collistan

High Desert

Bouge Mtns

Cape Ingmar

Eastath Ocean

Equator

Port Jamenk

Cham

Guelp Mtns

R. Mozal

Salalsav Mtns

Desert of Bone

Prerov

Ringtor

Portlynn

Colbal

Algory Mtns

Lamaran

Unca

Transo Mtns

Klev

Adeone

Pritwolds

Dios
Erond
R. Nubain

Gifhorn

R. Honorato

Alti Mtns

Helston

Peranthpoth

Cynton

Opole

R. Crisp

Port Chana

Polas Sea

South Eastern Ocean

Sansone Mtns

Bautzen

Straits of Tyree

Macbride Sound

N

1500 miles

Bienvenido

Prologue

The star was classified as an A7 on the Morgan–Keenan system, hotter and brighter than the G2-class star which humans had evolved under. At two and a half AUs out, where Zoreia orbited, Nigel Sheldon had to wear sunglasses; not even his modified green eyes could cope with the sharper light of his new world's sun.

He reached the top of a gentle rise, where he could see the lush green of terrestrial grass sweeping out across the landscape in all directions. Grass was always the easy part of terraforming a new world. After Zoreia's land had been seed-bombed, the colonists had waited thirty years for the roots and microbes and insects and worms and dead leaves to generate a deep enough layer of soil before starting on larger plants. Nigel stared at the forests that had spread out across the rumpled ground. Birds flocked among the higher branches, their nests safe from the predatory animals that stalked between the trunks. Now that the biosphere was complete, they were slowly introducing more sophisticated animals.

Zoreia was a modest triumph, given that only two hundred and fifty years ago, when the fleet of colony starships had come thundering into the star system, it had been an airless, barren rock. They had achieved so much, and not just on the planet. Oran and Bourke, two of the huge city habitats, were visible in the clear topaz sky, orbiting a hundred and fifty thousand kilometres out, far above the two small moons they'd manoeuvred into orbit to create some spectacular tides. And beyond that . . . Nigel smiled as his retinal filters activated. The surface of the blue-white star had three even brighter blemishes along the equator, like intense flowers of energy. The petals were vast streamers of plasma, pouring up into space at near-relativistic velocity, then twisting away into the J-nodes. Somewhere on the other side of the sun, the matter was streaming out of corresponding J-nodes, but changed, modified into the grid of their first Dyson shell, which would be over a million and a half kilometres across when it was finished in a couple of years.

An awareness seeped into the lowest level of his consciousness – knowledge coming from Central. There was a disturbance in hyperspace outside the star system, but approaching fast. The knowledge expanded up to full awareness, and he witnessed a line being drawn through the quantum fields that underpinned reality, driving straight for Zoreia. Its signature was familiar enough: a Commonwealth ultradrive. But this was a small ship, nothing like the behemoths of the colony fleet that had brought the Sheldon Dynasty to this place. Nigel sighed wryly as he drew up a list of who it might be carrying. It was a short list: just two names.

The ultradrive ship flashed through the star system and dropped out of hyperspace beside Oran.

'You have a visit request,' Central informed him.

'So I sense,' he replied drily. 'Well, it looks like my diary is clear for today. Let her in.' His biononic field function detected the planetary T-sphere engage and enact.

Paula Myo was teleported onto the ground barely four metres away.

Nigel almost laughed. It took just over five years for an ultradrive ship to fly from the Commonwealth to Zoreia. You had to *really* want to get here to attempt such a flight. And Paula had done it alone, in suspension. Yet here she stood wearing a grey business suit, her jet-black hair neatly styled. The amazing thing was, he knew that she'd consider this to be just another working day.

'Paula!' He gave her a hug and a platonic kiss on the cheek. 'Welcome to the Andromeda galaxy.'

'Stars are still stars. Only the distance is greater.'

'Oh, very profound.' He waited until she'd turned full circle to take in the vista. Then she tipped her head back and squinted at the dazzling sun.

'Coronal matter transference, now that is impressive,' she admitted.

'Why thank you.'

'You built yourself an ANA?'

'Central. It has the same technology base, yes, but we don't just download ourselves into it when we become jaded with life. The point of life is to avoid becoming jaded.'

'Profound,' she shot back.

Nigel chuckled. 'It's good to see you.'

'And you. This seems to be an interesting civilization you're building here. What would you call it?'

'I dunno. High-end pastoral?'

'Hmm. Slifen-lite, then?'

'Ouch.'

'Sorry.' She glanced about the wide empty landscape again. 'Do you have homes?'

'Those that want them have them.'

'Do you want one, Nigel?'

'Right now I'm happy just travelling around by myself. You realize no one has ever set foot on this ground before? I like that.'

'Doesn't sound like you. You were always so busy.'

'I help out with Central and our major projects. I don't have to be in the office. Not that we have one.'

'And what about people? Do you need to be with them?'

'You travelled between galaxies to ask me that?'

'No. The Void has gone.'

'*What?*' He'd thought he was of an age when nothing could surprise him, but that news was extraordinary. 'What do you mean, gone?'

'It transcended.'

'How the fuck did that happen?'

Paula's lips twitched. 'There was a small conflict.'

'Oh for—' He threw his hands up in dismay. 'The Living Dream morons, they finally went on their pilgrimage.'

'Yes. But they were being manipulated by the Advancers—'

'Son of a bitch. Ilanthe! I knew the Advancers were trouble. I told you all before I left.'

'Very prescient of you. Oh, and Gore played a big part, too. I have a summary of critical events on file if you'd like to access. It's quite large.'

'Of course it is. You were always thorough, Paula.'

'Thank you.' She turned and stared out across the sweeping grasslands. 'Our galaxy is safe now. The Raiel are considering what to do now their great vigil is over. The Commonwealth is changing, slowly as always. It's a new age of exploration and contact.'

'And yet here you are,' Nigel said wearily. 'Why is that, Paula? What could possibly be so important that you'd spend five years flying here – and five flying back.'

'You know why,' she said softly. 'My file isn't complete.'

'Our secret mission.'

'*Your* mission. You went into the Void, Nigel. Over two hundred and fifty years ago, you actually got inside. You're unique.'

'My clone went in.'

'And you dreamed his life.'

Nigel closed his eyes. Today was truly a day of emotional surprises. After so long, the pain of her loss was still as strong as it had been the day his clone had detonated the modified quantumbuster. 'Paula, it was a long time ago. Let it rest. She's gone now.'

'She?'

'It's personal.'

'You left us, Nigel. When the Raiel brought you home, you flew to another bloody galaxy to escape whatever happened to you in the Void. You didn't tell me what it was. The Raiel won't tell me either. I have stood in the real Makkathran, and confronted Torux, who was with you while you dreamed your clone's life – and he Would Not tell me.' Her voice rose. 'Torux said they were honouring your wishes.'

'Yes,' he said meekly. 'They are.'

'You owe me, Nigel. I helped you put that mission together. And more than that. It's personal for me, too; I have an investment in this. I don't just want to know about your mission. I want to know about the fallback. I have a right to know if you ever activated it. So now you tell me: what happened, Nigel? What happened to your clone in the Void?'

'I became a monster,' he said as tears began to leak down his cheeks.

'How?'

'I didn't land on Querencia.'

'But . . . then where?'

'There used to be another human world in the Void. It was called Bienvenido.'

'Oh crap. Used to be?'

'We never knew it existed. How could we? But it was where the rest of the lost Brandt colony fleet wound up. And me.'

'So you never made contact with Makkathran?'

'No. Once I landed on Bienvenido I had to stay; they were under attack from another alien species. The Fallers. Psychotic expansionists who would even frighten the Prime. I couldn't abandon Bienvenido – those people needed help. I thought I'd found a way. I was so fucking arrogant I just went right ahead. One of the Brandt colony ships survived – or rather, its armoury did.'

'Armoury?' Paula asked cautiously.

'Yes. I rebuilt a quantumbuster.'

'Oh no.'

'Oh yeah. Because I was right. I was always right. I thought I'd found a weakness in the Void's quantum structure. I believed, I really believed, I could blow it apart from the inside. I promised her I'd save them all. And she put all her trust in me.'

'Nigel.' Paula put her hand on his arm.

'So I detonated it. My clone was actually sitting next to it when it went off – how's that for a noble sacrifice? Only it didn't work. I should have known. The Raiel sent in a fucking armada of warships, with a technology orders of magnitude above Commonwealth weapons, and they couldn't defeat the Void – it destroyed them. You'd think I'd pause to take that into account – but oh no, I was so far up my own ass I never considered failure.'

'You thought you had an opportunity to terminate the Void. You wouldn't be human if you hadn't taken it.'

'Ha! We didn't know Bienvenido existed. Guess what else we didn't know? The Void has a defence mechanism, it's called Honious or Uracus – depending on which planet you're unlucky enough to be on. After my clone died in the blast, I was still dreaming my ANAdroids' life. I watched through their eyes as Uracus opened up and devoured the whole crudding world. They were standing beside her as it happened. I heard her screams.' He shook his head in angry frustration. 'I still hear them. The whole fucking planet, Paula – obliterated. It's been two and a half centuries now, and I still hear her. I deserve to hear her. There is no punishment – no suffering – great enough to fit my crime.'

'I'm sorry.'

'Don't be. Not for me.'

She studied him intently for a moment. 'Who was she?'

'Doesn't matter. She's dead.'

'A girl.' Paula gave him a forlorn smile. 'It's always a girl. Even you, in the end.'

'Even me. Who knew? I guess I'm human after all.'

BOOK ONE

Another Death For Laura Brandt

When it hit the planet's upper atmosphere, the starship *Vermillion* was still travelling at an appreciative fraction of orbital velocity. As with the majority of its onboard systems, the colony vessel's ingrav and regrav drives were glitching badly in the Void, leaving them unable to suspend the titanic bulk against gravity and lower it to a gentle landing as they were designed to. But they could still exert some resistance against the planet's hungry gravity, so they strained to slow the starship's otherwise-catastrophic speed. On the bridge, Captain Cornelius and the ten remaining volunteers from the crew did what they could to mitigate the impending disaster. Force fields, normally tough enough to deflect nuclear blasts with ease, headed towards breakdown as they expanded out from the hull. Redline instability warnings bloomed in Cornelius's exovision as they held *Vermillion* secure at the centre of a bubble of incandescent plasma five kilometres in diameter.

Vermillion curved around the planet, tearing a screaming hole through the atmosphere as it aerobraked to a manageable speed, its fiery hypersonic wake scoring a terrible furrow of destruction across every landmass it zoomed over. After seventy-two minutes of this torment it finally dropped to subsonic. They were still travelling at eighty kilometres an hour when their altitude reached zero. A last desperate burst of power was pumped into the fading drive units to brake their speed further. The force fields collapsed on impact, and *Vermillion*'s unprotected hull struck the ground.

Their wild flight had brought them to a rumpled stretch of land just beyond a massive river where the humidity was a constant mist twisting among the verdant trees. This was jungle territory, with a soft loamy ground. But soft was a relative term for a trans-galactic colony ship over a kilometre and a half long and massing hundreds of thousands of tonnes.

It hit at the foot of a small incline, pulverising vegetation and ripping out a deep gorge. Modules and compartments never designed to withstand such forces broke off, tumbling away to their ruin through the trees. But the main section kept surging onwards and upwards until it too came to rest.

Seventy-five per cent of *Vermillion* remained intact through a miraculous combination of good luck and steely nerves. Captain Cornelius was justifiably lauded by the passengers who'd flown down to the planet earlier in much safer shuttles with good old-fashioned solid wings. That hero-worship enabled him to retain his authority as the lost survivors slowly built their civilization in the strange environment of the Void. The threat of the Fallers who began to invade their world from space justified the formation of defensive regiments, of which Cornelius became commander-in-chief. The machines *Vermillion* had brought from the Commonwealth were largely useless in the Void, where electrical current was inhibited, and anything more complex than a steam engine was subject to constant glitches. Those resources which did work, especially the precious medical capsules, were guarded and restricted to the captain and his immediate family, enhancing his power and authority.

Vermillion's remains became the seat of power on the new, and somewhat ironically named, world of Bienvenido. To protect their declining technological advantage, the captain's family incorporated the starship's original sections into a working residence, then extended that out to embrace an executive complex and military headquarters as well as their private clinic. As the palace grew in size and splendour, so more and more of the ship was built around – but mainly on top of.

After three thousand years, nothing of the *Vermillion* was visible from outside. But by then it was no longer relevant; the nature of the Void had incapacitated even the simplest artefact of Commonwealth technology. The rule of the Captain's family had become established by law, political power, and a brutally effective secret police force.

Then – somehow – Nigel Sheldon arrived on Bienvenido. A quantumbuster was detonated, and the Void responded with the Great Transition, flinging Bienvenido out into the deepest gulf of intergalactic space. Technology worked again.

The great, gloomy warren of vaults underneath the ancient palace, built by the flickering light of yalseed oil lamps, were now illuminated by new electric bulbs. It was just as well, Laura Brandt thought as she hurried towards the crypt which housed the wormhole gateway she'd managed to renovate, as so many people were rushing round down here, all of them wearing a look of suppressed fear. Above ground, Fall alert sirens were shrieking a warning across the city of Varlan. That wasn't strictly accurate – those new lights in the sky above Bienvenido weren't a Fall, at least not in the usual sense. But it would do, warning people of an impending threat from space.

Marine guards in their smart black uniforms stood outside the big wooden doors that led into the wormhole crypt. For once the doors were wide open, allowing dozens of freshly laid telephone cables to snake inside. It also enabled technicians from the Manhattan Project to wheel in large metal trolleys. *Why ever did I call it that?* Laura wondered. *Probably the mental equivalent of comfort food.*

She stopped to let the trolleys clank past, staring at the black iron casing of the big cylinders they carried. The atom bombs weren't streamlined, but then she'd never intended for them to be dropped in the planet's atmosphere.

Inside the crypt, the sound of frantic voices dipped as technicians and officers from the People's Air Defence Force gave the weapons fearful glances. Their arrival was the final confirmation that the threat was terrifyingly real.

The Marine guards suddenly snapped off salutes. Laura turned to see Prime Minister Slvasta arriving behind her. He was wearing some kind of yellow and blue regimental dress tunic; she never could be bothered to remember which regiment had which colours. As always, Slvasta's empty sleeve was pinned prominently across his chest, the result of an encounter with a Faller. Of all Bienvenido's anachronisms, that was the oddest to Laura. Having spent the first three hundred years of her life in the Commonwealth, the concept of people walking round with missing limbs was unheard of. Even if some gross fluke accident did somehow maim a citizen, a replacement clone limb would be grown and attached within weeks. But not here. Here Slvasta was a physical reminder of how vigilance should never be allowed to falter.

She detested him, but needed his authority to instigate her desperate rescue plan for this benighted world. So the oppressive downside of his dictatorial rule had to be quietly overlooked. And her biononics (including full-body force field function) meant that he couldn't eliminate her. They were stuck with each other.

Slvasta's usual entourage of cronies formed a phalanx around him. Javier, a fellow leader of the revolution who'd slid smoothly into his role of Slvasta's political adviser, was a huge man who looked as sullen and angry as always; not even the emergency had broken his constant suspicion of Laura. Yannrith stood beside him – Slvasta's bodyguard during the revolution, and now the head of the People's Security Regiment. His appearance matched his job – stiff and forbidding, with a vivid scar on his throat giving his voice a sharp rasping quality. He remained ever alert for Faller nests and even more alert to counter-revolutionary forces – of which there were, apparently, a never-ending procession. Andricea completed the trio: a tall lean woman with a face Laura judged to be too cruel to be genuinely pretty. She was officially Slvasta's chief bodyguard, though rumour around the People's Congress said that she also shared his bed now that his wife had been sentenced to twenty years in the Pidrui mines.

'Laura, is everything working?' Slvasta asked.

'Seems to be,' she said grumpily. Fatigue was starting to take its toll, even on her biononics-enriched body.

'The floaters,' he said urgently. 'Did you repair the floaters?'

'Yes. They're working.' She closed her eyes, allowing the last five crazy days to flash past like a dream. Biononics had allowed her to keep going without sleep, but she could feel that body-debt lying in wait now. Nonetheless, she and her exhausted team of assistants had managed to refurbish two of the floaters, cannibalizing the others for spare parts. Her earlier experience rebuilding the gateway had provided plenty of insight into the procedure.

'If there's anything else you need, anything at all, just tell me,' he said sincerely. 'I'll make sure you get it.'

Democracy. Civil rights. Trial by jury. 'Sure.'

They walked into the crypt together. It was one of the largest chambers beneath the palace, with dusty brick walls curving up to an arched roof, supported by metal ribs that had come from *Vermillion*. Looking round it, Laura was always struck by the resemblance to a European-style church, albeit with a dark gothic quality. It had been abandoned for centuries before she found the ancient machines it housed.

Standing at the far end, instead of an altar, the circular gateway shimmered with the purple ghostlight of Cherenkov radiation. It was a CST BC5800d2 model, intended to create small-scale planetary and interplanetary wormhole connections that would transport bulk material about while a new settlement established its manufacturing base. *Vermillion* had carried five of them, all of which were still sealed in their transit shells when Laura had landed on Bienvenido eight years earlier. As the last survivor of the *Vermillion,* she was the only one who understood Commonwealth technology. Even so, getting the wormhole gateway to work had been a devilishly tricky job, especially given everything else she had to do.

Every day since she'd landed, Laura mused that she'd committed some terrible crime back in the Commonwealth and this was her punishment: first trapped in a weird temporal loop in the Void, then liberated by Nigel Sheldon only to fall into this hell populated by people she regarded as psychotic half-savages. She'd spent those last eight years trying to educate the mistrustful citizens of

Bienvenido, whose society had levelled out to something equivalent to Earth, circa 1850. That education had focused on raising their technology and engineering base by almost a century to combat the Fallers – a mission which had to be done carefully. Bienvenido was fighting for its life against the alien invaders, and the machines she showed them how to build needed to be reliable, something their very basic factories could produce dependably. So far they had aircraft powered by simple V12 engines, better guns, electricity, and radio. The planes of the new People's Air Force had proved sufficient to hold the Fallers at bay while she got to work renovating the wormholes stored below the palace. The idea behind that was to reach out to the ring of Trees orbiting high above Bienvenido – crystalline alien biotechnology hive spaceships (as near as she could determine) which produced the lethal eggs that Fell as a plague across the planet. Her plan was that once she could open a wormhole amid the Trees, she could nuke them with the primitive fission bombs which the Manhattan Project was painstakingly assembling under her direction. Once the Fallers were eliminated, Bienvenido could finally start to progress along standard socioeconomic lines, and hopefully one day re-establish contact with the Commonwealth. It was always a desperate notion, but it was all she had.

Now even that fantastical daydream was dying around her. The threat she'd uncovered on Ursell was closing fast on Bienvenido, and it was potent enough to obliterate humans and Fallers alike. A row of trestle tables had been set up along one side of the crypt. Senior officers from various regiments sat there, talking into the black Bakelite telephone handsets linking them to their various headquarters, their babbling voices rich with suppressed panic.

'Ma'am,' one of the officers called. 'The Space Vigilance Office has confirmed approach tracking. The first invasion fleet is going to reach the atmosphere above Fanrith in seven minutes.'

'Thank you,' Laura said as calmly as she could manage. She knew if she showed any weakness in front of these people, everything would be lost. They were all depending on her to save them. 'Can someone get me confirmation on the second fleet?'

'Estimated atmosphere entry over Tothland in twenty-eight minutes,' another of the officers announced.

'Okay. Chief air marshal, are you ready?'

'Our squadrons are over Fanrith, ma'am,' the marshal said, her face grim. 'We won't let you down.'

Laura gave her a quick nod, fighting to prevent tears from forming. They'd deployed just over four hundred IA-505 air-interceptor planes to the uninhabited Fanrith continent – two thirds of the planet's entire air force. The IA-505s were her own design, cobbled together out of her storage lacuna's basic encyclopaedia files of the Second World War: terribly flimsy things made from an alloy monocoque structure, with the skin riveted on. The V12 engines powering the props were just supercharged pistons; she hadn't got round to introducing turbines yet. Control surfaces moved when the pilot pulled on a joystick, which tugged wires connected to hydraulics. The planes were armed with four powerful pneumatic Gatling guns in the fore and aft turrets. And the crews, seven to a plane, were all proud and eager kids, fiercely loyal to their world, and determined to protect it no matter what. They were delighted with their radical flying war machines, smiling gamely when she went to meet squadrons at their aerodromes, promising her they'd do her proud when they took to the air to blast the Faller eggs apart with their guns.

And now she'd sent them into battle against interplanetary spaceships, crewed by the vilest aliens humans had ever encountered. She'd told Slvasta and the Air Force Regiment marshals it was almost certain suicide, but they ordered the squadrons into the air anyway. If they didn't, all Bienvenido would be lost.

Laura blamed herself for that.

It was a mere six months ago when she'd got the wormhole functioning again. After the utterly hellish time she'd endured since arriving on Bienvenido, desperately upgrading its primitive military technology to cope with the Fallers – struggling against a paranoid Slvasta's authoritarian regime – she had finally found the time to repair it. Her hope was that by exploring the other planets that shared this terrible exile with them she might find an ally against the Fallers. And for those brief months it looked as if the dream had come true.

She'd opened the wormhole five hundred kilometres above Aqueous – the most promising-looking of the nine other planets in orbit around this lonely sun. It was a beautiful oceanic world of deep turquoise scuffed by long white clouds, and possessing a standard oxygen–nitrogen atmosphere. If it wasn't for the complete absence of any landmass, it could have been another Earth. It was only when the wormhole opened just above the atmosphere that they saw the green and pink dots of tiny coral islands, not one of which was more than a hundred metres in diameter.

They'd made contact with the Vatni, who lived on and around the islands – a semi-aquatic species who, for all their willingness to be allies, didn't have any technological ability. However, thanks to the finite number of islands they did have a considerable population pressure problem, which gave Slvasta's diplomatic team an easy time during negotiations. It was agreed that Vatni families could come and live on Lamaran's coastline, in exchange for dealing with any Marine threat posed by the Fallers in a way humans never could.

After a month, during which thousands of eager Vatni came across to Bienvenido, Laura had switched the wormhole terminus to the second most viable planet: Ursell. The Vatni had told her that a thousand years earlier they'd seen spaceships flying from Ursell to explore every planet. After that, Ursell had undergone some kind of war, which had lasted for years. The flashes of explosions on the surface had been visible across interplanetary space.

Standing in this very crypt she and the observation team looked down on a planet swathed in a thick layer of dingy grey clouds. It wasn't really H-congruent any more, though it must have been centuries ago. Through the occasional gaps in the swaddling vapour they'd glimpsed a desolate landscape of brown semi-desert littered with wrecked towns. Background radiation was high – the inevitable result of nuclear weapons being detonated all over the planet – and the radio picked up a constant high-frequency *click click click* signal amid the heavy static. Something was still alive down there. They'd transmitted a message towards the source – a standard welcome sequence, devised by ancient Commonwealth alien contact specialists, and stored deep in her lacuna. And they got an answer back – a linguistic code also stored in her lacuna. A lot of red symbols had erupted across her exovision that day, for it was a species the Commonwealth knew well.

The Prime: the living embodiment of ruthless, with a single evolutionary imperative – to constantly expand. To the Prime, all other lifeforms were a threat to be exterminated.

Just as they were about to be exterminated now, if Laura's desperate plan failed.

'Ah bollocks,' Laura muttered under her breath. 'Here we go.' She went to stand alone in front of the wormhole. Her u-shadow sent a code to the ancient machine's smartcore. Schematics opened across her exovision, giving her a status review of the wormhole's systems. It was entirely self-contained, powered by a direct mass-to-energy converter. There had been plenty of component decay in the three thousand years it had lain here undisturbed, but by cannibalizing the other four BC5800d2s she'd got this one operational again – even if it was a bit quirky.

She ran through the exovision displays, checking there weren't too many amber warnings. Satisfied, she loaded in coordinates.

'Stand by,' she told everyone.

The four-metre circle of Cherenkov radiation was abruptly contaminated by serpent shadows. Then the haze cleared. The wormhole terminus was poised two thousand kilometres above the Fanrith continent, looking directly down. Laura's exovision displays showed her the terminus was juddering, which always happened to an open-ended wormhole; it needed to be anchored to be completely stable. But the movement was minimal, a few centimetres at worst. Looking through the opening she had an excellent view out over the landmass lying twelve hundred kilometres west of Lamaran, Bienvenido's major continent. Roughly oblong in shape, it straddled the equator, with a desert dominating a third of the interior. Dawn had reached its eastern coastline, shading the ground a pale ochre, fringed in the dark green of native vegetation. Thin clouds scudded slowly across it.

Laura was very aware of the awed silence behind her. 'Observers,' she called. 'Front and centre, please.'

Five young officers with perfect eyesight hurried forwards. The vista was slightly fuzzed by the wormhole's integral force field holding back the vacuum, but despite that, nine points of light were visible, descending slowly into the atmosphere. The exhaust was a high-temperature hydrocarbon that was extremely radio-active. Laura thought it might be some kind of nuclear gas-core rocket.

They'd tracked the Prime spaceships for six weeks, ever since they launched from Ursell. The ships massed about two thousand tonnes. Not huge then, but big enough to carry a significant threat. The Ursell Primes' technology certainly wasn't up to Common-wealth levels, and they didn't have force fields, which meant Bienvenido's more primitive forces stood a chance against them – a small one.

'They're well below orbital velocity now,' she said, checking the vector reading from the terminus. 'The descent trajectory is effect-ively vertical. Mark them.'

The observers started talking to the operators gathered round the big strategic map that took up two of the trestle tables. Wooden spaceships – simple cones – were pushed across the big map of Fanrith by long poles. The Air Force squadrons were already there, marked by model planes. She would have wept in frustration if it wasn't that she knew she'd end up laughing in hysterics at the monstrous futility of it.

Squadron communication officers talked urgently into their telephones. Poles began prodding the model planes as the IA-505s started to change course to intercept the descending spaceships.

'Let's hear it,' she said.

Tannoy speakers came alive, filling the crypt with distorted voices and a lot of static as the radio links played. Squadron leaders relayed instructions, receiving tight confirmations from the aircrews.

'I see them,' was repeated several times, jubilant cries riding the static. More voices crashed out of the tannoys – a confusing medley of navigation vectors and course-correction commands.

Laura turned back to the gateway. The spaceships were entering the atmosphere, their rocket plumes shrinking away. Even though they were travelling below orbital velocity, their size and blunt cone shape created a huge shockwave in the tenuous ionosphere, sending out annular waves of glowing atoms, as if phantom flowers were blooming high above Fanrith. The nine ships were holding a loose circular formation, no more than fifteen miles across.

Typically unimaginative, Laura thought. *No clever tactics. Just get down, establish a planetary beachhead and start attacking.*

The ships reached the chemosphere and the flares of superheated atmosphere began to elongate as they grew brighter. Chatter from the pilots grew louder and jumbled as they flew towards the invaders. Laura checked the tabletop map, seeing twelve squadrons clustering round the ships. They were coming down on the northern edge of Fanrith's central desert, just south of the equator.

'They need to get underneath,' Laura told the chief air marshal.

'Yes, ma'am.'

'Right underneath. That's their sensor blind spot.'

'They know that.' The chief air marshal's voice was level. 'Your briefings were very clear.'

Slvasta stepped up beside Laura. 'Let the aircrews do their job,' he said quietly.

Laura nodded, rubbing a hand across her forehead. She was worried now – worried for the planes and their crews, worried the invasion would succeed, worried she was making mistakes she was so tired.

'Something—' a tannoy spat out.

'Marco, Mar— Oh Uracus, they just disintegrated! There's nothing left!'

'Evelina. Evelina's gone!'

'Explosions, they're just exploding!'

'Three down.'

'Command, we're taking some kind of hit!'

'What are they using? Wha—'

'Nothing! There's nothing.'

Laura stared at the nine long glowing contrails that were streaking down through the stratosphere. 'Beam weapons,' she said. Then louder, trying to keep the anguish from her voice, 'They're hitting you with beam weapons. X-rays, or masers. Get underneath them!'

One of the officers at the end of the trestle tables was chalking numbers on a board. The tally of planes lost. When he put up twenty-seven, Laura looked away. The IA-505s weren't even in Gatling-gun range of the invaders yet.

'Portlynn and Siegen squadrons circling under intruder seven,' their liaison said.

The tannoys were broadcasting a barrage of screams. Orders were garbled shouts. Static grew louder.

On the table, the models of Gretz and Wurzen squadrons reached intruder three.

Laura's u-shadow ordered the wormhole terminus to descend. The panoramic view blurred as it lost altitude *fast*. Then the image steadied as it came to rest a hundred and ten kilometres above Fanrith, allowing them to look directly down on the fringe of the desert. There were no clouds. The only blemishes were the diminishing glimmers of distorted air ripped apart by the spaceships.

'Nineteen kilometres altitude,' Laura announced. 'Watch out for the rocket exhaust. It's as bad as any weapon.'

As she spoke, she saw the white spears of radioactive plasma emerging. More confusion and shouting erupted from the tannoys.

'Thirty-two confirmed lost,' a communications officer declared. No one in the crypt spoke.

'Stand by missiles,' Laura said, knowing it was all so wretchedly futile. They weren't guided missiles; she hadn't got Bienvenido's electronics up to that level yet. These were unguided, developed to be fired in clusters from pods under the wings at a Faller egg in mid-descent. Thirty IA-505s had been hurriedly modified to shoot them vertically. Laura didn't have any illusion that they'd hit the spaceships, but they would act as chaff, and hopefully divert some of the beam-weapon fire.

'Begin missile barrage,' the chief air marshal ordered.

The spaceship exhausts were now incandescent streaks, kilometres long. Coming down fast. Her u-shadow activated retinal filters, allowing her to see the tiny sparks of the cluster rockets swarming up at seven of the nine invaders. She wasn't sure, but she thought the cries of fury and pain surging out of the tannoys might have decreased slightly.

'Invaders two, three, and eight coming down to your altitude, and slowing,' Laura said. 'Four and six reaching attack altitude.'

'Converge,' the chief air marshal ordered.

'Giu bless you all,' Slvasta said in a strong clear voice. 'Go get them!'

'One and seven,' Laura said. Then: 'Five and nine. That's all of them.' There was nothing left now but to pray.

The tannoys were a continual blast of shouted warnings and curses mixed with the high-pitched whine of the pneumatically driven rotary barrels. She closed her eyes, seeing the flimsy propeller-driven planes banking, turning towards the monster invaders and diving in, their Gatling guns firing furiously. They were good, those Gatling guns she'd designed for them, slinging five and a half thousand rounds a minute – hundred-gram projectiles with a muzzle velocity close to nine hundred metres a second.

Individually, a strike by one round would be nothing to space-ships this size, but the IA-505s were slamming out a wall of metal, chewing up the hull and outer systems. There would be damage, and the invaders were still in the air with three kilometres to go. If anything harmed their rockets . . .

A massive cheer burst across the crypt as intruder seven's rockets failed. The spaceship began its long tumble to the unyielding desert below.

'Seventy-three per cent casualties on seven's attackers,' their liaison announced.

'Oh bollocks,' Laura groaned in anguish. She refused to glance at the tally board. It wouldn't be accurate anyway; they were losing planes so fast nobody could keep count. But she could see them through the terminus, small balls of flame flickering and dying in the hot air far above the desert.

On the map table, a pole ceremoniously knocked over the wooden rocket that represented intruder seven.

Intruder three's rocket exhaust dimmed and vanished. Intruder five began to wobble, scything its plasma around in long curves.

'We're killing them,' Slvasta said in satisfaction.

'Not enough,' Laura snapped back. *You don't understand. If just one of these bastards lands . . .*

'Attack on intruder two is over,' the communication officer announced.

'Over?' Javier asked. 'What do you mean, over? It's still flying. Send the planes back.'

'We can't,' the officer told him bleakly.

'Why not?'

'They're all gone. Wiped out.'

'Crudding Uracus!'

Laura tried to block it all out of her mind, the suffering and deaths. Suspend emotion, everything that made her human, and concentrate on the facts. Intruder three was plummeting now, spinning wildly as its erratic rockets sliced their lethal exhaust across the sky. Intruder one was abruptly knocked sideways as something exploded, sending out clouds of flame. Then it began to tilt, less than a kilometre from the ground, its blunt nose cone sweeping round to point directly at the scrub desert below. Its rockets continued firing, accelerating it down.

The spaceship struck hard, detonating in a massive seething mushroom of flame and smoke. Planes that were already retreating were caught in the blast wave. She saw wings crumpling, then the mangled fuselages began their long plummet.

The tannoys fell silent.

'Intruders two, four, eight, and nine are on the ground,' the chief air marshal said. 'We've taken the rest out. Confirmed kills.'

'Get the squadrons out of there,' Laura said urgently. 'Low and fast. If they're in the air, they're sitting ducks to the beam weapons.'

'Surely one last assault—'

'Would just be suicide. You'll achieve nothing and lose what remaining planes we have.'

Slvasta turned to look at the big atomic bombs on their trolleys, then back to the wormhole, which showed the edge of the desert where the invaders now sat. For kilometres in every direction the ground was smothered in flaming debris. 'You'll have to use the nukes.'

'We can't,' Laura said wearily. 'We only have three, and there are seven ships in the second invasion fleet heading for Tothland. *If* they fly close enough, and *if* I can open the terminus just right, three bombs might be able to take them all out while they're in the air.'

'But—' He gestured at the wormhole, which was still looking down on the edge of the desert where the invaders had landed. 'You said they would be unstoppable if they landed!'

'I know.' She took a breath and told her u-shadow to open a link. 'I need you,' she sent.

'You have a Commonwealth force field,' Javier said. 'Can you eliminate them?'

'I have to take out their planet,' Laura told him, pleased at how calmly she'd spoken that preposterous statement. 'I can't fight four ships here as well.'

'So it is down to the regiments to defend us yet again,' Slvasta said gravely. 'I will tell Master General Doyle to order full mobilization.'

'No,' Laura said.

'But we have nothing else! Bienvenido will be destroyed. You told us these aliens are worse than even Fallers. How can we—'

There was a commotion just outside the crypt doors. One of the Marine sentries called: 'Halt! You are not authorized to be here. I will shoot.'

'It's all right,' Laura said. 'Let them come in.'

Kysandra walked into the crypt – an entrance which brought complete silence with it. Biononics, the tiny machines permeating every cell in her body, barely had anything to do with maintaining her youthful looks. She was still in her twenties, her Celtic-pale skin rich with freckles, and thick Titian hair falling halfway down her back. She wore a long brown suede skirt and a white blouse;

a loose suede waistcoat with many pockets held a variety of small metal and plastic gadgets. A long black cylinder was carried on a shoulder strap – featureless, but everyone in the room knew it had to be some kind of Commonwealth weapon.

Marek and Fergus followed her in. They were both dressed in identical grey coveralls made from some slick fabric, and they carried the same cylinder weapon as Kysandra. Even their height and build were identical, though Marek had darker skin and looked a good thirty years older than Fergus.

Laura acknowledged the visitors with a wry grin. You had to use a full biononic field function scan to tell the men were ANAdroids, not actual people. And she'd never seen versions with morphic features quite so human; their creators had done an excellent job. But then, as they were part of Nigel's mission, she knew no effort would've been spared.

Yannrith and Andricea immediately drew their pistols and aimed them at the newcomers with a steady double-handed grip.

'Don't be ridiculous,' Laura said in her most contemptuous voice. 'They have integral force fields, like me. You can't shoot them.' Which was almost true. Kysandra's biononics did have that energy-field function, while the two ANAdroids wore force-field skeletons under their light armour suits.

'What in Uracus are *they* doing here?' Slvasta hissed.

'I asked them to help,' Laura said. 'Nobody else can take out the invaders on the ground. Now, will all the morons waving medieval weapons around please put them away before you hurt yourselves?'

Andricea flashed her a hateful glare before silently consulting Slvasta. He nodded, and the pistols were reluctantly holstered.

'Good to see you again, too,' Kysandra sneered at the prime minister. 'Imprisoned any innocents yet today? Some kid complaining his state-issue shoes are too tight, maybe?'

'Uracus take you, Faller-whore,' Slvasta spat back.

'Oh, for— Nigel was not a Faller, you bonehead cretin!'

'He has given this world to them,' Slvasta shouted, spittle flying from his lips.

'Nigel freed us from the Void,' Kysandra said coldly. 'He

sacrificed himself in that quantumbuster explosion so we would have a chance of a decent future.'

'Falls have increased tenfold since the Great Transition.'

'Because the Trees that survived the quantumbuster blast are no longer confined to the Forest formation they were locked into,' Marek said calmly. 'Now they have dispersed into a high-orbit ring, and the temporal loop is broken, so they can release their eggs with greater frequency. It was an inevitable consequence of liberation from the Void.'

'Liberation! You call this being free?'

The ANAdroid produced an expression of mild puzzlement. 'Yes.'

'Then I pity you.'

'It could have been freedom,' Kysandra said sweetly. 'But then you took over from the Captain.'

'I am nothing like—!'

'Ha! Even your own wife saw the truth – eventually.'

'You corrupted her. It was your fault.'

'Enough!' Laura said. 'Everybody, forget your political pissing contest. This is the day we face extinction, so let's not try to do that job for our enemies, shall we?'

Slvasta gave Kysandra a furious glare. She matched it with the most indolent stare, taunting . . .

'Kysandra, thank you for coming to help,' Laura said. 'Four spaceships made it past the IA-505s; numbers two, four, eight, and nine.'

'The squadrons did a good job then,' Kysandra said sympathetically.

'Yes.' Laura gestured at the wormhole. 'Can you handle them?'

Kysandra patted the cylinder she was carrying. 'Count on it.'

'Okay, where do you want us to put you down?'

Marek had been studying the table map. 'Are these landing positions accurate?'

'Yes,' the chief air marshal said.

'Okay, nine and four are close together. Laura, drop me between them. I can deal with both of them.'

'I'll take number eight,' Kysandra said.

Fergus grinned. 'So I guess that leaves me with number two.'

'All right, stand by.' Laura's u-shadow sent a stream of encoded instructions to the gateway. The terminus started to shift.

'Can you really do this?'

The voice was soft, but anxious. Almost everyone in the crypt looked at Javier. The big man was staring at Fergus.

'We can do this,' the ANAdroid said. 'Even Kysandra. She might look like an angel, but she can be quite the warrior when she needs to be.'

Kysandra winked at Javier.

The terminus shifted, coming down to ground level, revealing a level expanse of rock-strewn desert sand, with dunes rising high up ahead.

'Terminus is in the lee of a dune,' Laura said. 'No sensor coverage. Picking up some low-level radiation out there.'

'The exhaust,' Marek said. 'We believe they used nuclear gas-core rockets.'

'That was my conclusion, too.'

'Okay, my armour can cope with that. Let me through.'

Laura sent a code to the gateway, and the force field became porous. Marek took it at a run, jumping through onto the grainy sand beyond.

'Clear!'

Laura shifted the terminus to spaceship two. This time the ground was covered in scrub bushes, but all of them had wilted. Some were smouldering. Then the terminus jittered, shifting up several metres then sliding sideways. Laura sent a flurry of corrections through her u-shadow, and it stabilized again. She checked her exovision schematics.

'It's holding,' she said.

Fergus sprinted through. He ducked down behind some boulders as the terminus shifted away, but not before they all saw his coverall transform to the same colour as the rocks. It would be stealthed, too, Laura knew, keeping him hidden from any sensors the invaders could deploy.

'Then there was one,' Kysandra said quietly as the terminus settled a kilometre from number eight.

'Good luck,' Javier said.

She turned to Slvasta, her red hair flowing over her shoulders, and took her time placing a wide-brimmed leather hat on her head. 'I won't abandon these people you oppress,' she said. 'I will always be here to help them. But never you.' With that she walked calmly through the gateway, taking the cylinder off her shoulder as she went.

'Arrogant bitch,' Slvasta grunted – but not before Laura had shifted the wormhole terminus once again.

'Don't underestimate her,' Laura said without looking at him. 'And remember, I have exactly the same opinion of you.'

Nobody said anything; all the officers were suddenly busy studying their maps or clipboards.

'How are we doing with the second invasion fleet?' Laura asked.

'Estimated eleven minutes until landing,' the Space Vigilance Office liaison officer said. 'They're entering the chemosphere.'

Laura reconfigured the wormhole, opening the terminus above Tothland – an island in the Sibal Ocean not big enough to qualify as a continent. Seven crimson patches of light shone bright above the night-time landmass as the spaceships aerobraked. Her u-shadow analysed the positions and trajectories. Their rocket exhausts started to fire, sending pale splinters of luminescence shimmering across the hidden mountains far below.

'Weapons master,' Laura said. 'Please prepare the bombs.' Three keys were hanging on slim chains round her neck. She passed them to him.

Slvasta handed over his three keys as well. The weapons master opened the control hatch on the first of the three atomic bombs and put the keys in their twin sockets. Laura was almost tempted to activate her biononics force-field function, but if the damn thing did go off, a force field wouldn't protect her – not at this distance. The keys were turned simultaneously.

'Bomb one activated,' the weapons master announced solemnly.

Laura's u-shadow performed a quick calculation as she walked over to the crude metal cylinder, and she set the timer for a hundred seconds. She flicked the red switch, trying not to flinch. Three lights shone red, and she closed the little hatch.

Five Manhattan Project technicians wheeled the bomb into the middle of the crypt, directly in front of the gateway.

'Stand by,' she told them. The terminus shifted again, down into the stratosphere, close to the trajectories of three invaders. Silver light shone through, coming from somewhere above the opening. 'Go!'

The technicians were all young and fit, chosen for their strength. They pushed hard, building speed quickly across the ancient stone-paved floor. The bomb weighed nearly half a tonne, but it was moving fast when the trolley reached the gateway, and they gave it a final shove. Laura's u-shadow immediately moved the terminus away.

Theoretically, the bomb had a yield of forty-three kilotons. It would have been useless deployed in space against the invaders. For one, she couldn't hope to open the gateway terminus close to an accelerating spaceship and match velocity accurately enough. And second, even if they could deploy the bomb close enough, a nuclear explosion in a vacuum was unlikely to be effective. There would be no blast wave. Yes, the spaceship would suffer the radiation spike, and the electromagnetic pulse, but she couldn't be sure that would kill it.

An atmospheric strike, however, was different. The ships were vulnerable during their descent phase, and it was the blast wave which would cause the real damage. Supersonic winds smashing into the spaceships in tandem with the radiation deluge and the electromagnetic pulse knocking out unprotected electronics and power systems . . .

With only three bombs it was their best chance.

'Bomb two activated,' the weapons master said.

She set the timer for a minute. The short interval was used to confirm the location of the invader's ships. Looking down from four hundred kilometres above Bienvenido, they saw proof that the first bomb had exploded successfully, which brought a swift cheer round the crypt. The detonation flare was spent; now there was only a seething ball of star-hot plasma, cloaked in a shroud of ruined air. Tothland was fully illuminated by the devilish purple-white glare. Her u-shadow could just distinguish four spaceships still descending within the chaotic atmosphere.

The terminus switched position again. Bomb two was shoved through, six kilometres above the ground.

Bomb number three was deployed at a mere two and a half kilometres of altitude.

Please work, she prayed as the five determined technicians let go of the trolley handle. It seemed to be the mantra she lived her life with these days. Everything she'd done since she landed had been nick-of-time kludges in the face of adversity. Every time she thought she was making progress, something would come along to challenge her satisfaction.

In a bizarre way she almost welcomed this invasion. If they destroyed the Prime, it would buy Bienvenido time. The planet's society might just start to change as newer technologies began to make life easier. She might live to see the Commonwealth once more.

Unlikely.

Not that there was anyone left for her in the Commonwealth, anyway. The majority of her friends and family had all been on the colony fleet. *But it has to be better than this.*

The terminus opened again at five hundred kilometres above the radiation-saturated zone. Everyone watched anxiously as the three malevolent swirls of energy staining the air slowly subsided. Massive firestorms had broken out across Tothland as vegetation vaporized and entire forests ignited. Broiling hurricanes raced outwards, bringing ruin with them. There was no sign of any spaceship rocket exhausts.

'Did we do it?' Slvasta asked in trepidation.

'I think so,' she said. Her enhanced retinas scanned the area where the ships had been, unable to detect anything but the billowing ion haze.

'Thank you.'

She nodded acknowledgement. He'd actually meant it.

'Do we open the gateway back to Fanrith and bring *them* back?'

'No. Kysandra said they would find their own way home.'

'I see.'

'So how do we know if they've been successful?' Yannrith asked.

Always the suspicious one, Laura thought. 'You need to send the forward scouts into the landing zone to confirm the ships were destroyed. But Kysandra will have done the job. Trust me.' *I haven't told you half of the things biononics are capable of.*

'All right.' Slvasta turned to one of the regimental colonels. 'Send the scouts in.'

'Sir.' The colonel picked up a telephone and started talking into it.

'Time to finish this,' Laura said. 'Let's get the floaters in here.'

'Yes, ma'am,' the weapons master acknowledged.

Slvasta and Javier exchanged a glance.

'Are you sure about this?' the political adviser asked.

'I've never been more sure of anything,' Laura told him solemnly. 'If we don't eliminate Ursell, the Prime will just keep on coming. Once they confirm how vulnerable Bienvenido is, it won't be sixteen ships they send next, it'll be sixteen thousand.'

'I thought you said Ursell was ruined?' Slvasta asked.

'It is.'

'So surely the ships we've just defeated are all they can send?'

'No,' Laura told him firmly. 'What they've sent is just what they could put together in a hurry. The Prime that are left back on Ursell will expend whatever is left of their resources to transfer themselves here. They know they can survive and expand again on Bienvenido.'

'But the Fallers—' Javier began.

'What? They'll save us?' she asked scornfully. 'Even they can't stand against the Prime. No, this is something that must be done.'

'All right. Just . . . be careful,' Slvasta said.

'I always am.'

They continued to look through the gateway as the bombs' devastation slowly cleared, the devil's light draining from the sky above Tothland. The firestorms raged below them, pumping dense smoke into the tormented air. Then the next two trolleys were being wheeled into the crypt by the same technicians who'd delivered the atom bombs.

The floaters were another of *Vermillion*'s cargo which had lain undisturbed since the landing. Like the gateways, floaters also generated wormholes, but they were intended to support the new colony's burgeoning manufacturing industry rather than provide transport. Slightly smaller than the CST BC5800d2s, they were designed to be dropped into a gas giant's atmosphere, where their force fields would expand, acting as a buoyancy system so their altitude could be selected with a good level of accuracy. That was necessary in a gas giant, where the atmospheric density varied the chemical composition enormously, from almost pure hydrogen at the uppermost levels to complex hydrocarbons at the bottom. When the floater reached the required strata, its wormhole would open directly into a refinery, and a near-infinite supply of hydrocarbons would rush in, ready for conversion into whatever products the burgeoning colony needed.

The first time she saw them still in their protective transit shells, she'd thought she could use them to assist Bienvenido's petrochemical era, providing combustion engine fuel without the need for oil wells and shale mines. Then she'd hesitated, wondering if she could skip that entire stage by going directly to fusion and high-density batteries – and cut out decades of pollution. It was a good problem to have, taking her mind off the Faller threat and Slvasta's despicable regime.

The weapons technicians had to turn the floaters sideways to get them through the crypt's arched doorway. They were cylinders four metres in diameter and two deep, with a concave centre on one side. The casing was a grey metalloceramic mottled with turquoise blemishes, as if it was a living carapace. They'd been relatively easy to restore, with less component degradation than the gateways. She supposed that was due to the tough environment they were designed to work in.

Her u-shadow established a link to both of them, and interrogated their smartnets to run a final systems check. Like the CST BC5800d2, they were powered by a direct mass–energy converter that could be fed by the superpressurized atmosphere they were immersed in. Exovision displays showed her they were fully functional.

She stared at them as the trolleys came to rest. She'd done good work, aided by information from the ANAdroids. *So no reason to delay, then. Bollocks.*

'All right then,' she announced. 'Let's do this.'

'And there's no other way?' Javier asked.

'No.'

'You would kill an entire world?'

'Sonny, it's us or them.' *Again.*

Slvasta held up a hand and gave Javier a sharp glance. 'Laura knows what must be done. Without her . . .' He smiled ruefully. 'It's just the risk. Please allow me to send some Marines through with you.'

'They wouldn't be any help,' she said. 'But thanks anyway.' Her u-shadow sent a new series of instructions into the CST BC5800d2.

The terminus shifted again. Exovision displays showed her the gateway's increased power consumption as the wormhole extended its range by eighty million kilometres. This time, the terminus judder was more pronounced.

A wan heliotrope light shone through the gateway, but there was nothing to see, just a haze. The terminus had opened deep inside Valatare's atmosphere. Laura studied her exovision displays as 3D graphics fluctuated, with amber caution graphics streaming in. The force field was being subjected to a huge pressure. 'Odd,' she muttered.

'Something wrong?' Slvasta asked. There was an edge to his voice – not anger for once, but fear.

'Not specifically.' Her u-shadow sent a fresh batch of instructions to the gateway, and the terminus shifted. She monitored the pressure against the gateway's force field, which was reducing rapidly. Then the haze cleared. The terminus had risen out of a cloud layer. It was as if they were looking out across an infinite cyan sky, roofed by another unbroken cloud sheet tens of kilometres above them. Mammoth hurricane-whorls chased through the gulf at colossal speed. Phenomenal lightning bolts snapped between them, rivalling solar flares in power.

Valatare was the sole gas giant orbiting this lost sun, ten million kilometres further out than Bienvenido. At ninety-seven thousand kilometres in diameter, it was considerably smaller than Jupiter, but still massive. Whenever it was in conjunction, it created storms and tides the like of which Bienvenido had never known before.

Laura frowned at the readings she was getting from the gateway – not the force field, but the wormhole itself. 'That's not right.'

'What is it?' Slvasta asked. 'Are there more aliens?'

'It's not that,' she assured him and everyone else in the crypt. Aliens were now Bienvenido's ultimate nightmare. They had a justifiable collective paranoia of monsters swooping down on their planet, she acknowledged.

In truth she'd been worried by what might be lurking in Valatare's atmosphere. The theory she and the ANAdroids had come up with was that the Void used this lonely star as a place to banish the planet of any species who defied it in some way – a theory confirmed by the Vatni, who claimed to have seen Ursell emerge from nowhere over a thousand years ago.

The Vatni themselves, though amenable to strategic deals with humans, were stubborn to the extreme, refusing to have their nature consumed by whatever malevolent intelligence lay at the heart of the Void. Ursell was a semi-habitable wasteland, ruined by a nuclear war – so typical of the Prime, whose existence was one of constant belligerence.

Macule was in an even worse state than Ursell – whatever species used to live there must have wiped themselves out in a ferocious nuclear exchange millennia ago. Odd Trüb, a featureless barren planet with a thin atmosphere and a dozen tiny moons (the only ones in the system). She'd never had the time to work out its enigmatic presence. Asdil, orbiting much further out than Valatare, and completely frigid under its nitrogen–methane atmosphere. Laura didn't know what kind of alien that could support; the Commonwealth had never found any cryolife, and there was no electromagnetic signal or thermal emissions signalling any kind of civilization. The same went for Fjernt, which was visually encouraging, with water oceans and twenty per cent landmass, but the atmosphere was nitrogen and carbon dioxide – no free oxygen. As it was unscathed by any conflict, Laura liked to think its aliens had found their way back to wherever they'd come from. *And if they can do it . . .*

But from what she'd experienced so far, this isolated star system was turning out to be utterly lethal for humans.

'Then what's the problem? Javier asked.

'It's the gravity.'

'The what?'

'Valatare's gravity. It's wrong somehow. The gradient is steeper than it should be this close; that's what threw the terminus emergence point off. The pressure is all wrong as well. It might be the density – that blue colour is from methane – but there's not enough to . . . This is weird.'

'Does that affect your plan?'

'No.' She locked the terminus coordinates, and looked over her shoulder at the technicians clustered round the first floater. A final activation signal from her u-shadow – confirmed by the floater's smartnet – and she told them: 'Go.'

They pushed hard, but the floater weighed a lot more than the atom bombs. It trundled slowly over the floor towards the gateway. Javier went over and added his considerable strength, soon followed by Yannrith, and then Slvasta. Several Air Force officers joined them until it resembled a rugby scrum piled up against the floater's dark casing. The machine began to pick up speed.

'Careful,' she warned as the leading edge slipped through the force field. The bulk of it went through, and Valatare's gravity took over, pulling sharply. Everyone let go and lurched back. The floater fell through and dropped away fast.

Laura stood close to the gateway so her link to the floater's smartnet would be maintained. Secondary routines in her macrocellular clusters monitored the telemetry, seeing a force field expand out around the tumbling cylinder, increasing its buoyancy. The rate it dropped began to slow, then it stopped twenty kilometres below the terminus – a dark speck buffeted by the winds. 'Okay, that's good. External pressure at the floater is thirty-three times Earth standard. That should do it.'

She suddenly realized that it was *now*. The inevitable moment had just crept up, which was maybe for the best. Laura knew she wasn't the bravest person; her first encounter with Fallers had shown her that. But she'd accepted her fate then, so once again— 'Bring the second floater up, please,' she said.

'Can you really do this?' Andricea asked. 'Destroy a whole world?'

'Believe it,' Laura said. She activated her biononic force-field function. A thin layer of air shimmered around her, rippling like a heat haze before stabilizing. Her u-shadow delivered a new coordinate for the wormhole terminus.

It opened a hundred kilometres above Ursell. Laura looked down across an expanse of filthy clouds. Even the stratosphere above was clotted with particles, staining it a benign sulphurous yellow. The quick mapping run they'd performed weeks earlier had given them a rough outline of continents and seas, so the terminus should be above land – a region devoid of radio emissions and without any large ruins.

She told the gateway to lower the terminus. It slipped down through the clouds, kilometre after kilometre of dank grey vapour. Exovision displays showed her the radiation level rising as the terminus approached the ground. Then it was abruptly dropping through the base of the cloud. The ground was five hundred metres away – a wasteland of flinty stone cluttered with boulders. There was no vegetation, only ribbons of dark lichen clinging to fissures in the rock. Turgid rain drizzled down, giving every surface a dull oil-rainbow gleam.

Under Laura's direction, the terminus rotated to the vertical then turned three hundred and sixty degrees, allowing her to study the entire area. 'Looks clear,' she said.

'How long will you need?' Slvasta asked.

'Not long. A few minutes, maybe,' Laura said. She looked at the team standing behind the final trolley. 'Stand by.'

'Do you have to go through?'

'Yes,' she said firmly, and walked through the gateway onto Ursell. The light level was almost as bleak as it had been back in the crypt. Drizzle spluttered against her force field, dripping onto the sodden ground. Exovision displays showed her the atmospheric composition, the toxins and contaminants – all easily filtered by the force field. She turned full circle. There were hills in the distance, with tiny scarlet lights scattered along a deep valley. Her field scan function couldn't detect any electromagnetic signals, though there was a spray of radiation coming from the valley, and also some strong magnetic fields. Having the Prime this close was still a worry, though. 'Come on,' she muttered. 'Get it through.'

On the other side of the gateway, men pushed hard against the trolley. The floater began to trundle along the crypt's stone floor.

Something moved. Laura's secondary routines caught it – a flicker above the valley with the red lights. She turned and faced it, her enriched retinas scanning frantically. Infra-red was difficult; the cool rain wrecked the image. Light-amplification routines cut in.

Flying machines. Small, blunt hemispheres, maybe twenty metres across, eight deep. Stubby fin-wings. Strong magnetic field. Ducted fans tilted to power them forwards – heading straight for her.

'Bollocks,' she grunted. She twisted round. The floater was almost at the gateway. 'Move it!' she yelled. Nobody seemed to hear her. Her u-shadow transmitted a crude analogue radio signal. 'Hurry! They're coming. Push!'

The signal must have got through, roaring out of the tannoys. The scrum pushing the trolley strained hard. Slvasta and a half-dozen officers added their strength once again. The front of the floater emerged through the gateway.

A maser beam struck Laura. Her force field stiffened for an instant, flaring green. Amber warnings zipped across her exovision. Rain flash-vaporized around her, cloaking her in a seething steam squall.

'Double bollocks.' The beam was strong, but her force field

could withstand it relatively easily. *From this distance.* Another beam struck her. The flyers were still seven kilometres away. She faced them, frowning with determination, bringing her arms up like some pre-Commonwealth priest-queen. Her bionomic field function sent out a disrupter pulse. Ionization made the wet air flare purple-white as if a lightning bolt had just discharged. She fired again. Again.

Alien flyers tumbled out of the sky. The remaining flyers broke formation fast, shooting up away from the valley, accelerating into the dank camouflage of the rain and cloud base.

Behind her, the trolley carrying the floater cleared the rim of the gateway. It tilted down slightly and its small wheels dug into the wet ground. The team pushing it strained with all their might, but Laura could see it wasn't going to budge.

'Oh triple bollocks.'

Her u-shadow linked her to the CST BC5800d2's smartcore, and the terminus shot upwards thirty metres. The floater fell out, smashing onto the ground five metres away from her and crushing the trolley. She looked up to see Slvasta and Javier standing at the edge of the terminus, staring down anxiously. She gave them a quick wave, hoping to reassure them. Another maser blast hit her. Her field function scan backtracked it easily. The flyer was hovering in the cloud two kilometres above. She hit it with a disrupter pulse.

Her u-shadow established a link to the floater's smartnet. Its force field strengthened.

Pity there's no way of using it to kill the individual flyers, she thought. When she glanced back at the valley, she could see another flock of flyers shooting up into the clouds. These ones looked even bigger.

Laura activated the floater's wormhole, feeding in a coordinate that should see its terminus opening above Valatare. Somewhere from above, the flyers opened up a salvo of electronic warfare pulses. They were crude, but still managed to degrade her link with the floater. Smoking debris from the flyer she'd destroyed began to hail down around her. Her scan pinpointed the sources of the electronic-warfare pulses, and she responded with more disrupter fire.

Then the floater's wormhole opened: a sapphire haze streaked with white strands. Exovision displays showed her the terminus at the far end reaching for Valatare.

Eight flyers dropped from the base of the clouds. They were over a kilometre away and coming down fast. Another cohort dropped down on her other side. They were all emitting strong electronic-warfare distortion pulses, trying to fuzz whatever sensors she had. It was good, but not good enough to deflect Commonwealth systems. She blew the first group apart, its glaring fireball swelling out. The surging red light showed her *things* scampering over the drab wilderness.

Four stumpy legs, a fat pear-shaped body wearing some kind of black-glitter armour, with sensor stalks sprouting from the crown like whip antennae weighed down with electronic modules on their tips. No mistaking them: *Prime motiles.* The memory was ingrained into the human psyche after a war that had brought the Commonwealth to the brink of extinction.

No wonder the Void shat them out.

Laura blew up another flyer. Prime motiles were scuttling out of all the other hemispheres that had landed. The jerky way they moved, zigzagging from boulder to boulder, was like watching a charge of giant crustaceans. There was only silence around her, except for swift coded radio bursts. She emitted a powerful jamming signal, and watched with satisfaction as they all stopped moving for several seconds. The Prime weren't a hive mind, but the motiles certainly qualified as a herd, functioning best while under direct control from the immotiles – who were the herd brains as well as the egg layers.

The smartnet on the floater above her reported it had established a realtime link to the Valatare floater through the wormhole. Her u-shadow was in direct control of both of them.

Now for the tricky part. Laura directed the Ursell floater's terminus towards the Valatare floater, at the same time reconfiguring the Valatare floater's mechanism. She wanted to turn it into a stable anchor for the Ursell floater's wormhole rather than generate its own.

The motiles started to move again. Her field function scan detected small objects flying towards her on ballistic trajectories. The scan identified a small quantity of uranium inside each of them. 'Holy fuck!' Her secondary routines took over, running in parallel, identifying the mini-nukes arching through the air, and slammed out over a dozen disrupter pulses in less than two seconds.

Over twenty maser beams stabbed down, hitting the floater. Its force field resisted easily. She couldn't waste time targeting the flyers overhead, but this all-out saturation attack was going to overwhelm her pretty quickly.

Her exovision was showing her the wormhole terminus easing slowly to the Valatare floater. The engagement procedure was working, helping to reel it in. Just a couple more minutes, and the gateway to the crypt and safety was a simple jump away . . .

But she had to be here, had to maintain a direct link with the floaters so her u-shadow could manage the incredibly complicated procedure. More mini-nukes came streaking towards her. Her routines knocked each of them out.

A dazzling flash erupted five kilometres away. Her force field turned opaque to cope with the monstrous gamma pulse. Data flowed across her exovision: the yield was about four kilotons. *Survivable.*

She watched the mushroom cloud ascending, finding its grotesque seething shape oddly elegant, as if seeing a legend reborn. The ground around her was suddenly steaming. Then the blast wave reached her, a rolling eruption of sand and small stones hurtling across the wasteland. She flung herself down. Her force field strained into a dull rouge as it fought the pressure slam. The screaming storm began to tip the floater up. She ordered it to expand its force field, and watched it take off, dwindling away into the sky, flipping round and round in the violent air. Her link remained intact.

Laura rolled over, seeing the BC5800d2's terminus still hovering thirty metres above the ground, with long fronds of dust and vapour flashing across it. She couldn't risk its force field being overloaded by Prime weapons. The radiation and pressure surge would kill everyone in the crypt – and probably smash half the palace to pieces, too.

With a sense of bitter inevitability she knew what she'd have to do next.

Slvasta was there, pressed up against the force field, watching aghast. Her u-shadow transmitted an analogue signal again.

'For crud's sake, Slvasta, pardon Bethaneve!' she sent. 'This is a big bad universe – you've seen that for yourself now, so you can't go through it jumping at shadows. You have got to dial down your paranoia. Grow up, think logically, plan ahead. You have to defeat the Fallers, kill the bastard Trees. Build the atom bombs and get them up there into the Ring – any way you can. With the Trees gone there'll be no limits to what your world can achieve. Do it!'

She saw him shouting at her, saw the anger and fright on his face. Her u-shadow linked to the BC5800d2, shutting down the wormhole and codelocking its smartcore. The terminus shrank to nothing then winked out in a purple ember of Cherenkov radiation. Her field function scan caught five more mini-nukes in flight. Secondary targeting routines zapped them.

At last, the Valatare floater's smartnet reported it had anchored the wormhole from Ursell. The connection between the two planets was open and stable.

All right. Now we're getting somewhere!

Over two hundred Prime motiles were advancing on her from all directions. More fliers were ascending from the valley. Twenty-five accelerated after the floater as it spun lazily through the air, gradually rising – four hundred metres high already.

Another mini-nuke detonated on the ground three kilometres away. Then a third went off.

Laura sent another batch of instructions into the linked floaters. The final procedure had to be enacted. Then the first of the new blast waves struck her, sending her rolling helplessly across the sharp rocks until she crashed into a boulder.

Pinned there by the wailing superheated wind, with her force field fizzing aquamarine, she stared upwards. The blasts had torn the clouds from most of the sky, allowing her to see the floater and its shimmering force-field bubble. The explosions were swatting it about brutally, sending it skipping higher and higher. Her u-shadow initiated the final sequence, and the wormhole's diameter began to expand. She watched a plume of the gas giant's hydrogen atmosphere come squirting out – thin at first, then gradually getting wider, but still the colossal pressure was maintained. Her mouth split open in a smile. It was acting like a rocket exhaust, accelerating the floater upwards. And the wormhole diameter continued to expand – a hundred metres wide now. Then bigger. The flow of gas was fierce and undiminished, backed by the incredible pressure of the gas giant's atmosphere. And the fringes of the massive gas plume were bursting into stark blue flame as the hydrogen finally mixed with Ursell's oxygen, creating a fire halo.

Another mini-nuke detonated, the closest yet. Laura left the ground, spinning over and over in the glowing air before crashing down painfully. Her exovision medical readouts blinked up a series of amber warnings. Biononics shut down nerve paths, closing off the pain.

The immotiles must be using the motiles as carriers, she thought, sending them crawling along ridges and depressions to infiltrate her defensive perimeter, sacrificing them. Which was what the Primes did: individual motiles were valueless.

The wormhole was two hundred metres wide now, its roar rivalling the awesome soundwall of the nukes. Laura ran a systems diagnostic on the two floaters. Everything was functioning very smoothly, all components within tolerance, gas feeding easily into the mass–energy converter.

Four hundred metres wide, and the sky above her was a single layer of elegant indigo flame.

'It will never stop,' she broadcast to the Primes in their own neurological code – and started to laugh. It wasn't quite true, of course. Valatare's atmosphere wasn't infinite, but there was more than enough to crush and burn the Primes a thousand times over.

Her link to the Ursell floater was still working, which surprised her. She suspected the local immotile clusters were analysing what was happening, trying to decide what action to take. Demoting her priority status.

She started downloading her personal memory store into the floater's smartnet for safekeeping.

Which has to be the universe's most desperate roll of the dice.

The floater was seven kilometres in altitude, and its wormhole six hundred and eighty metres in diameter – and still widening. After analysing the component loading factors, she'd settled on halting the expansion at five kilometres in diameter. The floaters should be able to maintain that indefinitely.

The Primes launched a barrage of mini-nukes up at the catastrophic incursion.

'Pissing in the wind, boys,' Laura called out with manic cheerfulness as she deactivated her force field.

Ten mini-nukes exploded simultaneously above her—

BOOK TWO

Defence of the State

1

Captain Chaing, of the People's Security Regiment (PSR), saw *her* in the crowd not twenty metres in front of him, and froze in shock. It was a joyful noisy crowd spread out along Broadstreet – thousands of people determined to enjoy the night's festivities. Today was Fireyear Day: a public holiday for the whole world to celebrate the time when, two hundred and fifty-seven years ago, Ursell's entire atmosphere burned and dear Mother Laura sacrificed herself to save Bienvenido. That was an event worth celebrating, and Opole's residents were certainly going for it.

Chaing was new to the city; the PSR had only reassigned him from Portlynn two months ago. He thought it a drab provincial town, and spent those grim months wondering if he'd somehow pissed off his superiors and they'd sent him here as punishment. But today all that had changed. First there was the procession of big colourful floats through the city centre, then as dusk came bands claimed the street junctions, playing loud and fast music, and unlicensed stalls miraculously appeared to serve the excited people some truly throat-killing liquors. Half the city had turned out in bizarre and wondrous costumes, singing and dancing along the streets. The grand civic firework display was about to start.

It was a perfect time for any clandestine activity, which was why he'd arranged to meet the undercover agent in the Nenad Cafe on LowerGate Lane. His route took him along Broadstreet, and there she was, his own personal ghost – but in the flesh. He stood there numbly as the merry singing people swirled around him, watching her. She was side-on to him, face heavily shadowed under her wide-brimmed hat, with her red hair braided into a neat tail that fell down her back. But he knew that profile; he could recognize her anywhere. Just to confirm it, she wore her brown leather coat, the one that came down to her ankles. And now she was walking away from him. That jolted him into action. He hurried after her.

Will I finally see her smile?

Chaing had seen her just once before, three decades ago, but that vision had haunted him ever since. He couldn't stop it. Right from the start he'd been cursed with an excellent memory. And out of all the moments which made up his life, her face was the most vivid recollection. The rest of the incident he always pushed aside – too unpleasant. But her . . .

He'd been five years old, playing in the filthy alley behind their tenement block, when he tripped to sprawl across a mound of earth that turned out to be a bussalore nest. He'd screamed in terror as the vile rodents emerged from the dislodged dirt, squeaking and spitting.

Tiny stars of many colours sparkled behind his eyes, merging to form the picture of a beautiful lady with red hair. And abruptly a voice told him: *Stand up, darling. Bussalores are intimidated by anything larger than themselves.*

Chaing scrambled to his feet, and stared down at the nasty lean *things* slithering round his ankles. They regarded him for a moment, their noses twitching, sharp little teeth bared, before slinking away through a hole in the wall.

He was still standing in the same spot, trembling in shock, a minute later when his mother came hurrying out of the tenement.

'Are you all right?' she asked. 'You did the right thing standing up. Bussalores are horrible things, but they're basically cowards.'

'Was that you?' he asked incredulously. 'Did you tell me what to do?'

His mother smiled nervously. 'It's your clever memory again, darling. I've told you several times what to do if you see a nest of bussalores.'

She had never said anything of the sort. He knew that. He would have remembered.

'But there was a lady,' he said with a five-year-old's insistence. 'She was very pretty.'

His mother pointedly looked both ways along the alley. It was empty. 'Nobody here, darling. You must have imagined her.'

'I didn't,' he persisted, upset that Mummy wouldn't believe him.

She gave him a worried glance. His mother always looked harried or tired. He wished it wasn't so.

'There is a legend,' his mother said slowly. 'If I tell you about it, will you promise me not to repeat it, not to anyone, not even Daddy?'

'I promise,' he said solemnly.

'People say that there is a Warrior Angel who watches over this world. She protects us from the Fallers, among other things.'

'But I thought the regiments and the Liberty astronauts guard Bienvenido.'

'They do, darling, and they're magnificent. But sometimes we need a little extra help.' She put her hands on his shoulders and gave him a grave look. 'Now this is the important part: the government doesn't really approve of the Warrior Angel, because she's not one of them. And they get angry with her because she doesn't always do what they say. So that's why we don't tell them if we see her. And we don't tell Daddy, either, because we don't want to worry him, do we? This is our super secret, you and me, and we'll keep it forever, all right?'

Chaing didn't like the idea of upsetting Daddy – who had a short temper and never hesitated to use his belt to beat Chaing when he did something wrong. He seemed to do a lot of things wrong no matter how hard he tried not to. 'Yes,' he agreed solemnly. 'She's our secret.'

His mother died three years later. One night his father came home drunk again, and started hitting her. This night she was standing at the top of the stairs when the vicious punches began to land. She fell, breaking her neck before she'd tumbled halfway down.

A court took less than a day to find his father guilty of murder, and sentence him to life in the Pidrui mines.

Chaing was placed in an orphanage. By then, like all children on Bienvenido, he knew not to give away any secrets about himself – not his memory, not his vision of the Warrior Angel, nothing that might be regarded as suspect. On Bienvenido, suspicion was always followed by accusation – and soon after that the arrival of PSR officers.

Every child brought up by the state went on to be employed by the state; there was no question, no choice. You took the tests and waited for your assessment results when the career officer told you how the rest of your life would be spent. Chaing's IQ was measured as slightly above average (never high enough to be suspect), and his two-year compulsory regimental service was admirable, so he was sent to the PSR officer cadet training college – at which point he realized just how lucky he'd been escaping his new employer's attention.

Not that he was a filthy Eliter. But some distant ancestor must have made a bad marriage choice – which, by luck or chance, or more likely subterfuge, had escaped the PSR's comprehensive files.

So he'd inherited a good memory through no fault of his own. That just meant he could be a more effective PSR officer, and devote his life to tracking down Faller nests, saving citizens as he was sworn to do.

And as for the Warrior Angel: his mother was right. She was just a legend, one the Eliters incorporated into their criminal propaganda. Which was why he was always on the lookout for her.

Except . . . his recall was flawless. He really had seen her as a vision, wearing a long brown leather coat that moved with the ease of silk, her red hair falling over her shoulders as if she had a halo of fire. His memory held her lips forever poised on the verge of a smile. And that vision troubled him. Badly.

A lesser man might call it *obsession*.

Chaing started to push through the partying crowd, heedless of the annoyed looks as he knocked shoulders. The ghost girl was ten metres away now, slipping through clusters of laughing people with the greatest of ease. As he closed on her, his initial astonishment gave way to anger. She'd left him alone for thirty crudding years, until he'd practically convinced himself all she'd ever been was a child's stress-induced fantasy. Now here she was again – and, given he was now a captain in the PSR, she could end him.

A group of women dressed in cloaks of yellow feathers, and exorbitantly high gold and emerald headdresses, came along the road, all of them linking hands as they highstepped along. They shrieked at him with drunken delight as he tried to push through them. He snarled and ducked round; taking time to remonstrate, to pull out his PSR badge, would have taken even longer. He looked round frantically, seeing a plait of red hair swaying about behind some youths clustered furtively round what looked like a bong of narnik. Chaing was almost running now, and she was right ahead of him. Close enough to—

'Hey, you!' he reached out and closed his hand on her shoulder. His heart thudded at making physical contact. *She's real.*

Then she turned and he saw her face. It wasn't the vision, not as he knew her. The light and confusion of the bustling merry crowds had fooled him. This woman was approaching middle age, with rounded cheeks and a small mouth, her eyes painted in gold mascara. Her features creased up in annoyance. 'Whaddya want?' she demanded, and her accent was pure Rakwesh Province.

'Who are you?' he gasped. He could have sworn it had been her.

She laughed. 'I'm the Warrior Angel, and so's me friend.' She draped her arm over the shoulder of another girl, and tugged her close. The ebony-skinned friend was also wearing a brown coat; tufts of black hair protruded from below her skewed wig of red hair.

Chaing snatched his hand away as if it was burning.

'Wazzamatter?' the woman asked.

'You're not her,' was all Chaing could manage to say.

The second girl was giving him a sly appraising look. 'For you, fella, I could be.'

He frowned. 'Why are you doing this? This is a festival. A

celebration. It is not appropriate to dress as the Warrior Angel. She's just a reactionary legend. A criminal.'

'Screw you, dickhead,' the first woman snapped. 'We like the Warrior Angel. She's done more for this shitty world than any regiment ponce. What're yuooz anyhow? A Party git?'

'Bet he is,' sneered her friend. 'Bet his important daddy got him off proper regimental service, too. Didn't he, Party boy? Nice little office job in a supply depot instead, was it?'

Chaing backed off, knowing his cheeks would be colouring. 'It's not right, that's all. You shouldn't celebrate her.'

The woman gave him an obscene finger gesture.

Chaing turned away, embarrassed and annoyed – mostly with himself. People were supposed to respect the PSR, to show proper deference. But then he'd hardly behaved like a PSR officer. The first fireworks burst overhead, crowning the cloudless black sky with topaz and ruby scintillations. And there, on the other side of the wide thoroughfare, *she* was standing amid a bunch of revellers who were dressed in outsize silver astronaut pressure suits, staring right back at him – real this time. This was the face he knew from his vision, stippled by the weird multicoloured light of the fireworks.

His jaw dropped in amazement. Then a rowdy band of regiment troops jostled their way along the middle of the road, jeering and shouting among themselves. He craned his neck, desperate to keep sight of her, but there were only the carnival astronauts who were singing a badly out-of-tune rendition of 'Treefall Blues'. There was no sign of the ghost girl.

'Crudding Uracus!' One stupid mistaken glimpse and now he was seeing phantoms on every corner. He took a breath, and stomped off along Broadstreet, heading for the bulky Filbert Exchange two hundred metres away. Baysdale Road lay down the side of the covered market, and the crowd was considerably thinner here; he turned down it as more and more fireworks smothered the sky above in sizzling lightbursts. Baysdale Road led him into the Gates district, the original heart of the city, over three square kilometres built without any order or conformity. Two of the ancient founding families had clashed here, which is why the streets were all at angles to each other, as neither would adopt the other's grid. The buildings were slim and high, made from brick and stucco with wooden strapwork, and topped by steep-pitched tile roofs. They weren't particularly vertical any more, with some facades leaning alarmingly over the cobbled streets, as if their neighbours were squeezing them out of alignment.

The Fireyear celebrations here were mainly alcohol-based. Many ground floors in the buildings that made up the Gates were small state-licensed enterprises where families had followed the same crafts as their forebears for over two thousand years. Plenty of them revolved around brewing and distilling. Open windows showed him that the small pubs were teeming. Lively modern music was flowing out of the bigger clubs.

Even though he'd memorized the city layout, it took him a while to find LowerGate Lane amid the muddle of the Gates. It turned out to be uncomfortably narrow; if he extended both arms, his fingertips brushed the walls on both sides. You couldn't even drive a tuk-tuk along it, let alone a modern van. He wasn't entirely surprised to find the city council had clearly given up the idea of providing electrical streetlights here. The only illumination came from open windows and the occasional oil lamp hanging outside a doorway. It was like stepping back into pre-Transition times.

The Nenad Cafe was a student haunt, its alarmingly uneven ceiling ten centimetres too low for comfort. One wall was shelving for a 'free library' with a good selection of leather-bound books donated by alumni from the Opole University, which bordered the southern end of the Gates. He looked round the tables with their painted chessboards. At thirty-five, he was the oldest patron by a good ten years. Fortunately his family genes kept him relatively youthful. With his full head of hair, as yet unwrinkled pale-olive skin, and a trim figure, he liked to think he could pass for mid-twenties.

Once his eyes adjusted to the candlelight inside, he saw a short girl who didn't even look twenty sitting by herself, reading an unlicensed news-sheet, a mug of chocolate half-drunk on the table. Her legs were folded up yoga-style on the worn chair. Chaing just knew he could never manage to bend his limbs like that, and he prided himself in keeping in good shape. She wore a dark-blue corduroy jacket over a black waitress blouse, a uniform finished off with a short black skirt. Her oval face had hazel eyes that seemed far too large for someone so dainty, and her wavy raven hair was held back by a velvet band.

He hesitated. It was definitely Corporal Jenifa; he recognized her from her file photograph. But she looked a lot younger than her twenty-two years. *Which is probably the reason she was chosen for this mission.*

The sullen expression marring her features was also off-putting.

He eased himself into the seat opposite. 'Anything interesting in the news?' That was the identifying phrase.

She slapped the sheet onto the table, and regarded him in annoyance. 'Yes, I'm Jenifa.'

Which wasn't the kind of greeting he expected. 'Chaing.'

'Of course you are. Who else would you be?'

'Is something wrong?'

She rocked forwards, putting her face close to his. 'This is Fireyear Day, right?'

Chaing returned her gaze levelly. He wanted to issue an instant reprimand, yet undercover agents had to be given a certain amount of leeway. 'Yes.'

'Plenty of people about . . .' she paused as a couple of students squeezed past the table, 'so no one is going to notice or care about two strangers talking in a cafe. Not tonight.'

'Well, no.'

'Brilliant. Your idea?'

'Yes, actually. I wanted to meet you. The information you've provided has been helpful.'

She grunted dismissively. 'The information that I gathered from my job, waitressing at the Cannes Club. Waitressing! Nothing suspicious about me taking time off on the busiest night of the year, then. Right?'

'Oh.' Chaing didn't know what else to say. It had seemed clever when he'd had the instruction placed in her drop box.

'Forget it,' Jenifa said, abruptly dismissive. 'I'm here now, and I've got something for you. It's about the other girls. We may have been right about the gangs here.'

'Good.' Chaing was suddenly very interested. His predecessor had brought Jenifa in to infiltrate a probable trafficking operation. The PSR didn't usually bother chasing streetwalkers; that was the job of the local sheriffs. But inevitably when humans were treated like cattle, there was the chance that they'd wind up being shipped off to a Faller nest. Fallers who took human form ate human flesh. According to the Faller Research Institute manual, it was mainly to do with body chemistry. Fallers mimicked humans in such a way that the nutrient requirements of their human-shaped bodies required the proteins and vitamins contained within real human flesh. It was instinct at an individual and species level. Fallers had evolved themselves to conquer worlds by supplanting the dominant sentient species – and what better way to speed up the process than by literally consuming your opposition?

'The manager at the Cannes, he asks a lot of questions,' Jenifa said. 'Stuff like where a girl comes from, her family. Basically, if anyone's going to notice them missing.'

'I would have thought that was pretty standard.'

'Yeah, but this is more. Once a girl goes to work in the rooms upstairs, she belongs to the house. She's meat to them. All they're interested in is that she keeps herself clean and attracts enough customers.'

'Right.' He nodded. There was a big Opole county regiment camp on the edge of the city. Everyone on Bienvenido was conscripted into the regiments for two years on their eighteenth birthday. It was one of Slvasta's laws, designed to make people understand the reality of the Faller threat. But with the Air Defence Force planes successfully killing eggs in the sky, and the paratroops following them immediately into the area, there was less call for the regiments to sweep the land as there had been in Slvasta's time, which left the teenagers kicking their heels in the camps undergoing basic training. And with so many teenagers away from home for the first time, and with the regiment basic pay in their pocket, the town's clubs and bars and brothels received a large never-ending income stream.

'If the answer comes back that no one cares, they work for a few weeks and then get passed on to another house,' Jenifa told him. 'I've seen it three or four times now.'

'Are these other houses in Opole?'

'That's the thing. Girls working the pubs and clubs and houses move around a lot, but we all share lodgings – three or four to a room, sometimes. Some of these ones that don't have connections, nobody ever hears from them again. They certainly don't come back to their lodgings.'

'Okay. The manager who keeps asking these questions, what's his name?'

'Roscoe Caden.' Her clenched hand slid over the table. 'I managed to get a few shots of him for you.'

Chaing took the little cylinder of film from her. He looked at the corduroy jacket again: it was PSR issue, bulky to disguise the lump of the camera mechanism sewn in just behind the long broad collar. All the buttons were shiny black so as not to draw attention to the fact that the top button was actually a lens. The right-hand pocket contained the end of the shutter-release cable, allowing the wearer to take a photo without anyone seeing. 'If Caden is just managing girls at a club, he's not the top man. Do you know who he takes orders from?'

'Not really. But the name that keeps coming up is Roxwolf.'

'Roxwolf?' Chaing said scornfully. He knew the animals had been hunted out of the district over a millennium ago. They were nasty beasts, running in packs that would gang up on just about anything in the wild.

'Whatever. That's the name he goes by. He's Opole's biggest gang boss, by all accounts – has interests in every underground activity.'

'And where do I find him?'

'I don't know. Nobody does.'

'So how do they all get their instructions?'

'No idea. Could be Eliters linking privately.'

'Possible,' he mused. That ability to communicate unheard and unknown was one of the reasons the PSR mistrusted Eliters so badly. Somehow he couldn't imagine Eliters helping Fallers. But her comment was typical of PSR officers in the radical monitoring division, so he let it slide. 'Anything else?'

She gave him a cynical grin. 'You're hard to please.'

'I do my best.'

'There's a new girl in the Cannes, Noriah. Just a waitress for now, but she's a runaway like I'm supposed to be. Caden has started his getting-friendly routine with her. Normally he worms his way in, then puts the pressure on to force new girls upstairs if they're pretty enough. Noriah ran from her co-op farm. She fits the nobody-cares profile. Might be worth putting her under observation.'

'Right. Where's she staying?' He tried to think which officers he could request to watch Noriah. There were enough resources at the PSR office – once you'd gone through the paperwork to liberate them from their desks. Just the thought of that made him weary.

'The Mother Laura Hostel on Old Milton Street, same as me.'

'Is Caden showing an interest in you?'

'Don't worry about that. I can handle myself.'

I'm sure you can. 'What does Noriah look like?'

'Develop the film. You'll see.'

'Thank you. This is good work.'

'Be sure to write that on my report.' She got up and shrugged the jacket round her shoulders before walking out.

Chaing put the reel of film in an inside pocket on his own jacket, and zipped it up. If he took it back to the PSR office now, he could get it developed and printed inside an hour.

*

They came for Noriah two days later. Chaing was still setting up the surveillance operation. All he'd got after filling in a mound of forms was three extra officers in addition to Lieutenant Lurvri, his junior partner. It was ridiculous! You couldn't mount total coverage on someone with just five people.

'Find me useful intelligence, and I'll give you a bigger team,' Director Yaki had said simply when he'd gone up to her office to complain.

So he and Lurvri had spent the morning setting up a field office over a hardware shop in Old Milton Street that was opposite the Mother Laura Hostel. The family who held the shop's state enterprise licence cleared some space in their store room for the PSR officers, who sat on fold-up chairs by the grimy window, watching the hostel's entrance.

Noriah's photo was pinned up on the window frame, next to the camera with a long telephoto lens they'd aimed at the hostel's door. She was a slight girl who claimed she was fifteen, though Chaing had his doubts she was that old. Her thin face was almost lost in the centre of a massive frizzy ball of ebony hair.

According to Jenifa, her routine was a simple one. Noriah slept at the hostel until midday, then took a tram into town, sometimes with another girl from work; a couple of times it had been Jenifa. She had lunch at a cheap cafe, then took a look round stores before going back to the hostel to change for work. Another tram to the Gates, and she'd be in the Cannes Club by six. Her shift finished at four in the morning, when she took a tram back to Old Milton Street.

'Not much of a life, is it?' Lurvri said as they lugged their equipment cases up the stairs to the store room. 'What the hell did her parents do to her that she'd want this instead of the farm?'

Chaing shrugged. 'It's boring on a co-op farm. Kids want action and excitement. Always have.'

'I'd never let any of mine sink to this.'

Chaing suppressed any idea of commenting on Lurvri's parenting skills, or even on his relationships in general. Lurvri was an Opole local, fifty-seven years old, tall, with wiry limbs and a bald head – shaved meticulously twice a day. He was now on his third marriage, and had to support five children from the first two. His current wife had just given birth to their second, a boy. To be stuck at lieutenant at his age marked him as a by-the-book time server. Chaing had no problem with that; Lurvri wasn't particularly dynamic in his role, but he knew the city, knew everyone in the PSR office. He could even push things through its Uracus-begat bureaucracy. Best of all, he was never going to question Chaing's decisions or complain.

Just before midday a van drew up outside the squat brick edifice of the Mother Laura Hostel, its diesel engine growling. For a private individual to own a van on Bienvenido they needed to have a licensed enterprise that legitimately required one – something that involved hauling around a large quantity of goods. Even then, getting a purchase authorization from the county transport office was difficult, and normally involved an envelope stuffed with cash changing hands.

Chaing read the side of the van. 'Devora Fruit Nursery. Odd, there's no greengrocer on this street.'

'Never heard of them,' Lurvri said, writing it down in his notebook. 'I'll check it out.'

'Well, well, look who it's delivered,' Chaing said happily. The passenger door opened and Roscoe Caden got out. He was a sturdy man, wearing a brown jacket, his curly greying hair kept in place by a black leather cap. He looked both ways along Old Milton Street and went into the hostel.

'Let's go,' Chaing said, and snatched up the camera.

It was Lurvri who'd found them their transport in the PSR's garage: a small van similar to the one Caden was using, but older, a drab grey body with rusting edges. The city's water utility logo was painted on the doors. Chaing was more than satisfied – there were always dozens of them scuttling round the city's roads.

Lurvri drove; he knew the streets a lot better than Chaing. He had to adjust the choke as he kept turning the ignition key. The engine fired at the fifth go, then something made a terrible grinding sound.

'Crudding clutch,' Lurvri grunted, and pumped the pedal twice before shoving the gear lever forwards. The van crawled out of the alley and paused at the junction with Old Milton Street. They didn't have to wait long. Caden emerged from the hostel, his hand clamped round Noriah's arm. She didn't look scared; more like defeated, Chaing thought.

Caden opened the doors on the rear of the van, and got inside with Noriah. The doors were closed, and the Devora Fruit Nursery van drove off.

After another fight with the clutch, Lurvri started after them. The first few hundred metres were difficult. Apart from cyclists and a couple of tuk-tuks loaded up with boxes, there was no traffic on Old Milton Street. Then they were out into the wider, busier streets of the city centre, and more vans were driving, along with lorries and a river of tuk-tuks caught up in their eternal fist-shaking battle with cyclists, both of whom knew the right of way was theirs and theirs alone. Trams rattled along the centre of the wider streets, sparks flashing from their spindly pantographs overhead.

Lurvri kept back about fifty metres, surging forwards or dropping back depending on how many vehicles got between them.

Chaing searched the dashboard. 'Do we have a radio? We could do with some backup.'

'You're kidding, right? The transport manager got this van from the impound park. The sheriffs nabbed the utility guys using it to carry narnik wads around the city. It's not an official PSR vehicle.'

'Oh. Right.'

'Better for us. The gangs know all the official vans and cars in Opole, even the unmarked ones. They also monitor the sheriff radio bands.'

Chaing wanted to dispute that, but held his tongue. If Noriah was being taken to a nest, then it was likely Caden was a Faller. Having the PSR assault squad on call would be comforting.

'I don't think they know we're following,' Lurvri said. 'He's not trying any manoeuvres.'

They were heading north along Dunton Road, a duel carriageway lined with ulcca trees that would take them to the Yokon Bridge over the river Crisp. There were fewer bicycles here, and a lot more commercial vehicles – larger lorries hauling freight in and out of the warehouse district. The Devora Fruit Nursery van slotted in behind an empty coal lorry, and Lurvri stayed in the outer lane, keeping its tail lights in sight. Dunton Road curved round to run parallel with the railway tracks. Chaing could see the big marshalling yard up ahead, merging into the docks, whose tall iron cranes stood guard over the wharfs that extended for over three kilometres along the river.

Five hundred metres from the long stone arch bridge across the Crisp, the Devora Fruit Nursery van started indicating, and turned off onto a slip road. Lurvri followed it, receiving a series of sharp blasts from the lorry he swerved in front of.

They drove for another fifteen minutes along Fontaine Avenue, which ran parallel to the river, heading out of town. At first it led through an industrial district of big factories and long warehouses, even passing the fenced-off Opole Rocketry Plant where they manufactured vernier rocket engines for Silver Swords. It was a residential area next – acres of flat ground where the old buildings had been demolished, allowing the city council to build citizen tenement blocks. They were depressing concrete and brick cubes, fifteen storeys tall, marked by narrow balconies which wrapped round the whole structure. A dozen had already been built, with scaffolding for another five rising out of the dusty, rubble-strewn ground, but now abandoned and swamped by vegetation. Trees struggled to survive in the regimented parkland laid out between the aloof buildings.

As they entered the outskirts of Opole the houses grew larger. Walls began to line the road to shelter them from curious eyes, with gateways opening onto long driveways; none had gates any more. This was where the pre-Transition aristocrats and merchants used to live. Some families had managed to hang on to their ancestral homes providing they weren't too ostentatious, but the larger ones were deemed inappropriate for a single family and nationalized. They'd been divided up into apartments. Chaing caught glimpses of allotment strips covering the extensive gardens that surrounded the old houses.

'They're turning off,' Lurvri warned as they drove along Plamondon Avenue.

Up ahead, the Devora Fruit Nursery van was turning through a gateway.

'Keep going,' Chaing instructed.

They passed the entrance, which showed them a big old stone lodge. It looked dilapidated, with wisteria and roses swamping the walls and covering a good fraction of the roof. Windows, too, had been overgrown. The grounds were a wilderness of vines and lawns turned to meadow. A slate plaque on the stone gatepost read: Xander Manor.

'Okay, pull in to the next house,' Chaing said.

Lurvri turned up the next driveway. The villa facing them was small enough for the original family to retain ownership. A couple of children peered out of the sagging porch as the van pulled up in front of it.

'Right,' Chaing announced as he got out of the van. 'Let's find out what in Uracus is going on here.'

*

The seven-storey Opole PSR office was poised between an old bank and the County Guilds headquarters at the northern end of Broadstreet. It had an impressive stone facade that had blackened with city grime over the decades. Chaing considered that to be the most pleasant aspect of it. The windows were slim horizontal slits, protected by iron bars. While the front was stone, everything else was built from a drab grey-brown brick – floors, internal walls, arching ceilings, all of it, as if it was a building comprised entirely of cellars. Those thick solid walls soaked up sound, leaving it oddly quiet as you walked along the corridors with their caged electrical bulbs. That aspect was an architectural triumph considering the interrogations that went on in some of the specially equipped basement rooms.

However, Director Yaki's office on the seventh floor defied the general bleakness. The furniture was old-aristocrat style, with comfy leather wingback chairs, and a huge carved miroak desk that dated back centuries. Even her windows seemed to be wider than the others in the building.

Chaing stood in front of the desk, trying not to let himself be intimidated. Director Yaki herself was a tall woman, with her once-blonde hair now a lush silver-grey, and swept back from her forehead. The dark-pink scar on her face went from her right ear to the corner of her eye, then down to the mouth – a legacy of hand-to-hand combat with a Faller, so Lurvri had told Chaing, which she wore with more pride than any medal. When he arrived at Opole, Chaing had hoped her front-line experience would make her sympathetic to field operations – a hope that was rapidly dying.

'So a brothel owner moves his whores around?' Yaki said tonelessly. 'That's not PSR business.'

'Noriah isn't a whore. She's a waitress.'

'She's a waitress that they're pressuring to be a whore. So? It's not unique, sadly.'

'But this whole set-up, it's wrong.'

'Wrong how?'

'I talked to the Geale family – they live in the house next door to Xander Manor. They told me it's owned by the Elsdon family, who were wool mill owners pre-Transition. Slvasta's citizen-equity law changed all that. The state took possession of the mill and left them as managers. It didn't exactly incentivize the next generation, and most of them left. By the time the third generation came along, only the youngest daughter, Elyse, was interested in wool. She ran the old mill for a hundred and twenty years, until the Opole city council finally knocked it down twenty-eight years ago. The whole place was falling apart, and the looms were completely obsolete. Elyse was heartbroken. She became a classic recluse; she's barely left Xander Manor since. The Geales used to see her walking about on the grounds occasionally, but that's all. She's a hundred and ninety-seven now – if she's still alive.' Which he had his doubts about. Officially, the average lifespan for Bienvenido was around two hundred. Some lived longer, of course, though they tended to be Eliters. The Elsdon family wasn't on the PSR list of Eliter families.

Yaki nodded slowly. 'Infiltration?'

'Yes, I'm sure of it. Three years ago, the Elsdon family started to come back. Two supposed cousins, in their twenties, turned up to help look after the old matriarch and keep Xander Manor's title in the family. Or that's what they told the Geales.'

'Have the Geales seen Elyse in the last three years?'

'No, they have not. It's a classic nest set-up.'

'Uracus! All right, captain, what's your play?'

'We followed Caden back to the Cannes Club. Noriah wasn't in the van. So either Caden is being naive and thinks he's supplying young girls to the cousins for sex, or he's a Faller himself.'

'Nobody in that business is that naive,' Yaki said. 'Especially if the girls are never seen again.'

'Those are my thoughts as well, director.'

'Do you want to use the assault squad on Xander Manor?'

'Eventually, yes. But we need to know how big this is, how many there are in the nest. I want a proper team watching Caden, and another on Xander Manor. The Geales seemed to think one of the cousins, Valentin Murin, goes to Opole University.' The one word he wasn't going to mention in the director's office was apocalypse – which was just Eliter propaganda. That the government and PSR were actually useless at their job, and the Faller nests were expanding across Bienvenido, ready for the final genocidal assault. Every time the PSR uncovered a long-established nest, Chaing found himself disloyally wondering just how true it was.

'Crud! Are they snatching students as well?' Yaki asked.

'I don't know, but the university would make a good source of bodies. Kids drop out all the time and never tell their parents. The dean is supposed to monitor anyone leaving, just like all institutions, but I don't know vigilant they're being.'

'Same as the rest of Bienvenido,' Yaki said bitterly. 'They never think it's going to happen to them, and when it does they shout loud enough to be heard in the Ring, swearing it isn't their fault.'

'Typical.'

Yaki smiled, stretching her scar to a darker pink. 'I'll assign you two watcher teams. You'll have them by mid-morning tomorrow.'

'Thank you. Caden is my priority. The first team can follow him and report directly to Lurvri.'

'A duty that entails spending all night in a club. We shouldn't have any shortage of volunteers.'

'Yes. When the rest are allocated to me, they can watch Xander Manor. The Geales will cooperate.'

'Which team are you going to run?'

'The one watching Caden. But if you don't mind, I'd like to command it from here. I've got Lurvri and two of my team down in the basement, going through the Rolodexes to track down this Elsdon family, and find out if there actually are any cousins. And I want to talk to one of Major Gorlan's informants at the university, see if anyone there knows anything. When we send in the assault squad, they need to know how many and who the targets are.'

'What about Noriah?'

'I'm sorry. She's been in Xander Manor for four hours now. They've either eaten her or she's been eggsumed.'

Yaki gave him a sorrowful look and swung her chair round until it was facing the window. She had an excellent view along Broadstreet down to Ghalby Park, where tall weeping wanno trees encircled the central lake. 'Tough call.'

'Yes. But we have to look at the overall picture here.' It was the delicate way of saying it. If a nest had infiltrated Opole three years ago, that was a serious lapse of vigilance – one that was going to reflect badly on the PSR office when it came out – especially its director.

'All right,' she said. 'Keep me informed.'

*

Chaing took a tram around the Gates district to Opole's university. The campus sprawled across several acres in the middle of the city, a village in itself, composed of enormous ornate stone colleges accumulated over a millennium and a half, with turrets and halls and libraries and lecture theatres and residences donated by alumni keen to show off their wealth and charity. The grounds enclosing them resembled an exclusive parkland, with avenues of trees, and ponds, and statues.

Walking through it, Chaing thought how different it was to the rest of Opole. Here there was a sense of optimism, of looking to the future; even the colours and noises were enhanced somehow.

It was the students, of course, all of them seeming ridiculously young to his jaded gaze. They either smiled or looked intent as they milled around, inevitably laden with books and folders, or carrying elaborate shoulder bags. Groups sat on steps having earnest conversations, while others gathered around people reading out loud. Several impromptu ball games were underway, never lasting long before they were chased off by fierce college wardens in their scarlet and black uniforms.

Chaing headed for McKie College. At five hundred years old, the stone edifice was relatively new compared to the other buildings. There was a large paved area at the foot of one gable wall, below the central library's massive stained-glass window. Holat trees were planted around it, the long crimson and amber leaves spreading from their overhanging boughs creating a pleasant dapple over the wooden tables and benches set out on the slabs. Tea and coffee and cakes were served from a small wooden hut, invisible under a froth of climbing roses.

He spotted Corilla straight away. She was supposed to wait at the outdoor cafe for thirty minutes every day, and sure enough there she was by herself at one of the long tables, wearing a cheap baggy green sweater, with a hole in one elbow, scuffed black boots, and purple tights. Her jet-black hair was gathered into a side clump, which sprouted blue and red feathers. The informant was supposed to be wearing a hat with a red ribbon in it so a PSR control officer could identify her. None of the other girls in the cafe even had a hat. So it must be her.

'I can recommend Pinborough,' he said as he sat next to her. 'She's one of the best novelists Bienvenido has ever produced.'

Corilla looked up from her biology textbook, and flashed him a sullen expression – instantly reminding him of Jenifa's greeting. *What is it about covert meetings that makes everyone so grumpy?*

'Everyone says *Basement* is her best,' she recited.

'Pleased to meet you, Corilla. I'm Chaing. You'll be reporting to me for now.'

'Where's Gorlan?'

'Moved on to greater things.'

'On this planet?'

He couldn't reprimand Corilla; she was a reluctant PSR informant, not an officer. Major Gorlan, from the Eliter monitoring division, had offered her a deal when she applied to study physics at the university – guaranteed admission in return for divulging any radical activity on campus. As an Eliter, she would never normally get into a university, especially not to study physics.

'Probably not,' Chaing admitted.

'Well, you've wasted your time today, Officer Chaing. Nothing to report.'

'Good. And it's just Chaing. Don't risk blowing your cover with casual statements.'

She put her textbook down on the table. 'I don't get you people. Where does the paranoia come from? I mean, everyone complains about government. It's only natural. Don't tell me you think the People's Congress is doing a good job?'

He sighed. Eliters were always philosophers, and mostly angry ones at that; she was a genuine walking talking cliché. 'The Air Force clears Fallers from the sky, the regiments sweep them from the land, we pick up any nests that get through, and the Liberty astronauts are eliminating the Trees. I'd call that crudding good, wouldn't you?'

'That happens because we have to fight the Fallers. The only alternative is death. But I didn't mean them.'

'I know what you meant. But that strikes me as a very simplistic view.'

Corilla scowled and waved her hand dismissively. 'You prosper from the status quo, but the irony is your own actions are ridding us of Fallers. When they've gone, people will look round with new eyes. They won't like what they see. Mother Laura knew that.'

'I'm sure she did. But in the meantime I have a world to protect.'

'Well, still nothing to report, sir. Nobody planning to overthrow the People's Congress. Nobody plotting to sabotage the railways or blow up bridges, or cut off the city's water supply.'

'I don't care about that.'

Her hazel eyes narrowed suspiciously. 'Who the crud are you?'

'Not in the department that deals with political radicals, that's for sure.'

'A persecutor?' She was trying to sound defiant, but he could hear the worry in her voice.

'A what?'

'The PSR department that makes our lives a misery.'

'No. And that's not their name, either.'

'It's what they do,' she snapped back.

'You have to be monitored, that's all.'

'Why?'

'You're different. You're privileged, and privilege always leads to exploitation of the underclass.'

'Privileged? Us? That's a crudding joke. You have no idea what it's like, to be abused and shunned from the moment you're born, to be blamed for everything that goes wrong no matter what.'

'I don't blame you for anything.'

'Your kind always do. And then you wonder why we hate you.'

He didn't really have the time for this, but handling assets like Corilla in the past had taught him that appearing to tolerate their cause always got better results in the end. She was testing him, that was all, trying to find out how much of a Party man he was. 'There was good reason for Slvasta's Limiter Act,' he said. 'Eliters are a kind of aristocracy – no, not like the ones ruling Bienvenido in the Void, I admit – but your abilities set you apart. Above. Slvasta wanted a fair society. No one group could be allowed to take over again. If we hadn't been careful, you would have elevated yourselves into a new exclusive regime. Bethaneve was trying to do that – imagine that, Slvasta's own wife! We broke free of the Captain. Slvasta's revolution destroyed his dictatorship, and Democratic Unity is going to make damn sure nobody's going to replace it with another oligarchic regime.'

'Oh, get real,' she said. 'As soon as we're back in touch with the Commonwealth, every one of you will be begging to have Eliter genes.'

'Not me. I'm happy just the way I am.'

'Because you don't know any better! My macrocellular clusters have a hundred times the memory of your brain. I can communicate with others directly through a link. We can monitor our own health practically down to a cellular level. Eliter biology is liberating.'

'Yes, but it's your biology. You keep it for yourselves.'

'Set us free, give us the freedom to research genetics, and you can all share it with us. But no, because that's not the status quo. That would mean people having a say in power, in how their lives are run.'

Chaing sighed, suddenly weary of her. This argument was *so* old. 'I didn't come here for this.'

'So sorry. Was I getting uppity?'

'You were wrong about what I do for the regiment. I work for the Faller incursion division.'

'Then why are you here?'

'Because you may be able to help me. That is, if your ideals will permit you to help stop your fellow citizens from being eaten, or worse.'

Corilla's wide mouth lifted into a very sly smile. 'The enemy of my enemy is my friend.'

'What?'

'It means I am quite happy to help you with anything regarding Fallers.'

'Don't tell your . . . friends this, but I have reason to believe there's a nest in Opole.'

'Friends? You mean, *my type*? The filthy Eliters?'

He regarded her uncertainly. He hadn't quite expected an Eliter to be so hostile. She had confidence, too – also unusual. 'I mean anybody. We cannot afford a city-wide panic.'

'Yeah, I get it. Nice change for me to be on the side of the good guy *types* for once.'

'All right. Firstly, have you ever heard of Xander Manor? Has somebody mentioned it recently? Maybe a party being held there? Anything like that?'

'No. What is it, a club?'

'No, an old house on the edge of town. It may hold a nest. That's what I'm investigating.'

'First stage or a breeder?' she asked without hesitation.

'What?' he answered automatically.

'Is the nest made up of first-stage Fallers, or breeders?'

'I don't know what you're talking about,' he retorted automatically – standard PSR denial, slap down any mention hard and fast. Breeder Fallers, even more ferocious than ordinary Fallers, were another fiction the Eliters used to try and undermine confidence in government.

She quirked her lips. 'I thought you said Fallers are your speciality?'

'They are.' He got the uncomfortable impression she was trying to establish some kind of intellectual superiority. It wouldn't work, of course. *Typical Eliter mind game.*

'Well, you should know, or be briefed, that first-stage Fallers are the ones that emerge from the eggs. Breeders are the offspring of the first stage. They can be real brutes – or so I've heard. They'll lead the Faller Apocalypse, you'll see.'

'Stop it,' he said angrily. 'Nobody believes this pathetic propaganda.'

'Whose propaganda? The Fallers'? When did they ever get hold of a newspaper or a political platform?'

'They certainly seem to have infiltrated Eliter communication links,' he retorted sharply. 'Spreading mendacities like that can get you sent to the Pidrui mines.'

'You'll need more than one mine if you're going to round up everyone who knows about the breeders,' she muttered.

'You're not to repeat that. Understand? I won't have a PSR asset spreading sedition and damaging public morale.'

'But nobody knows I'm a PSR asset. It's not the kind of thing I can broadcast, now, is it? Face it, you'd throw me in prison for breaching state secrets if my fellow students didn't lynch me first.'

'Can we just get back to the point?' he said, alarmed at how he was losing control of the narrative. Assets, especially informers, weren't supposed to argue back.

'Sure.'

'Okay. Do you know Valentin Murin? He's registered as a

history and economics student here on campus. He lives at Xander Manor.'

'Again, no, I don't know him.'

'I'd like you to try and meet him. Find out who his friends are, if anyone he knew has left recently.'

'Crud, that's active undercover-agent work. I'm just supposed to betray radicals and their stupid notions of actual democracy!'

'Are you saying you won't do it?'

'No. I'm just pointing out what a good girl I'm being.'

'Noted. I also want to know—'

'Officially noted?'

'What?'

'Are you going to put that on my record? I could do with having a bit of credit from you people. You might even consider offering me some tolerance – although that's probably wishing for a miracle.'

'Yes, I'll put it on your record,' he grunted. 'Though I might put another entry on there about how everything is always an argument with you.'

Her grin was sardonic.

'Also,' he continued with some force, 'are there any missing persons on campus? Not students formally reported missing, but a rumour, perhaps, someone saying they've not seen a friend around for a while, and how odd that is?'

'That's easy enough. I'll keep alert for gossip.'

He nearly fell for it, nearly retorted to the not-quite-mockery. 'Good. You know your dead drop if you have urgent information?'

'I know my dead drop. I know my fallback dead drop. I know my contact time for this cafe. I know my cover-blown signal. I know my emergency telephone number. I even kept the midget camera Gorlan gave me. I'm still waiting for my secret-agent pen gun.'

'All right.' He stood up. 'Don't let me down. Don't let Bienvenido down. But be careful around Valentin Murin. Be very careful.'

She gave him a fast, derisive salute.

Chaing walked away, wondering how in the empty heavens

Gorlan had ever managed to get her to agree to being an informer. *I need to read her file. All of it.*

*

The PSR's records division belonged to Ashya Kukaida, a one-hundred-and-seventy-two-year-old who ruled the two extensive basement halls as if she was running a Void-era aristocrat's fiefdom. Office directors and department deputy-directors came and went, but Ashya Kukaida went on forever. Her phenomenal (natural) memory was the Opole office's greatest weapon in the fight against Faller incursions. Her obstinacy was legend, and the loyalty of her clerks fanatical. If you gained her disapproval, you had no future in the Opole PSR office. Any serious operation needed her cooperation to succeed.

Chaing knocked respectfully on her office door.

'Come,' she said.

Her office's brick walls were painted a gloss white. Double the usual number of caged bulbs were fitted to the arched ceiling, making it seem more like a solarium than an underground haunt. There was only one desk (also white), and one chair. She sat there in her usual grey suit and white blouse, her thinning hair arranged in a tight bun. Three middle-aged clerks in identical black suits were in attendance, holding files and boxes of photographs. The desktop had twenty-five photographs arranged in a neat square, which she was studying through her thick glasses.

'Colonel Kukaida.' Chaing gave a small bow.

'Ah yes, Captain Chaing.' She looked up from the photographs. 'You seem to have impressed Director Yaki. I was asked to prioritize your operation.'

'Yes, colonel. I believe a nest may have infiltrated Opole.'

'Well, of course you do. You're in the Faller incursion division; what else would you be investigating?'

'I am determined to expose and eliminate them.'

'I'm glad to hear it.'

'Could you please tell me if you know anything about the Elsdon family?'

'Let me see.' She drew a deep breath. 'Pre-Transition merchants, not true aristocrats like everyone thinks. You needed to have at least ten generations of wealth behind you to qualify for that. They were only on their third generation when we underwent the Great Transition. But they would have got there eventually. Their wool mills produced some exceptionally fine products. Half the houses in Opole will have one of their blankets on a bed somewhere. It was a shame the council shut down the mill.'

'Apparently it was out of date.'

'Age does not automatically imply obsolescence, captain.'

'No, colonel.' He finally saw the photos on the desk were the ones Jenifa had taken of Caden. 'That's one of my suspected Fallers. Do you recognize him?'

'We don't have a file on the gentleman in question, which is interesting. Normally someone in his profession will have encountered the sheriffs at some stage. Well, we do now. My clerks are contacting the City Registry to see if he's a native. A background will be compiled.'

'Thank you. Every detail will be helpful.'

Ashya Kukaida pushed her glasses back down and returned to the photographs. 'Lieutenant Lurvri is in the index office on the second level,' she said without looking up. 'I have assigned two clerks to assist your enquiries.'

Which was all Chaing really wanted to know. 'Thank you, colonel.'

Chaing made his way down the glass-walled central stairs. The record halls stretched out on every side, row after row of metal filing cabinets illuminated by stark electric bulbs hanging from the arched brick ceiling. Just looking at them made Chaing faintly depressed. The Opole office alone held over a million and a half files on citizens, and it was nowhere near the largest PSR office on the planet.

As he made his way to the second level's index office he found himself wondering how much of the information Corilla could hold in her macrocellular stores. Was a hundred times the memory of an ordinary brain enough to hold the files around him? Had she even been telling the truth about that? What if it was a thousand? Or ten thousand? He was fairly sure his memory, wonderful though it was, couldn't hold anything close to the stacks of information he was walking through. It was a shame. Having so much knowledge just a thought away would give him a phenom- enal advantage over the Fallers. For a start he wouldn't have to pander to the whims of a belligerent old woman who should have been retired decades ago.

The index office had floor-to-ceiling metal shelving which held hundreds of Rolodex drums. Ashya Kukaida had been true to her word. Two of the black-suited clerks were there, helping Lurvri – checking the Rolodexes for file numbers, then bringing the requisite folders to the table where he sat. They'd clearly had a busy afternoon. Files formed a half-metre tower beside Lurvri, their cardboard folders old and creased, faded to a uniform brown. The desk's anglepoise lamps cast a bright pool of light on the sheets of paper and old photos he was studying.

'What have you got?' Chaing asked, as he slid into a spare chair beside his partner.

'Elyse had two brothers and a sister,' Lurvri said, waving his hand over some of the files. 'The Geale family was right: they all left Opole. The sister went to Varlan, married a captain in the Marines. We don't know where the brothers went. I've sent out a priority-three request to other PSR offices to check residency regis- tration – which is a long shot, given they left damn near two hundred years ago. But I talked to the Opole city land and build- ings bureau. The so-called cousins, Valentin and Rashad, applied for an ownership-continuation certificate for Xander Manor three years ago. Their residency permits were issued by Gretz county.'

'Have you contacted the Gretz office?'

'Yes. Their records hall promised to get back to me before midday tomorrow.'

'Good work.' He signalled one of the clerks over. 'I want Opole's missing-persons statistics for the last fifteen years, and the files of everyone reported missing during the last three years.'

The clerk hesitated. 'The chief sheriff's office hasn't submitted their returns for the last six months.'

'Oh, for— Get me what you can now, and call the chief sheriff's office. I want their paperwork here by tomorrow morning.'

'Yes, captain.'

Chaing looked round. 'We're going to need a command office. This is too small.'

'Building management has the allocation forms,' Lurvri said.

'Yaki promised me more people.'

'Good!'

Chaing glanced out of the office's window. At the far end of the records hall aisle, jail-style metal bars protected the restricted files section. 'I want another file,' he told the clerk. 'An Eliter called Corilla. She's an active informant, handled by the political division.'

'Yes, captain.'

Lurvri was giving him a curious look. 'Problem?'

'I just want to know how reliable she is, that's all.'

'Right.' Lurvri lowered his head to study the spread of paper on the table, but not quick enough to hide the knowing smile elevating his lips.

Chaing let it go.

Within minutes the clerks had checked the Rolodexes and started bringing the files. Chaing was surprised by the number of missing persons – over twenty-five a year from the city alone. The county statistics were a lot higher. And this in a world where someone vanishing was always a cause for concern. Then, starting three years ago, the numbers had risen. 'Does no one ever check these?' he demanded.

'Statistics aren't terribly accurate predictors,' Lurvri said with a shrug.

'They're an ideal way to monitor possible nest activity.' He forced himself not to voice any more criticism in front of the clerks; no doubt a report of everything he said would be quietly delivered to Colonel Kukaida.

He was making notes on the locations people had gone missing from when Jenifa arrived, bursting through the index office door. She was out of breath, sweat beading on her face, blue cord jacket flapping open.

'What—?' began Chaing. For an undercover agent to break cover and turn up at the PSR office went against every operational rule.

'Something's happening,' she said urgently. 'I had to come.'

Chaing glanced at the clerks, who were watching attentively. He took Jenifa's arm and hustled her out of the office into the echoing cavern of the records hall. Lurvri followed, making sure no one else was within earshot.

'Did anyone see you come here?' Chaing asked.

'I was careful leaving the club. And I used the Warral Street entrance at the back of the store to get in here.'

'Okay, then. What's happened?'

'There were people in the Cannes Club tonight, a group of them. I marked five of them, maybe more.' Her hand juddered along her sweaty forehead. 'They were a team, I could see it. Really professional. They sat at three tables, which gave them full coverage of the club floor, ordered one drink and didn't drink it. They just watched the customers.'

'An observer team?'

'Yes, but they're not PSR. Caden talked to them. It was casual, like he was checking that they were having a good time, but that wasn't it. He knew them and they knew him.'

Chaing felt his throat muscles tighten. 'Fallers?'

'I think so, yes.'

'Uracus! How many of them are in this nest?'

'I don't know. But I managed to get some photos.'

'That was risky.' But even as he said it, he couldn't help admiring her. *If only everyone in the PSR had her guts and initiative.*

'I only got shots of two of them,' she said regretfully. 'They left before I could get them all. I had to be careful they didn't notice me. But, Chaing, they were following someone. A man. I've seen him in the Cannes Club before. He was by himself. Came in early, had a couple of drinks up near the stage, watched the girls for a few routines, then left. They went with him. Just like we'd do it – with two in front and three following. Next thing I know, Caden's gone, too.'

74

'Who was the target?'

'I don't know. He was well dressed, reasonable clothes, but nothing too flash. No one prominent.'

'You think they were waiting for him?'

'Yes, but it's weird. If all they need is a human for food or eggsumption, Caden can find them girls that no one cares about, so why risk a man who can fight back? And he must have a job; his office or workplace will notice him missing. It'll be reported.'

'Yeah, that doesn't make a lot of sense.' He was unnerved by the idea of Fallers having teams the same way the PSR had. 'We need to know who this man was, why he was important to them. I want you to work with the sketch artist, work up a likeness for me. Maybe Colonel Kukaida will recognize him.'

Jenifa grinned wryly and held up a roll of film. 'I can do you one better than a sketch. I got a shot of him.'

It was nine o'clock; most of the PSR office had gone home, leaving a small night shift working until breakfast. There was only one technician left in the photographic lab. Chaing took the roll of film there in person, and even went into the darkroom with him to watch it being developed. That way it was done quickly.

He stared at the glossy paper in the chemical tanks as the images slowly formed, willing the shadowy outlines to darken quicker. The dull crimson light from the solitary bulb overhead made the pictures curiously intense.

'I know him,' Chaing exclaimed as he pulled the first sheet from the liquid. 'That was the driver from this afternoon, the one who helped Caden take Noriah to Xander Manor.'

Jenifa pulled another sheet out. 'What about this one? He's the other watcher I snapped.'

'No.'

She pulled out the last photo, letting the reeking chemicals drip back into the tank. 'This one? He's the one they followed out of the club, the target.'

Chaing studied the man, almost disappointed by how ordinary he appeared – middle-aged, ebony skin with jowls just beginning. He was expecting some kind of feature that would make him understand why the Fallers wanted him. 'No,' he said in frustration. 'I want blow-ups of all three,' he told the photographic technician. 'Get them up to my office as fast as you can.'

Then, with Jenifa behind him, he knocked again on Colonel Kukaida's door, wishing he didn't feel so sheepish.

'Come.'

Only the photographs on the white desk were different. Kukaida hadn't moved, and the same clerks hovered in attendance.

'Sorry to bother you, colonel,' Chaing said, and held up the still-wet photograph of the Faller's target, 'but I was wondering if you know this man.'

Colonel Kukaida carefully cleared a space on her desk and studied the photo. Her glasses magnified the twitch of her eyebrows. 'I certainly do, Captain Chaing. This is Comrade Deneriov.'

The name meant nothing to Chaing. 'Who is he?'

'Deneriov is the general manager of the Opole Rocketry Plant.'

'Crudding Uracus!' He stared open-mouthed at an equally apprehensive Jenifa. 'They don't want food. They're after the factory.'

*

Chaing caught Jenifa giving his office a mildly disappointed appraisal as they hurried in. It made him realize just how small and shabby the room was for an officer of his rank (not that status or comfort should bother a PSR officer). The brick walls were painted a depressing grey-green. One of them had a big pinboard with a map of the city, and various photos of suspects from Chaing's five current operations. A lone high window looked out into the central courtyard, so even in daylight there was nothing to see but more walls with narrow barred windows. His desk was at an angle across a corner, while Lurvri's was crammed into the other side. None of the furniture matched, and one wall was lined with filing cabinets from different eras – all a disjointed legacy of careers that had been played out and absorbed by the bleak room.

Major Sorrell, the duty officer, was in there, waiting with Lurvri.

'We need the assault squad,' Chaing said immediately. 'We have to be ready to storm Xander Manor tonight.'

'I can put them on standby for you,' Sorrell said, 'but it's going to take a real emergency to authorize deployment.'

'A real emergency? How about Fallers sabotaging the rocketry plant?'

'Not a chance. There's no way a Faller could get past perimeter security. Our officers supervise the guards, and blood tests are compulsory for anyone going in. No exceptions.'

'The Fallers have captured Comrade Deneriov, the manager.'

Sorrell gave him a suspicious look. 'Have you confirmed that?'

The Bakelite phone on Chaing's desk started ringing, its red priority light flashing on the side.

'Corporal Jenifa saw him being followed by five suspected Fallers earlier this evening,' he told Sorrell.

'I need positive confirmation.'

Exasperated, Chaing picked up the phone. 'Yes?'

'Help me,' a frightened female voice said.

'What? Who is this?'

'It's me, Corilla. I need help.'

Chaing's back stiffened in surprise. 'What is it? What's happened?'

'They're here,' she whispered. 'They're at the campus looking for me.'

'Who are?'

Lurvri was frowning hard at him, wanting an explanation. Chaing waved him away.

'I don't know. There's three of them. They asked a friend about me. He warned me. I'm frightened. And, Chaing, they're using links to communicate with each other. We've picked up the transmissions.'

'So they're Eliters?'

'No. Their links are encrypted. It's something new, something different. We can't crack it.'

Chaing put his hand over the mouthpiece and turned to Sorrell. 'If Fallers eggsume an Eliter, do they have the same abilities?'

Sorrell gave him a blank stare. 'I've no idea. I've never heard of it.'

'They duplicate everything else,' Lurvri said.

'Except the human brain,' Jenifa said. 'Fallers have our organs, but their own neural structure.'

Chaing wanted the universe to slow down for a minute so he could make sense of it. There was too much happening. 'Corilla?'

'Yes.'

'I'm going to bring you in. Where are you?'

'I'm in a phone box on Rence Street.'

Chaing studied the map. 'That's too close to the university. Get out of there – now. I'll pick you up at the corner of Sedto Street and Frikal Alley in fifteen minutes. All right?'

'Just hurry. Please!'

The phone went dead.

'Who was that?' Sorrell demanded.

'An asset. She's in danger from Fallers.'

'Is this the same case?'

'I believe so, yes. Sir, this just got a whole lot bigger. We need to call in Director Yaki.'

'Yes.' Sorrell nodded slowly. 'Yes, I think we do.'

'I'm going to collect my asset. Lurvri, I want you at Deneriov's home. Confirm if he got back there tonight. Call it in as soon as you know anything.'

Lurvri shot a glance at Sorrell. 'Okay.'

'I'll come with you,' Jenifa said.

Chaing's automatic protest died before he could voice it. She looked so determined. 'Right.' He went over to the wall safe and took out a ten-millimetre pistol, along with a case of hollow-tip bullets – the same kind the PSR assault squad used in their carbines. He handed it to her. 'Here. You might need this.'

*

Chaing took a car from the underground garage, ignoring the transport manager's plea to sign for it.

'No time,' he barked, snatching the keys from a hook in the woman's cubicle.

The Cubar was a four-door saloon built at the Adice Motor

Industry factory. Its acceleration was notoriously sluggish, but the engine was reliable even in cold weather, and the squat metal bodywork sturdy enough to survive modest collisions. The government bought fleets of them.

It was raining when they emerged onto Broadstreet, a thin drizzle that created a lot of spray and degraded the tyres' grip. Chaing switched on the sirens and their blue flashing lights, driving as hard as he dared, forcing tuk-tuks out of his way. At least the weather had banished most of the city's cyclists.

'How could they know about her?' Jenifa asked, hands gripping the passenger seat as the Cubar slalomed across the road.

'I don't know. Maybe she asked the wrong person about Valentin Murin, or Xander Manor.'

She winced as he spun the wheel, dodging a couple crossing the street. 'I suppose. But that implies they're very well organized.'

'Yeah, it does. But they've been here for three years, and they're planning to sabotage or destroy the rocketry plant. You have to be organized to accomplish that.'

'They're organized, all right. Remember Kassell? They don't show any mercy, either.'

'I know.' The Kassel atrocity had been the PSR's lowest point. Sixty years ago, a nest of Fallers had managed to drive three trucks packed with explosives into the regiment's barracks for the Fireyear Day celebration ball. Over three hundred troops and support staff had died that day.

'So if they'd do that to troopers, what are they going to do to a factory that makes rocket engines for the Silver Sword?' she mused.

'What are you saying?'

'The Xander Manor nest has been established for three years that we know of. How much explosive can they put together in that time?'

He gripped the steering wheel tighter. 'Giu!'

They were four blocks out from Sedto Street when Chaing killed the lights and siren.

'Let me out,' Jenifa said. 'I'll cover you.'

It must have been her appearance, small and vulnerable looking; his immediate instinct was to protest. But she was a fully trained and qualified PSR officer. In fact, she was probably a lot more streetwise than him.

He braked at the top of Sedto Street and she hurried out, zipping her blue cord jacket against the miserable rain.

The wipers smeared water across the windscreen. This wasn't the best of the city's neighbourhoods. The streets were narrow, their timeworn buildings small and densely packed, but without the antique quirkiness of the Gates. This was where the poor sank to live their overlooked lives of no consequence. He drove along slowly, looking for the junction with Frikal Alley. The street lighting was inadequate, and his headlights struggled against the grey rain. A strange bass noise rose over the engine's low growl, thudding in the fast rhythm of an excited heart.

Chaing spotted the junction and pulled in just past it. He got out. The sound was music coming from an open club door that glowed red, as if its steps led down into a cave of lava. It was awful – the new electrically amplified guitars pounding out a fast beat that youngsters listened to these days. Further down Sedto Street, a group of youths loitered in another doorway, the glow of narnik pipes illuminating their faces in spectral shadows.

He unclipped the leather strap on his shoulder holster but didn't draw the pistol as he walked cautiously back towards Frikal Alley. He couldn't see Corilla anywhere.

Frikal Alley itself was a gulf of blackness as deep as the empty night sky. There were no street lights at all. A few glimmers came from windows that weren't properly shuttered, but that was all. He peered forwards, unpleasantly conscious of how he was presenting a clear silhouette to anyone in the alley.

His eyes adjusted quickly to the low light, revealing the outlines of walls and abandoned crates. Rubbish littered the uneven cobbles. Maybe this hadn't been the best place for a rendezvous.

'Corilla?' he said quietly. It was no use against the racket coming from the club. 'Corilla?' Louder this time.

A couple of the narnik youths looked his way.

Chaing took a few tentative steps down the alley. 'Are you there? Come on, let's go.'

Something moved up ahead – a black wraith emerging from the cover of a doorway.

'Corilla?'

The indistinct shape moved towards him.

'Chaing?'

He hadn't realized how tense he was until his shoulders sagged at the relief of hearing her voice. 'Yes. Come on. Hurry.'

His night-adapted eyes saw her nebulous shape resolve into a more solid outline as she quickened her pace. Then something else moved in the alley behind her – a smaller shape, lower to the ground, a liquid shadow flowing through the chilly drizzle. 'Who's that?' He tugged his pistol from its shoulder holster.

Beyond the spooky shape, a bright yellow muzzle flame flared. The pistol's discharge echoed down the narrow alley, overpowering the wretched music. Its muzzle flash illuminated Jenifa's intense face. She fired again, and again. Bullets whined as they ricocheted off walls.

Chaing shrank down instinctively, his own pistol waving round as it sought a target. He saw Corilla hit the cobbles, crying out in shock. And behind her, exposed by the flashes—

An animal, bigger than any terrestrial dog. Streamlined, brutal, its equine head half mouth, with sharp curving fangs. Powerful squat legs, ending in dark claws that could tear any human apart in seconds.

He managed a wordless shout of warning, trying to bring his pistol round. But though Jenifa had stopped shooting, his precious night vision was still impaired by the sharp flashes. He saw the creature jerk sideways as if it was bouncing, scooting up a low wall. There was a clatter of rubbish being dislodged. He shifted the pistol, lining directly onto the sound. Then glass shattered above the rubbish. The pistol went up. But there was nothing. No movement. No sounds.

Jenifa was running down the alley. 'Did you see that?'

'Yes.' Chaing hurried over to Corilla, who was curled up on the cobbles. 'Are you okay? Can you move?'

She let out a sob.

'Come on,' Jenifa snapped at the whimpering girl. 'We don't have time for this. Either get up or we leave you. Because we are out of here, *now.*'

Chaing bent down and grabbed the girl's shoulder. She half-cooperated as he pulled her up. She was groggy, swaying.

'Move!' he shouted.

The three of them came careering out of the alley. Chaing was swivelling round, trying to look in every direction at once. Trying to see if the creature was closing, ready to pounce. The narnik gang were standing perfectly still, staring at him.

'Get out of here,' he yelled. 'There's a . . . a roxwolf loose.'

They started jeering.

Chaing caught a slither of motion above – and froze. He scanned the roofline, his pistol in a two-handed grip, pointing up.

Nothing.

They ran for the Cubar. Jenifa and Corilla dived into the back seat and Chaing turned the ignition key, praying to Giu to smile on him just once this night. The wonderfully reliable engine caught immediately, and he slapped it into gear, shoving his foot down hard on the accelerator. The wheels spun, sending up small puffs of rubber smoke, and they lurched forwards.

'Is it there?' he yelled. 'Is it following?'

Jenifa was craning her neck, looking through the clouded rear window. 'I don't think so. I can't see anything.' Her pistol was held ready.

He slapped the switches for the siren and blue flashing lights. He shoved the gear stick into third, still accelerating. Sedto Street became a blur.

Corilla slowly sat up. 'Thank you.'

Chaing grunted in satisfaction. Despite it all, they'd done what they set out to do: save the asset. Score one for the PSR. 'You okay?'

'Crud, no! But I'm alive.'

He turned out of Sedto Street and eased off the accelerator slightly.

'We'll take you back to the office. You'll be safe there. I'll debrief you myself.'

'Safe from what?' Jenifa demanded angrily. 'What the crudding Uracus was that?'

'A roxwolf?' Chaing suggested. But he didn't believe it for a second.

'That's bollocks,' Jenifa retorted angrily. 'It was— Crud, I don't know what we saw, I was so hyped up. Could have been an Uracus-damned cat for all I know.'

'It was a breeder Faller,' Corilla said in a flat tone. 'That's what the bastards set on me.'

Jenifa gave her a sharp look. 'There's no such thing.'

Chaing glanced into the rear-view mirror. Corilla was staring right at him. He didn't say anything.

*

They made good time back to the PSR office.

'Take her to an interview room,' Chaing told Jenifa. 'She's not under arrest, but don't let her leave.'

'Got it, boss.'

'Chat to her, make friends, and keep the tape recorder running. I want to know everything she says.'

He found Major Sorrell in the command room – a grand name for a windowless room consisting of five desks with telephones, and two further desks with radios to talk to the PSR's mobile units. There was a bigger version of his office's city map on the wall behind them. He was surprised to see there were only three communication staff inside. *We'll need everybody at their stations to deploy the assault squad.*

The transport manager was just leaving the command room. She scowled at Chaing.

'What happened?' Sorrell asked. 'The sheriff patrol cars are reporting gunshots fired.'

'That was us,' Chaing said. He explained what had happened – what he'd seen.

'An animal?' Sorrell asked. 'What sort of animal?'

'I don't know. It was big.'

'So we don't know that the informant was being pursued by Fallers. You couldn't confirm that?'

Chaing felt his shoulders tensing up again. 'No, sir. But something was after her; that could not have been a coincidence. It wasn't any kind of natural Bienvenido animal. It had . . . purpose.' He couldn't quite bring himself to say *breeder Faller*, not here in the centre of the PSR office.

'I see.'

'I'd like to tell Director Yaki about the incident.'

'So would I, captain.' Sorrell gestured to one of the telephone operatives. 'But we haven't been able to get hold of her, yet. She seems to be between engagements.'

Chaing stared at him in astonishment. As director, Yaki was supposed to leave her itinerary with the command room so she could be contacted at any time, day or night. 'What about the assault squad?' he asked lamely.

'Right now they are officially on standby, but I've authorized their vehicles to be released. Major Borlog is their commander tonight. She's down in the armoury now.'

'Good. Thank you, sir. Has Lurvri checked in?'

Sorrell checked with one of the communication staff, who gave a small shake of her head.

Chaing frowned. 'But—' He looked at the big city map. Deneriov's flat on Veenar Avenue had a bright green pin stuck in it. 'Deneriov's residence is closer than Sedto Street; he should have been there a long time ago.'

Sorrell held up a clipboard, his index finger running down the entries. 'He confirmed his arrival at the address thirty-seven minutes ago.'

'And there's been nothing since?'

'No.'

'Sir, that's not right. Lurvri knows how urgent this is. All he had to do was see if Deneriov was at home. That's five minutes maximum.'

'He's one of us. He knows to radio for backup if there's any trouble.'

Chaing turned to the radio operator. 'Have the sheriff patrols reported any disturbance on Veenar Avenue?'

She lifted up her earpiece. 'No, sir.'

'Something's happened.' All Chaing could see was that weird savage creature moving with eerie grace, big mouth opening to expose those evil fangs. 'And we need to find out what.'

'Very well,' Sorrell said reluctantly. 'I'll order a sheriff patrol car to investigate.'

'No, sir! They're not equipped for this, and they're certainly not prepared. I'll go.'

*

He took the Cubar out again. This time he didn't use the siren or lights, but still drove fast. The rain was a lot heavier now. Even the tuk-tuks were off the roads, although the city's trams were still going, rattling down the centre of the major thoroughfares. The occasional car or truck passed, their headlights shimmering off the slick cobbles.

Chaing arrived at the address on Veenar Avenue eleven minutes after leaving the PSR office. He drew in behind a parked Cubar, and checked the number plate. It was the one Lurvri had signed out. The lights were off. Nobody was inside.

He pulled the radio microphone off its dashboard clip. 'This is car 37-B. Has my partner checked in yet?'

'Negative, car 37-B. No contact.'

Lurvri had been out of contact for almost an hour now. That was bad. Lurvri wasn't a man who took risks. 'Roger that. I'm at the address. Will contact you again in ten – one zero – minutes, no matter what.'

'Confirm received, car 37-B. Contact in ten minutes.'

Chaing glared at the radio as he slapped the microphone back onto its clip. *Confirm – my arse.*

There were no pedestrians on Veenar Avenue. Chaing stood on the pavement, taking his time as he surveyed the area, hunting for any sign of that unnatural beast. A tram trundled down the middle of the street, a disconnected row of bright yellow windows, revealing empty seats inside. Sparks scattered from the overhead cable as its pantograph crossed a junction.

He waited until it was gone before walking up to the broad doorway of a grand old apartment block. Deneriov lived on the second floor. The big lobby was all polished marble and ornate pillars, brightly lit by electric bulbs wired into the original chandeliers. There was no one behind the concierge desk, which was unusual for a well-to-do block like this. He walked across the tiles towards the stairs, leaving wet footprints as he went.

Deneriov's door was ajar. Chaing flattened himself against the wall at the side of it. No sound from within. He spun round, kicking the door open. Into the flat fast and low, identifying potential hostile locations, pistol held in front, moving smoothly from one threat point to another, just like he'd done in a hundred training exercises. Nobody there.

A low table had been overturned in the lounge. *Struggle?* He moved into Deneriov's study. It had been ransacked, papers strewn everywhere.

He jogged back out to the Cubar and plucked the microphone from its clip. 'This is car 37-B. There's been a fight at the flat. The opposition was here tonight. There's no sign of my partner. They must have taken him.'

'Do you have confirmation of that, car 37-B?'

'Oh, for Urac—' he grunted, then took a breath and pressed the microphone button. 'If he's been taken, we don't have much time. I am proceeding to the manor to verify. Request backup.'

'Negative, car 37-B. Duty officer will come to your location to assess the scene.'

'No time, control! I am proceeding to the manor. Request urgent backup!'

'Car 37-B, you do not have authoriza—'

'He's one of us. I'm going. Back me up!' Chaing switched the radio off, and pulled out from the kerb.

Anger made him a surprisingly calm driver. He was totally focused on getting there alive and quickly. Lurvri's life depended on that, so no risky charging across junctions, no reckless speeding on the rain-slicked road. Just *get there*.

It took nearly thirty minutes, which was a good time. The Fallers wouldn't have driven so fast, so he should have cut their lead down considerably. *Lurvri could still be alive. They'll want to know what we know. They'll ask – hard. But they won't kill him immediately.*

The siren and lights had been turned off for the last couple of kilometres. He drew up a hundred metres short of the gates leading to Xander Manor and hurried out. The rain soaked him within a minute. He took his jacket off; the wet cloth was just too restrictive. Reaction times were going to be critical. Fallers were a lot faster than humans; he'd seen that for himself both times he'd actually encountered them.

Streetlights on this road were few and far between. As before, his eyes adapted quickly to the darkness. Going through the gateway was out of the question, so he slung his jacket over the top of the unkempt nettlethorn hedge and scrambled over, cursing as the big spikes scratched his arms and legs.

Pistol held ready, safety catch off, he scurried across the wide unmown lawn to the big house beyond. Slim lines of light showed him windows that weren't entirely covered by curtains. Using them as a guide he worked out the shape of the house. There was one oddity, a light in some kind of annex. He crept towards it, and realized this was the stable block where the family's coach and horses would've been kept pre-Transition.

Chaing slowed his approach, always alert for the *thing* from Frikal Alley lurking somewhere in the gloomy grounds. The front of the stables boasted three big double doors. Light was spilling out from the one closest to the main house, which wasn't fully closed like the others. There was gravel under his boot soles now, but cushioned by moss and weeds so his feet were silent as he crept forwards.

His heart was hammering away fast in his chest. He could feel the adrenalin surge in his blood, chilling him, making it difficult to hold the pistol steady.

'Get a grip,' he whispered harshly, ashamed by how scared he was. *I should have waited for backup.*

Without warning tiny colourful stars were sparkling across his vision, yet strangely not interfering with what he saw. The breath caught in his mouth as he remembered exactly when he'd seen this phenomenon before. And – as before – the stars swarmed into a picture of *her*: the Warrior Angel. Exactly the same picture his five-year-old self had seen.

'Where are you?' a voice asked. It was a silent voice, speaking into his head.

Chaing spun round, his pistol trying to cover the whole world. There was nobody there, of course.

'Crudding Uracus!' he cursed under his ragged breath. *It's the pressure, it must be. Lurvri's life is on the line here.* He took a moment to quell his anger and fear. The phantom image of the Warrior Angel faded, and he walked unhesitatingly towards the stable.

There were no voices, no sign of movement in the fan of pale light that shone out across the mossy gravel. Chaing swivelled round the opening, presenting the smallest profile as he'd been trained – and his heart thudded, shock locking his muscles. The stable was a big open space, with a stone slab floor and empty wooden stalls at the back, illuminated by a single bare bulb hanging from a flex. And right in the middle was a Faller egg. He'd never seen one before; all the countryside sweeps he'd taken part in as a regimental conscript had been uneventful, and the times he'd encountered nests as a PSR officer, there had never been eggs involved.

Now he stood facing one, and it was exactly as the descriptions and photographs depicted it: a sphere three metres in diameter with a hard crinkled skin the colour of charcoal. It was eggsuming Comrade Deneriov.

Rule one in the Faller Institute manual was *never ever* touch the shell of a Faller egg. It responded to the slightest physical contact at a molecular level; skin stuck and adhered in an unbreakable bond. From that moment on, you had to be cut free. If your friends were quick enough, then you only lost a finger, or hand, or in the worst case an entire limb. For as soon as the adhesion process was triggered, the shell became permeable around the contact point, and began to drag the entire body inside.

Deneriov's naked body was too far gone for any rescue. He was being eggsumed sideways, so an arm, leg, and half of his torso were already inside. His head, too, was sinking below the shell, leaving just one eye and the corner of his mouth left outside as the shell slowly drew in more and more, a millimetre at a time. There was no expression on his remaining features, and his free limbs were hanging limply.

The parts of his body inside the egg were being broken down by the alien cells that made up the yolk. Once he was completely inside, those same cells that were consuming him would come together in a perfect replica of the lifeform they'd ensnared. But the only thing it shared with its original victim was form; its thoughts were pure Faller. And those thoughts were bent towards one thing – conquering whatever planet they had come to and making it their own.

Chaing didn't know how long he stared at the terrible scene. It was too late even to perform a mercy slaying. The yolk cells were already infiltrating Deneriov's brain, penetrating individual neurons. His memories were being extracted, drained away. He wasn't Deneriov any more. To shoot what was left of him would be to alert the nest.

There's only one egg, so where's Lurvri?

He slipped out of the barn and headed for the house. The front door was too obvious, so he tried one of the ground floor's sash windows. It opened a few centimetres, and he strained harder, forcing it upwards. Eventually it was wide enough for him to squeeze through.

The room inside was very dark, with a door outlined by thin cracks of light coming from the hallway beyond. He could see the shape of furniture – big chairs and sofas, a low table – and guessed at a lounge.

He paused by the door, but there was only silence. Pistol held ready, he turned the handle gingerly and opened it a fraction to peer out. The hallway was dilapidated, with faded wallpaper mouldering away, and dirt crowning every surface. The carpet was now a strip of furry grey grime, filling the air with a musty smell – and something more. He sniffed, not quite recognizing the scent.

Chaing pushed open the lounge door and walked slowly along the hall, pistol held rigidly out in front. One of the doors five metres ahead was open, with odd muffled sounds coming from within. He reached the door frame and knelt down to press his eye to the gap between the hinges. The instant lasted an eternity.

He knew the naked, dismembered corpse lying on the long dining table was Lurvri, because the vile beast from Frikal Alley chewing on his head hadn't yet bitten off every distinguishing feature. Caden was also in the room, along with another four Fallers, all of them feasting on chunks of limb.

No thought. No plan. Only pure rage.

Chaing burst into the room, shooting wildly. Two bullets caught the beast, punching it across the dining room. Blue blood squirted out of its gaping wounds. Then he swung the gun round, firing at Caden. A bullet caught his neck, blowing off a big chunk of flesh, sending blue blood splattering everywhere. The other Fallers roared in fury, jumping aside. Chaing tracked them, going for the nearest, his finger relentlessly pumping the trigger.

Then something slammed into his back with agonizing force, sending him flying. He thudded into a chair and tumbled to the floor. For a terrible second, he thought he'd been shot. But when he twisted his head round he saw a huge humanoid shape lumbering forwards from where it had been hidden behind the door. Blue-grey skin was stretched over impossibly bulging muscles. Its profile was the only remotely human thing about it. The head was clearly related to the beast, and it had six fat pincer claws on the end of each arm.

Chaing rolled desperately, trying to bring his pistol round. A foot stomped down on his wrist. Something snapped, and he screamed. He couldn't feel his fingers behind the hot pain.

'Mine,' the hulking humanoid creature grunted. It reached down, pincers flexing wide. The tips resembled horns.

Chaing wailed helplessly.

An explosion blew out half a wall, plunging the room into darkness as debris shattered the lights. Then the dreadful scene was lit by an electric-blue glare, as if every air molecule was fluorescing.

The Warrior Angel strode out of legend and in through the smouldering hole, surrounded by her own violet aurora. And she was just like she'd appeared in his vision. Silky Titian hair hanging down over her shoulders. Her sweet twenty-year-old face heavily freckled, wide-brimmed hat at a jaunty tilt. Long dark-brown leather coat flowing like a captured liquid.

Great Giu. She is *real.*

She raised her arm as if it was a weapon, and the air in front of her warped, emitting a dull *whoomp.* A purple-white flash smothered the room. And the giant Faller disintegrated, great globes of gore splatting outwards.

The Warrior Angel's splendorous blaze lashed out again. Then again. Again. Faller bodies ruptured violently, flinging steaming gobbets wide to coat the whole room in slick carrion.

Chaing was curled up in a foetal ball, trembling in shock. Finally, the awesome flares ended.

'Chaing?'

He tensed even tighter.

'Chaing, it's over. They're dead. The Fallers are dead. You're safe now.'

The words made no sense. *I can never be safe, not in this world, not any more.*

'Would you like a sedative? It'll help you cope.'

He risked looking up. The whole room glistened blue. Blood and tattered gore coated every surface. His shirt and trousers were saturated in warm, viscous Faller blood, as was his hair, his face. He held up dripping hands, staring at them numbly, then threw up.

'Easy there,' the Warrior Angel said. 'I know it's a shock, but you'll be okay.'

'What are you?' he managed to snivel.

'You know what I am, Chaing, you're the PSR, you know all about me.'

'Why did you haunt me? I was a child.'

'Haunt you? Don't flatter yourself, captain. I never even knew you existed before this week. As far as I know, tonight's the first time you linked to the general band.'

'Linked? I don't understand.'

'Okay, let's get blunt here. You have a Commonwealth Advancer heritage, Chaing. You're an Eliter.'

'No. No, I can't be!'

'Not fully, no. Genetic drift means your macrocellular clusters aren't integrated properly with your neural structure. But they're still there, in your head. Panic or fear put your brain into overload for a moment there, and your clusters went active – briefly.' She smiled, and it was enchanting. 'Lucky for you, huh? It allowed me to pinpoint your exact location.'

'You knew? You knew about the nest?'

'I knew there was one around here. Local Eliters have been monitoring their encrypted communication for a while. I've been in Opole for a few days, helping to track them down.'

'Why?'

'To protect the Liberty programme. There's a factory in town producing vernier rocket engines for the Silver Sword. I couldn't risk the nest damaging it.'

'You do this? You help us?'

'Of course. I promised Laura Brandt. Bienvenido needs protecting if we're ever going to grow into a society that can contact the Commonwealth. Sadly, your PSR isn't doing the best job defending us right now. You can help rectify that, Chaing. You can bring back some of the drive and determination the PSR has lost. You're a great officer, I'm sure, so climb the promotion ladder to where you have real influence and power. Help sweep away the dumb politics and prejudices that hinder the fight against Fallers.'

'Eliter sedition.'

She gave him a disappointed glance. 'That's a shame. I thought you were smarter than that. Look around you, Chaing. This world is decaying; human birth rates are in decline. The Fallers are expanding, and they're organizing to an alarming degree. You have to stop them. The Liberty programme alone can't save us, not now the Fallers are breeding down here. They're growing more dangerous, and the government is in denial about the apocalypse. You know it's all true. That ogre-thing nearly ate you tonight.'

'So breeder Fallers are real?' he murmured in defeat.

'Oh yes. Breeder Fallers don't have to copy the indigenous species like the eggs do; they can designate their offspring's physiology just like the old neuts and mods we had back in the Void. Don't your superiors tell you anything?'

'That's just—' In his head, Chaing could hear Corilla saying *whose propaganda?* 'We were told their existence was an Eliter lie,' he said, hating himself for being so weak.

'You might want to think about why you were told that.'

He looked up fearfully at her. 'I can't say these things.'

'No, but you can believe them. Right?'

'I . . .'

'Okay,' she said sorrowfully. 'Do what you have to, Chaing. But a word of advice. Some special political officers from Varlan will be debriefing you. Tell them I was here; don't hold that part back. Then agree to everything they order you to do. That way, they'll probably let you live.'

He watched the Warrior Angel turn away. Her disconcerting aurora shrank to nothing as she walked out through the blast hole, leaving him in pitch blackness. Somewhere in the distance, sirens were shrieking.

2

As custom dictated, the morning before his launch, pilot Major Ry Evine walked alone up the steep grassy slope to pay his respects to the grey stone statue of Comrade Demitri – the father of the Astronaut Regiment, chief designer of the Silver Sword rocket and Liberty spacecraft, and people's hero first class. The statue stood atop Arnice's Peak, a modest hillock that formed the tip of the promontory where Port Jamenk stretched along the steep inclines above the shoreline. Yigulls soared overhead as he walked, squealing loudly, their blue and white wings spread wide so they could ride the strong winds from the sea with minimal effort.

Ry reached the plinth of granite slabs that circled the statue, and took his cap off so he could perform the required solemn solitary deliberation, head bowed before Demitri, deep in thought and thanks. Even though the footpaths to the crown had been closed yesterday evening by the town authorities, he knew he wasn't really alone – there would be watchers from the People's Security Regiment. The PSR was always watching, always suspicious, always judging. Even him, with his prestigious family ancestry – a direct relation to Slvasta himself, no less. There was no aristocracy on Bienvenido any more, but he was about as close to the old concept as it was possible to be these days. It meant they'd watched him for all of his twenty-nine years, protectively at first, then with increasing interest as his flight drew near. He no longer cared; it was just another price to pay for being an astronaut, for being able *to slip the surly bonds of Bienvenido, and dance defiantly among the shining enemy.* Comrade Demitri himself had spoken that phrase the year he died, selflessly saving others from the horrific fuel-dump explosion.

He raised his head, and for once actually gave the statue a good look. The stone was old, over two hundred years now. Host to a cloak of dark lichen blooms, those slightly melancholic features – familiar from countless photos and coins – were badly weather-worn, while quallgull droppings adorned the head and shoulders. It was hardly the most noble of memorials, but he suspected that Comrade Demitri wouldn't have minded; he was supposedly a humble man, as the truly great always are.

'I won't fail you,' Ry promised softly. Then he put his cap back on and saluted before turning smartly and striding back down the path.

It was only a couple of hours after dawn, but the air was already muggy, making him sweat in his full dress uniform. Port Jamenk was thirty-five kilometres south of the equator on Lamaran's eastern coast. Built by the state, its core was a clutter of stone cottages bridging the saddle of land behind Arnice's Peak. Walls of thick granite blocks were painted white to help ward off the tropical heat, inset with broad shuttered arches to allow the air to flow, and they had roofs of red clay tiles crusted in sun-scorched yellow and green lichen. The cobbled roads were awkwardly narrow, roofed by vines and creepers that tangled around drainpipes and overhead power cables. They followed the inclines in zigzags and sharp curves, in contrast to the precise grids favoured by most of Bienvenido's post-Transition towns. But then Port Jamenk was an exception, born out of desperate necessity, its construction decreed by Prime Minister Slvasta himself, two hundred and fifty years ago. It housed the state engineers and regiment personnel who built and operated Cape Ingmar, Bienvenido's solitary rocket port. At first little more than dormitory barracks at the end of the new Eastern Equatorial railway line, it had grown over the centuries as the civilian population had expanded, their licensed enterprises slowly improving the comfort of the rocket port's workforce.

Ry looked across the jumble of rooftops as the severe sun burnt off the wisps of morning mist. Beyond the town, meadowland stretched back along the promontory, where broad fields contained flocks of goats and llamas and ostriches. Further west, where the promontory merged into the mainland, ramshackle banana and breadfruit plantations covered acres and acres of rumpled ground. They were about the only terrestrial crops that would grow in the poor flinty soil.

Beaches stretched along the bottom of the promontory's low cliffs, narrow strips of muddy grey sand where the water lapped gently – except for those times when Valatare was in conjunction. Then Bienvenido was subject to tides and hurricanes that the moonless planet had never known back in the Void.

A long curving stone harbour with a lighthouse on the far end had been built to protect the deep-water anchorage from those wild times. It had been built for the recovery fleet. Slvasta had commissioned nine big vessels capable of steaming across the Eastath Ocean in any weather so they could reach the splashdown sites, hauling the Liberty command modules out of the water and giving the victorious returning astronaut a well-deserved hero's welcome.

Today, there were only five ships. The oldest had been built seventy-eight years ago, and along with two other senior ships, it was anchored in the middle of the harbour, slowly rusting away. The three of them were mothballed, their fittings and cold engines constantly raided for spares by engineers to support the two operational ships.

General Delores, who commanded the Astronaut Regiment, assured her pilot corps that two was more than enough. These days, the return flight trajectory was known before launch, and re-entry was far more precise; there would always be a ship on station to pick them up. But talk around the astronaut mess was that five hours wasn't outside the norm, with some flights in the last decade waiting three days before a ship arrived.

Ry arrived at the fence at the bottom of Arnice's Peak. Pilot Major Anala Em Yulei was waiting by the gate, wearing her white

Astronaut Regiment dress uniform, chestnut hair tucked neatly into her cap. Her thin face was composed into a neutral expression, which her delicate features transformed to fierce disapproval. People who didn't know her often assumed she wore a permanent scowl. When she did smile, Ry always had to smile in tandem, because it was such a burst of cheeriness.

They'd known each other for years. Ry had left the cooperative farm in Cham county at eighteen to take a general engineering degree at Varlan University. From there he entered the Air Defence Force flight officer school where Anala was in the class above.

She was from a Gretz family, who before the revolution used to hold vast estates specializing in spice crops. That had all been nationalized by the state right after the Great Transition, but they got to keep the ancestral home and some farmland around it. She'd told him the big ancient building had been divided up into apartments where about fifteen branches of the family now lived. Despite all the institutional discrimination against her family legacy, they still had a strong tradition of regimental service. Anala joined up as soon as she finished her aeronautics degree.

After flight school they were posted to different squadrons – she back to Gretz, and he to Portlynn. Two years flying the new four-engine IA-509s on missions against Faller eggs had seen him notch up seven confirmed egg kills as testament to his piloting skill, before he applied to the Astronaut Academy – like every single pilot in the Air Defence Force always did.

Anala arrived at the academy as part of the same intake. Her small frame was always going to act in her favour, for the Astronaut Regiment didn't accept anyone over one metre seventy-five, and certainly nobody who weighed in above eighty kilos. Those were the limits for the command module. In his case some political pressure must have been brought to bear by Democratic Unity, who would have recognized the advantage from having someone related to Slvasta qualify as an astronaut.

They'd spent the next six years together in training, learning orbital mechanics, rocket systems engineering, electronics, atomic bomb design, physics, mathematics, astrogation, the entire layout

of the Liberty spaceship modules, and the nuclear missile operational margins – so much knowledge was crammed into his head
that, even with his phenomenal memory, he suspected his brain
must be leaking most of it away again. Then there was the physical
side of it: horrible survival training exercises on land and at sea,
punishing recurring medical evaluations, endless fitness workouts,
the divedown-upchuck flights in a modified transport plane to
familiarize them all with freefall, and the endless flight simulations
– most utterly boring, and the remainder so terrifyingly realistic
he'd thought more than once that he wouldn't get out alive.

All that they'd gone through together, enduring all the indignity and the strain and worry, the constant paranoid observation
by the PSR for loyalty to the Democratic Unity party. And all of
it endured because there, at the end, lay the greatest prize in the
world: *spaceflight*. Taking the fight against the Fallers up to the
Tree Ring. Six years of solid friendship, then last night they'd slept
together.

Astronauts got laid *a lot*. On a world as devoid of glamour as
Bienvenido, astronauts were more famous than even the prime
minister. Schoolkids collected playing cards of them, the news-
papers and cinema reels idolized them, and the whole planet kept
the Liberty tally against the Trees. They were all straight icons,
they were all gay icons – people just wanted them any way they
could get them, in fantasies or in the flesh. The astronaut office
had a whole building in Port Jamenk where two floors of clerks
did nothing else but deal with the fan mail from across the planet.

So six years of laughing together, travelling together, attending
parties, shared duties, covering each other's backs against the
training inspectors, total companionship, and then—

'I want to offer you a deal,' Anala had said in the middle of a
dance at his Commencing Countdown party yesterday evening.
They were swirling around gently as the band played old dance
tunes. Ry had been hoping for some of the newer faster songs that
were becoming fashionable in the cities, but this was Port Jamenk,
after all. 'I'll sleep with you tonight if you sleep with me on *my*
countdown night.'

It was a given for an astronaut to have someone (or more than one) sharing their bed the night before a launch. Officially eighty-nine per cent of missions returned – though if you actually did the maths, it was more like eighty per cent. Then there were the three per cent of rockets that didn't make it off the launch pad. And statistics about radiation damage to astronauts' bodies were never available outside of fearful whispers.

So nobody – not even the PSR – was going to object to astronauts spending their last night having plenty of sex.

Ry had enjoyed that particular benefit of his status during the tedious and numbing publicity and propaganda tours that the Astronaut Corps were sent on – speaking at factories, universities, town halls, Party rallies, and regiment headquarters right across the continent. Anala, he knew, wasn't as promiscuous, though she hadn't exactly been celibate.

'I . . . Me? Why?' he stammered in surprise.

'I'm going to want some human contact that night, same as everyone. I just don't want it to be some oaf I picked simply because he's got a hot body and a narnik bong.'

'You can choose anybody. You know that.'

'So can you.' She glanced pointedly round the hall, where there were a lot of amazingly pretty girls in very small dresses waiting impatiently round the dance floor. 'Most of these babes haven't even got a Port Jamenk permit; Giu alone knows how they got past security at the station.'

He grinned. Port Jamenk was a closed area, only open to state-approved residents and visitors. 'I guess our species can be just as determined as the Fallers.'

'Yeah. So?'

Ry didn't even have to think about it. 'I'd like that,' he said quietly.

She nuzzled up close. 'We don't have to have the sex, not if you don't want. I know a lot of astronauts are too tense, or drunk, or tired to actu—'

He kissed her. 'Oh, yes, we do.'

Anala opened the gate in the fence and saluted. Ry grinned

back at her. When he woke up that morning there'd been a moment when he worried that they'd be self-conscious around each other, that too much had changed. But actually being with a friend – someone who understood – on countdown night had been perfect. It didn't hurt that six years of intense physical training had made them as fit as marathon athletes, either.

'Respects paid, major?' she asked in a formal voice.

Ry glanced at the escort group around her. Three astronaut trainees from their own squad, two medical technicians, five reporters, two newsfilm camera operators, and Colonel Eades, a three-flight veteran. An experienced astronaut always mentored a rookie on their first flight.

'Indeed.' He looked back up at the grey statue. 'I think our father Demitri is smiling upon this launch.'

The group walked through Port Jamenk's convoluted streets to the town's small railway station. Bunting from the Fireyear celebration was still strung over the main street. There were few people about, though some had made the effort to gather along the route to quietly wish him luck. Fishermen on the way to their state-licensed boats stopped and applauded. When he looked out across the harbour, both the recovery ships were steaming away towards the horizon. He didn't say anything, but knew all the astronauts were thinking the same thing. *At least they both made it out of the harbour.*

The train in the station had a single passenger carriage – the same one that took Comrade Reshard, Bienvenido's first astronaut, on his momentous journey to the launch pad for the Liberty 1 flight. It had been refurbished many times so that it remained operational. Astronauts could be a conservative, superstitious bunch.

In the carriage it was just Ry, Anala, Colonel Eades and the medical techs. Ry sat down in Reshard's chair and took his uniform jacket off. The techs immediately wrapped a rubber cuff round his arm and took his blood pressure. A thermometer was stuck in his mouth. He was given a small bottle and told to give them a sample as soon as he could.

'I trust you didn't overdo it last night,' the colonel said.

100

'No, sir.'

Anala was staring solidly out of the window as the steam engine let out a whistle, and the pistons started to pump. The train pulled away from the platform.

'Good man. Glad you haven't forgotten your duty. Bienvenido comes before any personal indulgence. There'll be plenty of time for that when you come back. Giu, I remember my triumph parades. If you thought the girls were enthusiastic last night, you ain't seen nothing yet.' He slapped Ry's leg.

Ry gave Eades an embarrassed smile.

The train rattled along the track to Cape Ingmar, a raised stone-walled embankment that ran parallel to the coast a couple of kilometres inland. Outside, the ground was mainly jugobush swamp that had an ever-shifting boundary with the sea as gritty silt and vigorous fronds constantly pushed outwards, only to be washed back again. There were no settlements here; this land was too difficult to ever tame and farm. Nor were there any fishing villages. The swamp covered river inlets and possible harbours.

The only sign of life was a village of Vatni huts – long cylinders woven from dried jugobush branches, looking like some kind of exposed tunnel network. The aliens from Aqueous had slowly spread their family enclaves along Lamaran's coastlines since their arrival two and a half centuries ago, during the brief time Laura Brandt had opened a wormhole to their world. Some people muttered about their expanding population being as bad as a Faller incursion. Ry knew that was stupid paranoia. They were semi-aquatic; they didn't covet land. Besides, it was Slvasta himself who had negotiated the deal, allowing them new settlements on Bienvenido in exchange for protection. They had become invaluable in guarding the coastal waters from Marine-Fallers. Eggs Fell constantly into Bienvenido's oceans, where they eggsumed larger, more aggressive species of fish. Crewing a trawler, and even some of the smaller commercial boats, was a hazardous profession. Since the Vatni arrived and began patrolling along the coast, that risk had reduced considerably.

To the west, the imposing Salalsav mountains rose out of the horizon, snow sparkling on their upper slopes. The high range shielded the Desert of Bone from the clouds coming in off the ocean. Not even the post-Transition conjunction storms could break through their guard. Rain hadn't fallen on that desert for thousands of years.

Looking at the jagged pinnacles, he thought of his brief time on the edge of the desert. Astronauts underwent two weeks of desert survival training just in case they came down in one. After- wards, Ry decided he'd prefer a leaking command module adrift in the ocean to that.

The train whistled again as the raised track began to follow the coastal curve eastwards and start up a shallow incline. Ry and Anala stared out of the window. Cape Ingmar was a sight Ry knew he could never possibly tire of. The Cape itself was an oval of land protruding out from the low swamps, like a plateau that had never managed to rise more than thirty metres up from sea level. But its hundred and ninety square kilometres of scrub wasteland just south of the equator made it the perfect launch site.

The five assembly buildings occupied the neck of the Cape – massive metal hangars painted white to reflect the heat, with huge electrical air cooler boxes along the walls. A clutter of administra- tion and engineering buildings, equally white with silvered windows, were huddled in their shadow. The flight control centre out in front was a three-storey cylinder of white marble, topped by big radar dishes, and smaller radio aerial towers. The two base- ment levels were full of electrical computators that would guide his Liberty spacecraft up to the Tree ring, and back again.

Dominating the eastern side of the rocket port were the eight launch pads: big circles of concrete surrounding the deep blast pits, smothered in iron gantries. Seven of them were currently inactive, the gantry towers lying horizontally on their support columns as they underwent routine maintenance and refurbish- ment. But the eighth—

Ry couldn't help the sigh of satisfaction as he saw the Silver Sword rocket standing proud against the burning azure sky. It stood fifty metres high, including the escape rocket at the top. The four first-stage boosters were matt grey, clustering round the core stage. The third stage was a three-metre-diameter cylinder standing on a simple truss segment above the core, its insulation foam snow white, protecting the cryogenic propellant tanks from the brutal sunlight. (Even then, the rocket was only ever fuelled at night when the air was cooler.) Above that was the silver shroud, its aerodynamic segments encasing the Liberty spacecraft he was going to be riding tomorrow. Perched on top of the shroud was the spindly solid-fuel escape rocket.

Most of the Silver Sword was obscured by the four gantry towers that had levered up to clamp the fuselage and connect it to dozens of umbilical lines and fuel pipes. Hydraulic access platforms were extended all the way up, and he could see technicians crouched beside inspection hatches, running final tests.

'Now that is something beautiful,' Ry murmured.

'Certainly is,' Anala agreed. 'And it's all yours.'

'You get the next one.' Pilot assignments were made fifteen flights in advance, allowing mission-specific training.

'Six weeks,' she replied wistfully. 'It's going to seem like forever.'

The train pulled up at Cape Ingmar's solitary passenger platform. General Delores was waiting under the awning, heading the welcome committee of more officers and flight-veteran astronauts, several People's Congress representatives, more reporters, more photographers, and more newsfilm cameras. Ry put his jacket and cap back on, let Anala straighten them, and gave her a quick kiss when Eades wasn't looking. 'I don't want to wait six weeks,' he said.

Her grin was enigmatic, but promising. 'Me neither. So make sure you come back.'

'Deal.'

The carriage door opened. Ry stepped out and saluted the general amid the clicking of cameras and loud applause. The general formally presented him his mission badge – a platinum Liberty craft with a C-curve of exhaust wrapping round the planet, number two-six-seven-three.

With 2,672 Liberty missions already completed over the last two hundred and fifty years, the launch procedure at Cape Ingmar was now utterly rigid. There were no variables, no unknowns, no deviation from the long checklist.

Once his mission badge was pinned onto his uniform, Pilot Major Ry Evine became a piece of Cape Ingmar's property, a component to be inserted into the Silver Sword rocket when tests and preparations had been completed satisfactorily. There was the final mission briefing, hourly reports on the Silver Sword status, two hours of preflight medical checks, the formal handover of the bomb codes, and studying of the weather reports for tomorrow morning.

When dusk fell he went out onto the roof of the flight centre, where a small telescope had been set up. Trees of the Ring glimmered silver-white along their orbit, fifty thousand kilometres above Bienvenido. Laura Brandt had claimed they looked like stars in the Commonwealth galaxy, where they'd all come from originally. He looked through the eyepiece at his target, Tree 3,788-D. It hung just above the western horizon, magnified by the telescope to a small line of sparkling brilliance, with a hint of colour in its radiance.

'I'm coming for you, fucker,' he promised it.

He ate his last meal in the astronaut suite on the second floor of the flight centre: fillet steak, sautéed potatoes, grilled tomatoes, tolberry sauce. Chocolate ice cream with cherry sauce for pudding. Half a litre of water – no alcohol this close to the mission. Eades and Anala were his table companions. Talk was all trivia. One last weather report, predicting minimal wind at dawn. Silver Sword progress reports. At six thirty, the third-stage tanks were being chilled ready for fuelling with liquid hydrogen and oxygen. First- and core-stage fuelling was scheduled to commence in eighty minutes.

Six fifty: he changed into pyjamas and entered the bedroom. Lights out, seven o'clock – authenticated by Colonel Eades, who flicked the switch and shut the door.

Some veterans told the trainees they couldn't sleep. Others claimed they were so tired by the preflight procedures and their Commencing Countdown festivities they even asked to go to bed early. Ry lay on the bed, staring at the ceiling, convinced he was going to be an awake-all-night guy. There was so much running through his mind, the flight manuals flipping up behind closed eyelids, reviewing everything. Then they faded away to be replaced by Anala – her touch, her warmth, her lithe body writhing energetically against him. He wished there could be an exception about being alone tonight. And if anyone was going to break regulations and sneak in, it would be Anala. But the door remained closed. It was going to be a long night—

Colonel Eades opened the door and switched the light on at three o'clock precisely.

'Flight control has issued a pilot ingress go,' he announced.

Cape Ingmar's chief medical officer was waiting. Ry extended his hand, and the doctor jabbed his thumb with a needle. A drop of blood welled up.

'Confirmed red,' the doctor reported officially. 'Pilot Major Ry Evine is human.' He smiled. 'Good luck, major.'

Fallers had a dark-blue blood. There'd never been an attempt by a nest to hijack a Liberty flight in the two hundred and fifty years of the programme, and General Delores was determined there wouldn't be one on her watch.

Breakfast. Yogurt, then bacon, eggs, toast. Orange juice. Colonel Matej, the mission controller – a five-flight veteran and living legend to the Astronaut Corps – came in for his briefing. The fuelling had been completed during the night; all they were doing now was topping up the tanks. Tracking and communication stations around the planet were on line. The recovery ships had reached the splashdown zone, two hundred kilometres east of Cape Ingmar. Weather planes were up, reporting excellent conditions. Two Falls were in progress, neither of which would come close to his projected orbit.

Down a floor to the suit room. The indignity of the fluid waste disposal tube, its tight rubber cap squeezing his cock, bladder sac strapped to his right thigh. Further indignity of the solid-waste absorber pants – basically an adult nappy. Medical electrodes were stuck to his chest, a thermometer strapped into his armpit. Then they dressed him in a bright-blue one-piece cotton garment. Over that came the silver pressure suit. Tight gloves. Big bowl helmet, clicked into the metal ring round his neck. Thick flexible air tubes were plugged into the sockets on his chest, leading to a suitcase-sized personal environment module – carried by Colonel Eades as he walked out of the door.

People were lining the corridor, applauding. Camera flashbulbs going off. Outside doors opening. The transfer van. Drive to the pad. Rocket and gantries illuminated against the dark predawn sky by powerful arc lights. Ride up the gantry in a cage lift. No nerves. Not yet. Just eagerness. And pride.

Five flight engineers were grinning in welcome. They were used to this. It was nothing special to them, just another spaceflight. Open hatch in the shroud, exposing the smaller circular command module hatch. Ingress: an incredibly difficult gymnastic manoeuvre while wearing the pressure suit, holding the rail and wiggling in horizontally. But then he was snug in the acceleration couch, looking up at a console wall that was all switches and dials and the orange glow of Nixie tube numbers.

The inside of the command module was a simple hemisphere two and a half metres in diameter at the base, most of which was taken up by the controls, instruments, and various lockers. When the Liberty was in freefall, he would have just over two and a half cubic metres of space to move around it. On the ground it was like wearing a coffin, especially for him: one metre eighty-one tall, and eighty-four kilos. This capsule had to have customized fittings, and not even those could mitigate the way his legs were bent up to accommodate his height.

The engineers plugged his air tubes into the command module environmental circuit. Colonel Eades reached in and gave his hand a quick, firm shake.

Ry switched on the com circuit.

'Good morning, Liberty two-six-seven-three,' Anala's voice said in his earphones.

'Good morning, flight com,' Ry replied with a smile. It was comforting to have her as his flight com, and not just because of what had happened between them. Flight com was always the astronaut scheduled for the next flight – the intense shared training over the previous months helped them become familiar with each other, reducing the chance of misunderstanding.

He scanned the console, checking the lights and dials. 'Ready to commence pre-launch checklist.'

'Roger that. The flight controller has given a go for hatch closure.'

A hand slapped his helmet, then the hatch shut.

Ninety minutes spent confirming instrument data, putting switches in the correct position, watching the Liberty systems stabilize. Dawn light started to shine in through the tiny hatch port behind his head.

He became the machine he'd been trained to be: a piloting mechanism. Observing and responding correctly as the tanks were pressurized, the umbilicals withdrawn. Gantry retraction. First-stage booster motors' turbine ignition. Not even when all twenty rocket motors of the boosters and core stage ignited simultaneously did he take a second out from the procedures.

Liberty mission 2,673 lifted smoothly from the pad as the rocket engines burned four hundred kilograms of liquid oxygen and eleven hundred kilograms of highly refined kerosene every second, delivering a combined thrust of four and a half thousand kilonewtons. Acceleration in the command module reached four gees, shoving Ry down hard into the couch. The instrument console blurred from the vibration and he couldn't read anything; he just gritted his teeth and concentrated on trying to breathe.

Booster separation came at a hundred and twenty seconds – a judder that made him yell half in fright, half in delight. Now he started to relax and take in the experience. Thirty seconds later the Liberty shroud split apart, and the segments peeled away from the spaceship amid a vigorous shaking. The guidance computator steered the core's four small vernier rockets, keeping the trajectory steady, and the Silver Sword continued to power upwards for a further hundred and forty seconds until the core stage was exhausted, and the third stage ignited. The hydrogen–oxygen rocket produced two hundred and fifty kilonewtons and burned for a further two hundred and seventy seconds, putting the Liberty into orbit two hundred and twenty-five kilometres above Bienvenido.

Ry Evine finally got to experience real freefall, not just the twenty-second interludes delivered by the divedown-upchuck flights. When he confirmed the Liberty's systems were all fully operational, he took his helmet off and loosened the acceleration couch's straps and looked out of the larger port that had been covered by the shroud. The crescent of the planet glowed brightly below. Ry flicked the safety guards off the Reaction Control System (RCS) joystick, confirmed the system readiness, and tipped the joystick slightly. The Liberty began to roll, responding just like it did in the training simulations. With the third stage still attached it was sluggish, but he turned it so the port on his right was aligned on Bienvenido, all the while checking the spherical attitude indicator as he stabilized the spaceship.

Now he could look down directly. An astonishing amount of glaring white cloud was smeared across the planet. The Eastath Ocean was a deep enticing blue, and so smooth; some astronauts claimed they could see individual waves. The Liberty approached Fanrith's western coast and Ry grinned at the coastal outline – silly thought, that it was just like all the maps. He was surprised by how brown the land appeared; this section of Fanrith had plenty of tropical vegetation. He caught sight of rivers, silver veins slicing across the land. At least they were surrounded by the darker hues of vegetation. Further east was the central desert. He touched two gloved fingers to his forehead in a respectful salute. So many Air Defence Force crews had died defending Bienvenido that day the Prime invaded – thirty-nine planes just from the Portlynn squadron he'd served with during his Air Force duty.

A light on the communication section of the console turned from amber to green as the spaceship came in range of the tracking station on the west coast of the Aflar Peninsula.

'Do you copy, Liberty two-six-seven-three?' Anala asked.

'Roger that, flight com, communication link operational. Good to hear you again.'

'Stand by for course tracking data.'

Radar stations across Lamaran locked on to the spaceship as it orbited, checking course and velocity with meticulous precision – data which he fed into the tiny onboard guidance computator. He had completed a full orbit, passing over Cape Ingmar again, when flight com gave him a go for the apogee kick burn. He checked the Liberty's orientation, correcting its attitude with a series of RCS burns. Then when he was stable and aligned, the guidance computator took over. Numbers blurred in its display row of seven Nixie tubes, counting him down. The ullage rockets fired first – small solid rocket engines around the base of the third stage, pushing the liquid fuel to the bottom of the tanks where the turbopumps could suck it in. Then the main rocket took over, firing for a hundred and thirty-five seconds, thrusting the Liberty up away from Bienvenido.

The third stage shut down and separated. Ry fired the service module engines, moving the Liberty away from its spent third stage.

Flight com confirmed his course track was good. Liberty 2,673 was in a highly elliptical orbit, on its way up to the Ring, fifty thousand kilometres above Bienvenido.

It took a long time to take his pressure suit off, banging elbows and knees against the capsule's equipment and console as he struggled, but eventually he stowed it in the locker. And he finally had a few moments to himself.

Everyone called it freefall, but to Ry it was *flying*, pure and simple. He didn't even feel nauseous. Instead, he felt unshackled, as if space was where he'd been born to live. And through the main port, beautiful Bienvenido was visibly growing smaller as the Liberty rose further and further away on an elliptical orbit which would peak at the Ring.

Flight com asked for updates on systems. With a sigh he strapped himself loosely into the acceleration couch and began to run through another checklist. He had to establish a thermal roll, setting the Liberty rotating around its long axis, so that the heat from the sun was evenly distributed. The sextant was used to confirm the position of the other planets and fed into the guidance computator to check his position. Then he sighted the crosshairs on Tree 3,788-D. Flight time to bomb release was verified at seventeen hours, nineteen minutes.

Food had no taste; veteran astronauts had warned him about that. Fluid was pooling in his head as if he had a cold. His fingers swelled up until they resembled sausages. Systems whirred and buzzed loudly. Thick sunbeams stabbed through the ports, moving across the cabin like bizarre clock hands as the Liberty continued its stately thermal roll. Ry didn't care. Out there beyond the port, Bienvenido dominated space. And the other planets glimmered excitingly. The blue jewel of Aqueous, the closest world to Bienvenido, sharing the same orbit but trailing by seventeen million kilometres. Weird Trüb, sliding along its orbit fourteen million kilometres closer to the G1 star, its elegant necklace of twelve moonlets glinting against the infinite black. Valatare, the cool, shining rose-coloured giant in its outer orbit. And hated Ursell, whose murky atmosphere was now over a thousand kilometres thick; its tenuous upper layers toyed with the sunlight to crown it with an oddly beautiful haze that extended for hundreds of kilometres further still.

Ry spent every spare second staring at the planets, tying to visualize the day Bienvenido would finally be free of the Trees and their vile Faller spawn. A future without fear of aliens, where spacecraft would fly across the gulf between worlds, and astronauts would land on those exotic planets. He allowed himself to believe he might live to exist in those times. Slvasta, in his historic speech after the Prime invasion was defeated, had declared that they could rid Bienvenido of Trees within three human lifetimes. Most people could live past two hundred years, and there were only three thousand two hundred and twenty-three Trees left in the Ring. If they could increase their launch rate to fifteen or twenty a year, the Ring would be gone and the skies open before Ry passed his two-hundredth birthday. It was a pleasant daydream to carry him along to apogee. But the factories were going flat out to meet current Silver Sword and Liberty delivery schedules, and the current defence budget was a huge economic strain on the whole world.

Three hours from apogee, when Liberty 2,673 would reach the top of its elliptical orbit, flight com told him to start activating the bomb carrier missile.

Ry pulled his head back from the sextant. 'Roger that, flight com. I'll pull the manual out.' The sextant folded back neatly into its storage position. He'd been examining Tree 3,788-D with the device on full magnification. Trees were usually about eleven kilometres long, with little variance: slender spires of crystal with a tip at one end always pointing planetwards, while the other flared out into a broad bulb over a kilometre wide. Their surface was made from deep folds and wrinkles in the crystal, which hosted slow blooms of moire light that slithered along their length in random surges.

Laura Brandt said Captain Cornelius's ship had estimated up to thirty thousand Trees in the Forest that hung above Bienvenido back in the Void. Nigel Sheldon had destroyed about twenty-four thousand when he set off the quantumbuster in the centre of the Forest – collateral damage to the distortion applied to the fabric of the Void. After the Great Transition, the surviving Trees had dispersed into the Ring, using what Laura said was some kind of gravity-manipulation propulsion, like that of the Skylords, left behind in the Void. Some of them had taken longer than others. The newly formed Space Vigilance Office had catalogued their movements, then started to observe them closely with telescopes and Bienvenido's newly built radars. They kept a file on every Tree, classifying them into two distinct types: S for standard, and D for damaged.

First-flight astronauts were always assigned to D Trees, as they were usually easier targets. 3,788-D was short, barely nine kilometres long, indicating a good two kilometres had broken off during the quantumbuster blast. Broad sections of it were permanently dark. The Space Vigilance Office had only recorded it releasing seventy-eight Faller eggs in two hundred and fifty years – well below average.

According to the sextant observations, it wasn't moving. *Not yet, anyway*, Ry corrected himself. That made the mission so much easier. Trees inevitably moved when the missiles got close.

Ry unlocked the console's missile section and took the thick manual from its recess. He didn't really need to; every page was perfectly clear in his memory. But the microphones in the command module were picking up every sound, and transmitting it continually to mission control where tape recorders faithfully documented each cough, knock, and fart he made. If there was no sound of the manual's pages being turned, someone might get suspicious about just how good his memory was – and why. It was a high level of paranoia, he acknowledged wryly, but with the PSR you could never be sure. And he certainly wasn't going to take the risk. So the manual was opened with a soft rustling sound, and he started down the checklist.

Prepping the missile took ninety minutes – powering up its systems and loading the inertial guidance system with the data from the command module guidance computator. The missile itself rode above the command module: a cylinder with the same two-and-a-half-metre diameter as the rest of the Liberty. At the front was a radar dish, then the electrical instrument section. Below that was the actual warhead: a fission bomb with a yield of three hundred kilotons, the largest practical size Bienvenido's bomb factories could make. Propulsion was dual stage, with a hypergolic-fuel rocket for launching it from the command module, and a clustered solid rocket motor stack for final high-velocity delivery. The total mass was two point two tonnes.

'Missile systems at preflight stage five, and holding steady,' Ry reported an hour from apogee. The Liberty was close enough now that he could make out the shape of Tree 3,788-D without any magnification. Even the dark areas were visible, slim fissures amid the bright entrancing shimmer.

'Good to hear that, Ry,' Anala replied.

It was probably his imagination, but her voice seemed fainter – maybe just the static crackle that came with such a long-distance radio beam.

'Taking final radar reading of target,' he said. A muted mechanical clanking reverberated through the command module's frame as the radar dish scanned round. Nixie numbers shifted and settled, sending a warm orange glow across his face as he floated over to that section of the console. 'Navigation data locked and transferred. Flight profile confirmed. Requesting final missile sequence initiation.'

'You have a green light for missile fuel-tank pressurization, Liberty two-six-seven-three.'

Ry went back to the port, where he could see the Tree – noticeably larger now. Radar gave him a separation distance of three hundred and twenty-seven kilometres. He flicked three switches on the missile console, moving them to mid-position. 'Commencing propellant-tank pressurization.'

'SVO reports Tree movement,' Anala said. 'One per cent gee.'

Ry pulled himself over to the port, and swung the sextant out of its recess. Two readings a minute apart, centring the crosshairs on the bulbous end of 3,788-D. The coordinates were different. Sure enough Tree 3,788-D was on the move, accelerating at just under one per cent of Bienvenido gravity.

He grinned savagely through the port. You can run,' he told Tree 3,788-D, 'but you can't hide.'

Most Trees moved when a Liberty spacecraft approached. That was the thing Ry found most amazing about them. Something so *huge* being able to move. The Silver Sword had burned two hundred and seventy-five tonnes of propellant in order to lift a six-and-a-half-tonne Liberty into space. Tree 3,788-D was *nine kilometres* long, and it was accelerating. A small acceleration, true, but he couldn't even visualize the energy level necessary for such a motor. And some Trees accelerated at up to five per cent gee. Seventeen Liberty astronauts had burned all the fuel in the service module so they could still intercept their fleeing target, completely altering the spacecraft's orbit and thus throwing away their chance of a successful re-entry. Only one of them – Matej – had ever made it back.

The next twenty minutes were spent calculating the catch-up burn that would change the Liberty's course to give the missile its highest strike probability. Ry fed the figures flight com gave him into the guidance computator, and fired the service module's main rocket for sixteen seconds.

The missile's guidance data had to be reloaded to take the new course into account. Then it was time; the Tree was only seventy-five kilometres away. He entered the bomb arm code on the missile console's red keyboard, and confirmed three green lights. A final check of missile systems, and he turned the launch key. The Liberty shuddered as the missile detached. Ry saw sparkling gas flowing past the ports, and used the joystick to turn the Liberty, aligning it for the retro burn. He caught sight of the missile through the port, its exhaust flaring wide from the small rocket nozzle at its base, accelerating towards the Tree. Radar confirmed its course was steady.

Ry fired the service module rocket again, retro burning to build distance between him and the impending blast, and putting him back onto his original re-entry trajectory. It was a busy time, requiring two further short burns.

'Course correction verified,' Anala told him after the second one. 'Good burn, Liberty two-six-seven-three.'

'Thank you, flight com. Appreciate that.'

'Flight control wants you to put Liberty into shield one orientation.'

'Roger. Beginning RCS manoeuvre for shield one.'

He reached for the joystick. Basically, shield one was positioning the Liberty so the back of the service module was pointing directly at the Tree, so when the atom bomb went off, the bulk of the spaceship would be between him and the blast, shielding him from the brutal gamma-ray pulse. He cancelled the thermal roll and began to turn the Liberty.

The missile panel buzzed a warning. Ry scanned it quickly, not quite understanding. That particular warning sound was for attitude correction. The numbers in the Nixie tubes were slowly changing, as if he was updating the missile's guidance computator.

'Flight com, I have a problem,' Ry said. He started flicking switches, trying to cancel the error. The numbers kept on changing.

'Say again, please?' Anala asked.

'There's a malfunction in the missile guidance system. Course vectors are changing.' He growled in frustration as the numbers locked. Nothing he was doing was making any difference.

'Wait, please. Missile command is analysing your telemetry.'

'They're going to have to hurry,' Ry muttered. He tried to reload the original vector, but it wasn't registering. An amber light came on at the side of the missile control panel. 'No, no, no. Don't do that!' The light turned green, indicating the missile's tiny RCS nozzles were belching out cold gas, changing its attitude in accordance with the new data. 'Uracus!'

'Liberty two-six-seven-three, telemetry is showing you transmitting a new course to the missile.'

'Negative! I'm not! It's changing. Oh crud.' Another light turned amber, the missile's engine was preparing to fire. 'It's going to course correct. Flight control, do I abort? Do I abort?' His thumb hovered above the red key.

'Liberty two-six-seven-three, cancel your update to the missile.'

'I haven't updated! It's malfu— Crud!' Ry stared helplessly at the console as the light changed to green. The missile was fifty kilometres from the Tree, and the engine burnt for three seconds. He read the new numbers again, and instantly worked out the course that would take the missile on. Procedure always had the strike aimed at the base of the bulbous end, the biggest target, but this new trajectory would take it to the midpoint – so it wasn't going to miss. 'It's still aimed at the Tree,' he said numbly.

'Major Evine, what's happening?'

Ry recognized the new voice in his headphones: Colonel Matej. That was a severe break with protocol.

'Something changed the missile's course,' Ry said, hating how inadequate that sounded.

'Did you change the missile course, Liberty two-six-seven-three?'

'No, I did not.' Ry took a breath and made an effort to calm down. His medical telemetry would be showing them his quickened heartbeat and respiration – rising temperature, too. 'There's some kind of malfunction. I'm going to attempt to regain control of the missile.'

His fingers flew over the missile panel, flicking switches in a sequence he knew should work, wiping the computator's memory ready for a clean reload.

'What are you doing?' Colonel Matej asked.

'Clearing the false data from the missile. I can reload the correct course.'

'Negative. Missile desk has confirmed the new track. It *is* still on course for the Tree.' There was a short pause. 'But how did you know that?'

Ry grimaced, furious with himself. It took the big electrical computator sitting in the basement of the Cape Ingmar flight control building to work out orbital vectors. No normal human brain could perform that kind of calculation. 'I guessed the burn wasn't long enough to divert it,' he said. *Come on, Matej, you know an astronaut could make that guess.*

'Okay. Consensus down here is to let it run. If the kill burn doesn't initiate as programmed, we'll consider a data reload.'

'Roger that.' Ry stopped trying to correct the anomaly, and looked at the missile countdown clock. They were seven minutes away from the kill burn, when the solid rocket cluster would ignite and send the missile streaking in towards the Tree. 'Can I have an update on Tree 3,788-D, please, flight com?'

It took a moment, but Anala's voice returned to his headphones. 'SVO is saying the Tree acceleration is holding constant. Its course is stable. Missile will not require a further update.'

He nearly said it hadn't had an update – that something very strange was happening. The new data had to come from somewhere, and flight control had an override channel for the Liberty's computator in case anything happened to an astronaut; they could continue the missile launch by remote. *But why would anyone change the impact point?* He just couldn't understand that. Unless— *Fallers!*

They would be the only beneficiaries from a sabotaged Liberty mission. But the missile is still going to hit the Tree. So it can't be them. Who, then?

'Ry, are you all right?' Anala asked.

He realized his heart must have jumped at the thought. *If they can alter the missile course from the ground, what else could they change? But the flight centre team gets blood checked almost as often as astronauts.* 'I'm fine,' he said, eyes tracking across every readout on the console, trying to spot any anomaly, but everything seemed to be functioning normally. The Liberty's battery power was lower than he would have liked at sixty-two per cent, but still well inside mission parameters. His eyes were fixed on the missile countdown display as the numbers wound down.

'The doctors would like to remind you to pull the viewport blinds down,' Anala said.

'Roger that, flight com.' He reached out and pulled the silver blinds across each of the command module's ports. It was to protect his eyes from the explosion. 'Strapping in, and locking down guidance data.' The electromagnetic pulse from an atom bomb explosion was fierce, and had knocked out circuits and instruments in the early Liberty craft until Demitri and his team came up with methods of hardening the electrical components on board. But even then, the protection wasn't always a hundred per cent effective. Ry began copying the readouts onto a pad – not that he needed to, but the technicians who recovered the capsule might notice the absence. If the computator did get knocked out, he could reload it quickly enough.

'Stand by, one minute,' he said. His gaze was fixed on the missile panel. If anything happened now, there'd be no chance of correcting it. The numbers flicked downwards. On ten seconds, a green light indicated separation of the missile's hypergolic-rocket engine module. Then, right on time, the green light for the solid rocket ignition lit up.

Ry let out a soft breath of release. He watched the radar, seeing the missile's velocity build as the solid rocket cluster accelerated it at seven gees. The distance from the Tree shrank rapidly.

'Looking good,' Anala said.

Twenty seconds.

All his console readouts were stable. 'Switching on external cameras,' he announced. Footage of the Ring Trees exploding in nuclear fury always played well in the newsreels.

Ten seconds. The solid rockets were spent. Missile acceleration dropped to zero. The radar return was perfect, the Nixie numbers measuring distance to the Tree merged together as they wound down to zero.

His earphones emitted a loud hissing, then went silent. Tiny cracks of intense light shone around the edge of the port blinds. Needles in the dials connected to the hull radiation instruments flipped over to maximum. Lights dipped from the bomb's electo-magnetic pulse. He held his breath, scanning the console. There were two amber lights. One for an RCS tank pressure valve, which didn't matter – the valve was triple redundant. And a second for a radar servo – again, the backup could cope. A red light glowed for the omnidirectional radio antenna receiver. He switched the backup set on immediately. His earphones started hissing again.

'Clean detonation,' Anala called through the static. 'Visible down here.'

'Good to hear, flight com. Tell everyone to go ahead and start their Treefall parties. Systems nominal up here.' He checked the flight director attitude indicator and fired the RCS.

'It looks like you're manoeuvring, Liberty two-six-seven-three,' Anala said, and there was a note of strain in her voice which was evident even through the static.

'That's confirmed, flight com: manoeuvring. I want to see,' he said simply.

He stabilized the Liberty side-on to the Tree, and put on dark sunglasses before opening a blind.

There it was, a perfect sphere of dazzling white plasma – Bienvenido's latest and very temporary secondary sun. It expanded fast, dimming as it went. A slender flare extended out from the northern surface. Ry frowned at it. Then the tip began to curve over. 'What the crud . . . ?' The tenuous line across the infinite blackness began to dwindle. 'I can see something,' Ry gasped. He snatched the camera from its locker and tugged at the lens cap with comic ineptitude.

'What is your visual, Liberty two-six-seven-three?'

'Something's moving.' The explosion's plasma shell was shading down to a purple-blue, becoming translucent as its luminosity faded. The tenuous trail of ions had almost vanished. He managed to click off three fast shots. 'Something came out of the plasma shell.'

'Repeat, please.'

'There's something out there.' He peered through the camera's viewfinder, trying to focus the lens properly. The tip of the dying streak was meandering aimlessly as it dissipated.

'SVO will begin tracking the debris constellation when the plasma shell scatters. There's too much ionization interference right now.'

'That wasn't debris, flight com. The trail the object left in the plasma shell curved. Whatever made it was changing course. It was under acceleration. It's a spaceship of some kind.'

There was a long pause. 'Liberty two-six-seven-three, please confirm you said there is an alien spacecraft in the Ring.'

Ry didn't like the way all emotion had vanished from Anala's voice. In his mind he could see the flight control centre, all the dozens of technicians sitting at their desks, looking round at Anala with nervous astonishment, none of them saying a word.

'Affirmative, flight com. I don't think I'm alone out here.'

'Can you see the anomaly now?'

Ry pressed his face against the cool glass of the port, twisting round so he could scan as much of the empty panorama as he could. There were definitely some chunks of Tree visible out there now the plasma shell had dissolved, faint-glowing splinters tumbling slowly across the blackness. One segment must have been a kilometre long – presumably the end of the spire. But all of them formed a central cluster, expanding slowly. *At least I did kill 3,788-D.*

'Negative.' Now he began to doubt himself – up until he replayed his own memory. With his eyes closed, the tenuous strand of glowing ions was pushed out of the seething shell, energetic gases stretched along by some invisible force. *Something created that wake, something accelerating. Something that could survive a three-hundred-kiloton atomic bomb. But what?*

He glided back into the acceleration couch. 'Flight com, I'm activating the radar. It might find something.'

'Roger that, Liberty two-six-seven-three. Nice thinking.'

119

Ry watched the tiny circular scope for several minutes. The cluster of Tree remnants showed as a faint fuzz at the radar's extreme range. There was nothing else – and certainly nothing close or accelerating.

'All right, Ry,' Anala said. 'We've alerted SVO; their radars will scan for it. If there's a Prime ship hiding up there, they'll find it.'

He blinked in surprise at the almost-heresy. *There are no Prime, not any more. Mother Laura sacrificed herself to destroy them and save us. Besides, the Prime ships had a vast exhaust plume.*

His training took over, and he strapped himself in, barely realizing what he was doing. The more he thought about it, the less he understood what any kind of spaceship would be doing so close to the Tree. Research? Attack? But he was damn sure that it was the cause of the missile going awry. Nothing else could have done it.

So where did you come from? Which planet? Is there going to be another invasion?

Despite his urgency to find the intruder, Liberty continued its constant demands on his attention. He had to restart the thermal roll. Systems needed resetting. Readings taken. Updates entered. Flight control's astrogation team wanted Liberty to perform a course-correction burn.

Two hours after the strike, the Liberty's orbit took it out of Bienvenido's umbra. Sunlight shone into the command module as the spacecraft slipped back into the full glare of the G1 star. Ry always wondered why Laura Brandt had bothered classifying the star at all; it wasn't like they had anything to compare it to. Apart from the planets, the sky above Bienvenido was completely empty.

Of course he'd seen pictures of the smudges the SVO and university observatories had photographed. Galaxies: so far away that even Commonwealth starships would take decades to reach the closest. Invisible to the naked eye. Bienvenido was alone forever. The Void had made sure of that, banishing its woebegone exiles beyond any hope of return.

Something glinted amid the eternal black out there on the other side of the viewport – a tiny point of light far above the planet's distant crescent. Not a Tree. The Liberty wasn't oriented to let him see the Ring.

Ry unclipped his couch straps and slid over to the port. Sunlight was shining on *something*. An object in space. Distance undetermined. He grabbed the camera again and clicked off a few pictures before the thermal roll carried it out of view.

'Liberty two-six-seven-three, telemetry is showing you cancelling the thermal roll. Do you have a problem?'

'It's here,' he said, inanely using a near-whisper. 'It's with me. I can see it.'

'What is there? What are you seeing, Liberty two-six-seven-three?'

'I have visual contact. The alien . . . it's following me down.' Ry watched the flight attitude indicator, and stabilized the Liberty's attitude. When he looked out of the viewport he found the grey glimmer where he'd seen it before.

His fingers moved over the console as if he was playing some complex piano music, flicking switches and clicking knobs round, always knowing what to do. Turning the radar towards the alien. The round scope lit up with a slight phosphorescent sheen. There was nothing there. He glanced out of the viewport, seeing the faint glimmer point. It wasn't bright, not like the refraction you got off the crystal substance Trees were made from, but certainly not dark like a Faller egg. There was still nothing on the radar. 'Crud!'

'Ry, we're not getting any reports of anything near you from SVO.'

'Roger that; it's immune to radar.' Ry pushed himself back to the port. *Far away and big, or close and small?* He brought the camera back up, and took more shots. The rangefinder wasn't helping. He pulled the sextant out of its recess and lined up the crosshairs. Read the figures. Checked the guidance computator display.

'Can you describe it?' Anala asked. 'Is it a Faller egg?'

'Negative. It's a solid material that's reflecting sunlight. I'm assuming that means it's relatively small and close by. If it was big, the SVO observatories would spot it. Giu, they can see a Faller egg, and they're dark.'

'Is it accelerating?'

'Taking a reading now.' He lined up the sextant crosshairs again, and read the figures. Compared them to the glowing numbers of the guidance computator. 'I think it might be. A very small acceleration. This is right on the error margin.' Even with his eyes, he couldn't see any kind of exhaust plume. *Trees don't have rocket exhausts.*

'Roger. We'll ask SVO to attempt visual observation of the anomaly.'

'Thank you, flight com.' Another sextant reading, and the figures were slightly different again. *It is under power – which means something is controlling it.*

He took a deep breath, considering his options if it moved closer. *What if it attacks me?* Now that he had fired the nuclear missile, Liberty boasted a single pistol, and that was in the emergency-landing survival pack. His gaze darted to the base of the console where it was stowed, and he grunted in exasperation at how desperate that was. A Liberty spacecraft was expendable, he'd always known that; he just hadn't faced up to that situation ever becoming real.

He stayed by the viewport, determined not to let the enigmatic glint of light out of his sight. It was drifting slowly towards the base of the port. Ry checked it through the sextant again. Difficult now – it was definitely dimmer.

'Ry, the Prerov observatory has visual acquisition of the Liberty,' Anala said. 'They're using their main telescope.'

Ry knew from her tone it wasn't good news. 'Glad to hear that, flight com.'

'They report empty skies. There are no Faller eggs around you.'

'It is not a Faller egg,' he said firmly. 'It is a vehicle, under acceleration.'

'Stand by, Liberty two-six-seven-three.'

He knew what that meant. Flight control had become worried he was cracking up. Medical 'incidents' were another rumour spoken about in hushed tones around the astronaut quarters – the unique stress of spaceflight with its cabin claustrophobia and simultaneous exposure to the infinite nothing of intergalactic space. It didn't happen often, but even the best pilots had been known to get *quirky* out here, all alone.

'Ry, engineering believes the object you're seeing may be a part of your third stage,' Anala was saying. 'Possibly a section of the inter-stage fairing. That would account for the similar orbit.'

'Roger that, flight com. Could be.' He almost laughed with contempt at the amount of crud they were expecting him to swallow. After separation, the third stage would carry on along a similar elliptical orbit, true. But the third stage automatically vented the gas left in all its tanks, to avoid any later rupture producing a fragment cascade which might endanger a Liberty mission, and that venting alone would diverge their orbital tracks. And his continuing correction burns would add further distance and velocity difference. It would be impossible for any part of the third stage to run parallel with his own course by this time in the mission.

Ry grimaced and turned his attention back outside. The alien was still there, but very faint. 'Flight com, the intruder is definitely darker now. Liberty is moving away from it.' He swung the sextant round, centred the crosshairs, and took another reading. It turned out to be the last. Less than a minute later, the speck had vanished.

Routine and training reclaimed him for the rest of the flight.

There was the seventeen-second mid-course-correction burn. He needed to eat. He needed to sleep; flight com said the doctors were insisting on that.

For fifteen uneventful hours the Liberty spaceship glided along its elliptical orbit, back down towards perigee, two hundred and fifteen kilometres above Bienvenido.

After he woke from a troubled three-hour doze, Ry started working through the atmosphere re-entry checklist. Now he was approaching the planet, SVO's radars were tracking him with greater precision. It was a critical time. The command module had to hit the ionosphere at the perfect angle. Too steep and it would burn up, too shallow and it would skip across the tenuous gas and pick up an unstoppable tumble.

Ry laboriously entered new data into the guidance computator.

Everything checked out for his final course-correction burn. It lasted nine seconds, and flight com confirmed its accuracy.

'We need to start the checklist for command module separation,' Anala said.

Ry was staring out of the viewport, half-expecting to see the alien ship out there, a black splinter silhouetted by Bienvenido's glaring blue and white panorama. 'Roger that, flight com. I'm opening the manual now.'

He had to switch the command module power over to its own internal batteries. They could keep the spacecraft's instruments and life support running for ninety minutes. Ry was back in the pressure suit for the descent.

The command module separated from the service module while the Liberty was three hundred kilometres above Nilsson Sound. Seven minutes later, Ry experienced the first effects of gravity reclaiming the spaceship when crumbs and scraps of food packets, a lost pen, all drifted gently down out of the air to settle on the rear bulkhead around him. Static built up in his headphones.

'See you on the other side of the sky,' Anala said encouragingly just before contact was lost.

Gravity was increasing now. The sky outside the ports began to glow a faint orange, swiftly rising to a brighter cherry red. Then the sound started – a low moan building fast to a full hurricane roar. Ry could see solar-bright streamers flaring for kilometres along the plummeting command module's wake, clogging the air with the dazzling embers burning off its blunt heat-shield base. Inside of a minute, gravity reached one gee, then continued to climb. The whole command module started shaking, far worse than it did during launch. In front of him, the console was a blue-grey blur as he fought to inhale, gulping down air in short frantic bursts. After forty hours in freefall, the six-gee force which re-entry exerted on his body was excruciating.

Finally the deceleration force began to ease off, and the brilliance of the tormented air died away. Blue sky was visible above as the command module sank through the lower atmosphere at terminal velocity. There was a terrific bang, and a yellow flash streaked across the port.

'Drogue chute deployed,' Ry managed to croak, not even knowing if he had regained radio communication.

Another giant impulse crushed him painfully down into the acceleration couch. He saw the three bright orange main chutes opening across the sky, clumped together like a bunch of flowers.

'Welcome home, Liberty two-six-seven-three,' Anala said solemnly. 'Recovery fleet reports they have a visual on your chutes.'

Ry scanned the console. His altitude was five hundred metres. Gravity was back to normal. He braced himself as the altimeter wound down to zero. The command module thudded down into the water – which, after the trauma of re-entry, seemed quite mild. Spray sloshed over the viewports, and the floatation ring inflated out from the top of the command module. He began to bob about in the ocean swell. In his earphones, he could hear the flight control staff cheering.

'Great Giu,' he groaned, and started to laugh. 'I made it. I actually crudding made it!'

3

The small, well-equipped clinic was on the second floor of the Opole PSR office. As well as the five treatment bays, it had a bath-room with a shower. Chaing stood under the thick stream of hot water for a long time, despite the acute pain from his damaged wrist, washing the carnage off his skin. Soap took care of the physical contamination. As for the mental pollution – well, that was a whole different thing.

The trauma of losing Lurvri, the butchery, those were events he could come to terms with eventually. That was an honourable part of the fight against the Fallers. But the Warrior Angel . . .

I am completely compromised. Everything she told me, my heritage, it leaves me exposed. She did that deliberately.

The nurse bandaged his discoloured, swelling wrist, and told him he would have to get an X-ray. It was probably broken. He would need a cast for a couple of months.

She offered him some painkillers. Chaing almost refused, but that would be churlish. *And possibly out of character. I can't risk that.*

He swallowed the pills and dressed in a set of spare clothes someone had brought from his locker. That was when he realized his PSR badge was missing, removed along with his ruined clothes.

Two mildly embarrassed guards were waiting for him, as he knew they would be. He knew them – he knew everybody in the office – but said nothing as they led him down into the basement. It was indignation he felt, rather than anger or fear, when they put him in one of the interrogation cells. Humiliatingly, it was a cell for interrogating renegades and reactionaries: three metres by three, the universal bricks painted a dull grey-green. Table in the middle, and a plain wooden chair on each side, facing each other.

At least it wasn't one of the cells down on level five. The ones with benches where the suspect was strapped down. Where instruments and injections were used to extract truths.

Not yet, anyway.

He'd completely lost track of time when the door finally swung open again. The man who came in was well over a century old, wearing a perfectly tailored charcoal-grey suit, a white shirt, and a slim dark-red tie. Chaing didn't know him; he wasn't from the Opole office. But he was definitely PSR. He possessed the air of cold authority Chaing always strove to project.

He settled himself in the chair opposite Chaing and adjusted his steel-rimmed spectacles. A thick cardboard folder was placed on the table.

Chaing looked at the label. His name was printed on it. *If there is any hint of an Eliter ancestor in there, I'm dead.*

'Captain Chaing.'

'Yes. And you are?'

'Stonal. I am the director of Section Seven. And I've flown in from Varlan specifically to talk to you.'

Chaing nodded. 'Of course you have.' Everyone knew about Section Seven, the PSR's internal security office. But . . . *The director himself?*

'Given you are a fellow PSR officer, you understand how this interview will proceed? I don't have to go through the whole threats-and-promises routine, do I?'

'No. You don't have to do that.'

'Good. I'm not interested in the nest, nor their plans to sabotage the rocketry plant. I don't care about Lurvri, though I'm saddened that the regiment lost a good officer. Nor am I bothered by Comrade Deneriov.'

'So what does interest you?'

Stonal pursed his lips in a grudging approval. 'Right now? Only one thing. So tell me . . . What was *she* like?'

Chaing didn't hesitate. 'Very frightening. Her weapons were powerful. Those Fallers, she just . . . shredded them.'

'Did you see her weapons?'

Chaing cocked his head to one side, trying to recall the slaughter. Not easy, even for his recall – he'd spent the last couple of hours suppressing the horror. 'Actually, no, now I think about it. The air wobbled, like a heat shimmer, and there was a flash. But her hands were empty; there was no hardware.'

'Her timing was perfect, from your point of view. Did she say how she knew about the nest?'

'She said the Eliters had intercepted some encrypted signals, so they knew there was a nest in Opole. They'd been watching for it.'

'They? She'd been working with radicals?'

'She said she'd been in Opole for a few days, helping local Eliters track down the signals.'

'What else did she say?'

'One thing I found interesting: that she'd promised Mother Laura she would protect Bienvenido.'

'I'm told that's true.'

Which almost threw Chaing. He shot Stonal a suspicious glare. 'How could it be true? She looks about twenty. The legends say she was alive back then, so she must be the last person alive to see Bienvenido undergo the Great Transition.'

'Kysandra was born in the Void. Nigel gave her some form of Commonwealth medicine which allows her to stay young – apparently.'

'Oh.'

'Indeed. And she chooses to keep that medicine for herself, as she does a lot of things. Uniqueness helps consolidate her quasi-mythical status among the Eliters and other reactionaries.'

'But she is helping us.'

'When it suits her, yes.'

'Then why the secrecy? If she has Commonwealth technology, why not let her aid us openly?'

'That's simple: Nigel Sheldon. Kysandra was his . . . companion. Prime Minister Slvasta, quite rightly, did not trust her. She had assisted the revolution not to right injustice, but purely as a subterfuge enabling Nigel to steal the Captain's old quantumbuster. Then she collaborated with Slvasta's own wife to secretly influence the new People's Congress. She cannot be trusted. We still do not understand what Nigel's ultimate aim was. In the Void we were at least the equals of the Fallers. Looking back, we may even have had a slight advantage due to the mental powers the Void gave us. Here, in the infinite dark, we are barely holding our own. In the Void, our souls were taken into the loving embrace of the Heart: we had immortality. Out here, when we die, it is forever. This is not liberation, as Nigel and the Warrior Angel claim. This is one short step from damnation.'

'She killed those Fallers. She saved me.'

'If we Fall, she Falls with us. For all her weapons and her technology, she is alone. She cannot hold off an entire planet of Fallers.'

Chaing let out a long breath. 'All right. We can't eliminate her, and she won't cooperate with us. So, now what?'

'Now that you know about her, you have a choice. Or rather, I do.'

Exactly as she said, Uracus damn her. 'And that is?'

'I understand you saw breeder Fallers at Xander Manor?'

'Yes. I did.'

'Their existence would be extremely detrimental to the morale of Bienvenido's citizens. Do you agree?'

'They scared the crud out of me.'

'Contrary to rumour, Section Seven isn't concerned with internal security matters. My cadre of officers are fully informed about breeder Fallers and work to eliminate not just them, but any public knowledge of their existence. You know first hand how deadly they are, so you have passed the first entry requirement of that cadre. But I only accept officers with an excellent record.' Stonal patted the file. 'Which you have been, except for one regrettable lapse.'

Chaing frowned. 'What lapse?'

'Earlier this evening you brought Corilla to this very PSR office.'

'Yes. We rescued her from a breeder Faller. We needed to get out of that situation fast and bring her in for debriefing.'

'There are perfectly clear standing orders governing Eliters – the first of which is that they cannot be brought into PSR offices; they may be broadcasting what they find to their own kind. It is a massive security breach. She should have been taken to the specialist holding cells. That's why we have them.'

'There was an active nest which I knew was targeting the rocketry plant. That was my priority. I didn't have time for anything else.'

'Cutting corners, captain?'

Chaing knew the man was trying to provoke him, testing his temperament. 'I acted to save the factory,' he replied levelly. 'It might not be your priority, but it is, and remains, mine.'

Stonal took his glasses off and placed them on top of the file. His sunken eyes regarded Chaing thoughtfully. 'I like your dedication, Captain Chaing, and I appreciate the difficulty of active operations, which is why I'm inclined to elevate you to Section Seven.'

'There is no going back, is there, not now?' Chaing said, trying not to tense up.

'No. None.'

'Then I'd better re-read the rule book.'

Stonal chuckled. 'I don't think that's necessary. Welcome to Section Seven, Captain Chaing.'

'Thank you, sir. I won't let you down.'

'No, you won't. Nobody does.'

'So what now?'

'You carry on exactly as before, except you have an additional reporting channel, directly to my office in Varlan, and a little extra authority to invoke when you have to deal with your local superiors. You will receive a full briefing package.' He hesitated, putting his spectacles back on. 'It makes uncomfortable reading. We have hunted down and killed an extraordinary variety of breeder Fallers over the years. They can make themselves take on practically any animal form they wish.'

'How? That's . . . incredible.'

'It's some innate ability to reshape their embryos, which naturally fascinates the Faller Research Institute. But I don't care about the science, only the end result.'

'Understood. And the Warrior Angel?'

'See that she remains legendary. Knowledge of any activity must be suppressed. That same information will be passed on to us.'

'So you are interested in her?'

'I'm extremely interested in everything Kysandra does. I have a whole team of Section Seven staff devoted to compiling her movements and abilities, drawing up lists of suspected sympathizers – mostly Eliters. One day we will know enough to track her down.'

'Then what? I've seen what she can do. I expect she could defeat an entire regiment.'

'Yes, but she has limits. We know that from Mother Laura, who had the same level of inbuilt Commonwealth technology. It is unlikely she could survive an atomic explosion.'

'Crud! Nuke her? On the planet's surface? You're kidding?'

'Our exact response will be determined at the appropriate time. For now I am content maintaining the status quo, for all our sakes.'

Chaing hoped no flicker of surprise escaped to mar his features. *Just like Corilla called it.* 'It's how we've survived this long.'

Stonal reached into a pocket and took Chaing's PSR badge out. He examined it for a moment, then slid it over the table. 'I'm glad you agree. Reducing our local exposure will be your first assignment for me.'

'Sir?' He didn't snatch the badge back; that would just be sad.

'Corporal Jenifa, the undercover officer, she saw the breeder Faller in Frikal Alley. Yes?'

'She did, yes,' Chaing said cautiously. 'But only a glimpse. It was dark.'

'Then it won't be hard for you to convince her it was a wild dog, or something equally mundane.'

'I'll see to it. There will be no mention of it on her official report.'

'Good.'

'What about Corilla? Do I talk to her as well?'

'The Eliter? She's an irritation, not worth your time. Eliters are always droning on about their beloved Warrior Angel, and breeder Fallers, and the coming apocalypse. I've withdrawn her university permit so she doesn't continue spreading that kind of sedition among impressionable young minds. She'll be assigned to a people's collective farm where she'll live a productive life for the state – better for everyone all round.'

Chaing put on a thoughtful expression, knowing Stonal would be searching for any hint of disapproval. It was so monstrously unfair. Corilla had cooperated with the PSR, risked herself to warn them about the extent of the nest, and for that she had her dream of a real education taken from her. *No wonder Eliters all hate the PSR.* 'Yes, that tidies it up neatly.' He used his good hand to pick up the badge and put it in his pocket.

Stonal stood and reclaimed the file. 'It's nearly dawn. You'd better get that injury seen to.'

Chaing climbed to his feet and winced. The movement had triggered a hot throb of pain from his damaged wrist, despite the painkillers. 'I will. Er, sir?'

Stonal was about to knock on the door. He turned with some surprise. 'Yes?'

'How did you get recruited, sir? Did you see a breeder Faller?'

'No. This has been my function right from the start. Bienvenido needs people who will ensure that Slvasta's great work continues, that we don't turn aside from the goal he set us: to destroy the Fallers and make our liberation real. It is a difficult, wearying road we are on, and not everyone agrees with it. I have devoted my life to eradicating that domestic threat, and I will not fail. I promised him that. All of us did.'

'Promised who?'

'Why, Slvasta, or course. He couldn't have children of his own, you know. Quanda, the Faller he encountered when he lost his arm, she *damaged* him. Instead, in later life, he took in children who had lost their parents to Fallers. I was fortunate to be one of them. He treated me like a son, he put his faith in me, and I will not let him down.'

'You knew Slvasta himself?' Chaing asked in astonishment. The leader of the revolution had died over eighty years ago.

'I did. He was a remarkable, inspiring man. His passion that the people of Bienvenido should ultimately triumph was breath-taking. Almost as great as his contempt for the treachery of Nigel and Kysandra. Once the Fallers are defeated, he was determined that we should be free to build our own destiny, free from the Commonwealth that Eliters claim is so wonderful. If it is wonder-ful, then why did they inflict Nigel upon us? Slvasta did not want us contaminated by them. Our battle against the Fallers has now been fought for over three thousand achingly long years. First on our planet, and now, triumphantly, in space. We have never wavered in all that time. The people of Bienvenido are the most indomitable in the universe, making tremendous sacrifices for the sake of gener-ations unborn. Our victory should belong to us alone, for we will have earned it as no humans before. Only we should have a say in our future thereafter.'

'Crudding right,' Chaing agreed; he didn't have to fake sincerity for that sentiment. Eliter whispers of impending glories and wonders when Bienvenido regained contact with the Common-wealth had always sounded fanciful, the envy-promise of a desperate politician.

Stonal rapped his knuckles on the door, which opened almost immediately. 'Good night, Captain Chaing. I expect my trust in you to be rewarded.'

Chaing raised his damaged hand to his forehead in a salute, gritting his teeth against the pain. 'It will be, sir.'

*

It was Jenifa who was waiting for him on the ground floor when he finally made it up the stairs, weary from lack of sleep and the constant pain inflicted by his wrist. Disillusioned by the subterfuge the PSR practised to suppress knowledge of the breeder Fallers.

Mourning Lurvri more than he ever expected to. *There simply isn't a worse way to die.*

She got up from the bench in the entrance hall and put her arms round him. 'I know about Lurvri. Everybody does. I'm sorry. He was one of us, and nobody deserves that.'

'Thanks.'

She gave him a searching gaze. 'You okay?'

'I think I might be.'

'Good, come on. I'm driving you to the hospital.' An idiosyncratic smile touched her lips for a moment. 'I volunteered for that duty. Well, insisted, actually.'

4

Ry Evine hadn't known the PSR office even existed. It was a nonde-script concrete block in among Cape Ingmar's scattered collection of administration and engineering buildings, not half a kilometre from the grand white-marble control centre.

He found out about it three hours after splashdown. Ninety minutes after the recovery ships had picked him up, a dinghy had transferred him to a seaplane which flew him back to Cape Ingmar. That was when he realized something was badly wrong. The seaplane taxied into a hangar, and there was no reception commit-tee, no cheering crowd of Astronaut Corps and Cape workers, no reporters; even General Delores was nowhere to be seen. Instead three armed PSR officers in smart khaki fatigues escorted him to a car which drove him to the PSR office.

The quarters he was shown to were comfortable enough, like a hotel room, with a lounge and bathroom – but no windows, and the door had no handle on the inside. It was a cell.

He stripped out of his flight suit and went into the shower. There were clean clothes (his own) laid out on the bed when he finished. His flight suit was gone, and with it his platinum mission badge.

'Hey!' Ry banged on the door. 'Hey, there's no crudding authority on this planet that lets you take my badge. Give that back!'

No response.

He smashed his fist on the door again. 'You pissy little bastards!'

Then all he could do was wait. There were no books. No radio.

He grew angry. He grew impatient. He grew tired. The flight had been exhausting. He was running on adrenalin alone now, and that was never going to last.

The door opened, and Ry lifted his head from the table. He had no idea how long he'd been asleep. His body was telling him: not nearly long enough.

A man came in. Ry guessed his age somewhere between a hundred and a hundred and thirty. Old – the heavy eyes behind small steel-rimmed spectacles gave that away – but sprightly with it, a man who clearly kept active and busy. He wore a dark-grey suit, even in the tropical heat of the Cape, with a white shirt. A slim burgundy tie, for Giu's sake. Then Ry caught the discreet lapel pin, a pale blue rectangle with a gold stripe down the centre.

PSR political division.

The man pulled a chair over to the table, and sat opposite him. 'You recognized my insignia, Pilot Major Evine?'

'Yes.'

'Good. You are an intelligent man. That will make this easier.'

'Make what easier? Who are you?'

'Do you think you need to know my name?'

'Looks like I don't.'

'And why am I here?'

Ry tried to keep his voice level. Losing his temper now wasn't going to help – in fact, it might be dangerous. 'Because of what I saw.'

'Precisely. So let us examine that, shall we? Liberty mission two-six-seven-three encountered some anomalies. The first was you entering an unauthorized course alteration into your nuclear carrier missile.'

'I did not! Something changed the missile guidance data.'

'As I understand it, once the missile has detached from the command module, a course correction can only be entered by a radio signal. Correct?'

'Yes.'

'And that signal is coded?'

'Yes.'

'The encryption is changed for every mission. So to amend the guidance data you have to know the code. There are only two sources that can transmit a coded signal – the Liberty spaceship and the flight control centre here at Cape Ingmar. Did you accidentally strike a button, Major Evine? Was an erroneous signal transmitted to the missile?'

'No!'

'To pilot a Liberty mission is an incredible achievement. You are the very pinnacle of mental and physical excellence, but even astronauts are subject to human error. It is a cramped capsule, movement in freefall is tricky. A careless wave of a hand, perhaps? A simple cough that knocked you against the console?'

'I was in the acceleration couch, looking at the console. The numbers started to change without warning.'

'Very well, I accept that.'

'You do?'

'Indeed. Do you accept that this rogue signal could not have been transmitted from the ground without someone in flight control or the communication crew knowing?'

Ry couldn't answer honestly; he didn't know the entire system of the communication division, just the basic layout. But it wouldn't be easy, that was for sure. 'Unlikely,' he admitted.

'Good. So, logically, that leaves us with a third source. And yet, the missile still hit Tree 3,788-D. Therefore it wasn't sabotage, was it? The course change was too minute.'

'Well . . . yes.'

'Is it possible solar activity caused a small disruption to the missile guidance circuits?'

'Theoretically, I suppose.'

'So if you didn't alter the course, and the Astronaut Regiment communication division hasn't been infiltrated by Fallers – which it assuredly has *not* – is that not the most likely cause of the minute anomaly?'

Ry leant back in his chair, and fixed the man with a resigned stare. 'Yes. It's possible.'

'Do you enjoy being an astronaut, Major Evine? Of course you do; nobody would put themselves through that gruelling training process without being utterly committed. A successful first flight opens the door for further flights, does it not?'

'Is that a threat?'

'Certainly not. If I considered you a genuine danger to the state, we would not be sitting here talking.'

The hairs along Ry's spine reacted as if they'd been stroked by an ice spike. 'Astronaut is not a job, it's a calling. It's what I am.'

'And you are prepared to sacrifice anything to achieve it, I see that. Then answer me this: why did you argue?'

'Argue what?'

'You were told by flight control, with all their considerable resources, that your third stage was following you on the same orbital track. Yet you chose to disagree with them.'

'I said it was possible. I agreed with them.'

'To quote you: *the intruder is definitely darker now. Liberty is moving away from it.* The intruder, Major Evine? That doesn't sound like an agreement to me.'

'There was something out there,' Ry growled in exasperation, *and Uracus, take the risk.* 'Why don't you take a look at the photographs I took?'

'I have.'

Ry sat up fast. 'And?'

'Empty space, Major Evine. Empty space.'

'Really?'

'You sound dubious. Do you have a problem with authority?'

'No. Do you have a problem with facts?'

'I have issues with interpretation. That, major, is my calling. We are fighting a war. It is long and brutal, and phenomenally expensive. We cannot afford anything that will undermine public support.'

'You think I don't know that? I've visited the factories building the Silver Swords; I know how much they cost. I've also killed a Tree, so I know better than you how vital it is that we continue this struggle until the very last one of those bastards is nuked out of existence. Then we can finish them on this planet and finally be free. No matter how much your kind twist the truth, I will fight that fight. I will play the biggest part I can in destroying the Fallers.'

The man seemed almost surprised. 'And how do you think Bienvenido would react to news of another possible alien enemy? Would resolve fail or strengthen? We nearly fell once before, when the Prime came. It took everything we had, including Mother Laura's life, to survive them. A repeat of that would be catastrophic. I've seen the reports of dissent from across Lamaran. I've interviewed reactionary leaders, I've interviewed rebels. They have support; we are grown-up enough to admit that. What we cannot do is give them credibility. If our vigilance falters, we die – all of us. So I will not allow our fragile society to be distracted, or demoralized to the point of submission. That is the part I play in all this. Do you understand that, major?'

Ry nodded roughly. 'What do you want me to say? I know what I saw. And you know what I saw. There's something else out there.'

'An enigma. A glitch. One we will investigate to our full ability. But not in public, and not in panic. Someone of your unique status should be aware of that.'

'Status, Comrade? This is an equal society for all.'

'Is it? Did you really qualify for the Astronaut Regiment without political support?'

'You know how keen Democratic Unity was for me to join the Astronaut Corps. I am Slvasta's half-brother's great-great-great-grandson. That earns everyone publicity and support, which can only help the Liberty programme. So yes, me qualifying for the Astronaut Corps was a political decision. But don't you ever imply I'm not qualified.'

'I wouldn't do that. I know how hard you worked to earn your flight. And ultimately General Delores would never let you launch if she believed you weren't capable of carrying out the mission.'

'Good, then you can return my badge.'

The man smiled without humour. Then the door opened, and he gave the PSR officer who came in a disapproving look. Both of them retreated into the corridor.

Ry wondered just how much of this was theatrics. Some new piece of evidence of his complicity uncovered with miraculous good timing – so please confess, Comrade, and we will go easy on you.

The PSR man returned and gave Ry a long appraisal.

'What?' Ry asked belligerently. He didn't care about caution any more. This was too much of a farce.

'I have to leave now, so this will be short. You have just completed a successful Liberty flight, Major Evine. Did you see an alien spaceship in the Ring?'

Ry took a moment. 'No.' *Uracus, I'm pathetic.*

'Will you mention your suspicions to anyone?'

'No.'

'Will you dismiss any questions that your Astronaut Corps friends will ask you? And ask they certainly will.'

'Yes.'

'Thank you. You are a good Comrade, major. Your esteemed ancestor would be proud. I am glad this time in the hospital has enabled you to recover from re-entry sickness so you can resume your duties. I wish you many more successful flights.'

The man stood up and dropped Ry's platinum flight badge on the table before leaving the room.

Ry picked up the badge and pinned it on his fatigues. It shone in the room's electric light. *So why does it seem so tarnished?*

5

Chaing woke up in his own bed. That was comforting. He hadn't been able to quash the nagging worry that somehow he'd failed Stonal's requirements, or that the director of Section Seven had seen right through him. *Uracus, I'm paranoid. If he ever suspected I had some kind of broken Eliter ability, I wouldn't have left the cells.*

As if to confirm he was above suspicion, Jenifa was on the bed beside him. She was still fully clothed, and lying above the blankets. But still . . . She was sleeping with her knees up against her chest, which was endearingly girlish. His movement woke her, and she gave him a bleary gaze.

'Morning.'

'Afternoon, I think,' he said. Bright daylight was pouring through the bedroom's thin red and blue curtains.

'How's the wrist?'

He lifted his arm, staring at the white plaster cast encasing his forearm and hand. His memory of the hospital was vague, he'd been so exhausted. 'It aches,' he admitted.

'You can take some more painkillers. It's been six hours.'

'I have painkillers?'

Her grin faded. 'I drove out to Xander Manor with the assault squad; you were only fifteen minutes ahead of us. We found the egg first. Then we went into the manor. Crudding Uracus! That room. I'm never going to forget that room! It was a slaughterhouse. Even the assault squad was puking their guts up. What happened, Chaing?'

'I used grenades on them.'

'Grenades? Come on!'

He reached out with his good arm, and grasped the hair on the back of her head, making her look at him. 'Grenades.'

'I thought you were dead,' she whispered. 'I thought that creature had come back. It nearly got us in the alley. I was so scared—'

'The Fallers are dead, the whole nest of them. I saw them die. You're safe.'

'We're never going to be safe. Not with those things Falling on us . . .'

He kissed her. It wasn't gentle. He wanted her, and she responded with the same hot urgency. When they broke off, they were both breathing harshly. Getting their clothes off became a frantic scramble. She had to help him with his shirtsleeve, tugging it over the cast.

'Ow!'

They both paused, then laughed before embracing eagerly. He was intrigued by the physique he exposed as he pulled her clothes off. It was as if she was compensating for her short stature by building muscle mass. He couldn't even guess what her daily workout must be like to become so brawny. Her strength was tremendously exciting. Their unrestrained rutting tangled up the blankets and sent the headboard slamming repeatedly against the wall, making the eventual release all the sweeter.

Jenifa finally rolled off him to smirk up at the ceiling as if she'd just heard a wicked secret. 'I needed that,' she confessed. 'Undercover work is constant crudding stress. And then last night hit us.'

'Like an egg on the head,' he agreed. His good hand carefully stroked strands of sweat-damped hair from her face. Looking at those hazel eyes, he felt absurdly content.

'It's been a strange week,' she said. 'I mean, this is what we're trained for, yes? But when it actually happens and we discover a nest, it seems . . . wrong. I guess, deep down, I wanted an operation that was all paperwork and bitching about my boss. Not this.'

'It was real. And I'm your boss.'

'Yeah. And quite a good one, too.' Her hand gripped his as he was tracing curving lines of muscle down her arm. 'So what was this?'

'This was . . . good.'

'Don't deflect, captain.'

'All right. We've just been through Uracus together, so this was kind of inevitable. But I don't want to throw it away in a counter-reaction.'

'Fair enough. We'll see where we go.' She kissed him.

'There's two things I need to deal with immediately.'

'What?'

'One: painkillers,' he said, letting the urgency filter into his voice. His wrist was throbbing badly inside the cast as a result of all their exertion.

'Oh, Chaing!' she was instantly all concern. 'Stupid!' She scrambled off the bed and walked over to her bag, which was lying beside the door.

He watched her keenly. Her sculpted frame made her seem like some idealized image of girlish vitality. *Does she have an Eliter heritage to look so perfect?*

'Here.' She returned with a small bottle of pills.

Chaing swallowed a couple of them.

'What's the second thing?' she asked.

He sat up and patted the mattress beside him. 'Your report,' he said as she sat beside him.

'What about it?'

'It has to confirm my report. When we were in Frikal Alley, we were both on edge. We saw a stray cat and thought it was something else. That's all. There was no creature.'

She pulled away slightly as she turned to give him a concerned look. 'Are you in trouble? That man who interviewed you last night, who was he?'

'Just a standard debrief. Nothing to worry about. I only want to make sure the paperwork is right, that's all.'

'He was from Varlan, wasn't he?'

'There was no creature.'

'Oh, great Giu, it's Section Seven!'

'A cat,' he said softly. 'It was a black cat. Understand?'

Jenifa nodded reluctantly. But the happiness had drained from her spry face, to be replaced by real worry. 'Yes. Yes, you're right. It probably was.'

Thank you, he mouthed.

She started hunting round for her clothes. 'I need something to eat.'

'There's some milk in the fridge. I think.' He was a bit hazy on details, like how long it'd been there.

'Ha! I saw your kitchen when we got back here. I'm not going anywhere near it.'

Chaing produced a mock frown. The second-floor flat was a decent size, with two bedrooms and a bathroom. The kitchen appliances all worked; the block's manager had demonstrated them when he moved in. Admittedly, he ate most of his meals out. 'There's a hot stall at the end of the road. He's not got an enterprise licence, but the food's decent.'

'Okay.'

'Don't get the rice, it sits there for days. Order the noodles.'

'You just said he was good.'

'Good apart from the rice.'

'Okay. No rice. Got it.'

'You're coming back?' He winced at how needy that sounded.

'Yes. I'm coming back. If nothing else, I need a shower before I go into the office. They're reassigning me.' She pursed her lips. 'Hopefully not undercover work again. It wasn't exactly what I was expecting. I want to do something that'll get me noticed.'

'You did good work. That's what my report will say.'

She bent over and gave him a kiss. 'Thanks.'

The front door closed behind her with a loud thunk. Now that he had a moment, he looked round the bedroom, not liking how messy it was. Unwashed clothes piled up against the full laundry basket. Chest with the drawers open and clothes hanging out as if burglars had rejected them. A narrow threadbare rug on worn floorboards. His three big suitcases standing by the door, as if he'd just arrived.

He sighed. When he'd moved in, he had solid plans to smarten the place up. *When did I stop caring about how I lived?*

Although he already knew that answer: the day he left Portlynn. It was a pleasant town, built on hundreds of silt islands in the Nilsson Sound, all of them linked by an eclectic array of footbridges. It was clean, with a leisurely pace, and a fleet of boats coming and going all day long. It also had Sazkar, a deputy manager at the train station – though in the end, she was one of the main reasons he'd accepted the Opole posting. The rows over his job and PSR activities had just become too great.

At least that won't happen with Jenifa.

Jenifa didn't have any of Sazkar's inhibitions, either. He was still smiling fondly at how good the sex had been when there was a knock at the door. He put on his bathrobe, and tried to tie the belt as he hurried down the short dark hallway. 'What did you forget? I can give you a key,' he announced as he opened the door.

It wasn't Jenifa. The man standing there was wearing a dark suit, like one of the clerks from the records hall. He shoved a brown paper package at Chaing.

'You'll need to sign for this, sir.'

Chaing had to balance the package on his cast as he tried to sign the clipboard with his left hand. The signature was illegible. 'What is it?'

'Restricted documents from your new section, sir. Don't allow anyone else to read them.'

Chaing made it to the living room before he realized the timing wasn't accidental. *They knew she was here. Uracus! They're watching me. How many of them are there that they can afford the manpower to do that? I can't be that important. Or . . . Oh great Giu, is Jenifa one of them? Did she tell them she'd left?*

That was the thing with Section Seven: you never knew who was a part of it. They supposedly had members in every PSR office on Bienvenido, at every level.

But that's just rumour. Stonal said they're only interested in breeder Fallers. Chaing laughed at himself. *Yeah, the planet's chief super spook told me that, so it must be true.*

He looked down at the package and pulled the string off. There were three thick folders inside, along with a lapel pin – a pale blue rectangle with a gold stripe down the centre: the insignia of the political division. That pin gave its wearer the authority to question or give orders to anyone, even regional directors. He looked round the living room, almost guilty. Jenifa would be back soon, and she wasn't authorized to see the folders. *Is this a test? Uracus, I'm getting paranoid.* He shoved the folders in his briefcase, locked it, and went to the bathroom for a wash.

*

'We missed a Treefall,' Jenifa announced as she arrived back, holding several brown paper bags full of food from the stall. 'Ten o'clock this morning. Must've slept right through it. The stall owner said the bomb flash was visible, even against the sunlight. Loads of people saw it.'

Chaing poured some hot water from the kettle into a teapot, and brought it over to the table. He wished he'd had more time to clear up; the living room was almost as disorganized as the bed-room. But it'd taken longer than he'd expected to wash, standing in the bath using a sponge; the doctor who'd put his cast on had warned him not to get it wet. At least he'd managed to find some clean plates. 'I'd forgotten there's a Liberty mission flying,' he admitted.

'Yeah. To be fair, we've been kind of busy. The astronaut was one of Slvasta's relatives, apparently.'

Chaing couldn't help it; he started chuckling.

'What's funny?' she asked.

'Nothing. But I'm glad he's having a better time than I am.'

They doled out the food. She'd bought some deep-fried coi prawns with cashew nuts, he saw. *This could work out very well.*

'No chopsticks?' she asked as she lifted a tangle of noodles with bean sprouts onto her plate.

'No. I'm a cutlery kind of man. Problem?'

She clicked her chopsticks together, and grinned. 'Deal-breaker.'

'Have you still got the car outside?' he asked.

'Sure.'

'I'd like to drive out to Xander Manor when we're finished.'

'Urrgh. Really? Why?'

'It's still my case. Yaki should have sent a scene examination team out there to see what evidence they can find. I want to check they're doing it right, that's all.'

'You sure you're up to that?'

He held up his cast. 'It's just a fracture. I'll come into the office with you after the manor.'

She chewed on some of the duck in ginger and gralula sauce, giving him a disapproving glance. 'Okay. But don't overdo it.'

*

Jenifa turned off Plamondon Avenue and braked sharply. There was a sheriff standing outside the gateway to Xander Manor. A chain had been slung between the two old stone pillars, with a sign hanging in the middle: Crime Scene. No Entry By Unauthorized Persons.

'Screw this,' Chaing grunted softly. He climbed out of the car, staring disbelievingly ahead.

'Hey, can't you idiots read—' the sheriff began. His voice died away as he saw Chaing's PSR uniform. 'Uh, sorry, sir.'

'What happened?' Chaing asked.

The grand old manor had been reduced to a pile of rubble, with charred timbers sticking out at odd angles. Wisps of smoke continued to rise from the smouldering wood.

'It was a nest, sir,' the sheriff said. 'Your people, they got 'em all. Filthy scum.'

'I know we got them. I was here last night. What happened afterwards?'

The young man shrugged lamely. 'The Marines said this was a standard decontamination procedure.'

'Marines?' Jenifa asked as she joined Chaing.

'Yes, they were leaving when I started my shift. Aren't they great? Tough buggers. Nothing gets past them.'

Chaing blinked heavily as he gazed at the scorched debris. 'Nothing at all, it would seem,' he murmured.

*

They hadn't announced they were coming in, yet word got out as soon as Jenifa drove into the office's underground car park. News of his arrival raced on ahead of him. It was a building full of spies, after all, Chaing reflected in amusement as people came hurrying out of their offices to line the brick corridors, applauding him approvingly. Colleagues he barely knew smiled wide in welcome, telling him *well done*, shaking his uninjured hand enthusiastically, offering a few words of sorrow and commiseration about Lurvri. *PSR one, Fallers nil. We showed the bastards.*

Yaki was standing outside her office to give him an animated greeting for everyone watching. Jenifa mouthed *later* and disappeared back down the corridor as Yaki guided him inside.

'Sit,' the director said, her public good humour fading. 'Are you okay? I wasn't expecting you in today.'

'It's just a plaster cast. Nothing too bad.'

She grunted and sat behind her desk. Chaing waited in the silence which followed, slightly unnerved. It was her fault she hadn't been available last night. *Is she going to try and blame me?* Then Yaki produced a small mirthless smile and turned over her right lapel. She wore a Section Seven pin on the underside, identical to his own.

'Ah,' Chaing said, and clicked the lock on his briefcase. He took out the pin.

'I thought so,' Yaki said. 'It would take something like a breeder to bring Stonal down here.'

'So . . . ?'

'Yeah.' She pointed to her scar. 'Brute had claws the size of fingers. It was as big as a crudding horse, too. I was lucky – emptied my entire magazine into the bastard before it died.'

'There were two creatures there last night. One was like a panther, and the other was human-shaped, but huge. I was going to be eaten, then the Warrior Angel arrived.'

148

Yaki's eyebrows rose. 'You seriously want to keep that part quiet. Even from me. Read your Section Seven briefing.'

'Understood.'

'Sorry I wasn't there. Lapse of protocol. My fault; I was travelling between functions and stopped off with some councillors for a drink. I didn't phone in a contact number, because nothing ever happens in Opole. And you got lumbered with Stonal because of it.'

'I've just been out to the manor. There's nothing left.'

'That'll be the Marines. They're pretty thorough.'

'There could have been more members in that nest. But the Marines have destroyed any evidence. I've got nothing to go on.'

'Yes, so you're going to have to work the case from another angle. If there are any survivors, they'll sneak into another nest. You had other active cases, didn't you?'

Chaing shrugged. 'A few leads.'

'Then go get them. I won't be stopping you.'

'There was one thing. Corilla mentioned the Fallers were communicating like Eliters, but the signals were encrypted.'

'I haven't heard that one before.'

'I'd like to bring in some technicians from the Eliter division. They have receivers that monitor the Eliter frequencies. If they do pick up weird signals, we could triangulate on them.'

'You haven't ever heard Eliter signals before, have you? I have. If you play them through a speaker, they're like a long whistle. It's "digital", apparently; they turn sound into binary code, which itself is coded. We don't have the electronics to unravel it all; not even the big computators at Port Ingmar are good enough. As far as the rest of us are concerned, all the Eliter transmissions are encrypted. So what your Eliter friend was saying is that *they* can't understand them. Which means the Fallers probably have eggsumed Eliters, and duplicated their macrocellular clusters.'

'Crud.'

'So asking PSR Eliter division techs to monitor transmissions is a dead end.'

But not Eliters, he thought. *They could scan for them. Except*

Stonal sent Corilla away. Stupid move. 'All right. I'll need a new team to hunt for nests. I'd like Corporal Jenifa assigned as my partner to replace Lurvri.'

'Are you sure about that? It's generally not a good idea to have someone you're screwing working under you. Emotional attachment can lead to hesitation, among other problems.'

Crud, how did she know that? 'I wasn't emotionally attached to Lurvri, and that didn't help him.'

'All right,' she said. 'You can have Jenifa. Your call.'

'Thank you.'

*

Early-morning light was just starting to shine round the red and blue curtains when Chaing woke up. It revealed Jenifa lying beside him. She was under the bedclothes this time, and naked – like him. He looked at her for a while, enjoying the memory of last night. His wrist still ached from that, so he moved his arm trying to ease it.

She woke at the motion, disorientated at first as she glanced round his bedroom, then she saw him watching her and grinned. 'Morning.'

He kissed her, using it to huddle up closer. 'Morning to you.'

'You're very eager . . .' A curious frown, and her hand was snaking down his stomach to find how stiff he was. She giggled. 'Men in the morning. It's like a crudding alarm clock.'

He nibbled her ear and moved down to her throat, which made her squeak.

'Tickles,' she protested. Then she shoved the bedclothes away and slung a leg over his hips, rising up to straddle him. Instead of taking him inside herself, she began to toy with him. He groaned in frustration. The wan beams of light stippled her skin, bestowing her robust figure with a rich gold hue. Anticipation became unbearable.

'Please,' he moaned.

Smirking, she leant forwards so her mouth was a centimetre from his ear, a hot whisper telling him the wicked things he'd have to do before she'd let him inside her.

The phone on the bedside cabinet started ringing.

'No crudding way!' Chaing cried.

Jenifa nearly fell off the bed, she was laughing so hard.

He glared at the phone, but of course it was no good. He wouldn't be getting a phone call at home and at this time unless it was extremely important. 'Yes?' he snapped into the handset.

'Am I interrupting something?' Stonal's voice asked.

Once again Chaing wondered if his flat was being bugged. 'No, sir.'

'We have a problem. You'll be helping me control a regiment operation.'

'Er . . . Yes, of course. What regiment operation?'

'I'm conducting a search of the countryside not far from Opole. A car will pick you up in ten minutes. There'll be a helicopter for you at the Air Defence Force aerodrome.'

'I'll be ready, sir.'

6

They reversed Ry's furtive arrival – a procedure he would have laughed at if it hadn't been so ridiculous. The same escort took him back out of the anonymous PSR office block and into the car, which retraced its route to the hangar with the seaplane. He got in, and one of the aircraft crew handed him the crumpled flight suit he'd worn during the mission. Nobody said anything as he changed back into it, making sure his mission badge was prominent on his chest. Then they all sat and waited.

Sure enough, base personnel started to appear in the hangar soon after – colleagues from the Astronaut Corps, flight controllers, Cape workers, a regiment band, reporters and the newsreel camera crews. Finally the radio operator looked up and said: 'They're ready for you, sir.'

The band was playing when he stuck his head out of the seaplane door. A grand cheer went up; flashbulbs went off. Ry raised an arm to wave. At the foot of the airstairs, General Delores saluted. He walked down and saluted her back. A ten-year-old girl in a pretty red and green dress gave him a bunch of flowers and smiled up shyly. He looked round the hangar at the enthusiastic faces, returning their smiles. Then stopped. Anala was standing two rows back from the front, giving him a mocking slow handclap, an icily contemptuous expression on her face.

Ry didn't get back to his private quarters until after midnight. There had been the official press interviews, carefully monitored and guided by the Astronaut Corps political officers; then the formal splashdown banquet in the mess hall. Followed by a less formal, but still traditional, session in the Astronaut Corps bar, drinking the same shots of Dirantio Comrade Demitri had downed after the first successful Silver Arrow launch – during which no one, *absolutely no one*, had mentioned anything about any part of the mission having difficulties. Nothing about the delay after he arrived, and the welcome-home ceremony in the hangar. A whole evening of talk which said nothing. It was quite remarkable, really.

He took his dress uniform off and got into a pair of shorts and a T-shirt – another change of clothes; he'd lost track of how many there'd been today – and gave the bed a longing look. Yet he knew he wouldn't be sleeping any time soon.

And there it was: a discreet knock on the door. Just before he opened it, he wondered if he'd got this wrong and it would be another armed escort, and the last anyone would know or see of Pilot Major Ry Evine would be the newsreel films of his splashdown banquet. But it was Anala, looking rather sexy in her tailored dress uniform with the top three buttons on her white blouse undone.

Ry gestured her in with an exaggerated motion, realizing he'd had quite a lot of Dirantio shots. Then he put his finger to his lips, and gave his quarters an embellished glance round.

She responded with an exasperated scowl, but nodded in understanding. 'Good to see you.'

'And you.' He started to kiss her, then discovered it wasn't being returned. 'Oh,' he grunted.

'Come on,' she said, more sympathetically. 'I think you need a proper sleep. You can tell me all about it in the morning.'

'You're probably right.' Ry looked round for the bed—

*

He woke up with that uncomfortable fading ache which told him he'd slept through a hangover. Anala was moving round in the little galley kitchen which all the astronaut quarters had. All she wore was the white blouse, which barely came down over her hips. It was a fantastic sight to wake up to.

She brought a mug of coffee over to the bed. 'I thought you might need this.'

'Thanks. I'm not too bad actually.'

'Lucky you. Astronauts and parties! No wonder none of us ever worry about making it to old age; alcohol poisoning is going to get us long before a faulty capsule.'

'Right.' He was looking at the bed with its rumpled sheets, wondering if she'd spent the night beside him. *Perhaps she'd like to spend the morning on the mattress as well?* Then he remembered the welcome in the hangar, and decided not to push his luck. Besides . . .

'Drink your coffee,' she told him, 'and we'll walk to the canteen for breakfast.'

Something in her voice . . . 'Okay.'

All of Cape Ingmar's accommodation blocks were on the north side, well away from the engineering hangars and rocket-assembly facilities. Concrete paths between the military-style buildings were lined with shrubs that struggled to produce any flowers in the sandy soil. When they stepped out of the astronaut quarters, a warm wind was blowing in off the sea. Humidity hadn't yet reached its usual hostile peak. Ry took some deep breaths, finally starting to feel the tension slacken off as he inhaled the fresh air.

'So are we safe to talk out here?' Anala asked.

'If we're not, we might as well pack for the Pidrui mines right now and save them the trouble of a show trial.'

'I'm not sure you'd even get that,' she said. 'All of Cape Ingmar was in lockdown while the political officers talked to you.'

'Officer – not officers. Just one. He didn't give me his name, but he had to be from Section Seven.'

'Figures. So what the crud happened up there?'

'There was *something*. I saw it. Some kind of craft. I think it was hiding behind Tree 3,788-D.'

'Really? Not debris from the Tree?'

'It was a spacecraft.' He closed his eyes, his perfect memory bringing back the image of the bomb's plasma shell, the slim contrail spiking out from it, the tip curving round. 'I saw it manoeuvre.

154

But there wasn't any rocket exhaust. It was alien, Anala, and it was heading down to Bienvenido. And those bastards from Section Seven don't give a crud. All they're worried about is suppressing the knowledge.'

'They won't supress this. Not at the highest levels. They can't ignore this.'

'They've got the photos I took. There's no evidence. If I say anything, they'll tell everyone I tried to sabotage the missile.'

'Yeah, and how *did* that happen?'

'It must have been the alien. Anything with that level of technology could interfere with our communications.'

'The only aliens I know that can fly without a reaction drive are the Skylords. Do you think they're coming back? The Church of the Return would love that.'

'No, the Skylords were as big as mountains. This thing was small, probably about the same size as the Liberty capsule.'

'Not an egg. Not a Skylord. Not a Prime. What, then?'

'The only species other than the Skylords that don't need rockets to fly through space is us: humans.'

Alana gave him a shocked look. 'The Commonwealth?'

'That's the only possibility left.'

'It can't be them.'

'Why not?'

'Because they'd . . . show themselves?'

'Maybe, maybe not. I don't know.'

'What are you going to do?'

Ry's hand went automatically to his mission badge, fingertips stroking its small hard curves. 'What I swore to do when I joined this regiment: to protect Bienvenido from aliens. All aliens. Not just the Fallers.'

'Same as everyone else on this planet, then.'

'I have to know, Anala. I have got to find out what I saw up there.'

She stood still and brushed at the hair the wind was blowing across her face, revealing a troubled expression on her sharp features. 'I know you. That's trouble coming.'

'Whatever it takes. I don't care. They don't frighten me. They can stop me if they catch me, but they can't intimidate me into silence.'

'Fine words. Slvasta would be proud.'

Ry saw the old political officer's face, emotionless and calculating in the interview room, waiting for the *correct* answers. 'I doubt it.'

She grinned cheerfully. 'So what have you got in mind?'

'I need ten minutes with the flight centre's computator. When are you due an orbital mechanics training session?'

Teaching room 3-B was one of several identical rooms in the astronavigation department. A small window provided a view out over the shallow dunes along the neck of Cape Ingmar's plateau. Ry had spent weeks of his life in this very room, sitting at one of the three wooden tables, trying to keep interested as the instructor droned on behind the lectern. The big blackboard was covered in curving vectors, like giant arrows stabbing out from a small chalk representation of Bienvenido, each with a series of equations running along them.

He ignored that and walked over to the chunky teleprinter standing beside the lectern. The machine resembled an oversized typewriter, with a near-inexhaustible supply of paper that kept spooling out of the top. Its printer head was a small electrically powered globe that bobbed about like some badly neurotic creature.

Anala pulled the blind down over the glass pane in the door. 'You're going to have to hurry.'

'I know.' It was six in the evening, and the trainee astronauts were taking a break, which meant the department was almost deserted. Still, it was a risk.

Ry bent down to switch the teleprinter on. The button was on the side of the metal pedestal. He flicked it across. Nothing happened. 'There's a lock,' he said in surprise. In all the years he'd been using teleprinters at the Cape, he'd never had to actually switch one on. The machines were always up and running when the teachers began their training sessions.

'What do you mean, a lock?' Alana asked.

'It's locked. You need a key to switch it on. Crudding Uracus!'

She hurried over to check for herself. 'Damn. Okay, let's go.'

'Go?'

'Get out of here.'

'But—'

'Ry, think! You're only going to have one chance. We can't afford time to try and hotwire this. Now let's go. We'll work out how to get a key for you – after we're out.'

'Right,' he hissed through clenched teeth.

The door opened. General Delores walked in.

Shock and guilt froze Ry's legs. *This is it; crash and burn.* 'General,' he began. 'This is my idea, not Anala's.'

'You're an idiot,' the general snapped. 'One day after Stonal interviewed you, and you're breaking into restricted facilities.'

'Stonal?' Ry blurted inanely.

'The Section Seven director with a very long sharp stick up his arse. The man who controls every PSR officer and informant in the Cape. And that's a lot of informants.'

'Oh.'

The general narrowed her eyes. 'What do you want with a teleprinter?'

'I'm going to use the computator to work out a course vector.'

'The intruder's?'

She knows! She knows it's real! 'Yes.'

'Here.' General Delores held up a fat cylindrical key. 'Be quick. Even I can be held to account by the PSR.'

Ry's throat was contracting from the burst of relief and grati-tude. Just knowing he wasn't alone against the PSR was—

'Get on with it!'

He took the key and switched on the teleprinter. There were a number of programmes available on the computator. He typed in the activation sequence for the navigation vector plot, and waited until the manic jerky ball printed READY.

Two columns: one with the fixed coordinates, the second with the sextant reading. Ry started typing out the fifteen-digit coord-inates for both. He'd managed seven readings before the intruder had disappeared from sight, and each time he'd meticulously checked the Liberty capsule's own location on the console display.

Anala blinked and peered forwards to read the printout paper when she realized what he was doing. 'You remember all those coordinates?'

Ry nodded silently. They would know what that meant, what he was. His *other* heritage. *As if that matters now.*

He finished typing the numbers, and entered COMPUTE.

The ball hopped up and down for a few seconds, then started to whirr noisily again as it printed out numbers for latitude and longitude. Ry tore the paper off the teleprinter. It wouldn't be exact, he knew that; there were too many variables. But he had the rough area where it would have landed – which was all he needed.

'Now what?' General Delores asked as she shut down the teleprinter and retrieved her key.

'This is where it was heading,' Ry said, holding up the paper. 'So it's where I go.'

'I can't cover for you,' she warned him.

'I know. Thank you, general.'

'I'm coming with you,' Anala said.

'No, you're not. I won't be coming back. This has finished my career here. But the Liberty programme needs good astronauts. That's you, Anala. You've earned your flight. Don't throw that away. I don't know what this thing is, but we still have to kill the Trees.'

'Ry . . .'

'I'll get word back to you. I'll tell you what I find. Somehow. I promise.'

*

An hour later, Ry was on the train out of Cape Ingmar, a non-stop journey which took a day to curve around the edge of the Desert of Bone before heading south to terminate at Portlynn. At the big station there, he bought a single ticket for the express to Opole.

BOOK THREE

Running From a Fall

1

It rained for most of the day in the Albina valley, as it did for the majority of days on the northern fringes of the Sansone mountains. Florian was used to the microclimate of the foothills. Seven years he'd spent as the valley's forest warden, looking after the trees that grew up the broad slopes, maintaining the firebreak lanes, watching out for roxwolf packs. So he'd learned that for eight months each year, chaotic southern winds would push the clouds through the high snow-capped peaks before sending them slithering over the foothills where they coated the forested slopes in a persistent drizzle. Then the summer months arrived, and the sea winds died down. That was when a more intermittent rain came in from the north, carried by the warm air from the heart of the continent.

He'd known the rain would end by mid-afternoon, recognizing the weather pattern as soon as he rose that morning. So after breakfast he stayed close to the little lodge with its shaggy thatch roof and shifted stodgy clumps of dalfrond from the big pile to the metal trailer ready to take to the trenches that afternoon. It was the Vatni who brought the stuff to him, dredging the dark-green water weed from the lake at the bottom of the valley where they had a village. Teal, his springer spaniel, trotted along behind him, curved bushy tail wagging about and soaking up its usual quantity of mud.

Once the trailer was full, he backed the four-wheel-drive SMI (Siegen Motor Industry) Openland truck up to it and hitched the two together. The trailer's left tyre looked slightly flat again. It'd been three weeks since he filed a report of the slow puncture with the county office of the forest warden service. Jackso, the warden two valleys to the west, had loaned him a compressor, which now sat in the lean-to shed on the side of the lodge. He unwound the air hose and screwed it onto the tyre's valve. The compressor's electric motor started with a vigorous whirring sound, and the tyre inflated.

That the cottage had an electrical supply had come as a surprise to Florian back when he arrived, but the full electrification of Bienvenido had been one of Slvasta's prestige projects, giving everybody the same benefit of the new and modern post-Transition civilization, no matter where they lived. Dams were built across hundreds of valleys, bringing employment to tens of thousands in every county, while newly nationalized factories re-tooled and re-educated their workforce to build the hydro-turbines Mother Laura had designed before she sacrificed herself to exterminate the Prime.

Not that there were many uses for electricity in the warden's lonely lodge. Each of his four rooms had an electric light bulb. There was a radio. A pump shunted water from the rainwater tank through to the back boiler on the wood-fired cooking range, allowing him to have hot water in the sink and shower. He also had some woodworking tools in the lean-to.

That was all Florian needed. Ever since Lurji, his brother, had fled the PSR – supposedly to Port Chana, where the Eliter radical movement was strongest – Florian had wanted to be by himself. He never had got on very well with people – a situation exacerbated by his Eliter status, condemning him to constant taunts and bullying at school, and even worse victimization during his time as a conscript for the county regiment.

It was maths which interested him, and he was good at it – an ability magnified thanks to his macrocellular clusters. He even made a few modifications to the binary codes of the operating system they all used, improving the file search function. The Eliter community, of course, was eager to have him work on refining and expanding their routines, which was an ongoing project. But for all their solidarity, they endured relentless persecution, driving angry people like his brother into more open acts of defiance. That was a life he knew would bring him nothing but misery. And outside the Eliter community, there were no intellectually challenging jobs available, not for the likes of him. He could never escape his heritage. Eliter status was on your birth certificate and identity papers, condemning your life. It didn't even matter if an Eliter's children didn't have functioning macrocellular clusters, they were still deemed Elite – just another injustice perpetrated by the government, of which there were many. Some Eliters had managed to hide their family's abilities from the PSR, but not many in this day and age. If he joined the civil service, he would never rise above grade five – junior management level. The university wouldn't allow him to study. And he would certainly never be allowed to join the Astronaut Regiment, whose Liberty missions he'd worshiped from an early age.

Most would consider the forest warden job, with its isolation, to be a curse, but to Florian it was a blessing. He joined the warden service the same week he was discharged from his national service. They accepted him without question; these days, few people were interested in such a career. He'd heard nearly a third of the valleys under their stewardship lacked a warden.

Out here in the seclusion of Albina valley, he could spend a few hours each day doing the actual job, while the rest of the time he could sit and think. His macrocellular clusters allowed him to become an even greater recluse, giving him the ability to live quite literally inside his own head to the exclusion of everything else.

In the afternoon, when the cloud had lifted to form a dank roof over the valley and the drizzle had abated, he drove the Openland truck up the eastern slope with Teal sitting in the passenger seat. The Openland's fat tyres had deep treads, giving it plenty of traction on the spindly lingrass which covered the ground between the trees. Albina valley was covered in a mix of terrestrial pine and native browfrey, a deciduous tree sprouting long trains of grey-blue leaves that dangled like a spindly moss from its whip-thin branches.

The main tracks were cut vertically up the slope, with firebreak paths extending outwards at ninety degrees every hundred and fifty metres, dividing the entire valley wall into a grid. Some tracks were quite overgrown, which he dutifully logged in his memory files. He would come back with a chainsaw on a dry day and trim down the worst of the overhanging branches. Then there were the other paths through the trees, produced by wild goats and shal-sheiks meandering along gradients. Even his memory log didn't have all of them mapped out yet.

Twenty minutes after leaving the lodge, he turned off the main track and rumbled along firebreak AJ54 (in his private designation). The firebreak was narrow, and the lingrass thick and cloying. There was a small circular clearing five hundred metres in, which the Openland could just turn round in – if you knew how and took it slowly. He kept a hard lock on the steering wheel as the fronds of browfrey slapped against the windscreen.

When he killed the motor, silence engulfed him like a benign presence. He sat still for a moment, relishing the seclusion. It simply wasn't possible to get further away from people than here, which made these times away from the lodge quite precious.

'Go on, boy,' he told Teal. 'Find me some rabbits.' Teal obediently jumped out of the Openland and started pushing through the tangled undergrowth. The forest's rabbit population had been increasing a lot lately, despite the native bussalores preying on them. Knapsvine and jibracken, which grew in abundance between the tree trunks, were excellent foods for them. Unfortunately it meant the newly planted saplings on the western slopes were getting badly chewed. Again, the county's warden service office had known about it for the last two years. Nothing had been done.

Waxed leather trousers tucked into knee-high boots kept the water from the lingrass off his legs as he gathered up bundles of dalfrond from the trailer and carried them down to the trench. There were eighteen identical trenches scattered at random around the valley. He'd methodically dug them out during the first eighteen months, his spade making light work of the soft peaty soil – a metre and a half deep, two wide, and twenty long. The bottom was covered in lengths of wood that proved too spindly for logs that he could use in the lodge's range stove. Nothing odd or suspicious about that, if anyone stumbled across them. Nor the layer of smelly dalfrond scattered on top; that was applied to accelerate the wood's decay.

Florian scanned the trench and smiled as he counted eleven waltan fungi that had fallen in. The waltan was a strange thing – a fan-shaped nodule of fungus that was mobile. It didn't move fast, but it could sense the rotting wood it fed on, and moved inexorably towards it. And the trenches, with their decomposing branches and bark, were a rich source. Unfortunately, once the fungus fell in and began to leach the nutrients it thrived on, it then had no way of climbing up the trench's vertical walls afterwards. The trenches were the most basic trap it was possible to create.

When he'd finished scattering the fresh dalfrond weeds over the wood, Florian picked up the tough fibrous waltans, the smallest of which was the size of his head, and dumped them in the trailer.

Teal reappeared, his head hanging low, and his muddy coat snagged with tiny twigs and knapsvine burrs.

'Nothing, huh?' Florian said. 'Don't know why I bother with you.'

Teal clambered back into the passenger seat and gave him a forlorn look.

Florian drove to the drying shed, hidden in a dense clump of pines along firebreak FB39, and hung the waltans up in net bags. It took at least three months to dry one out properly in Albina valley's humid atmosphere. There were a couple of batches that had withered to the point they were starting to crumble through the netting, so he carried those back to the trailer before heading home.

*

Evening was Florian's favourite time, and he had a very specific routine. As the sun began to sink below the horizon he loaded several logs into the range cooker, and put the big pot of rabbit stew back onto the hotplate. His kitchen took up half of the living room. Over the years he'd added several pots and pans, along with a drawer full of new utensils. Crockery pots with rubber-seal lids held his flour and sugar. Herbs from the garden hung on a rack above the range cooker, drying out. One day, when savings from his minuscule wages had grown enough, he planned on buying an electrical refrigerator, which would probably double his electricity bill.

First there was the chicken coop to check. Three new eggs there.

'They'll do for breakfast, boy,' he told Teal happily. Teal wagged his tail on the other side of the wire mesh. Teal was no longer allowed inside the pen after getting a little bit carried away two years ago. It was for his own good; a chicken claw had left quite a graze on his nose.

Goat pen next. Florian sat on the stool and milked Embella. He got just over half a litre from her, which was one reason he wasn't hurrying for the refrigerator.

Inside again, and he began to mix a new batch of bread dough for tomorrow, scattering in a few rosemary leaves then kneading it for a good ten minutes before shaping it into a hemisphere. The proved dough from yesterday was taken out of the bowl, and the fresh one put in. He draped the bowl with a damp cloth, and checked the temperature of the oven, which was up to two hundred degrees Celsius.

The bread was put in the oven, and the stew stirred. There wasn't much left.

'Be taking a trip tonight, boy,' he told Teal. 'Fancy myself some lamb for next week.'

A subroutine in his macrocellular clusters began counting down. The timer was one he'd written extra code for, so it could count down as well as up. He settled into the comfy chair, switched off the electric bulb, and closed his eyes.

The routines squirted coloured sparks into the darkness which rapidly coalesced into the image of the Warrior Angel – the Eliter's standard activation symbol. Icographics, the Eliters called them – strips of translucent colour, like malleable glass, that could be bent and twisted and stretched to provide illustration, mainly for graphs. He'd welcomed them when he was younger, using them to help structure equations. You could create three-dimensional fields of them, and punch them with dark alphanumerics, creating matrices of numbers governed by equations, transforming the physical into mathematics, explaining so much of the world. He'd achieved a lot with them back then, before growing frustrated with their limitations. So he'd dug back through the icographic formatting routine and begun to add code of his own, enhancing functionality.

Florian's mindscape unfolded. He was no longer in a dark lodge in Albina valley. Now he was sitting on a beach of some tropical island. His skin felt the warmth of the sun, he smelt the sea air – or what he determined sea air would smell like from the descriptions he'd read: sort of like sweet rose perfume. Waves lapped against the snow-white sand. It was the world of *Danivan's Voyage*, the book he'd read when he was eleven, captivating him because it described Bienvenido after the Fallers had been purged – a glimpse of the future he had clung to throughout all the bad days, then years.

It wasn't perfect. There were areas which lacked colour. Some sections weren't three-dimensional, or flickered between the two. But he was making progress, exploring the abilities of his macrocellular clusters, the effects that could be generated within his mind. And the code that made it possible. Code was king. Code was his true life now.

He settled back and summoned up the audio routines. They opened round him, column after column written by his own designator subroutines. He could play music from a file now. It wasn't particularly clear, and there were lulls. A lot of that was to do with his radio; reception in Albina valley wasn't good. Atmospherics affected the short-wave signals, and the new medium-wave services broadcast out of Opole were blocked by the valley walls.

He had plans for all that. Plans for a routine that could take the meagre music files and use them as a basis to compose new music, with him as a conductor. Plans to build a medium-wave radio with an aerial on the peak of the valley. Plans to build a converter that would change analogue signals to digital, so that his macrocellular clusters could receive them directly; that way, he wouldn't have to rely on inefficient old ears. So many ideas. Terannia sent him books about mathematics and electrical circuits when she could, but they were all mimeographed copies of originals and didn't tell him what he really needed to know. But they gave him the fundamentals, so code could be written to solve the problems. Code could do anything. Code could save the world.

*

It had been dark for three hours when Florian drove the Openland down to the lake at the base of the valley. His eyes provided him with a grainy green-tinged vision of the landscape, allowing him to keep the headlights off. The only people likely to see the four-by-four would be people doing the same thing as him, but avoiding attention was second nature for Eliters.

The lake was seven kilometres long and three at the widest. Nine streams fed into it, with the river Kellehar running out the far end. It was one of the hundreds of tributary rivers that merged into the river Crisp that drained the lands to the north of the Sansone mountains all the way up to the Pritwolds, and from the coast to the west of Opole.

Florian drew up on the edge of the Vatni village and switched the engine off. The aliens had been here for over sixty years, swimming upstream from the coast to spread down several tributaries. They tended to settle on lakes like this one, which weren't close to any main human towns. Their huts were long cylindrical affairs woven out of pine and browfrey branches that seemed to be connected into a single chaotic maze.

Infra-red vision showed him the bright scarlet blobs of fires burning on hearths in the centre of the larger huts, the cooler amber haze of smoke rising up through long clay flues. The Vatni didn't have much to trade with humans; the cultures were too different. Back on Aqueous they didn't even have fire. The tiny islands on that world of water had never evolved any kind of woody vegetation; the best their biosphere had come up with was a kind of spiky coral lichen. Yet once those initial Vatni families arrived on Bienvenido, they'd readily taken to the innovation, and now cooked a lot of food. They said their ancestral memories showed them they'd once had fire back on whatever world they'd originated from prior to the Void. Knives were also a popular item to be traded, along with basic tools. Some of the larger coastal settlements even had electricity, supplied from Bienvenido's grid.

Most Vatni settlements exchanged fish for human goods. The village in Albina valley supplied Florian with fish from the lake, but mainly he paid them cash for the dalfrond. Cash which he then used to buy them what they wanted from the general store in Wymondon on his fortnightly trips for his own supplies.

It was Mooray that came out to greet him. Like all his kind, the Vatni was nearly three and a half metres long from his nose to the tip of his dorsal tail. His body was a fat cylinder weighing in at nearly a thousand kilograms. Yet despite their bulk, the Vatni were surprisingly lithe, even out of the water. Mooray's hide was a dense grey-brown fur, like bristles that had fused together, which shone with a waxy oil that made it look like he was permanently damp. That colour showed he was in his early middle age. As a Vatni got older, the hide would tinge into blotchy rust-red.

He waddled towards Florian on his three flattened tentacle-like tails that wriggled across the compacted ground like synchronized snakes. The thick dorsal tail was the shortest, used for balance alone when Mooray was out of the water, with the lower two providing traction. The trisymmetrical limb configuration was repeated for the mid-body flippers. His dorsal flipper was purely a fin for when he was in the water, while the remaining pair of serpentine flippers were longer and had pincer tips. There were also three tusks protruding from Mooray's triangular mouth, with the longest one at the top, curving down.

Three large gold-hued multi-segment eyes peered down at Florian, and Mooray emitted a lengthy liquid squealing sound, as if he was gurgling a thick syrup, interspaced with fast clicking as his tusks drummed together.

Florian brought up his translation routine.

'Greetings, my friend Florian of the land,' Mooray was saying. 'Are you meat hunting again this night?'

Florian took the modified flute out of his pocket and positioned the castanets carefully in his right hand. Using Vatni speech was a prolonged operation, even for an Eliter, but the routines governed his lips and tongue movements, allowing him a decent stab at speaking Vatni directly. 'My gratitude to you for seeing me, friend Mooray of the water. You are correct in thinking I would hunt this night. Will you honour me with your presence?'

'I will be delighted to go with you. Have you made progress with the killing apparatus?'

'Progress is slow, for which I apologize. I think you would require a pump handle to pull the string back.' Modifying a crossbow for Mooray had been an ongoing project for over a year now. Shaping it to be held by Vatni flippers had been relatively easy, but those pincers didn't really have the strength to crank the string back. An additional mechanism was needed for that. Routines could create basic three-dimensional designs, but Florian's carpentry skills didn't quite match his ambitions.

'No apology is required,' Mooray chirruped and thrummed. 'Your attempts are a demonstration of friendship which I find most honourable.'

'I will succeed eventually,' Florian warbled back.

'All things will be in the end.'

They walked around the huts to the stubby wharf the Vatni had built into the lake. Very occasionally anglers and other coun- tryfolk would visit to trade. The Vatni were anxious to make them feel welcome.

The boat waiting at the end had been built for Florian by the Vatni, more rounded than a human rowing boat, but very stable. Florian climbed in and sat on the bench. Teal curled up behind him, while Mooray made the whole thing rock about as he lumbered in and lay at the prow, with his head over the gunwales.

'I'm going to go up to Naxian valley,' Florian said.

'A good choice for the land meat creatures.'

Florian cast off and swung the long oars out over the side. The

Naxian valley stream which fed into the lake was a good eight hundred metres around the shore. He began rowing.

'It is a clear night,' Florian remarked. Above them, the northern sky revealed the Ring Trees glittering silver-white in a mighty curve around the planet. One less tonight. He'd seen the atomic flash through the drab clouds as Liberty 2,673 successfully destroyed another enemy.

'It is an empty night,' Mooray replied.

'Aqueous should be rising soon. And Trüb is coming back into view from behind the sun. Even Ursell will shine bright before morning, so we can enjoy Mother Laura's triumph.'

'A full sky is a glorious sight.'

Florian smiled to himself. This was how he always got the Vatni talking about other worlds. There weren't many humans who took the time to get to know the Vatni. Contact was mainly limited to official meetings about guarding the coastlines, and merchants looking to trade. But he couldn't get enough of these stories, and their racial memory was extraordinary. Somehow the females passed knowledge on to their offspring while they were still in the second womb (of three).

It was the Vatni's knowledge that he used to embellish his most precious file, the astronomy one. A mindscape of the whole solar system, where he could tour around the planets at will – as he'd dreamed of doing as an astronaut. Images from telescopes had been incorporated to map out planetary surfaces with great accuracy. Aunt Terannia had even found him an old book which had photographs taken by Mother Laura's team when she opened the wormhole to survey the strange star system the Void had banished them to.

But it was the stories of the Vatni which allowed him to animate them, to make them live. Ursell before the Fireyear, a world with dark seas and wasteland continents, speckled with lights coming from Prime fortress enclaves – then the glorious blue fire enveloping the entire planet, the still-expanding atmosphere. Macule, with its vast ice caps and berg-cluttered equatorial ocean, the ominous craters pocking its bare sterile lands, carved by nuclear explosions millennia ago. Trüb, the strange uniform grey world, devoid of surface features, circled by its twelve tiny moons – but to the Vatni memory, a world of extraordinary colour.

Even the moons had been larger in the past, engulfed by mighty petals like a solid rainbow flower. Until the day, over a thousand years ago, when spaceships from the recently arrived Ursell landed on its smooth surface. The day Trüb's colours died, never to blossom again.

The Vatni, with their remarkable eyes, had spotted Ursell as soon as it appeared in orbit around this star. A century later the white sparks of the Prime ships had risen from its continents and flown across space. First they went to Trüb. Within days of their landing the surface had darkened, and the petals of the moons withered to nothing. The ships never came back, and the Prime sent no more to Trüb. Instead the next wave of Prime ships headed straight to Aqueous.

They had orbited the ocean globe for several days before departing.

'We know now we had a lucky escape,' Mooray said. 'Your great and wise Mother Laura told us the Prime need land not water to dwell on.'

The Vatni had watched the ships depart and fly to Macule next – which was also unsuitable for the Prime. They visited Asdil after that, briefly, then went on to examine every world orbiting their new star, an epic two-year voyage that saw them returning to Ursell at the end.

Then four centuries after the ships went home, Ursell began to flash with very bright explosions. Its atmosphere turned sour, and the cloud cover swelled to cover most of the surface.

'And what of Fjernt?' Florian asked. 'What do you remember seeing there?' Fjernt was a planet in the same orbit as Bienvenido and Aqueous, but in conjunction behind the sun, which meant it could never be seen from Bienvenido. All Florian knew was it had no oxygen in its atmosphere, and eighty per cent of the surface was water. Laura Brandt's brief survey had detected no radio emissions nor seen anything that could be a city.

'Clouds,' Mooray said. 'White as ice. Towers of cloud taller than a dozen land mountains. They spin and they dance as the world turns.'

'All the lands?' he asked, captivated.

As Mooray gurgled his flowery descriptions of the hidden planet, Florian turned the boat up into the stream that ran along the floor of the Naxian valley. It was wide for a stream, with plenty of water surging along its stony bed, but not quite big enough to qualify as a river in its own right. Rowing against the swift current was hard work. Florian was soon sweating.

A couple of hundred metres from the water, the well-maintained track up into the valley curved in from the west and began to follow the stream. It was easy enough to see, even without his superior Eliter vision. Like all country roads on Bienvenido, it was lined with trees in accordance with Captain Iain's law, passed seven hundred years after Landing, so that travellers would always be able to see the way ahead.

The huge ancient larches marched away into the night, all the way up to the Ealton family's farmhouse – a large stone mansion at the centre of half a dozen barns, stables, and yards.

Florian kept rowing, methodically pushing the boat along parallel to the avenue. Naxian was a lot wider than the Albina valley; its shallow slopes were predominantly pasture, with long swathes of jibracken clinging to the boggy folds. It was excellent terrain for raising herds of mountain sheep. The Ealton family had been doing just that for generations, dating back a thousand years before the Great Transition. Now they carried on under the People's Congress as they had done when the Captains ruled, only they did it under state licence – a difference which made no difference.

The road slowly split away from the stream, angling westwards. When they were a kilometre apart, Florian eventually turned the boat into the shallows and clambered out. Tall, stiff volreeds lined the swift water, and he secured the painter to a big rock jutting out of the bank.

The Ealton family farmhouse was another four kilometres upstream. On full magnification, Florian's eyes could just make out a small glimmer of red where the stone walls were a couple of degrees warmer than the night air.

'Can you see anything?' he asked Mooray.

'No people of the land are close.'

Florian reduced his zoom and started to scan the surrounding landscape. The centuries of work which generations of Ealtons had devoted to the valley had resulted in long drystone walls dividing the meadowland into regular pastures, extending across the valley floor and halfway up the slopes, almost reaching the high wild forests. A lot of the walls were in need of repair, with long sections crumbling away – just as they always had been. Strips of temporary wire fencing had been set up to block the bigger gaps.

Flocks of sheep showed up in his infra-red vision, red lumps clustered together for security and warmth. He picked the crossbow out of the boat. 'This way.'

They set off towards a walled-off pasture a couple of hundred metres away, which contained at least eighty sheep that he could see. The gate was held shut by a simple chain, which he removed quietly. None of the sheep moved when he pushed it open. Mooray and Teal slipped through the gap.

'Wait here,' he told them. Teal let out a tiny whine, but sat obediently next to the Vatni.

Florian loaded a quarrel into the crossbow as he walked towards a pack of seven sheep. They started to stir when he was about twenty metres away. He stood still and took careful aim.

The quarrel shot into the sheep's skull, killing it instantly. The others scattered, bleating in panic as it collapsed onto the ground. Florian scanned round carefully. If any of the shepherds were close, that would attract them. Apart from the sheep, and some smaller creatures he guessed were bussalores, nothing was moving. He let out a low whistle.

Rustling wasn't a huge problem for the valleys, and Florian didn't sneak into the Naxian valley often enough to draw attention. The Ealtons would likely write off the occasional missing sheep to roxwolves, not that he ever saw much of them; the lean predators tended to stay within the treeline.

Mooray lumbered up out of the darkness as Florian finished strapping a rope harness to the sheep. Between the two of them, the carcass was easy to drag.

They'd almost made it to the bank of the stream when Florian's communication routine flashed a spectral green icographic of a general ping request across his vision. He started at the unexpected connection.

'Is something wrong, friend?' Mooray asked.

Florian held up a hand for silence. The signal was gaining strength. His auditory nerves plagued him with a distorted whistle which quickly calmed and began to stutter before becoming coherent.

'Urgent request for assistance. Urgent request for assistance. If you are receiving this, please respond. Urgent request for assistance. Urgent—'

The message carried on with methodical insistence. *An Eliter!* Florian let out a small groan of dismay. Some hothead radical on the run had ended up in the valley, one step ahead of the sheriffs or PSR officers. But scanning the larch-tree avenue in infra-red, he couldn't see any kind of vehicle, not even a bicycle. *I don't need this.*

'Is there a problem?' Mooray asked in a fast clatter of tusks.

'I hope not.' Slumping his shoulders, Florian ordered his communication routine to open a link. 'Nobody here can help you. You need to keep moving.'

The signal strength multiplied by an order of magnitude. Florian hadn't known anyone could transmit at such strength. 'Not an option, I'm afraid. I'm locking on to your position. That's good; nice and remote. I can make that easily. Hang on, I'm decelerating.'

'What?' Spoken aloud as well as transmitted along the link.

'Three minutes out. You'll hear me real soon. Don't be afraid.'

Which was completely the wrong thing to say. And still there was nothing visible between the larch trees.

Mooray's tusks clattered wildly. Teal barked.

'Look, look,' Mooray was saying. His heavy body was rocking about in agitation, flippers extended rigidly, pointing up into the air.

With blood thudding in his ears, Florian slowly looked up into the sky, dreading what he would see, telling himself there could be nothing. *Please.* 'Oh great crudding Giu!' he moaned.

Something blazing with heat was moving across the northern sky, curving round. *Fast, so fast!* Lining up on the Naxian valley as if the wide open slopes were some kind of welcome embrace.

'Go away!' Florian pleaded. He knew he was watching the end of his life zooming towards him. Nothing was ever going to be the same again. He whimpered in dismay. The urge to wrap himself in a pleasant faraway mindscape until the *thing* was gone was almost overwhelming.

'Way too late for that, pal. I've been waiting for a long time now. And anyway, my systems ain't what they used to be.'

Then *it* was dipping down, and slowing. Getting bigger. But actually, it wasn't that big. Florian had been expecting something the size of an IA-509. What he saw now was a cylinder with slightly bulbous ends, which his optical-analysis routines were classifying at three metres long, and two wide. The incredibly hot air surrounding it was not moving, which was impossible. He could see the turbulence in the sky behind it, a long line of warm twisting air.

'What is that?' Mooray asked. 'A new type of Faller?'

'No,' Florian told his friend. 'I don't know what it is. But it's trouble.'

The cylinder passed fifty metres overhead, descending rapidly now. Somehow it wasn't as hot. Its halo of fiery air was dissipating, a spherical ripple gushing away.

Florian felt it, a gust of heat as if someone had opened an oven right in front of him. Teal barked in dismay, jumping about. Then thunder rolled into the valley – a weird crackling boom from the north that went on and on. And Florian just knew that had to be the cylinder's wake, ripping through the sky.

The whole county's going to know it's here!

Teal was howling with fright now as the thunder echoed off the valley walls. Sheep were charging across their pastures. Infra-red vision showed him flocks of panicked birds rising from the trees they'd been sleeping in.

'Down and safe. Well, sort of. Get yourself over here, my new friend. I have something for you.'

'What?' Florian replied automatically as he tried to soothe Teal.

'As of now, the most precious thing on the planet. Come on, get your arse over here.'

Florian looked at Mooray and pulled out the flute. 'The thing that Fell from the sky; it wants us.'

'How do you know this?'

'It's speaking to me, the way my kind speak, over distances.'

'What is it?'

'I don't know.'

'Then we will adventure this night. Hunt more than stupid land meat. Hunt the knowing, friend Florian. This is good.'

The cylinder had landed about eight hundred metres away, at the edge of a spinney of silver birch that crowned a small rise. Florian hurried towards it, torn between wanting to know what the cylinder was and simple fear of the unknown. Teal bounded along beside him, while Mooray struggled to keep up.

'Who are you?' he asked.

'Joey . . . well, I used to be. I'm not any more.'

'I don't understand. What are you now?'

'Good question. Technically, this is an independent life-support system.'

'Life support . . . ? You mean you're in a spaceship, like a Liberty capsule?'

'Not so much in it, as: it. I'm resident in the smartnet nowadays.'

'What?'

'I'm the electronics.'

'You're the machine itself? I'm talking to an electrical machine?'

'Yeah, that's it. You are.'

'Then what is your function?'

'Okay, that's the complicated part. You'll see in a minute when you get here.'

Florian saw the lights in the farmhouse come on. They would have been woken by the thunder of the cylinder's flight. But the Ealton family weren't Eliters; they wouldn't be able to see the cylinder's radiant heat, and know something had come from the sky. He still had some safe time.

'You said you required assistance?' Florian enquired.

'Yeah. I was trying to reach a big concentration of Advancers. I scanned from orbit and picked up their link chatter; there's an area near the coast with a lot of them there. I figured they'd be my best bet.'

'What are Advancers?'

'Crap. You have forgotten a lot. Advancers are people like you, with functioning macrocellular clusters.'

'We call ourselves Eliters. Bethaneve founded our movement during the revolution, but it became so much more. Now it is used by the government to denigrate us. But we use it with pride.'

'Ah. I wondered about that. I've picked up some radio over the centuries, but it's been intermittent. Eliters got mentioned, but never in a good way.'

'Centuries? You have been orbiting for centuries?'

'Not through choice. I got stuck. Long story, and irrelevant tonight.'

'Joey, where are you from?' Florian asked in trepidation. There was one answer he wanted to hear above everything.

'Again: complicated. But originally I'm from the Common-wealth.'

'You've found us!' he yelled joyfully.

'No. Sorry, pal, I've been here all along, and I'm completely alone. But that should end soon.'

'How?'

'Look, I'm not sure how long we've got, so let's just cut short the— Holy shit! What is that with you?'

Florian glanced sideways at Mooray, uncertain how to respond. 'This is Mooray, my friend of the water.'

'It's an alien? A sentient one?'

'Yes.'

'I didn't know there were more aliens on Bienvenido.'

'The Vatni come from Aqueous. They came across through the wormhole Mother Laura opened.'

'Sonofabitch! I've missed so fucking much. Bastard Tree. Nuking was too good for it. Is Laura Brandt still alive?'

'Mother Laura sacrificed herself to defeat the Prime.'

'Sweet Jesus! The Prime are here? The *Prime*? This is a fucking nightmare!'

'The Prime were exterminated. Mother Laura killed their world. She flooded it with the atmosphere from Valatare.'

'Valatare? That's got to be the gas giant, right?'

'Yes.'

'Flooded . . . ? So she left you working wormholes?'

'No. The wormhole closed behind her. We think she did it to protect us.'

'Oh, that stupid smart woman. I always thought she was the best.'

Florian had arrived at the bottom of the slope. He looked up at the pale slim trees on top; several of them had been knocked down when the cylinder landed. There was a short gash in the ground as it had torn through the lingrass to end up with one blunt end embedded in the steaming mound of peaty soil it had ploughed up. Once again, his enhanced vision revealed a strange layer of air cloaking the thing's skin.

'Joey, did you know Mother Laura?' he asked in bewilderment.

'Yes, I knew her. Long time ago, now.'

'But—'

'Look, I know you've got a bazillion questions, but we're kind of short on time. From what I did manage to catch from your radio, Bienvenido has some kind of totalitarian government, right?'

'Depends how you look at it.'

'Should have asked before. What's your name?'

'Florian.'

'Okay, Florian. My sensors are showing you're a young man. So you're full of ideals, right?'

'Not really.'

'Dump the modesty; this is extremely important. Is your government totalitarian? Think carefully about your answer, please. I need you to be completely honest with me, okay? No pressure, but the fate of every human on Bienvenido may depend on it. There are some big decisions that have to be made in the next minute, and this net isn't really wired for that. I need my choices to be as simple as possible.'

Florian stared at the cylindrical space machine that used to know Mother Laura. *Dear Giu, how do I answer? I should just walk away, let someone else deal with this.* But of course he couldn't. *A friend of Mother Laura!* 'The government can be quite oppressive, yes.'

'Shit! Okay. Right. Thanks, Florian. Do you live around here?'

'In the next valley.'

'So I'm not going to ask what you're doing here at this time of night.'

Too late, Florian realized the crossbow was still hanging from its shoulder strap. He shifted in embarrassment. Was the space machine judging him? It felt like it.

'Now listen,' Joey said. 'This is the way these things always play. The government is going to come looking for me – and looking hard. I managed to deflect their radars; that's easy enough. But there was nothing I could do about the hypersonic boom. They'll figure that out soon enough. I'm already picking up some pretty paranoid communications, and I'm guessing those are search planes they're launching from that city to the north. Then there was that astronaut who saw me, clever bugger. They'll know what they're looking for.'

'What astronaut?' Florian was angry with himself for not understanding what was going on, but even more upset with the space machine for not explaining anything properly.

'The one in the Liberty spaceship – and how you wound up building Soyuz copies is a story I'm really going to enjoy hearing some day! Irrelevant – sorry. But this is how it is: I can't fly again. My ingrav units took a pounding in the quantumbuster blast, and didn't get any better while I was tussling with that motherfucking Tree.'

'You've been fighting the Trees?'

'Sort of. This life-support system used to be part of Nigel's ship—'

'Nigel!'

'Yes.'

'You knew Nigel as well?'

'Briefly. Focus, please. The life-support package was damaged by the quantumbuster Nigel detonated. The Trees don't have force fields, so chunks had snapped off, and the surface was heated to plasticity, jetting vapour like a comet.'

'A what?'

'Ah, yes, you don't get them here, do you? Think chunk of ice and rock that starts to boil when it gets near a star. They shoot out huge vapour trails— Never mind. Point is, the Tree surface was molten. When I hit, I was embedded deep. Ever since then the bastard Tree has been trying to engulf me. It was a slow process, and I fought back by manipulating my force field. Neither of us could ever get the upper hand. Then along came your Liberty mission.'

'Two hundred and fifty years fighting a Tree! That is a truly heroic battle, Joey.'

'Yeah – whatever. Let's concentrate on the now, shall we? I have something for you, Florian. Something I need you to keep out of harm's way for a month. There is nothing more vital in the universe right now. Capish?'

'What?' Florian hated the way he'd been reduced to repeating that one word over and over, like he was too dumb to say anything else.

'This gift has to be kept out of government hands. They'll be . . . unpleasant. Can you do that? Or if not you, can you find someone who can?'

'I . . . I suppose. Yes.'

'Thank you. I mean that from the bottom of my heart.'

'You have a heart?'

'Used to. Come up here now, please.'

Florian walked slowly up the incline towards the space machine. He urgently wanted to be holding the crossbow ready, but that was plain ridiculous. His enhanced vision showed him how smooth the space machine's skin was. There was no way of knowing what it was made from, except he didn't think it was metal.

'Do you know what it is yet?' Mooray asked from just behind him.

Florian raised the flute once more. 'I think it came from the place where humans lived before the Void.'

'Is it a good thing?'

'Giu, I hope so.'

A circular hole appeared in the centre of the space machine, expanding rapidly and silently until it was a metre wide. Florian watched it in fascination; it was as if that section of the shell had turned to liquid.

Not mechanical then.

Pale blue light spilled out. He frowned and peered into the small chamber it exposed. 'Crud! That's a . . .'

The naked baby wiggled, her chubby face wrinkling up into a distressed frown as the cool night air washed over her.

'Take her,' Joey said.

'Oh, no. Joey, no. I can't. Not that.'

Teal nuzzled forwards to see the baby. He barked excitedly.

'You have to,' Joey said. 'She's alive now. I cannot care for her.'

'This is insane!'

'Wrong. This is the greatest dose of sanity to hit this world since we fell into the Void.'

'I don't know anything about babies,' Florian protested frantically.

'They're simple. Feed 'em, change 'em. Repeat. And she's going to need a lot of specialist richmilk. I synthesized a few bladders for you to start with.'

'What?' Florian could feel his heart hammering that way it always did when things got bad. His skin was growing hot – then icy. Breathing difficult. He always had to sit down for a while when these attacks came on . . .

'Shit! Kid, are you okay? Florian!'

Florian gulped, his throat constricting.

'I don't fucking believe this! Okay, this is from my medic kit. It'll help. Florian!'

He whimpered.

'Beside the baby. Look! See it?'

Something had risen up out of the white cushion-stuff the baby was wiggling about on – a gloss-green hemisphere three centimetres across.

'Put it on your neck, Florian. Do it now. It's medicine. Oh, crap, he's going to pass out. Florian, put it on your neck. *Now!*'

Florian sank to his knees in front of the opening. Shaking hands scrabbling for the little hemisphere. Eyesight blurring. Fingers grasped the object.

'Go on. Up. That's my boy! Flat side on, and press firm—'

It was like a mild pinch on his skin, barely noticeable among the horrible sensations shuddering through the rest of his beleaguered body.

Then—

Pure ice water blasted through every artery under immense pressure, streaking through capillaries, zapping every cell in his body to full power. He sprang to his feet. Wanting to run. Wanting to fight. Wanting to fuck. Tears flooded his eyes. 'Crudding Uracus!'

'Good stuff, huh?'

His heart was still hammering, but for completely different reasons now. 'What . . .'

'Okay. Take a breath. And again.'

Florian's hand scrambled round wildly for the green hemisphere, peeling it off to stare at it. 'What *was* that?'

'Just a little pick-me-up. Welcome to Commonwealth medical technology.'

'I can't— That's amazing!'

'Right. Now let's focus on the problem at hand, shall we?'

Florian gave the infant girl a guilty glance; she was starting to snivel.

'Oh crud. Joey . . .'

'Don't worry. You're doing fine.'

He blinked and looked properly. The girl had something attached to the side of her head behind her right ear, a glistening oval of dark-red tissue, as if some strange organ had formed outside her body. 'Is she ill?'

'That is the healthiest person on the planet right now,' Joey replied. 'And you have to keep her that way.'

'But—' He reached out to touch the glistening tumour-thing, then drew his fingers away. 'That's not right. I know it's not.'

'That's an organic secure store; it contains all her personality and memories. They will flow into her as her neural structure grows.'

'What?'

'It's her fairy godmother. Let me have an input access to your lacunae. I can send over some files that'll make sense of all this for you.'

'My what?'

'Hell. What kind of semi-sentient are you guys running?'

'What?' Florian ground his teeth together. *Stop saying what!*

'You know what macrocellular clusters are, right? The thing in your head you're using to talk to me with?'

'I know that,' he said defensively.

'Okay. So what runs them? Can you connect me to it, please?'

'Connect you to my routines? I don't see how.'

There was a long pause. Florian kept staring at the baby, terrified she'd start crying. If that happened, he'd have no option but to lift her out and try to soothe her. That wouldn't end well.

'Right,' Joey said. 'Let's start at the beginning. The routines you have, where did they come from?'

'We've written them. They are shared between all Eliters.'

'You write your own operating code?'

'Yes.'

'But how do you— No, scratch that; the Void must have stopped Advancers from linking. You lost the original Commonwealth u-shadow operating software. Then why didn't Laura . . . Forget it! I have to work with what I've got now. Kid, I'm going to give you another gift. It's going to come into your head, and start helping you understand a lot more about who you are and what you can do, okay?'

'Are you talking about code?'

'Oh yeah. This is the biggest upgrade you're ever going to have.'

Florian gave the space machine a tentative smile. 'I think I would like that.'

'Okay. Here we go. I'm going to keep the bandwidth down; I don't know your limits. When the package is in, it will run parameter tests on your secondary neural system – the macrocellular structure – and modify itself accordingly. It might take a while.'

'How long?' Florian could hear some strange whistling in the background, like a chorus of very high-pitched musical instruments, but discordant. At the same time, something flickered in his vision – rainbow spectres he knew were there but couldn't quite focus on.

'Couple of hours, maybe,' the space machine told him. 'Now let's concentrate on the baby, shall we?'

'Oh.' Florian gave her a guilty glance again. In his joy at the gift of sophisticated new code, he'd managed to forget that part.

'I've microfactured a couple of nutrient processors for her. When the bladders have run out, just chuck food in one end and they'll do the rest. There's an instruction file in the data I'm sending you, which tells you what kind of food to use – the processors will help a lot there. There's another file that tells you what to give her when she can take solids, but keep giving her the richmilk. Okay? That's important.'

'Er . . . I guess?'

'I'm kind of limited in the things I can synthesize for you, but I'll give you some protection. Nothing that's going to blow cities to shit, mind. Just something you can use to avoid trouble if they're closing in on you.'

'I really don't want any trouble.'

'That's good. Stay ahead of the hunters and you'll be fine.'

'Hunters?'

'The secret police, or whatever they're called here.'

'The People's Security Regiment,' he said automatically.

'Yeah. Figures. That type are always real imaginative.'

'Joey, I don't understand what you want. Why can't the government look after the baby?'

'Because they'll be scared of her. People are always scared of change. And nobody more so than undemocratic officials who can see their power and their world being taken from them.'

'She'll do that?'

'If anyone can get Bienvenido out of this mess, it'll be her.'

The baby yawned, fat little fists clenched.

'But . . . How?' Florian asked in amazement.

'If I knew that, I'd do it myself. But this girl . . . Once you give her a problem, she will not stop until she's solved it. Not ever. Now come on, it's time for you to go. I've produced a backpack. Shove everything else in it, then take the baby and go.'

Quite how the padding in the chamber parted Florian never did catch. He just saw a simple dark-green canvas backpack slide up next to the baby. When he lifted it out, it didn't seem anything different to one you could buy in Opole – except, perhaps lighter? Next, a brushed metal cylinder half a metre long appeared. He'd started to put it in the bag, surprised by how heavy it was, when another identical cylinder emerged.

'This is the richmilk,' Joey said as the space machine conjured up five plastic bulbs twice the size of his fist. 'It'll last you until tomorrow morning. You'll have to start the processors after that to replenish them.'

Florian gave the space machine a questioning glance. He didn't know much about babies, but he was pretty sure one wouldn't drink that much.

'I can give you a medical kit, too. Your new files will show you how to use it.'

Florian frowned at the neutral grey oblong box that didn't appear to have any lid, but he stuffed it in the bag anyway.

'Wipes,' Joey went on. 'Trust me, you're going to need a lot of those. Nappies. Very absorbent. Enough to last until tomorrow, then you'll have to improvise. Same with clothes. Use this shawl to swaddle her in. After that, you'll have to find some bigger bits of cloth.'

It seemed to Florian that Joey knew as much about looking after a baby as he did – and possibly even less. But he pushed everything down into the backpack without mentioning that.

'Now put this round your wrist.'

This was a wide featureless bracelet made from some pearl-white substance that resembled wax. Florian picked it up, surprised to find it was quite flexible. He slipped it over his hand, then gave a start as it tightened around his arm above the wrist. It gripped tight but not painfully so, like it had become part of his flesh. 'What is it?'

'That's the protection I told you about. The new routines will give you full access when they're integrated.'

Florian held the bracelet up and gave it a suspicious examination. He'd been expecting some kind of gun.

'Now pick up the baby, wrap her in the cloth. And go.'

'That's it?' Florian asked. The rush from the drug had worn off. He was getting a headache now – an odd one, like a dull itch behind his temple. That had to be whatever code the space machine had given him. 'That's all you're going to tell me?'

'You know this land. I don't. Look, I get that this is a huge ask, and I'm sorry. But fate brought you here – if you believe in such a thing. Just keep her safe. Keep moving, keep ahead of them. You can do this. It's only for a month.'

'What's going to happen in a month?'

'You'll see. Trust me. Now pick her up. She's going to need feeding soon.'

'Is someone else going to come and collect her?'

'Go, Florian. My sensors are showing me some kind of vehicles leaving that big house.'

'Crud!' Florian had forgotten the Ealtons. Very, *very* carefully, he picked up the baby, terrified he was going to drop her. Then there was the delicate operation of putting on the nappy – which had sticky tabs on each side, so it wasn't too difficult. After that he had to wrap her in the square of soft cloth. She started to cry.

'Nooo!' he told her. 'No, don't do that. It's all right.' He tried rocking her, like he'd seen mothers do.

'Whoa. Gently, kid!' Joey said. 'She's not made of metal.'

'Sorry,' he blurted above the baby's cries, and slowed the motion down. He was sure the farm trucks pulling out of the yard must have heard the wailing, it was so loud! 'Easy there; easy.' He held her a little closer, and carried on rocking her in a gentle swaying motion. By some miracle, the crying subsided.

'Thank you, Florian,' Joey said. 'Remember, keep ahead of them. Keep her safe. Just for a month.' The hole in the side of the space machine closed up as silently and quickly as it opened, leaving them in the dark.

'What happens in a month?' Florian asked again, but there was no answer; the link was dead. The baby wriggled round. She was fully awake. He looked down at her, still not understanding how he had wound up holding her, how he'd agreed to any of this. It was madness. *I should wait until the sheriffs get here, give her to the authorities.* But he knew he'd never actually do that.

'What now, friend Florian?' Mooray asked.

Florian took a look at the headlights from the farm trucks. One set was heading down the long larch-tree avenue. The other was driving along a track that would bring them close to the little hillock where he was standing.

'Now we leave. I'll think about what I'm going to do with her later.' *Aunt Terannia will know what to do. And if she doesn't, she knows people who will.*

They set off back down the small slope, heading to the boat. After a minute the baby started crying again, and no amount of soothing and rocking would stop her.

'Is it in pain?' Mooray asked.

'I don't think so. She might be hungry.' The high-pitched wailing wasn't helping his headache. 'I'll feed her as soon as we get to the boat.'

'Should we not use the boat to speed from this place?'

'Yes, but I don't think she really wants to wait.'

'Throw away your fear. I will propel us.'

'Thank you.' Florian had never asked Mooray to give the boat a push; the whole idea was too much like hitching a horse to a cart. Mooray wasn't a farm animal. It would be demeaning. But the baby was getting even louder.

Florian settled himself in the boat and scrabbled hurriedly

round in the backpack for one of the richmilk bladders. The teat had a twist cap protecting it, which took a moment for him to work out. Then he was proffering it to the baby. She seemed reluctant at first, too busy crying to start sucking. He remembered something he'd seen one of his cousin's friends do and squeezed out a few drops of the richmilk, rubbing the liquid on the rubbery teat, then put that in the baby's mouth. There was a surprised gurgle, and she started sucking fast. The sudden absence of crying was a blessed relief.

Mooray, meanwhile, had slipped into the water. His tails were flicking about with deceptive force, pushing them along with the current, travelling a lot faster than Florian had ever managed to row.

The lights from the farmhouse and the trucks quickly fell behind. The empty night sky and dark land merged into one, leaving him alone. And for the first time he could actually stop to consider what had happened, the crazy thing he'd agreed to do: hide a Commonwealth baby for a month by avoiding the PSR, the most ruthless, most efficient force on the planet?

'Oh crud, what have I done?' It had all happened so fast.

Of course, the whole encounter was madly exciting, and he was defying the PSR bastards. But that burst of exhilaration, the yearning for defiance, might well be a side effect of the Commonwealth drug.

I'll never know now.

The baby finished guzzling the bladder and let the teat drop from her slack mouth with a contented smile. Florian held the flaccid bladder up in puzzlement. It was practically empty. The baby couldn't possibly have drunk that much. *Has the bladder got a leak?*

'What are you going to do?' Mooray asked.

Holding the child very carefully under one arm, Florian put the flute between his lips and blew a quiet answer. 'I'm not sure. Keep her safe like I told the Commonwealth machine I would. I really don't want the government to get her.'

'Why not?'

'I suppose because she's from the Commonwealth. Government people don't like that. They're always saying how bad it is.'

'How do they know?'

'They don't. The last person from the Commonwealth was Nigel and he triggered the Great Transition, which Slvasta hated. But then Eliters always claim we should make contact with the Commonwealth because it will save us. Only they don't know that for sure, either, if I'm being honest.'

'What do you think?'

'I guess I just want things to change.' He looked down at the baby in the crook of his arm. 'And it sounds like she might do that for us.'

*

They were halfway across the lake to the Vatni village when the baby woke and started crying – really bawling. The noise was incredible. Florian was convinced she'd wake the whole county. Any Air Force planes searching would hear her above their propeller roar.

'Is she ill? Have you damaged her?' Mooray asked.

'I don't know,' Florian replied. He held the baby up, looking beseechingly into her scrunched-up, distraught face, hoping beyond reason she'd give him some kind of clue what was wrong. *That weird thing stuck to her head?*

He bounced her softly on his knee. 'What is it? What's wrong, sweetheart?'

The wailing continued. He began to move her a little more. 'Please, please. It's all right. Just . . . What is it?'

She came down on his knee – and let out the biggest burp he'd ever heard. A mouthful of richmilk splattered on his hand. It was disgustingly warm and tacky. He couldn't move his hand to wipe it off, or she might topple over.

'Oh.' Now he understood. *Wind. You have to wind babies after they've had milk*, he remembered.

She still didn't look happy, so he tentatively bounced her about again. Two burps later, she seemed calmer. So he supposed he ought to check the nappy—

'Oh, great crudding Giu!' Florian thought he might throw up. The *smell*. And surely it shouldn't be so *liquid*? He winced, and looked away, trying to inhale some clean lake air.

'Friend—'

'Don't ask! Just . . . get us to the village. Fast, please!'

But it had to be dealt with. So balancing the baby on one knee, which was now suspiciously damp, he felt round in the bag for the wipes and a fresh nappy.

It took forever, and the unsteady boat didn't help. But just before they reached the little jetty she was clean and dry and wrapped in a new nappy. He actually felt rather pleased with himself for coping. And he'd know how to do it better next time.

The boat knocked into the jetty and Mooray heaved himself out of the water. 'What now?' the Vatni asked. 'Do you wish to stay here with us?'

'No. You have been more than kind, my friend. But I cannot stay here, for to do so would be to put you in danger. My government would not take kindly to you aiding me.'

'Please be careful.'

'Don't worry, I will be the most careful person on the planet.' He lifted his head, looking to the north. The breeze was growing stronger. Thin scattered clouds were starting to build across the horizon. The weather would slow any search. He would have time to prepare, to work out what he was going to do, and where to go. *Aunt Terannia first. She'll know what to do.*

He drove the Openland back up to his lodge, again not switching on the headlights. By the time he got back, he was exhausted and the headache was getting even worse. All he wanted was to crawl into bed and sleep.

The baby was fitful when he took her from the passenger seat. When he bent over her, he caught a whiff of— 'Not again? I just changed you.'

But when he got her inside and unwrapped the cloth on the kitchen table, sure enough the nappy was full. He cleaned her up, quicker and more efficiently this time.

The baby lay on her back, wide awake. Her little arms were

raised, hands clawing at the air, as if she was searching for something. The beginnings of a frown crinkled up her face.

'Now what?'

Her mouth was opening and closing like a fish.

'What? More milk?' It didn't seem possible. But when he produced the second bladder she started guzzling immediately. Teal curled up on his blanket beside the range cooker and watched quietly.

And of course, after the feed, she needed to be burped. It wasn't anything like as easy as last time. Then, just as she seemed to settle, she had to be changed.

'Great Giu.' Florian could barely keep his eyes open; he'd never been so tired before. Dawn was only a couple of hours away now. His headache had evolved to a hot burn that thumped away behind his eyes with every heartbeat.

He put the baby down in the middle of his bed. Then, worried she'd wiggle her way off, he put the pillow on one side and lay down on the other. Sleep came fast.

Equally fast, he was awake as soon as she started crying. Another change!

Sleep.

Dawn and more crying combined. The headache had mercifully abated, but his neck was stiff from not having a pillow. And he couldn't have had more than an hour's sleep in total.

'All right, all right,' he groaned, close to weeping himself now. The third bladder of richmilk. *Crud, I've only got two left. How can she drink so much?*

When he held her in the crook of his arm to feed, he saw the cloth she was wrapped in was uncomfortably tight around her skin. *Must be from squirming round in her sleep.*

Change her. Wrap her up again – but there wasn't as much cloth. 'Huh?' Looking at her, he could have sworn she'd grown several centimetres overnight, which was weird. But . . . *Kids have growth spurts . . . I think?* Nothing else could explain it, and Joey said he would need more cloth soon, so nothing was wrong. She'd survived the night. 'I did it right,' he told the dozing infant with a proud smile. 'I actually did it.' Then he thought about having an entire month of nights identical to the one he'd just survived, and his skin turned cold.

It was raining. A low cloud roofed the valley, reducing the morning sunlight to a dour grey glimmer as if twilight had already arrived. Florian switched on the light in the living room. The range cooker was cooling, but the embers were still glowing, so he put some fresh logs in. Before long they'd caught, and he left the air vent fully open so they would burn fast and hot.

The baby was asleep on the ancient sofa, safely surrounded by cushions to make a kind of nest. He knew he'd only have an hour at most before she'd need changing again. Probably a feed too.

There was still some of yesterday's bread left, so he cut some slices and spread raspberry jam over them. Only then did he realize how hungry he was. The kettle took a long time to boil. He put some more logs on, knowing the oven temperature would be all wrong – and just not caring.

He sat on the rocking chair and stared at the baby. The enormity of what he'd done was starting to register. He'd be lucky if he could manage to look after her, never mind keep her away from the PSR.

That drug. It must have been the drug. I'd never agree—

There was a mild flash. Florian looked up at the window, thinking lightning was plaguing the valley, but it was a very weak flash and there was no thunder.

'What?'

More flashes – but they were coming from behind his eyes. Like a broken icographic, except this was brighter. The flashes quickly stabilized into five stars in a pentagon formation.

'Huh?'

Shapes began to emerge from each of the stars, so much sharper and clearer than the icographics he was used to. A green pyramid, turning slowly in mid-air. Spheres made up of smaller spheres, multiplying from the centre. A sinkhole of concentric lavender circles that led back to infinity. A sphere of rippling yellow sine waves. Rainbow star cluster.

The space machine's code.

Florian smiled, entranced. Then someone spoke fractured, juddering words that made no sense, fading in and out like short-wave radio in a storm. He twisted round in shock, but there was nobody in the room. It was inside his head, part of the new code.

The voice spoke again, and this time the fragments came together in a mellow tone. 'Can you understand this? If you can, please say yes out loud.'

'Yes!'

'I am the basic operational memory package for macrocellular cluster operation. I have run tests on your neural functionality, and configured myself accordingly. There is a red diamond icon positioned at the top of the display in your exovision. Please locate it.'

'Sure. I got it.'

'In order for this package to download from your lacuna and into your main cluster, you must visualize the diamond expanding. When it has done this, please rotate it one hundred and eighty degrees clockwise. To cancel the download, please rotate it the other way. Please confirm you understand.'

'Yeah. Uh, right.' He needed to take a breath. This commitment was as big as picking up the baby. *Commonwealth knowledge! The one thing the Eliters have wanted for centuries.* 'I understand.'

'Please make your choice.'

Florian concentrated on the diamond, wanting it to be bigger. When it expanded, he thought of it turning rapidly clockwise.

The sensation which followed was akin to the drug he'd taken last night, but confined to his skull. Information like silver light was glowing inside him, shining through his grey matter to nestle snugly inside a billion neurons, elevating them. It was as if his brain had never been truly alive before, and now it sang with knowledge.

The operating system downloaded and installed, bringing a revelation of *understanding*. Instinctively, he grasped the functions behind the exovision icons. There were formatting tools for sight, sound, and sensation. There were files decompressing into his storage lacuna. Encyclopaedia files. Specialist files. Even enter-tainment files. Medical routines started monitoring his physiology, showing him body temperature, heart rate, blood-oxygen levels, toxin levels, hormone secretion, muscle performance, nerve paths, neural activity.

'Oh crudding Uracus,' he breathed in glorious amazement.

The baby started crying.

'Seriously?' he growled at her. 'Now?'

But she needed feeding, and was as insistent about it as only she could be. With a small martyred sigh, he postponed exploring his newfound wealth and reached for the next bladder. *Crud, only one left after this.* So while she sucked down the entire contents, he sat on the settee and accessed the file on richmilk. It was like ordinary milk, but with a massively high protein and vitamin content, along with concentrated specialist fats and hormones. He started to cross-index their functions with encyclopaedia files, and quickly got lost in terms he didn't understand. For all the infor-mation now filling his storage lacuna, comprehension was lacking. The space machine hadn't given him any education packages.

'Uracus!' It was like being able to see an orchestra playing, but not hearing it.

So the Commonwealth baby needed richmilk. He didn't know why she was different to Bienvenido babies, but that explanation was probably somewhere in the files, too. He could work on refining the search function later. He called up operational files on the nutrient processors, and shot an activation code at one of them. The top opened, its malmetal expanding, allowing the plyplastic hopper to swell up and form a big cone. Florian laughed in delight and made the cylinder repeat that several times before he sheepishly admitted to himself it was a bit childish.

He burped the baby while looking up what kind of food to put in the hopper. Plenty of vegetation, the goat's milk would also do, some protein (there was a little bit of rabbit stew left), water, jam for sugar.

While she was sleeping – it wouldn't be long before another change was due – he ran round collecting the ingredients and dropping them in the smooth conical hopper. The nutrient processor's micronet asked for a bladder to be attached. Florian had to use all the water he'd boiled to sterilize the used bladders, so he still hadn't managed to make a cup of tea for himself. The kettle went on again. He sterilized the used bladders in a big copper pot, and connected one to the bottom of the nutrient processor. Then he watched in satisfaction as the mush of food in the hopper was slowly ingested, and a trickle of richmilk filled the bladder.

I made it work!

Then the baby needed changing, and then the bladder on the nutrient processor was full, so he attached a second one. And he realized Teal hadn't been fed, so he took care of that. And the kettle was whistling loudly, which woke the baby. So he soothed her back to sleep. Then the hopper needed cleaning, the undigested slop flushing out of the processor ready for the next batch.

It was midday already (how did that happen?), and Florian hadn't eaten anything but three slices of bread. Three weeks ago, on his trip to the general store in Wymondon, he'd bought a cured ham. There was still some left, which was a relief. He had to eat something before he set off to visit Aunt Terannia. Exactly when he was going to pack for his forthcoming trip, he didn't know – nor what to take. The baby would need feeding again soon. And—

Teal raised his head, ears twitching. Then he was on his feet, nose close to the door, barking. The baby started whimpering.

'Quiet, boy,' Florian told the dog; the last thing he wanted right now was the baby waking up again.

He looked out of the window. Three black-painted regiment Terrain Trucks (bigger versions of his Openland) were driving up the track to his lodge.

2

The Albina valley forest warden's lodge was Chaing's seventh visit of the day. A helicopter had brought him out to the big farmhouse in Naxian valley an hour after leaving the Opole aerodrome. Chaing had never flown in one of the contraptions before. The lack of wings was profoundly disturbing, though the pilot's cheery attitude went some way to building up his confidence as they took off. Then they flew into the dismal low clouds which plagued the foothills of the Sansone mountains and he gripped the seat hard, relieved that the painkillers for his wrist were keeping a lid on his anxiety.

For over twenty minutes they flew on in rain, the big inflated rubber landing skis just skimming the treetops. Naxian valley was easy enough to distinguish; it seemed as if half of the county regiment's vehicles were parked along the larch avenue, spilling out into the expansive fields on either side. Twenty troop carriers were parked in the various farmyards along with a mobile Fall command post, while a knot of big lorries and tracked trucks were clustered together beside a spinney of silver birch.

As soon as they landed, a flustered lieutenant escorted him to the command post. Stonal was inside, talking to the regiment's brigadier. They stood beside a table that was covered with maps of the surrounding area, where pins representing deployment were already stuck in. One wall of the command post was taken up with a bank of radio equipment, manned by seven operators.

'Good to see you again so soon,' Stonal said without any noticeable insincerity.

The brigadier gave Chaing a moderately disapproving glance before leaving to talk to a group of officers at the other end of the table.

'Has there been a Fall?' Chaing asked.

'Yes and no. The latest Liberty mission might have caused more than the usual Treefall.'

'What do you mean?'

'Pilot Major Evine claimed to have seen some kind of alien spaceship directly after the warhead detonated. Naturally, we discourage such flights of fancy; it could as easily have been a chunk of Tree debris. But it seems he may have been right. Ironically, while I was interviewing him last night, something flew into the atmosphere over the Gulf of Meor at very high speed. A lot of people heard it.'

'I see.'

'No, no one did. There was no radar trace. Just noise.'

'Noise?'

'Air Force boffins describe it as a sonic boom. Apparently if you fly faster than the speed of sound, it makes a terrific noise, like a thunderclap, but continuous. They put the reports together and found a trail heading in from the coast, travelling just south of Opole and ending here.'

Chaing frowned. 'That's unusual for an egg.'

'It wasn't an egg. The Ealton family, who live in this valley, reported finding the "object" at first light this morning. It crashed to the ground a few kilometres from where we're standing.'

'What is it?'

'Good question. We have no idea. It's a manufactured artefact. Cylindrical, not particularly large, but potentially revolutionary in impact.'

A giddy combination of fear and fascination created a tingling along Chaing's spine. 'The Prime?'

'No. It appears to be protected by a force field, just like Mother Laura could create around herself.'

'You mean . . .' Chaing gave the huddled officers a guilty glance before lowering his voice. 'It's from the Commonwealth?'

'First conclusion, certainly.'

'Is it communicating?'

'Not yet. Or at least, not with us. If it is of Commonwealth origin, then it is reasonable to assume it can talk to the Eliters.'

'Have the radio operators picked up a signal?'

'Not now, but it's been here a while. Who knows what it was doing last night? Captain, I need this area fully secured, and that's where you come in. There aren't many people living around here, but I need them checked out. The brigadier has assigned us – well, you – a squad of seasoned troopers. Visit the nearby crofts and farms, find out if they know anything. Some are Eliters. Did they receive a signal? Did it talk to them? That kind of thing.'

'Yes, sir.'

'There's also a Vatni village down at the end of the valley. Possibly coincidence, but make certain. They can be quite obscure and evasive when they want to be.'

'I understand.'

So five minutes later he was in the cab of a Terrain Truck, driving fast along the larch avenue out of the valley, a map on his knee and a list in his good hand. The foothills weren't quite as empty as they'd seemed when he flew in. Several crofts were scattered about on the lower slopes, their occupants all surly types, struggling to make a living by themselves in the harsh landscape. They weren't welcoming, or particularly talkative. However, his own badge, backed up with armed troopers, enabled him to elicit answers quickly enough. Everyone had heard the long thunder last night, but that was all they knew. Chaing was familiar enough with people who had something to hide to spot any subterfuge.

Then there was the Vatni village. Two of the squad assigned to him knew how to use the flute and maracas that enabled them to talk to the Vatni in their own language. The Vatni always co-operated with the regiments conducting a sweep; they hated Fallers just as much as humans did. So through the interpreters, they told

Chaing that they'd all heard the strange thunder last night, but nothing else.

After that, the Terrain Trucks drove up into Albina valley as the clouds sank lower and the rain grew heavier. They pulled up outside the forest warden's lodge and Chaing shook his head, not understanding how anybody could live out here by themselves, cut off from the rest of the world. The front door opened, and the forest warden waited for them just inside. Chaing and a couple of troopers hurried over the short distance. His clothes were already damp from the earlier drizzle; by the time he reached the lodge he was completely soaked, his nice black leather shoes ruined by mud. A dog growled at him, to be swiftly shushed by the waiting man.

Chaing flashed his badge as he checked the soggy list on his clipboard; the warden's name had a star pencilled beside it: Eliter. 'You're warden Florian?'

'Yeah. What is this? I didn't know there'd been a Fall. The radio never said anything.'

'There may have been. Did you hear a noise last night?'

Florian tipped his head to one side, as if consulting something. *Presumably his memory files*, Chaing decided.

'There was a lot of thunder. It was strange. Like they all merged together into one big blast.'

'So I understand.' He gave Florian a closer look. The list said he was twenty-eight, which given his appearance was hard to believe. Sure enough, he had the lean, well-muscled frame of someone in their twenties, but his face was so haggard under several days' stubble he could have been fifty. 'Are you all right?'

'Didn't sleep much. I think I'm coming down with Cham flu.'

'Who've you seen recently?'

'What?'

'You can only catch Cham flu from other people. So who have you seen?'

'No one. Well . . . The storekeeper. I go down to Wymondon every couple of weeks to stock up. But that's all.'

'Right.' Chaing studied the living room. The kitchen end with the range was slightly surprising – it had a lot of pots and implements; he hadn't been expecting that. However, the rest of the living room was a bit of a shambles. Still, Florian was a bachelor living all by himself, and had been for years. In truth the state of the lodge wasn't much worse than Chaing's own apartment. There was the heavy scent of wood smoke in the air from the logs burning away in the range stove. But that couldn't disguise another, quite unpleasant, smell. Even the troopers were wrinkling up their noses. *Privy not working properly, probably overflowing in the rain*, Chaing thought, and suddenly didn't want to look at his shoes to make sure it was mud . . . 'So is that the store in Wymondon?'

'Yes.'

'Are any of your friends around here?'

Florian yawned; his eyes blinked slowly as if he could barely stay awake. 'I don't have friends.'

'You know who I mean,' Chaing said, letting some displeasure show. There was something not quite right about this. Everything looked as it should do. The warden was a recluse – a little wild, nervous and uncertain around other people. Again perfectly acceptable, and yet— *Could he be sick with some disease from space? Uracus, I'm paranoid, but he does look like crud.*

'I know who you mean,' Florian said belligerently, 'and I don't have any friends. I'm here to get away from everybody. Them. You . . .'

'Very well. Your thumb, please.'

The troopers put their hands on their carbines as Florian extended his hand. Chaing took out the slim box all PSR personnel carried, took out a needle, and pricked Florian's skin. A drop of red blood welled up.

The troopers visibly relaxed.

'Happy now?' Florian asked.

'Happy you're not a Faller. You're sure you didn't see anything last night?'

'What are you people looking for?'

'Hey! I ask the questions. Did you see anything?'

Florian bowed his head, unable to meet Chaing's stare. 'There wasn't anything happening last night,' he mumbled sourly.

Chaing's problem was the man's reserve. Florian was clearly a natural introvert, which wasn't quite a crime, but PSR technique was to encourage suspects to talk. The more they talked, the more inconsistencies would inevitably build up, condemning them. Florian clearly wasn't going to utter a single word more than he had to.

Chaing glanced down at the dog, who was standing at Florian's side, tail wagging. He carried on looking round the living room, but there really was nothing out of place. 'All right. We're going now. But if you hear anything, or pick up a link signal – anything – you report it, okay?'

'Yeah,' Florian grunted, still not looking directly at Chaing.

Chaing dashed back to the Terrain Truck, getting even wetter. It was only mud on the ground outside the lodge.

'Where now?' the driver asked.

Chaing consulted the list. 'The Mellhoff farm. That's at the far end of the lake.'

*

Three hours later they were driving back up the larch avenue into Naxian valley. The driver had to brake and pull off the side of the track to make room for a convoy heading the other way. Three tracked troop carriers trundled past in the rain, followed by two big covered lorries, then another three troop carriers made up the rear.

Chaing saw the brigadier sitting in the cab of the first troop carrier. Then he watched the two lorries carefully, wondering which one was carrying the alien cylinder. His driver so clearly wanted to ask *What is going on?* but managed to stay quiet.

'Just take us up to the farm,' Chaing said, not without sympathy.

When they arrived, the helicopter's blades were starting to turn. Stonal walked down out of the command post, holding up an umbrella to ward off the persistent rain. 'Anything?' he asked.

'No,' Chaing reported, trying to hide his disappointment. 'They all heard the thunder it made, but that's all.' He waited while Stonal considered this. The Section Seven director made no attempt to include him under the umbrella's cover.

'Very well,' Stonal said eventually. 'I'm taking the Commonwealth device back to Varlan for proper examination.'

'Is that wise, sir? Suppose it's a bomb?'

'The evidence is against it being a weapon, captain. For a start, it's too big. The quantumbuster that knocked us out of the Void wasn't even a quarter of its size.'

Chaing thought that was a nonsense, but held his tongue.

'Captain Philious described the quantumbusters to my father,' Stonal said in mild censure. 'Who went on to describe them to me in great detail.'

'I understand, sir.' Chaing began to wonder if the telepathic ability that everyone had in the Void had somehow stayed with Stonal.

'Indeed, it is that very size which does concern me. In volume, the object is actually close to the space pod which Mother Laura arrived in.'

'Yes,' Chaing said, not really knowing what he was agreeing with.

'Therefore, the object is quite large enough to contain a human.'

'Ah.'

'Ah, indeed, Captain Chaing. So if it has brought a Commonwealth citizen to Bienvenido, they will either still be inside it, or . . .' He raised an eyebrow expectantly.

Chaing turned to gaze across at the slopes of the valley, the big square fields and scattered clumps of trees, the oppressive cloud obscuring the tops of the mountains beyond. 'Oh crud. He could be out there, hiding in the trees.'

'It is a possibility we have to consider until such time as we can disprove it. There are bloodhounds on their way from the regiment headquarters. If someone did get out of the object, the dogs should pick up his trace.'

'In this rain?' Chaing said dubiously. 'I'm not sure—'

'You have my full support to begin a search.'

'Sir?'

Stonal pointed to the helicopter. 'I am accompanying the space object back to Varlan. You are now in charge here. Colonel Hokianga has been informed of that.'

'But—'

Stonal raised an eyebrow and Chaing sighed. Senior officers didn't change no matter what branch of government they served in. To qualify, you simply had to be able to dump a pile of steaming turds on your juniors from a great height without warning. 'If he's here, I'll find him.'

'Excellent. You know how to contact me if you do,' Stonal said, and walked over to the helicopter. The blades began to spin faster. Chaing hurriedly backed away as the machine took off amid a hurricane spray of rain.

*

It was still raining when the bloodhounds arrived an hour later – ten of the big animals, barking and howling inside the back of a converted troop carrier. Chaing met their handlers, and took them up the small hillock to the silver birch spinney where the space object had come down. There were still some of the big vehicles parked there, including a mobile crane which had got stuck in the mud. He stood in the middle of a small quagmire which feet and tyres had churned up and explained what he wanted, ignoring the glances the handlers exchanged.

'I know it's difficult,' he told them, 'but you have to try. See if the dogs can pick up anything.'

The handlers set off in pairs, with a large squad of troopers following each one. Chaing watched them go, slipping and sliding down the wet lingrass, knowing it was all useless. The rain would've obliterated any spoor hours ago. Consequently, he'd had a difficult conversation with Hokianga about mounting a proper sweep. The colonel had been against it, but Chaing insisted. Once he'd written off the bloodhounds, a visual sighting was all he was left with. And besides, a full-on sweep covered his arse with Stonal.

Hokianga reluctantly agreed, and called his officers together. Despite their disapproval, they carried out the operation professionally. Troopers were sent out along the length of the Naxian valley where they formed up into two lines. When the order was given, those lines would separate and walk up into the foothills on both sides. A classic, simple sweep, although the regiment didn't usually conduct it on such a scale. Nor in such poor conditions – at night and in the rain, moving through trees. But then again, someone might spot something.

This event was too momentous for timidity and caution. *A Commonwealth spacecraft!*

All the time he'd spent driving about in the Terrain Truck that morning, he'd tried to understand what it would mean for Bienvenido if the Commonwealth did make contact. Eliter propaganda – handed down from Nigel and doubtless encouraged by the Warrior Angel – claimed contact would bring about the end of all struggle: a profound liberation not just from the Fallers, but for society as a whole. Like going to live in Giu's glory. Which made Chaing certain of one thing – that kind of deliverance did not start with a small cylinder dropping into a remote valley.

But then, that was how Nigel arrived.

He went into the mobile command post, where almost all conversation stopped as the officers glanced at him. They resented him being placed in charge, he knew that, but no one argued with a Section Seven officer. He almost laughed at the bitter irony – that the one person who he wanted to be here right now, the one person who might actually know what to do, was the Warrior Angel.

She must know something had happened. The regimental deployment wasn't a secret. And the space machine's sonic boom had been heard across a thousand kilometres. She'd be on her way, if she wasn't already lurking close by. And he had no idea what to do if he encountered her again.

Chaing looked at the large-scale map spread out over the command post's table. Hokianga's people had put together a decent ground plan. Coloured lines and pins showed deployment patterns, stretching the regiment out across the Naxian valley. The communication staff were chattering away constantly, keeping the map updated. The lines were almost complete.

'We'll be lucky if we get another three hours of daylight,' Colonel Hokianga said.

'Conditions are as bad for him as they are for us.'

'Very well. But I am officially on record as advising against this.'

'Understood.'

'The squads are all in position. I'll give the order for them to start.'

'Thank you.' Chaing looked at the map again, but couldn't really focus. Inside the cast, his wrist was throbbing badly, as if it was attempting the break through the thick plaster. He couldn't remember the last time he'd taken his painkillers. Holding the little bottle in his bad hand, he managed to unscrew the top; no way was he going to ask the regiment officers for help.

He swallowed a couple of the pills, then went outside where he could actually see the operation. The gloomy light and thick rain closed visibility down to little more than a couple of kilometres, but he could make out the line of troopers beyond the sprawling farmhouse, stretching off into the dreary grey haze that clotted the far end of the valley. Forlorn figures huddled in long brown oilskin ponchos, their bulky packs making them all look like hunchbacks. As he watched they began to move, splitting into two lines that slowly moved apart as they trudged across the wet fields towards the slopes beyond.

The sight wasn't nearly as satisfying as he'd hoped it would be.

In front of him, two headquarters troopers carried a dead sheep across the farmyard to the mess tent that had been set up in the corner.

Chaing watched them for a moment, slightly baffled, before asking:

'What are you doing with that?'

'It's for the cook, sir,' one of them replied. 'He's going to use it for the headquarters staff meal tonight.'

'Did the Ealton family say you could kill one of their sheep?'

'No, sir. It was dead anyway. Garrel's squad found it down by the stream this morning.'

'That's even worse. You don't know what it died from. It could be diseased.'

'It wasn't ill. Someone shot it with a crossbow.'

Despite the cold rain, Chaing felt the skin along his spine chill down. 'What?'

'Somebody shot it. It's only been dead a few hours. Chef said it'll be fine to eat.'

Chaing ran across the yard to examine the sheep. Sure enough, the quarrel was still sticking out of its skull. And he'd seen that type of quarrel once already today. 'Oh crudding Uracus.'

*

Five Terrain Trucks and two troop carriers roared back along the rough track up Albina valley. The front wheels in the lead Terrain Truck weren't getting much traction at the speed the driver was going. Chaing winced as the bulky vehicle slewed about, snapping off browfrey saplings that lined the track. They came to a halt outside the warden's lodge, spraying up fantails of mud. The other vehicles carried on past them, surrounding the low building. Troops leapt out, forming a tight ring. Over thirty carbines were levelled at the lodge, safeties off.

'The Openland has gone,' Chaing observed through the windscreen. 'The little tit's on the run.'

'He won't get far,' Hokianga said. He turned to the radio operator in the back of the cab. 'Signal to all our units. The target is running. Vehicle type confirmed as an Openland. Harden all roadblocks. Pursuit vehicles continue on assigned patrol routes.'

'Yes, sir,' the radio operator confirmed.

'This whole region is covered,' the colonel assured Chaing. 'That Eliter's not going anywhere. I know Openlanders. Top speed eighty klicks, and that's when they're factory fresh. These brutes,' he banged the Terrain Truck's door, 'can make a hundred and ten, no trouble.'

In these conditions? Chaing held his tongue and climbed out of the cab, walking towards the lodge with his pistol held ready in his good hand. Five troopers crashed through the door ahead of him, immediately spreading out through the rooms inside.

'Empty,' came the cry.

Chaing went into the living room, with Colonel Hokianga right behind him. He went straight over to the wall where the crossbow was still hanging and held up the quarrel he'd removed from the sheep. It was identical to the others clipped to the crossbow's stock.

'So he was in Naxian valley last night, then,' Hokianga said.

'Yeah.' Chaing glanced over at the kitchen with its big collection of pots and pans. The biggest pot of all held the remnants of a stew. 'Stealing a sheep. Probably does it every week. So my real question is: why leave the sheep?'

'Because he wanted to get out of there fast? If there was a Fall next to me, it's what I'd do.'

'But it wasn't a Fall, and if he saw it land he'd know that. So maybe he needed space in his Openland.'

'Crud!' the colonel exclaimed. 'Is Stonal right? Did that thing bring someone here?'

Chaing stared round the cluttered, disorganized living room again, trying to understand what had happened. *If Florian had met the space machine's pilot, would he have brought them back here?* But there was only the same old mess, and the smell. No sign of anyone from the Commonwealth being there – not that he had a clue how he'd know that. He started a proper search, opening drawers and cupboards. Nothing. He went into the bedroom, and the smell of faeces was stronger in there. He sniffed, trying to determine where it was coming from.

A wicker basket next to the bed. There were a lot of scrunched-up tissues in there, smeared with faeces, along with a mound of odd podgy triangles of a sponge-like cloth. Grimacing, he picked one up, surprised by how heavy it was.

'What is that?' Hokianga asked.

'Oh great Giu,' an aghast Chaing whispered. 'It's a nappy.'

3

As soon as the scary PSR captain and his thug troopers left, Florian pushed all the Commonwealth stuff into his backpack and picked up the baby, who had been sleeping on his bed. It was impossible, but she seemed to have grown again. The cloth he'd wrapped round her was already starting to constrict her limbs. So he loosened it, and of course she needed changing.

It was pouring outside, but he knew he couldn't wait. He'd been lucky this time, but Chaing would be back. He settled the baby in the Openland's passenger seat, and set off up the valley to firebreak FB39. Of all the waltan fungi hanging up in the shed, there were maybe a dozen that were completely dry and good enough for Joffler, the buyer he supplied. He unhooked the biggest six and shoved them down into an old duffel bag. It was heavy, but he stowed it in the back of the Openland, then drove back down the valley past the lodge.

The whole way he was expecting to see the regiment vehicles coming for him, but the track was clear. He turned off half a kilometre from the lake and headed up into firebreak CR42. It was getting badly overgrown, top of his list to clear, thus ideal to hide the Openland in. They'd find it easily enough if they searched the valley, but until they did they'd assume he was fleeing along the roads. That was where they'd devote their resources to finding him.

With the backpack on, and the duffel bag slung over one shoulder, he picked up the baby. She grizzled a bit. 'You'll just have to wait,' he told her sternly. He'd got an old cloak to wrap her in, which should keep the worst of the rain off her.

He had to walk carefully. The lingrass was dangerously slippy, and the weight of everything was a strain. His new exovision displays showed him his blood sugar energy reserves being eaten up at an alarming rate by the relatively short walk back down to the Vatni village.

Most of the Vatni were out in the lake when he arrived. He didn't waste any time on politeness, just walked along the jetty to the boat that he'd used last night and put the baby down on the decking boards. Teal jumped in beside her and barked at the splash he made. The amount of water sloshing round in the bottom of the boat made Florian pause for a moment, but he didn't have any options. He dropped the duffel bag and dumped the backpack, pressing his fists into the base of his spine as he straightened and winced at the ache which had spread into every muscle. Unencumbered by the weight, he felt he could fly, or at least float.

The baby started to get more agitated as he used the bucket to bail rainwater out, reducing it to a level that wasn't quite so worrying. She was crying when he finally pushed off. For once he ignored her and started rowing, hoping that would be enough to draw Mooray's attention. Sure enough, he saw the Vatni's distortion ripple surging across the dark water towards the boat, and Mooray's snout broke surface ten metres away.

'Friend Florian of the land, you are honouring us with another visit. I am joyful.'

Florian pulled the oars back into the boat. 'You are honouring me with your kindness, friend Mooray of the water. I know I am a burden to you.'

'Not at all. I was waiting for you. Your land regiment people came to us today. They asked many questions of many of us. They did not want to be friends.'

'I'm sorry you have been caught up in this.'

'I was with you by my own choice. We have a fruitful friendship.'

'It makes me happy to hear you say that, friend Mooray. It is with sadness that all I can offer you this day is to leave, but that will mean you and your village will be left in peace. The regiment people are only interested in me and the baby. When I am gone, so will they be.'

'In a great swarm across the land hunting you, friend Florian.'

'They haven't got me yet. I'm going to go downstream. I know some people who might be able to help me.'

'This gladdens me. Can I help?'

'I will tell you the truth, friend Mooray, I was hoping you would ask. It is difficult to look after the baby and row at the same time.'

'I hear her. Does she ever stop?'

Florian was tempted, but Vatni never quite got irony. 'She cries when she is in discomfort. All human young do this.'

'I am glad I am not human, friend Florian. Where do you wish to go?'

'Down the river Kellehar, please.'

Mooray ducked round to the back of the boat, and once again Florian found himself moving along far faster than he could ever row. He started dealing with the baby, who wanted feeding and changing. She didn't like the cloak being opened and the raindrops splashing her skin. She was reluctant to take the bladder teat. Didn't burp well. Wouldn't go to sleep afterwards. So he hunched over her, protecting her from the worst of the rain as the boat slid swiftly across the lake to the start of the river Kellehar.

The Kellehar was one of a multitude of tributaries winding sinuously out of the Sansone mountains before merging into the river Crisp to flow in a potent surge eastwards to the distant coast. Wide and shallow as it emptied out of the boggy floodland at the end of the lake, it soon narrowed down to a fast-flowing channel that carried the boat rapidly northwards. Beyond the valley, the landscape flattened out into larger, more leisurely folds. Florian had driven along the adjacent lanes enough times to know farms were prevalent here – an irregular chequerboard of arable fields and grazing meadows that extended over all but the roughest elevations and ravines. Today the dull clouds and persistent rain kept most of the countryside veiled from him, even with his Eliter sight and new vision-enhancement routines.

The current became strong enough that Mooray hardly bothered pushing the boat at all, but simply steered them past snags and kept away from the banks. They passed under several stone bridges, which made Florian nervous. He was expecting regiment patrols to be watching the river, but every time they were deserted. A river from the west ran into the Kellehar, then two large streams from the east added their power to the flow.

After a couple of hours he leaned over the stern, and put the flute to his lips. 'I can manage from here. You should go home, my friend. Return upriver to be with your pack family, be happy.'

'Do you believe you are safe now, friend Florian?'

'As much as I can be. You can help no further. To expose you to any further danger would sadden me greatly.'

'I believe you, friend. I would wish you return soon.'

'I should be safe to return in a month. Goodbye, friend Mooray of the water.'

The Vatni let go of the boat and slipped easily below the surface. A V-shaped ripple swelled against the current for a few seconds before being washed out.

Florian settled the oars again, and began to scan the water ahead. He dipped the oars in and out slowly and carefully, using them primarily to steer with, keeping the boat centred in the current. His exovision threw up a map of the area – as best remembered from studying an atlas several years ago. The new management code, which called itself a u-shadow, was reformatting all his old memory files. Half of his time on the boat had been spent talking to the u-shadow, which responded in a way that reminded himself of his own questions and eagerness when he'd been about five. Having a semi-sentient (its nomenclature) resident in his head was something that took some getting used to.

The map showed him the Kellehar would curve sharply to the west in a few kilometres, taking him away from Opole, where Aunt Terannia lived. But the land which it curved round was where he wanted to be tonight – an odd rocky highland where Joffler lived in a place called Letroy. If anywhere was safe from Captain Chaing and the regiment, it was there.

As the dour light faded from the sky Florian checked the baby again. She was bigger still. Her growth was no longer something he could just gloss over as his own ignorance of babies. It was real and worrying. He reckoned she'd grown nearly eight centimetres since he'd lifted her out of the space machine, and she certainly weighed a lot more. *It must be the richmilk.* But why Commonwealth babies grew like that was still beyond him. He determined to try and find a file on it that night, when he had a moment.

As the daylight faded, his concern about being spotted withered in tandem. He'd already passed a couple of small villages sitting on the side of the river. No one had seen him sail by, as the rain was keeping a lot of people indoors. But thankfully, it was starting to lift. He was soaked, even wearing his oilskin coat. He just hoped the duffel bag had kept the fungi dry.

Steering in the dark was unnerving, even though his night vision gave him a decent view of the river ahead. Land on both sides began to rise. Before long he saw what had to be Letroy.

Florian had never visited before, but Joffler had described it enough times when they met up in Wymondon to pass on the waltans. There was a long cliff a couple of kilometres beyond the crumbling riverbank, with a swathe of weather-worn stone outcrops descending from it all the way to the water. From a distance you could mistake Letroy for some weird alien village, with fat tower buildings standing atop flinty mounds. Back in the Void, the settlers to this region had used their telekinesis and servant animals to expand and smooth the existing caves in the outcrops, creating homes in the living rock. In its heyday it had a population of nearly six thousand – a quirky artists' community that attracted painters, writers and musicians from all over Bienvenido. It flourished for centuries.

After the Great Transition, the arts suffered a general malaise. In this new, harsher existence, there was less leisure time, not so much money, and fewer patrons. But Letroy's traditions persisted, though its reputation for quality gently declined. Despite this, the majority of residents still followed some kind of artistic vocation. Several of the most popular new-style music bands with their electrically amplified instruments had emerged from Letroy, playing to growing crowds in the cities.

Wide ovals pocking the strange pinnacles glowed with a yellow-shaded light that Florian found incredibly welcoming while sitting in a boat with a cold drizzle swirling round him. There were two substantial wooden jetties protruding from the bank, with several boats moored to them. He rowed his boat into the lee of the first and secured it.

The baby was crying yet again as Florian put his backpack on and hoisted the duffel bag over his shoulder. He just hoped that Joffler lived somewhere close.

Once he was on the jetty he cut the painter and watched the boat drift away. The current caught it soon enough, propelling it downriver. It was carried out of sight within two minutes.

'No going back now,' he told Teal. The dog wagged its tail.

It was five minutes before he met anyone. Five minutes wandering rather aimlessly along the crushed stone paths that twined round the outcrops, looking for anyone who might be about this wretched night. They were an old couple who were curious about the wailing baby, and they clearly didn't approve of Joffler; he could tell that from the way their attitude became stiffer at the mention of the buyer's name. But they pointed at the outcrop Joffler had claimed for himself and gave instructions on which paths to follow.

Ten minutes later, with aching legs and a sore shoulder, Florian trudged up a curving incline that was set with steps too far apart to use comfortably. The mound skirting the outcrop was planted with fig trees that were getting choked by vines. He had to stop halfway up, it was such an effort, even though he was barely fifteen metres above the ground.

The path completed a full circuit of the outcrop, ending at a broad entrance chamber that had iron railings stretched across it. Joffler was standing behind the gate, staring out suspiciously. The only light was from a bulb hanging from the apex, just behind the railings.

'I heard the noise,' he said, peering at the baby. 'Who are you?'

'It's me, Florian. I'm knackered, Joffler; I need to come in. I brought you some waltans.' He dropped the duffel bag beside the gate.

'Crud!' Joffler exclaimed. He unlocked the gate and swung it open. 'Come on in. You shocked the piss out of me, turning up like this!'

Florian staggered through the gate, noting the way Joffler looked round carefully to see if anyone else was on the path before picking up the duffel bag.

The entrance cavern had three openings at the back, each one covered by a thick curtain. Joffler pushed one aside and led Florian into the stone house's main chamber. It was roughly circular, twenty metres across, with an irregular ceiling. A big oval opening, looking out over Letroy, was covered by a white woollen sheet that swayed about in the damp breeze. Opposite that, lumps of peat burned in a raised hearth, with a curving cowl above it, blackened by centuries of smoke. There was a spicy aroma pervading the air that Florian didn't recognize, but it certainly wasn't coming from the peat. The low settees were ancient, even older than the pieces in Florian's living room back in the lodge. He suspected the furnishings had all been made long ago by some Letroy artisan with a zeal for chunky carvings.

He sat close to the fire and pulled a bladder out of the backpack. The baby started guzzling the richmilk straight away.

Joffler stood looking down at him. He was a lanky man in his forties, with alarmingly thin limbs that poked out of his grubby fur-lined kaftan. His skin, which five years ago when they first met had been a silky dark olive, was now an unsavoury pallor, as if he'd devoted those years to a bad diet and avoiding sunlight. Long black hair was tied back with a rainbow band, which only emphasized how much his hairline had receded.

'Why didn't you tell me you were coming, fella?' he asked. 'Gave me quite a shock there, turning up like this.'

'I didn't know until a couple of days ago,' Florian said. He hadn't actually thought much about how he was going to explain things to Joffler; he just knew Letroy was the best place to lie low for a few days. And Joffler should know how to arrange transport to Aunt Terannia.

'Okay,' Joffler said. 'So who's this then? You the daddy? You been having some fun up there in the valley, you bad boy? What happened? Did Mummy turn up and dump her on you?'

'Uh, yes.' Florian couldn't meet his eye. 'Something like that.'

'So what's her name?'

'What?'

'Her name, fella? What's your daughter's name?'

'Essie,' Florian said without thinking. Essie had featured quite heavily in his life before he did his regimental service – the one person he could overcome his chronic shyness for, and actually talk to. And unfortunately the girl who'd turned down his narnik-fuelled pass the day he was decommissioned from the regiment. He hadn't smoked the Uracus-cursed stuff since.

'Cool.' Joffler leaned in closer, and frowned. 'Uracus, what's wrong with her?'

'Nothing,' Florian exclaimed defensively.

'Fella, her head! It's like half her brain's hanging out.'

'That? It's just a growth. The doctor said not to worry.' He improvised boldly. 'That's what he told her mother anyway.'

'That is such a lump of crud. She's dumped a broken kid on you. What a cold-hearted bitch.'

'Look, the baby's going to be okay. I just need somewhere to stay for a few days. You can manage that, can't you? We have a good arrangement.'

'Well, okay, fella. Ah, you are, like, going to go back after this, aren't you?'

'To the valley? Sure. Don't worry, I've got plenty more waltans drying.'

The curtain to the main chamber was pushed aside and a woman came in. Florian looked up, then immediately lowered his head to the baby, feeling his cheeks flush hotly. The woman was probably about his age; the hair hanging down to her hips had been dyed a vivid emerald-green, into which she'd woven long colourful ribbons. Her cheesecloth skirt was a vivid sky-blue, its hem swirling round her ankles. Apart from the bangles on her wrists it was the only piece of clothing she wore.

'Joffie, what's happening?' she asked in a high voice.

'Hey, babe, this is Florian. He's an okay fella.'

'Hi, Florian,' she said. 'I'm Rohanna.'

'Um, pleased to meet you,' Florian mumbled. He was aware of the girl padding over the stone floor to the settee where he was sitting. He glanced up – though not to her naked torso! Something glinted in her navel. Before he realized it, his retinas zoomed in, which was another autoimpulse function his u-shadow had bestowed. There was some kind of gold ring piercing her navel, like an earring in completely the wrong place.

'Oww,' she cooed. 'Poor darling baby. What's wrong with her?'

'It's just a growth, that's all. It's fine.'

'Oh, that's so woeful. She's not going to live long, is she? Not with that much cancer.'

'It's not cancer, and she's not dying,' Florian snapped, incensed. It made him look Rohanna straight in her face. Her expression was curious and sad. She was very pretty, he realized, but with dilated pupils. Exovision displays offered an analysis of visual data: her increased heart rate, skin temperature two degrees above normal, slightly sluggish limb motion.

She's high, he realized, which didn't really surprise him.

'Not cancer? If you say so.' She almost giggled.

The baby finished her feed. As always, the bladder was empty. Florian started bouncing her gently on his knee, to be rewarded by a burp. That did make Rohanna giggle.

'Is there anything to eat?' Florian asked. 'I'm kind of hungry. Haven't had much food today.'

'Sure thing, fella. Uh, where did you leave your Openland?'

'I came on a boat.'

'A boat? What, from Albina valley?'

'Yes.'

'Sweet crud. She really worked a number on you, didn't she?'

Rohanna was wiggling her fingers in front of the baby's face,

217

making chuckling sounds. It annoyed Florian, but he didn't want to cause a scene. 'The food?'

'This way.'

One of the other curtains in the entrance cavern led to a corridor that ran through the centre of the outcrop. More chambers had been hollowed out on either side. Joffler led him into the kitchen. Its fittings had clearly been made by the same artisan who had furnished the living room. A clay oven stood beside the outside opening, surrounded by a little skirt of cold ash, which had damped down to a sludge from the drizzle eddying in.

'Some fruit somewhere,' Joffler mumbled as he pulled drawers out. 'And I know we have bread.'

Florian's stomach grumbled in protest; he'd been looking forward to a decent meal. 'Fruit?' he complained.

Joffler grinned sheepishly, and gave a wide-armed shrug. His kaftan swayed open at the gesture, and he was wearing nothing underneath. Once again, Florian found himself quickly looking the other way. After seven wonderful years alone in Albina valley he wasn't used to people, let alone ones who were comfortable exhibiting their bodies.

'Rohanna doesn't like eating dead animal flesh. She says it contaminates our souls; that its one big reason why the Skylords have never come back.'

'Right.'

'I know, fella.' Joffler lowered his voice and smirked. 'Who wants to listen to all that Church of the Return bollocks? But I'm not arguing. She just wants to screw all the time. Say's the body's blessings are a gift from Giu that shouldn't be wasted – some crud like that. I'm not complaining. Good job you're bringing in all those waltans, huh?'

'You're using granddad's delight?' Florian asked in surprise. Waltan fungus, when refined by a chemist who knew what they were doing, produced a drug that helped older men with their erections. That's why he didn't mind setting traps for the fungus. The county sheriffs were really only interested in busting narnik farmers.

'Like I said: all the time.' Joffler pulled a loaf of bread from a metal bin. 'Got some jam around here somewhere, too.'

Florian stopped himself from sighing. 'Don't worry, I'll manage.' The baby still hadn't settled properly. *Probably needs changing.*

'Sure thing. If you need anything and can't find it, just give a shout. My home is yours, so make yourself comfy and get those clothes dried out. I'll see you in the morning, yeah? And don't worry, I'll get you some eggs for breakfast. Rohanna doesn't object to them.'

'Thanks, Joffler.'

Joffler winked, then threw a slightly troubled glance at the baby before leaving Florian alone.

Back in the main chamber, Florian took off his shirt and trousers and hung them on a chair next to the fire. Teal curled up next to them. 'I'll get you something to eat in the morning, promise,' he told the dog.

He changed the baby – she must have grown another couple of centimetres during the river trip – but that didn't make her any happier. She was whimpering almost constantly.

'What's up?' he asked gently. She stared up at him with unnerving focus, then her face screwed up and she started to wail. 'Oh, for crud—' He reached for yet another bladder of richmilk, but she refused to take it. When her mouth opened wide for another yell, he saw a flash of white. 'Teeth?' he asked incredulously. 'You're teething?' Close inspection showed about six teeth had broken through sore red gums. 'Oh, you poor thing. But I haven't got anything for that. Or have I?'

He got his u-shadow to link to the medical kit the space machine had given him, and list the contents. A quick check with his new medical files showed one of the salves would help.

The plyplastic top of the medical kit parted and a small bulb poked up. He squeezed out a little blob of the clear salve and rubbed it on her gums. The baby seemed so outraged that his finger was in her mouth the crying actually stopped for a moment. Then she resumed her bawling.

He cuddled her, crooning soothingly for another couple of

minutes. The crying slowly subsided and she fell asleep. Florian grinned down contentedly at her. Night two. And actually he was doing all right.

Two hours later he was woken up by her cries. But that was okay, because that was the hungry cry. Feed, change. There were eleven teeth showing now, so a touch more salve.

With only two full bladders left, he went back into the kitchen and scrounged some food to fill the processor's hopper. An hour later, with the bladders refilled, he dozed off only to be woken by more demands for feeding.

*

'Doo-da,' the baby said after Florian finished her dawn feed. He blinked at her in surprise.

'You talk now?' As before, he felt he'd had about ten minutes' sleep in the whole night. When he rubbed some more salve into her gums he counted twenty teeth, and the front ones looked fully developed now.

Overnight? A quick check in the medical files showed that wasn't normal, not even by Commonwealth standards. But she'd grown another three centimetres since they'd arrived in Letroy – that was undeniable. *So if she keeps this up, then in a month she'll be* . . . 'Oh great Giu!' *That's what Joey meant.* He stared at her with a smile of wonder lifting his lips.

Teal let out a mournful whine.

Florian tore his gaze away from the baby. 'Yes! I'll get you something to eat.'

His shirt and trousers had dried, so he put them on. A sniff confirmed they needed a wash after yesterday. So did he.

There were so many things he should be doing. He hadn't stopped running since he'd taken the baby out of the space machine. What he needed was a couple of days' peace to plan and prepare.

The white wool sheet over the big opening was easy to pull aside, allowing the warm morning sun into the chamber. He looked out at Letroy in the daylight. All the primeval stone spires were pocked by oval openings, the majority covered with curtains or wooden shutters. He was surprised that most of them lacked any sort of safety rail. Behind them, the cliff was also studded with homes. Wooden walkways hung precariously on ropes, zigzagging up the vertical rock. He saw several of them were broken, swinging gently on their last surviving anchor points, the openings they once led to now dark and cold, the stone hive-houses abandoned.

Food. He needed food for himself and the richmilk processors, and poor old Teal. Clothes, washed or new. Cloth for the baby, to wear and use as nappies. Some cash, maybe. And transport, a quiet way to get to Opole, two hundred and seventy kilometres to the west. No way was he going to attempt that in a boat, rowing against the river Crisp.

Florian exhaled pensively, realizing just how dependent on Joffler he'd become.

Behind him the baby cooed. He turned round and gasped. She wasn't in the settee's nest of cushions. 'Giu! Where—?'

She was on the stone floor beside Teal, little hand gripping the dog's ear and tugging hard as she smiled.

'No!' he rushed forwards and picked her up. 'How did you get there?' He put her down again, and watched as she started crawling eagerly back towards Teal.

'Oh great Giu,' he moaned in dismay. It had been bad enough when she couldn't move.

'Morning.' Joffler walked in, scratching his hair, which had escaped the band. He wasn't even wearing the kaftan.

Florian averted his eyes. 'Morning.'

'Hey, she's crawling. Hiya there, Essie.'

The baby cooed again, and changed course towards Joffler. Florian picked her up, and immediately wished he hadn't. She wriggled about enthusiastically in his precarious hold. 'Eggs,' he said. 'You said we could have eggs for breakfast.'

'Sure thing, fella. It's just a bit early—'

'And Teal needs something to eat as well.'

'All right, all right. Let me put some clothes on.'

'Is there somewhere here that sells clothes?'

'Yeah. Uh . . .' Joffler looked him up and down. 'Clothes in Letroy, they're not so . . . well, like yours, you know?'

'What do you mean?'

*

'How do they get the dye like this?' a perplexed Florian asked. He was holding up a cotton shirt that Gemain had made. Gemain was a friend of Joffler who made *funky* clothes to sell in his store, which was a narrow cavern in the base of the cliff.

'You need to blend in,' Joffler insisted. 'No offence, fella, but the whole forest-worker-gear thing is going to draw a crud-load of attention here. Nobody wants that.'

Florian had planned on spending as much time as possible in Joffler's stone house, so he quashed down an argument. He only had a few shillings; it was Joffler who was paying for everything. 'I can send you the money,' he promised the dealer. 'As soon as I get to Opole.' All the money from the waltan fungi was going into a safe deposit box; fifteen dollars for each one, which had been agreed with Billop in advance. Billop was the contact who sold granddad's delight in the city. It was Rasschaert who had arranged the deal for him when he announced he'd been accepted for the forest warden service. Rasschaert worked in Aunt Terannia's club, which was where they'd met, but had a lot of contacts within the local gangs.

Joffler pulled a face and said: 'Don't worry about it,' whenever he brought up the subject of money and buying supplies.

Gemain's shirt was purple and red, with weird blotchy green and blue spirals all over it. The baby tried to grab it. Florian was holding her under one arm, while he held up the shirt for critical examination. It looked like a rainbow had melted across it while it was spinning round.

'It's called tie dye,' Gemain explained proudly.

'We'll take a couple,' Joffler said quickly. 'And those trousers, too.'

Florian nearly yelped: *not the trousers*. They were denim, but not like any dungarees he'd ever worn before. These were black,

222

unnaturally tight across his bottom, and had red suede tassels running down the outside leg seams. Instead of arguing he just gritted his teeth. He'd get back to Joffler's stone house quicker if he said nothing.

They were on their second foray into Letroy this morning. The first was for food, which had been traumatic enough. Florian had folded up a towel to make a papoose for Essie, who welcomed it as some kind of escapology challenge while they walked among the rock outcrops. He was already looking back fondly to the previous day, when all she did was sleep, feed, and require changing.

As well as the trousers and shirt, Joffler bought a kaftan for Florian, and some fresh underwear. 'I don't need boots,' Florian said firmly as they passed Kani's shoe shop in the base of the cliff. The shoes and boots in the window were all made from strips of different colours, or sprinkled with small brass stars and rings. Not one of them had a heel less than six centimetres high. 'Why would anyone want those?' he asked plaintively. 'They're not remotely practical.'

'They look kinda neat,' Joffler replied. 'I've got a couple of Kani's myself. And you don't wear them to work, fella, you wear them to be you.'

'To be me?'

'Yeah. When you go out in the evening to a bar or a party, what else are you going to—' He stopped and gave Florian a long look. 'Ah, never mind.'

*

Back at the stone house, Florian had a quick wash in the bathroom (the water wasn't very warm) and changed into the new clothes. He enjoyed how clean they were, but the style was just awful. He knew he looked ridiculous, like a dancer from a Fireyear carnival.

Joffler and Rohanna were playing with the baby in the living room. She was crawling across the floor between them as they rolled a soft ball to each other. When Florian came in, she immediately scuttled over to him. 'Doo-da!'

'Looking good, fella,' Joffler exclaimed.

Rohanna walked over to him. She was wearing a plain white cotton robe that was almost translucent. A small fat cigarette was cupped in her hand, leaking a bittersweet scent. 'Nice,' she murmured. 'Forest warden's a very physical job. I bet you're really fit.'

'I, er . . .'

'Was it lonely in the valley? I can make the loneliness go away for you, if you'd like. Joffie won't be jealous, will you, baby?'

Florian looked round desperately at Joffler, whose smile had become very forced.

'Love is free and beautiful,' Rohanna continued. 'Isn't that right?'

'Absolutely,' Joffler said.

Florian started to back away from her. 'No! That is, er, I'm very flattered and everything, but no. I have someone. A girl. She's special. I can't. I promised.'

Rohanna pouted. 'A mother and a girl. I dig you're hot on the mattress. I think I'm jealous, which is so wrong. The Skylords wouldn't like how that colours my soul.'

Florian instinctively stopped backing away and looked down. The baby was at his ankle looking up. 'Doo-da!' she smiled. He picked her up so he could use her as a shield. Tiny fingers closed round his nose – surprisingly tight.

'Come on, Joffie baby, you're on,' Rohanna said, and sauntered out of the living chamber.

Joffler started after her.

'Joffler?' Florian asked quietly. 'What is it she does? I mean, does she have a job or something?'

'She's a kinetic performance poet,' Joffler said, his cheeks flushing slightly.

'A . . . A what?'

'Just don't ask her to do one for you. Trust me, fella. Some of them last for hours.' And with that he was gone, hurrying after Rohanna.

Florian looked at the baby. Her black hair, which until now had been a wispy fuzz, was starting to thicken. 'Well,' he said to her. 'A kinetic performance poet. How about that? You know what Mother Laura would call it?'

The baby went for his nose again. Florian ducked away, smiling. 'She would call it: total bollocks. Yes, she would. She would. Yes.'

'Goo-da,' went the baby. She opened her mouth and sucked air.

'Quite right. You're hungry again, aren't you? And nothing is more important than that.'

'Hung-gee.'

'Yeah. Hungry. Come on, let's see if there are any bladders left.'

There were still two bladders with richmilk in his backpack. Florian let her have both of them. She could hold them up herself now. He grinned at the sight of her sitting on the kitchen floor in just her makeshift nappy, looking like a miniature alcoholic tipping back a bottle of booze.

He chopped up an apple, and cautiously offered her a thin slice.

'Hung-gee,' she said after she chomped it down, and clapped her hands.

'More?'

'HUNG-gee!'

'Uracus. All right. Here we go.' He started feeding her the rest of the slices.

With the sounds of heated rutting from Joffler's bedroom echoing through the stone house, Florian opened up both richmilk processors, and filled their conical hoppers, talking all the while so young ears wouldn't hear the bad noises. Once all five bladders were full, his u-shadow switched the nozzles to open-discharge and the richmilk started to trickle out into jugs. 'That should be enough for the rest of the day,' he decided after the third jug. 'And you can have fruit now, too. Solids, clever girl.'

She needed changing. Of course.

Florian made himself a simple lunch, then went back into the living chamber. The open oval window gave him nightmares of the baby falling off the ledge. He pulled and shoved at the biggest settee until it was across the opening, acting like a safety barrier.

The infant yawned, so he cuddled her in his lap until she was asleep. The odd dark tumour-thing on the side of her head hadn't grown like she did. It still looked awful, but not as bad as it had to start with. Not as life-threatening.

'It has all your memories, Joey said,' he told the sleeping baby. 'They'll download into your brain. So you must have lived before, back in the Commonwealth. How weird is that? I wonder who you are? Do you know how to build a real spaceship? Is that it? Is that why you're here? Are you going to lead us all back there?'

His secondary routines highlighted starship files in his lacuna and he gave in to the impulse. The first one opened; blueprints and images surged into his exovision, surrounding him with the most glorious construct. *Great Giu, a Commonwealth starship!*

*

'Hey, fella, you okay?'

The exovision folded away neatly and Florian felt a profound sense of loss.

Joffler was poised over him, frowning. 'Are you like, *crying*?'

'What?' Florian wiped the moisture from his eyes. 'No. I just . . . It's dust. I got some dust in my eye.'

'If you say so, fella. Are you smelling that, too?'

Florian sniffed, and looked down at the baby sleeping in his lap. 'Oh Uracus!'

'Takes some doing, being a dad, huh?'

'Yeah.'

'She grows fast, doesn't she?'

'I guess. I've never had one before.'

'Sure. But— Ah, to Uracus with it. I'm going to fire up the boiler properly. You can give her a bath.'

'Thanks, Joffler.'

'Hey, it's nothing.'

'Do you think—' Florian paused. 'Do you reckon the Skylords ever will come and take us back into the Void?'

'Who the crud knows, fella? Why are you asking?'

'If they don't, we have to find the Commonwealth. We can't go on living like this.'

'Are you an Eliter?'

'What? No!' Even as he said it, he was surprised by how guilty he felt at the denial.

'Sounds like Eliter bollocks to me. Look, fella, the Church of the Return wants us back in the Void, the Eliters want us to go back to the Commonwealth. Why can't everyone just chill out, and be happy with what we've got here and now? We've got narnik, there's a sweet new music scene coming on strong, and more and more people are telling the PSR to crud off. This is a cool and beautiful world, and it could be more so.'

'Apart from the Fallers, you mean?' Florian scoffed.

'The regiments stop them spreading, and all those super-duper tightarse astronauts are nuking the Trees for us. We're beating the Fallers, fella. Another fifty years, maybe a hundred, and there won't be any more of them. Dig that?'

Florian frowned. Didn't Joffler know about the Faller Apocalypse? *I guess he's not the type to think about stuff like that. Or maybe it's just the Eliters who worry about it.* 'Yeah. Maybe you're right.'

'You know I am.'

'Joffler, I have to get to Opole. Do you know someone who can take me? Someone who won't ask questions?'

Joffler glanced down at the baby. 'Just how big is this trouble you're in, fella?'

'I'm not in trouble, not big trouble. I just want to lie low for a month. That's all I have to do. One month. Then it's over.'

'Over, huh? Did you take her from the mother?'

'No! Really, no. It's just complicated, that's all. I need to get to Opole. I've got money there, and people I know. Uracus, in a month I'll be back in the valley and things will all be normal again. I swear to Giu.'

Joffler scratched the back of his neck and gave the toddler another curious glance. 'Okay, fella. There's someone I know, Lukan. He runs cargo all over the county for the city boys. He's the one who takes the waltans back to Billop for me. Drives a big old Coperearl saloon car – crudding thing is as rusty as Uracus, but you've got to dig that engine. He and his cousins rebuilt that thing from the ground up; you wait till you hear it purring like the king of the beasts. On the flat he can top that machine out at two hundred klicks per hour, easy. The sheriffs don't have a single thing on the road that can catch him. He'll get you to Opole.'

'That sounds . . . flashy. I don't want any fuss.'

'No fuss. He will get you there or your money back. Guaranteed.'

'I don't have any money on me.'

'Figure of speech. Lighten up, fella. We just need to get you and the waltans to Billop and everything will be fine. Trust me. I've got a stake in this too, remember? I want you happy and back in the valley. I really do.'

'Okay.'

'I'll make a phone call.'

*

Florian gave the toddler her first ever bath that afternoon – in the kitchen sink. She loved it, splashing water and suds everywhere. He was as wet as her by the end. For her afternoon meal she drank two bladders of richmilk and chomped down seven carrot sticks.

When she was clean and dry he took her back into the living cavern. She crawled over to the settee. Florian watched nervously, but she hauled herself up and used the settee to cruise, walking along beside it, holding on to the cushions with a marvellously serious expression of concentration on her plump little face.

'You're going to be walking by yourself tomorrow, aren't you?' he said softly.

She turned to face him. 'Dada play?'

'You bet.' He smiled happily, and held up the soft ball. 'Catch?'

The evening meal saw her eating a bowl of chopped vegetables he'd prepared, along with a bladder of richmilk. Florian had to feed the little cubes to her, and a good quantity wound up mashed over her face, her bib, the table, the floor . . . But she ate it eagerly enough. Then she got it into her head that she should be using the spoon.

Florian had to wash the stuff out of his hair before he went to bed. She slept fitfully, crying out several times in the night as if she was in pain. He soothed her back to sleep, cuddling up to her in the bed, holding her tight, murmuring soft promises that he

228

was there and everything was going to be all right. She needed feeding twice, just straight richmilk.

He was woken just before dawn by demands of: 'Hunquee, hunquee, Dada. Hunquee!' She'd grown another five centimetres, but was starting to get quite podgy with it. Her breakfast was porridge made with richmilk, two full bowls.

After that he took her into the living room so they wouldn't wake Joffler and Rohanna. When he drew back the curtain, dawn was just starting to create a pale haze above the horizon. Essie left cruising the furniture behind and began to walk, managing a few steps each time before falling over in a fit of giggles. The third time she landed on her bottom there was a ghastly squishing sound. Mortified, Florian knew it was time for potty training.

4

The big mobile command post arrived at the Albina valley warden's lodge forty minutes after Chaing discovered the nappy, roaring along the chewed-up mud of the track. It was followed by a long procession of regiment vehicles, bringing a lot of troopers who had just been ordered to stop their sweep of the Naxian valley.

Colonel Hokianga had spent most of the intervening time in the Terrain Truck, issuing orders through the radio operator. The vehicles he'd dispatched across roads and tracks beyond the lake were told to make for the next junction and establish a roadblock, locking down the whole area's traffic. Nothing was to pass, and use of deadly force was authorized.

Chaing spent the time going through the lodge. Picking through the contents of the wicker basket in the bedroom wasn't fun, but he laid out the tissues and nappies on a table in the living room. The nappies were a kind of shiny absorbent substance that he'd never seen before – which helped confirm that the baby had been brought to this world in the space machine.

With that settled in his own mind, he set about examining the living room. The two bookcases were large, which wasn't entirely unexpected for a man who lived completely by himself. Chaing started pulling books off the shelves. Nearly a third of them were folders containing mimeographed copies of technical manuals, mostly mathematics texts and electrical systems.

'Find every machine and electrical device,' he told the troopers.

'I want to inspect them. He must have been building some kind of gadget.'

'Communicating with the alien?' Hokianga asked.

'There's no such thing as coincidence,' Chaing said automatically. Even so, the man he'd met in this lodge earlier didn't strike him as some kind of Commonwealth secret agent. *But then what does one look like? And if he is, then he managed to fool me easily.*

Chaing fetched a screwdriver from the work shed on the side of the lodge and started to take the radio apart. He wasn't an expert, but the valves and capacitors inside didn't look like they had any other function. The troopers started to pile up the power tools they'd found.

He'd opened up about half of them, and was just unscrewing a big air compressor when the mobile command post showed up. It parked in front of the lodge, along with a dozen support vehicles. The chief communication officer plugged the command post into the sweep-coms box. Every farm and isolated home on Bienvenido had one. It gave regiments multiple telephone lines to the local exchange, enabling them to talk directly to their county headquarters, allowing them to coordinate sweeps with district authorities and reserve platoons.

'I'll call in a Fall alert to headquarters,' Hokianga said when the communication officer gave him the thumbs-up.

'No,' Chaing said. 'This is now a nest alert. It'll provide us with a plausible cover story and gives us the authority to call in the sheriffs.'

For a moment he thought Hokianga might argue, but the colonel gave him a tight nod, and made the call.

Regiments were tasked with finding and eliminating Faller eggs – motionless targets. But a nest alert, with Fallers moving about, that put the PSR in charge.

The plan he and Hokianga came up with would see sheriff offices in every town out to a hundred kilometres from Albina valley establish roadblocks on the major roads that evening. Off-duty sheriffs were to be alerted overnight, who would then set up more roadblocks at dawn. Once that was organized, a second tier of sheriffs, from a hundred to two hundred kilometres away, were to repeat the procedure. They would have to be run by the regiment headquarters in conjunction with the Opole PSR office; that size of operation was just too big for the mobile command centre.

Also at dawn, the troopers would start sweeping the entire Albina valley.

'He's gone,' Hokianga protested. 'They should be helping extend the roadblocks.'

'He fooled me once,' Chaing replied. 'This time we are going to be completely certain.'

After that it was the *bad* phone call. The communication staff managed to track down Stonal at the Opole Air Force squadron aerodrome, where a transport plane was assigned to take him and his consignment back to Varlan. Chaing accepted the telephone handset from the operator with a sinking sensation; the wretched thing felt as heavy as lead.

'What is it?' Stonal asked.

'Sir, your suspicions were correct. The machine had someone in it.' Chaing closed his eyes, waiting – the pause lasted several seconds.

'Do you have them in custody?'

'Not yet, no. Sir, I believe it's a baby.' He didn't want to say anything more; it was a regiment telephone line, but he had no idea how many people could overhear the conversation.

'A baby?'

'Yes, sir. An Eliter called Florian is on the run with it.'

'Florian? Isn't that the forest warden in the next valley?'

'Yes, sir.'

'I thought you visited him?'

Chaing grimaced. 'I did, sir. But the baby was hidden when I was here, and he misled me completely; by the time I realized what had happened, he'd gone. I apologize for the mistake. I've instigated a county-wide nest alert.'

'I see.'

Chaing waited, wondering if he was going to be relieved of

duty on the spot. Perhaps Hokianga would get a phone call and the troopers would line up in a firing squad . . .

'Who else was involved, captain?' Stonal asked.

'I'm at the warden's lodge now, sir. We're examining the whole place. So far there's no evidence of anyone else working with Florian. He was in the Naxian valley last night rustling sheep. It's looking like his encounter was purely chance.'

'If this visitor is from where we think, then Florian must not reach the radical Eliter movement. That is imperative. Understood?'

'Yes, sir.'

'Good. So what is your course of action?'

'It's unlikely he'll head south; that's into the mountains. But I've ordered the colonel to deploy the regiment in a sweep through Albina valley starting first light. Florian's Openland is missing, so the regiment and sheriffs are coordinating roadblocks to the north. Regimental vehicles will patrol all night, trying to spot him on the roads.'

'How long has he been a warden?'

'Seven years.'

'He'll know all the back routes in the area.'

'Yes, sir. But if he uses them, he'll be travelling slowly. The roadblocks are being set up for a hundred kilometres outside the Albina valley. Tomorrow I'll extend them further.'

'Do it tonight, captain.'

'Yes, sir.'

'Anything else?'

'I'm going to requisition all the Opole PSR office's files on this Florian, find out who his friends and family are. Who he's likely to turn to for help.'

'Proceed, captain. The Air Force plane should take eight hours to reach Varlan. I want a progress report as soon as I arrive. Don't use radio to contact the plane unless it's urgent.'

'Yes, sir.' Chaing took a moment to steady his nerves after the phone went dead. 'Get me the Opole PSR office,' he told the operator.

*

His name was Minskal, and according to Yaki he was the leader of the three-strong Section Seven team Stonal had brought to Opole to monitor Captain Chaing. Jenifa stood beside the dresser in his hotel room, with her bare back pressed to the wall, and watched him screwing the teenage Eliter girl. For a forty-two-year-old he had plenty of stamina.

The honeytrap had been closed perfectly. It shouldn't have been, not on anyone from Section Seven. But Jenifa had been wearing her PSR uniform when she and the Eliter girl had walked into the hotel bar where Minskal was sitting by himself. With Chaing called out to the countryside so unexpectedly, the team had been left with nothing to do. Minskal was killing time with a drink and a news-sheet while he waited for instructions.

Jenifa chose the table next to him. He knew her, of course – that helped close the trap. The junior corporal who had been in Frikal Alley, who had obediently excluded any mention of a strange creature from her report (the Section Seven team had checked the records division), the corporal who had slept with Chaing (they'd been watching his flat). A good little PSR agent. No risk – and her young friend was very pretty, too.

There were smiles. A few tentative words exchanged, quickly becoming a conversation. Drinks ordered.

An hour later they were upstairs in Minskal's hotel room. It was a suite, of course, befitting someone of his status, with a high bay window in the bedroom. Jenifa made sure the curtains were open, allowing bright afternoon sunlight to splash across the bed. Then she and the Eliter girl put on a show undressing each other that matched any you could find in Opole's private clubs.

Jenifa took him first, delighting in using her strength to excite him, and through that to control him. Her only regret was that he didn't realize how much she'd played him, how superior she was – but that knowledge would come later, and she would get to see his stricken realization.

When she finished with Minskal she rolled off the mattress so the other girl could begin. There was a mirror fixed to the wall above the dresser, overlooking the bed. Jenifa stood beside it, watching for a while to see if she would have to intervene, but the girl did what she'd been instructed, and started talking, admitting how turned on she was by him being a PSR officer, and what did he do exactly . . . ? *Tell me about the bad guys you've caught. Have you actually seen a Faller?*

Jenifa slipped away into the suite's lounge, and picked up her clothes. Carrying them, she walked down the corridor to the next room. It had a number on the door, but it was never used by residents. There was no furniture other than a couple of wooden chairs. The curtains were closed, keeping it dark.

She went into what used to be the bathroom. The plumbing had all been taken out, providing space for the substantial cine-camera on its tripod. Its wide lens was pointing through the small square hole in the wall which had the mirror on the other side. Thanks to the bright sunlight pouring through the bay windows, Minskal's bed was perfectly illuminated even through the misty one-way glass.

Major Gorlan was peering through the camera's viewfinder, one hand clamped on her headphones so she could hear everything the concealed microphone was picking up. She gave Jenifa a sardonic look.

'Has he given away any state secrets?' Jenifa asked as she started putting her underwear back on.

'No. He might be crazy-horny but he's not completely stupid. Besides, I made it very clear to Lauraine: don't press for anything detailed, keep it to generalities.'

'Lauraine?'

Gorlan pointed through the mirror. 'Your new best friend on Bienvenido.'

'Oh. Right.'

Gorlan patted the film drum contentedly. 'He's said enough to make him ours. Yaki will be satisfied.'

'Good.' Jenifa buttoned up her blouse. 'You didn't film me, did you?'

'No.'

'I want to see the film after you have it developed.'

'Don't you trust me?'

'No.'

*

Jenifa put a civilian coat on over her uniform, and slipped out of the back of the hotel. One of Yaki's fleet of private cars drove her home – her real home, not the small flat she maintained, which was appropriate for her corporal's salary.

Real home was an elegant, old four-storey townhouse on Deral Avenue, where she had her own apartment on the third floor. After she handed her uniform over to a maid for laundering and showered, she went down to the gym in the basement.

That was where Yaki found her that evening, straining away on the bench press.

'You need to be careful,' Yaki said as she checked the weight Jenifa had loaded. 'This is very heavy.'

'I can take it,' Jenifa shot back, and defiantly lifted again. 'And you take risks.'

'Do I?'

'That Lauraine girl is an Eliter. You can't trust them, no matter how much pressure Gorlan applies. Suppose she linked to the radicals and gave them Minskal's identity, or even mine?'

'She can't. This operation was a strategic advance, not a risk. Lauraine is a mule. Just because you have Eliter parents doesn't mean your macrocellular clusters actually work. The PSR has plotted a small but noticeable decline in functionality in the Eliter population over the past century.'

'I didn't know.'

'Did we get what we wanted?'

'Yes. Once I'd banged him his brain was so fevered he couldn't stop bragging to Lauraine about the Fallers he'd killed. It's total bollocks, I reckon; he's internal security, not a field agent. But we have it all on film.'

'A Section Seven officer telling an Eliter about his missions. Excellent.'

'But you just said she's a mule.'

236

'That part isn't on her official file.'

Jenifa grinned maliciously. 'Neat. So how are you going to use him?'

'Strategically. Someone in his position hears a great deal more than his pay grade clears him for. I need eyes and ears in the capital.'

'What's in the capital?'

'Power.'

'You have power. You run this city, not the mayor or Democratic Unity.'

'The crudding Eliters were on to that nest,' Yaki snarled angrily. Her scar throbbed dark red. 'Do you have any idea how bad that makes me look? There was a nest in Opole for years without the PSR office getting a hint of it. My office! It's a weakness I can't afford.'

'Oh.'

'It's crudding humiliating. And it should never have happened. But the PSR has gone soft, we're starved of resources and authority. People like Stonal have lost sight of our true objective. He's old and weak, grown comfortable in the capital where everything is about politics. His generation has lost its relevance to this world. He'll be departing it soon enough.' She jabbed a forefinger at her scar for emphasis. 'And this is what he's leaving us to face: the Faller Apocalypse. It's real and it's happening. And what's he done to prepare us? Nothing! He sits around on his arse and tries to cover up any evidence that he's doing a piss-poor job. That has to change, we have to be ready for them. We have to be strong, and take the right decisions, not just build bunkers in Byarn to retreat to. But that's not going to happen with him in charge. That's why I need assets like Minskal.'

'So I don't need to see Chaing again? Good.'

'No. I want you to keep screwing him.'

'For Giu's sake, he's not even a proper Section Seven officer. He's weak, too. You know I hate that. The only reason Stonal gave him the badge was because he was in the wrong place.'

'But he found the wrong place, didn't he? And he met the Warrior Angel there.'

'What?'

'You heard.'

'He never said. Crud, it was her that slaughtered all the Fallers like that, wasn't it?'

'So he's not quite as weak as you thought, then, is he?'

Jenifa stood up and admired herself in the full-length mirrors on the wall. 'He doesn't deserve me.'

'That's what makes you so effective. None of them can believe their luck.'

'All right.'

'And the first thing I need to know from him is what's going on in the Sansone mountains. Stonal has half the Opole Regiment out there running some kind of high-priority sweep. But there was no Fall.'

'I don't understand. What is it, then?'

'I haven't been briefed, which is crudding insulting. So you're going to find that out. Chaing is helping Stonal. A test, presumably, to see if he's up to Section Seven standards. So he'll know everything.'

Jenifa ran a hand back through her black hair and sneered. 'Getting that out of him isn't even a challenge.'

The phone rang. Yaki picked it up and dialled in the secure code. A blue light on the side lit up.

Jenifa watched her listening to the voice on the other end. Then Yaki smirked and held out the handset. 'Speak of the Uracus,' she said. 'It's your lovely new boyfriend. He wants you.'

*

It was ninety minutes before dawn, and Chaing was asleep in a chair when the mobile command centre door swung open. Jenifa walked in, wearing a long leather PSR uniform coat with a broad fur collar.

The command centre's officers threw some dubious looks at her, but kept silent.

'Busy night?' she asked archly as Chaing peered up at her with bleary eyes.

'Oh, yeah.' He levered himself out of the chair, scowling at how stiff his joints were, the twinges of pain coming from his wrist. Yesterday's rain hadn't done his cast any good; it'd got soaking wet and now it was starting to crumble round his fingers. 'Coffee, please,' he told the centre's young orderly. 'And one for the corporal.'

'So there's a nest Faller on the loose with an egg?' she asked.

'Almost.' He lowered his voice. 'It's an Eliter, Florian, who's run off with a Commonwealth artefact that fell from space last night.'

Jenifa's delicate eyebrows shot up. 'What sort of artefact?'

'A baby.'

'Bab—?' she squeaked, then clamped her lips together. 'For real?'

'Oh yeah.'

Her finger pointed at the command centre roof. 'So have they finally arrived? Are their spaceships . . . ?' The finger jabbed upwards urgently.

'I don't think so. Section Seven believes it was the latest Tree-fall that started this.'

'What?'

'I know. I don't understand, either. But right now all I'm worried about is making sure we take Florian into custody.'

Jenifa held up a slim black-leather briefcase. 'Okay, these may help. Files on Florian. Not many.' She grinned. 'Last night was something to watch. Yaki had Kukaida brought back in after midnight to oversee your search request.'

'Ouch.'

'Oh yes,' Jenifa said maliciously. 'But it worked. Florian's a non-entity, but his family's interesting.'

The orderly came in, carrying a tray with two mugs of coffee. Chaing took his gratefully.

Jenifa waited until the orderly left the command centre before continuing. 'His mother is Castillito. Father unknown; she refused to name anyone on the birth certificate – and paid the fine. Brother—' She gave him an expectant look. 'Lurji.'

'No crud?' Chaing grinned, and used his coffee to wash down a couple of painkillers. 'Even I've heard of the graffito lord of Opole. That was, what? Ten years ago?'

'Yes. Some of his artwork is still there.'

'Didn't I hear he also burnt down the mayor's residence?'

'To be fair,' she said with a smirk, 'only the expensively refurbished wing the mayor's mistress used. That's when he took off. Democratic Unity and the sheriffs didn't appreciate the anti-corruption statement.'

'So do we know where Lurji is now?'

'There haven't been any verified sightings for years. PSR believes he's gone to ground in Port Chana, like all of them.'

'Good call. But . . . this valley is big, isolated. The perfect place to hide, especially when your brother is the warden.'

'Any evidence for that?'

'No,' he admitted. 'But I am starting to wonder if this is coincidence after all.'

'If it was planned, it was very long term. I read the files on the drive over. Florian's regiment service was completely unremarkable. He got bullied a lot, but then he's an Eliter, so what do you expect? He's been in Albina valley for seven years, never taken his holidays, always here when the supervisor turns up for an inspection. He signed up right after he left the regiment – and I mean within a couple of days. There are no entries after that day. He's been a good boy.'

'Seven years without a break? No one's that good.'

'Kukaida made her clerks dig in the right places. There was a ten-year-old intelligence file in Gorlan's department. One of our informants reckoned Florian was some kind of hotshot at writing instructions to control those specialist cells Eliters have in their brains. His kind wanted him to carry on, but he turned them down. That was right around the time Lurji was getting down and dirty with Opole's sheriffs.'

'So he didn't want to follow his brother's path, then?'

'Maybe not. But you're right: it's incredibly convenient that he's got contacts with the serious Eliter radicals.'

'Yeah.' Chaing stared at the new maps on the central table. There were over seventy red pins stuck in the largest, showing the area to the north, each one a roadblock.

'How big a start has he got?' Jenifa asked.

'Half of yesterday afternoon, and all last night.'

She wrinkled her nose up. 'I would have been here ninety minutes earlier if we hadn't been stopped at all those roadblocks. The troopers are good. He won't get far.'

'Yeah. We need to catch him, and the baby.'

'Your pride got hurt bad, huh?'

'I keep thinking about it. What he was when I questioned him – a shy, awkward loner – that wasn't an act.' He tapped the files with his index finger. 'We're seeing connections that maybe aren't there.'

'What do you mean?'

'It could just be that he really is acting on his own. It's not cunning and planning and determination that's got him this far, just sheer blundering luck. We weren't prepared for this, not a Commonwealth spaceship – and certainly not for one that's brought a baby. I mean, a baby? Why? What's it here for?'

'To give the Eliters some kind of leader they can rally round. Their greatest weakness is how fragmented they are.'

'We can't see the Commonwealth galaxy with a naked eye, and according to Mother Laura they don't know we even exist, never mind where we are. If they have found us, they have a power beyond even how Eliter propaganda tells it. They're not going to sneak around making contact with a pissy little radical movement. They'll arrive in a hundred spaceships the size of Skylords, and order us around like we're cattle. And if they truly are this big super-powerful benevolent society like Eliters claim, they certainly won't stand for humans being eaten by Fallers; they would've blasted every Tree out of the Ring.'

'I don't know.' She shrugged. 'Maybe this is just the first scouting mission taking a look round?'

'A baby is not a scout.'

'I haven't got the answers, Chaing.'

'I know,' he said wearily. 'This is just all so frustrating. I'm so sure we're missing something, that's all. Something obvious.'

'Then we'll get there eventually.'

'Thanks for the vote of confidence. Did you bring me some clothes?'

'Yes. So what now?'

He checked the clocks on the wall. 'The troopers are having breakfast at the moment. At first light, they start a sweep of Albina valley. We have bloodhounds, too.'

'Looking for what, exactly?'

'Florian, or maybe Lurji. I'd settle for something that'll tell me where I can find him and that baby.'

'I thought you said he's charging away from here as fast as his Openland can go.'

'He's not stupid. I've already underestimated him once. That isn't going to happen again.'

'Ah,' she said appreciatively. 'Misdirection?'

'We'll know soon enough.'

*

At one o'clock, the sweep found Florian's Openland truck. Chaing and Jenifa got to it nine minutes after the discovery was radioed in. Their Terrain Truck plunged along the overgrown firebreak track and came to a halt ten metres short of the Openland.

'Did it break down?' Chaing asked the corporal.

'Er, sir?'

'Never mind.' Chaing brushed past the confused man, and clambered into the cab. There was no key in the ignition. He pulled out a pocket knife and cut the wire bundle below the steering column.

Jenifa leaned against the open door frame. 'And where did you learn to do that?' she asked coyly as he stripped the end of two wires.

'Misspent youth.' He touched the two bare wires together, and the starter motor growled. The engine caught with a clatter. Black smoke belched out of the exhaust. 'He abandoned it,' Chaing announced.

'Misdirection,' Jenifa said. 'You were right. That's impressive. We've got half the regiment and every sheriff for two hundred kilometres searching the roads. And he's on foot.'

Chaing climbed out of the cab and stared along the overgrown firebreak track. 'Get the bloodhounds up here,' he told the corporal.

'Yes, sir.'

Jenifa gave the lush lingrass and thick pine trees a sceptical glance. Raindrops still beaded every leaf, giving the forest a glossy texture. 'Do you think they'll pick up a scent?'

'I don't know. But probably not.' Chaing looked back into the Openland cab. It was dirty and worn, and the leather on the driver's seat had several holes in. The passenger seat was covered in dog hairs. He checked the fuel gauge, which was showing the tank half full. 'This doesn't make sense,' he said slowly.

'What doesn't?' Jenifa asked.

'I get that he parked it here so we'd start off thinking he was driving away. But, actually, why not drive away?'

'Because the roadblocks and patrols would catch him.'

'Yes. But he had four or five hours' head start on the roadblocks. He could park the Openland in a shed thirty kilometres away and switch vehicles. Or take a train, or a bus.'

'Nearest train station is Collsterworth; that's fifty klicks away. And the local sheriff was there last night, right after you started putting out the alarm.'

Chaing pointed along the firebreak track. 'How fast could you walk up here?'

'Average walking speed is five kilometres an hour. Florian is young, so he could probably make seven for the first couple of hours. But . . . it's uphill and overgrown, so that'll take him back down to maybe four.'

'And he's carrying a child. So four maximum. The Terrain Trucks can push through this stuff easily. We'll catch him in a day and he knows it.'

'That's good—'

'No. Somebody has collected him, or there was another vehicle in the valley. Crud!' He drove away, but not in the Openland.'

'Makes sense,' she said.

'I need to get back to the command centre.'

The Terrain Truck driver backed down the firebreak, snapping several low branches as he went. When they pulled clear of the treeline, he turned them round and started heading down the slope. Chaing looked back. The trees extended all the way up the valley slope behind them. No way could Florian have contemplated walking out. The abandoned Openland had to be a double bluff.

To the north, where the valley opened out, the lake glimmered in the warm afternoon sun. He could make out the lone track winding along the floor of the valley, following the stream that fed into the lake.

'Stop!' he snapped at the driver. The Terrain Truck lurched to a halt, slipping on the mud.

'What the crud?' Jenifa demanded; she'd nearly been thrown out of her seat.

Chaing pointed through the windscreen. 'The Vatni village. Of course! We've been going about this from the wrong angle.'

'You mean the Vatni would have seen whatever vehicle he used to drive away in?'

'No.' Chaing smiled coldly. 'The troopers found the sheep by the stream in Naxian valley. Why drag it there from the field it was killed in?'

'You're speaking in riddles.'

'No, I'm not. He's a sheep rustler, so he needs to get into Naxian valley without being seen. No matter how late at night he goes, there's always a chance the Ealton family could see the Openland's headlights. So he doesn't use it. Why?'

'Oh,' she groaned. 'Because he's got another method of transport.'

'A boat. There was a boat at the Vatni village yesterday when I asked them about the space machine. Vatni don't need boats; they're aquatic. He's not walking. He's not driving on the roads. He's on the crudding water.'

'That lake feeds into the river Kellehar,' she said. 'Which is a tributary to the Crisp.'

'Which goes all the way to Opole!' His good fist hit the dashboard. 'Get us down to the village,' he told the driver. 'Now!' He picked up the microphone. 'Hokianga, I'm en route to the Vatni village. Send me some backup.'

The Terrain Truck pulled up twenty metres short of the intricate woven branches of the Vatni's tunnel-like buildings. Chaing climbed down and frowned at them. More Terrain Trucks were coming up behind him, as well as a couple of tracked carriers. Squads began to jump out of the vehicles.

'Give me a flamethrower,' he told a sergeant. He didn't want to, but everyone knew how stubborn the Vatni could be. After all, they didn't have to detonate a quantumbuster to be rejected by the Void.

'Er . . . sir?'

'You heard.'

The sergeant wasn't going to argue. He signalled one of his squad members, who went round to the tracked carrier's armoury locker.

It had been a long time since Chaing had used a flamethrower, and that was only in training. They were standard issue for regiments conducting a sweep. Procedure was for any Faller eggs they found to be broken open, and the yolk incinerated. The backpack with the fuel cylinders felt a lot heavier than he remembered.

A dozen adult Vatni had gathered by the edge of the village to watch the humans. Chaing strode right past them and walked the length of the jetty to where he'd seen the rowing boat. They whistled in short low notes as their tusks rattled. He ignored what was undoubtedly their version of gossip, and beckoned the trooper who was equipped with a flute and maracas. She looked young, probably still in her teens, which made him suspicious. 'Are you an Eliter?' he asked.

She scowled at him. 'Yes, sir.'

'So you know Vatni language perfectly. That's one of your kind's memory files, right?'

'Sir?'

'What happens here is classified. If it leaks out, I will make sure it goes bad for you and your family. Understand?'

'Yes, sir.'

'Good. Translate this: Who speaks for you?'

'Can we help you, land friend?' came the reply from one of the bigger adults.

'I came here yesterday to ask your help. I wanted to know if you had seen a Fall the previous night. You told me you hadn't. You lied.'

He looked at the gathering of Vatni, who had now fallen silent. For a moment he hesitated, but this had to be done, they had to understand he was *desperate* to find Florian . . . He turned to the nearest of their huts, and fired the flamethrower at it. For wood so close to water and recently rained on, it burned well. The gel which the flamethrower squirted out helped considerably, clinging to the curving branches, and enveloping them in flame, dripping through onto the earth floor inside. Flames roared several metres into the air.

The Vatni bellowed loudly, shuffling about in alarm. Their low-pitched whistling carried across the whole village. He saw several of them dive straight into the water, shoving youngsters ahead of them.

'Uracus, Chaing!' Jenifa exclaimed. 'What are you doing?'

'My job,' he told her calmly, refusing to let any hint of emotion contaminate his voice. 'You,' to the Eliter girl, 'tell them this: There was a boat tied up to this jetty yesterday. I believe one of my kind left in it. Is that correct?'

She looked scared as she turned to the group of Vatni and began blowing a series of notes on the flute. The aliens shuffled closer together and hooted softly among themselves, their tusk *clicks* subdued. Then one of them, a big male, waddled forwards to stand in front of Chaing. At another time, Chaing might have felt intimidated by the alien's size and strength. Not today. Today he was going to face them down. *This* was the point where Florian's luck ran out.

'Why do you do this, human of the land?'

'What's this one's name?' Chaing asked.

'Mooray,' the translator told him.

'Well, Mooray, did Florian take your boat into the next valley two nights ago?'

'Yes.'

'Did he use your boat to sneak away yesterday afternoon?'

'Why do you want to know this?'

Chaing spun round, and fired the flamethrower again, sweeping the long horizontal jet of flame over one of the bigger huts until it was completely ablaze.

'Did you help him escape?'

'Friend Florian left this place in a boat yesterday afternoon.'

'You would be better off not making friends with people like him. Where was he going?'

'I do not know.'

Chaing turned and raised the flamethrower nozzle again.

A furious hooting came from the Vatni.

'He doesn't know,' the translator said frantically. 'Florian went down the Kellehar. That was the last Mooray saw of him. But . . .'

'Yes?' Chaing asked darkly.

She frowned, and played some fast notes, clicking the maracas. The Vatni replied.

'Florian said he'd be back in a month.'

'Why a month?'

'It would be safe to return then. He didn't say why.'

*

'You're sure this time?' Stonal asked.

'Yes, sir.' Chaing was standing in the mobile command centre, looking at the new maps Hokianga's officers were unrolling across the table. These were a smaller scale than the ones illustrating the roadblocks and road patrols, but they showed the entire river Crisp tributary network in detail from the coast to the west of Opole. Some of the northern rivers reached almost up to the Pritwolds. He hadn't realized how many subsidiary rivers there were, nor their multitude of feeder streams. Most of them were large enough for boats to use. Apparently back in the Void, a lot of the region's commerce had been carried by cargo barges. Then after the Great

Transition and the advent of combustion engines, most of those goods shifted to road transport. 'He's in a Vatni boat heading downriver. Or at least he was yesterday. I don't think he'll be able to make it all the way to Opole. The Kellehar will take him down to the Crisp, but after that he'd have to row against the current to get to the city. And he's got a baby to take care of. He'll switch to an alternative route soon enough. There are two possibilities – the Eliter underground or his gang connections.'

'Very well. Your course of action?'

'I've got regiment troopers heading for every town and village along the Kellehar. They'll ask the portmasters if they've seen the rowing boat. They'll also commandeer motor boats to patrol the river. Colonel Hokianga is in contact with the river sheriff's office at Opole. They're going to send their boats downriver to the Kellehar. It's a pincer movement. If he's on the river, we'll get him. If the boat is berthed somewhere, we'll find it.'

'Very good, Chaing.'

'I'd like to use Section Seven authority to deploy that Air Force helicopter from the Opole squadron. That can cover the Kellehar a lot quicker than boats.'

'You have that authority. Don't keep referring back to me; I'm not here to cover your arse. Carry on.'

Chaing put the telephone receiver down, and let out a breath of relief.

'So now what?' Jenifa asked.

'Get the helicopter up. We've got a few hours of daylight left. And I need those files from Opole prioritized.'

'Yes, sir.' She grinned and picked up the telephone.

*

It was seven o'clock when the radio call came in from one of the boats the regiment troopers were using. They'd found an empty Vatni-made rowing boat snagged on the banks of the Kellehar, seventeen kilometres downstream from a town called Letroy.

5

The sewing kit didn't have much thread in it, and the needles were bigger than the ones Florian was used to. He was also having trouble cutting up the curtains from the spare room; the kitchen scissors were blunt. But he was determined the toddler should have a decent dress – at least for one day. Besides, a dress was a lot easier to lift up when she needed the toilet. So he started stitching just as the rose-gold sun rose above the cliff, sending a thick light pouring through the living chamber's opening.

'How long is this going to last you?' Florian muttered to himself; already she was larger than when he'd woken up. He glanced over at the toddler, who was now standing beside the raised fireplace. She was naked except for her nappy – a strip of faded red towel held together by four large safety pins. Her fingers raked through the mound of cold ash. Small puffs of the stuff clotted the air round her, swirling like miniature snowflakes to dust her black hair.

Florian sighed, but didn't try to stop her. She laughed as she flung a handful of ash into the air – then sneezed.

He turned back to the dress. The cloth was too thick really, and the faded green flower print wouldn't have been his first choice. His stitching was crude; he was used to sewing on buttons and patches, not whole seams.

'You're going to look really gorgeous in this. Yes, you are.'

'Dada!' She grinned and began to totter across the floor, trailing ash in her wake. 'Hunquee. Hunquee very, Dada.'

'Oh, look at the state of you. We'll give you another bath, and then you can wear the pretty dress.'

'Bath! Bubbles!'

'Yes. Bubbles. Lots of bubbles before we go.'

'That needs to be real soon,' a man's voice said.

Florian whirled round, knocking several cotton bobbins off the table. The man was standing in the entranceway to the hall, dressed in a worn check shirt and dirty grey jeans. He wasn't tall, but had a rangy physique, emphasized by exceptionally long arms. His face had a long jaw, with wide eyes and small grey-blue irises, making it hard to see what he was looking at. Just by standing there he was managing to intimidate Florian.

Teal barked at the intruder.

'Who . . . ?' Florian grunted.

'Name's Lukan. Billop said you needed a ride into Opole.'

'Oh. Um. Yes.'

'Let's move it then, guys.' He walked into the chamber, and glanced quizzically at the half-completed dress. 'Sweet.'

Florian scooped up the toddler, ignoring the ash that smeared down his tie-dye shirt. 'I didn't know you were here already. Joffler didn't say.' He glanced back at the entranceway, wondering where the crud the buyer had got to.

'Well, here I am.' Lukan eyed Teal. 'Nobody mentioned a dog.'

'Teal comes with us,' Florian insisted stubbornly.

'Okay. But it's going to be kind of crowded on your side of the car, what with the girl and all.'

'I've got some bags we need to take as well.'

'Really? Buddy, you might want to take a look outside.'

Florian gave him a worried look, then went over to the big oval window. 'Oh crud,' he groaned. His retinas zoomed in on the road that led out of Letroy to the west. A long convoy of black Terrain Trucks was rumbling along it. To the east, the other road that led into the town had a similar regiment convoy heading in.

'I spent the whole night avoiding their roadblocks to get here,' Lukan said, sounding almost amused. 'They're sure riled up hot over something. You want to wait around and find out what?'

'N-no.'

'Good.' Lukan clapped his hands loudly. 'Come on, then.'

Joffler appeared behind him, still pulling on his kaftan. 'Lukan. Hi there, fella, wasn't expecting you for a while. Uh—' He looked back into the hallway. 'I thought the gate was locked?'

Lukan grinned, showing off three missing teeth, and slapped a hand down hard on Joffler's shoulder. Joffler winced.

'No cage is ever going to hold me.' Lukan laughed. 'Told you that enough times, fella!'

'We have to go,' Florian said anxiously.

'What's happen—' Joffler caught sight of the convoys. 'Holy crud!' He stared at Florian, his jaw open. 'Are they coming for *you*? All of them? Crudding Uracus, fella, I thought you were in trouble with her mother! Not . . . Oh crud, what have you done?'

'Rule one: never ask,' Lukan said. 'If you don't know anything, you can't tell the sheriffs squat when they come a-knocking.' He pulled a huge hunting knife out of a sheath on his belt.

Florian took a step back, hugging the toddler tighter.

'Rule two: I don't drive no Fallers.' He beckoned. 'Come on, buddy, blood-check time.'

Very reluctantly, Florian held out a hand. The blade wasn't just long, it was amazingly sharp. 'Oww!'

'Had to be sure,' Lukan said without sympathy, and pushed the blade back into its sheath. 'You really sure you want to take a bag?'

'Yes. We have to; it's for Billop.' Florian started to suck his thumb. The cut stung.

'You got one minute, then I'm outta here, with or without you.'

Florian ran into the spare room and struggled to get his backpack on, then shouldered the duffel bag. Into the kitchen, and basically took every piece of food he could find – not much. Finally, he picked up the toddler.

'Dada? Hunquee, Dada. Very hunquee.'

'It's all right,' he promised. 'We're going for a big fun ride. Bouncy bouncy along in a car. You and me.'

'Dada.' She hugged him, and giggled. 'Still hunquee.'

'I've got your milk. But we have to go.'

Lukan and Joffler were talking in low, heated voices when he arrived back in the living chamber. Florian went over to the table and picked up the half-made dress and the sewing kit.

'You've gotta be kidding me,' Lukan said.

'She doesn't have any clothes,' Florian said, hating how whiny he sounded.

'Give me the bag.' Lukan took the duffel bag from him. 'These are all Billop's going to care about anyway.'

Florian squared up to Joffler. 'Thanks. For everything. I mean it.'

The buyer couldn't quite meet Florian's earnest gaze. 'Sure thing, fella.'

'I'll see you in a month. Back at the Wymondon store for a handover, yeah? There's going to be a lot of waltans ready by then.'

'At the store it is, fella.' Joffler hurried forwards and hugged him, then kissed the toddler. 'Look after her, okay?'

'Okay.'

'We need to move it, buddy,' Lukan said as they hurried away from the outcrop. 'Once those troopers' boots hit the street, we are dead men walking.'

'What do you think they're going to do?' Florian asked apprehensively. Teal was bounding along beside him, happy to be outside again.

'I was listening to their radio chatter last night,' Lukan said. 'They found a boat downriver from here, yesterday afternoon late on. Lots of big noise about that, like someone shoved a hot needle up their arse. Their mobile command centre came down out of the mountains and set up there. Been squawking ever since. Turns out they're looking for a man and a baby travelling together.' He raised his pale eyebrows. 'Fancy that, huh? So they're hitting Letroy and three other villages along the river this morning. They've got orders to visit every house and ask questions, and Giu help anyone that doesn't let them in or answer. They can just break the door down and cart them off for PSR interrogation. They can do that because this is an official nest alert.'

'Oh crud,' Florian said. He clutched the toddler harder. 'But I'm not! I'm not a Faller.'

Lukan grinned. 'I know that. Why do you think I checked your blood? I'm a driver; I get cargo where it's supposed to go, is all. Never failed to deliver. Ain't about to start now. I got me a reputation to think about.'

Florian nodded, too scared to say anything.

There weren't many people about as they hurried along the paths that wound round the rock outcrops. Florian could hear the engines of the Terrain Trucks grumbling across Letroy. *If they're still moving, that's good, right? It means they haven't let the troopers out yet.*

'Hunquee!'

'All right, all right,' Florian said as the toddler squirmed about in his arms.

'What's wrong with her?' Lukan asked. 'That thing on her head, gotta be bad news, right?'

'No,' Florian said, keeping it casual. 'It's a submandibular-gland tumour, but non-cancerous. The doctor said they'll remove it when she's older.' His u-shadow had accessed files of similar-looking natural tumours, and it was a nicely complicated name – the kind that if you say it authoritatively no one would question.

'Uh, right. So how old is she?' Lukan asked.

'I . . . I'm not sure when she was born. Her mother didn't tell me.'

'Oh man, that has to hurt. But you win, coz she's a real cutie. What's her name?'

'Hunquee! Hunquee! Hunquee!'

'Essie,' Florian said proudly.

They headed away from the river towards the cliff that dominated the town.

'Where's the car?' Florian asked. 'Do you think you can get past the regiment? There are a lot of them.'

'You worry about your girl. Leave the delivery to me.'

Florian wanted to ask a whole lot more questions, but didn't have the nerve. There was something about Lukan that reassured him. If anyone could drive them to Opole, it was him. Yet at the same time Florian felt thoroughly daunted by the man.

Lukan stopped outside Gemain's store, which still had the shutters down. He checked round to see if anyone was about, then used a key to open the wooden door.

Gemain was waiting inside. He nodded tersely to Florian and showed them through the back of the narrow chamber that made up the store. There were stairs carved into the stone, leading up to his home above. Another locked door that led into the store room, which he opened for them.

'Thanks, buddy,' Lukan said, and shook his hand as they went through. The cavern was filled with storage racks holding bales of cloth, and big drums of dye. Lukan went right to the back, and pushed at the rack. It pivoted neatly away from the stone wall, revealing a circular opening a metre and a half wide. Wherever it led to was hidden by darkness.

'This'll take us to the top,' Lukan said. 'This old cliff is riddled with natural caves. The people who built their homes here opened up a few, but the rest, the deeper ones, are unused and unmapped. Well, most of them, anyway.' There were five torches on the ground just inside the opening. He gave one to Florian and switched on his own.

Teal didn't like the narrow caves at all. Florian had to coax him along the whole way, even carrying him when they had to work their way up vertically. Some of the passageways were oppressive; when he shone his torch into some fissures the beam couldn't find the far end.

The toddler's cries got so bad that after forty minutes Florian had to stop and give her one of the richmilk bladders. Lukan took the delay well, but he did complain the torch batteries might not last.

Eventually they made it to the highest cave, which Lukan explained was part of a rock ridge several hundred metres behind the top of the cliff. He used it as a hidden garage and small-scale repair shop. It was wide, over twenty metres, and not particularly high, three metres at the apex. Parked in the middle of the rumpled stone floor was the big old Coperearl saloon Joffler had told him about. The bodywork had started out as a light blue, but now had various different-coloured patches where some new metal sheet had been riveted on and painted with whatever colour had been available. There was some kind of fat air intake sticking up out of the centre of the bonnet. But it was the tyres that drew Florian's attention; they belonged on something a lot bigger. Lukan had extended the wheel arches considerably to cope with them, and the hefty suspension was now lowered below the base of the car, lifting it forty centimetres higher than when it rolled off the production line.

'Great Giu,' Florian muttered. Even the toddler stared at the machine with interest.

Lukan lit an oil lamp and grinned back at them. 'She's something else, huh?'

'Certainly is,' Florian admitted. He'd enjoyed doing his own maintenance work on the Openland, but the Coperearl was beyond anything he'd ever be able to build.

'I calls her Sandy-J, after a girl I was hot on. Hell of a ride.' He winked then gave the toddler a guilty glance.

'Right.'

'Hunquee!'

Little hands were tugging urgently at the tassels on Florian's tight black trousers. 'Coming, sweetheart,' he promised, and shrugged out of the backpack. The toddler grabbed the bladder from him.

'She'll be finished in a minute,' Florian said as Lukan walked towards the gloomy shadows that shrouded the front of the cave. He could see the entrance had been blocked off by a wall of wooden planks at a steep angle. Most of them were supported by thick posts, while in the middle a rectangular door was held in place by a complicated pulley-and-chain arrangement, and two counterweights. It looked like the whole section could hinge up horizontally. Florian was quite curious what the other side of the door looked like – some kind of camouflage?

'No matter,' Lukan said as he examined the door. 'We're here till night now.'

'We are?'

'Buddy, they got troopers and sheriffs crawling the ground like a bussalore apocalypse. They even had them a helicopter buzzing about yesterday, so sure as Uracus shits, they'll use it again today. Now there's a lot of open land between here and Opole; if they see us, we are royally screwed. I can get us past the usual sheriff patrols, but this . . . Let's just say my bragging rights are going to skyrocket if I zip us on through this one without getting burned.'

Waiting should have bothered Florian, but he found it oddly reassuring; Lukan clearly knew what he was doing. He used the time to finish sewing the dress together. When he put it on Essie, she smiled happily. 'Pretty.' She toddled over to show Teal, not nearly as unsteady on her feet as she had been back in Joffler's house. 'Dada—'

'Yes! I know. Hungry.' He pulled some of the food from the backpack.

Lukan used the time to fix big extension tubing to the exhaust pipes (which were pretty large already). 'It'll reduce our power a fraction,' he said as he started threading the bolts on the first one. 'But we're not going to be counting on speed tonight. I need quiet for this, and my Sandy-J, she's not a modest girl.'

So Florian spent half the afternoon lying on his back on the cold hard rock, holding the big cylinders in place while Lukan made various connections, and added support brackets. When they finished, the old Coperearl looked like it had a pair of rocket engines screwed on the back.

Essie drank down more richmilk, and ate all the fruit Florian had brought. Then she curled up on his kaftan and went to sleep. He watched her in the light of the oil lamp. She must have been at least twice as big as she was when he lifted her out of the Commonwealth machine – in fact, the dress was almost too small already. He could see her eyes moving constantly beneath her eyelids – REM sleep, his medical files called it. She whimpered a lot, which he found distressing. She was such a wonderful little girl; she didn't deserve any kind of suffering.

*

After the mobile command centre had driven to the riverside where the boat had been abandoned, Chaing and Hokianga had spent most of the night planning the next day's urban sweep. They identified four villages and towns where Florian could have gone ashore and set the boat adrift. The roadblocks around them were immediately strengthened, with nothing allowed in or out. Troops were assigned and moved into position, their officers and NCOs briefed, a mimeographed photo of Florian (taken seven years ago for his valley warden service application form) distributed.

They moved in just after dawn. Terrain Trucks dropped off their squads, then drove round the streets with loudspeakers blaring, officially declaring the nest alert and ordering everyone to remain inside. The squads started moving from home to home.

It was one of the grocery store assistants that identified Florian, and confirmed he had a small child with him. The corporal in charge of the squad immediately radioed it in.

Chaing arrived in Letroy eleven minutes later, the Terrain Truck bouncing along the narrow tracks that wound between the weird rock outcrops. By then, the captain in charge of that sector had confirmed Florian was accompanied by a local citizen called Joffler.

Joffler's rock home was surrounded by a ring of troops, using the scattered boulders and lush vegetation to deploy without being seen. Heavy machine guns were set up, and trained on the openings in the outcrop, most of which were covered by curtains or shutters.

Chaing and Jenifa led two squads of troopers along the spiral path that wound up to the entrance of Joffler's home. He was confronted by iron railings with a locked gate, so he nodded to the engineer, who came forwards and jammed a small explosive pack onto the lock.

'Remember: he has to be taken alive,' he told the troopers – though it was more of a warning.

The charge blew the lock, and troopers rushed in, carbines held ready.

'Bedroom, sir,' called Kavris, the captain in charge of the assault. 'Two hostiles.'

Troopers were ripping the home's fittings apart as Chaing walked along the curving stone passage that linked all the chambers. The bedroom was clogged with a thick smell – narnik smoke, and something like ammonia. The place was a tip. The big bed's sheets obviously hadn't been washed for a long time, and clothes spilled out from chests and a couple of hefty wardrobes.

A man and a woman were on their knees beside the bed, hands behind their necks with fingers linked. Three troopers stood beside them, carbines pressing into their necks while Kavris watched them, his expression one of disgusted contempt.

'Name of the woman?' Chaing snapped.

She was naked and clearly heavily stoned, judging by the way she was swaying about and humming under her breath. Her long green hair had dozens of ribbons woven in, which helped to curtain her body.

'She hasn't spoken,' Kavris said. 'Crudding narnik addict.'

'She's Rohanna,' Joffler said, looking up.

Chaing backhanded him with his good arm and he yelped in shock.

'Speak only when you're spoken to, is that clear?' Chaing said coldly.

A badly frightened Joffler nodded quickly.

The humming from Rohanna grew louder. Her eyes were squeezed shut.

'Check her,' Chaing told Jenifa.

Rohanna squealed as Jenifa stuck a needle in her arm. A drop of red blood welled up.

'Human,' Jenifa concluded.

Tears trickled down Rohanna's cheeks.

'You,' Chaing told Joffler. 'Arm out.' He jabbed a needle into the fleshy part of the man's upper arm. Red blood.

'Where's Florian?'

'He's not a Faller!' Joffler exclaimed.

Chaing paused, allowing Joffler to register his disappointed expression. The man was clearly going to need some hard facts explaining to him.

But before Chaing registered what was happening, Jenifa stepped forwards and kicked Joffler in the groin. Joffler screamed, collapsing onto the rug, curling up, hands clutching desperately at his testicles. Jenifa grinned, watching keenly.

Chaing turned to her and mouthed: 'What?'

Rohanna wailed and started rocking back and forth. 'The Skylords will come. The Skylords will come,' she chanted. 'My soul is pure, my soul is pure—'

'Get her out of here,' Chaing told the troopers.

They dragged the young woman away.

'Bad cop,' Jenifa said in a quiet voice to Chaing. Then she crouched down beside Joffler, studying the man's agonized expression. Seeing the fear. 'I'm not interested in your smartmouth opinions. The only thing I want to hear from you is answers to my questions. Next time you say something wrong to me, I will have these boys hold you down with your legs apart and I'll keep kicking your balls until I've ruined you.'

'Oh Giu, help me,' Joffler sobbed.

'Enough!' Chaing said. He took her by the shoulder and pulled her away. 'This is my operation.'

'Fine. You ask, then. But he won't tell you crud. I've seen his type before. They're tough. They need to be softened up.'

'I don't!' Joffler wailed. 'I'll tell you whatever you want to know. Just don't . . .'

'All right,' Chaing said. He pointed at Jenifa. 'You wait there.'

'You're going to need me,' she said angrily.

'Maybe, maybe not.' He knelt beside a snivelling Joffler. 'I'm going to give you one chance. Where. Is. Florian?'

'He left this morning with Lukan.'

'Okay, good. And who is Lukan?'

'Driver. He takes my cargo to the city.'

'You mean Opole?'

'Yes.'

'So you're a nasty little criminal drug dealer?'

'Yes, I am.'

'How do you know Florian?'

'It was set up by Billop. Florian brought the waltans he trapped to me and I'd ship them back to the city. We'd meet at the Wymondon store every month for the handover.'

'Florian supplies you with waltans?' Chaing tried to keep the surprise from his voice.

'Yes.'

'How long has he been doing that for?'

'Seven years. Ever since he started at Albina valley.'

'Okay, so you bring the waltans back here, and Lukan takes them on to this Billop person?'

'Yes.'

'Are you an Eliter, Joffler?'

'No! Crud, no. I swear it, no.'

'What was Florian doing here? What did he tell you had happened?'

'It was some girl he'd got pregnant or something. She dumped the baby on him. He wanted to get to the city. He's got family there who'd look after him for the month. After that he'd be back.'

'A month? He was only going for a month?'

'Yes, he said it would be over by then.'

'What would be over?'

'I don't know. Just: over.'

'Was someone coming to collect the baby from him?'

'He never said. I thought he meant she'd be dead by then.'

'Now why would you think that?'

'Because she was ill. Cancer, I guess. There was this tumour thing on her head. It looked awful.'

'So the baby was sick?'

'Well, it was seriously weird, you know?'

'No, I don't know! Tell me.'

'It was like she was growing up too fast. I mean, she could walk when they left, and she couldn't when Florian arrived. I don't know crud about babies, but I'm telling you that one wasn't right. She ate more than I do, and grew like a beanstalk. It kind of creeped me out, really. I didn't tell Florian that.'

Chaing stood up and turned to Jenifa. 'A fast-growing baby,' he said in amazement.

'If she grows that quickly,' Jenifa said slowly, 'then in a month . . .'

'She'll be an adult.' *Great Giu! A Commonwealth adult, with all their capabilities.* He closed his eyes and saw her again, the Warrior Angel, her phenomenal invisible weapons wiping out an entire nest without any effort.

'What does Lukan drive?' he asked Joffler.

'It's an old Coperearl. But he rebuilt it for speed.'

'I'm sure he did. Where was it parked?'

'He didn't tell me. He never does.'

'Smart man.'

*

'Don't do that again,' Chaing said as they hurried down the slope below Joffler's house. 'Not without consulting me first.'

'Why?' Jenifa said cheerfully. 'We're PSR, we're not weak or squeamish. I'm not, and now we know where he's going, who's taking him, and how they're travelling.'

'Direct application of pain is only useful when the subject is determined to hold out. Joffler was never one of those.'

'You misread Florian,' she countered.

'Maybe. Once. I know him now.'

'Good cop, bad cop got you a fast result, didn't it? We have a description of Lukan's Coperearl. No way he'll ever get past our roadblocks; he's only got an hour's head start, if that.'

'I hope you're right.' He glanced over at her, as always misled by her stature and young looks. It wasn't just the strength she'd used when she kicked Joffler, it was the pleasure he'd seen animating her at the man's pain. He'd been shocked. Yes, good cop, bad cop was still an effective interrogation technique – and he'd got the right information. But they hadn't discussed it before; she'd just taken the lead. That wasn't good. Weakening the interrogation subject psychologically, the fear of the threat, was always more effective than any physical pain – so he thought. More efficient.

'My problem is that we're back to apparent coincidences again,' he told her. 'I don't like that.'

'What coincidence?'

'Florian supplies waltan fungus.'

'He's a forest warden who catches waltans for a little extra cash. So what? I expect most of them do. It's not like he's a real drug dealer – you need a chemistry lab to process them into granddad's delight.'

'The point is, Florian has connections with Opole's gangs. That gave him a driver into the city. How many civilians have contacts like this? It put him ahead of us again. I don't like it.'

'He's got lucky, that's all. He can't escape the PSR. Nobody can.'

'But he's smart. And his contacts – radicals *and* criminals . . . That's not a good combination, not for us. If he's been supplying the gangs with waltans, he'll have money, too, that'll help him disappear. Seven years of drug money, and he hasn't spent any – I saw his lodge.'

'Get a grip. If you're a proper PSR officer, you have to be positive. We're going to catch him. Lukan can't outrun an entire regiment, not to mention the helicopter. They're only an hour ahead of us.'

'Right. But we have to be certain. When we get back to the command centre I want you to call the Opole office. We need to know all about the city's trade in granddad's delight. Which gangs supply it, where they operate from, known members.'

She nodded – approvingly, for once. 'I'm on it.'

*

Florian had to admit, he was expecting the Sandy-J to start with a roar, maybe sounding like an Air Defence Force IA-509. Instead the engine came to life with the *purr* of a happy kitten. Whoever designed the exhaust's silencer extensions really knew what they were doing.

Behind the windscreen, Lukan gave him a thumbs-up. Florian turned out the oil lamp and started pulling the door winch chain; its rattling was louder than the engine, reverberating round the cavern. Slowly, the big wooden door levered its way up. The night outside was as dark as the interior of the cavern. Florian carried on tugging the loop of chain.

When the door was fully open, the Sandy-J whispered past him. He pulled the release lever, and ran out into the open as the door hinged silently back down. The car kept on going.

'What the . . . ?' Florian gazed helplessly at it as it rolled across the gritty sand, past some low boulders. 'Hey, stop. Stop!' He ran after it, waving his arms about. Teal barked excitedly, bounding along beside him. Essie was in the car!

Sandy-J curved round a small clump of rock, and dipped down into a stone hollow before braking. Florian came skidding to a halt beside it, breathing heavily.

'You okay, buddy?' Lukan asked as he climbed out of the car.

'Where were you going?' Florian demanded. Shock was making him lightheaded again. Exovision medical displays showed him his heart-rate was one-fifty. He felt giddy, and ducked his head in through the open door to see Essie. She was sitting in the passenger seat, leaning forwards so her hands rested on the dashboard, going: 'Vroom vroom!'

'You okay, sweetheart?'

'Dadda, I's hunquee.'

'I know.'

'Come on,' Lukan said, and started walking back to the hidden cave.

'What were you doing?'

'What?'

'You drove off!'

'Buddy, you gotta be— Oh, you thought I was snatching the baby from you, didn't you?'

'No. I just— I . . .'

'You did! Man oh man, you are one paranoid ass.' He pointed at the ground. 'See where Sandy-J is parked up? She's on naked rock. But here, this is earth she's driven over. Sandy-J leaves tracks in this crud, especially after the rain we've just had. So you and I, we go back to the door and cover our tracks. If we didn't do that, we might as well send up a big red flare to show your PSR friends where we are.'

'Oh. Yes. I get it.'

The door was camouflaged by a layer of soil on the outside, leaving it almost invisible amid a sloping pile of gritty dirt that lay against a long rock ridge. It even had weeds growing in the middle of it. Florian and Lukan used branches from scrub bushes to sweep the earth back over the edges of the door, then wipe the car's tracks away.

'Now we go,' Lukan announced as they got back into the Coperearl.

Essie clung to Florian. 'Legs stiff, Dada. Stiff.' Her tiny nose was wrinkled up as if she was about to cry.

'Okay, sweetheart. Daddy will fix it.' He began massaging her legs, slightly surprised by how chubby they were. Essie had been walking around the garage cave that afternoon, exploring while he helped Lukan; along with her accelerated growth it must be putting a strain on her muscles and joints.

It was only after a minute he realized Lukan was driving without the headlights on. His own Eliter retinas with the u-shadow enhancer routines allowed him to see at night, which must mean Lukan . . .

'Are you an Eliter?' he blurted.

Lukan flashed him a wide grin. 'I am surely not, buddy. I am a proud believer.'

'A believer?'

'In the Church of the Return.'

'Oh, right. Yeah.'

'So you don't believe?'

'I've not really thought about it.'

Lukan laughed softly and turned on the radio. The car was filled with the crackle of the speakers and the occasional garbled word of the regiment communication staff.

Florian was still massaging Essie's legs. He stared out over the bonnet, watching the landscape. Sandy-J was driving along a shallow stone gully. A narrow trickle of water ran along the bottom, almost invisible in the darkness.

Lukan has to have an Eliter heritage, Florian decided. *No way could ordinary eyes see well enough to drive at night.* He almost pinged the driver just to find out, but decided against. Not all Eliters embraced their 'community'.

After a couple of kilometres, Lukan turned off, and drove along a farm track. Florian could see fields of tall wheat on either side of them. On the left, in the far distance, his infra-red sight revealed a small spot glowing dull pink. *Farmhouse?*

Whatever the source, Lukan kept well away from it. He knew every track across the land and through woodland – knew where the gates in the fences were. The only time they saw a main tree-lined road was when they dashed across it to vanish up another country lane.

Essie fell asleep after a couple of hours and plenty more richmilk, cosy in Florian's lap, his arms around her. Then the whimpering began again.

'So do you think we'll reach Opole before dawn?' Florian asked.

'Sure thing. Look, a normal run would take me maybe three hours. This route, we're looking at ten. And if we do come up short, I've got me some holes to crawl into. We can wait the day out snug and secure. Quit worrying.'

'Sorry. I've never done anything like this before.'

'Well, I have. Wouldn't have life any other way.'

'But . . . I thought you believed in the Church of the Return?'

'I do. The Skylords are the only way our souls can find their way to Giu. They are the guiders through the dark.'

'But this life . . .'

Lukan laughed. 'The Skylords don't judge how our life is lived in accordance with all the petty laws and restrictions we invent for ourselves. They judge only if you have led a full life, if you have lived in a way that makes you happy. They care that you have not wasted your mortal existence. And, buddy, this is not a waste. I bring people what they want, and have fun doing it. It don't get much better than that. Take yourself now. How would you like it if I wasn't around?'

'Good point.'

'We were all better off in the Void. We belong there. Our minds were strong there. I truly believe that this is a temporary exile, that Giu is punishing us for the crimes Nigel committed. But the Skylords will find us again, because they are the compassionate angels who have always guided us. It is why they exist. And when they do finally come to Bienvenido, we must show them that we have learned our lesson, and be humble in the face of their glory. If we can do that, if we show that we are worthy again, then they will guide us back.'

Florian didn't argue, much as it galled him. All the files he had in his head, all the superior Commonwealth knowledge, told him what an utter load of crud the Church of the Return was. Yet he held back. He'd learned long ago that logic and facts never meant anything to true believers – of anything. And now he was slightly scared of Lukan, too – not just because he was completely dependent on him, but how the man would react if he learned what the child was, the hope she was bringing to Bienvenido.

How many more people like him will she have to face? How much anger and fear?

Smiling down at her little face, he brushed strands of hair from her forehead. *It's not fair, not fair at all.*

The radio messages faded to almost nothing after midnight. By then they were driving through broad open countryside, where the farm tracks stretched on for kilometres, and Lukan rarely changed direction. Progress was good.

It was only when they drew closer to Opole that the regiment chatter started to build again. And this time there were sheriffs out there as well, reinforcing the roadblocks.

'—definitely going for the city—'

'—Coperearl is modified—'

'—high speed—'

'—chased Lukan before—'

'—looks all battered, but—'

Lukan sucked down a breath. 'Now how about that? They know we're coming.'

'Joffler!' Florian grunted in dismay. 'He betrayed us.'

Lukan's answering laughter was shocking. 'He's a drug dealer, buddy. What did you expect?'

'Yeah, but—'

'You think all he does is pass waltans along to the city? He's got deep connections, and Letroy is his territory. He supplies a lot of small local dealers. You weren't five per cent of his traffic. Means he's got a lot to protect when those troopers came a-knocking.'

'Crud!'

'You betcha. Now from what I've heard on the radio, they've got every road into the city staked out and blocked.'

Florian instinctively hugged the girl tighter. No way could he let the PSR get her now. Not now he'd seen how they reacted to the space machine, how desperate they were to get their hands on him. *Crud, it's going to have to be Port Chana.* He dreaded having to face Lurji again after all these years and those terrible words spoken at the end. But for the girl's sake he was just going to have to swallow his pride – assuming he could find his brother. After all, the sheriffs never had.

'I suppose I might know some people in Port Chana,' he said miserably.

'It's a dump,' Lukan said flatly. 'Besides, I'm due to deliver you to Opole.'

'But they've got it surrounded.'

'They've got the roads covered, sure, but there's plenty of rail tracks into the city.'

'They'll be covering the stations as well!'

Lukan laughed again. 'I said rail tracks, not trains.'

*

Less than an hour later, the Sandy-J was sitting atop a steep railway cutting. The lights of Opole were creating a pale haze in the predawn sky, five kilometres away to the west.

'You ready?' Lukan asked with a manic grin.

'Oh Uracus.'

'Come on, buddy. This is what I was talking about before. *This* is living.'

'Yeah,' Florian muttered. 'But for how long?' Clearly, Lukan was crazy.

'Oh yeah, here we go!' Lukan gunned Sandy-J down the slope.

Florian squeezed himself back into the seat, holding the girl firmly. They must have been tilting at fifty degrees, though it seemed they were only one degree off vertical as they dropped. He could feel Sandy-J's back end starting to slide sideways. Lukan spun the steering wheel enthusiastically, fighting the skid, keeping them stable.

Then they reached the bottom of the cutting, levelling out with a lurch. Essie moaned in her sleep as she was jolted around. Florian shushed her, stroking her face softly.

Lukan steered Sandy-J onto the tracks. The metal rails stretched out ahead of them, perfectly straight lines reaching into the heart of the city.

'Do you know the train timetable?' Florian asked nervously.

'Nope! Just hoping the Skylords are smiling on me tonight.'

'Oh crudding Uracus.'

'Hey! Young ears, buddy.' Lukan slipped the car into third gear, and accelerated. The big tyres thrummed monotonously over the sleepers as they raced forwards. For the first time, Sandy-J showed off the kind of speed she was capable of.

Florian desperately wanted to shut his eyes, to disconnect from what was happening until such time as Lukan announced they were in the city and turning off the track. But instead, panic made him sit bolt upright, his eyes scanning round for any hint of a train – ahead or behind.

After five kilometres, the cutting walls suddenly grew higher and they shot into a tunnel.

'How long?' Florian demanded.

'Dunno.' But Lukan did floor the accelerator. Sandy-J leapt forwards.

Florian's enhanced eyes found the soft semicircular glimmer

of light that was the end of the tunnel up ahead. Then a pinpoint of bright light was shining in the rear-view mirror.

'Train!' he yelped.

Lukan chuckled. 'Oh yeah, baby, this is what it's all about!'

Sandy-J raced out of the tunnel. The cutting walls sank down on either side, and Lukan twisted the wheel. They bounced off the tracks and sped along parallel to them.

'Need a place to hide,' Lukan said. 'See anything?'

'There. On the left. Shed.'

'Got it.' Lukan started braking. Behind them, the tunnel mouth was a bright white semicircle as the train approached.

There wasn't much room between the shed and the cutting wall. Sandy-J wound up tilted at thirty degrees, wedged in behind the shed as the train roared past, belching out steam and smoke, pistons pounding. A long line of goods wagons followed. Then silence.

'Skylords,' Lukan said knowingly.

Utter crud! Florian thought.

A kilometre and a half further on, they reached an intersection where more tracks joined the ones they were following. The land on both sides flattened out. Sidings branched away from the main tracks. Old abandoned wagons stood on rusting wheels, while buddleia bushes grew tall and spindly between them. Lukan turned off the tracks and found a service road. Two minutes later they were driving carefully through the back streets of Opole's Bingham district.

*

It was a small brick warehouse along Connolyn Street. Lukan stopped outside, and flashed his lights twice. The double doors were opened, and he drove in.

With the headlights off, there wasn't much light inside. A couple of low-wattage bulbs hung from the age-blackened rafters high overhead. The warehouse was practically empty, with just some old wooden packing crates along one side.

Lukan took a moment in the silence after the engine had died, staring through the windscreen. 'Careful around these guys,' he said softly.

Three men were waiting for them. Florian knew it was an ancient prejudice, but he didn't like the look of them. They were dressed sharply, suits of expensive fabrics, cut well. Heavyset – a bulk that wasn't all fat. And gold jewellery worn prominently: thick rings, bracelets, necklace chains outside their shirts, earrings.

Earlier he'd been intimidated by Lukan; now he was glad the driver was sitting beside him.

Essie woke, blinking, as Florian climbed awkwardly out of the car. Incredibly, she'd grown again while curled up in his lap overnight. The dress was far too tight across her shoulders. Teal lolloped out behind him. Lukan was climbing out on his side, smiling welcome at the men, reaching out a hand. 'Perrick, good to see you, buddy.'

The taller of the three men smiled and shook hands. 'Impressive, my man,' Perrick said in a throaty rasp. 'The sheriffs have the whole city sealed up. My boys here said it was pointless waiting for you. But me? I said no, we will wait. The mighty Lukan has never missed a delivery. And see, here you are.'

'Yep, here I am. And this here is my friend, Florian.'

'Greetings, Florian.'

'Hello.' He wanted to say more, but Essie was snivelling.

'Dress tight, Dada. Everything hurts. I's hungree.'

'Okay, sweetheart. Daddy will sort this out. There's some milk in my backpack. I'll take the dress off and wrap you in my coat. Be nice and cosy, yes?'

'Hungree! Need toilet.'

The men sniggered. Florian tried to ignore that as he went back into the car and retrieved his backpack.

'You got the cargo?' Perrick asked.

'Sure,' Lukan said. 'In the boot.'

While Florian was trying to pull the last richmilk bladder out of his backpack, one of the men opened Sandy-J's boot, and retrieved the duffel bag.

'Um, I need to go with you to Billop,' Florian said as Essie snatched the bladder of richmilk from his hands. 'I need my money.'

Perrick directed a neat implacable smile at him. 'No, you don't go see Billop. Not now. Not ever. We've been listening to the sheriffs and the PSR on the radio. You are way too hot, my friend – that's if you're even human. We don't need dangerous liabilities like you fouling our territory.'

'Of course I'm crudding human! Lukan, tell them!'

Lukan raised his hands in a sorrowful gesture. 'I'm just the driver.'

'You're crudding kidding,' Florian cried in outrage. He turned to Perrick. 'But I need my money.' Teal picked up on his anger and barked.

'What money is that?' Perrick asked, feigning curiosity.

'My money! Seven years I've been trapping waltans for you. I want my money. It's mine!'

'You should go to the sheriffs, then. Put a complaint in.'

All of them laughed at that.

'Those are my waltans,' Florian shouted. He started towards the man carrying the duffel bag, ready to snatch back what was rightfully his.

'Don't!' Lukan warned.

The third man took two quick steps forwards and punched Florian hard in the gut. He doubled up as the breath was slammed out of him and toppled onto the hard stone floor. Essie wailed. Teal barked, and charged forwards, snarling.

'Crudding dog!'

Teal leapt, jaws closing on the arm of the man with the duffel bag.

Medical alerts sprang up in Florian's exovision. He couldn't get enough oxygen, and his heart was doing its panicked flutter again. Concentrating was hard. There was a lot of angry shouting. Teal's snarls.

A pistol shot rang out. Incredibly loud.

And Teal was lying on the ground, blood pouring from the huge hole in his neck.

Florian yelled out in anguish.

Perrick swung his pistol round to point it directly at Florian's head. 'Faller bastard.'

'Imminent threat identified,' Florian's u-shadow declared. 'Suggest immediate neutralization.' More displays slipped up into his exovision as the defence bracelet armed itself. Target circles captured all four men, shrinking around them like coloured shadows.

'Do it!' Florian wheezed.

Four slim, dazzling blue-white lines ripped out from the bracelet, stabbing the men. A ferocious bang accompanied the discharge. And all four of them were flying backwards through the air as if they'd been struck by a sledgehammer.

'Crudding Uracus,' Florian whimpered. The silence in the warehouse was as shocking as the beams' thunder had been a second ago. Then Essie started wailing at the top of her lungs, tears flooding down her cheeks.

Florian patted the smouldering holes in his shirt cuff as new files popped up in his exovision, explaining the bracelet stun-pulse function.

Mostly harmless, the summary read. Targets usually recover after a few minutes. Not recommended for targets with a weak heart.

Lukan was twitching where he lay, so he was still alive. Perrick and the man with the duffel bag were unconscious, but groaning as if having nightmares. The third man was completely inert.

Florian staggered over to Essie and picked her up, hugging her close. 'It's over,' he soothed. 'It's over, sweetheart. Daddy promises. It's all over. Only good things are going to happen now.'

She went rigid in his hold. 'Leave, Dada,' she said in a clear voice. 'Bad people will come. Always more bad people.' Then she slumped down lethargically and started trembling.

'Oh great Giu, help me,' Florian moaned. He looked at Teal's body for a while, holding back the anger and tears, then picked up his backpack and headed for the door.

*

It was seven years since Florian had been in the Gates district. As dawn washed its narrow crooked streets in a pastel light, he found the old memory triggers oddly reassuring. Nothing had changed. The sweet shop his mother used to take him and Lurji to. The second-hand clothes store. TollGate, a long bent lane where he and Lurji had fled a gang of lads who'd shouted out 'Eliters!' and run at them with clubs. Six Bells pub where, aged thirteen and goaded by his brother, he'd tried to buy a beer, only to be thrown out by the jeering barmaid; Lurji had laughed and taunted him the whole way home.

Most of all, he was reassured by the links. The Gates was full of link pings, buzzing around him like invisible bees as Eliters called to one another with address codes, then began talking. Encrypted files filled the electromagnetic spectrum. The general band was full of data packets with the Warrior Angel's icon.

It was music to his mind. *I'm home.*

And the broad green-painted door halfway along MistleGate – Aunt Terannia's club. The door was smaller than memory had it. Drab paint, old and scuffed.

He stood in front of it for a long moment. Then knocked. Nothing. The club had probably only shut a couple of hours ago.

Knocked again, more forcefully this time.

Heavy bolts thudded back, and the door swung open. Aunt Terannia stood there – a formidable woman in her nineties, dyed ebony hair dishevelled, wrapped in a threadbare burgundy towelling robe, blinking in amazement. 'Florian? Oh Uracus, it *is* you. Come in, my boy, come in.'

To his absolute horror, he burst into tears.

BOOK FOUR

A Long Fast Week

1

The Opole General Hospital was a nine-storey grey stone building on the edge of the Jaminth district, built over four hundred years ago. Designed to provide the comfortable Void-era middle-classes with individual rooms where they could be treated privately, the management board had struggled to adapt it for the requirements of modern medicine and the massive post-Transition political shift of the state providing equal medical treatment for all. But it persevered through funding crises and staff shortages, giving local citizens a basic medical safety net.

Ambulances delivered urgent cases to the Emergency Treatment Centre, a newly built brick annex at the back. To get to it, you had to turn off Roturan Road, which ran along the front of the hospital, and down Vilgor Alley – a narrow backstreet that had a sharp turn at the end, which was difficult for ordinary vans, let alone anything as big as an ambulance.

When Chaing's Cubar pulled up outside the hospital late in the afternoon, his PSR driver didn't even have the option of turning down into Vilgor Alley: it was blocked off by three sheriff patrol cars. He and Jenifa got out quickly and barged through the cluster of reporters outside the main entrance. They were both wearing their PSR uniforms, which quashed any complaints before they were made.

The Emergency Treatment Centre was divided into three wards. The sheriffs had taken over one of them, with two officers standing guard outside the door. They exchanged a glance as Chaing advanced on them and reluctantly let him past unchallenged.

Inside, the long ward was lined with assessment bays that could be curtained off. Most of the curtains were open, showing several injured sheriffs on the trolleys. Arms were in slings. Foreheads were grazed and gashed, wrapped crudely in bandages. Pressure dressings were bound over abdominal wounds. One had badly blooded torn trousers, her foot at an impossible angle. The ward's team of harried doctors and nurses were treating the casualties, conferring with a couple of surgeons.

More sheriffs milled about in the centre of the ward, looking angry and anxious – wanting to help and not wanting to get in the way.

'Where is he?' Chaing asked the first one.

The sheriff pointed along the ward, scowling. 'We should have just left the piece of shit in the wreck.'

'No, Comrade,' Jenifa said levelly. 'You shouldn't. He's ours.'

That earned her plenty of animosity from the other sheriffs.

'You did a good job catching him,' Chaing said.

'Yeah? Five of our patrol cars got smashed up in the chase before we rammed that bastard off the road. It's a crudding miracle nobody was killed.'

'The PSR appreciates what you did, Comrade.' Chaing carried on down to the main trauma suite. It was a bigger area than the assessment bays, with solid walls and double doors big enough to wheel surgical trolleys in and out. Three armed sheriffs stood outside. He ignored them, pushed the doors open, and strode in.

Two doctors and three nurses were in attendance. Chaing glanced at the man on the trolley. There were a lot of grazes and facial bruising, but he didn't even have to compare what he was seeing with the file photo: it was Lukan. His clothes had been cut away, allowing bandages to be applied to both legs; blood was already soaking through them. One long arm was in a splint. His wrist was crushed, wrapped in a bloody dressing. A doctor was stitching up gashes on his torso.

'Get out,' Chaing ordered.

'But—'

'OUT!'

They went, cowed and sullen. Jenifa held the doors open for them.

'Don't let anyone in,' Chaing told her, though he was more concerned that she wouldn't be in the room when he began. He didn't want a repeat of what she'd done to Joffler.

She nodded, and went out to stand guard.

Chaing studied Lukan for a moment. The driver was barely conscious. An intravenous drip of amanarnik had been set up, feeding the drug into his good arm to banish the pain. There was a supply regulator tap underneath the bag. Chaing turned it off.

One of the cupboards contained the trauma suite's supply of bandages. He took out several and wound them round Lukan's arms, binding him securely to the trolley. Once he'd finished that, he opened the man's mouth and began feeding a bandage in.

As the drug wore off and the pain returned, Lukan began to moan. His awareness returned slowly. Head turning weakly from side to side. Eyes blinking into focus. His moans grew louder, confused as he realized his mouth was full of bandage. He frowned up at Chaing and tried to lift his arms. Another muffled protest emerged when he found he couldn't move.

Chaing stared down at him. 'You know, I've often heard my colleagues claim the worst possible thing that could happen to anyone is that they wake up to find themselves in a PSR basement, strapped down on an interrogation bench, with one of our professional torturers standing over them, lighting his blowtorch.'

Lukan strained against the bonds, trying to shout, the cords in his neck standing out in sharp relief. The wad of bandage crammed into his mouth prevented anything but a frantic mewling.

Chaing held up a scalpel in his good hand. Lukan froze, mesmerized by the blade. Chaing began to carefully cut along the bandages around Lukan's leg, exposing the badly damaged flesh. 'Personally, I disagree,' Chaing said. 'I think the worst thing that could happen to you would be if you woke up, strapped to a trolley

– much like this one, in fact – with an *amateur* torturer standing over you. What do you think?'

*

Director Yaki had assigned Chaing to a big operations room on the third floor of the PSR's Opole office. It had three long barred windows along one brick wall, and with typical PSR thoroughness the glass was misted to prevent the minute chance of anyone from looking in. Metal desks for the investigators were arranged in a long row, each with two telephones; the secretaries' typing tables were smaller, and lined up behind them. Pinboards occupied the wall behind the chief investigator's desk, which was the biggest in the room, and made of wood.

So far the boards had a standard street map of the city, and several photos arranged in a pyramid with Billop at the top, and his suspected senior lieutenants below. There were two further photos, one of Florian, and one of Lukan, over which someone had scrawled *gotcha* in red felt tip.

Chaing resisted a grin at that when he and Jenifa walked in that evening. He'd been appointed ten PSR investigators. Three records division clerks stood ready, with direct lines down to their basement offices to summon up whatever files the investigators wanted. Captain Franzal from the PSR assault squad had also been given a desk; Chaing and Yaki had agreed that the assault squad should be on standby throughout the investigation – and this time he didn't need senior-officer authorization before deploying them. Even the transport pool was represented by a manager.

The only person not in a PSR uniform was Nathalie Guyot, a senior detective on secondment from the city's sheriff office, who ran their gang investigation bureau. Yaki had brought her in as liaison; apparently no one knew more about Opole's gangs than her.

When it came to running a case, Chaing couldn't ask for a better support team. The only person missing was Lurvri. *Damn, he would have relished working a case like this.*

Yaki was waiting for him. 'You have the floor,' she told him quietly. 'I'll keep the county commander off your back for now, but given the scale this is running at, we're going to need results. Stonal won't take any responsibility for this.'

'Understood,' Chaing told her, and turned to face the room. 'We have fresh information,' he announced as the heavy door swung shut behind him. 'Lukan was very eager to cooperate with the PSR.' Knowing smiles appeared round the room. 'He told me he delivered Florian to a warehouse on Connolyn Street early this morning. I want a team over there to check it out right away. The reception committee was three of Billop's people: Perrick, terVask, and Bulron. I want their files up here within the hour.

'Now, being the lowlife crud he is, Billop was going to dump Florian on the street and hold on to his money. Even the gangs realized Florian is too hot for them. According to Lukan, there was a fight. It was a short one, because Florian has some kind of Faller weapon. It's like a gun that shoots lightning bolts.' He paused for that to sink in. Stonal was adamant there was to be no mention of a Commonwealth connection, so they were still running with the nest-alert cover story.

'That means,' he continued, 'when we do catch up with him, we will be taking extra precautions. Franzal and I will be drawing up an assault procedure later. In the meantime, our priority is bringing in Billop.' He raised a hand as Nathalie Guyot gathered herself to speak. 'Yes, I know he's hard to find, so first I want to talk to our friends Perrick, terVask, and Bulron. We have a clock running on this, so I need them here by tomorrow midday at the latest. Draw up their full profiles, families, friends, where they hang out. Liaise with the sheriffs on this. Nathalie, what do we need to know about gangs?'

She nodded and stood up. At a hundred and ten years old, her hair was mostly silver, but her grey-blue eyes were still alert, and she was clearly enjoying her moment as part of the investigation. 'Thank you, captain. Some background for you all. There are four main gangs in Opole. The largest is run by Roxwolf, who I'm embarrassed to say we still haven't shut down after fifteen years. He is the smartest, most ruthless gang boss we've had in the last hundred years; we've never been able to pin a damn thing on him. I can't even give you a likeness, let alone a photo. Witnesses vanish, and it's impossible to turn anyone. We've tried sending in under-cover sheriffs, but he always spots them. Any illegal activity in this city runs with his approval. The other three gangs are nominally independent, but in reality he tolerates them, and most of their rackets are run jointly, with Roxwolf's boys taking the lion's share. Billop is the smallest of these.' She put her hand on the map, tracing an outline. 'The last gang territory war was three years ago, which saw a whole lot of the smaller operators wiped out, and left Billop with the eastern half of the Gates, extending out into the Veralson and Guntas districts. That's his turf, as agreed with Roxwolf. After the warehouse fight, he'll have gone to ground somewhere in that area. Captain Chaing is right: Perrick is our best way to him. And that leaves terVask and Bulron as the best way to Perrick; the three of them are a solid crew.'

'Okay then,' Chaing said. 'It is imperative we get Billop into custody as soon as possible. Someone arranged for Florian to deliver waltans to Billop, and that someone is the best connection we have to Florian right now. Joffler doesn't know who it was; he was told to collect the waltans and arrange shipment. Which means it's Billop who has that name. So go and get me Billop.'

With the investigators given specific assignments, Chaing pulled Jenifa and Yaki aside. 'I don't like Billop being our only lead.'

'I'd be disappointed if he was,' Yaki said. 'What have you got for me?'

'Jenifa had the records division draw up a list of all Florian's known family and associates from when he was growing up. I want to bring them in.'

'All of them?'

'Yes.'

'How many?'

'Seventeen. And that's really scraping the connections barrel. Florian wasn't a sociable person.'

'Okay, do it.'

'His mother is Castillito.'

'Crud. The civil-rights activist?'

'Yes.'

Yaki clenched her jaw, which made her scar lighten. 'Irrelevant, especially in this case. She doesn't get any special treatment.'

'I'd like to send the assault squad to carry out the arrest. They can search her home and offices too.'

'Florian won't have gone to her. That's too obvious.'

'Florian is very good at doing what we don't expect.'

She raised an eyebrow. 'Is he getting to you?'

'Absolutely not. I'm just trying to think like him.'

'I'm glad to hear it.'

*

Like most buildings in the Gates, Aunt Terannia's club was high and narrow, its wooden beams warping over the centuries, leaving walls and floors without any level surface. The ground floor was given over to the club itself, with a small raised stage for musicians facing a floor with twenty tables. A bar along the rear served a good selection of beer, with more casks stored in a tiny cellar underneath. Steep, awkwardly angled stairs at the side of the bar led up to the first floor, which had the green room, cluttered with crates of glasses and spare furniture. The staff room was next door and even smaller, with a row of ancient lockers and a cracked porcelain sink. There was also the tiny manager's office, where the desk covered half of the floor space, and boxes of spirits took up most of the rest.

The floor above that was Aunt Terannia's apartment. Florian sat at the dining table in the living room, with Essie beside him, greedily scooping up porridge from a bowl. Dull thirty-year-old egg-blue paint on the cracked walls seemed to absorb light from the two electric bulbs hanging overhead, adding to the sense of decline, of no one caring. He tried not to look round because he knew he'd start judging, but he reckoned his lodge back in Albina valley was a better place to live.

Aunt Terannia poured herself some tea from a big pot glazed

with an orange and green floral design into a matching cup. Florian remembered that crockery from his childhood. He and Lurji used to come visiting Aunt Terannia a lot when they were growing up; she was actually their mother's second cousin, which made her about the only family they had in Opole.

'What's her name?' Aunt Terannia asked; she was watching Essie closely.

'Essie.'

'Really? I remember another Essie. You were keen on her, as I recall.'

Florian blushed heavily. 'I haven't seen her since I left.'

'Yet you called this girl Essie.'

'It's a good name.'

'She calls you Daddy. Is she yours, Florian?'

'Not exactly. Please. I can't explain.'

'This is me, Florian. Talk to me.'

Florian couldn't meet her gaze. He'd forgotten how firm Aunt Terannia could be.

'Where did this little sweetie come from, Florian?'

'She was given to me by someone who trusted me. Please, I just need somewhere to stay for a few days.'

'A few days? How did you get into the city, Florian? Every road is blocked by the sheriffs. Yesterday, the queues were kilometres long. It was all anyone was talking about in the club last night. Is it you they're looking for?'

He nodded miserably.

'They're saying it's a nest alert,' Aunt Terannia continued. 'We haven't had one of those for a decade, and never on this scale. Is she a Faller?'

'No!'

Terannia slammed a palm down on the table. 'Then what is going on?'

'I can't tell you,' he said wretchedly. 'It's for your own good.'

'I decide what I do and do not need to hear.' She narrowed her eyes to give him a fierce stare. 'Is she Lurji's?'

'What? No. Please, stop asking!'

284

A man appeared in the doorway, dressed in blue and red striped pyjamas. He was probably a couple of decades older than Terannia, with ebony skin that was thick with wrinkles, and short curly hair that was nearly all silver. His beard was trimmed elaborately. A long gold earring hung from his right ear. 'Asking what?' he enquired lightly.

Florian looked at him, then back to Terannia. He blushed again.

'Oh, Florian,' she said in a disappointed tone. 'Age doesn't mean people can't be happy together. It actually helps, being long past the time of exuberant youth's foolishness.' She grinned up and took the man's hand. 'Matthieu, this is my dearest nephew, Florian.'

'Ah, the one you send all the textbook copies to. Pleased to meet you, Florian. Nice threads, by the way.'

Florian shook the hand he was offered. There was something wrong with Matthieu's fingers. They weren't straight, and the joints seemed swollen. 'Pleased to meet you,' he mumbled.

'Florian needs somewhere to stay for a few days,' Terannia said. 'Half the government is hunting him, but he won't tell me why.'

'Quite right, Florian.' Matthieu grinned as he sat down. 'A man is entitled to his secrets. Don't let her bully you.'

'I might have known you'd take his side.'

'We all share the same side,' Matthieu chided. 'Know your friends. Trust your friends. Love your friends,' he chanted softly, and gave Florian an expectant look.

'Florian doesn't know any of your songs,' Terannia said.

'You're a songwriter?' Florian asked.

'I'm a musician. Or I used to be.'

'Matthieu plays drums with his jazz band here once a week. They've joined the electric trend. Even so, it's very good.'

'Not professional,' Matthieu assured him. 'Just amateurs having a good time jamming together. If you do stay, perhaps you'd like to come and hear us play?'

'Yes, thank you,' said Florian, who didn't like jazz at all.

'Are you going to call your mother?' Terannia asked.

'I don't want her involved.'

'She will be, Florian. They're blocking the roads, searching the train stations and the port. You think they're going to leave your mother alone?'

Florian dropped his head into his hands. 'Oh crud.'

'Your mother is a very tough lady,' Matthieu said. 'If they cross her, they'll regret it.'

'They'll come here!'

'I doubt they know we're related, so this is safe. I'm more worried about your future. Do you actually have a plan? Are you trying to meet someone to hand the girl on?'

'No. It's not like that. I just have to stay away from the PSR for a month. It'll all be over then.'

'The PSR won't stop, Florian. They never stop. I don't know what you've done, but it must have really pissed them off.'

'I didn't do anything,' he whispered fiercely.

Terannia and Matthieu both looked at Essie, who had now started munching down buttered toast.

'Who is she, Florian?'

'I can't. I'm sorry. If you can loan me some money, I'll go.'

'Don't be ridiculous. You wouldn't last ten minutes out there. Every sheriff in the city is looking for you; that means every informer, too.'

Florian hung his head. 'That's not all,' he admitted.

'Go on,' Terannia groaned. 'If I'm going to protect you, I need to know.'

'The man I take the waltans to, Joffler. He contacted a driver called Lukan, who got me into Opole this morning.'

'I've heard of Lukan,' Matthieu said. 'He's quite a legend – in his own eyes.'

'Yes. But the thing is, they all work for Billop. And Billop's people were waiting for me. There was this . . . sort-of fight.'

'Oh great Giu,' Terannia said. 'And I always thought Lurji was the problem one!'

'I'm sorry, Aunt Terannia. I didn't mean for any of this to happen.'

'I'm kidding, Florian. There was a fight, then? With Billop's lieutenant? And you got away free?'

'Did you shoot him?' Matthieu asked quickly.

'What? No! Well, not exactly. They did get hurt. I knocked them out.'

'They? How many are we talking about?'

'Three. Well, four if you count Lukan.'

'You knocked out four gang thugs?' Terannia said in astonishment. 'Singlehanded? Crud, Florian. That warden's job turned you into a real tough guy.'

'So it's the PSR, the sheriffs, *and* Billop's people who are going to be looking for you?' Matthieu said.

Florian exhaled loudly. 'Yes.'

'Wow.'

Terannia and Matthieu exchanged a glance.

'What is it that you need, Florian?' she asked. 'From us, I mean.'

'Just somewhere peaceful to stay. It'll only be for a month, I swear. After that, it won't matter.'

'So you've said. Can you at least tell me what happens in a month?'

He gave Essie a fond glance. 'I don't really know. But it will only be a month. I know that.'

She nodded ruefully. 'If that's all there is to it, you can stay in the mod stable.'

*

The office on the first floor was wood-panelled. Matthieu led him in and immediately started rearranging the cases of spirits, clearing them away from the wall.

Florian stood in the doorway, watching him as he held Essie's hand.

'Essie needs some new clothes,' Terannia said, in a disapproving tone. 'That dress is far too tight – and short.'

'I know. Just some sheets or something will do. I can sew them into a new dress.'

Terannia gave the existing dress a closer look. 'Did you make this one?'

'Yes.' Florian braced himself for criticism.

'Not bad.'

'Here we go,' Matthieu said. He pressed a section of panelling. There was a *click*, and a small door swung back.

Florian stared at the lightless passage it revealed. 'What's that?'

'A little bit of quiet privacy in a bad, noisy world,' Matthieu chortled. He took a couple of torches from a drawer in the desk.

'You take them,' Terannia said. 'I'm not dressed for it.'

Matthieu gave her a pained look. 'Because my old bones are just built for this.'

'Is it difficult?' Florian asked.

'No. Just not built for our height, that's all,' Matthieu said. 'Essie will be fine.' He switched the torch on, and crawled in.

Essie followed him, a delighted expression on her face. Florian brought up the rear, shining the torch forwards so Essie would be able to see where she was going.

The corridor was about a metre and a half high, one wide. It had floorboards, and the walls were a reddish brick that had been worn smooth and dark by something rubbing along them for a very long time. There were small doorways at regular intervals, all of them blocked off, some with hurriedly laid brick, others with wooden planks.

'What is this?' he asked.

'Mod-dwarf passage,' Matthieu said. 'Back in the Void there were millions of the creatures. They were a slave species that started out as neuts, then got changed somehow by telepathy. Modified, hence mods. You could get mod-horses, mod-dogs, mod-apes – things that helped with all the tough manual labour. You also got mod-dwarfs, who were house servants.'

'I have heard of them; we learned about them at school. But the teacher never said much.'

'I'm not surprised. Slvasta had them all slaughtered after the Great Transition. There was no telepathy any more, so we couldn't order them around, and they were supposed to be related to the Fallers, somehow. Anyway . . . all houses had them to do the drudge work. So their stables were part of every building back in the Void, along with these passages so they could move between human rooms without getting in the way.'

'Every building?'

'Yes. Trouble is, the passages are all so small there's no use for them – no human use, anyway – so down the years they gradually got blocked off.'

They reached the end of the corridor, and climbed some small wooden steps into a larger room that Florian could just stand upright in. It was semicircular, with the curving wall inset with two rows of deep alcoves. A single window at the top of the flat wall was glazed with a white glass which allowed a reasonable amount of sunlight to shine in.

'The mod stable,' Matthieu announced; he pointed at the alcoves. 'They slept in those. But no worries, you've got these.' He took a couple of sleeping bags from one alcove. 'Toilet in that corner. Sink over there. It does work – not that there's any hot water, mind.'

Florian turned a complete circle, trying not to show his dismay.

'Hungree, Daddy,' Essie said.

'I'll bring you some food,' Matthieu said. 'And I'll see what I can do about some picture books or something for Essie.'

'Thank you.' Florian picked up one of the sleeping bags. There were more in other alcoves, he saw. 'Who are these for?'

'Ah.' Matthieu gave him a soft smile. 'Your aunt helps a lot of people who need to get out of town. I don't need to tell you how much crud Eliters get given here, do I? That bitch in charge of the PSR office has a real animosity going for us. So if someone crosses them, they stay in here for a while to let the heat die down, then we send them along to Port Chana. I think your brother stayed in here for a while before he left.'

'Lurji? He was here?'

'Yeah. And the PSR never caught up with him, did they? So you're perfectly safe – just so long as you remember not to make too much noise. The Gates are kind of crowded, and you're only ever five metres away from your neighbours.'

*

There were eight cells in the Opole PSR office that were specific-ally designed to hold Eliters. They were in the first level of the basement, with their own external access from the alley at the back. A corridor led away from the bottom of the stairs, directly underneath the building, so that none of the cells had a window, or even an outside wall. Inside each cell, the walls, floor, and ceiling had been covered in a metal mesh, turning it into a Faraday cage that blocked any link broadcast, then another layer of bricks had been laid on top to make the cage secure.

The cells were the only part of the building Eliters were allowed in – even the informers run by Gorlan's division. Chaing was very aware of that as he stepped through the big iron gate which separated it from the rest of the basement. *I should have put Corilla in here. If I had, she'd still be at university.*

Ironically, he realized now, it was also the place he would be taken to if Section Seven ever found out that he had an Eliter heritage as the Warrior Angel claimed. But now he'd finally read the Section Seven briefing documents, he realized the odds of them ever catching her were remote verging on zero. The best Section Seven could do was contain and discredit rumours of her activities.

There was plenty of shouting going on inside seven of the eight cells – the usual shouts of abuse and demands for lawyers – the protests leaking out through the grilles in the doors. So far, they'd managed to bring in fifteen of the seventeen suspects connected to Florian. Chaing didn't hold out much hope; most of them hadn't seen Florian since senior school. Two had served in the same regiment conscript unit, but that was seven years ago.

He was really only interested in cell one.

The prisoner chief rose from his desk at the end of the corridor, and saluted.

'Open it up,' Chaing told him. 'And turn off the tape recorder.'
'Sir?'
'You heard.'
'Sir, the logs . . .'
'You're changing a reel over. Understand? That's the log entry.'
'Yes, sir.' The chief went over to a tall cupboard and opened the top door. Inside, eight tape recorders were sitting on two shelves,

their big spools turning slowly. The chief switched off the machine recording cell one.

'Thank you, Comrade.'

The door had two separate keys. Chaing waited until they were unlocked and the bolts slid back. It was all excessive; the danger from Eliters was never physical.

Castillito was sitting behind the small table in the cell. She was in her late sixties, a beret of close-cut hair coloured a strange violet. Her clothes were the kind modern electric bands favoured, a white blouse and suede waistcoat, inlaid with colourful glass jewels and beaded tassels. The maroon leather skirt came down to her knees, leaving a couple of centimetres of skin visible above her sky-blue boots.

If Chaing had seen that voguish combination on anyone else, he would have assumed they were narnik-heads, smoking away a vacant life. On Castillito, it simply looked elegant.

'Captain Chaing,' she said. Her gaze lingered on the frayed edge of the cast sticking out of his tunic sleeve. 'Glad to see you've recovered.'

'Very good, Comrade,' he said, sitting across the table. 'Try and throw me right from the start. Was I supposed to ask: how do you know my name?'

'Every Eliter in Opole knows your name, captain – especially after Xander Manor.'

'Yes, I thought *you* might be aware of that case. After all, you are the head of the Eliter radical movement here in Opole.'

'You are misinformed, I'm a civil-rights advocate. However, for what it's worth, I am genuinely sorry about poor Lieutenant Lurvri.'

'Thank you.'

'It couldn't have been easy going up against breeder Fallers.'

'There's no such thing.'

She laughed in his face.

'Tell me about your son,' he said when she'd finished.

'Tell me why you brought me in here? It must be terrifically important; they wouldn't even let me have breakfast before they dragged me off.'

'It is. Your son is the most important person on Bienvenido right now. Where is he?'

'Am I under arrest? The officer – the very excitable, unprofessional officer, I might add – didn't have a warrant.'

'He doesn't need one. This is a matter of state security.'

'Really? Has there been a Fall? That's your only authority to claim that, and the Space Vigilance Office hasn't declared one – not here.'

'It's not a Fall. We are operating under nest-alert procedures. That gives me a wide range of special powers.'

'A nest alert? Just after you've cleared up all those breeder Faller monsters at Xander Manor? That doesn't inspire confidence in the PSR.'

'Without us, Bienvenido would Fall.'

'Keep telling yourself that. It might comfort you at night. Nothing else will. The Faller Apocalypse is coming, and you're wasting your time oppressing Eliters when you should be chasing down nests.'

'Just tell me about Florian, Comrade.'

'My son left the city seven years ago. He was driven out by the persecution of our people as perpetrated by your organization. I haven't seen him since.'

'Has he contacted you?'

'Who?'

Chaing brought a fist down hard on the table and Castillito flinched. 'Don't,' he cautioned. 'Right now I'm being nice to you because I think your son is an idiot who is caught up in something he doesn't understand. But you need to know this: I will find him. And how I treat him when I do depends a lot on how much trouble he causes me. So I'll ask again, has he contacted you?'

'You weren't quick enough, you know.'

'Quick enough for what?'

'When your gangsters with badges came for me, they didn't stop me from linking to my friends. I was giving them a running commentary all the way here. And it isn't just me you've snatched illegally, is it? Lawyers have already filed motions for release with a judge. There's going to be a citizens' protest outside. A lot of citizens. It's not just Eliters that you antagonize.'

'Imagine how frightened I am.'

'You know, one day you really should consider doing the maths. There are more Eliters in Opole than there are PSR personnel. Check with Kukaida if you don't believe me. In fact, there are more Eliters on Bienvenido than there are PSR; we outnumber you quite heavily.'

Chaing sat back in his chair. 'I saw him, you know. I actually talked to him four days ago. He made me think he was a simple forest warden. Very clever, your son. Smart.'

He almost missed it – a flicker of uncertainty showed in her eyes for an instant. 'You've seen Florian?'

'Yes. That is one pitiful life he chose for himself. Mind you, I can see how he'd think it was preferable to living at home with you.'

'Oh. Gosh. Ouch. I'm so devastated. Please, let me confess everything to you.'

'Florian *is* the nest alert.'

She pursed her lips as she stared at him. 'If Florian has Fallen, you wouldn't be asking me for help. A Faller-copy of Florian isn't going to come running to his human mother. So what is this about?'

'State secret. But it's bad. If you help me, I can go easy on him.'

'Really? Are you going to put that in writing for me?'

'No, because you're completely dependent on me. This all boils down to my whims. So you have to work really hard on not annoying me.'

'He hasn't Fallen, yet you've declared a nest alert. Dear me, have you been lying, Comrade captain? Have you abused your position and the state apparatus for another purpose? What really happened out there in the valley?'

'Who is his father?'

'A very high-ranking PSR officer. He bribed me not to reveal his name on the birth certificate, paid the fine and everything. Oops, did that go on the recording?'

Chaing grinned at her, despising her smug expression. His

usual technique wasn't going to work on her, he could see that. 'Funny.' He slapped her across the face. Hard.

Castillito went over backwards, crying in shock. Chaing came round the table slowly and watched her squirm around on the floor. Blood was dripping from the corner of her mouth. He bent down to deliver the ultimatum, to make it very clear what a piece of subhuman filth she was. How he *owned* her.

Her hand lashed up *fast*. A rigid forefinger jabbed into his eye. He roared in pain and shock, staggering backwards. Castillito was up after him, spinning round, a leg extending. The heel of her boot struck his cast. It cracked, and the pain-flash of the impact was incredible. He couldn't see anything but a red haze. Nausea made him dizzy, and his legs nearly gave way.

'Crudding Uracus!' He tottered back and banged into the wall, almost slumping to the ground. Eliters were fast. Eliters were strong. He'd forgotten the very basics of his profession, he'd been so angry with her defiance.

'Sir?' The prisoner chief was knocking on the door. 'Sir, is everything all right?'

Castillito was standing still, staring at him in contempt as she dabbed at her split lip. 'Well, is it?' she asked mockingly. 'Or are you hoping the Warrior Angel will come and save you? Again.'

Chaing gaped at her. *She does know! I crudding knew it. She is the head radical, she must be.*

'Sir?' The key started to rattle in the lock.

'Go away, Comrade,' Chaing shouted. 'I'm fine.'

'Now, let me tell you what's going to happen,' Castillito said, righting her chair. 'If I don't walk out of here within another two hours, details of your Eliter heritage will be anonymously delivered to Gorlan and your precious Stonal.'

'I'm not an Eliter,' he growled, his undamaged hand pressing against his eye. The pain was bad. He worried she'd damaged the eye permanently. *Bitch!*

'The way you react to Eliters shows how much you're over-compensating, Chaing. Self-loathing isn't healthy. In the end, it'll eat you up. I've seen it happen before. Accept what you are. It's not like I'm asking you to help us. When the Faller Apocalypse strikes, you'll need us.'

'The day after Uracus closes up for good!'

'You know you're an Eliter. You know there are breeder Fallers. You've met the Warrior Angel. Just how much truth can you keep on denying to yourself? We're on the same side, Chaing. We want to defeat the Fallers. Why can't you acknowledge that?'

'If you want to help me, tell me where your son is.'

Castillito sighed as she sat down. Her expression was like the one his primary school teacher used when she was disappointed with him. 'Exposing you isn't a bluff. I sent a time-coded file about you to several friends when your people came for me. And as I can't link to my friends from in here, I can't stop the file from opening in two hours.'

He rubbed his eye, which just made it worse. 'I don't trust you.'

'You don't have a choice. Do you know what they do to Eliters who've wormed their way into the very heart of the PSR? There's a furnace in the lowest basement level of this building for the central heating and hot water. They will throw you into it alive. You can trust me on that, because that's what you'd do to a traitor. Isn't it?'

'I have friends, too. If you ever make them suspicious of me, I'll know about it, because they won't believe you. That gives me time. And I will use it to come for you. A furnace will be the least of your worries.'

'I don't want to hurt you in any way, Chaing. It's clearly going to take you a while for you to come to terms with what you are: one of us. But despite that, I have hopes for you, great hopes. One day you might even sit in the director's chair.'

'I will never betray the PSR!'

'The PSR does a good job fighting the Faller nests. That's what you need to focus on.'

He gave her a weary look. 'That's what she said.'

'I know.'

'You've met her, haven't you?'

'No. Not in the flesh. I'm not important enough. But friends receive communications occasionally. And we send stuff back. Who do you think alerted her about the new kind of encrypted links in Opole? Who alerted her that you'd found a nest? Who do you owe your pitiful life to?'

'I owe you nothing!'

'What has my son done to bring all this down on him? Florian hasn't Fallen. You would have tested his blood when you talked to him – the PSR always does that. So what has happened?' The way she said it made it a rhetorical question. 'The regiment was deployed in Albina valley, and you've been chasing him ever since. Why?'

'You're the head of the Opole radicals,' he countered. 'That's not coincidence. Did you send him out there seven years ago? Has he been waiting for this?'

'For what? And for the record, I'm not the leader of the Opole radicals. I am exactly what those precious files of yours say I am: a civil-rights activist. A good one, but that's all. There is no conspiracy, Chaing. There never is. It's all part of the lie Yaki feeds you on Stonal's behalf.'

'If Florian contacts you, the first – the only – thing you are going to do is call me.'

Castillito's victory smile was modest. 'Of course. Do you have a link code yet, Comrade?'

*

It was the middle of the second day when the pings with Florian's address code started to appear. Matthieu had been back to the mod stable several times, bringing Florian baskets of food, then yesterday afternoon he handed over some cloth and a sewing kit. It was a much better sewing kit than Joffler's, and Florian set about stitching together a new dress, with shoulder straps that had buttons so they could be extended as Essie grew.

After gorging on more bread and fruit, and drinking a lot of water, Essie had gone to sleep on top of the sleeping bag, snuggled up in his kaftan. It seemed to ease her somehow, and he was pleased to be rid of the garish thing. As always, her sleep was beset with nightmares. She moaned and snivelled continually. Several times she cried out and sat up, with wide frightened eyes. Florian soothed her back to a quiet slumber every time, unsure if she was actually awake during those episodes. That night she slept for a straight ten hours, waking up ravenous as always. The first thing he did was lengthen the dress straps by three buttons.

He began to review the general-band forums while he worked on another new dress. All anyone talked about was the nest alert. Retina-image files of the queues at the roadblocks showed stationary lines of vans and lorries for kilometres along the roads, their drivers either stoic or furious. Yesterday he'd seen a few files showing the Coperearl smashed up between a wall and two sheriff cars. He wondered if Lukan was all right, but after the ambush in the warehouse, he didn't really care much.

The next morning the general band was full of news about people being arrested and carted off by the sheriffs without warrants. Florian recognized most of the names of those being taken to the PSR offices, even though he hadn't thought of them in years. The PSR must have been pretty desperate to include them. In truth he'd not considered asking any one of them for help.

With the newest dress finished, he pulled the food processor cylinders out of the backpack. Most of the food Matthieu had given him went into the hoppers, with water from the tap. This time he set the menu to a paste which slowly extruded from the lower nozzle, directly into a bowl. It had all the same specialist fats and vitamins as the richmilk, but with a thicker constituency and a mix of flavours, from apple to beef, so he could give Essie some variety. He found another setting that produced hard pellets that she could suck on between meals like sweets.

It was while these were starting to emerge, rattling onto a plate as if they were pebbles, that the first ping with his code came in. Reception in the mod stable wasn't great; the walls were thick, and there was only the one window. But his u-shadow had some excellent filters and its new subroutines had increased his reception sensitivity. He told it not to acknowledge any pings directed at him, but began reading the message headings. Opole's Eliter community had discovered he was the reason the PSR had declared a nest alert. There was a lot of confusion about that; no one knew

297

if he had Fallen or not. Some urged him to give himself in: 'We're suffering because of you.' Most offered support and told him to run, to screw with the PSR bastards as best he could. Streaming in parallel to the pings for him, the general-band conversations were saying that all this was nothing to do with a Fall, that he'd struck some blow against the PSR. There were plenty of theories about that, from him burning down the PSR headquarters in Varlan (an impressive step up from his brother's arson), to the development of some new kind of weapon which could wipe out Fallers with a single shot – with a whole lot of criminal acts in between proposed.

Essie woke up mid-afternoon, crying. 'Legs hurt, Dada,' she sniffled.

'I'll sort it out,' he said as he always did. He massaged her calves and ankles while she sucked on the pellets. 'I have a new dress for you.'

'You best, Dada.'

Her simple love triggered a burst of emotions that made his throat constrict. 'We'll be safe here,' he told her as his fingertips dug into her stiff gastrocnemius muscles. 'You and me together.'

'Hungree, Dada.'

He grinned. 'Yeah, me, too.' That was when Captain Chaing's name popped up in the general access. Florian scowled at the mention of the captain. There were a lot of protestors outside the PSR office on Broadstreet, waving placards and chanting, holding up traffic. Surprisingly, the majority weren't Eliters. The restrictions of the nest alert were antagonizing a lot of people. Encouraged by a fearless core of civil-rights activists, they were becoming bold, protesting against the cause of the disruption.

Matthieu turned up again in the late afternoon. He blinked in mild surprise when he saw the food basket was empty. 'I'd better get you some more,' he said in a mildly sarcastic tone.

'Thank you,' Florian said.

'She doesn't do much else, does she?' Matthieu said as he gazed down at Essie, who was asleep on the kaftan again.

'No,' Florian said proudly.

'Is she yours?'

298

'No, she's not.'

'We've got a band playing tonight. Who's MacLeod.'

'What?'

'That's their name: Who's MacLeod. They're going to be loud. That's how the kids like it these days. And there's other clubs as well.' He pointed to the window. 'You might not get much sleep.'

'That's okay. It wasn't too loud last night. Are you playing tonight?'

''Fraid not,' Matthieu said sadly, and glanced at his hands. 'Not that I don't want to, but I can't play so much now. I used to play guitar, but drums and singing are the best I can manage these days.'

'Arthritis?'

'No, actually. The PSR didn't like the protest songs I used to perform. One night they came for me after a gig; they used wooden posts to break my hands.'

'Oh, great Giu. Matthieu, I'm so sorry.'

'You didn't do it. That's why I'm pleased you're here. Whatever you've done, I'm glad of the opportunity to help you. It's another blow against them. And besides, people still play my songs.'

'I'm glad.'

'We fight them in a thousand small ways each day, my young friend. That is how decent people will triumph in the end.'

Florian had never been more tempted to tell someone what had happened, who Essie really was. 'You're right. We will,' he said fiercely.

Matthieu nodded in understanding. 'I have some good and bad news for you.'

'What?'

'Castillito was taken into custody this morning.'

'Mum?'

'Don't worry, they released her. I have friends who were outside the PSR office on Broadstreet. They saw her coming out.'

'Oh, thank Giu.'

'But it does mean they will be watching her. Closely, I suspect. She is their only true connection to you now. That means you cannot see her, Florian. You understand that. Don't you?'

'Yes. I . . . I guess so.' In a way he was relieved. The fact that the one person who had never sent out a ping for him was his mother had been bothering him. Badly.

'Good man.'

'So she'll understand why I came to Aunt Terannia and not her, won't she?'

'Of course.' Matthieu hesitated for a moment. 'I know you said you will only need shelter for a month, but have you considered what will happen if they start to get close? I'm not saying they will,' he said quickly, 'but I've never seen anything like this hunt. And they're looking for Billop now. Florian, he's a nasty piece of work who'll do anything to save his own skin; he might be able to point them here.'

'I'll leave. I swear I'll not put Terannia and you in danger.'

'That wasn't quite what I was getting at. Florian, there may be one person who can help you, but I don't know how you'd feel about asking her.'

'Her? Her, who?'

'Why, the Warrior Angel, of course.'

'The Warr— But she's not . . . Oh, *is* she real?'

'Very much.'

'Crud.' There were a hundred questions he wanted to ask about that. For his whole childhood, the stories of the Warrior Angel and how she protected Eliters had been a fascination and a comfort. It was her face that was the icon of every general-band file, a constant reminder to Eliters that they had a champion. She was a myth he so wanted to be real. 'Do you know her?'

'Me? Crud, no. But there are some Eliters that do, or at least know how to get a message to her. Or so they say. There's no direct link, no ping code; it's more like shouting into haunted fog and waiting to see what comes out of it. And there's no way of telling if she'll come, or even if she's there listening.'

'So do you think I should ask?'

'Right now, maybe not, but I'd like you to at least consider it if things get . . . heated. If I get dragged into the PSR dungeons, I'm not likely to hold out for long. Not at my age.'

'Don't,' Florian said quickly. 'Don't hold out at all. Please. If they come for you, or Terannia, don't antagonize them. I'll go quietly if that happens.'

The old musician shook his head. 'I'm not saying that's going to happen. I'm just outlining a few options if things take a turn for the worse. You're not necessarily as alone as you think you are.'

'Thanks, Matthieu.'

'You're a good lad, Florian. Your aunt thinks the world of you.'

'She was always here for us growing up,' he said sheepishly. 'She helped both of us. It wasn't easy in those days.'

'I know. And it's never easy, not for us Eliters.' He gave the sleeping girl a soft look. 'Funny, she looks like she's grown again, even since this morning.'

'Um, Matthieu, she does grow. A lot. You need to be ready for that.'

'Riiight.' Matthieu glanced at him, then back to Essie. 'Okay, I'll get you some more food now. Then you're on your own for the night. Can't risk anyone coming into Terannia's office while that secret door's open.'

'I have some songs,' Florian blurted. He hated how much danger he was putting Terannia and Matthieu in, and there amid all the wondrous knowledge Joey had given him were music catalogues. It wasn't much, but it was all he had to thank the man with.

'Good for you, Florian. I didn't know you liked music.'

'I . . . They're part of the mindscape files I code,' he said meekly.

'The what files?'

'The . . . Oh, I make images you can play in your macrocellular clusters, sort of like dreams, I guess.' His u-shadow was assembling a file of titles based on a simple search request. He'd sampled a few tracks out of the thousands and thousands that the space machine had given him. Even he, who never really thought much of music, had to admit Commonwealth music was extraordinary. There was so much of it, and it varied enormously, from orchestras of hundreds to soloists, from bands, to single songsculpters creating directly through their technology. And the catalogue stretched back centuries, right back to the first recorded songs – further back if you counted the sheet music the truly ancient composers had written. The request he'd loaded into the secondary routine that handled simple searches was for songs that protested about injustice and gave people hope for the future, but also about love (there were an incredible amount of them), and there were plenty of lively tunes that were just plain fun. The last criterion was that they had to be written for guitars and drums and piano in any combination.

A list of several thousand slipped up into his exovision, dating from the mid-twentieth century on Earth. Data supplements told him Earth was the original home of the human race.

'Show me,' he instructed the u-shadow. And Earth appeared in his exovision. Earth from orbit – as if he was an astronaut! And a real vision, not the constructs he featured in his simple mindscapes. Earth had huge brown and green continents, and oceans smothered in exotic whorls of pristine white cloud. A world crowned by ice at both poles. The night-time continents glittered with the lights of cities – vast conurbations that stretched for hundreds of kilometres, especially along coasts. It was *so* beautiful he yearned to reach out and touch it.

'Oh great Giu,' he moaned. Tears started to fill his eyes.

'Florian?' Matthieu asked. 'Are you all right?'

'Yes. Yes, I'm fine.' He wiped at his eyes, ordering his u-shadow to shrink the list of songs down to ten. 'These are for you,' he told Matthieu, and sent the files over. 'Your band can play them if they're any good. I don't mind if you don't.'

'That's very kind, Florian,' the old musician said with a soft smile. 'I know how hard it can be to show your work in public, especially something as personal as a song. These are very big files, so I'll listen to them tonight, and we can talk about them in the morning. How's that?'

'Um, yes.' He hadn't expected to have to discuss them. 'That's fine.'

*

Chaing walked out of the clinic on the second floor of the PSR office and went down to basement level five, three levels below the records division. The operation had made progress during the morning. Perrick and terVask were now in custody and on their way in. The sheriffs were still hunting Bulron, but it was no longer a priority now Chaing had the other two.

Level five was where they were headed. The cells here were smaller than the Eliter cells up above, the corridors narrower, unpainted brick soaking up the light from the small bulbs in their caged glass holders. Iron doors on both sides of the central corridor had a central grille with a sliding panel covering them.

At the end of the central corridor was a junction with two other corridors leading off at right angles. It had a desk for this level's cell chief, and a normal door into the guard office behind him.

Jenifa was standing beside the desk talking to the cell chief and a couple of guards when Chaing arrived. She turned, and the start of a smile swiftly turned to a concerned frown. 'What the crud happened to your eye?'

'Nothing,' he said. The clinic nurse had been worried as she bathed it clean and applied a sticky ointment. She'd wanted him to go to the hospital optometrist – as if he had the time. So he settled for a small dressing and an eyepatch. One of the clinic's orderlies had removed his broken cast, and put on a fresh one, which was larger than the first and still setting. It meant he had to cut off his shirtsleeve and wear his uniform jacket with its sleeve pinned across his side.

'Just like Slvasta,' the orderly had said when he finished helping Chaing back into his clothes. His humour vanished fast when he caught Chaing's expression.

'Nothing?' Jenifa exclaimed. 'But—'

'I tripped. Hit my face on a door. Now move on,' he snapped. The painkillers weren't quite strong enough to stop the ache from his damaged wrist, and he was worried that Castillito's kick had shifted the broken bone out of alignment. It just didn't feel right somehow; the pain was sharper now.

Jenifa's expression hardened. 'Yes, sir.'

'When are they due?' Chaing asked.

'The sheriff cars are pulling up outside in a couple of minutes, sir,' the cell chief said.

'Right. I want interrogation room three cleared out. Remove all the furniture. Then put Lukan and his cot in there.'

'Er . . . sir?'

'You heard, Comrade. And when the prisoners come down here, put them both in with Lukan. Clear?'

The cell chief clearly didn't like any kind of shift in procedure, let alone this. But he nodded and said, 'Yes, sir,' almost as if he meant it.

Guards were summoned and started carrying the chairs and table out of interrogation room three. Chaing and Jenifa went into the observation room, which looked into the interrogation room through a big one-way mirror.

'Are you going to tell me what's happening?' she asked coldly. 'Nobody on the third floor knew where the crud you went after you interviewed Castillito.'

'Sorry.' Chaing gave her an awkward smile. He waved his hand at the eyepatch. 'I had to go to the clinic. I did trip when I was hitting Castillito. I feel ridiculous. What kind of interrogator does that?'

She pushed her lips together in bemusement. 'So is that why you let her go? To avoid the embarrassment?'

Chaing could practically feel her judging him; he was starting to get resentful about the way he had to justify himself the whole time. 'Not quite. She's still our best hope of a lead after Billop. Florian might contact her. I've got her under constant observation. If he comes within a kilometre of her, we'll spot him.'

'He's not going to go anywhere near her. She's his mother, for crud's sake; he doesn't want her involved. At best he'll do that Eliter link thing – how would we ever know?'

'Some of Gorlan's informers are watching for that.'

Jenifa gave him a puzzled glance. 'You're relying on them?'

'What else have I got? Locked up here in a cell, out of contact with her kind, she was no use at all to me. This way at least I've opened up a possibility. And yes, I know how slim it is, but Florian might risk it.'

'So this . . . ?' she indicated the room on the other side of the shaded glass. Three guards were carrying in Lukan's cot, with him on it. The driver was moaning feebly, barely conscious.

'This is to encourage attitude adjustment. Information volunteered through fear is always more reliable—'

'—than information extracted under duress. Yes, I know that's your preferred method.' She watched Lukan for a moment. 'He's not going to last much longer if you don't get him back to a hospital. You know that, right?'

'Know and don't care. He helped a known nest-alert subject get into the city. I find that kind of behaviour beyond understanding. It's treason against his whole species. Like this, he's useful to me.'

For once her expression was almost approving.

They had to wait for a couple of minutes, then the door of interrogation room three opened again and PSR guards shoved Perrick and terVask in. Their shackles were unlocked, and the guards left.

'What the crud?' Perrick exclaimed, and went over to the cot. 'Uracus, it's Lukan!'

'What?' TerVask hurried over. He paled as Perrick pulled the blankets back, revealing the driver's ruined legs wrapped in bloody bandages. Most of the cot's blankets were stained with urine and faeces.

Perrick swung round to stare at the mirror, his round face showing signs of panic. 'What did you do to him?' he growled.

Chaing chortled quietly.

'Lukan,' terVask called anxiously. 'Lukan, pal, what happened to you? What did you tell them?'

Lukan tried to say something, which emerged from his battered lips like a hissing cough.

'What's he say?' Perrick asked.

'I think he wants some water,' terVask said.

Perrick turned a full circle, then fastened his gaze on the mirror again. 'I don't know where Florian went,' he said loudly. 'The bastard shot us with some kind of gun. Ain't never seen anything like it before. It was like it was firing lightning bolts, or something. My legs still ain't right, I's got trouble walking half the time. But listen, anything I can do to help you catch him, and I'll do it.' He gave Lukan another concerned look.

'Glad to hear it,' Chaing muttered.

'Honour among thieves,' Jenifa said in contempt.

'These aren't thieves,' Chaing told her. 'These are gang thugs. Tough as Uracus on the outside, but no brains.'

'Which one are you going to question first?'

'Well, terVask is the weaker one, but Perrick is senior, so he's more likely to know where Billop is. But he might just get stubborn when he knows it's his boss that he's got to give up.'

'Perrick, then. We can't afford to waste time on terVask. The longer it takes to get Billop, the more distance Florian can put between himself and us.'

Chaing gave her an approving grin. 'You're right. Perrick it is.'

*

Interrogation rooms one to five were for people who could be intimidated or misled into revealing what the PSR wanted to know. Rooms six to nine were equipped for prisoners who were tough and stubborn. The centrepiece of number seven was a big wooden X set into the brick floor, with manacles at each extremity. Four bright spotlights on the ceiling shone on it constantly, turning the rest of the room into a glare through which sinister shadows moved, and the relentless questions emerged. The only time that light stopped punishing the prisoner's face was when one of the interrogators stepped forwards carrying electrodes, or sharp instruments, or heavy cudgels. These tools of the trade were always laid out neatly on a bench at the start, so that the smarter prisoner could see them when they were brought in, before they were fastened to the cross and the big lights turned on. If they were truly smart, they would know just how utterly hopeless their situation was.

Billop was smart, but then Chaing had expected him to be; you didn't get to be a gang boss by thuggery alone. He'd put up quite a fight when the sheriffs came for him, resisting arrest right up to the end. Now, though, it was different; now the screaming and struggling was from fear as the guards ripped his clothes from him, beating him with leather truncheons every time he resisted. He screamed a lot more as the manacles closed round his wrists and ankles.

The lights came on, and he stiffened as if the illumination was a physical force pinning him to the cross. He squinted into the glare as he pissed himself.

A mocking chuckle came out of the dazzling brilliance as his urine splattered onto the brick floor and trickled into the drain grille between his feet.

'What do you want from me?' he sobbed as his body began to shake.

There was only unnerving silence.

'What is it? What do you want? Please.'

This time there was an answer. 'I want a name.'

'Yes. Yes!'

'You know Florian, don't you?'

'Yes, I do. I didn't know he was a Faller. I swear on Giu itself, I didn't know that.'

'You worked with him? You paid him for the waltans he caught?'

'I did. It's just for granddad's delight; there's no harm in that. But I never actually paid him. He has no money.'

'The name I want—'

'Yes?'

'Who introduced you? Who told you he was going to be a warden? That he was the kind who would trap waltans? Who is his friend in Opole? Who will he go to here when he's in trouble?'

'Rasschaert!' Billop yelled at the top of his voice, as if he was expelling something evil from his body. 'It was Rasschaert! He came to me; he fixed it all up. It was Rasschaert. Rasschaert!'

'Good. Now, where is Rasschaert?'

'Huh?' Billop froze up again.

'Where. Is. Rasschaert?'

'He's . . . He's . . .' Tears started to dribble down Billop's cheeks as he shook his head. 'Oh Giu, please.'

'Use the cutters. Remove his toes.'

'HE'S DEAD,' Billop screeched. 'He's dead. I swear it. Please, that's the truth. He's dead. Rasschaert is dead.'

*

The whole team looked at Chaing with eager faces as he stomped into the third-floor operations room just after midnight. He kicked his desk. Hard.

Expressions changed fast. Everyone was abruptly busy with work, heads down at their desks.

Chaing kicked the desk again. 'Crudding Uracus.' He sat down, and so nearly swiped his good arm across all the files and folders on the top of the desk, sending them flying. Instead he took a breath and made a pained groaning sound from deep inside his chest.

Jenifa hurried in and slapped a thin folder down in front of him. It had DECEASED stamped in scarlet ink across the front. 'Billop was telling the truth. Rasschaert was killed three years ago. There was some kind of power struggle with neighbouring gangs.'

'Yeah. Nathalie mentioned it. Crud! We had him, Jenifa; there was a connection. Rasschaert would have known where he would go, who would take him in. He might even have sheltered Florian himself.'

'There will be others who know.'

He glared at her. She endured it calmly.

'Who?' he demanded with all the petulance of a five-year-old.

'We're the PSR. Finding out dirty little secrets is what we do.'

Chaing nodded slowly. The pain in his wrist was just awful. He opened the top drawer and fished out the little bottle of pain-killers.

'You have to come up with a new line of investigation before Yaki gets in tomorrow morning,' Jenifa said. 'You have to show you're on top of this.'

'I know.' He tipped four pills into his hand, and swallowed them without water, grimacing as they slid down slowly and awkwardly. For a bad second he thought he might choke. 'All right, let's think this through. The positive: we've identified Rasschaert

308

as a close acquaintance, close enough to know Florian would be willing to catch waltans for a drug dealer.'

'But he wasn't on our original friends-and-family list,' Jenifa said. Her finger tapped the folder. 'He was an Eliter, of course. That's why records division had this file.'

Chaing gave the drab cardboard folder a weary look. 'Florian won't have old friends outside the Eliters. We've both read his file; he didn't get on well with anyone at school, and his time in the regiment was a disaster. But Eliters stick with their own.'

'So it will be an Eliter sheltering him.'

'Yeah, and the PSR knows every one of them.' *Not true. They don't know about me.* His hand came down on the folder. 'So let's start with Rasschaert. Get Kukaida's people to run a cross-reference. I want everyone Florian knew around the time he was in Opole. Bring them in.'

'I'll get on to records division,' she said briskly.

'Every time,' he muttered sullenly.

'What?'

'Every crudding time we're closing in on him, luck snatches him away again. How can *anyone* be this lucky?'

'You still think this isn't a coincidence?'

'I don't know. You couldn't plan to have Lukan smuggle you into the city, not seven years ago. But Florian isn't stupid, that much is obvious. And he certainly knows someone who can shelter him. Anyone else – *anyone* – and they'd be in custody by now, and that Commonwealth girl would be alone in a cell with Stonal.'

'Not sure anyone deserves that,' she said with a raised eyebrow.

'I've been there.'

'Yes. How was that?'

He grinned lamely. 'I might tell you one day.'

'I'll get working on this,' she said, and picked up Rasschaert's folder.

Chaing watched her walk across the operations room and gather a couple of investigators together at her own desk. A records division clerk joined them as they started poring over the pages in the folder.

He was sure that they'd come up with a decent list. More possibilities. More arrests and interrogations in the basement. He ought to be satisfied, but it would take time. And the girl, the fast-growing girl from the Commonwealth, was getting older with every day. He wasn't sure why he feared that so much. *Instinct?* And maybe the memory of the incredible Warrior Angel.

Perhaps I should throw in the towel and join the other side? Castillito would welcome me, that's for sure. And they certainly seem to be winning right now. But winning what? The Warrior Angel has had two hundred and fifty years, and she's not accomplished anything different. Helped us, yes. But a significant victory? Uracus, even she said the Liberty flights were our only hope of survival.

Chaing went over to Gorlan and sat down in front of her desk. It wasn't that they didn't get on, simply that their paths rarely crossed. But now Gorlan was pissed off that a hunt for an Eliter was being conducted by someone from the nest investigation division – and a mere captain at that. As far as she was concerned, his appointment as operation commander was a monumental and deliberate vote of no confidence from Yaki. There would be payback for that, later. A bureaucratic ally in the office's vicious political jungle would no doubt leak some critical piece of knowledge at a strategic time. A detrimental comment would be placed on his permanent administration file. His promotion prospects would be hurt. That's how it always went. But Gorlan didn't know he was now with Section Seven.

Just the thought of all that office politics made Chaing weary.

'Didn't go well with Billop, then?' Gorlan asked sardonically.

'He told me everything I wanted to know, thank you, Comrade. The trouble was, the information wasn't any use. The only connection between him and Florian is dead. Gang turf war.'

'Yeah, when they happen, they're short and nasty. You should talk to Nathalie Guyot. These are not the people who take prisoners.'

'I didn't realize Eliters were part of the gangs, too.'

'Gang bosses aren't like us, Comrade; they don't discriminate. And Eliters can be quite an asset to gangs, as their links provide unbreakable communication. Very useful for criminal activities.'

'Okay.' Chaing leaned back in the chair. 'Question for you, Comrade.'

'Go on.'

'Say I'm a radical Eliter. I've done something bad, struck a victorious blow against the terrible government, and now the PSR is really mad about it. They're using every trick they have to hunt me down, calling in every favour, every asset, every informer. Every road and rail line and river traffic route out of the city is blocked to me. What do I do?'

'They'll catch you eventually,' Gorlan mused. 'So there's only one thing you can do. Like all your hothead friends before you: leave.'

'Leave to go where?'

'Port Chana is where rumour has it – a hotbed of Eliter radicals. But we both know the PSR has a disproportionately large office there precisely because of that. So it's not actually the destination which matters, because it could be anywhere.'

'An isolated valley in the Sansone foothills, for instance?'

'Quite. But it's how you get there which is important. Concentrate on the route.'

'Ah. I use the equally legendary underground railway.'

'A little less of the legendary, Comrade. It's not a formal organization, but the Eliters do stick together and help each other out. Sometimes they use people like Lukan.'

'Non-Eliters? For this? Really?'

'It's been known. You've seen people like Lukan don't care what their cargo is, only that it pays.'

'So the radical Eliters will get Florian out of Opole?'

'Every Eliter knows someone who knows someone. Then there's anonymous links – the general band, it's called. It's how they operate. So eventually, when the pressure gets too much – yes, they'll get him out.'

'Then all we have to do is find which Eliters are more helpful than others, and make them show us their secret routes out of the city.'

'Yes.' Gorlan laughed benevolently. 'It's that simple.'

'Thank you, Comrade.' Chaing got up to leave, then hesitated. 'How many Eliters are there in Opole?'

'Records division will give you the exact number, but it's in the thousands. Ten thousand, probably, maybe a few more. Why?'

'So there are more Eliters than there are PSR officers?'

'Yes.' Gorlan smiled knowingly. 'But don't forget, we have all the guns.'

Chaing nodded thoughtfully, as if reassured by her assessment. *And that's exactly what Captain Philious thought before Slvasta's revolution.*

2

Ry Evine watched the crowds ebb and flow along the street below his wide sash window. As soon as he arrived in Opole, he'd rented a one-bedroom flat above a clothing store on Broadstreet, almost directly opposite the imposing grey-stone monolith that was the PSR office. As far as sheer chutzpah went, he doubted it could be beaten. Watching the people who would be on the alert for him, separated by sixty metres of road, two tramlines – and, on the second day of his vigil, a throng of angry protesters.

Their chanting and singing had been persistent and inventive. He'd never known there were so many songs about freedom, and what had happened to Slvasta's balls. The banners they waved were direct, too. Demands for the release of prisoners, insults, lewd caricatures . . .

In a strange way he found it rather pleasing that so many people were prepared to stand up to the PSR. His incredibly sheltered life in the Astronaut Regiment had fostered the assumption that the PSR's power was unchallenged, that they were somehow invincible, infallible. His interview with Stonal had certainly reinforced that view; even the Astronaut Regiment was subject to PSR authority.

It had taken his mad trip to Opole to make him realize just how much of his life had been governed by fear. First, twenty-six years concealing his own precious secret from them, and now defying their deceit. That first day's train journey he'd sat hunched up on his seat, silent and numb, waiting to be caught.

But it seemed the PSR weren't so fearsomely efficient as he'd been led to believe. After all, they'd need to be told he'd gone missing – and who was going to do that? Certainly not General Delores, nor Anala. All government organizations were heavy with bureaucracy, even the Astronaut Regiment. And with everyone jittery about the PSR's strong interest in Liberty flight 2,673, his absence at events and training sessions would not be remarked on; nobody wanted to ask questions about things they shouldn't be asking. With luck, it might take a week before his absence was officially noticed.

By the time the Opole express pulled in to Gifhorn for refuelling, he'd been gone for nearly two days. With that much time to think, he'd realized his initial flight from Cape Ingmar had been far too impulsive, and he was actually woefully unprepared – anathema to an astronaut. To confuse his tracks a little, he booked into a hotel using his own name, and had his first shower in way too long. He never went back to the hotel, but the registration form would be forwarded to the local PSR office as a matter of routine. When the alert was finally raised, they would waste a great deal of time following that false lead.

After the hotel, he visited three banks and wrote himself a cheque for cash at each one. Only one cashier – at the County Agricultural Bank – recognized him (which he had mixed feelings about). She asked for an autograph for her son, which he obliged, then put his finger to his lips. 'I'm here on a break,' he told her quietly, 'before the whole Treefall triumph tour kicks off next week. They always give us a few days to ourselves after a flight.'

'I understand, Comrade,' she whispered back, delighted to be his confidante.

The cheques gave him enough cash to see him through a few weeks, if he was careful, maybe even a month. If he hadn't found any trace of the alien spaceship by then, he knew it was all over anyway.

In the bank, he committed his first theft. A man in his mid-thirties with a full beard was getting irate with the next cashier – something about payments on a tractor trailer. A whole array of papers were spread out across the counter to prove his point. Ry walked past him, fussing with his jacket – and deftly lifted the man's ID papers from the counter as the argument over finance grew even more heated. A fast, confident, conjuring motion, as if he'd been practising for years. *Maybe I missed my calling.*

Back at the city's train station he opened the papers and studied them. His victim was Tarial, from some small rural town Ry had never even heard of. The small black and white photo on the ID might be a problem, but Ry hadn't shaved for four days now, so his stubble should give him a reasonable chance of passing a courtesy inspection. It wasn't going to get any better.

The ticket clerk never even looked at the proffered ID when he bought a ticket for the Bautzen express. Forty-two minutes later his train was pulling out of the station at the beginning of a journey that travelled the first thousand kilometres overnight to Opole, before starting on its final twelve-hundred-kilometre leg south to Bautzen.

They were still a hundred and twenty kilometres north of Opole as dawn broke, shining its fresh rosy light into the carriage. The guard switched on the tannoy and announced that Opole had enacted a nest alert, and that all passengers would be inspected by the PSR before they were allowed to leave the station.

It was an anxious fifteen minutes in the queue that wound along the platform at the side of the express before he reached the barrier. A very bored and tired junior PSR officer took a fast look at his ID papers, barely glanced at his heavily stubbled face, and waved him on past the armed guards.

*

Opole had come as something of a revelation to Ry. Cape Ingmar and Port Jamenk were completely devoid of Eliters. Here in a much older city, where the Eliter community was large and well established, their pings and links were thick in the air. Ry had never sent out a ping in his life. The closest he'd ever come to embracing his heritage was accepting basic management routines from the general communication bands, which allowed him to organize his memory in a more orderly fashion. After that, he'd closed himself off to all electromagnetic communication.

Once he was in Opole, practical considerations overcame his lifelong refusal to involve himself with the Eliter community. He still wasn't going to link with anyone, but he did search through the general communication bands for upgrades to the routines he already had. To his delight, he discovered a whole section given over to the free distribution of files containing education bundles and upgrades for secondary thought routines. Intriguingly, every file's identity icon had the visual image of the legendary Warrior Angel. She was still a huge idol for the Eliters.

With some of those new routines operating in his macrocellular clusters, he began to filter the news and gossip that were flung about so gleefully by the city's maligned and abused underdogs.

The first thing he learned was that none of them believed the nest alert was actually about a nest. There had been a regiment deployment among the Sansone foothills the previous week, but oddly no corresponding Fall warning had been issued.

That's my alien spacecraft landing, it has to be.

The main focus of the nest alert was an Eliter called Florian, who according to the few Opole residents who remembered him was a harmless nonentity. Florian had been a forest warden in the valley where the regiment had been deployed. Speculation as to whether he had now Fallen reached a fever. Some pointed out there was no evidence; they were countered by others who suggested the PSR simply wouldn't mount an operation of this scale for anything other than a nest.

Florian's the key, then, Ry decided. *He must have encountered the alien spaceship. It must have given him something – information or a piece of technology the PSR are desperate to recover, to make sure nothing on Bienvenido changes.*

News leaked that it was Captain Chaing himself who'd been appointed to lead the hunt. Chaing: the one who'd recently faced down a whole nest of Fallers at Xander Manor. So the threat was real and serious. Then it came out that Florian was Lurji's younger brother. *Okay, so maybe he hasn't Fallen, but he's certainly pissed off someone high up in government. Typical of that family; no thought as to how the rest of us will suffer. To Uracus with that defeatism; go, Florian.*

At the time that argument broke out, Ry had just moved into his rented flat on Broadstreet and was settling down to watch the PSR. The general band was alive with stories about a car chase in the city. Visual files showed some kind of ancient, battered saloon moving at dangerous speed along narrow streets, being chased by sheriff patrol cars. It ended in a spectacular pile-up.

Nothing much happened after that. But early the next morning, joint PSR and sheriff teams started to systematically arrest Florian's old friends, hauling them from their homes without any valid charge or even a warrant. Then Florian's mother was arrested. Almost immediately a crowd appeared in Broadstreet below Ry's flat, their chants growing louder. Within an hour, their numbers had expanded dramatically. Traffic was blocked. Even the trams had to slow to a crawl. The sheriffs hung back, unwilling to intervene and make it worse. It was perfect for Ry; their presence put him next to the heart of Eliter gossip about the whole nest alert. And they didn't hold back what they were broadcasting across the general band.

Sometime around midday, Castillito was released to a huge outbreak of cheering as she emerged from the front entrance. After that, the crowd thinned out considerably.

Fresh gossip had it that the PSR was shifting their attention to gang members, specifically Billop's crews. Ry sat patiently by his window, meticulously organizing and indexing all the information accumulating in his storage lacuna, noting who was wanted, what their position and relevance was. Watching, waiting.

It was evening, with an erubescent twilight claiming Broadstreet, when the man came down the short steps out of the PSR office. He hunched his shoulders, as if frightened by the hard core of protesters who were still stubbornly clustered on the opposite side of the road, and immediately slunk off along the pavement away from the big domineering building.

Ry was interested; that was certainly no PSR officer coming out at the end of his shift; the furtive behaviour simply didn't match. His eyes strained against the dim illumination, filter and magnification routines sharpening the image. Then a couple of men got out of a van parked further along Broadstreet. The man stopped and looked round at them. Ry finally got a reasonable look at his face. His new visual-recognition routines kicked in, zipping through files and general-band streams to find a match. Perrick: one of Billop's senior lieutenants, arrested earlier for questioning.

The two men from the van now stood on either side of Perrick, who was severely discomforted. Ry could see that in his body language.

Crudding Uracus, they're snatching him! In the middle of the street, outside the PSR headquarters!

It was so incongruous, so *wrong*, that Ry knew it was important. Without thinking, he ran out of the flat and down the rear stairs to the alley at the back. Renting the tuk-tuk had taken over half of his cash, but as soon as he climbed into it at Opole station, he'd known it was the perfect way to get around the city unnoticed. They were everywhere all of the time, yet completely unseen.

The little three-wheeled vehicle trundled out of the alley spluttering oily smoke as all its kind did. Nobody paid him any attention at all. He was just in time to see the van doors shut. He turned towards it as it pulled out from the kerb.

A street map of Opole was another gift from the general band. He tracked his own position as the van drove steadily out of the city centre and headed north towards the river Crisp. After twenty minutes they turned into Midville Avenue, which ran parallel to the old Hawley Docks along the waterfront. Back in the Void days, those docks had been a source of great wealth for the district's merchants, who had spent their money lavishly along Midville Avenue, creating an extravagant mix of high-rise tenements, plush homes, fancy offices, and commercial properties. After the Great Transition, the nature of trade and commerce changed drastically as the economic equality laws were brought in, and Hawley Docks was designated as part of the state rationalization plan. Fewer ships used them, wealth and jobs drained away to the city's central docks, and the neighbourhood declined in every sense.

Ry stared up at the once-elegant facades as he followed the van. Judging by the number of windows that were lit, nearly half of the tenement flats were unoccupied. Several of the commercial buildings were boarded up; offices had heavy iron bars over their grimy windows, doors protected by equally sturdy metal gates. The huge old walwallow trees that lined the avenue hadn't been pruned in decades, allowing their thick boughs to spread over the street to create an intermittent roof of furry ginger leaves. Trunks and roots were now so thick they were lifting the pavement slabs and cobbles, making the ride bumpy.

The van pulled up outside a five-storey townhouse of dark red brick. Ry rode past, taking in as much as he could. The upper levels of the townhouse were invisible behind the walwallow, while the big bay windows on the ground floor shone with light. There was a discreet scarlet and violet neon sign curving over the broad door: Cameron's. A couple of beefy men in smart black suits stood outside.

The van doors opened, and Perrick was escorted to a narrow set of iron stairs at the corner of the house that led down into a narrow sunken courtyard running along the side of the building. Then Ry had to stop looking back before it became obvious.

He studied the street map in his exovision and turned off down Yenkoy Street, seventy metres further along from the club on the other side. Half of the alleys and service lanes behind Midville Avenue were so narrow and decrepit they didn't even feature on his street map. Weeds and creepers were colonizing every wall and mound of refuse, producing a decaying arena for bussalores and feral cats to fight over. The tuk-tuk puttered along the confined maze of dank passages until Ry was behind one of the larger tenements. He wheeled the tuk-tuk into one of its many deserted outbuildings, and made his way cautiously to the rear door.

A second-floor tenement had no door; the rooms inside looked like a domestic battlefield of broken furniture and mouldy carpets. Something smelt really bad, and Ry had no desire to investigate the source. The lounge was down a short corridor, which shielded it from any view from the tenement's central stairwell. Several panes in the tall window were empty. He peered up over the rim and had a perfect view of Cameron's. Even better, he could see right down the iron stairs that led to the sunken courtyard. The van which had delivered Perrick had gone.

Ry had visited clubs like Cameron's many times during his interminable astronaut tours. Civic dignitaries and Democratic Unity party officials would invite him and his fellow astronauts along after the formal functions were concluded, their glamour adding to the establishment's prestige. A lot of clubs and pubs on Bienvenido had connections with gangs, mainly because they were perfect for money laundering, supplying drugs, and human trafficking. High-end establishments, like Cameron's, tended to have friends in the local party, so their patrons weren't blatantly shaken down. Nonetheless, they remained the business of choice for gangs, so Ry was sure that whoever Perrick had been taken downstairs to meet was well placed in the Opole underworld.

All the files he'd acquired while he waited on Broadstreet said the same thing – Roxwolf was Opole's major player. No one else would have the audacity to have a man snatched from outside the PSR office – or a reason. So it looked like the gang chief himself was taking an interest in Florian's whereabouts.

That gave Ry two possible routes to Florian: Chaing and Roxwolf. He gathered some torn cushions into a pile and settled down to wait.

3

Florian gave up on making dresses on the third day in the mod stable. Essie was now growing so quickly there was no point. Anything he made in the morning was too small by midnight. So instead of dresses he fashioned the cloth into a kind of toga robe which she could button together down the side. That ought to last two or three days.

There was a change to Essie's daily pattern now. She used to eat and sleep with short times between spent playing; she'd never been much of a talker. Now, though, there was no more play. She just cried or whimpered, complaining about the pain. It was more than ordinary growing pains. Every joint was sore, so even the slightest movement made her wince, and her legs cramped constantly.

That afternoon, Florian had spent two hours trying to massage the cramp away, with little effect. Exhausted as she guzzled some paste from the processor, tears trickled down his own cheeks in sympathy for her suffering. He felt utterly useless, and worse, completely to blame. He was such a monumental failure. The space machine should have entrusted her to the Vatni; they would have done a much better job caring for her. She deserved better than him.

'Don't cry, Dada,' Essie said mournfully.

He pressed his lips together in shame as he looked at her. That delightful, pretty little face was smeared with gooey paste, her jet-black hair had become matted, and she looked so tired, exhausted by her fight against the pain. Even the weird memory organ fused to her skull was flushed a dark purple, as if it was bruised.

'Sorry, sweetheart,' he croaked. 'I don't like it when you hurt, that's all.'

'Do grown-ups hurt?'

'Not like this, no.'

'Then it will stop when I'm old.'

'Yes, sweetheart. Yes, it will.' He was probably lying, because how could anybody know what her strange body was going to do? But his guilt didn't matter, because the lie offered her some hope. Anything he suffered was inconsequential, and probably well deserved.

'Is it time for pill?' she asked hopefully.

'Yes,' he said. It wasn't, not for another hour, but he couldn't take much more of her woe. He'd been alternating types of pain-killers produced by the Commonwealth medical kit, so she could gain some relief. But of course he was fearful what a constant supply of drugs would do to her, if they'd damage her in the long term. The files said no, but still it was against his nature. At least he wasn't so panicky about the salves he rubbed into her joints and muscles, which did give some relief, albeit temporary. The trouble was, there wasn't an infinite amount; he'd already used up sixty per cent of the kit's chemical supplies, and he was worried how much longer she'd be suffering.

His u-shadow instructed the kit to produce some basic karacetami – a lower dose than before because of the shorter time. She'd taken some ibuprofen less than two hours ago.

'Thank you, Dada,' she said as she gulped down some water to swallow the little green capsules. Then she put her arms round him and hugged him until she began to grow drowsy. Florian stroked her gently as her eyes slowly closed.

'I never knew anyone who was a bigger pain than Dudley Bose,' Essie said softly.

Florian gave her a startled look, but her eyelids were shut. 'What's that, sweetheart?' he murmured.

'Ozzie took his motile down the Silfen paths. I wonder what became of him.'

'What?' But the girl was finally sleeping, and he wasn't going to do anything that might wake her up and plunge her back into her own private world of torment.

Matthieu arrived ninety minutes later. That was unusual enough to kick off a whole new plague of worry in Florian. It was late in the afternoon, with a single yalseed lamp replacing the fading sunlight with a meagre yellow glow. The rule was nobody visited him once the club's staff started to arrive.

'What is it?' Florian asked anxiously.

'They just arrested Terannia.'

'Oh Uracus.' He stared down at the sleeping girl, close to tears again. 'Okay. If I go to the PSR, can you take Essie away from here? I don't want to know where. Just somewhere safe.'

'Florian, just calm down a moment. First off, they are gathering in a whole load of people; there's forty so far. Most of them are Eliters, but we can't work out what the connection is, other than quite a few of them are musicians.'

'They know; they must. Why else would they take her?'

'Because they're desperate. The first group they took in were the ones you knew, or went to school with. Now they're going for an even more tenuous association. This is people who might know people who knew you. Maybe. They won't even know what questions to ask her. You don't know forty people in Opole, do you?'

'No.' He shook his head miserably.

'Then we're probably in the clear. They'll try and intimidate her for a day, and when that fails they'll let her go. Because fail it will.' He gripped Florian's knee, and gave him a little shake. 'It won't be the first time they've tried to pin something on her, lad. She'll be all right. This time.'

'This time?' Florian asked in a panic.

'I told you, nobody's ever seen a hunt like this before. They pulled in Billop last night.'

'But . . . He doesn't know Aunt Terannia. Does he?'

'No, but he probably told them about Rasschaert. That might be the connection. The point is, they aren't going to stop.'

'What do I do, Matthieu? I don't know what to do.'

Matthieu was gazing at Essie, his expression uneasy. 'She must be over a metre tall now.'

'I guess, yes.'

'Florian, what is going on? Who is she?'

'I don't know. I swear to Mother Laura, I don't know.'

'What happened in Albina valley, Florian?'

'Please, don't ask.'

'We want to help, Florian. We're not going to turn you over to the PSR.'

'You can't help. I just have to stay ahead of the PSR for a month – well, it's only about three weeks now.'

'You keep saying that. What happens at the end of that month?'

'I'm not sure. I'm guessing that's when she'll be old enough to take care of herself.'

'Florian. Lad, you do get how strange she is, don't you? The way she's growing: it's just not natural. What is she?'

Florian gave Essie a guilty glance. 'I don't know. But she was given to me. I have to look after her, I promised I would. She's going to help us all. Really, she is.'

'She's not from this world, is she?' Matthieu asked gently.

Florian shook his head.

'All right. Is she human, Florian?'

'Yes! Just different.'

'And the music. Where did the music come from, Florian? Don't tell me you created that. There are notes played on those tunes that have come from instruments that I've never even heard before. They are instruments that don't exist. Not here.'

Florian buried his head in his hands, furious with himself for being so stupid. Of course Matthieu would know the songs were different to anything Bienvenido had produced. 'Don't know,' he grunted sullenly.

'Are they here, Florian? Has the Commonwealth found us?'

'No. It was one machine, that's all. I think it was left behind by Nigel. The PSR took it away.'

Matthieu rocked back on his heels. 'But it gave you the girl before they took it?' he whispered.

'Yes.'

'Crud!' He ran a hand over his forehead. His fingers were shaking badly. 'Uracus, Florian, do you even realize what's at stake here? This is too big for us. This is . . . This is going to change all of Bienvenido. You must know that.'

'I'm frightened, Matthieu. What if they find me? What if they take her? She can save us. The machine said she can. She's not done anything wrong.'

'The Warrior Angel. She'll know what to do. We have to call for her, Florian. We can't do this alone. The Warrior Angel will be able to keep Essie safe.'

It took a moment, but Florian realized Matthieu was waiting for him to agree. 'All right. If you think she'll come. But you can't tell anyone else about Essie. You can't! Promise me, Matthieu.'

'I'll not mention her; you have my word. I'm betting the Warrior Angel will be quite interested in the nest alert anyway.'

'How long will it take her to get here?'

'I've no idea. Hopefully not long.'

*

When he crawled out of the old mod passage into the club's office, Matthieu closed the concealed door. It had been well crafted into the panelling, making it practically impossible to tell it was there. Nonetheless, he still stacked the liqueur boxes back up in front of it. The mod stable was such a perfect bolthole; neither he nor Terannia wanted to risk it being exposed. Over fifty Eliters had used it at the start of their urgent journey out of Opole.

He knew there was something wrong as soon as he went downstairs. The club's bar manager was unnaturally still behind the counter, with a perfectly composed blank expression – which didn't stop him sweating heavily.

'What is it?' Matthieu asked. They still had a couple of hours until the club opened.

'Someone to see you.'

Matthieu turned slowly to find Shaham sitting at a table up by the stage, a shot of hazelnut vodka in front of him. He'd been bracing himself for a PSR officer, but having Roxwolf's senior lieutenant show up at the club was probably worse. Everyone knew Shaham, of course. He was a painfully thin man, with a shaved scalp, and narrow wire-rimmed glasses that had strange amber-coloured lenses. The little finger from his right hand was missing – from a knife fight as a teenager, according to local rumour. If so, it was probably the last fight he'd ever lost. These days he was the voice of Roxwolf among Opole's gangs, speaking with total authority. So much so that some people had even whispered that he might actually be Roxwolf. After all, no one had ever actually seen the gang boss – and lived to tell of the encounter.

'We've paid this month's protection,' Matthieu said. He didn't like the way it sounded – all whiny defensive, as if he had something to hide.

Shaham smiled, which made his head look even more skeletal. 'Relax, Matthieu.' He drained the shot glass in one and stood up.

It was all Matthieu could do not to take a step back. The lieutenant was a good head taller, and so thin Matthieu was sure he must be ill – either a voracious parasite in his gut or a bad cancer.

'I don't make personal visits for arrears,' Shaham said. 'This is almost a social call.'

'Almost?'

'Roxwolf considers Terannia a good partner. This is an excellent club, and you and Terannia are always on time with your payments to Billop. We appreciate that.'

'He's welcome to visit any night and enjoy the music.'

Shaham chortled softly. 'I'll tell him; I'm sure he'll be amused by the invitation.'

'So what can I do for you?'

'A favour. It's always good to have Roxwolf owe you a favour, don't you agree?'

'I imagine it's better than owing him one.'

'Indeed. Is Terannia here?'

Matthieu shook his head, wondering if he was being toyed with. Shaham was normally *very* well informed. 'The PSR took her in for questioning.'

'Yes. This nest alert is proving rather tiresome. In fact, it's the reason I'm here. One of our associates is extremely concerned he might be scooped up in the next wave of arrests. He's a first-class accountant, so given his extensive knowledge of Roxwolf's commercial enterprises that would be . . . detrimental to a great many people.'

'Why would the PSR be interested in him?'

'Apparently this current sweep is for anyone who knew an Eliter called Rasschaert. Are you familiar with him?'

'No.'

'Well, our associate used to be. And once they have him in custody . . . The questions might not be limited to Rasschaert.'

'Yeah. Right. So where do we come in?'

'He's one of yours, our accountant.'

'What do you mean, one of ours?'

'An Eliter. Probably why he's so good at figures. So Roxwolf and I were hoping you could help out. You've got contacts in the underground railway. We'd like him out of the city.'

Refusal wasn't an option, not with Shaham; even delaying could be dangerous. 'I'll see what I can do. There's a friend who knows somebody.'

'I'm sure there is. We want him gone by tomorrow.'

'What?' Matthieu blurted. 'I don't know if we can—'

'That's settled, then.' Shaham leant forwards, stooping slightly to give Matthieu a level stare. 'We'll bring him round here at ten o'clock in the morning. So if the PSR come knocking tomorrow evening, he won't be here. Is that all right?'

'Yes,' Matthieu stammered. 'Yes, okay.'

'Good man.' Shaham turned and walked out.

Matthieu sat down hard in the nearest chair, and realized he was sweating as badly as the bar manager.

4

It was Jenifa's third interview that morning. They were using two of the eight cells on basement level one for interviews, with the Eliter suspects crammed into the remaining six. Rasschaert had known a surprising number of people, so after spending a night with nine other people in a small space with only two cots and one shared toilet, the suspects were now crabby as well as frightened. It wasn't a good combination.

Terannia was led in, and the handcuffs removed before the guard pushed her down into a chair. The club owner was taller than Jenifa, and probably weighed twice as much. If their positions around the table had been reversed, Jenifa might have been quite intimidated by that. As it was she took a minute to check through Terannia's file again, make the suspect wait. It didn't seem to unsettle Terannia. She looked tired and bored rather than cowed – which was interesting.

'Do you know why you're here?' Jenifa asked.

'I can think of several reasons. But everyone you're half-suffocating in the cell says it's about Rasschaert.'

'What are the other reasons?'

'The PSR doesn't have a gram of imagination, so you blame Eliters for everything. It's pathetic, you know.'

Jenifa glanced at the file, seeing Terannia had been brought in for questioning a dozen times in the last fifty years. No charges had ever been brought. They were all routine investigations into

Eliter radicals. 'The PSR protects Bienvenido. If you've done nothing wrong, you have nothing to fear.'

Terannia let out a bitter laugh. 'I'm being told that by a brain-washed child. Giu help us all.'

'Do you deny you knew Rasschaert?'

'I don't remember him specifically, but if you say he's been in the club, I'm not going to dispute it.'

Jenifa slid a photograph of Rasschaert over the table. 'To help your Eliter memory. He didn't simply visit your club; he worked there for three months. I also have a copy of his employment record, which you filed.'

Terannia glanced down at the photo, and cocked her head to one side. 'Nine years ago. He was behind the bar. Not much good.'

'Is that why he left?'

'Seriously, girlie? A reason from nine years ago? How many people have worked at the club since then? Is that in your records?'

'Seventy-two,' Jenifa answered immediately, enjoying the startled look that sprang across the woman's face. 'Actually, I don't care why you got rid of him, but I'm pleased you do remember, because this next question is critical.' She took out the photo of Florian. 'Did Rasschaert bring this man into the club? Did they ever meet there?'

Terannia stared at Jenifa for a long moment before studying the photo. 'This is Florian, isn't it? The one you're all after. He looks young, just a bit older than you.'

'Yes, that's Florian. Did he visit your club?'

'No.' She sighed. 'He's never been to the club.'

Jenifa studied her keenly. 'You're sure?'

'Yes,' Terannia said decisively, then hesitated. 'This picture was taken nine years ago?'

'Seven. It's from his regimental service file. Why?'

'So what does he look like now?'

'Much the same, apparently.'

'Oh. Okay. Still a no, then.'

'So what about this week?' Jenifa asked. 'Has there been any talk about him in the club?'

'Ha! Are you kidding, girlie? The way you lot have disrupted the city, nobody's talking about anything else.'

'Did anyone say where he might be?'

'It's got to be Port Chana.'

Jenifa lifted an eyebrow. 'Really?'

'Well, he must be, right? Nobody would stay in Opole with this kind of hunt going on. You'd be crazy.'

'The city is sealed.'

'He got in, didn't he?' Terannia smirked. 'He beat you, girlie.'

'One, he has not beaten us; we are preventing him from carrying out his subversion. Two, don't ever call me girlie again. You can go back to your cell now.'

The amusement vanished from Terannia's eyes. 'How long for? I have a business to run. I answered all your questions.'

'Until I say you can go. Which will be when we've finished cross-referencing everyone's statements.'

'But there's dozens of us. It'll take you all day.'

'Yes.' Jenifa tidied the papers on the table. 'It will. The PSR is very thorough. Don't ever forget that.'

*

The phone on Yaki's desk had a speaker attachment. Chaing sat on one side of the desk, trying not to show Yaki how discomforted he was by Stonal's voice.

'Do you even know if Florian and the girl are still in Opole?' the director of Section Seven asked.

'I'm reasonably certain,' Chaing said. 'The checkpoints around the city are secure.'

'It's a wide perimeter, and you have the river to consider as well. A small boat at night could go unnoticed, as Florian has already demonstrated.'

Chaing glared at the innocuous Bakelite speaker grille with the blue secure-line light shining below it. 'It's not possible to guard the exit routes with any greater degree of security, sir. If he's got past us, it was with considerable help.'

'Opole has a large Eliter population.'

'It does, sir,' Yaki said. 'But there is one piece of information we received last night which would indicate Captain Chaing is correct.'

'Which is?' Stonal asked.

Chaing gave Yaki a grateful nod. 'Gorlan's assets reported that the Eliters have started broadcasting general calls for the Warrior Angel to help Florian. They're telling her the PSR is persecuting him.'

'I see. Interesting.'

'She might be coming here.'

'Which is inconvenient, to say the least. I cannot leave the capital right now. Besides, we would require a considerably longer lead time to lay a trap for her.'

Chaing shuffled to the edge of his seat. 'Sir. With respect, I don't think we can afford her coming to Florian's aid. They cannot be allowed to join up.'

'Then you have a simple task, don't you, captain? You must acquire Florian before the Warrior Angel.'

'Yes, sir.'

'I find it hard to comprehend why you released Castillito. She is his major possible contact point in Opole.'

'He can't contact her if she's in our custody,' Chaing shot back. 'I have her under constant surveillance.'

'If Florian hasn't contacted her by now, after four days in Opole, he isn't going to. Someone else is sheltering him. Someone who is willing to risk everything. To me that speaks of a very close bond.'

'We have had considerable success bringing in Rasschaert's known associates,' Yaki said.

'And have they produced any leads? No? Then bring Castillito in again. Extract the name of Florian's father from her. That's where you'll find him.'

'Yes, sir,' Chaing said. *Crud!*

*

The tenement block was on Quilswith Road, just off Broadstreet, but at the opposite end of the thoroughfare to the PSR offices. *Ironic*, Jenifa thought as the car pulled up outside. She got out and

331

looked up at the blue-brick facade of the elegant old building. Unlike a lot of the city's tenements, this one was fully occupied and well maintained. *Perfect for a civil rights so-called leader; no living in the slum-zones with the lower orders for her.*

A van parked down the road had a couple of PSR officers inside, watching the front of the block. She knew another van was covering the alley at the back. A command post had been set up opposite, with cine-camera lenses focused on Castillito's window. Neighbouring apartments had been used to place listening devices against her walls. The sound wasn't good, but they could still hear most of what went on. And a tape recorder in the basement was wired into her telephone line.

Jenifa went into the big lobby. The floor was black and white marble tiling; large brass and crystal lights hung on long chains from a high ceiling. A house manager came out from his office to stand at the polished reception counter.

'Can I help you?'

Jenifa simply held up her PSR badge. 'Castillito. Which apartment?'

'Second floor, number four.'

She climbed the wide curving stairs. Far above, the afternoon sunlight was shining brightly through a circular lantern window. It was easy to imagine Void-era aristocrats living their decadent lives in such a place. Her disapproval of Castillito grew with every step climbed.

Jenifa took a second to straighten her uniform and compose herself before knocking on the door to number four. People always judged her by her size and youthful features, never quite respecting her, which was a constant source of anger – although the PSR uniform sometimes mitigated that casual disregard.

Not with Castillito, who looked her up and down with a dismissive expression. 'Yes?'

'You really want to do this in the corridor?' Jenifa asked flatly.

'Come in, why don't you.'

The apartment was as Jenifa expected – large, clean and bright, furnished with perfect antiques.

Castillito walked into the lounge, standing in front of the tall balcony windows, preferring to look out onto the street rather than at Jenifa. 'What is it now?'

'We need more information from you, and we need it fast. So this is how it goes. You either tell me now, or I take you in to the PSR office where I will personally extract the information from you.'

'What was it with you, I wonder?'

'Excuse me?'

'You're all very damaged people, so I'm wondering what happened to you to make you like this. A relative abused you during your childhood, perhaps? That's quite common.'

'It's not me sheltering a Faller! That's what I call damage.'

Castillito turned from the window and smiled contemptuously. 'The recruiters deliberately seek you out. Did you know that?'

'What are you talking about?'

'The PSR recruiters. They sift through court cases, looking for a specific type of victim. People who have had their moral compass broken. They're no different to your original abusers, you know; you're still being used.'

'This is ridiculous,' Jenifa said. 'The only reason I joined up is to protect Bienvenido from Fallers.'

'Really? In that case, look me in the eye and tell me Florian is now a Faller. Can you do that?'

Jenifa was instantly cross with herself for the traitorous flush colouring her cheeks. 'Who is his father?'

'Is that what all this is about? One of your forms I didn't fill in properly?'

'His father must be sheltering him. Who is it?'

Castillito chuckled. 'That's the best the PSR can come up with to excuse your failure to find him?'

'Who is the father?'

'All right. I can see you're serious about this, so I'll offer you a deal.'

'We don't make deals, especially not with you. Florian will face the full consequences of his actions.'

'The deal doesn't concern Florian.'

'What?'

'I'll tell you here and now on one simple condition. Aren't you even going to ask what it is? Even you won't be able to force the answer out of me straight away in your torture chambers. Can you afford to lose that time?'

'What's the condition?' Jenifa ground out.

'I want you to deliver a message to your boss, Captain Chaing.'

'What message?'

'So you will do it?'

'I'll report everything you say to me. Believe that.'

'Very good. The message is this: I know why Chaing sent you instead of coming himself.'

'That's it?'

Castillito gave her a sardonic grin. 'See, that wasn't so difficult, now was it?'

'The father!'

'Rafferty.'

*

Chaing, Yaki and Jenifa stood in Ashya Kukaida's shiny white office as clerks hurried in with files she'd requested. Each folder was opened, and the contents spread methodically across her pristine desk. When they were all laid out, she would put on her thick glasses and slowly scan the paperwork.

Chaing knew that, just like him, Yaki wanted to shout at the old woman to get a move on, but even she held her tongue in this realm. Everything depended on Kukaida.

What do we do when she gets too old for this? he wondered. *Is she even training a successor?* And there was another, more uncomfortable, thought nagging away in his head. *Does she have that amazing memory because she's an Eliter?*

He watched as Kukaida ran a finger down a column of reference numbers, then beckoned a clerk over. The man was given an index code, and hurried off into the records hall.

She can't be. Can she?

He'd been tense ever since Jenifa had returned in triumph from Castillito's with the name. And the message. She'd been puzzled by it, but Chaing knew all too well what it meant. Castillito wasn't letting him off the hook that easily.

The clerk returned with another grey cardboard folder. Kukaida painstakingly gathered up the sheets on her desk and returned them to their file before the new paperwork was put out for examination.

'Ah,' she exclaimed. An index finger tapped the guilty line of typing.

'Who is he?' Yaki demanded.

'Fetch this one,' Kukaida told a clerk before looking up. 'Rafferty isn't an Eliter, which is why we didn't have an open file on him. I thought that was odd.'

'But Florian and Lurji are still Eliters, aren't they?' Jenifa asked.

'In eighty per cent of cases, when an Eliter has a child with a non-Eliter, the offspring are functioning Eliters,' Kukaida said. 'The other twenty per cent are mules; their macrocellular clusters don't work. They're dying out, you know: Eliters. In a thousand years there'll be none left.'

Which explains a lot, Chaing thought miserably. *It must have been Mother who was the Eliter.*

'Irrelevant to this case,' Yaki said sharply. 'What's Rafferty's story?'

'Castillito defended him in three court cases. Standard acts of petty civil disobedience. It would seem Rafferty was something of a hothead thirty years ago.'

'Like father like son,' Jenifa muttered.

'That's Lurji,' Chaing said. 'Not Florian.'

'Where is he now?' Yaki asked patiently.

'The Cannik mine in the Transo mountains, that's a yellow-cake operation. Castillito couldn't get him off the last case; he was organizing a blockade at the rocket engine factory to call attention to some perceived injustice against Eliters. The judge took a very dim view of that. It was a fifty-year sentence.'

'Crud, so he's still there?'

Kukaida pulled a face. The clerk came back into her office,

holding a slim folder. Chaing groaned when he saw it; the cover had a big scarlet DECEASED stamp on the front.

'He was buried there,' Kukaida said, opening the proffered folder. 'Yellowcake is radioactive. Not many survive ten years, let alone fifty. He died from radiation sickness seventeen years ago.'

'Again!' Chaing protested. 'That crudding Florian has done it to us again.'

'I don't think having your father die of radiation poisoning is exactly a victory,' Jenifa said.

'But it helps him.'

'Not for long,' Yaki said. 'There are records. Not as detailed as the ones we keep on Eliters, but we can track down Rafferty's family. It has to be one of them sheltering Florian. There's no one else.'

'There's another possibility,' Jenifa said. 'Rafferty was Castillito's client. She'd probably know he was dead. And now we can't confirm he was the father. Not from his mouth.'

'She did it to deflect us,' Yaki said. 'Florian is her son, after all.'

'No,' Chaing said, as a sudden sense of guilty relief flooded through him. This was going to be a disaster for the case, but with Castillito gone . . .

'Why not?' Yaki said. 'It makes perfect sense to me.'

'She knew we'd suspect the parentage as soon as we discovered Rafferty is dead,' he said. 'So she knows what we'll do to her now. She wouldn't risk that.'

'Unless . . .' Jenifa groaned as she realized the deception. 'She knows how desperate we are to find the father. I made that pretty clear. This was all to buy herself time.'

'Time for what?' Chaing asked, trying to sound genuinely bewildered. Then he made a show of wincing. 'Oh crud!'

*

Chaing and Yaki were in the lead car, with the rest of the convoy following hot behind, all of them racing along Broadstreet with lights flashing and sirens wailing. They'd already radioed ahead to the surveillance team to check if Castillito was still in her apartment.

Strangely enough, Chaing felt remarkably calm. Even the pain in his wrist seemed subdued. With Castillito gone, the threat to him had vanished with her. Ruining one PSR officer wouldn't save her now; she would have to stay in hiding for the rest of her life. He was in the clear.

So he kept a calm expression in place as they pulled up outside the tenement on Quilswith Road. One of the surveillance team officers was hurrying out of the entrance, looking scared.

She's gone! And she has the contacts to make sure there's no trace of her.

'I'm sorry, sir,' the officer blurted. 'We were watching the building the whole time. I don't know how she got out.'

'I need your operation logs. Now!' Chaing shouted at him. 'We need to trace every vehicle that used this road this morning,' he told Yaki.

'On top of hunting Florian?' Yaki muttered darkly. 'We don't have the resources. Not for a fast result.'

'Crudding Uracus!'

Yaki watched the other PSR cars pulling up, blocking the street. 'Get our people inside. I want every apartment, every room, every bussalore hole in that building ripped apart.'

'I'm on it.'

'Stonal will go crudding crazy! You were specifically told to bring her in.'

From some weird distance, Chaing heard himself saying: 'Yes, that's what Corporal Jenifa was ordered to do.'

Yaki stiffened, giving him a surprised glance. Both of them looked at the second car; Jenifa was just climbing out of the back.

'Seriously?' Yaki asked.

'I logged the order,' Chaing said. Making it official that the order was to be carried out as Stonal instructed. What wasn't in the log was his suggestion that Jenifa threaten Castillito to get the father's name quickly. That would now be her own initiative.

Jenifa hurried over to them.

'She's gone,' Yaki said. 'Corporal, were you told to bring the suspect in for questioning?'

'I . . .' Jenifa gave Chaing a sideways glance. 'I was told to find the father's name.'

'Castillito was our last valid lead to the fugitive,' Yaki said coldly. 'She fed you false information in order to escape.'

'You were perfectly happy with what I did,' Jenifa said hotly.

'Until I realized just how big a mistake you made. Corporal Jenifa, as of now you are suspended, pending an inquiry into your actions.'

'That's—' Jenifa stopped herself from saying anything more. Her face was flushed with anger. 'Yes, director,' she said formally.

'Report back to the office. We'll try and salvage something from this mess.'

Jenifa turned, not making eye contact with Chaing, and walked back to the convoy of cars. She stumbled on the kerb.

'Too harsh?' Yaki asked.

'Not at all,' Chaing assured her.

'So what the crud do we do now?'

'What the PSR is good at. All those people Rasschaert knew that we have in custody, stop playing nice with them.'

Yaki gave him an intrigued look. 'You want to begin increased interrogation on all of them?'

'No. Just send a sheriff team to each of their homes. Tear them apart. Florian has to be somewhere.'

*

Essie had spent most of the day eating. She had always been hungry, but this new phase was worrying Florian badly. The cravings were strong enough to overcome the constant growing pains and joint aches. She ate her food, then his. Matthieu brought some more, then a further batch.

The food processors were working almost non-stop, and they were struggling to keep up. She now ate all the fruit directly, using it to graze between the batches that the cylinders churned out.

'Perhaps you should stop for a bit,' Florian suggested at midday. Her stomach was badly distended, making him think of a pregnant eight-year-old – a perturbing thought, given her body wasn't exactly normal. She was sweating copiously, too. And the med kit reported her temperature was high.

Essie's lower lip trembled as she gave him a remorseful stare. 'I's so hungreee, Dad.'

'I know, sweetheart, but you'll make yourself ill if you eat too much. Don't do that, please.'

'I'm hardly Daniel Lambert,' she said in a suddenly clear voice.

'Who?' She was doing that several times a day now, coming out with strange little phrases or names in a perfectly rational voice that made him question if he was the stupid one for not understanding.

'One more apple, Dad, please. I'll stop then. Promise.'

The pleading, adorable smile she hit him with was an unstoppable force. 'One, then, that's all.'

'Thank you. You're the best dad ever, much better than Marcus.'

'And you're the best daughter in the world. Uh, who's Marcus?'

'Dadeee,' she crooned, and snuggled up against him.

He took an apple out of the wicker basket and handed it to her. As she munched slowly he gathered her hair up into cute braids and used a strip of fabric as a ribbon to tie it. 'You look lovely,' he told her.

Her hair was matted and greasy, like his. Washing was tricky in the mod stable, and Matthieu hadn't brought a lot of soap to them since they'd arrived. And the sink in the corner was tiny, anyway.

She finished the apple and lay on the sleeping bag, wheezing. Another cause for concern – though when he applied the diagnostic sensor pad from the medical kit, it reported her lungs were okay.

You're getting far too paranoid, he scolded himself.

As the afternoon wore on, Florian became aware of loud noises echoing along the passage back to the office. It sounded like furniture was being smashed up. He held his breath while Essie slept on blissfully. Sure enough: the distinctive sound of glass breaking. Raised voices, one of them Matthieu's.

They're in the club! They're here for us.

His u-shadow armed the defence bracelet. Its targeting

programme went active, and he pulled up his shirtsleeve. Staring at the pearl-white alien band round his wrist made him all the more determined not to let them capture Essie. He was wearing a weapon from the Commonwealth. *It's all real. She can save us, if she just has the chance.*

Tactically, the mod stable was a disaster. Only one way in or out – and even with the Commonwealth weapon, breaking through a room of armed PSR officers would be nearly impossible. He glanced up at the window. Essie could fit through; he probably wouldn't. He started examining the floor. The old wooden boards were firm and dry. He had no idea what was underneath. If he had an axe, it would take barely a minute to chop through. If he had an axe . . . He glanced at the bracelet again. *Will it be able to shoot through wood? If it can, they'll hear it.*

But the sounds of the club being broken up were diminishing; they hadn't found the passage entrance. He sat at the top of the short ladder into the mod stable and listened for a long time. All the noise had died.

Essie woke up an hour later. He let her eat another meal from the processors, which finished the last of the food Matthieu had brought. He was getting hungry himself now.

Light was starting to fade from the window above when he heard the distinctive sound of the panel door in the office being opened. He woke Essie, who looked round in concern when he put his finger to his lips. Someone was crawling along the passage. He pushed Essie behind him and held his arm out rigid, ready for battle. Slim violet exovision targeting graphics sprang up around the top of the short ladder.

Aunt Terannia stuck her head up through the hole. 'Only me,' she said briskly. Then blinked. 'What is that on your arm?'

'E-beam pulsor,' Essie said matter-of-factly. 'Far Away's favoured Saturday-night special.'

Florian hurried over to help his aunt up. 'Are you all right? Matthieu said the PSR had taken you.'

'They did. I met a nasty little girl in there who'd better pray to Giu she never sees me again. They let me go an hour ago.'

'What did they want?'

'As we suspected, Billop ratted Rasschaert out. But that's not surprising. Nobody can hold out against the PSR in the end. So they rounded up everyone Rasschaert knew to see if they know where you are.'

'Crudding bastards!'

'Smart and efficient bastards, actually. They got close this time, Florian. Next time . . .'

'I heard people in the club earlier. It sounded like they were smashing the place up.'

'A sheriff raid; they did the same for everyone they'd taken into custody. And yeah, they knocked the club about.'

'I'm so sorry. It's all my fault.'

'Stop saying that. It's not their first visit here; it won't be the last.' She gave him a gentle hug. 'You can't stay here, Florian. Not any more. They came close today. And if they take me in again and go to work on me, I won't be able to hold out. It's not safe for you and Essie.'

'Are bad people coming?' Essie asked.

'Not here, darling, but we have to get you away to be sure.' Terannia gave Florian an anxious look. 'Besides, Matthieu and I don't think it's only the PSR that's looking for you now.'

'What do you mean?' he asked.

'There's been an upsurge in encrypted file traffic, similar to just before Chaing exposed Xander Manor.'

'There are Fallers hunting me?'

'Nobody can say for sure, but it's best to be safe.'

'They can't be that well organized, can they?'

'Come on, Florian, you're not a kid any more. We all know the Faller Apocalypse is coming.'

'But . . . That's the one thing the PSR are good for, taking out nests.'

'Yes,' Terannia said. 'And they probably uncover ten a year, have been for decades. It's a good record they have, no one is disputing that. But, tell me, where do those nests come from?'

'What do you mean? It's the eggs. There's a Fall from the Tree Ring just about every week somewhere on Bienvenido.'

'Yes, there is. And you served in a regiment. How many eggs did you find?'

'I didn't. But one of the squads on our sweep did, once. They're real, Aunt Terannia.'

'Very real. So is our Air Defence Force. They're good, those flyboys, and the Space Vigilance Office as well. Nothing lands on Bienvenido these days without us knowing about it. The squadrons are scrambled in time to reach the eggs when they Fall through the atmosphere, and the guns blessed Mother Laura designed for us blast the alien cruds apart before they even reach the ground. Officially, it's only about one in fifty that ever actually land intact.'

'Yeah.' Florian nodded earnestly. 'It's true, too, not just propaganda.'

'So where are all the nests coming from? Do the maths, Florian.'

'Well, they're . . .' He stopped, frowning, suddenly and unnervingly uncertain. 'Uh, the breeder Fallers?'

'Yes. The Fallers that are here are reproducing, Florian; they were doing that even back in the Void. Their numbers are growing despite everything the Air Force and regiments are doing; even the Liberty flights are just about irrelevant. They're *here*, Florian; they've been here for centuries. Back in the Void we were better off. Our telekinesis and psychic sight gave us an advantage, and we managed to contain them. Without those assets out here in the real universe, all we have is guns and PSR paranoia. It's not enough.'

'Great Giu,' Florian groaned.

'We don't even know how many Fallers there are. Worst-case figures the Eliter Council came up with are terrifying. And they're organized, Florian. There are nests in every city. Their children are spreading out, safely – because everyone knows the eggs are destroyed before they land and the PSR is just mopping up any stragglers. But they're not stragglers, they're the vanguard. The nests that orchestrate the attacks on places like the rocket factory, they're the expendable ones. Take out one, and three more quietly start up to finish their work.'

342

'But the government . . .'

'Is truly terrified. Prime Minister Adolphus even has an evacuation plan for the People's Congress and their families; the Varlan Regiment and three squadrons will retreat with them to Byarn. They think – they hope – the island's free of them. They've been building fortified bunkers there for the last thirty years.'

'That's . . . How can they do that? What about everyone else?'

'We think the IA-509s will atom-bomb the whole Lamaran continent if the Fallers have overridden it. It's called Operation Reclaim, which is a big fat stupid government lie-name. It's actually a scorched-earth policy. Bienvenido will wind up like Macule, all radioactive desert and glaciers.'

'They wouldn't!'

'Survival makes people desperate – not that it'll do them any good. Faller eggs must have been landing on all the uninhabited islands like Rachweith and Tonari while we were in the Void, and we know Fallers mimic the bigger animals the same as they do us, so presumably they can copy the creatures that live on the polar continents, too. Crud knows how established they are across the rest of this world, because we don't venture outside of Lamaran. Even the old Captain's government had an isolationist policy; Slvasta just carried that on. For all we know, humans are already in a minority on Bienvenido.'

Florian shook his head, feeling the tears welling behind his eyes. 'No. That can't be right.'

Terannia glanced at Essie. 'She really is our last chance. Matthieu told me where she came from. She and the Warrior Angel are all we've got left.'

Florian let out a long breath; there really wasn't a decision to make. 'All right. We'll go. Keeping her safe is the only thing that's important. Another three weeks, that's all.' He put his arm round Essie. 'Did you hear that, sweetheart? We're going to go somewhere else. Somewhere nice.'

'Where, Daddy?'

'Near the seaside,' Terannia said. 'You'll like that.'

Florian bowed his head. 'Okay. When can you do it?'

'Tomorrow. Matthieu had to get someone else out fast today, but our friends in the underground railway will be back in place in the morning.'

'Thank you.'

This time she hugged him tight. 'You stay ahead of them, you hear me? And when the time is right, you and Essie shake this world so hard it rattles.'

'I will. I promise.'

*

Chaing opened the door to his flat and saw Jenifa sitting at the small kitchen table. *Crud!*

She glared at him. 'You never said a crudding word to help me. Not one, you bastard!'

He closed the door and took a few steps towards her. She'd risen to stand rigid-backed, her face all belligerent. Seeing her like this, so angry, with her body all tense, he was surprised to find he was getting very turned on. 'Half the office was there outside Castillito's place,' he retorted, refusing to give ground. 'What else could I do? If I'd had an argument with Director Yaki in front of everyone, we would both have been backed into a corner with no way out. Is that what you wanted? Because you damn well know what the inquiry is going to find. You shouldn't have left Castillito; you shouldn't have given her the chance to escape. She made you look ridiculous. The PSR is a laughing stock because of you.'

'Me? It was your crudding idea!'

Chaing ducked forwards and kissed her. Jenifa pushed him away hard, then grinned viciously as she slowly unbuttoned her uniform blouse. 'That bitch has got something on you, hasn't she? That was the real message I carried back.'

Chaing never took his eyes from her small black bra. 'You screwed up, corporal. Don't try and blame me.'

'You messed up somewhere and she knows about it,' Jenifa sneered back at him. 'You're running scared from a filthy Eliter, captain.'

He grimaced at the raw truth, then grunted in shock as her

hand closed around his balls, squeezing roughly. With a yell he tugged her bra off, tearing the clips. She slapped him. He lunged forwards.

They fucked right there on the kitchen table. It was anger sex, hot and turbulent, both trying to climax first, to win. The table legs scraped across the floor as they writhed about, a screeching sound blotted out by her sharp cries and his animal grunts.

Chaing didn't care about the noise, or who heard them; he laughed in triumph as an orgasm claimed him. Losing Florian, being outsmarted by Castillito, none of that mattered now. This was real victory. Beneath him, Jenifa spasmed in pleasure.

They lay on the tabletop for a long time, panting almost in unison, clothes tangled, sweaty skin pressed together, limbs at awkward angles. Then the slow extrication began, like undoing a tricky knot of sticky flesh.

'So what happened after I was dismissed?' Jenifa asked. She frowned in annoyance at the ripped buttons on her uniform skirt as she slipped it off.

'Nothing,' he admitted as he eased his ruined shirt over the cast on his arm. 'Castillito made a very clean getaway. It was impressive considering how tight the observation team was.'

'What about the raids? I heard the sheriffs were starting as I left the office.'

'A few of them turned up some petty crud, but nothing connected with Florian. We still haven't got a clue where he is.'

'And Castillito's friends and associates? Are you bringing them in?'

'Procedure says we should, but we both know that's going to be a waste of time. First, there's hundreds of them. And she won't have implicated anyone.'

'This is falling into a grade-A crudstorm.' She shook off her blouse so she was standing completely naked in front of him.

'Somebody knows where he is. I'll find them,' Chaing said resolutely. His eyepatch had slid round to his cheek; he took it off carefully, fingers probing at the sore flesh round the eye where the bruise was now colouring up.

'Uracus, you look terrible.'

'Thanks.'

She pressed her fists into the small of her back, arching her spine as she tried to work the knots out of her muscles.

He enjoyed the sight of her flexing body for a while, then asked, 'Why do you do it?' genuinely curious.

'Do what?'

'Build your muscles up like that.'

She looked down proudly at herself. 'I want to be strong, to be exceptional. Not just my body, but my mind too. This job we have, if we're weak we fail. It's that simple.'

'And being physically strong . . .'

'The two are connected; one feeds the other. I need to be strong enough to withstand anything that can happen to me. And I am.' She tossed her head, and put her hands on her hips, staring at him defiantly with her wide hazel eyes. 'Why? Don't you like it?'

'I like it very much.'

'I admire you, Chaing.'

'Admire me? Is that all?'

'What do you think? I'm crudding furious with you, right now. But yes, you're so obsessed with catching Florian, you even sacrificed me. That's a kind of strength.'

'I didn't sacrifice you, I diverted Yaki, that's all,' he lied. 'The only testimony that'll matter at your inquiry will be mine.'

'I can't be pushed out of the PSR. You know that, right? It's everything to me, my whole life. We're all that stands between Bienvenido and the Faller Apocalypse.'

'You'll be fine. I'll make sure of it.'

'You want to screw again?' she taunted. 'Are you strong enough for that?'

Chaing gave her a greedy look. He was playing with fire now, and he knew it – which was what made it so exciting. 'Oh yeah.'

'Get onto the bed.'

He lay down, trying not to smirk.

Jenifa clambered onto the mattress beside him. With a dirty

grin, she licked the length of his cock. 'When are you going to talk to Yaki about me?'

'Tomorrow.'

'I want to be reinstated.'

'I know you do.' He sighed in delight as her tongue flicked out again.

'And fully vindicated.'

'Oh Giu! Yes. Yes you will be. Just . . . don't stop.'

5

Ry took the tenement steps two at a time on his way to the back door. For the first time since he started watching Cameron's, there was someone else using the stairwell – a woman holding hands with her young son as they climbed up, both dressed in faded clothes. Her face was tired and beaten down by the life this part of the city offered.

She gave him a sullen look as he hurried past; nobody acknowledged anyone in the tenement. The boy cocked his head to one side, blinking in amazement. Then he smiled.

Ry reached the bottom of the stairs. Above him he heard the boy saying: 'It's him, Mum. It's him! Really.'

'Who?'

'The astronaut. Major Evine. He just flew a Liberty mission.'

'Don't be so stupid.'

'I'm not stupid. It is him, it is, honest. I recognize him from the magazine.'

Ry grinned to himself as the boy carried on protesting, but it was an uncomfortable reminder of how precarious his own position was. His beard was thickening nicely, but he was still out of place here and very much on his own.

He retrieved the tuk-tuk and drove onto the east end of Midville Avenue, where the deep shade from the walwallow trees made it difficult to see anything – especially if you were standing in the bright morning sunlight outside Cameron's.

The van was outside the club, with Shaham just climbing into the front passenger seat. Ry's visual-recognition routine had extracted Shaham's identity from the general-band streams even quicker than it tagged Perrick.

There were two other goons accompanying Roxwolf's senior lieutenant, just visible in the back of the van. It pulled out from the kerb and did a U-turn. Ry cursed, and throttled the tuk-tuk hard, turning down the first alley on the left. Following Shaham and the van for a couple of days had left him as familiar with the crumbling dockland area as any of its hard-up residents.

He did a fast circle through the tangle of backstreets, catching up with the van on Krestol Street, which was one of the main thoroughfares heading back into the centre of Opole. Twenty minutes later they were in the Jollarn district, which was made up of neat streets lined by solidly average houses. The electromagnetic spectrum chittered with link transmissions – Jollarn was an area favoured by Eliters. But then Ry already knew that; he'd followed Shaham to the same district yesterday afternoon. The gangster's van had cruised round for a while, moving up and down Stower Road for no reason Ry could make out. Presumably it was some kind of inspection, scouting out the street.

As they turned onto Stower Road that morning, three motor-bikes raced past the tuk-tuk, all three with pillion passengers. Ry instinctively reduced speed to let them go. Up ahead the van was slowing, pulling in to park in front of the last house in a neat two-storey terrace at the far end of the road.

Ry turned into a side road and got off to watch. One of the bikes rode down the alley behind the terrace. Then the entire electromagnetic spectrum used by Eliters to communicate was flooded by a blast of white-noise signal. All the people on bikes and the two goons from the back of the van hurried into the house. Pistols were drawn from holsters that had been covered by bulky jackets. Two minutes later Shaham joined them inside the house.

The few pedestrians on Stower Road were looking round in puzzlement as the jamming signal continued to blast out its inter-ference. A couple of the goons emerged from the house and opened the back of the van. Boxes were carried inside. One of them tucked a big roll of what looked like chicken-wire mesh under his arm.

Ry simply could not work out what was happening. It didn't look like part of a protection racket. *Is that the house Florian is hiding in?* His retinas zoomed in for a better look. That was when he got lucky. One of the goons half-tripped on the kerb, the box he was carrying slipping from his grip. Even from where he was, seventy metres away, Ry could hear the other man's cry of fear. The box fell to the ground and tipped over, its top flapping open. Both goons froze. Then they were both scrambling round on the pavement, picking up the small grey cylinders that had spilled out of the box.

A chill crept along Ry's skin, and he quickly retreated back down the street to sit on the tuk-tuk while his racing heart slowly calmed. He recognized those innocuous waxed-cardboard cylinders: dynamite.

*

'It's time,' Aunt Terannia said.

Florian took a last look round the dank mod stable. It was a wretched place to hide, but it had been safe. This was the fifth day they'd spent here, which meant Essie had now spent half her life in the gloomy room. And that wasn't fair, not at all. He wanted so much more for her.

'We're ready,' he said.

'I brought you something,' Terannia told Essie, and held up a green dress. 'For the journey, sweetie. Can't have you going outside dressed in rags, now, can we.'

A huge smile broke across Essie's face. 'Thank you so much, auntie.'

Terannia swallowed something in her throat. 'You're welcome. Got you some shoes, too – well, sandals.'

Essie grinned and went over to the far end of the mod stable to change out of the robe she was wrapped in.

Florian smiled awkwardly. 'Thanks.'

'Like I was going to do anything else,' Terannia said. 'I care about her, and not just because of where she's from.'

'How's my mother? Do you know?' He'd spent most of the previous evening accessing the general band, hearing about Castillito's disappearance, the fury of the PSR.

'I don't know. And if *I* don't, you can be crudding sure the PSR hasn't got a clue where she is. So don't you worry about her, or us. You focus on your job, you keep that girl safe for the next three weeks.'

'I will.'

'She looks about eight or nine now. Damn, it makes my head hurt just thinking what the Commonwealth can do, even though stuff like this is defying nature. They're like gods.'

'They're not gods, but they're not backwards like us, either. If we can just talk to them, they'll help. I know they will.'

'I hope you're right, Florian. I really do.'

Florian heard crying, and turned to see Essie shuffling slowly towards them. She'd over-eaten again last night, bloating up her limbs so she had trouble moving her joints. The new dress only emphasized how grubby her skin was despite a half-hearted attempt to wash that morning. Ebony hair hung oily and limp against her head; for whatever reason, it didn't grow at the same rate as the rest of her, leaving it disturbingly thin. The memory organ was prominent beneath the lank strands, its livid colour vivid against her pale skin.

'Dad,' she whimpered. 'It hurts.'

Florian ran over, and swept her up in his arms. 'It's all right, sweetheart. I'll get you some medicine. It'll take the pain away. I promise.'

He sat her down and collected the medical kit. Terannia's eyebrows lifted at the sight of the smooth box extruding tablets. Essie swallowed them eagerly.

'I'm sorry, Dad. It just hurts!'

'Hey.' He stroked her brow. 'It's okay. It's going to stop soon, I promise.'

'Thank you, Dad. I love you.'

'And I love you too, sweetheart.'

He cuddled her for another couple of minutes, waiting for the painkillers to take hold. Then they made their way back along the narrow, low passage to Terannia's office.

Most of the boxes of bottles had gone. The floorboards were wet with wine and spirits, and the air carried their smell. There was no chair behind the desk any more. The top of the desk was covered in tall piles of paper.

'The sheriffs did this?' Florian asked.

'Let's just concentrate on getting you out of Opole, shall we?' Terannia said.

Downstairs, the club was missing half its tables and chairs. Matthieu was waiting by the bar, a big dressing taped on his cheek. Anger brought a flush to Florian's face as he saw the injury.

'I'm fine,' Matthieu said quickly.

'No you're not! Who did this?'

'It happens.'

'It shouldn't!'

'I know,' Matthieu smiled softly. 'And you're going to put a stop to it, aren't you, my boy?'

'Yes!'

He smiled at Essie. 'Looking mighty fine today, young lady.'

Essie sniffed and managed a sheepish grin.

'What now?' Florian asked.

'Well, you don't leave by the front door, that's for certain,' Terannia said.

There was a trapdoor in the cellar, concealed in the floorboards as cleverly as the doorway in the office panelling. Florian guessed it was the same carpenter who'd made both of them.

Matthieu handed Florian and Essie torches, and climbed down the ladder.

'You take care,' Terannia said, giving Florian a hug. She gave him a velvet hat with a broad rim. 'There, that should keep anyone from getting a good look at you. It'll only be a few paces in the open to the van.'

'Thank you. Without you—'

'Go,' she croaked. 'We'll be waiting to hear about you.'

'The whole world is going to know what she does,' he said solemnly.

Essie climbed down the stairs slowly, trying not to wince at every movement. Florian followed her down.

It was another cellar underneath, made of stone rather than brick. Florian knew it was older. The walls bulged in places, and the wooden beams were starting to crumble.

'The whole city is built on the remains of previous buildings,' Matthieu said. 'It's been here for over fifteen hundred years, after all. And the Gates is the oldest part. Giu knows how old some of these chambers are.'

Florian followed him through sagging archways, and rough holes knocked through thick walls, trying not to think of the weight of the Gates above them, nor the age of the catacombs and their cracked, decaying pillars. Matthieu seemed very sure of their route. The torch beams probed through numerous doors and arches they passed, sometimes illuminating chamber after chamber, occasionally falling on piles of rubble. There were even a few stone stairs curving down to lower levels. Bussalores squeaked somewhere in the darkness, their tiny paws scampering along unseen. Essie pressed up against him and his arm went round her shoulders.

'Here we go,' Matthieu announced at the foot of some crumbling stairs that led upwards. Each stone step was worn from age.

Florian's u-shadow told him Matthieu was sending out a ping. There was an answering ping from above. A trapdoor was open, sending a fan of yellow light sweeping down.

The steps came up into another cellar, where a man called Euphal was waiting for them. He ran the greengrocer's above, he explained. They were on Coal Gate Lane, which ran along the south edge of the Gates. Florian realized they must have travelled nearly a kilometre through the catacombs. He shook his kaftan vigorously, trying to get rid of the dust and grime that the fur lining had soaked up underground. Essie's nice new dress was streaked with dirt, too.

'This is as far as I go,' Matthieu announced as they slipped into the back of the cluttered shop. 'Redrith should be waiting outside.'

'Who's Redrith?'

'A friend. He'll take you down to the docks in his van. There are way too many ships for the PSR to check properly. We've fixed it for you to sail with the *Takiti*; she's a river barge that hauls grain up and down the Crisp. There are some compartments that aren't on the plans. The captain's one of us. You'll be fine.'

'I guess the Warrior Angel didn't come to help, then?'

Matthieu pulled a face. 'No, sorry, man. You're on your own. You and a world full of friends.' He went to the front of the shop and peered out through the window. 'He's there. I see him. He's in the van marked Redrith Maritime Supplies.'

Florian's u-shadow reported a quick exchange between Matthieu and the van parked outside. Now that the time had come, he was reluctant to go. 'I won't let you down,' he said.

Matthieu gripped his arm. 'Oh, I know you won't. Now go on; it'll look odd if he's there too long.'

'Bye bye,' Essie said solemnly.

'You take care,' Matthieu told her.

There was a moment by the door, when Florian looked at Matthieu. There was so much he wanted to say, but as always he didn't really know how to say what he felt.

Matthieu was clearly having a similar moment. He opened the shop door, and tipped Florian's hat down so the rim obscured his face. 'Go on; go!'

And Florian was out in the open air, which smelt so sweet after too many days in the mod stable. The sun was bright and warm on his skin, making the colours of the street so vivid after poorly illuminated drab walls. The noise and bustle of the city centre embraced him.

His arm went round Essie, who was wincing as she walked. Her round, heavy face was glancing round curiously as vans and cars and tuk-tuks drove past. Up ahead at the junction with Mill-Coate Street, a tram rattled along its tracks, bell clanging to shoo cyclists out of the way. 'Combustion engines?' she muttered in what sounded like dismay.

In front of them, the side door on the Redrith Maritime Supplies van slid open. The interior was empty, lined in stained plywood. The engine coughed into life, making the whole vehicle shake.

'Come on,' Redrith called from the driver's seat.

Florian noticed there was someone sitting in the front passenger seat as he helped Essie into the van. Then he was inside, and the door was sliding shut, pushed by the man in the back of the van – a tall man who was perturbingly thin. His eyes were obscured by glasses with dark-yellow lenses.

'Who are you?' Florian asked.

'More to the point, do you know what this is?' The man held up a small Bakelite stick with a red button on the top. His thumb was pressed down on it. A thick electrical cable snaked out of the stick and disappeared into the plywood panelling which coated the van.

Everyone swayed as the van pulled out from the kerb.

Florian stared at the switch stick. The man was missing his little finger. 'No.' He told his u-shadow to arm the bracelet.

'It's a dead man's switch. If you use the weapon on your wrist to shoot me, it will release and the ten kilograms of dynamite packed into the van around you will detonate.'

Florian instinctively put his arms round Essie, who whimpered and buried her head in his chest. 'I won't use the weapon. Let the girl out. It's me you want.'

The man smiled, which with the way his taut skin revealed every facial muscle, made it extremely creepy. 'No, and no.'

'What?'

'No, I won't let the girl out. No, it's not you I want. Is there anything else you need explaining?'

'Who are you?' Florian sent out a desperate ping to Matthieu, but his u-shadow reported no signal could get out. The van was a very effective Faraday cage. When he looked round at Redrith he could see a wire mesh taped across the windscreen and door windows. Then he saw the pistol the passenger was sticking into Redrith's ribs.

'My name is Shaham.'

'What do you want?'

'My boss would like to talk to the girl.'

'Captain Chaing?'

Shaham laughed softly. 'Oh no, I think we'll leave the good captain out of this.'

*

Florian cradled Essie for the whole journey. She sobbed for the first few minutes, then spent the rest of the time hugging him tight. 'It's all right,' he kept telling her. 'We'll be fine. It's not the PSR.'

From where he was on the floor in the back, he had a bad angle of visibility through the windscreen. All he could see was trees and the top halves of the taller city buildings. Traffic growled around them. They juddered to a halt at junctions, then the clutch snarl started them off again. Trams clattered along. None of which gave him a clue where they were headed.

The u-shadow ran through tactical options for him, which concluded he had to wait for the scenario to alter.

Then the van drove into what looked like a tunnel of leafy walwallow branches, dropping them into a cosy peach-hued shade. They stopped, and the van door slid back.

Florian immediately tried to send out a ping, a call for help directly into the general bands. It was no use. There was a powerful white-noise signal jamming communications.

'Don't move,' Shaham ordered.

Florian did as he was told, but he turned his head to glare at Redrith. 'How could you do this? She's a child!'

The man looked to be on the verge of tears. 'I had to,' he moaned.

'You could have warned us, warned Matthieu. You're an Eliter. Just like us.'

'I'm afraid we had to use some persuasion on your friend,' Shaham said. 'His family is the bond for his good behaviour.'

'Let them go,' Redrith said. 'Please.'

'Of course.'

Two more goons appeared in the open doorway. One climbed in. Very carefully, Shaham gave him the dead man's switch. In return he was given a pistol. The muzzle was pressed into the back of Essie's neck. She squealed and tried to squirm away.

'Control her,' Shaham warned. 'Me not blowing her brains out is your good-behaviour bond.'

Florian nodded numbly. 'Come on, Essie.'

'Can't move,' she wept. 'Everything hurts. Hurts so much, Dad. Hurts in my head. Please, I need more pills.'

'All right, you can have some. Let's get out of here, first.' He scooped her up in his arms, and with Shaham still keeping the muzzle up against her neck, staggered out of the van. 'I need my backpack.'

'Move,' Shaham said.

Florian glanced round. They were in a quiet street lined by giant shaggy walwallows, with the pavement littered in crisp husks of their furry leaves. Two trunks were missing in front of the elegant five-storey townhouse. It had a neon sign – Cameron's – above the wide front door. Shaham was waving him to some cast-iron stairs that led down the side of it to a basement door.

'My backpack has Commonwealth machines in it,' Florian said. 'Do you really want to lose them? Does your boss?'

Amber glasses lined up inquisitively on him. 'Bring it,' Shaham ordered one of the goons.

Florian took the iron stairs one at a time, worried he'd drop Essie. She weighed far more than he expected. Her skin was slick with sweat.

Three goons were waiting at the bottom, each carrying a semi-automatic rifle. Florian recognized the weapon from his regiment days. He'd even fired them a few times on the range. They caused a lot of damage. Targeting graphics silhouetted each goon. The bracelet was armed, ready. But Shaham wasn't letting him have the opportunity.

They went through the door. Two more goons with semi-automatics were inside. They walked backwards slowly, the rifles levelled on Florian's chest. He wanted to laugh at how ridiculous it was, but knew he'd only start crying if he let his control go.

There was a flight of stairs going down, leading to another corridor. The doors on either side were heavy polished wood, all closed.

No ordinary cellar, Florian knew.

At the end of the corridor, a door opened into a large plush lounge, with another five goons inside, all armed with semi-automatics. The walls were hung with long velvet curtains even though there couldn't possibly be any windows; they must have been at least two floors underground. And by Florian's reckoning, directly under the middle of the townhouse. It was lit by bright electric bulbs in three large crystal chandeliers. The furniture was heavy and expensive, putting him in mind of a high-class hotel lobby. The only odd thing was a metal pipe as thick as his thigh coming out of the wall at head-height. It ended in a mechanism with a short lens protruding horizontally.

As Florian went over to a leather settee, the lens turned smoothly to track him. Shaham let him lay Essie down, then backed away, holding the pistol up. A circle of nine semi-automatic rifles were pointing at Florian. The bracelet could only shoot seven e-beams simultaneously. Elapsed time between salvos, point four of a second. The u-shadow's tactical analysis gave a low probability of hitting everyone in time.

'Before you try and shoot us, you should know something,' Shaham said.

'What?' Every muscle in Florian's body was rigid. He didn't know if he was furious or terrified. Either way, he knew his usual logic was gone.

Shaham pointed at the lens. 'You're being observed.'

'So?'

'This room and the corridor outside are both rigged with dynamite. The corridor is the only way in or out.'

'What do you want?'

'Mr Roxwolf would like a word.'

Florian stared at the lens, then looked round the circle of rifles. Started. 'I thought you were dead.'

'Not yet,' Rasschaert said. 'Just switched sides, that's all.'

'You told Roxwolf about me and Terannia. That's why—' He started to raise his hand. The targeting graphic assigned Rasschaert as first strike.

'Let's get some focus here,' Shaham said. 'We all want to get out of this alive, so let's keep calm. We all agree Rasschaert is a total arsehole. Nothing you or anyone else can do about it. Florian, you need to think about the girl. Is what you're doing going to help her?'

Florian kept staring at Rasschaert, though his arm did sink back down. The tactical analysis still wasn't giving him a way out.

A telephone rang, making them all jump.

'I'm going to get that,' Shaham said. 'Okay? Moving to the table. No need to worry.'

He walked over to the phone and picked up the handset. 'Sir? Yes, I know. Yes, sir, right away.' The handset was placed back in the cradle. 'Mr Roxwolf will see you now.'

'Suppose I don't want to see him?'

'Then I guess we all die in a blast of bullets and explosions. Except Mr Roxwolf, of course; he's safe through there.' Shaham gestured at one of the curtains

Florian risked a glance. 'What's there?'

Shaham pulled the lush red velvet aside to reveal a huge steel and brass vault door, with a spoked wheel in the centre. 'This is Mr Roxwolf's residence. It's a double-lock system, mechanically linked, so both doors cannot be opened at the same time. There is nowhere safer on the whole planet.'

There was a loud buzz, followed by the heavy *clunk* of bolts withdrawing. Shaham started to turn the wheel, and the door slowly hinged open. He slung the backpack in.

Florian knew he didn't really have a choice. He picked up a semi-conscious Essie and walked into the plain room behind the vault door. Brick walls, floor and ceiling made a simple four-metre cube, with another identical vault door in the opposite wall.

Shaham started to close the one behind him.

'Aren't you coming with us?' Florian asked.

'Not likely.'

'But—'

Shaham's pale face was just visible in the shrinking gap, his glasses reflecting the chandelier light as dull-gold circles. 'Nobody who is summoned to see Mr Roxwolf ever comes out.'

Florian let out a wordless cry and took a step towards the door. It clanged shut. The bolts engaged.

6

The operations room was busy when Jenifa walked in just before midday. She glanced round at the rows of desks, each with an investigating officer deeply involved in sifting through paperwork. Clerks from the records division were bringing yet more files in. The air was filled with the clatter of typewriters as the secretaries typed up reports, which more clerks smoothly carried away.

To someone who didn't know better, it would have looked like the nest-alert case was proceeding efficiently to a successful conclusion.

Chaing was standing beside the wall map, arm in a sling, uniform tunic sleeve pinned neatly on the side, eyepatch in place. She'd made sure he looked right when he left the flat this morning, as smart as a high-flying PSR officer should be.

Major Gorlan was with him, sticking a purple pin into the map. Jenifa went over to them and saluted. 'Sir, reporting for duty.'

'Corporal,' Chaing said tonelessly. 'Welcome back. Director Yaki has reinstated you pending the report on your conduct yesterday.'

'Thank you, sir.' *If only you knew*, she thought. *I am going to enjoy taking you down when this is over. I'm going to enjoy it a lot. Because Castillito has something on you, and I want to know what it is. Rotten officers cannot be allowed to contaminate the PSR.*

'We need all hands on this,' Chaing said.

'Has there been any progress?'

'We're concentrating our efforts on Eliters known to be connected to the underground railway.'

'Good idea.'

'Thank you, corporal,' Major Gorlan said scornfully.

'But we're getting some strange reports,' Chaing said.

Jenifa frowned. 'Strange, sir?'

'My informants have reported a jamming signal has been operating in the city this morning,' Gorlan said.

'Jamming signal?' Even as she said it, Jenifa cursed herself; repeating things just made her sound stupid.

'Someone is blocking Eliters from communicating with each other. It's localized, but apparently one hundred per cent effective.' The major pointed at a purple pin, which was stuck into Stower Road. 'First one appeared here a couple of hours ago.'

'I've sent a team to investigate,' Chaing said. 'And in the meantime I told technical services to scan the bands the Eliters use. They've just notified us that another jamming signal was transmitting here.' His finger tapped the second purple pin.

'Midville Avenue,' Jenifa read. She studied the old dock area. 'Nothing much there.'

'The signal didn't last long,' Chaing said. 'They only just managed to triangulate before it switched off.'

'Why would anyone want to block Eliter gossip?'

Chaing pulled a face. 'We're searching for anomalies. This is unusual.'

'And Florian is an Eliter,' Gorlan said. 'It might be something for you to look into,' she told Jenifa.

'Go and talk to technical support, corporal,' Chaing said. 'Get me a report. We need to know more.'

'Yes, sir.' Jenifa didn't know if she was being sidelined or not.

'Sir!' One of the secretaries was standing up, holding a telephone. 'Captain Chaing, sir.'

'What is it?'

'Phone call for you, sir. It's urgent. The main switchboard put it through.'

'Who's calling?'

'Says he's Major Ry Evine, sir. He knows something about Florian, but he'll only talk to you.'

The operations room fell quiet. There had been a notification about Major Evine three days ago, that he was AWOL. All PSR officers were required to apprehend on sight. Force was authorized.

Chaing hurried across the room and snatched the telephone. He put his hand over the mouthpiece. 'Tell the switchboard to trace the call,' he told the secretary, then took his hand away. 'This is Captain Chaing.'

'Captain, I have some information for you.'

'Who is this?'

'Ry Evine, but that's irrelevant. I've just seen Florian. He had a few days' of stubble, but I'm sure it was him.'

'I see. Why don't you come in and tell us about it?'

'Don't patronize me, captain. There's a girl with him, a young girl. She looked ill. They've both been forced into a club called Cameron's by very well-armed gangsters. I'm really worried. I think it's Roxwolf's headquarters.'

'Crudding Uracus! Where are you?'

'Midville Avenue.'

*

The bolts on the inner vault door withdrew almost immediately and it slowly swung open. Florian peered into the chamber beyond.

He was expecting something like the lounge he'd just left, but this was almost like the nave of a Church of the Return – a wide double-vaulted hall, with a line of pillars running down the centre. Electric lights hung on long hoops of cable strung between the pillars, sending out a sharp blue-white glare. Bizarrely out-of-place household furniture was clustered together on one side, while on the other side of the pillars, long benches had been laid out, cluttered by what appeared to be laboratory equipment, both chemical and electrical. Next to them was a telephone-exchange cabinet, studded with buttons, winking lights, sockets, and braided cables ending in jacks. Ten telephones were lined up on a shelf underneath it, and below them was a row of tape recorders, their big reels turning slowly.

At the far end of the hall, a stream ran along a channel set into the flagstone floor, emerging from and vanishing into low arches. A three-metre-wide wooden waterwheel was fixed to the wall, turning slowly as the stream shoved its paddles round. Gears linked it to a dynamo.

'Come in,' a voice said.

Florian took a few nervous steps, passing through the vault door. That voice was wrong somehow, husky and gurgling, as if the speaker had a cold.

An electric motor hummed, closing the vault door. The bolts clunked into place.

'Just so you understand, I am the only person on this planet who has the combination for those doors. If you shoot me, this will become your tomb.'

'Okay.' Florian tottered over to the nearest settee and put Essie down on the cushions. She curled up, her eyes closed.

'Good,' the voice said. 'Now, please don't get hysterical.'

'What?'

Roxwolf emerged from behind a pillar. Florian couldn't help it. He let out a wail and stumbled backwards.

The figure that emerged was human in shape, although an easy head taller than Florian. He had lopsided shoulders, and walked with an odd limp, one leg dragging behind the other. His head was misshapen, the back of the bald skull distended, curving down-wards over the top of the neck. A wide mouth had lips that could never fully close over a massive set of fangs.

But it was the arms that drew Florian's attention. The man-thing was wearing a loose red shirt. One arm was normal, though the skin was shaded a faint blue, as if his flesh was freezing. The other arm was an animal limb, covered in grey-bronze fur, and ending in a paw with four thick claws.

A Roxwolf foreleg, Florian realized. He'd caught glimpses of them in Albina valley, skulking about amid the deeper forests, preying on the native wildlife and terrestrial goats. Heavily muscled, yet incredibly graceful; some had been timed sprinting at ninety kilometres an hour on their attack run.

Now he was clued in, Florian glanced at the creature's legs. Sure enough, one was a regular human limb and the other a roxwolf hind leg.

'What the crud are you?' Florian shouted.

Roxwolf laughed. It sounded like a beast tearing flesh apart. 'A mistake.'

Florian brought his arm up, fist clenched. Targeting graphics circled the creature. 'Stay back.'

'Ah. The lightning-bolt weapon. And you claimed your back-pack has Commonwealth machines. The same source, I take it? The spaceship that fell into your valley?'

'What are you?' Florian yelled. He gasped as his u-shadow reported a link opening.

'The same as you,' Roxwolf sent through the link.

'No!'

'The Eliter macrocellular clusters are interesting,' Roxwolf continued over the link. 'Humans added them to their DNA at some point. They're unnatural. Like us.'

'Us?'

'You call us Fallers.'

Florian's arm trembled. 'Stay back!'

'Or what?' Roxwolf asked. 'You'll condemn yourself and the child to a slow miserable death by starvation?'

'I'll not be eaten, not by you. You— You're a breeder Faller, aren't you?'

'I'm not going to argue semantics with you, so I'll just say yes. But as I told you: I'm a mistake.'

'What do you mean?'

'My species has the biological ability to shape ourselves. When we encounter a world, we mimic the dominant lifeform, then eliminate it. It's a war that takes many forms; therefore, we need to constantly adapt. So somewhere deep in our history, we gave ourselves this chameleon ability. We can consciously shape our offspring, providing we have a template. And to obtain a local

365

template, our first colonization wave absorbs the local animals, giving us their physiological pattern.'

'You eggsume us,' Florian groaned, his arm had dropped to his side as he made the connection. 'Rasschaert.'

'Yes. The version you saw outside is a Faller.'

'You're not gangsters. You're a nest.'

'No. Not true. Most of the infamous Roxwolf gang are genuine humans.'

'You're lying. You *eat us*. No human would work with you – not even gangsters.'

'The human members of my organization are unaware of their colleagues' nature, obviously. Their reaction would be the same as yours. That's why I rule them through lieutenants like Shaham. I am the guiding hand; the smart one. The one with the political insights; the one with insider knowledge. The one who is unafraid to order hits against our opponents.'

'How can this happen?' Florian implored. 'The PSR should have discovered you.'

'Ah, but you see Roxwolf hides in plain sight. Everyone knows I am a mere gangster, including the PSR. I find it ironic, as much as I can understand the concept. For at the heart, I remain unseen, at least by my criminal associates.' He gestured at the telephone-exchange cabinet. 'They receive all their orders by telephone.'

'They'll work it out in the end. They'll expose you.'

'Several already have. They were all taken out by rival gangs – apparently.'

'You . . . You—'

'Ate them? Yes. I worked hard to achieve this position. I'm not going to relinquish it.'

'Why? What's the point?'

'Colonizing a new world is a complex process, especially one with a dominant sentient species. First we must learn of you, and mimicking you is only part of the solution. Once we've arrived, we move invisible among you, to explore your civilization, to seek out its strengths and weaknesses. There are specific tasks that require specific forms. Strength, agility, intelligence – all these can be crafted. We gave ourselves that flexibility. I am a product of it.'

'So which are you? Strength?'

'Parentals normally craft and gestate two embryos in their wombs, but we are not parthenogenetic. Two adults exchange and create the new templates within a neural connection. This mental pattern is transferred to the embryo, which incorporates its structure. A neurological equivalent of your DNA, if you like.'

'Mods,' Florian said suddenly. 'We had neuts back in the Void. Our telepathy allowed us to shape their embryos.'

'One of our more useful servant species,' Roxwolf acknowledged. 'Designed to be redesigned in whatever fashion we required. The seeders bring them with us.'

'Seeders?'

'The Trees you see in the Ring. Before we were captured by the Void, they flew between stars, expanding our species across the galaxy. The Skylords you so venerate are merely versions who self-evolved, adapting to the strange conditions in the Void. Ironic, no?'

'The Ring Trees are starships?' Florian asked weakly. 'Faller starships?' He didn't want to believe it.

'Yes, but our kind of starship; they're nothing like your Commonwealth's technological vehicles. These are living entities that embody our essence. They are the pinnacle of our species. Our triumph. They carry us forwards forever.'

'Oh great Giu! You really are monsters.'

Roxwolf laughed again. 'Especially in my case. I told you I was a mistake. My parentals messed up the pattern they were formulating. They wanted a roxwolf for an established nest of the animals; they also wanted a human-mimic with Eliter macrocellular abilities. The patterns were merged somehow, for even our biology is not perfect. I am the result. An abomination.' He snarled, his long fangs clashing. 'I am nothing – not to them, not to anybody. They discarded me. Now I reject them as I reject you.'

'What do you want with us?'

Roxwolf stared at Essie as she lay shivering on the settee. 'This girl is the end of the world. That makes her the most important person alive.'

Florian sat on the edge of the settee and stroked Essie. 'What do you mean *the end of the world*? She's going to save it.'

'For humans, possibly. What about Fallers?'

'This is our world. We will burn you from it.'

'She might well do that. That is why she is so valuable.'

'I won't let you touch her.' He deliberately avoided looking at the backpack. The power cells in the Commonwealth gadgets still had a large charge left in them, and the roof of this underground lair couldn't be that thick. 'Can the food-processor power cells be rigged to explode?' he asked his u-shadow.

'Yes,' it replied.

'Assume the stone ceiling is a metre thick. If I detonate the power cells against it, could they blast a hole through?'

'Yes, assuming you placed them correctly. But the concussion wave within the hall would present a considerable danger to you.'

'But it's possible?'

'Yes.'

The knowledge allowed Florian to gather some confidence. There was a possible way out; that gave him an edge.

'I'm sure you're an excellent protector,' Roxwolf said. 'After all, not everyone could elude the PSR for nearly ten days. Congratulations.' He began to walk around the edge of the furniture, keeping the same distance from Florian and Essie.

Florian watched him carefully; he felt like he was being stalked. 'What do you want?'

'I offer you a deal. I am in touch with my own kind. My current activities make me extremely useful to them. They consider me completely expendable, of course, but I can achieve many of their goals – for a price. By now they will know I have acquired her.'

'Rasschaert,' Florian murmured.

'Indeed. An interesting constant is Rasschaert, an arsehole in both his incarnations.'

'So what do the Fallers want with Essie?'

Roxwolf emitted a soft hiss of amusement. 'Why, they will feast triumphantly on her flesh, of course.'

'They are monsters!'

'When faced with genocide, a species will do whatever it needs to in order to survive. And to me, your death is necessary; it is how the universe works. You occupy a planet where we could be living. There is no question, no ambiguity. Our life is superior in so many ways. It is right that we emerge victorious.'

'Monster!'

'I love studying humans. So few of my kind bother. I love your anger. It is supremely irrelevant, yet you all possess it. I find that so curious. Why has evolution not eradicated it? It is not a survival trait, not in a true sentient. Do you know what my conclusion is?'

'Do I crudding care?'

'I believe it is a short circuit. It allows you to overcome your vaunted ethics, to justify your own horrific behaviour in extreme situations.' Roxwolf smiled, exposing even more of his fangs. 'And I have seen a great many of you *in extremis*.'

'You think you're so clever?' Florian raised his arm. Targeting graphics focused on Roxwolf. 'Think you can outsmart me?'

'You haven't heard my deal. But I'm interested in this development, your resurgence of confidence. Do you believe you have a way out? What could it be?' He turned to the backpack. 'What are the machines you said were in there, I wonder? Weapons? No. Something you can modify after you've killed me?'

'What deal?'

'Ah, now that, you see, my creepy alien friend, that is your survival instinct coming to the fore. Sentience mixed with animal desperation, analysing the options. But first you need to know all those options. So you tell me, what is it that you want, Florian? I live in both worlds, human and Faller. There is nothing I cannot acquire for you.'

'You know what I want: to be free.'

'Free of what, though? The PSR? The Fallers? Me?'

'Yes! All of you. Just let us go. Leave Essie alone.'

Roxwolf nodded. 'A reasonable request. I presume this freedom is for the duration of your infamous "month", until Essie has finished growing. Until she is a fully developed Commonwealth human. Until she declares war on the Fallers.'

'How do you know about the month?' Florian gasped.

'My position is not dependent on violence and intimidation alone.' Roxwolf gestured at the telephone-exchange cabinet with his animal arm. 'Knowledge, you see, is the true power in any society. And that power is how I survive. I've been listening to Captain Chaing's phone calls to his Section Seven superior, Stonal. You should hear Chaing making the most pathetic excuses for his lack of progress finding you; I can play you the tapes if you'd like. Essie was mentioned a lot. Someone called Joffler said she grew quickly.'

Florian gave the tape recorders with their slowly revolving reels an astonished glance. 'You bug the PSR phones?'

'Absolutely. Among others. A most useful source of information. The PSR's arrogance forbids them to believe anyone would dare attempt such an action.' Roxwolf bent down and picked up the backpack.

'Hey,' Florian cried. 'You leave that alone.'

'Would you like to hear my offer?' Roxwolf held out his human arm, dangling the backpack by one of its straps.

Florian stared at him, breathing heavily. His old anxiety reaction was returning; he could hear his heart hammering. Exovision medical displays were flicking to a mild amber. A list of suggested medications popped up. 'What's your offer?'

'The spacecraft. It gave you Essie and the machines. What else?'

'Nothing. That's it.'

'You're lying again, Florian. For a start, it gave you the weapon. Perrick described it in great detail for me.'

Florian shrugged, wishing he didn't feel so lightheaded. The stress of negotiating with Roxwolf was terrible; his skin was growing ice cold as he started to sweat. 'Well, yeah.' He shrugged.

'What did it tell you, Florian? You have Eliter abilities for communication and memory. It gave you information, didn't it? It gave you files that came from the Commonwealth itself.'

'No.'

Roxwolf raised the backpack. 'Then how do you know how to operate the machines?'

The blood was roaring in his head, heartbeat pounding like a hammer. 'Well, it gave me those instructions, but that's all.'

'They'll do for a start.'

'What?'

'You have information which is unique, Florian. Knowledge which humans lost when they were captured by the Void. Technology that has passed into legend. Tell me what you have.'

'None of those things,' he said, starting to panic.

'You are a terrible liar. Think what we could build together. Anything Opole's factories can produce can be brought to us here within a day – any piece of engineering, any electrical component; chemicals, metals. I can acquire it all. First we make the tools that make the tools. You just have to share the knowledge.'

'I don't want to build anything.'

'Are you sure, Florian? Look into your heart. Look into your Commonwealth knowledge. What could be done to improve the life of every human on Bienvenido? Are there medicines in there? Eliters always claim Commonwealth humans can live forever. Can you give that to your family, your friends? Would they thank you for keeping it to yourself?'

'If I had that kind of knowledge, it would be used to destroy the Fallers!'

'Yes, but if I had it, I would be able to survive. I told you, that's what I am. Every day of my life is a battle to survive. And I have won. I am *alive*. I live against every obstacle and challenge this world has thrown at me, despised and shunned by my own kind, hunted by yours. I will not give up my life simply because *she* has arrived. Why should I?'

Tremors were running along Florian's limbs as Roxwolf's words beat against him. It would be so easy to give in, to make some kind of deal. Say anything just to make this torment stop, to walk out with Essie. 'You can't offer us sanctuary.'

'Oh, but I can.' Roxwolf threw the backpack. It took Florian completely by surprise. He cried wordlessly as it tumbled through the air. It was a powerful throw, taking it the length of the hall. Exovision graphics sprang up, projecting the territory. 'Nooo!' The backpack landed in the stream with a loud splash. It sank as the current carried it sluggishly to the drain arch.

Florian sprinted along the line of pillars, desperate to reach it before it was swallowed by the black drain hole at the end of the channel. His targeting routines picked up Roxwolf's movements from his peripheral vision. The malformed Faller was leaping towards Essie as she lay dozing on the settee.

Florian fired a stun pulse. *I can't kill him, he's the only way out now!* The slender dazzling beam flashed out, missing Roxwolf by centimetres. It hit the wall, blowing a small crater out of the stone.

Roxwolf landed beside the settee and rolled fast, his animal arm curling round Essie, pulling her with him, using her to shield himself from Florian. There was a pistol in his human hand, swinging round to slap its muzzle against her head.

Jerked so savagely from her slumber, Essie started to wail.

'She would have wiped us out,' Roxwolf said. He pulled the trigger.

Florian began to scream. His u-shadow accelerated his perception. There was a flash from the pistol muzzle which seemed to ripple out at right angles, rising to a searing white wavefront. The sound of the shot pummelled his ears, numbing him. Then Roxwolf's hand was snapping backwards, breaking the wrist bone. Confusion bloomed across the Faller's features as his grisly mouth opened; the roar that emerged was almost as loud as the pistol shot, combining pain and dismay. He staggered backwards.

And Essie was standing there in her dishevelled green dress, completely unharmed. A tiny haze of purple light covered her entire body.

'Force field,' Florian said dumbly as secondary routines dumped the information into his mind.

He shot Roxwolf with another stun pulse. The Faller shrieked, and collapsed to the ground, spasming.

An incredulous smile lifted Florian's face. 'You have an integral force field. Biononics!' Then his knees gave way, pitching him onto all fours, and he threw up.

*

There were seven cars and four vans in the convoy that raced across Opole. The cars carried most of the investigation team while the vans held Captain Franzal's entire assault squad.

Chaing sat in the front passenger seat of the lead Cubar, urging his driver on through the traffic on the main road to the river Crisp.

'Do we sneak up on them?' Jenifa asked from the rear seat as they neared the intersection with Midville Avenue.

Chaing looked round. She was sitting on the back seat next to Nathalie Guyot. When he mobilized the assault squad, she'd eagerly exclaimed: 'I'm coming with you.' But the deal he'd made with Yaki was that she'd be restricted to office duties. He hadn't mentioned that to her as they all hurried down to the garage.

'Nathalie?' he asked.

'This is Roxwolf,' Nathalie Guyot said. 'He'll know you're coming by now. Most of the city knows with this racket.'

'Okay.' He raised the radio microphone to his mouth and pressed the button on top. 'Franzal, we're going in hot.'

'Roger that,' Franzal's voice crackled out of the dashboard speaker.

The driver turned into Midville Avenue.

'Crud,' Chaing grunted as he tried to study the tall buildings that were obscured by the big walwallows. 'Which one is it?'

Nathalie pointed ahead. 'There.'

Chaing saw the gap where a couple of the trees had been removed. 'Pull in just past it,' he told the driver. That would allow the vans to stop directly in front of the club, allowing Franzal's people to deploy quickly.

He had a brief flash of a nice old brick townhouse with a stylish neon sign above the front door. Then the Cubar stopped with a hard lurch. He opened the door as fast as he could and got out, pulling his pistol from its holster. Behind him, the vans were braking to a halt. 'Move in,' he called.

'Chaing!' Jenifa yelled. She barrelled into him, knocking him to the ground. As he went down he saw three men racing off the top of some metal stairs that led down into a narrow sunken courtyard at the side of the townhouse. They were carrying semi-automatic rifles.

As his shoulder slammed painfully into the cobbles, the rifles opened fire, strafing the assault-squad vans. Answering fire erupted from the PSR officers and squad members already out of the vans.

Glass shattered above Chaing as the Cubar's windscreen was hit by bullets. He cowered down, pressing himself into the uneven cobbles as gunfire raged and agonized screams cut through the air. His pistol had skittered away. He could see it a metre away, and reached for it.

The gunfire ended. Chaing snatched up the pistol, then risked a glance round the front of the car.

He saw five black-clad, helmeted members of the assault squad lying on the road, one of them with his legs still inside the van. Screams were coming from inside the vans, which were riddled with bullet holes. Two PSR officers were face down on the street, unmoving.

The three gangsters were dead, their bodies torn apart by bullets, blood spreading around them. 'Oh great Giu,' he moaned. One of them was surrounded by a pool of blue blood. 'Nest. It's a crudding nest!' Then he saw the face of the Faller gangster, and started in shock as he recognized it from the records division photo. 'Rasschaert?'

'What do we do?' Jenifa shouted. She was still crouched down behind the car, shaking violently.

'Cover the club,' Chaing said. He realized he could barely hear his own voice above the ringing in his ears, and shouted: 'Cover the club. All active squad members, cover the club! Jenifa, find a radio. Call for ambulances. And get us some crudding backup. Franzal? Franzal!'

'Here.' The assault squad captain scuttled out from behind one of the vans, keeping low.

'We've got to get down there.'

374

'Okay.' Franzal started shouting orders to survivors. Four squad members took cover behind the vans and watched the club, carbines held ready for any sign of movement – hostile or otherwise. Chaing split the PSR officers. Half were designated to help the wounded, the rest were to provide cover as Franzal led ten of the assault squad down the metal stairs.

They deployed perfectly, the two taking point duty edging up to the railings along the top of the sunken courtyard, swinging their carbines over the top as they scanned round.

'Clear!'

Franzal led eight squad members down the metal stairs. A shotgun took out the hinges on the door at the bottom. A barrage of semi-automatic fire slammed out from the gangsters in the basement corridor.

Chaing flinched back from the railing along the top of the sunken courtyard. Franzal himself flung two grenades through the ruined door. Chaing took a couple of paces back, waiting for them to go off.

The explosion was immense. A lethal high-velocity plume of smoke and debris slammed out of the basement doorway, billowing upwards. Chaing felt the ground quake, knocking him down. Cars and vans rocked about. Every window in the front of the townhouse shattered, and the entire building sagged downwards. Cracks split the brickwork, ripping right up to the eves.

'What the crudding Uracus?'

A dustcloud was mushrooming up from the sunken courtyard, shooting out across Midville Avenue. He staggered over to the buckled railing, and leaned over. 'Franzal?' His ears were ringing, but he thought he heard cries from somewhere below. The seething dust was too thick to see through. He started to cough as he breathed it in. A couple of roof tiles smashed on the pavement barely a metre away.

'Crud!' He looked up through the haze to see more slates skidding off the roof. The building let out an ominous creak. A second wave of fissures were splitting open, multiplying out from the initial cracks.

'Back,' he yelled and started to run. 'Get back. It's going to go!'

Jenifa came running though the swirling cloud, dust coating her uniform and hair a sickly grey. 'What happened?'

'Grenades,' Chaing coughed. 'Franzal used grenades.'

'Grenades?' she bellowed. 'Crudding grenades didn't do this.'

The old townhouse collapsed in on itself with a drawn-out rumble. Shattered chunks of masonry went flying across the street, smashing into the PSR's cars and vans. More dust flooded out to choke the air.

*

Someone was calling his name. It was a sweet voice, filled with anxiety and fright, coming from a long way away.

'Florian? Florian, help me.'

Florian sucked down some air, an action which made his whole body judder. Two more breaths, and his heart began to calm. The blurs of orange in his exovision started to come into focus. He jerked his head up. 'Essie?'

She was sprawled on the floor five metres in front of him. The ion haze of the force field was gone. He scurried over to her, and cradled her, a hand stroking her head where Roxwolf's pistol had fired. There was no damage.

'Oh great Giu, are you okay? Sweetheart, speak to me.'

'Everything fucking hurts,' she said, and started sobbing. 'I can't switch off the pain. I'm not fully integrated yet. Oh fuck. It's too soon. Fuckity fuck.' Her mouth opened to let out a pitiful mewl.

The sight of her anguish made Florian weep. 'I wish I could take your pain from you.'

A bell started ringing. Up on the wall beside the telephone exchange, a red bulb flashed.

'What now?' Florian grunted.

'Alert,' Roxwolf grunted.

'You bastard!' Florian shouted. His arm came round, targeting graphics locking on the teratoid Faller. Hot thoughts ordered the bracelet power up to maximum, ready to kill this time. Ready. Yes, ready.

376

No way out! He yelled wordlessly in frustration.

Roxwolf rolled over and sneered at Florian. 'You know the routine, moron. Kill me and you die, slow and bad.'

'What alert?' Essie moaned.

'Can I find out?' Roxwolf mocked. 'Please?'

'What do I do?' Florian pleaded.

'Let him ask,' Essie said.

Roxwolf walked unsteadily over to the telephone-exchange cabinet and flicked a switch that killed the bell and flashing light. He picked up a telephone. 'Speak to me.'

Florian hugged Essie. 'He threw the medical kit into the stream. I'm sorry, sweetheart.'

'Ozzie fucking wept.'

Florian was about to chide her for using that kind of language, but gave up with a bitter snort. She seemed different somehow, more aware – more *controlled.*

The memories, Florian realized; *her true memories must be waking up.*

'Crud!' Roxwolf exclaimed. 'Don't let them get in or you'll be visiting me first,' he bawled into the handset. Then he was hurrying over to a set of thick brass pipes that emerged from the wall to one side of the vault door. Each of them ended in what looked like a set of binoculars.

'What is it?' Florian said.

Roxwolf bent down and peered into the lenses. He spun a small iron wheel at one side of the pipe, which turned the whole apparatus. 'Your friend Captain Chaing has found us.'

'Chaing?' Amazingly, that actually seemed like a welcome development.

'Yeah. Come on, boys, hit them – oh yes! Go, go! That's it. And again. Ah, crud!'

'What's happening?'

'My people are defending their turf.' Roxwolf stood up. 'They have to; there's no way out past Chaing now, and the only other door is into here.'

'You're trapped,' Florian said victoriously.

'And you're a crudding moron. Last chance to deal. I can get you to a safe haven. Just give me the spaceship's files, everything you've got.'

'There is a way out,' Essie said. 'Nobody locks themselves into a place like this without an escape route.'

Roxwolf gave Essie an admiring stare. 'Smart girl.'

'Where is it?' Florian demanded.

'Even if you use it, you've got nowhere to go,' Roxwolf said. 'Without me helping you, the PSR will grab you within an hour.'

'You tried to kill Essie!'

'You're not going to hold that against me, are you? I failed. So now go to plan B.'

'Not going to hold . . .' Florian spluttered in outrage.

'How safe?' Essie asked.

'No!' Florian shouted. 'Absolutely not.'

'Ten years in preparation,' Roxwolf said. 'But I want the files. I want to be able to protect myself from the Commonwealth fury you're going to unleash on my kind.'

'So Fallers can fight back!' Florian said.

'To Uracus with them! I want the knowledge for me.'

'I can offer you a degree of protection,' Essie said.

'You can't do that!' Florian said. 'Not him.'

'I want the knowledge,' Roxwolf insisted.

'No!'

There was a tremendous bass *thud* that Florian felt as much as heard, and the ground juddered. A web of splits appeared in the wall round the vault door. Dust and flakes of stone snowed down from the vaulting ceiling. One of the pillars snapped with a violent *crack*, the bottom third shifting out of alignment. The lights flickered and went out as the waterwheel's axis emitted a terminal metallic grinding. Small emergency bulbs in each corner came on, casting a pale yellow glow that left most of the hall in shadow.

'What the crud—?' Florian gasped.

'You were told the lounge was rigged with explosives,' Roxwolf said. 'I wasn't bluffing. Chaing and his team have set them off. Some stray bullets, no doubt.'

More flakes of stone fell from the ceiling. Florian noticed Essie was wrapped snugly in the pale violet glow again. 'Are you okay?' he asked.

'Yes, but we need to get out. I can't protect you as well.'

Roxwolf was heading towards the far end of the hall. 'Last chance to make a deal, Florian.'

'Never!'

'Moron to the end.' He did something to the base of a pillar. A flagstone dropped out of the floor, and Roxwolf jumped into the hole it exposed.

A deep rumbling started somewhere above. Rivulets of gritty mortar poured down out of widening gaps.

'Quick!' Florian shouted. He gripped Essie's hand tight and started to drag her along towards the hole in the floor.

She stumbled, crying out in pain. 'Oh crap, it hurts!'

Florian scooped her up and ran for it across the shuddering ground. The rumbling became a constant roar. Large lumps of stone rained down.

His enhanced eyesight revealed practically nothing below the hole. He jumped in, bending his knees, praying it wouldn't be too far. Infra-red gave him a brief glimpse of a grey surface that had to be the floor. He hit painfully, toppling to one side and letting go of Essie, who shrieked as she went tumbling. His legs were agony, and he was sure one ankle was cracked; the pain signals the exovision displayed were peaking. Nausea rose in his gullet.

'Essie?'

She groaned somewhere in the gloom. Infra-red revealed her – a salmon glow, huddled on the floor a couple of metres away. Above them the hall collapsed. Debris plummeted down through the hole. Florian crawled desperately across the slimy ground, feeling stones hit his back. He curled round Essie to try and protect her. All he could think was that the hall's floor would surely collapse, crushing them.

The cascade of rubble stopped. He looked up. All his infra-red showed was an indistinct grey smear in every direction, except for the mound of debris that had come through the hole, and that glowed a feeble amber. Dust swarmed up his nose and down his throat. He started coughing.

His u-shadow reported Essie was opening a link. 'Don't try to talk,' she sent. 'Put some fabric over your mouth to breathe through. The dust density is getting dangerous in here.'

'Okay,' he sent back, and brought up a corner of the furry kaftan to wrap over his nose.

'We need to move. Ozzie knows how long this cellar will last. The whole house must have collapsed on top of us.'

'Okay. Where?'

'Just follow Roxwolf's footprints.'

'How in Uracus do I do that?'

'Can't you see them in infra-red?'

'No.'

'Okay, I'll feed you my vision.'

A small pink icon popped up in his exovision, and he allowed it to open. It showed him the cellar in grainy green and black detail. It was about two and a half metres high, with pillars in every direction like a forest of brick trunks. The viewpoint swung round, and he saw himself lying on the ground, kaftan over half his face. The picture wasn't favourable. Another shift as she turned her head. And there on the dank floor was a series of dimming red patches snaking off into the distance.

'See them now?' she asked.

'Yes.'

'Florian, I'm really sorry, but can you help me again, please? My limbs are agony.'

'No problem.' He tried to stand. Pain shot up from his damaged ankle – pain so strong he had to open his mouth in a soundless shout, determined she shouldn't know just how much he was hurting. Steeling himself, he hoisted her up, grimacing at the additional weight. Then he started tottering off, following the glimmering footprints.

He had to stop and lean against several pillars, steadying himself, building up the determination to overcome the pain every time. Then launching himself forwards again, sometimes managing seven or eight steps before he had to rest again.

'Florian, what's wrong?'

'Nothing. The dust, and I picked up some bruises. That's all.'

There was a wall ahead that was covered in a thick web of tough roots. The footprints led to a ragged gap. When Roxwolf had forced his way through, some of his body heat had transferred to the gnarled woody fronds. Essie's superior infra-red vision showed them flushed as if they were smouldering embers.

They had to duck down and squeeze their way past the clawing vertical thicket. The corridor on the other side was completely covered in the same roots, turning it into a knotty arboreal tunnel. The air was damp, but finally devoid of rubble dust. Roxwolf's footsteps led straight for ten metres over the tangled cords before twisting off through another gap.

'We're not going to catch him,' Essie said. 'You're hurt.'

'I'm fine,' he said, even as he faltered, his ankle giving way on the treacherous snarled surface.

'Let go of me,' she said.

'No.' He gritted his teeth, and carried her another few metres before pitching forwards onto his knees.

'Florian!'

'I'm sorry. I'm so sorry, sweetheart.'

'This is ridiculous. We can get into an underground culvert through that hole on the left. It has to be the main one under the road.'

'How do you know that?'

'Field function scan.'

Secondary routines produced the appropriate files. He dismissed them. *Irrelevant.*

'Let's go,' she said. 'I can break us out from there.'

'You can do what?'

'Come on, together now.'

He tried supporting her as best he could. They staggered forwards, pressed against each other, no longer trying to hurry, just to minimise the discomfort.

It was a thin hole. Florian went first, pushing at the thicker roots, tearing the smaller lace-like filigrees.

The culvert was about three metres high and five wide. It must have been larger when it was built, but the original brickwork was smothered by the ubiquitous roots. Drains and sewers emptied into it through slimed apertures in the chaotic weave. Half a metre of water gurgled along the bottom.

Mostly water, he realized in disgust as his feet squelched down.

Essie wiggled through the hole, and he helped her lower herself down.

'Stay here,' she said, and shuffled forwards a little. 'Face away from me and curl up tight.'

'Why?'

Her force field came on.

'Oh.' Florian did as he was told.

There was a bright flash of light, and something exploded. The pressure wave sent Florian sprawling. Cold fetid water soaked into all his clothes.

'Hold on,' she said. 'Another coming.'

He gripped one of the roots.

The second explosion slapped him hard. There was a colossal crashing sound, and sunlight was abruptly shining all around him. He turned to see a ragged hole in the apex of the culvert, with a pile of smouldering roots and rubble forming a steep ramp up to the surface.

They clambered up together, coming out in Midville Avenue about a hundred metres past the ruins of Cameron's. Languid swirls of dust hazed the air, caged between the giant walwallow trees. A cluster of PSR officers were tending their wounded colleagues beside a line of smashed-up cars and vans. They were all staring at Florian and Essie. Standing slightly apart from the others, caked in ochre dust, his arm in a sling and wearing a black eyepatch, Captain Chaing was pointing a trembling finger.

'Florian!' he bellowed.

*

Ry Evine had been impressed by how quickly the PSR arrived. After he phoned them from a grocery shop at the end of Midville Avenue, he'd parked the tuk-tuk in an alley along from the club where he had a reasonable view. The position gave him plenty of opportunity to leave fast if anyone spotted him.

The convoy arrived with the arrogance of all PSR operations, sirens wailing and lights flashing, demanding total priority from hapless citizens. And all Uracus erupted. Ry hit the ground fast as stray bullets zipped through the air. A couple struck the tenement on the corner of the alley, *wheee*ing away in ricochets. Then just as he peered round the corner again, there was a massive explosion. Nearby windows cracked. Walwallow branches flapped as if caught in a zephyr. He watched in stunned awe as the whole townhouse came tumbling down. Dust obscured most of the carnage. There was a lot of shouting.

He could hear sirens in the distance, getting louder. The dust thinned, revealing the bodies and their traumatized Comrades.

Another dull crump of an explosion sent Ry cowering. It sounded close, but muffled somehow. He could feel the vibration through his boot soles, but there was no sign of a fireball anywhere. Then another detonation came, and ten metres away the middle of the road suddenly cratered down. It split open to reveal a deep pit. Dust jetted up.

Ry watched in trepidation as two figures clambered up out of the hole. He recognized Florian and the fleshy girl who'd been in the van with him earlier. Both of them were soaking wet and smeared in shit. Something was badly wrong; they didn't seem able to stand up properly. The girl was snivelling as if she was in far too much pain for one so young.

'Florian!' Chaing shouted furiously. The PSR captain started to run forwards.

Ry saw Florian thrust his hand out. A slender incandescent beam stabbed out from his dripping wrist and a big walwallow branch crashed down in front of Chaing, who had to fling himself out of the way.

Florian looked round wildly. Ry was close enough to see the

383

desperation in his face. The rest of the PSR officers started to move. It was like watching the start of an avalanche.

'Need a lift?' Ry sent across the general band.

Florian and the girl turned to gape at him, and Ry smiled in mad exhilaration as he slung a leg over the tuk-tuk saddle and twisted the throttle. The little machine zoomed out into Midville Avenue and skidded round beside the fugitives. Behind him, the PSR officers were shouting in anger, pelting forwards en masse.

'Zap more trees,' Ry yelled.

Three white beams flashed out simultaneously. Then three more. Branches smashed down, forcing the officers to scatter for safety.

Florian lifted the girl onto the tuk-tuk behind Ry. She groaned in distress as she flopped against Ry's back. He could feel her whole body shaking. Then Florian was clinging to Ry, sandwiching the girl between them.

'Hold tight!' Ry gunned the throttle, sending the tuk-tuk angling across the road. There were gunshots behind. A bullet thudded into a walwallow trunk as they flashed past it, bumping up the kerb and slaloming along the pavement. Ry jerked the handlebars hard, and they careered down an alley, more bullets slamming into the wall behind them. He turned again, then they were racing down one of the back roads, bursting out onto Tolsune Road with its busy traffic. A sheriff car swerved to avoid them, horn blaring. Ry could hear its brakes squealing.

'Take it out,' he yelled.

Florian raised his arm, and the beam punched through the sheriff car's bonnet as it was in the middle of a U-turn.

'Where to?' Ry called out.

'I don't know,' Florian replied. 'Everyone's hunting us. And who are you?'

'Ry Evine. Ex-astronaut. Pleased to meet you. I followed the alien spaceship here.'

'Crudding Uracus,' Florian grunted.

'Who's she?'

'Essie. She's from the Commonwealth, I think. Sort of.'

Vindication was the sweetest ever feeling, Ry decided. 'Is there a plan?'

'No. Sorry.'

Behind the tuk-tuk, the sirens were getting louder. With the wind blasting Ry's face, the little machine felt as fast as a Silver Sword burning into orbit. *Poor illusion*, Ry thought; in truth, any sheriff car could catch it easily. And every sheriff car in the city was about to attempt just that.

Then the strongest link transmission he'd ever known broadcast a signal right into Ry's macrocellular clusters.

'Talk about upsetting a warren of mad bussalores,' the general link announced. 'You three have the city's entire sheriff department heading your way.'

'Who is this?' Ry and Florian demanded together.

'The one person who can help you. Here.'

A file downloaded into Ry's storage lacuna. It opened into his exovision, displaying a map.

'Head for Hawley Docks. I'm waiting there. And hurry. I'm listening to some very aggravated radio chatter.'

Ry studied the map. Hawley Docks was barely a kilometre away, a tiny green icon winking at one end of it. Red route-guidance lines sprang out from their current position, snaking their way through the streets to it. His mirror showed him a sheriff car streaking out of a side road and curving round in pursuit. 'Do I go for it?' he asked Florian.

'There's nothing else.'

Ry dodged round some cars, ignoring the blast from their horns. Tuk-tuk drivers glared at him as he weaved through them. Pedestrians were stopping to stare. Flashing red and blue lights filled the tuk-tuk's wing mirrors as more sheriff cars joined the pursuit.

The route guidance led them off Tolsune Road, into Marine Drive. Ry followed it loyally. Marine Drive was the original thoroughfare to Hawley Docks, a wide road with rusting tramlines running down the centre. Old merchant offices and warehouses loomed up on both sides, their windows boarded up, grass and long woody weeds sprouting from clogged gutters.

And it was completely deserted. The sheriff cars seized the moment and surged forwards.

'Pull over,' a tannoy-boosted voice demanded over the howling sirens.

Two sheriff cars drew level with the tuk-tuk. Ry tried to turn the throttle further, but it was already fully open. The cars actually began to pull ahead. He knew what was coming next: they'd box him in.

Florian shot the rear tyre out of the one on the left. It veered sharply and began a skid. Then the other car was slowing. Ry could see the anger on the driver's face.

A hundred and fifty metres ahead, a tall chain-link fence had been thrown across Marine Drive, sealing off the disused Hawley Docks. Sturdy gates in the middle were closed, a heavy padlocked chain holding them secure.

'Florian,' Ry shouted. 'Gates!'

The beam took out the chain and padlock.

Ry couldn't help it – he actually closed his eyes as the tuk-tuk smashed into the gates. He heard the front tyre blow, and the handlebars were almost ripped from his grasp. The tuk-tuk wobbled forwards on its bent wheel as the gates were shoved aside, and he regained control, throttling back drastically. His body was being shaken so violently he was worried he was going to fall off.

'What now?' he broadcast into the general link band.

'I see you,' the stranger replied. 'Keep going.'

The exovision map showed him the green icon, two hundred metres ahead. He looked up. A pair of big cranes stood at the end of wharf three, their rusting arms drooping. The icon marked a spot between them.

A procession of sheriff cars poured through the open gates and spread out to form a line. They slowed, keeping level with each other to follow the damaged tuk-tuk as if herding an injured animal.

Cracked concrete and tufts of grass continued to punish the tuk-tuk as Ry drove it to the end of wharf three. He braked four metres from the edge, exactly where the icon glowed in his exovision.

In front of him and ten metres below, the deep muddy waters of the river Crisp flowed past wharf three. Yigulls flapped languidly overhead, squawking in complaint at their usual peace being wrecked by the massive intrusion of sheriff cars.

'But there's nothing here,' Florian said.

*

Jenifa drove. Chaing didn't complain about that; his cast meant he wasn't able. But he did want to shout at her to drive faster, despite how unfair that was. Wind shrieked through the Cubar. Bullets and the explosion had taken out all the glass; he seemed to be sitting on half of the shards. The front left tyre was getting progressively flatter, and something had happened to the stalwart engine. It was misfiring constantly, sending sooty smoke belching from the exhaust.

Despite all that, she kept her nerve, steering perfectly round the traffic that had stalled in the wake of the pursuit, even over-taking a couple of the sheriff cars as they turned into Marine Drive.

Up ahead, the white beam weapon struck the gates.

Chaing thumbed the button on his microphone. 'We've got him; there's no way out of the docks. Spread out and block him. Don't overtake, just corner him. And don't get too close.'

They drove into Hawley Docks and joined the rank of sheriff cars advancing along wharf three. He watched the juddering tuk-tuk come to a halt between the two rusting cranes.

'Stop here,' he ordered. 'Cover the targets. Do not shoot. Repeat, do *not* shoot. They are to be taken alive.'

Jenifa stopped the Cubar. Chaing climbed out. On either side, sheriffs were crouching behind their cars, aiming pistols, carbines, and shotguns on their trapped quarry sixty metres ahead. A second batch of patrol cars halted behind the first; more guns were lined up.

'Make crudding sure no one gets over-excited,' he instructed Jenifa.

'Got it.'

He turned to face Florian and held his good arm up. 'I'm coming over,' he announced clearly. 'Unarmed. I only want to talk.'

387

Very conscious of just how many guns were deployed behind him, he walked slowly forwards. Ry Evine was standing beside the tuk-tuk. The little Commonwealth girl was slumped in the saddle, with Florian holding her.

'It's finished,' Chaing said. 'You understand that, don't you?' He kept walking, only fifty metres short of them now. 'That's an amazing weapon you have, Florian, but look what you're facing. And I've got reinforcements coming. I can bring the whole crudding Opole Regiment down here, if that's what it takes. So why don't you just come with me? Nobody's going to hurt you. You have my word on that.'

Forty metres. Close enough to see the anguish and uncertainty on Florian's grimy face.

Chaing smiled. 'Come on. What do you say?'

The Warrior Angel rose up from nowhere at the end of wharf three and stepped onto the decrepit concrete. Dark leather coat open to flutter behind her in the breeze, hat at an angle. Exactly the same as she'd appeared at Xander Manor. Long red hair rippled gently as she walked towards the three startled fugitives.

'I say they're with me, captain,' she said.

Chaing whirled round to face the shaken sheriffs. 'Hold your fire,' he demanded. The memory of the Warrior Angel's weapons, the slaughter she could unleash, was chilling him to the bone. And the sheriffs were abruptly, shockingly confronted with the nemesis of myth. It would only take one petrified, trigger-happy kid . . . 'Do not shoot. Put your weapons down. Down! Now!'

And Jenifa was shouting, too. Ordering them to stand down.

Chaing turned back to face the Warrior Angel. 'What's happening?' he implored.

She was going to talk to him, to explain, he was sure of it. Then he saw her frown, her face hardening. He followed her gaze and saw two sheriffs lifting a long tube out of their patrol car's boot. *Bazooka!* 'No!' he yelled, and started to run. 'No, no! Stand down. Do not fire!' Other sheriffs were turning to stare. Jenifa was yelling at the two mavericks. But Chaing could see they weren't listening, faces rigid with determination. One of them knelt, the bazooka resting on his shoulder – levelling it at the Warrior Angel.

'No!'

The bazooka fired. Chaing saw the explosion bloom. It surged wide across an invisible wall that materialized round the tuk-tuk, flame and thick black smoke churning ineffectually three metres away from a cowering Florian.

It was strange. He witnessed the whole scene unfolding, but there was no sound. He was flying back through the air, arms and legs flailing, yet he felt nothing. Then the ground descended on him, and there was only blackness.

*

Glass from the windscreens of the patrol cars shattered in a blizzard of shards. Jenifa was knocked off her feet by the blast as the tiny crystalline splinters scythed through the air. Several of them sliced through her uniform to slash her skin.

A mushroom of flame and smoke surged up into the sky where the bazooka shell had detonated. She squinted, trying to bring the world back into focus. The Warrior Angel was carrying the girl, while Florian was leaning on Ry Evine for support. They walked to the end of wharf three and jumped off.

Jenifa groaned. Every part of her ached. Her ears were ringing painfully. Around her, sheriffs were clambering to their feet. She blinked, seeing Chaing's prone body lying on the concrete. His left leg was bent at an impossible angle. 'Oh great Giu,' she moaned, and slowly stood up.

'We need an ambulance,' she announced, but no one paid any attention.

Angry, frightened shouting broke out. She turned, seeing the sheriff who was still holding the bazooka. The glass swarm had cut his face, leaving blood to run down his cheek. Blue blood.

Jenifa snatched her pistol up and started firing – her and ten other sheriffs, pulling the trigger again and again and again until the pistol was empty. The two Fallers bucked and juddered as the bullets ripped into them, then toppled to the ground. Sheriffs gathered round, pistols pointing down at the dead bodies, still cautious. Everybody was looking round, hunting for anyone else with blue blood leaking from a cut.

Jenifa hurried over to Chaing. A bone was sticking up out of his left leg, just above the knee, but he was still breathing. Medic-trained sheriffs arrived and started to sort out the leg. An ambulance was on its way, they assured her.

When she looked round she saw the abandoned tuk-tuk, completely unharmed by the bazooka. She walked to the end of wharf three, and peered over where she'd seen the Warrior Angel disappear.

There was nothing there, no boat, nobody swimming. Just the calm brown water of the Crisp flowing smoothly past the disused docks. 'Impossible,' she whispered.

*

The submarine's cabin was small, about the same size as the inside of a car, but with much more elaborate chairs. Florian sat in one, looking round with a goofy, delighted smile lifting his lips. *A submarine! The Warrior Angel! Great Giu, Essie will finally be safe.*

The Warrior Angel was bending over Essie, applying a small green hemisphere to the side of her neck. Essie let out a long sigh of relief.

'Thank you,' Florian said. 'For everything.'

The Warrior Angel turned to him. 'I think that ankle of yours could do with some medical help, too. And then a shower – big priority for you there.'

He smiled shyly. 'Yes, but don't worry about me. I know how to operate a medical kit.'

'Really?'

'The space machine gave me copies of all its files when it asked me to protect Essie.'

'So, let me get this straight. A Commonwealth spaceship just dropped out of the sky one day and asked you for help?'

'Um, well . . . Yes.'

'Ha! I had a day like that myself, once. Long time ago.'

390

'You did?'

'Yep.' She winked and dropped a medical kit box on his lap – a larger version of the one the space machine had given him. 'I'll leave it to your *expertise*, then, while I concentrate on getting us out of here.'

'Where are we going?' Ry Evine asked.

'Port Chana,' the Warrior Angel told him. 'You'll be perfectly safe there with me.'

Florian stuck a diagnostic pad on his badly swollen ankle. Even that featherlight touch was painful. Results zipped across his exovision. He selected a series of treatments for the medical kit to produce. 'Essie, sweetheart, how are you doing?'

Essie gave him a sad little smile. She reached up and slowly peeled the shrivelled memory organ from the side of her head. It left a nasty-looking weal on her skin. 'I'm sorry, Florian. I know you meant well, but that's not actually my name.'

'Oh. What is your name, then?'

'Paula Myo.'

BOOK FIVE

Safe Haven

1

For three thousand years it had been called Walton Boulevard – a wide, straight thoroughfare in the centre of Varlan, stretching from Bromwell Park all the way up the incline to the Captain's Palace. Although the capital's later residents had long forgotten its origin, it followed the giant furrow which the *Vermillion* had ploughed upon its chaotic landing. Big ten-storey government buildings flanked the broad road, each with their own neat skirt of grass and trees.

That was two and a half centuries ago. The statues and fountains that had once graced most of the intersections had been taken away after they'd been smashed and defaced during Slvasta's revolution. They'd never been replaced, thus allowing the new democratic city council to run modern tramlines straight and true up the centre of the cobbles of what was now Bryan-Anthony Boulevard – named after some forgotten hero of the revolution.

Stonal watched the long burgundy-coloured tram carriages slide past as his official armoured Zikker limousine drove up Bryan-Anthony Boulevard's gentle slope, leading a convoy of unmarked PSR cars, five Varlan Regiment troop carriers, and two big regiment lorries. The passengers inside the tram barely glanced through the long grimy windows at the government vehicles as they passed.

Typical of the capital's citizens, he thought. *Stoic and jaded. Government officials are always racing round on some important mission. Who cares? Nothing changes. Life goes on.* He gave the bovine tram passengers a disgruntled sigh. *If only you knew.*

A glance in the Zikker's wide wing mirror confirmed the lorry carrying the Commonwealth space machine was still moving. That was a mild surprise. He had no idea of the thing's capabilities, but he was fairly sure that if it wanted to stop the lorry, it could. He'd spent the plane journey from Opole in a numb fear, thinking they would tumble out of the sky at any moment. The Air Defence Force people had thought him mad when he insisted they give him a parachute, which spent the whole flight on the seat next to him. Stonal ignored their poorly concealed amusement at his paranoia. In his profession, you didn't live to a hundred and thirty-two if you didn't possess a very healthy suspicion, coupled with an exceptional political aptitude.

The Zikker arrived at the colossal People's Palace. Before the revolution, the wide parade ground in front of the palace had been protected by a fence of tall iron railings, allowing tourists and Varlan residents alike to watch the spectacle of ceremonial Palace Guards dressed in their splendid uniforms marching with amazing precision between their posts. Those rails were gone now, replaced by a thick four-metre-high wall. Steel-reinforced gates opened to allow the convoy through.

They drove through a huge archway in the palace's facade to the main courtyard, then under another archway to the smaller rose courtyard. The Zikker stopped there, while the lorry slowly backed down a cobbled ramp to a set of open wooden doors and disappeared inside.

Stonal walked down the ramp to the old stables. Faustina was already waiting there at the head of a small team of assistants. The chief scientist of Section Seven's advanced research division was a hundred and fifty-four years old, but still quite sprightly. Thinning white hair was styled to resemble a tight beret, framing heavily wrinkled porcelain skin that sagged around her broad features – an appearance that too many mistakenly believed reflected an equally declining intellect. Her eyes were gazing at the back of the lorry, more alert than any twenty-year-old.

Troopers opened the lorry doors. Faustina peered eagerly into the gloomy interior. 'Up you go,' she told one of her assistants.

A big forklift truck rolled up to the tailgate, the long prongs sliding slowly inside. The assistant inside waved directions to the driver.

'Director Stonal,' she said. 'This is all very exciting.'

'I thought you'd enjoy it,' he said.

'And it's been inert since it landed?'

'Completely. Apart from the protection layer, of course.'

'Yes, that sounds like a Commonwealth force field. So it is still active. There's a functioning power generator inside, and also a computator of some kind which governs its systems.'

'Well, yes. We think it might have brought someone to Bienvenido.'

'Really. Who?'

Stonal almost smiled at the offhand question. Faustina hadn't even looked round as she asked. She was only truly interested in science. People, politics, they couldn't hold her attention like machines and electrical circuits. It made her ideal for her job. He had personally approved her appointment sixty years ago, bringing her over from the Varlan University mathematics department. She had an exceptional mind, but on campus she would never have risen further than a tenured professorship. He didn't need someone who could play the academic advancement game, or who had Party contacts – just someone who was focused on the job.

The advanced research department wasn't huge, but in those sixty years under her leadership it had produced a steady trickle of results. And he had no worries anything she discovered would leak to the Eliters. The world outside her domain simply didn't register with her.

'A child, we think,' he said. 'One of my people is tracking her.'

That, at least, got her attention. 'A child? Isn't that an odd thing for the Commonwealth to send to Bienvenido?'

'Very.'

The forklift truck started to move away from the tailgate. Stonal watched Faustina suck on her lower lip in anticipation. The space

397

machine slowly emerged. In the glaring electrical lights, its sleek fuselage shone with a pearly sheen. Back in Naxian valley, the regiment engineers had built a sturdy wooden frame around the cylinder, allowing the crane to hoist it up. The forklift's prongs had slipped under the planks, but the weight of the contraption was almost enough to topple the truck. A big flatbed trolley was hurriedly shoved into place, and the crate lowered onto it.

'Superb,' Faustina said. She beckoned one of her assistants over. The man was carrying several electrical boxes with silver aerials sticking out like strange insect antennae. 'It's not broadcasting in any spectrum,' she said, studying the dials on the boxes. 'And it flew supersonically, too, the Air Force said?'

'So they said, yes,' Stonal agreed. 'They tracked the sound it made.'

'Interesting. It's not very aerodynamic, is it? Those bulbous ends might make atmospheric entry easier than a blunt surface, but I can't believe that's their purpose. There isn't an aero-surface of any kind. What was the size of the impact crater?'

'There wasn't really a crater, more a scar in the earth. It slid along, like an airplane landing badly.' He held up a briefcase. 'I have photographs of the landing site, measurements the engineers took. Anything we could think of, really.' He glanced at the technician who was now waving a Geiger counter around the cylinder. 'We checked that, too. No radioactivity.'

'Interesting. Space is full of radiation, solar-wind particles, high-energy electromagnetic waves from the sun. Any surface exposed to such a bombardment should have residual traces. Liberty capsules certainly do.'

'The force field protected it from radiation?'

'Undoubtedly.' She finally turned to face him. 'So what do you want my department to analyse?'

'All of it.'

'Really. Not asking for much, are you?'

Stonal gave a modest shrug. There were few who would dare talk to him like that, which was why he respected the science chief. 'I need to know what it's capable of.'

'I'll do what I can.'

A small tractor was coupled to the trolley, and began to tow it into a tunnel at the back of the stable. Stonal and Faustina walked behind it. After twenty metres the tractor turned off down a side corridor, which soon became a ramp spiralling down.

The lower level of cellars had vaulted ceilings just as high as the palace's state rooms above. Stonal always felt slightly uneasy down here. In part because of all the dungeons he'd been in, supervising increased interrogations. But this subterranean area of the palace was where the Captains had stored the Commonwealth machines that survived the landing – the core of the old order. And then there was the wormhole generator.

The tractor rolled slowly into the big brick-walled crypt where Faustina did so much of her work. It was the site of Mother Laura's triumph and sacrifice. Stonal had seen the old black and white photographs of the day Bienvenido defeated the Prime, with the Fanrith map table surrounded by junior officers, their poles moving squadron models to intercept spaceships; trestle tables of telephones and radio equipment. Armed guards stood by the doors, trolleys with Bienvenido's first crude atom bombs in a line before the eerie open wormhole. Slvasta himself had been there (he was the one who showed Stonal the super-classified photos), and his friends and fellow heroes were all present and correct – Javier, Yannrith, Andricea. A pivotal moment in history.

Today the crypt was very different. The wormhole still stood at the far end, unmoved since Mother Laura had shut it down. But not inert; its force field still encased it, like a layer of clear crystal stronger than the toughest steel, preventing any kind of analysis. The trestle tables had long gone, replaced by lab benches covered in strange chunks of machinery, analysis instruments, and chemical arrays. Half of the science division's investigatory power was devoted to analysing chunks of Tree that were either held in metal clamps or hanging inside tanks full of liquid. They were splinters that had come whirling out of Treefall explosions to crash onto Bienvenido. Stonal always thought they looked like tarnished quartz, though Faustina assured him they were far more complex than that. They'd discovered channels of different molecules running through them, like seams in ore. Some conducted electricity, although most didn't.

'It's not the same as the Commonwealth's solid-state circuits,' Faustina had explained once. 'They have different properties. One day we'll understand them. Once we have more refined instruments.'

Stonal had made no comment. Section Seven's advanced science division had a lot of leeway when it came to researching and utilizing new technology, but he had to impose limits. Unrestricted technology had too much potential to impact on Bienvenido society, betraying all they had achieved for themselves. It was everything Slvasta had warned them of. To this day, Democratic Unity's core policy was to keep Bienvenido society stable, which meant very little industrial or technological development was licensed.

To remind him of the danger, right in the centre of the vault, a new section of clean white flooring had been laid half a metre above the old stones – a perfect circle that always made him think of a club's dance floor. Sitting on it was the exopod which had brought Mother Laura safely to Bienvenido. It was a spherical space capsule only slightly larger than a Liberty command module, but *oh so* different in terms of capability. Nearly half of the fuselage had been gingerly removed to lie carefully on the floor, each bit in a precise relationship to the others, like mechanical orange segments peeled from their technological core. Some sections were original access panels, while other parts had been carefully cut away. The sophisticated machinery and electrical systems underneath had also been dismantled and extracted, forming a second jigsaw ring around the exopod. Each piece had a printed label, with an index and a brief description of the function it performed (where known).

The tractor left the space machine's flatbed trolley next to the exopod floor, and trundled out of the crypt. Both large doors swung shut behind it with a loud *thud*; the bolts were thrown.

Faustina gave her new prize a thoughtful look for a while, then picked up a large screwdriver from one of the benches. She bent down to examine the wooden frame it was resting on, wincing as her joints protested.

'About a centimetre and a half clearance,' she muttered. One of her assistants started writing on a clipboard. 'See the gap?' she asked Stonal.

He bent down beside her. There was a clear gap between the space machine's surface and the wood, as if it was floating. Faustina poked the gap with the tip of the screwdriver. The slim edge was unable to get through.

'Invisible glass or solid air,' she muttered, climbing up again. 'Take your pick.'

He glanced over at the imposing wormhole generator. 'Same as that, then?'

'Yes. And the wormhole force field has remained functional for two and a half centuries. The Commonwealth build their machines to last.'

'So what's your first step?'

'You tell me what you want me to do. How much damage do you want to risk? We know the wormhole force field is strong enough to resist an atomic explosion – from a distance. Slvasta himself witnessed that, when the Prime were detonating them all around Mother Laura.'

'So there's no way we can break through to find out what that thing is?'

'Everything has a breaking point, director,' she said archly.

It surprised Stonal. He'd never heard her say anything remotely ambiguous before. 'Meaning?'

'A nuclear explosion up close might do the trick.' She grinned at his disapproving frown. 'But instead of a uniform blitz of energy, we can concentrate our assault on a tiny area, perhaps a centimetre across. We need to puncture it, not vaporize it. This is not something we've ever attempted with the wormhole.'

'Of course not. No Section Seven director is going to be responsible for the wormhole's destruction – it was Mother Laura's last gift to us. My dear father assumed she left it active as a warning not to meddle with the other planets again. What sort of assault were you thinking of?'

'We'll start with a simple electrical discharge and monitor the effects, if any. Next, a thermal lance, perhaps. Personally, I would like to use the maser beam we developed. That can emit a great deal of energy on a small area.'

'I remember,' he said.

The maser projector had been impressive, derived from one of the exopod's sensor instruments; but he and the security cabinet had vetoed making it available to the regiments. It required too much power to be truly portable, and the Gatling guns could smash a Faller egg apart for a fraction of the cost. There was also the problem of what else masers could be adapted to once factories became accustomed to producing them. *Spinoffs*, Faustina called such unpredictable consequences.

'I can probably get you permission to use the maser again,' Stonal told her.

'Thank you, director,' she said. 'I'll need to modify the weapon when we remove it from storage. We did some theoretical work on increasing its power rating.'

'I'm sure you did. I will speak to the prime minister about it right away.'

'In the meantime, we'll see what we can do with passive scans,' Faustina said. 'Now we know how to activate most of the exopod's sensors, it might be able to reveal some of the space machine's secrets to us. How's that for irony?'

'Ironic indeed,' Stonal agreed. Again he had that little feeling of unease. She was talking about machines they knew practically nothing about other than how to switch them on. 'I don't need to tell you to be careful, I'm sure.'

'Hmm?' Faustina was staring at the smooth surface of the Commonwealth machine, practically oblivious to him. 'No, no, we'll be very careful,' she said absently.

Stonal made his way back upstairs through the maze of service corridors and grand cloisters until he reached the second floor of the palace's state wing. After the revolution, there had been a big debate among Democratic Unity over razing the whole place to the ground. Practicality won out, pitched as sentiment. *Tens of thousands of workers have spent three millennia crafting the most impressive building on Bienvenido; smashing it down would be insulting their memory and achievement.*

A senior aide ushered him directly into the prime minister's study, walking him through the antechamber full of officials and politicians who started to glare at his privileged progress until they recognized the slightly stooped figure in the grey suit. The study was always too bright for Stonal's taste, with tall arched windows letting in a flood of sunlight which glared off the white marble floor and walls. He had to squint as he walked the length of the ballroom-sized chamber. Overhead, big eight-blade fans turned slowly as their electrical motors whirred, stirring the warm air.

All the glitz and finery of the Captains' era had been stripped out of the palace during the revolution, with every one of the family's possessions redistributed to Varlan's poorer citizens in an inspired public-relations exercise. So the plinths in the alcoves where the busts of past Captains used to sit now held Faller skulls aloft, and the paintings on the wall depicted crowd scenes from the revolution itself, along with squadrons of aeroplanes shooting at Falling eggs, and hydroelectric dams in various stages of construction.

Prime Minister Adolphus sat at a broad desk at the far end, surrounded by a cluttered nest of bookcases and cheap metal filing cabinets. It always made Stonal think of a boy living in an adult room, trying to comfort himself with familiar furniture from his own bedroom.

Adolphus pushed aside the pile of files he was reading, and stood up. At seventy-nine he already had the posture of a hundred-and-fifty-year-old, and he'd only held the office of prime minister for seven years. When the People's Congress voted his affirmation, he'd clawed his way up from the local Adice party to county senator and then into the cabinet itself at sixty-two – quite an achievement, given the average age of the cabinet was ninety-eight. But he was a good public speaker, popular with the Party's grass roots, had a strong regional powerbase in the north, and knew how to make deals and alliances, abandoning old allies with a ruthlessness which even impressed Stonal.

A glad-handed voter being given his smile would be inspired, confident he was the right man to lead their world – whereas Stonal could see the deep worry it shielded. Even the prime minister's rich ebony colour had shaded paler over the last couple of years. His aides whispered to the right ears that the stress of his high workload, tirelessly advocating for the people, was affecting his health; they begged him to slow down, of course, but he selflessly refused to reduce the burden he was humbled by. Stonal, who had read his private medical reports, knew what a load of crud that was.

Terese, the deputy prime minister, was sitting patiently in front of the desk, wrapped in a colourful toga-like robe edged in gold thread. At a hundred and twelve, she was a more experienced politician than Adolphus, but hadn't quite got the votes necessary to claim the prize when the last prime minister stepped down. The deal for supporting Adolphus gave her the chairmanship of the Joint Regimental Council as well as being the treasury's chief officer.

Stonal approved of that. Their power-split in the cabinet was almost equal, meaning their continual battle for supremacy limited both of them.

'So?' Adolphus asked as Stonal settled in one of the plain chairs beside Terese.

'The machine isn't doing anything. I've turned it over to the advanced science division to see what they can find out. But we do know it had a Commonwealth citizen on board.'

'Giufucking bastards! Are they coming for us?'

'No. Not directly, anyhow. It was a girl, a child.'

'What?' a startled Terese asked. 'What's the point in sending a child?'

'One of my officers is pursuing her. He's just reported from Letroy where an Eliter radical had taken her for safety. She might be young, but she is growing at an unnatural rate. Apparently she will be an adult within a month.'

'Crud! Then what?'

Stonal took off his glasses and pinched the top of his nose as he looked at her. 'Best-case scenario, it's Laura Brandt all over again. She's all alone and has Commonwealth knowledge, but has to work through us.'

'And the worst case?' Adolphus demanded.

'She's some kind of scout, a prelude to their true arrival. The end of our entire society, a culture over three thousand years in the making.'

'After so long, though! Why now?'

'I don't believe she came from the Commonwealth. Not directly anyway.'

'How do you conclude that?'

'Liberty flight 2,673. Something strange happened up there at the moment of Treefall; we still don't understand what. But that's when the Commonwealth machine appeared. It was photographed by the astronaut, Ry Evine.'

Terese frowned. 'He's from Slvasta's family, I remember. One of your relatives?'

'In a manner of speaking, yes. Interestingly, he's also gone missing. Our last verified sighting is at a bank in Gifhorn. He may be trying to contact the machine.'

'So he was in on this? He's a Commonwealth agent?'

Stonal sighed as he put his glasses back on; politicians did see conspiracy everywhere. 'No, I believe the machine has been there all along.'

'You mean since the *Vermillion*?'

'Unlikely, but certainly since the Great Transition. Perhaps the Liberty missile's atomic explosion knocked it out of orbit.'

'I don't get it,' Adolphus said. 'If this girl is still a child, how could it have been there for two hundred and fifty years?'

'The *Vermillion* had some kind of suspended-animation chambers for its passengers. Laura Brandt was sleeping for most of the voyage, she told us. My theory is that this is some kind of lifeboat.'

'And now the crudding Eliters have her,' Terese snapped. 'How could this happen?'

'To be fair, this isn't something we were expecting,' Stonal said patiently.

'She can't tell them what she knows. Great Giu, they'd wind up with technology more advanced than us. They'd take over.'

'I have authorized my officer to use whatever resources he needs.'

'And he's good?' Adolphus pressed. 'Your best?'

'Very good. He fought breeder Fallers and survived. And he's actually met the Warrior Angel.'

'Crudding Uracus!' Terese sat up straight. 'Is he loyal?'

'Without Section Seven support he is nothing. He knows that.'

'You have to find this child. She has to be brought here so we can decide what to do with her.' Terese and Adolphus exchanged a glance. 'Some of the knowledge she has might be valuable.'

'Indeed.' Stonal marvelled at the way they saw everything in terms of political advantage alone.

'How long until you have her in custody?' Adolphus asked.

'Soon. We know she is on her way to Opole. There's a large Eliter population there who will doubtless shelter her. I suspect the Warrior Angel will soon be showing an interest.'

'That can never happen,' Terese said firmly.

'Whatever you need to apprehend her,' Adolphus said flatly. 'Whatever needs to be done. You have my complete support on this.'

'I understand.'

*

The ellipsoid-shaped submarine surfaced in a small cave lit by bright spotlights. It nosed forwards onto a cradle. Plyplastic arms curved round the hull, securing it, and the cradle's tank treads trundled their way up a slipway.

Kysandra climbed out of the upper deck hatch and took a deep breath. As always, the humid cave air smelt of slightly rancid seaweed, but right now that was pretty good after three days in a submarine cabin designed for three, sharing it with Florian, Ry, and Paula. Life support had always provided enough oxygen. The filters, on the other hand, had struggled.

Demitri and Marek were standing on the top of the stone

406

slipway, grinning up at her. Kysandra hurried down the ladder that was welded to one of the cradle's support girders.

'Welcome back,' Marek said, and gave her a quick hug.

'Any problem?' Demitri asked.

'Not for me,' she admitted. 'But poor old Captain Chaing has got another round of explaining to do.'

'Well, I never did thunk – thunk – *think* he's be our new Slvasta,' Marek said.

Kysandra kept her smile in place. The poor old ANAdroid's bioware brain was becoming more glitch-prone these days. The semiorganic synthesizers Nigel had left behind for her could produce spares for most ANAdroid body parts, but a duplicate brain was a hugely complex component. Back in the Commonwealth, they were extruded by specialist synthesizers. As the glitches were only affecting his vocal routines so far, she was content to keep him running.

Both ANAdroids looked back at the submarine. Kysandra saw Paula carefully climbing down the ladder. Her body was now aged about twelve or thirteen. The fast growth process had been very weird to watch during the voyage. Fortunately, the pain in her limbs seemed to be reducing as she drew closer to maturity. Her biononics were also coming close to full integration, which helped.

'Hello, Paula,' Demitri said with a lopsided smile. 'Long time.'

Paula flinched as her bare feet touched the rock floor. 'You're the Sheldon ANAdroids.' She glanced up at Demitri. 'Interesting features you morphed for yourselves.'

'Thank you.'

'Asian traits, very sweet.' She turned to Marek. 'And North Mediterranean by the look of it, though I don't understand why you went for old age on top of that.'

'Italian,' Marek said. 'My great-great-grandmother came from Naples.'

'You believe you have an ancestor?' Paula queried.

'Nigel and I infiltrated the ANAdroids into various parts of society,' Kysandra said. 'They needed to look different, obviously. I helped them put together their appearance.'

'I understand,' Paula said.

Kysandra pressed her lips together in mild disapproval. The dismissive tone Paula was using with the ANAdroids was verging on disrespectful. And then there had been all the questions during the voyage as she familiarized herself with Bienvenido's basic history – especially the revolution and the Great Transition. It wasn't Paula's fault, of course, but those questions had brought out Kysandra's defensive side. Nor did it help that she constantly felt as though she had to explain herself to a twelve-year-old. The whole accelerated-growth thing was troubling at some deep instinctive level. No one likes a kid smarter than them; it triggered all sorts of insecurity. *And I had quite enough of that with Nigel, thank you.*

'We're glad you're here,' Demitri said.

'Better late than never,' Paula said.

Ry climbed down the ladder. He was looking round the cave with a great deal of interest, particularly the small engineering section at the top of the slipway where the sub was serviced.

'Uh, I think Florian's going to need some help down,' he said. 'He's not going to manage the ladder with that ankle of his.'

'We have a mobile access platform,' Demitri said. 'I'll call it over.'

'Thanks, that—' Ry broke off and stared at the ANAdroid. 'You? But you can't be here. You're dead!'

Kysandra grinned mischievously. 'Major Ry Evine, this is Demitri.'

'No, that's not right!' Ry grunted. 'You died. The fuel-dump explosion.'

'A convenience,' Demitri said. 'The Liberty programme was up and running. There was nothing more I could add.'

'It was two hundred years ago. You can't possibly still be alive.'

'I am an ANAdroid,' Demitri said. 'A biological machine in human form. I came with Nigel Sheldon from the Commonwealth.'

'Oh Great Giu,' Ry said. 'But you were the one who made it all possible. You designed the Liberty and Silver Sword. I've been in space because of you. I flew in the spaceship you designed.'

'The Liberty is not original,' Demitri told him. 'Although we are human in many respects, ANAdroids do not have a creative ability.

We cannot innovate. I simply modified the existing blueprints for the Russian Soyuz launcher system, and showed Bienvenido's managers and engineers how to put together the requisite factory production lines. Soyuz was the most successful rocket-launched manned vehicle ever built, and also the most reliable of its type.'

'You saved us,' Ry said, looking between Demitri and Kysandra. 'The Liberty flights are wiping out the Trees. That's all that stands between us and annihilation.'

'We do what we can to help,' Kysandra said, feeling embarrassed at the worshipful gaze he was directing at her. 'But it's not enough.' She turned to Paula. 'The Fallers are going to win, and I don't know how to stop them.'

*

The farmhouse was perched close to the clifftop on the eastern side of the Honorato estuary. It was a modest two-storey building with rendered brick walls to withstand the battering it got from the wintertime weather coming off the Polas Sea. Several barns and smaller outbuildings sprawled around it, all in reasonable repair but due some maintenance – exactly what anyone would expect from a goat farm in such a rugged location. The windswept grassland that spread back behind the cliff was scattered with boulders and jutting rock outcrops. Its soil too thin and poor to support arable crops; goats were about the only animals that could succeed commercially in such a location, and even they couldn't be said to thrive.

Kysandra had leased just over a thousand acres from the National Land Office, who had assumed ownership of all land on the Lamaran continent after the revolution. It was a typical joint-enterprise venture, with the State Agriculture Board owning thirty-five per cent of the business. According to their records, she had been at the farm for twenty-seven years; before that it had been run for fifty-seven years by 'Larkitt' who was actually Valeri, another ANAdroid; before that it had been Marek who had run the farm for nearly seventy years. Nobody from the board ever showed up to check. Eliters, under Kysandra's guidance, had acquired positions in every government office in and around Port

Chana; they also formed a strategic part of the local Democratic Unity party. It was done with quiet efficiency, maintaining the urban myth that Port Chana was a hotbed of radical Eliters on the edge of society, while in fact they actually ran the county.

Port Chana itself was just visible from the farmhouse. Kysandra glanced at it from the first-floor landing window as the sun sank below the horizon. It was on the other side of the estuary. There was no cliff over there, no stony plateau country, just rumpled lowlands that had once been an expanse of marshes and orango bushes, now long-drained to produce some of the most fertile farmland on the continent, with a geometric network of dykes keeping the rich black loam drained in winter and irrigated in summer. It was Bienvenido's fruit basin, with kilometre after kilometre of orchards and berry fields stretching all the way north to the edge of the Pritwolds.

Farm trucks rattled along the raised roads, their headlights casting weak beams in the twilight as they headed into town, where the silos and warehouses waited, wedged into the commercial sector between the docks and the railway station. Port Chana's streetlights were coming on, marking out the crooked web of roads, along with the more colourful neon signs of the waterfront clubs. At the end of the harbour wall, the lighthouse beam was flashing in an imperiously slow tempo. It was a flourishing little city which, from her vantage point atop the cliff, was easy to imagine being slowly, methodically encircled by the Faller hordes as their numbers grew.

She shook her head, angry with herself for letting the old doubts gain traction. *Paula's here now. She might know what to do.* The ANAdroids seemed to think so, anyway.

Florian was in one of the three guest bedrooms. Kysandra knocked on the door and went right in. Since they'd arrived back at the farmhouse, he'd had a very long hot shower, shaved, and spent half an hour in the medical chamber. Now he was lying on the bed, dressed in a white T-shirt and a pair of navy-blue shorts, eyes closed.

'Sorry,' she said as he stirred, blinking as though being woken. 'Didn't realize you were sleeping.'

'I wasn't. I was accessing your files. I just can't access enough of the Commonwealth.'

'I know that feeling. What were you accessing?'

'The Starflyer War. The Primes . . . Wow, I know Laura Brandt was scared of them and they were invading us, but I didn't realize just how bad they were. MorningLightMountain took out entire Commonwealth star systems!'

She sat on the end of the bed and tucked some strands of hair behind her ear. 'It's been a while since I checked those out. How's the ankle?'

'Perfect. There's nothing wrong with it.' He glanced down at his foot and moved it round. 'I can't believe it. I thought the kit Joey gave me was good, but your medical capsule . . .'

'It can handle a damaged ankle easily enough. You need to keep your weight off it overnight; that'll allow the cells to knit back together properly. But the capsule is getting a bit quirky now. It came from Nigel's starship two and a half centuries ago. He left it behind for me when he flew into the Forest.'

'So is that why you—' He flushed slightly, avoiding eye contact. 'Well, you look – you know – amazing, actually. If I didn't know, I'd have said you were younger than me.'

'Yeah, not bad for a girl over two and a half centuries, huh? If I say so myself.'

'Yes.' He swallowed, still unable to look at her.

Knowing she was being terribly unfair – and rather enjoying it – she leaned in a fraction closer. 'It's mainly biononics that keep me like this, but a few colleagues do use the capsule for rejuvenation when they have to.'

'Uh, right. How many people are in your organization?'

'Organization is a strong word. Let's just say I know people I can rely on. And, Florian, I count you as one of them now.'

'Really? I mean, yes. Yes, you can count on me. Of course you can.'

'Oh, you've already proved yourself. Keeping Paula safe like that with every PSR officer on the planet hunting you . . . And the Fallers, too. That was remarkable.'

He gave a not-very-modest grin and propped himself up on his elbows. 'You did the same thing.'

'Hardly. Nigel was fully grown, and he arrived with the ANAdroids and a starship. I was just a junior member of the organization he put together.'

'Organization? You mean the revolution! What was it like, overthrowing the Captain? And you went through the Great Transition, too.'

'One was terrifying, and one was awful. I'll leave you to guess which was which.'

'I don't believe you were just a junior. You're the Warrior Angel. Everyone talks about Mother Laura's sacrifice that day, but you fought the Prime, too. You're our saviour as much as her.'

She ran a hand back through her hair and chuckled. 'Giu, but you're young.' His crestfallen expression was enough to make her grin. 'I wasn't complaining, Florian. Quite the opposite.'

'Oh.'

'Fate's a strange thing. I often wonder what would have happened to me if Nigel had landed at the next farm along. Actually, I know what was supposed to happen, and it wasn't anything nice.'

'What?'

'Arranged marriage. My mother had a lot of . . . debts.'

'That's awful. Did that kind of thing really happen back then?'

'Yes. And what about you? What would have happened if the package came down in the next valley?'

'It did, actually. I was there rustling sheep.'

'Florian!' She laughed. 'You're very literal, aren't you?'

'I guess. Sorry.'

'Don't be. It's quite cute. But tell me this: you do know there's no going back for you, don't you?'

'I knew that the moment the space machine arrived.'

Kysandra cocked her head to one side and studied him. 'Interesting; there's more to you than meets the eye. I don't know why I'm surprised by that. I'm just used to egomaniacs with loud opinions.'

He shrugged.

'This is a different life we live here, Florian. And it's coming to an end now, one way or another.'

'I understand.'

'Do you? Then answer me this: would you like me to stay here with you tonight?'

His mouth parted, but it took him a moment before he finally managed to croak: 'Yes.'

She stood up and began to unbutton her blouse. 'One thing.'

'What?'

'Your poor ankle. You're not to put any weight on it, so that means I get to go on top.'

*

It was midnight when Kysandra giggled.

'What?' Florian asked.

She'd been staring out of the window at the terrible emptiness of the night sky, trying to remember what the nebulas had been like in the Void. Without secondary routines activating some correctly filed memories, it was difficult now. So she snuggled up a bit closer, and stroked his chest gently. Seven years' manual labour as a forest warden had given him a nicely muscled frame, which she'd spent an enjoyably long time exploring. 'I don't get many chances to relax like this, that's all.'

'Oh. Okay.'

But she'd felt his abdomen tense up anyway, so she took his hand and guided it to her breasts. Once again she felt his breathing quicken. *Men, always so simple.* 'You do get that this is just fun, don't you?'

'Yes.'

'It doesn't finish with us walking off into the sunset. For a start, I'm ten times older than you.'

'Your body is younger. And I've probably got as much memory loaded into my storage lacuna as you now.'

'I'm not sure if that's gallant or crazy, but I appreciate the thought you put into it.'

'You're welcome.'

413

'Ooh, smugness. Tell me, did you really spend seven years alone in that valley?' Although, she already knew the answer to that. He'd been so endearingly inexperienced. At the start of the night, anyway. *Crud, I'm growing old disgracefully. Thank Giu.*

'Yes,' Florian said.

'Why?'

'My life was a pile of crud. I didn't see any other way out. I just wanted to be away from people.'

'You poor thing.' She traced her forefinger along his chin. 'That's some discipline you've got there to stick it out for so long. I guess that's something else we have in common. But I'm glad you're out of it now.'

'Me too. What's going to happen next?'

'There's some very naughty positions I'm going to teach you just as soon as you're hard again.'

'Uh, right. Um, actually—'

She laughed. 'Giu, you're so easy to tease. I love that.'

'I don't want tonight to end. Not ever.'

'I know. I also know what you meant. So: we wait until Paula hits her late teens at the end of the week, then we find out what she suggests.'

'That's what I don't get. You have biononics like her. The smart-core you've got here has more data stored in it than a thousand Eliter humans. And you know this world; you're the Warrior Angel, for Giu's sake. You're the one who should be deciding what to do. Why don't you just march into Varlan and take charge? I saw what you did at Hawley Docks. You could be prime minister if you wanted to be.'

'Been there, done that. It finished up with Nigel dead and that psychotic lunatic Slvasta running the world. Bienvenido was a bad place after the Great Transition, Florian. Government was in chaos, and the Trees were flying down into the Ring formation. And nobody realized how bad the nest situation was.

'I was being hunted by Slvasta's people and Laura Brandt seemed to be turning things around, so I just waited while things settled down. Then the Prime came: that was an utter crudding disaster.

After Laura sacrificed herself, we didn't have many options, so we decided to push Laura's plans forwards. They made a lot of sense back then. Laura had already taught them to build atom bombs. Demitri went undercover and showed them how to build their space rockets. The Liberty flights worked. We thought it was just a matter of time – and biononics eliminate time as a problem for me. So we sat back and waited for the Trees to be wiped out. The thinking went that once the Fallers are gone, society won't be on this permanent war footing. Humans will be able to start progressing again, just like they always do when they're not constantly living under a threat. Bienvenido would evolve into a real democratic society. And when that happened, we'd be here with the seeds of advanced technology. We'd go back into space, and build starships again. That was always Laura's goal, to make contact with the Commonwealth.'

'Why don't you just release the technology now?'

'Even if I released it universally, the Eliters are the only ones who can utilize it effectively, at least to begin with. The general population would have to undergo gene therapy, or receive OC-tattoos, to interface with Commonwealth technology. And those concepts would trigger every PSR paranoia going. Society as a whole has to change, to liberalize. Plus, Commonwealth-level technology can be badly abused. The Captains showed that, and they only had a residual number of functioning systems.' She let out a long sigh. 'In any case, I was wrong to take this course, and it's too late for me to correct now. Liberty missions are irrelevant; the Fallers are too well established. They have nests everywhere. We think they're already dominant across the rest of the planet.'

'The Faller Apocalypse,' he said gloomily. 'How could we have let that happen?'

'My mistake.'

'No! You can't blame yourself for everything.'

'You're so sweet. And actually I don't. The Captains and Slvasta have a huge responsibility with their Lamaran isolationist policy. I just didn't make the effort to try and break that convention. I've done the best I can, Florian, I really have. But it's not good enough, and I don't know enough to try anything else. That damn revolution haunts me every crudding day. We never had a plan for what happened afterwards, because Nigel was so ridiculously confident the Void would be destroyed and the Commonwealth would come zooming in to help. But that didn't happen. We were left hanging on by our fingertips. That's the world I really grew up in. Biononics gives me a lot of power, but I do not know how to change the path of a whole society; I don't have that experience – ironic, considering I'm over two hundred and fifty years old.'

'And that's where Paula comes in?'

'All I know is: Paula was the fallback. Plan B. The ANAdroids told me she and Nigel prepared the package in case his mission failed and a different approach was needed. Not that he even began the mission he entered the Void to do.'

Florian rolled onto his side and frowned at her. 'What was his mission, then?'

'There was another planet in the Void, Querencia, which was settled by the ships that accompanied the *Vermillion*. They managed to get some sort of message out to the Commonwealth – though it turned into a religion or something. Anyway, Nigel came looking for Querencia. Nobody in the Commonwealth knew we existed.'

'So they'll never look for us?'

'I thought they would,' she said forlornly. 'I thought that for over a century, which is another reason I failed to change anything here. It's complicated, but the Nigel who came here was only a copy. The real Nigel is still out there somewhere in the Commonwealth. He wouldn't give up on us, I know he wouldn't. But we're so achingly far from the Commonwealth galaxy, and he must have thought Uracus destroyed us rather than simply expelling us. So we're on our own.' She gave him a sad smile. 'Sorry.'

'Hey.' He cupped her cheeks. 'Everything you've done is magnificent. Really. Think of the lives you've saved, the Fallers you've eliminated. Bienvenido practically worships you for that – the real Bienvenido, not the government bollocks. I did when I was growing up.'

'Thank you, Florian.'

They kissed. She liked the way he kissed – fearful and excited at the same time, so anxious to please.

'And when Paula's old enough she'll give us a different perspective,' he said, all eager with reassurance. 'You'll see. Maybe we can build a starship and fly to the Commonwealth galaxy.'

'Now you're starting to sound like Ry.' Who had spent the whole submarine trip talking about Commonwealth starships – so much so, she'd almost regretted letting him access her files on them.

'We'll find an answer,' he insisted. 'Humans can do anything if they have enough determination. And knowledge. Knowledge is the key to everything.'

Which is what I really want from him. All that beautiful youthful optimism. 'Well, we'll know soon enough.' She rubbed her nose softly against his and returned his hands to her breasts. 'And in the meantime, we'll start with the first of those positions I mentioned . . .'

*

At one o'clock in the morning, Opole General Hospital was quiet. Ward lights were out, night-shift staff sat in their offices chatting softly, janitors mopped corridors with the listless movements of everybody working while the rest of the city slept.

The receptionist barely glanced up when Jenifa came through the main entrance. Despite the balmy night, she wore her full-length uniform coat, buttoned up to the top, and long black boots. Her cap completed the appearance of an aloof PSR officer. 'Comrade,' she said coldly to the startled receptionist, and carried on up the central stairs.

The private wards for Party members and senior government officials took up their own wing on the second floor. Two sheriffs were sitting on chairs on either side of the double doors. She waved them down when they started to rise and salute her. 'No one else is to come in until I leave,' she told them. Pointed at their logbook. 'I am not here. Understood?'

They nodded silently. She went through the doors into the long corridor. Chaing's room was the third door along. She locked it behind her as she went in.

A soft night light glowed on the wall, bathing the room in a warm yellow glow. There was a single metal-framed bed under the window with a thick mattress. Chaing was asleep on it. An IV bag hung from the frame, feeding a painkiller into his arm. Jenifa gazed down at him for a long moment. A bandage held a fat gauze dressing against his eye, and his face had a few light grazes. Despite that he looked very peaceful, she thought.

She moved the call button out of his reach, then folded the sheet and blanket down until they made a tidy roll below his feet. He was dressed in a green, short-sleeved hospital gown that came down to his knees. There was another new cast on his arm. His left leg was heavily bandaged from thigh to ankle, with sturdy wooden splints bound on to hold it rigid.

Chaing stirred slightly as the weight of the blanket was lifted. Jenifa took a syringe from her coat pocket and slipped its needle into the rubber IV tube, just above his arm. She didn't know his exact body weight and he had a sharp mind, so she'd measured out a maximum dose of sodium pentothal. The second syringe contained a liquid form of granddad's delight – which wasn't easy to come by, but her time working the Cannes Club meant she knew who to go to. That was a maximum dose as well. Her tongue slowly moistened her lips as she watched the plunger go down. 'Do you like that, captain?' she whispered.

The empty syringes went back into her coat pocket. Carefully, so she didn't wake him too soon, she gripped the hem of his hospital gown, and worked it up until his torso was completely exposed.

Chaing let out a low moan. Not of pain. The sodium pentothal would be reaching his brain now, disorientating him.

Jenifa climbed onto the bed, and stood there with her boots on either side of his hips. 'Oh captain. Wake up, captain.'

It took a little while, but Chaing began to regain consciousness. Sighing again, shoulders moving.

'Look at me,' she commanded. 'Look up, captain.'

His unbandaged eye fluttered open. She could see how dazed he was, but aware of her at some level.

'Can you see me?'

'What?' he mumbled.

'Look at me.' She undid the coat buttons, working from the top down. Her own heart was pounding with exhilaration now. 'I'm here for you, captain. Here for you any way you want.'

Chaing was definitely focusing on her through his drug stupor as the coat fell open. With an impish grin she loomed over him, and pulled the coat apart to show off her naked body underneath.

'Oh yes,' she cooed as she watched his cock stiffen. 'You're going to take your reward, aren't you, captain?'

Fever sweat started to ooze across his brow as she knelt down. Her hand curled round his iron-hard erection, impressed with just how well granddad's delight worked.

'What?' he groaned.

Jenifa joyfully impaled herself on him. 'Oh, that is so good,' she sighed. Her weight was pressing him down, pinning him to the bed. The dominance was a spike of pure pleasure direct into her brain.

'Jenifa,' he grunted. Tears were leaking from his eye. 'Lovely Jenifa.'

'Yes, it's me, it's Jenifa. And I want you to screw me. I always want you to screw me.'

'Giu yes.'

'I'm your reward, captain. This is what you get for a mission accomplished.' She began to move up and down, trying to concentrate through the blaze of physical delight. 'You found Florian. We all saw him, and the girl. You did so well.'

'Yes, yes.'

'And better than that, you outsmarted Castillito, didn't you?'

'Yes! Crudding yes.'

'She threatened you, didn't she? That's so insulting for a PSR officer, so shameful. Especially one as fantastic as you. But she got what she deserved. She's in exile now, she can never come back. You made that happen. You!'

'Yeah. Yeah, I did that. That'll teach the bitch.'

Jenifa felt sweat trickling down her skin as she rode him faster and faster. 'Tell me. Celebrate your victory over Castillito. It'll be our secret. Tell me, tell me so I can never confess it to anyone. What did she know about you?'

'She told Castillito!' He yelled vehemently. 'She betrayed me.'

'Who, captain? Who betrayed you?'

'The Warrior Angel.'

Ecstasy claimed her, and she cried out in glory. When her body and mind finally calmed, she saw Chaing had lost consciousness beneath her. She smiled victoriously, and bent forwards to whisper in his ear. 'I am the strongest. I am the best.'

*

The black Zikker was parked on the other side of Roturan Road from the General Hospital's entrance, its engine running with a low purr. Jenifa walked over the street and climbed in the back.

'So?' Yaki asked. 'How did that go?'

Jenifa looked through the darkened side window as the limousine pulled away, watching the big old grey-stone hospital disappear behind them. 'You need to eliminate him. He's been compromised. The Eliters can manipulate him.'

'Really? How?'

'The Warrior Angel knows some secret about him.'

'Interesting. What secret?'

Jenifa pouted. 'I don't know yet.'

'You need to improve your interrogation technique, my dear.'

'There's nothing wrong with my technique, thank you. Castillito knows whatever the Warrior Angel discovered about him. That's the hold the Eliters have on him.'

'But you don't know what it is the Warrior Angel has on him.'

'I can go back and ask.'

'Any more sodium pentothal tonight and you'll fry his brain.'

'So? He's a traitor.'

'Hmm.' Yaki settled back into the thick leather cushioning. 'And yet he ran a very effective hunt for Florian.'

420

'We didn't catch him, though, did we?'

'You were just a few metres away on the docks.'

'And then the Warrior Angel appeared. Convenient, that. She must have tracked Chaing. Or more likely he told her where we were.'

'Maybe. But there's something odd about this. He's not a double agent, not in the traditional sense.'

'He's compromised!'

'Did you ever see him put in less than a hundred-per-cent effort? Did he ever come over as less than genuine?'

Jenifa gritted her teeth. 'No.'

'He even threw you under the proverbial tram so he could stay on the operation. Now that's dedication.'

'Thank you for that reminder.'

Yaki paused, closing her eyes for a moment. 'We can use this. Stonal rushed into recruiting him for Section Seven after Xander Manor. If Chaing is truly compromised, that calls Stonal's judgement into question.'

'Is this good enough to take out Stonal?' Jenifa asked.

'I know people in Varlan. If questions are asked in the right places, he'll be damaged. Nobody wants a damaged director of Section Seven.'

'Crudding Uracus! You're really going to do this, aren't you?'

'It's for the good of Bienvenido. This world needs strong people in charge. But before we can even think of that, we need to know what the Warrior Angel has on Chaing.'

'I can do that,' she said eagerly.

'No. At least, not the way you're thinking. I want to keep Chaing in play. He'll write off one night like tonight to painkiller nightmares, but any more and he'll grow suspicious. So . . . I know the director of the PSR Portlynn office; I'll have Chaing's old case files forwarded to us. Go through them; find his vulnerability.'

'Yes, Mother.'

*

Stonal walked the long length of the prime minister's study, taking care not to appear any different to all the other times he'd had a meeting here – poised, slightly contemptuous of politicians. It was difficult, which it shouldn't have been; not for him. This time he was bringing bad news, which in itself was unusual, but the magnitude of the failure took this to a whole new level. When he'd been younger, growing up in Kassel before Slvasta took him in, there had been an earthquake. A minor one, but even now he could still remember his fear and confusion as the uncanny noise roared through the house. There was nowhere to go to shut it out, nowhere safe. It was exactly the same noise he imagined Bienvenido's last two and a half centuries of stability would make if it started to fracture. And there it was resonating inside his head, a possibility now.

Adolphus and Terese were sitting in their usual places. Instead of the routine farce of him going through paperwork and her waiting impatiently, they were both watching him approach. He understood that look: he'd relinquished his status as ally, become a potential opponent. Given the files he had on both of them, that arrogance was almost amusing.

He stopped in front of Adolphus's desk, and nodded politely. 'Prime minister. Deputy.'

'What the crud happened?' Adolphus demanded.

'My officer had Florian and the Commonwealth girl contained. He was actually taking them into custody when the Warrior Angel appeared. There was nothing anybody could do.'

'I understand there were Fallers present,' Terese said.

'Yes. They were impersonating sheriffs. They used a bazooka to shoot the Warrior Angel. It was spectacularly ineffective.'

'That's it?' Adolphus said, incredulously. 'She's gone? We're just supposed to accept that?'

'Hardly gone. I suspect we'll be hearing from her in the near future.'

'No. Oh, no. That is not acceptable, on any level.'

Stonal sat himself down, ignoring the prime minister's aggravated stare. 'We lost, Adolphus. It's that simple.'

'Lost? This wasn't a crudding vote in the Congress. What's she going to do to Bienvenido?'

'I have absolutely no idea. But I can't imagine it will be wholly beneficial to the government.'

'Then we have to stop her,' Adolphus growled out. '*You* have to stop her.'

'Me? She's under the Warrior Angel's protection now.'

'Operation Overload,' Terese said quietly.

Stonal turned to glance at the deputy, surprised she would suggest it. Both politicians were more desperate than he'd realized. 'I see.'

'You must have some idea where the Warrior Angel hides out,' Adolphus said. 'Section Seven has had crudding centuries!'

'It's most likely Port Chana, or somewhere in that area. However, that might be a double bluff. We'd need to be *extremely* certain about her exact location before we even think of detonating a three-hundred-kiloton atomic bomb on the planet. And she may well be living in Port Chana itself. The civilian casualties would be enormous.'

'But we know an atomic explosion will break a Commonwealth force field,' Adolphus insisted. 'That's how the Primes killed Mother Laura.'

'My father saw her being overrun by them, yes,' he answered carefully. 'But it has to go off close to the Warrior Angel, very close.'

'Okay, then,' Terese said.

'Okay what?' Stonal asked.

'Proceed with Operation Overload,' Adolphus said. 'Find them; eliminate them.'

'Operation Overload was drawn up as a last resort in case the Warrior Angel tried to overthrow the government.'

'And now this Commonwealth girl is here, that's become a whole lot more likely.'

'Has it? How so? If the Warrior Angel had established the kind of revolutionary cell network necessary to overthrow the government, she would have used it by now. She's not a political creature; all she has is the tacit support of Eliters. And we watch them closely. There is not going to be a revolution just because this girl has arrived.'

'What then?'

'I told you I don't believe that the girl is the vanguard of the Commonwealth's arrival. It is most likely she is a refugee.'

'So you're saying she's not a danger?'

'Not a physical one,' Stonal contended. 'But potentially a political one, yes. The Warrior Angel has never released any of the Commonwealth's technological knowledge, despite an infinite number of opportunities to do so. We know why; she was in agreement with Mother Laura on this. They both believed that, after the Trees were destroyed, our government would have to be – as she put it – less authoritarian, and society would change because of that.'

'Crudding insulting,' Terese muttered.

'Yes, but it has been a principle the Warrior Angel has thankfully stuck to. Consequently, we have maintained order for two hundred and fifty very difficult years.'

'Exactly!' Adolphus said. 'And now this wretched girl has arrived to upset everything. Suppose she doesn't agree with the Warrior Angel?'

'She is very limited in her options. If she wants to build any advanced machinery, or even a starship to take her home, she will need resources. Vigilance will uncover that; my father knew what he was doing when he introduced the joint-enterprise law. The state has a stake in every commercial venture on the planet no matter what size; the movement of raw materials and finished products cannot be hidden from us in the same fashion Nigel did before. If she wants to achieve anything, she has to negotiate with us.'

Adolphus and Terese exchanged one of their knowing looks.

'So you're saying we're safe?'

'Not at all. Change is coming; it is inevitable. But if the girl comes forwards, we can cooperate with her and manage the situation. That's the good news.'

'But you just said she has limited options,' Terese said.

'She is no longer my primary concern.'

'Who is then?'

'The Fallers. They took a big risk appearing openly in Opole and trying to take out the Warrior Angel. It was a suicide mission and they knew it. That it failed is even more cause for alarm. They will be extremely worried, which in turn worries me. The nests know that Commonwealth technology poses the greatest threat to them and their ambition to conquer Bienvenido. This might be the event which forces them into desperate measures.'

'The apocalypse?' Adolphus asked anxiously, glancing round the vast study as if fearing being overheard. 'You think they can launch it?'

'We have not attempted to send any exploration parties out to other islands since the disastrous Marine scout trip to Fanrith eighteen years ago,' Stonal reminded him. 'There is an increase in the disappearance of coastal ships, small but significant, despite the Vatni's vigilance. We do not know their strength beyond our shores.'

'We know Byarn is clear of the bastards,' Terese said.

'We certainly do, yes.'

'What the crud do you expect us to do, then?'

'If this Commonwealth girl comes to us, we have to find a solution that will satisfy not just ourselves, but also the Fallers.'

'Operation Overload is Giudamned satisfactory,' Adolphus said. 'I am not going to have my premiership remembered for appeasing the crudding Fallers.'

'And if she physically comes to Varlan, do we still use Operation Overload?' Stonal asked contemptuously. 'But consider this: for all she was difficult with Slvasta, Mother Laura had a basic level of integrity. We can only assume this girl will have a similar outlook. Even if she doesn't, I cannot believe she will want to endanger an entire planet of humans.'

'All right,' Adolphus said angrily. 'If she contacts us, we'll consider offering her a deal. In the meantime—'

'My people will continue looking for her. Of course.'

'I was going to say: we should move Byarn's status up to level four. Purely as a precaution. Terese?'

'Agreed,' she said. 'We'll both sign the order tonight.'

'That needs to be kept very quiet,' Stonal said, trying not to show how perturbed he was by the extremes Adolphus was thinking in. 'If any hint of that leaks out, it might just push the Fallers into irreversible action.'

'I'll talk to the chief of the Joint Regimental Council,' Terese said. 'As far as anyone will know it's going to be just another irritating logistics exercise.'

2

The tailor on JermanGate had taken an impressive eighteen hours to produce the new uniform. Jenifa had picked it up the morning Chaing was released from hospital. The jacket sleeve folded neatly to be pinned at the side, while the front could be buttoned over the sling which held his arm. Instead of a seam on his left trouser leg, there were buttons he could do up after he'd slipped them on, covering the bandages and splints. Even the shirts were customized, with the right sleeve missing, and a larger than usual shoulder hole.

Despite the ease of wearing it, Chaing was sweating when he got to the top of the third-floor stairs. He had to use a crutch on his left side and it was exhausting work; he often found his left arm shaking from the strain. But he'd flat-out refused to accept the wheelchair the hospital offered. It would make him look too much like a failure.

In his mind, he'd prepared the scene that would greet him in the operations room. A week from the firefight outside Cameron's would see several of the metal desks sitting empty, their investigators either killed or still in hospital. But there'd be a full complement of secretaries, typewriters clattering away, gossipy voices talking down the telephones. Clerks would be moving silently among them like swans across a lake, gathering and distributing files. The pinboards would have new photos, and ribbons stretching between them forming a thick unsymmetrical web.

He stood in front of the door and used the crutch to push it open, a smile lifting his face, ready to greet his team. Instead, there were two janitors inside, stacking chairs on a trolley. Half of the desks had already been taken away, the remainder were empty. All the boards were clear.

'Where's it gone?' he asked numbly.

'Oh, hello, captain,' one of the janitors said. 'Welcome back, sir. Nice to see you on your feet.'

'Where's the operation gone?'

'Sir?'

'My crudding operation! Where's it gone?'

'Chaing.'

He turned to find Gorlan standing behind him. 'What's going on?'

'Director Yaki would like a word.'

Chaing wasn't sure he could make it up to the seventh floor. He had to stop a couple of times on the stairs to take a breath. Gorlan didn't say anything, just waited patiently for him to recover. He could feel how damp his shirt was from perspiration when he finally arrived at Yaki's office.

She looked up from behind her antique miroak desk, and frowned when she saw the state he was in. 'For Giu's sake,' she muttered.

Chaing sank down onto one of the chairs, ashamed to find his vision tunnelling. A glass of water and crushed ice was put into his hand. He drank it gratefully.

Gorlan gave him a disdainful look as she left.

'So I don't need to ask if you're fit for duty,' Yaki grumbled.

'I wasn't going to do any field work,' he countered. 'I was going to sit behind *my* desk. In *my* operations room!'

'Great Giu, Chaing. It's over. You were there, for crud's sake. You saw the Warrior Angel take the pair of them.'

'Someone alerted her. The Eliter radicals. Castillito's associates. They might not know where she's taken them, but it's a start.'

'They vanished,' Yaki said. 'Thirty-seven sheriffs and Corporal

428

Jenifa searched wharf three within seconds of the bazooka explosion. There was nothing, no sign of them. This is beyond us.'

'It can't be,' he implored, fearful he would lose it in front of her. 'Florian was there in front of me, and so was the girl. I had them!'

'And she took them from you.'

'Uracus be damned!'

'There were Fallers there, Chaing. Masquerading as sheriffs – the balls of it! Another nest in Opole that we knew nothing about. Some of Roxwolf's gangsters were Fallers. How did that ever happen? And how did Roxwolf know so much about what was going on? I need answers to all of this, because Varlan is asking me some very pointed questions. You can get those answers for me. Finding that new nest is my top priority now; in fact, it's my only priority.'

He almost nodded, almost gave in to her. 'I want to talk to Stonal.'

'I see.' Her eyebrows rose up at his insubordination. She pulled the black phone across her desk and dialled. Once the connection was made, she dialled the scrambler code and the blue light came on. She flicked the toggle switch for the speakerphone.

'Director Yaki,' Stonal's voice crackled out of the speaker.

'I have Captain Chaing with me,' Yaki said. 'He insisted on talking to you.'

'Really? Hello, captain.'

Chaing wasn't sure, but there may have been a hint of amusement in Stonal's tone. 'Sir, I'd like your permission to carry on hunting Florian and the girl.'

'Do you have any reason to think they're still in Opole?'

'No, sir. They'll be in Port Chana.'

'What in Giu's name makes you say that?'

'Major Evine said Florian and the girl had been forced into Roxwolf's headquarters. Forced. That implies they'd been kidnapped. Then they escaped Roxwolf, and the Warrior Angel was there to snatch them to safety. The fact that she was in Opole implies they were about to be moved, presumably along the underground railway. That always takes wanted Eliters to Port Chana.'

'Well, it certainly takes a lot of them there. But you can't know for certain that's where Florian and the girl are.'

'It's our best lead.'

'Florian's brother left Opole ten years ago. He's never been found, and he's only one of hundreds.'

'You have to let me try, sir.'

'The Port Chana office is already looking for him.'

'She nearly talked to me,' Chaing said in desperation.

'Who?'

'The Warrior Angel. On Hawley Docks. I asked her what was happening. She was going to answer me, I swear she was, then the crudding Fallers fired their bazooka.'

'So you think she'll . . . what? Take pity on you if you show up, and surrender?'

'Not surrender, no. But . . . I've faced her twice now, and I'm still alive.'

'Pick up the handset.'

'Sir?'

'Pick up the handset. I want to talk to you in private.'

Chaing gave Yaki a guilty look and lumbered up out of his chair. She watched him with an impassive expression, but her scar was a hot red jag against her cheek.

'Here, sir,' he said with the handset pressed to his face.

'We're in a difficult situation politically. This Commonwealth girl, we don't know what she's capable of. Unofficially, the government is willing to negotiate with her. That's why I'm going to let you go to Port Chana. You're bait. That is your only value.'

'Yes, sir!' He smiled like a buffoon.

'Make yourself known down there, see if the Warrior Angel gets in touch with you. If she does, the message you will deliver is very simple: we want to talk. That is all you will do.'

'I understand.'

'There's another thing. I don't trust the Port Chana PSR office.'

'Sir?'

'Port Chana is the last stop on the underground railway; you're quite right about that. But the office there is singularly useless in apprehending radical Eliters, and has been for some time. I have to ask why.'

'Oh.' He glanced at Yaki, wanting to ask a whole load of questions about that. 'Got it.'

'I'll clear it for you to run an independent operation there; the local director will provide all the services you require. But take some of your own people, keep them inconspicuous, and run the real search in parallel from our safe house.'

'Yes, sir.'

'Good luck, captain.'

*

It was two fifteen in the morning. The phone rang.

Anala sat upright in bed, focusing hard. All astronauts got used to interrupted sleep; it was part of the training. *Glitches can happen at any time.*

She picked up the phone. 'Yes?'

'This is Sergeant Rebara.'

'Uh, yes?' She clearly wasn't as alert as she thought; the only Sergeant Rebara she could think of was the drill master at the Air Defence Force flight officer school, who specialized in making cadets' lives a total misery.

'I have the results of your last training exercise in teaching room 3-B.'

Now Anala was very awake. The voice . . . It was *him*. She came so close to yelling: *Ry*? Instead she got a grip like a good astronaut.

'Yes?' she said cautiously. 'What was the result?'

'The landing coordinates you worked out were correct, and a full recovery was enacted. Well done.'

'Great Giu,' she whispered. Her gaze went directly to the three-day-old *Varlan Times* newspaper on the table, with its headline: Opole Nest Destroyed.

'I'll call you when your next training session is allocated.' The phone went dead in her hand.

*

Paula's last memory was of the elegant lake house on the Sheldon estate on Augusta. She'd been staying there with Nigel and Vallar, a Raiel; the three of them were preparing Nigel's covert mission into the Void. The plan was a simple one. Humans in the Void had found Makkathran, an ancient Raiel warship that had somehow survived their vanquished invasion a million years earlier. Now the Raiel were desperate for the knowledge Makkathran had acquired during its million-year purgatory. Nigel had agreed to go inside the Void and attempt contact with Makkathran. Paula had been concerned he wasn't right for the mission. There were humans living in Makkathran, a primitive society with a very rigid class structure, where people possessed strong mental powers and weren't afraid to use them. An interloper would need to be subtle, infiltrating them slowly and quietly.

That *so* wasn't Nigel – in her opinion.

So, with acute reluctance, she'd suggested the backup. If Nigel failed, she would carry on with the mission. But it had to be an *extreme* last resort, she insisted . . . and Nigel and Vallar had agreed. Because Nigel considered it so unlikely he would fail, and she personally disapproved of going multiple, she wasn't going to grow an adult clone of herself like he was doing. Instead, there would be an embryo and an external memory lacuna. So she'd gone into the estate's clinic for a secure memory download—

The growth phase from infant to child was a vague period of laughter and tears and deep affection for her father, the one person who was constantly there for her. And pain. Pain that plagued her relentlessly, integral to a body which was being forced to grow far too quickly. She knew frights, too, from some of the people who lurched into her life, only for Daddy to fend them off.

Then finally she'd integrated her memory and become herself again – to find she wasn't in Makkathran, that Nigel had never made it to Querencia. Her home galaxy was millions of lightyears away, and for some reason the package smartcore had taken two hundred and fifty years to activate her.

So: she and Nigel drinking a pleasant vintage burgundy on the lake house terrace that evening just before she'd gone for the download, chatting away in such a civilized fashion about times past and possible options – cut to a nonhuman monster threatening to eat her before trying to blow her brains out in its underground lair. As disorientating events went, she was now the all-time universe champion.

The semiorganic synthesizers in the extensive underground chambers (*why were people on Bienvenido obsessed with putting their secret bases underground; didn't they understand how that limited their escape routes?*) carved into the rock below the farmhouse had produced a decent grey suit for her. The cut was weirdly old-fashioned, which Fergus (*who names an ANAdroid Fergus?*) assured her would go unremarked in any of Bienvenido's towns. She looked at herself in the bedroom's full-length mirror. It had been a long time since she had rejuvenated herself all the way down to eighteen. Despite rejuve being commonplace, Commonwealth society still placed their trust in more distinguished elderly figures, so the most clinics had ever taken her back to was her mid-twenties. Then biononics had come along and she maintained her appearance at a constant thirty.

Now that the forced maturation was complete, she wasn't about to dive right in and use biononics to adjust and tweak her physiology. Nature could take its proper course for the next twenty-two years. *If Bienvenido lasts that long.*

Her ebony hair had been cut by Fergus. He'd actually done a reasonable job. It was still too short for her usual style, so he'd trimmed where necessary, and crimped tightly. The result looked a bit shaggy-wild, but was perfectly in keeping with her teenage features. The suit, too, was reassuringly comfortable. She felt she was finally coming to terms with her new body and circumstances.

It was seven o'clock in the evening when she made her way downstairs. She paused at the first-floor landing window. Kysandra was on the small lawn outside, looking through a long telescope. That starless night sky was something that Paula still wasn't acclimatized to; it alarmed her at some instinctive animal level.

The ANAdroids were all waiting for her at the bottom of the stairs. 'Now that is the Paula we remember,' Valeri said.

She raised an eyebrow at the artificial man. It was understandable that Kysandra had used the ANAdroids as a social support mechanism, accepting them as people, but there was no way she could ever think of them as human. However, she was the outsider here. *As always.* Her lips lifted in a tiny wry smile at the true familiar. 'Thank you,' she said. 'Would you like to call Kysandra in? We should get started.'

'Give her this moment,' Demitri said. 'She'll be in shortly.'

'Of course.' Paula went into the dining room.

Ry Evine was already there, along with Florian. She hadn't seen much of them in the four days they'd been at the farmhouse, preferring to stay quietly in her room with the occasional trips down to the medical capsule when her joints were at their worst. Most of that time she'd spent assimilating the memories which the ANAdroids had prepared for her, detailing a comprehensive breakdown of Bienvenido's history, and information on the Fallers.

Florian got to his feet, a nervous smile on his face. His arms came up, but he clearly didn't know what to do next – hug, kiss, shake hands . . . Paula saved him, giving him a swift hug and a quick kiss that could almost be classed as paternal. He was dressed in a simple dark-orange shirt and navy-blue trousers; she almost missed the colourful shirts and extravagant, furry kaftan he'd worn in Letroy and the mod stable. But he looked a lot smarter now, and quite respectable. Ironically, now that he'd cleaned up and shaved and had some decent sleep, he actually seemed to have lost several years while she was going the other way. 'How are you?' she asked.

'Uh, fine.'

Paula quashed her grin; it was clearly going to take him a while to get over the experience of being a father for ten days. She just hoped he wouldn't carry on feeling all protective of her.

Ry Evine was a lot easier. They shook hands briskly. He was easy to categorize – the epitome of alpha-class human. She'd met so many just like him back in the Commonwealth, the forward crews from CST's exploratory division, and latterly survey starship personnel. They all exuded that same self-confidence, coupled with wanderlust enchantment. Focused dreamers, all of them. She just hoped he wouldn't open with another barrage of questions about Commonwealth spaceflight. It seemed to be about his only topic of conversation.

'Thank you for helping out,' she said as she took a seat at the dining room's big polished walnut table.

'Pleasure,' Ry said as he sat to her right. 'Though I'm not sure I'll be much use.'

'We're going to need as many viewpoints as we can get.'

'Good to know,' Kysandra said as she came in. She was wearing a leaf-green summer dress, with her red hair falling loosely down her back. Her beautiful face was heavily freckled, making her smile even more prominent.

Paula caught Florian's response to this girlish vision as she ran her hand lightly across his shoulders before sitting next to him – opposite Paula and Ry. Florian was clearly a man besotted, and – if she was any judge – hopelessly out of his depth. She wondered if she should warn him, repaying the kindness and devotion he'd shown her. *But he won't thank me, let alone believe me.*

'I think we's reed – red – ready,' Marek said, sitting at the head of the table. Demitri and Fergus sat on either side of their batch brother.

'So what do we do?' Paula said.

'That's why you're here,' Kysandra said. 'You tell us.'

A tad defensive, Paula thought. 'It's not why I'm here at all. I am as unprepared for this as it's possible to be, frankly.'

'But you must have some idea what we can do?'

'I can offer advice based on the situation as I see it. As I understand it, our primary worry is now the reaction of the Faller nests to my arrival. Certainly that was Roxwolf's concern.'

'Are you sure the Commonwealth won't help us?' Ry asked.

'Very sure. When Nigel and I put our mission together, no one in the Commonwealth knew Bienvenido existed. And even if Nigel and the Raiel released the knowledge, they have no way of knowing where we are now.'

'If they knew, would they help?' Florian asked.

'They would help,' Paula said solemnly. 'They would do whatever it takes to rescue us.'

'So we have to get a message to them,' Ry said. 'Somehow.'

'We've examined this,' Kysandra said. 'We can't build a starship, not with the facilities we have. And even if Democratic Unity agreed we could and helped, we're still twenty-three million light-years from the Commonwealth galaxy. An ultradrive would take almost fifty years to reach them. And then there's an equal return time. Whatever we do, we have to do it ourselves.'

'That's what will be scaring the Fallers,' Demitri said. 'They will assume you have brought weapons or knowledge that will allow us to wipe them out.'

'Which I have, of course,' Paula said. 'But building sophisticated weapons on a scale that will eliminate them will take time.'

'We don't have time,' Kysandra said.

'Sensors,' Florian said. 'That's what we need, not weapons.'

'What sort of sensors?' Paula asked.

'Ones that can pick out Fallers. We don't need new weapons; our carbines and Gatling guns can kill a Faller very effectively. What we need are verifiable targets.'

'Nice idea,' Paula said, mildly impressed with the way he'd analysed the situation.

'Forget sensors,' Ry said. 'People need biononics.'

'Also a valid solution, but there's an even bigger problem introducing them. Biononic organelles do replicate in tandem with cellular mitosis, so the new cell also contains one. Which is fine for embryos; when the child reaches maturity they are embedded and ready to begin full functionality. However, to implant them into an adult requires time.'

'It took three years for our medical module to enrich my cells with them,' Kysandra said. 'Admittedly I had to stagger the treatment sessions, we were so busy. But at best it would take eighteen months per adult.'

'And for those without functioning Advancer traits, it would take even longer,' Paula said. 'The biononics would have to be manipulated to create a neural interface within the brain. I remember the upheaval it caused in the Commonwealth when the Sheldon Dynasty released the technology. There was a fundamental schism which to some degree still exists. In this case, I expect it will increase the divide between natural humans and Eliters. Besides, it doesn't solve the time-critical problem.'

'Plus, we don't have anything like the resources for that,' Kysandra said. 'All we've got is a single medical module and three functioning semiorganic synthesizers – though functioning is pushing it for one of them. We can release the knowledge of how to build anything, but the actual construction process requires an industrial base which simply does not exist on Bienvenido.'

'Some kind of political agreement will have to be made,' Paula said. 'The government must understand how severe the Faller threat is.'

'They do. That's why they fortified Byarn,' Kysandra said. 'It's their refuge from which they'll reclaim Bienvenido. Uracus, they even call it Operation Reclaim.'

'Nuking this continent won't reclaim it,' Paula said, recalling the files the ANAdroids had prepared for her. 'Surely they know that?'

'Operation Reclaim uses low-yield bombs. The thinking goes that the land will take a century or so to recover, and after that they'll spread out from Byarn to repopulate the planet.'

'That's crazy.'

'Yes,' Demitri said. 'But like everything on the planet, it all goes back to Slvasta. The government has always known Fallers are prevalent on the other landmasses. His idea was that after the last Tree was blown up, the Air Force would use low-yield bombs on the islands and continents to wipe out the nests. And when the radiation decayed to safe levels, we could claim them for ourselves, and occupy the whole planet.'

'Didn't he understand what Macule was?' Paula asked in annoyance. 'That planet is a perfect example of why you don't use nukes – period. Never mind for some ethnic-cleansing programme.'

'You don't quite appreciate how much Slvasta feared the Fallers,' Kysandra said with a regretful sigh. 'He wasn't rational on the subject. To him, widespread nuclear bombing was a risk worth taking if it resulted in eliminating Fallers from Bienvenido. This is how the government still thinks.'

'Then I should probably talk to them,' Paula said. 'Come to an agreement over us accelerating the planet's technology base.'

'Good luck with that,' Kysandra muttered.

'Politicians will always talk.'

'Democratic Unity are crudding fanatics; the only thing they hate and fear more than Fallers is the Commonwealth. Nigel's legacy here is toxic like you wouldn't believe.'

'I have some experience in this field,' Paula told her, 'and we have the entire knowledge of the human race to trade with. There will be something they want; at the most basic level they need to survive. That is ultimately the hope that I can offer them.'

'But we have no time,' Kysandra said heatedly. 'If we're going to defend this planet, we need all these advanced manufacturing facilities yesterday. It took Nigel years to build the solid rocket boosters to get *Skylady* back into space. And you're not Nigel.'

'Kysandra—' Florian said uneasily.

'No, I'm right. The whole reason Paula is here is because she's not Nigel.'

'Correct,' Paula said. 'So we have to find a different solution. At the extreme, we might consider offering the Fallers an evacuation deal.'

'What do you mean?' Ry asked.

'They hold off any further attempts to take over Bienvenido while we build ark starships.'

'Crudding Uracus,' Florian exclaimed. 'But there's millions of humans! How long would that take?'

'A century, probably,' Paula said.

'The Fallers aren't going to agree to that. You heard Roxwolf. All we are to them is a mealtime on the road to their civilization dominating the planet.'

'Florian is possibly correct,' Valeri said. 'Such an arrangement does not fit with Faller psychology.'

'I'm outlining options,' Paula said, unperturbed. 'Do you have any line of communication to Democratic Unity?'

'No.'

'Then I need to open one.'

Kysandra nodded reluctantly. 'I know someone who has direct access to the head of Section Seven, and in turn he has the confidence of the prime minister. We've just heard he's coming to Port Chana. I'll ask him.'

*

It was a two-hour drive south-west from Opole. The Adleton collective farm was nestled in the saddle of a low valley, the first of eight farms stretching along its thirty-two-kilometre length. The valley floor was mathematically flat, potato fields alternating with sugar beet and broad beans. Up on the slopes, pines and bluewoods covered the rumpled ground all the way up to the stony crests, above which huge mantahawks soared on the thermals, their kite-wings keeping them aloft for days at a time as they soundlessly stalked their prey below.

The farm compound was a big square area surrounded by a high wooden fence in bad repair. Twenty single-storey log cabins formed a neat row on one side, where the families and farm workers slept. Larger communal buildings formed another side, while opposite them were the barns and silos.

The ground was muddy, churned up by tractors and hooves. Chaing's crutch kept slipping about in the stuff, slowing his walk from the car to the administration building, where Shanagu, the farm manager, had his office.

Shanagu – a middle-aged man who spent most of his time behind a desk rather than working outside in the fields – greeted them with the same cautious enthusiasm that everyone affected when the PSR came knocking. Chaing and Jenifa warded off all his offers of drink and food.

'We're here to see Corilla,' Chaing said when he was sitting in a leather wingback chair. *It must be a prosperous collective*, he thought; Shanagu's office had expensive furnishings and a heavy gold and blue rug on the floorboards – a decor which to Chaing spoke of a pre-Transition aristocrat's hunting lodge.

'I see,' Shanagu said guardedly.

'Problem?' Jenifa asked. She was wearing her PSR uniform, jacket and trousers perfectly pressed, peaked cap holding her short hair out of view, which made her look beguilingly young. That youthfulness – combined with her unsmiling, clearly humourless persona as she stood rigid-backed beside Chaing's chair – was guaranteed to make the most innocent citizen feel guilty about something.

'No more than usual for her kind,' Shanagu said.

'Her kind?'

'Eliters.' Shanagu went for the conciliatory angle. 'Look, we're not a prison; we just do some correctional work for the county justice office.'

'I wasn't aware Corilla had been sentenced,' Chaing said.

'She's not a justice office case. It's like this, nearly a third of our Comrade workers have been assigned here by the Department of Labour – the usual layabouts and hotheads. It's our duty to the state to install a sense of worthiness, show them their place in society, make them understand they are valuable. Eliters are always such a pain. They consider themselves better than everyone else – the arrogant cruds. She's just the same, young and condescending; thinks she's an intellectual and shouldn't be working with her hands. But good, honest physical labour will make her come around in the end, you'll see. We have a good record here handling recidivists.'

'I'm sure you do,' Chaing said. 'If you could call her in, now, please? And we'll need to talk to her alone.'

'Is she in trouble?'

'If she is, it's happened since she arrived here,' Jenifa said curtly.

It took twenty painfully long minutes before Corilla arrived. Chaing almost laughed as she stomped into the office. The feathers had vanished from her black hair, which was now gathered into a practical braid. She wore dungarees which were smeared in mud and grime; knee-high boots were thick with muck that wasn't a hundred per cent mud. Shanagu tried to keep his face composed as she trod the dirt into his fancy rug.

'You two,' she grunted, her hostile gaze sweeping from Jenifa to Chaing, lingering on his straight leg and crutch. 'What happened to you?'

'The Warrior Angel happened.'

'Is that a slogan? I thought your people said she doesn't exist.'

'Thank you,' Chaing said to Shanagu. 'We'll take it from here.'

Jenifa closed the door behind him and stood in front of it, arms folded over her chest.

Corilla ignored the belligerent stare she was being given and sat herself down in Shanagu's chair. She started opening the desk drawers. 'He keeps the good booze in here somewhere, I know he does.'

'Corilla,' Chaing said patiently.

She looked up. 'Paid for from all the illegal deals the commune makes with local merchants, if you're interested.'

'Not in the slightest. How would you like to get out of here?'

'What I'd like would be for you two to eat crud and die.'

'You're angry with me.'

'Wow, nothing escapes the mighty PSR, does it?'

'I didn't send you here.'

'The PSR did. Whose uniform are you wearing?'

'I can get you out,' he repeated levelly.

Corilla pulled a fat oval-shaped bottle of Dirantio out of the lowest drawer. 'Gotcha!'

'I need your help.'

She finally looked right at him, her face animated with naked fury. 'I helped you before. Now see where I am. Where I'm going to be for the rest of my life if I'm crudding lucky. This is the future I so *dreamed* of when I went to university.'

'I'm sorry.'

'Yeah, it just oozes from you.'

'Do you want to leave or not?' Jenifa snapped.

Corilla glared at her for a moment before flipping the bottle neatly so she was holding it by the neck. 'Hey, bitch, how bad do you think I could rip your face up before your cripple boyfriend limps to the rescue?'

Jenifa pushed away from the door, hands becoming fists.

'Enough,' Chaing said. 'I get it; you're pissed off. Third and last time I ask: do you want me to get you out of here?'

Corilla inhaled deeply. 'To where?'

'Port Chana.'

'You're crudding kidding me!'

'No.'

'Why there?' Corilla asked suspiciously.

'You heard there was a new nest alert?'

'Yeah, we get news even here. And the non-existent Warrior Angel brought that alert to a very public end at Hawley Docks, didn't she? Good job someone is genuinely helping the people of this world.'

'She and the people she helped escape have probably gone to Port Chana. I need to find them. I thought you'd like to help.'

'Help you do what?'

'Find the Warrior Angel. You'll be an informant, same as before. Tell us what's in all those messages the Port Chana Eliters are sending to each other.'

'You want me to betray the Warrior Angel to the PSR? Could my life get any better?'

'It's not her I'm interested in, it's the people she's protecting. The Fallers want them badly, and there's no telling what lengths they'll go to.'

'What people?'

'A man called Florian; we think he's developed some kind of weapon. The Fallers are reacting badly. Very badly.'

'You mean they're going to launch their apocalypse?'

'I have no idea how they'll react. But,' he tapped the splints on the side of his leg, 'they're serious enough to try and take on the Warrior Angel in broad daylight. We have to try and calm the situation. And to do that, I have to locate Florian and determine exactly what he's up to.'

'Right,' she said uncertainly.

'I have the authority to reinstate you at Opole University. But of course, there has to be a university left for you to return to . . .'

'Ha! Some choice, then.'

'I guess so.'

She held up the bottle. 'I get to keep this.'

'Deal. Go and pack. You've got ten minutes before we drive out of here.'

Corilla sauntered past Jenifa, giving her a smug victory smile as she passed.

'Seriously?' Jenifa asked as the door shut behind Corilla. 'She'll be broadcasting everything she knows about us to the radicals the second we arrive in Port Chana.'

'I sincerely hope so,' Chaing said, holding his crutch firmly, ready to lift himself from the chair.

'You expect her to betray you?'

'I'd be disappointed if she didn't. I want the Warrior Angel to know who's hunting her.'

'You want to meet her *again*?'

'Correct.'

'Why, Chaing? Look what happened last time.'

Chaing shoved down hard on the crutch, levering himself upright. 'Next time will be different. I know it's coming.'

*

Supper, served by the ANAdroids, was braised beef short ribs with portobello mushrooms, dusted in shallots and smoked folal cheese with a red wine jus, and served with buttered korril rice and steamed vegetables picked that afternoon from the farmhouse's garden.

Paula ate about half of her plate, enormously relieved that the impulse to completely stuff herself with whatever food she could grab had finally subsided. She did manage all of her raspberry crème brûlée, though.

The formal meal seemed oddly momentous, which she supposed was a realistic appraisal. What they were proposing was essentially going to usher in the end of an era.

While the ANAdroids were clearing away she followed Kysandra outside, back to the telescope. A gentle breeze was blowing in off the sea, playing soft discordant notes as it eddied up the tall cliff.

'I'm sorry about before,' Kysandra said sheepishly. 'I was being unhelpful.'

Paula stared out across the estuary, where Port Chana glowed with a bright twinkling haze against the darkness. 'You've spent two and a half centuries defending this world, then I come along and advise you to change everything. You're entitled to an emotional reaction.'

'Quite.' Kysandra took a sip of her dessert wine and peered into the telescope's eyepiece. 'Although it was going to change anyway.'

'I'd like to ask you a favour.'

'What's that?'

'Florian. Let him down gently.'

Kysandra stood up and gave her a surprised glance. 'You're concerned about Florian's love life? Why? Do you . . .'

'No. My feelings towards him are purely maternal.'

'That's – weird. He's just spent a fortnight being your father.'

'Welcome to Commonwealth ageing issues.'

'Crud.'

'He's a good man. He stood up for me against incredible odds.'

'Then he deserves some happiness, surely.'

'He certainly does. I don't want him hurt, that's all. His emotional involvement is a lot higher than yours. You're his first true love.'

'He is rather sweet. And he might well be my last love. It's funny, how they all genuinely think you're going to save us.'

'And you don't?'

Kysandra shrugged and went back to the eyepiece. 'Maybe if you'd turned up even fifty years ago, we might have had time. But you know as well as I do that we don't have the resources to achieve anything now. When the Fallers come, they will come in their millions. Tens of millions, probably.'

'So what do you suggest?'

'Oh no, I'm clean out of ideas. I made my mistakes a long time ago. Now I'll live with them. And die with them, I expect. But if you make a deal with Prime Minister Adolphus, it will just confirm the Fallers' fears.'

'Damned if I do, damned if I don't.'

'Is that a quote?'

'It is. I just don't know where from.'

'That's quite comforting, that you admit you don't know everything.' Kysandra lifted her head. 'Do you want to see?'

'Certainly.' Paula walked over to the telescope, and put her eye to the lens. It was centred on a faint swirl of light. 'A galaxy?'

'The Commonwealth galaxy,' Kysandra confirmed. 'Your home. I look at it every night it's in the sky. I get a silly degree of comfort knowing there are humans living there, that they'll carry on living even after we're wiped out. And . . . Sometimes I imagine him, looking up into the night from that planet he owns. I believe he's there, searching for Bienvenido, wondering where we are.'

'Him?'

'Nigel. Am I being stupid?'

'You're being human. That's never stupid.'

'Is he looking for us?'

'I can't answer that.'

'Yeah. I know. Don't want to dash my hopes.'

Paula straightened up and looked into the blank, black sky where the telescope was pointing. There was nothing there, nothing at all. 'Twenty-three million lightyears.'

'So the ANAdroids say.'

She looked towards the east, where the bright point of Ursell had risen. With her retinas on enhanced focus, she could actually see the solar-energized haze shimmering around its unnaturally thick atmosphere. 'Laura certainly wasn't doing things by halves, was she?'

'Fireyear Day is an annual celebration,' Kysandra said. 'It's a grand carnival in all the towns and cities.'

'Laura came up with a simple swift solution. Using floaters like that was inspired.' Paula searched across the sky, seeing blue Aqueous, the grey-white glimmer that was Trüb, then almost directly overhead the pale pink gleam that was Valatare. 'And none of the other planets have native species we can ask for help?'

'No. At least, not that Laura could find while the wormhole

was active, and the Space Vigilance Office hasn't picked up any signals since. They keep a good watch, too.'

'I could probably break the wormhole's codelock. I have routines that weren't even around when it was built.'

'What good would that do?'

'We could evacuate some people to Aqueous. Children and some guardians.'

'The island areas are small. You could only take a few thousand at best.'

'And Macule is a radioactive desert?'

Kysandra nodded and drank some more wine. 'Yes. The ANAdroids call it nuclear winter. They had the really big dumb war – the one Earth managed to avoid.'

'We're all here because we were too belligerent or stubborn for the Void to tame.' Paula fixed Aqueous with a pensive stare. 'We could send boats through the wormhole to Aqueous. They could anchor together, form a floating city. If we give every Eliter that goes with them Commonwealth technology files, they might be able to bootstrap their way up to a spacefaring civilization. Once they're in space they could build starships. Trouble is, most solar systems have asteroids and comets that can be mined. This has nothing.'

'Trüb has twelve tiny moons,' Kysandra said. 'If your spaceships get there, they could mine them.'

Paula's secondary routines called up all the information the ANAdroids had on Trüb. 'That's a strange one,' she murmured. Trüb was completely featureless, it had no mountains or basins; no oceans nor even polar caps. Just a uniform grey wasteland – presumably of dust or sand, but even with a low-pressure argon–carbon dioxide atmosphere, there were no storms. And the twelve moons . . . It wasn't impossible for a planet Trüb's size to have twelve natural moons like that – but highly unlikely. 'There is no ecosystem at all; no life. So if nothing lives on it, what's it doing here?'

'I have no idea.'

She began to review the other planets. Asdil: a solid world larger than Bienvenido, orbiting seven hundred and forty seven million kilometres out from the sun, with a thick, cold nitrogen–methane

446

atmosphere clotted with many cloud layers, denying any glimpse of the surface. Radio silent.

Fjernt: forever in conjunction with Bienvenido on the other side of the sun. Another solid world, but with no free oxygen in its nitrogen–carbon dioxide atmosphere. Laura Brandt hadn't detected any radio transmissions on her brief exploration mission. Which was the only thing Paula cared about. The cellular bio-chemistry of a species was irrelevant; she wanted a technological civilization, someone who could help. If there were any sentients living on the worlds Bienvenido shared this lonely sun with, they weren't developed enough to come to their aid. All she was really doing was confirming what Laura Brandt had discovered when she drew up her plan to fight the Prime.

'Why do you need asteroids to mine?' Kysandra asked.

'Actually, we don't. If we can build ingrav and regrav systems, we could start mining the other planets directly and not have to come back here.' Paula sighed. 'I'm not an industrialist. And it's all purely theoretical right now.'

'The floaters were intended for mining, weren't they?'

'Yes.'

'The two Laura used to kill Ursell are still working.'

'We'd have to get to them to change their operation. I wonder – the package that brought me must have some kind of ingrav. Using it might have to be part of the deal I offer Adolphus.'

Kysandra smiled dryly. 'Old times, getting Commonwealth spaceships back into space. But it would have to be careful orbiting Valatare; Laura said the gravity was wrong.'

'She said what?'

'Valatare's gravity is wrong.'

'Wrong how?'

'I think . . . the gradient was too steep.'

'How can—? When did she find this out?'

'When she opened the wormhole.' Kysandra grinned. 'Actually, you can see for yourself if you want.'

'How?'

'One of the "technicians" helping Laura develop the atom bombs was Valeri. He was there in the crypt the day we defeated the Prime. Slvasta and his cronies didn't know what he was, so he was able to go on and work with the Manhattan Project. He offered some subtle guidance to build bigger bombs until they got the yield up to three hundred kilotons. Those are the ones the Liberty flights take up to the Ring to kill the Trees.'

Paula couldn't help the small twitch of her lips at Laura using the name Manhattan Project. 'So you were behind the bombs and the Silver Sword?'

'This is my world, Paula. I'll defend it to the end.'

'I know. I do admire what you've done.' Her u-shadow opened a link to Valeri. 'Could you show me your memory of Laura opening the wormhole to Valatare, please?'

The farmhouse's terrace rippled away, replaced by the crypt below the palace. A tense, tired Laura Brandt stood in front of the wormhole.

'Well?' Kysandra asked eventually.

Paula had to grip the telescope hard for balance; she thought her knees might give way. Her personality might be over a thousand years old, but her brand-new teenage body was still remarkably susceptible to emotional surges. 'The baddest of them all,' she whispered.

'Excuse me?'

'Every planet here is home to a belligerent, untameable species. The Void saw all of us as a danger. But some are a lot more dangerous than others.'

'Oh crudding bollocks, are you saying Valatare is worse than the Fallers?'

'No, not if I'm right.' She couldn't keep the smile from her face. For the first time she actually began to feel hopeful. 'I just have a theory, that's all. But it changes everything. Come on.' She hurried back towards the farmhouse. Her u-shadow called Florian and Ry, telling them to come to the dining room.

'What are we doing?' Kysandra asked.

'We need a new plan. Because, let's face it, just asking the government for help is fairly pathetic.'

Fergus and Valeri followed Florian and Ry into the dining room.

'What's happened?' Florian asked, looking intently at Paula's face.

Paula made an effort to rein back her exhilaration. She sat down and took a moment as the others reclaimed their chairs. 'Two things. Firstly, an emergency survival option. If the Fallers do launch their mass attack against humans, we need to evacuate as many people as possible.'

'Evacuate?' Florian asked. 'You mean, to Byarn?'

'No, I mean to Aqueous.'

'How are we going to get there?' Ry asked.

'I may be able to open the wormhole in the palace vaults. If I can, we send boats through for people to live on. We'll take mostly children with some adult guardians. They'll need to be Eliters, and we provide them with all the files we have. We also send through all the equipment from here. My hope is that a colony nucleus can elevate themselves up to a level that can at the very least build an ultradrive starship, one capable of making it back to the Commonwealth with a message. It's not a great plan, but it does save Bienvenido's humans from complete extinction.'

'I can imagine the price Adolphus will demand for giving you access to the wormhole,' Kysandra mused.

'If he comes with us, then so be it. He will not be in charge when we get there. That is something he will have to accept.'

'You'll be admitting to the government that the situation is hopeless,' Ry said bitterly. 'That even you can't stop the Fallers.'

'Not quite. I'm hoping all Aqueous will ever be is a contingency. We need to open the wormhole to Valatare.'

'Valatare? What the crud is on Valatare?'

'The theory behind this star existing is that the Void banished all the planets here because the species living on them inside the Void were either a threat or refused to submit to the Heart. Right?'

Kysandra nodded. 'We're here because of the quantumbuster. The Vatni are as obstinate as Uracus, they always refused to be guided by the Skylords. The Prime – well, we all know about them. And whoever used to be on Macule were clearly hugely antagonistic

– they blew themselves up once they regained their industrial technology base.'

'Trüb and Asdil we're not clear about,' Paula said, ticking them off on her fingers. 'But they don't seem to have any active aliens. Same goes for Fjernt, which is unscathed.'

'Laura assumed the Fjernt species managed to build starships and went home,' Kysandra said.

'Reasonable,' Paula said. 'Because you'd have done that if it wasn't for the Fallers. Which leaves us with Valatare. As far as I'm aware, the Commonwealth never found a native sentient species in any gas giant. There are various microbes in the atmosphere of some of them, but a sentient evolving there – it's not impossible, but it's very unlikely. And Valatare's gravity is wrong, which implies it's artificial.'

'Artificial?' Ry barked. 'A whole planet?'

'Not a planet,' Paula said. 'A prison.'

There was silence in the dining room. She looked round at all of them, resisting the impulse to smile at their surprised expressions. 'There is one other species that we know is extremely hostile to the Void: the Raiel. So hostile, they've kept a million-year vigil to prevent other aliens being ensnared by the Void. So enraged that the Void's expansion could one day consume the entire galaxy they sent an armada of their greatest warships through the barrier to destroy it.'

'The armada was defeated,' Demitri said.

Paula cocked her head to one side and smiled at him. 'Exactly. And where does the Void send its beaten enemies?'

'Oh crudding Uracus,' Kysandra whispered. 'You think they're in Valatare?'

'The Void beat them, yes, but the Raiel warships are formidable. I know, I've been on one. So it sent them here, but the distance back to our galaxy is nothing to the Raiel – a moderately inconvenient few decades of flight, if that. So to be sure they never posed a threat again, the Void imprisoned them. That's what I believe Valatare to be. Underneath the atmosphere there's some kind of barrier holding them in.'

'The gravity gradient,' Fergus said quickly. 'It's like a miniature Void barrier.'

'It probably works on the same principle,' Demitri said. 'It's just the scale which is different. The Void consumes stars to power itself; Valatare consumes the hydrocarbon atmosphere.'

'Good,' Paula said. The ANAdroids couldn't come up with ideas of their own, but set them a problem and they'd use logic and a process of elimination to force-compute a solution.

'Will they still be alive after a million years?' Florian asked apprehensively.

'I suspect they won't be a day older,' Paula said. 'A major component of the Void's internal spacetime was the variable temporal flow. Humans were living on Bienvenido for three thousand years, yet out in the galaxy only two hundred years went by. The Void wouldn't want the Raiel to be active inside their prison, not with the resources available to those warships. They'd probably manage to find a way to break out. I may be wrong . . .'

'But you're not, are you?' Kysandra said softly. 'There's a file on you in the smartcore Nigel left behind.'

'Checking up on me?' Paula enquired.

Kysandra smiled thinly. 'Very thoroughly.'

'Would the Raiel help us?' Ry asked.

'They will help us,' Paula assured him. 'Even if it wasn't us breaking them out, they'd help. That's what they're like. Besides, they owe me a few favours.'

Kysandra poured herself the last of the dessert wine. 'I'll bet they do,' she mumbled.

'So how do we do it?' Florian asked eagerly. 'How do we jailbreak the armada?'

'With difficulty,' Paula said. 'Are we absolutely sure there's no more Commonwealth technology left? Valeri, your memory showed me nothing apart from the wormhole under the palace. What else did the Captains hang on to? Is there anything else left of *Vermillion*'s cargo?'

'Effectively nothing,' Valeri said. 'The wormhole Laura Brandt reactivated is still there, but codelocked. All the others were cannibalized to repair it and the two floaters. There are no synthesizers or extruders left.'

'Nigel cleared all the quantumbusters out of the armoury,' Kysandra said. 'I helped him do it. The medical modules the Captains hung on to broke down two and a half thousand years ago. All that's left now are some components which the Section Seven advanced science division is scratching its head over. I have an asset in that department, who has supplied us with an inventory, but if you're looking for something to bootstrap our manufacturing base up to Commonwealth levels, it's not in the palace.'

'Three colony starships came to Bienvenido,' Paula said calmly. '*Vermillion* landed to found Varlan. What happened to the other two?'

'The *Verdant* splashed down in the Gulf of St Ives, seventeen kilometres off what is now New Angeles,' Fergus said. 'They salvaged what they could, which wasn't much; it took them months just to build wooden-hulled boats back then. That was more than thirty-two hundred years ago. There's nothing left of it now.'

'And the *Viscount*?'

'Nobody knows.'

Paula checked the faces at the table, startled at how they all seemed perfectly content with that statement. 'The starships the Brandts built for this colony attempt were a kilometre and a half long. How can they *not know* what happened to one?'

'According to the *Landing Chronicles*, they never found it,' Ry said. 'Their auxiliary flying craft carried on working for up to a fortnight after they arrived, so they managed to gather everyone together at the *Vermillion*'s landing site. Once that was done, they made some over-flights of the islands, but there was no sign of it.'

Paula rested her elbows on the table and tented her fingers. 'If *Viscount* had left orbit for another star, they would have seen it go. I take it there have been expeditions to all the landmasses on Bienvenido?'

'Yes,' Fergus confirmed. 'In the first couple of centuries the Geographical Association sent expeditions to every landmass on the planet. They never found a crash site.'

'It has always been assumed *Viscount* came down in water,' Valeri said. 'Presumably the Eastath Ocean; it is the largest.'

'No tsunami? And nothing ever washed ashore?' Paula asked. 'Ever? If it broke up on impact, there would have been thousands of tonnes of debris which floated. If it didn't break up, the crew would have had time to escape.'

'So where is it?' Florian asked.

'There's only two places it can be,' Paula said. 'One of the polar continents.'

Fergus and Valeri looked at each other, then at Kysandra.

'Logical,' Fergus conceded.

'Which pole, though?' an intrigued Ry asked.

An image taken from the Captain's Cartography Institute slid up into Paula's exovision. 'The southern polar continent, Lukarticar, is the largest. It also has an unmapped interior, so those ancient expeditions probably only charted the coastal areas. That makes it the most likely.'

'Lukarticar is unmapped because it's big and desolate,' Kysandra said. 'If the *Viscount* did come down there over three thousand years ago, it'll be underneath at least fifty metres of snow and ice by now. How are we going to find it? This is needle-in-a-haystack territory.'

'Your semiorganic synthesizers can still produce ge-eagles,' Paula said. 'Fabricate a new batch with upgraded sensors and communications and take them to Lukarticar. They'll find it.'

'That's quite an expedition,' Kysandra said with a sly smile growing on her lips. 'Too big for the sub. We'll need a proper ship. And I just happen to know an obliging captain.'

3

Chaing was surprised by how small Port Chana was. Given how prominently it featured in his life – with the endless rumours of its status as the capital of radical Eliter activity, the probable hometown of the Warrior Angel and the final destination of the underground railway – he'd been expecting something altogether more grandiose. The buildings were made from thick granite blocks to withstand the winter winds blowing in off the sea, which made them imposing but hardly significant. Industry was mainly ware-house storage for all the farm produce harvested across the rich lands of the county to the west, and the docks, where bulk cargo ships competed with the rail freight companies to ship all that food out to the rest of Bienvenido.

The PSR office was on Haigal Avenue, a commercial street which ran back directly from the waterfront marina where all the smaller, more prestigious stores were clustered. Buses roared along it, belching out thick fumes, elbowing their way through the cars and vans. Unlicensed food stalls cluttered the pavement, tipping pedestrians over into the dedicated cycle lanes, creating a constant chorus of angry bells. The pace of life here was more like one of the larger cities, Chaing decided, everybody busy and rushing.

He made his way carefully across the pavement. Most people moved out of the way when they saw his uniform and crutch, but some had to be stared away. There were several youths strolling along in their outlandish clothes; he'd noticed them about the city, inevitably in their twenties, dressed like colourful tramps with long unkempt hair, looking like they were high on narnik half the time. Talk in the PSR office was that they did it in reaction to the strictness of their regiment service.

Port Chana's temperature was lower than in Opole, so he'd felt the chill in his customized uniform with its thin cloth. Today, his third day, he'd worn a sweater under the jacket – which had to be cut to fit over the cast. But at least he'd finally got rid of the eyepatch and dressing on his face.

Decent vision allowed him to see the taxi with its green 'for hire' light on sixty metres away. He raised his crutch. The taxi shot over two lanes with other vehicles tooting angrily. It wasn't much bigger than an Opole tuk-tuk, but it had four wheels and two passengers could fit in the back. Just.

Chaing climbed in and told the young driver to take him to Empale Street. He couldn't drive himself, and he'd politely turned down all Director Husnan's offers of providing a car and driver. Officially he had a room at the Raffiat Hotel on the waterfront and he didn't want the local office knowing different.

He spent most of the journey pulling on an ankle-length raincoat. As disguises went it was pretty ineffectual for a man with an arm in a cast and using a crutch, but it would cover the fact that a PSR officer was going into a house on Empale Street every day.

The Section Seven safe house was a typical Port Chana two-storey, three-bedroom fisherman's cottage, one in a long row of similar homes with tiny back yards making up the winding street that rose up a gentle slope. Chaing paid off the taxi, and waited until it had driven round the corner before crossing the road and walking back five houses to number seventy-three.

Jenifa was in the ground-floor living room, jacket off, sleeves rolled up as she read through reports. The long table was covered in files, as were most of the chairs.

'Good news,' he said, and dropped the thick briefcase down on the table in front of her.

'What?'

'More reports.'

She gave him a sour look. 'Funny.'

Under Stonal's direction, every PSR office on Lamaran was now running an investigative analysis operation, compiling reports of 'unusual' commercial or engineering activity. Stonal was hunting any clue that might indicate the Commonwealth girl was building something. So far a team of Port Chana investigators working under Captain Fajie had found nothing. But that wasn't good enough for Stonal, so every evening Chaing would bring back the team's reports, and he and Jenifa would go through them all again. In addition to that paperwork, Corilla was supplying them with any suspicious cargo invoices she could find from the railway yard, where she'd been placed in the handling office.

'We're not getting anywhere, are we?' he said.

'No.'

'I just wish I could come up with a new angle.'

'Section Seven has been hunting the Warrior Angel since the Great Transition,' she said. 'We've been here three days.'

'I know, but the situation has changed now.'

'Are you going to tell me you can "feel" it?'

Chaing gave her an annoyed glance, wishing she'd keep barbs like that for the bedroom. 'I'm acting on instinct *and* logic,' he said patiently. 'This is the most likely place she'll be.'

'Have you seen anything to suggest Stonal is right about the local office being compromised?'

'No. Director Husnan doesn't like me being there, but that's to be expected. And Fajie is a straight arrow; her team are doing their best.'

Jenifa pushed the paper away and leaned back in the chair, yawning. 'I don't like it here.'

'Take a break; I'll make some coffee. Then we can go through the rest of this crud together.'

'No.' She stood up, stretching. 'I'll get the coffee. I don't want you in the kitchen.'

'Okay.' Chaing couldn't judge the tone. Was she saying she didn't want him to risk a boiling-water accident because he had his arm in a cast, or that he couldn't make decent coffee? It was strange: each night they went up to the bedroom and had the best sex ever, but the rest of the time it was almost as if she didn't like him. He was always slightly on edge around her, never forgetting her suspicions about the whole Castillito incident. While he was in the hospital, recovering from the explosion, he'd had the most vivid dream of her taunting him.

The smart thing would have been to leave her behind in Opole. He just couldn't bring himself to make the break.

Chaing shook his head to clear it. *Just concentrate on getting the job done.* He sat down at the table and opened the briefcase. Two dozen files spilled out.

*

Florian had a fast shower in the small en-suite, then put on a towelling robe and went back out to the bedroom. It had been a long day, with the whole farmhouse a bustle of activity. He'd taken part, of course; the ANAdroids always found some task for him, though he suspected they could do it themselves in a tenth of the time. Today they'd had him making up lists of food to take on the expedition. He'd quite enjoyed that, even though it wasn't fancy food. The farmhouse's smartcore had catalogues of every supplier in the county on file, so after the lists were compiled, he'd gone on to place orders. They couldn't be large orders, nothing that could attract attention, and they had to be shipped to a warehouse company on the edge of Port Chana, sometimes via intermediaries. There were a dozen different bank accounts, false invoices, different delivery firms, never the same route. The farmhouse had a secure cable down to the town's three telephone exchanges, wired in to circumvent PSR monitors. He'd thought about putting on different voices on the phone, but that was taking it a stage too far. Besides, his false accents were seriously cruddy.

It had been a rewarding day; he'd achieved a lot. Probably not as much as everyone else, but they wouldn't starve on the trip. And now there was going to be sex.

He hopped onto the bed and looked expectantly at the half-open door. Lots of sex. Great sex. Like every night since he'd arrived, and sometimes during the day, too. Kysandra was so utterly divine. He didn't even think about the risks facing them on the expedition, how the Faller Apocalypse was going to come crashing down on them very soon now, nor did he care that Captain Chaing had arrived in town to continue his hunt. Those things were just intervals between his time with Kysandra, endured and enjoyed as much as filling in all those eternal warden office reports.

'Florian,' Kysandra's voice called from the landing.

He smiled in anticipation and rolled over on the bed, feeling his erection growing. 'In here.'

'I've got a surprise for you.'

'Is it that little black lace number, the one that makes you look really hot and dirty?'

'Er . . .'

'Hello, Florian.'

'Mum!' Florian yelped in horrified surprise as Castillito peered round the door.

'Oh Giu, you really are here.' There were tears in her eyes.

'Mum.' He hurried over and hugged her – still blushing furiously. He saw Kysandra standing on the landing, an unreadable expression on her face. Then her lips twitched, and she gave him a little finger wave. A link opened from her u-shadow. 'See you later,' she told him.

Then his mother was stroking his face, needing the reassurance of touch. He was surprised she was so anxious. She'd been such a force of stability and calm throughout his life, always supportive, always encouraging, understanding and tolerant with his coding obsession. She hadn't even shown any disappointment at him signing up for the warden service, though he knew it was a bitter blow to her. She'd aged, too, which shocked him. It had only been seven years. Guiltily he realized his letters home had gradually become fewer and fewer.

'They told me the PSR had arrested you,' he said.

'Captain Chaing himself,' she said with what sounded suspiciously like pride. 'I was the one who gave him a black eye.'

Florian remembered Chaing walking towards them at Hawley Docks, wearing an eyepatch. 'Really? That was you?'

'I guess we've both surprised each other.'

'I didn't visit you in Opole,' he blurted. 'I wanted to keep you safe from the PSR.'

'I know. I guessed you'd be with Terannia.'

'I was. They smashed up her club. And they arrested her as well for a bit. I really messed up.'

'Silly boy. You made it here.'

'And you,' he said in wonder. 'How are you here?'

'Underground railway, of course. I've dispatched enough people along it. It was an interesting experience. Not exactly first class the whole way.'

'You're safe; that's all that counts.'

'Safe from the PSR, for now. From what I understand, that isn't going to last for long.'

'No, it probably won't.'

'The Warrior Angel said you'd tell me what's going on.'

'Oh. Did she?'

'Yes. It was quite overwhelming finally meeting her. Such a pretty girl, too.'

Florian gave his mother a curious look. She'd never used that teasing tone on him before. 'Yes, she certainly is.'

'Well done, you.' She pinched his cheek playfully. 'So what has been happening? Why was the entire PSR going crazy hunting you?'

'Let's go downstairs. I'd like you to meet Paula. And you're going to need a drink.'

*

The log fire in the lounge was still blazing away, so they sat on the sofa and chatted away in a fashion which surprised Florian. He tried to tell his mother everything that'd happened without bragging too much, but she seemed genuinely impressed by what he'd done. She actually stumbled over her words when he introduced her to Paula, which she never did.

459

'So,' he said when his story was over. 'Do you know where Lurji is? They'll be looking for him now.'

'Lurji is fine,' Castillito said. 'And you're an uncle, by the way. He has a daughter: Zoanne. She's eighteen months old.'

'Really? That's amazing.'

'Yeah. He calmed down a lot after he left Opole; I think burning down the mayor's residence made him realize how he'd run too wild. He lives on a farm about a hundred kilometres away. I'm going to visit him next. I want to see my grandchild before—' She sucked on her lip.

'Not going to happen,' he said, gripping her hand for emphasis. 'Paula is amazing. And the team here . . . equally cool. We'll find the *Viscount*, don't you worry.'

'My son,' she shook her head ruefully. 'Always the quiet ones.'

'Tell Lurji hello from me.'

'Will do.'

'And, Mum. Who's my father?'

'Oh, Florian.'

'This is the end coming, Mum. We either die in the Faller Apocalypse or the Raiel will take us home to live in the Commonwealth like we always dreamed of. Either way, I deserve to know.'

'You do, yes. His name is Salvatore.'

Florian was surprised by his own reaction: he felt nothing. The name was just some syllables; it didn't mean anything. He'd been expecting it to resonate somehow, to connect him. 'Thank you, Mum. Is he still alive?'

'I honestly don't know. We agreed not to stay in contact – to protect you and Lurji.'

'When this is all over, I want to find him.'

'You want to ask me why, don't you? Why we split up? Why I never told you? Why I never registered your father at the birth?'

Florian nodded meekly, keeping his gaze away from his mother's face.

'Well, don't worry; we weren't one of those couples who split up and are so bitter we can't stand each other afterwards. It's actually rather special. You see, your father's great-grandmother was Dionene.'

'But—' There was only one person he knew called that, and he didn't need his secondary routines to run a file search for that, either. 'She . . . I don't . . . No! Really?' His heart was beating faster. 'The Dionene?'

Castillito was smiling sheepishly. 'Yes, Florian. Your great-great-grandmother is the youngest daughter of Captain Philious. She escaped the revolution and Andricea's psychotic massacre of her family. That makes you and Lurji the direct descendants of the Captains of Bienvenido. The last of the line.'

'Crudding Uracus!'

'Which means there are quite a few people, not just in the PSR, who would like to exterminate you simply because you exist.'

Florian started to chuckle, and it soon became a full laugh.

'What's so funny?' Castillito asked curiously.

'You know Ry Evine saved me? He snatched me and Paula away from Chaing.'

'Yes. You said.'

'Ry is related directly to Slvasta.'

She grinned. 'I never knew Giu had such a sense of irony.'

'Thank you for telling me, Mum.' He embraced her. 'I missed you. If you'd asked me to stay, I would have done. You know that, don't you?'

'That's why I never did, darling. It's not easy being a mother; we all know we have to let go at some time. And you couldn't have stayed in Opole. You were so miserable it was killing me to see you like that. You had to leave to grow. And how you have grown!'

Florian was worried he was going to start crying.

'We're going to save Bienvenido. You'll see.'

'I know, darling.' She patted his leg. 'Just don't go thinking you're invincible. You're not.'

*

The Ankatra Cafe was at the western end of Port Chana's waterfront, with a hedge of bushy heliotrope-shaded trasla trees marking out a snug area for their pavement tables outside. Jenifa walked along the edge of the marina at midday, where the rigging ropes slapped constantly on the masts of the yachts and yigulls circled overhead, vigilant for unwary sightseers leaving their pasties or ice creams unguarded. Her legs still ached from last night's hot athleticisms; with Chaing practically immobile, she had to exert her splendid body to thrilling extremes. In bed he was completely obedient, so much so she sometimes wondered if he did remember what she'd done to him in the Opole hospital. Uncertainty heightened the whole experience quite deliciously.

She walked past the outside tables into the cafe. It was darker inside, with traditional yalseed oil lamps hanging from the beams, casting a shady jasmine illumination across the small black tables. Corilla was sitting in her usual corner, munching on an almond croissant, with a glass of hot chocolate with whipped cream in front of her.

Jenifa sat opposite her, keeping her face rigid with disapproval. 'Have you got anything for me?' she asked the Eliter.

Corilla shrugged pugnaciously. 'Plenty. It's all crud, though.' She slid a brown paper store bag out from under her seat.

Jenifa dropped it into her own bigger, woven shoulder bag. The weight of the dockets from the rail freight office meant a couple of extra hours tonight. She almost asked: *then why did you bring it*? But that would have been an excuse for Corilla to start bitching. So instead she asked: 'What are the Eliters talking about today?'

'Same as yesterday. Everyone's worried about the Faller Apocalypse. They know what happened on Hawley Docks was important.'

'Did they say how it was important?'

'No, just that the Warrior Angel wouldn't show herself unless something really heavy was going down. People are speculating about Florian.'

'In what way?'

'Saying he has weapons. Does he?'

'No. He's a forest warden, for crud's sake!'

'Okay. No need to bite my head off.'

'Are they saying anything about the Warrior Angel?'

'Not much. No one knows if she can hold off the Fallers if they do overwhelm the rest of Lamaran. Talk is, probably not. Unless we use nukes.'

'There's too much talk of the Faller Apocalypse,' Jenifa grunted disapprovingly. 'Too much like traitor propaganda.'

Corilla rolled her eyes. 'One day you'll learn: we're all in this together. The only people who discriminate between humans are you. What kind of person would ever ally themselves to Fallers?'

The image which immediately dominated Jenifa's sight was the firefight outside Cameron's, where gangsters had fought alongside Fallers. 'Bad ones,' she said softly.

'You're crazy. No human would do that. We'll be fighting against them just as hard as you, despite everything you've done to us.'

'Faller Apocalypse is just more Eliter lies.'

'Like breeder Fallers and the Warrior Angel? So what was that attacking us in Frikal Alley?'

'A cat.'

'Like bollocks was it!'

'You would be wise to focus on your job.'

'I'm working ten-hour shifts in that cruddy office. Those are dockets that I thought you might want to see. It's not me that breaks deals.'

Jenifa picked up her shoulder bag and stood up. 'I'll see you tomorrow.'

'Already looking forward to it.'

Jenifa smiled thinly, imagining how Corilla would look, stripped naked and strapped to the frame in the safe-house inter-rogation cell. *Not so smug, I'll bet.* She wondered if Chaing would agree to that. He'd enjoy watching; she'd make sure of that. 'And if you hear anything—'

'Emergency phone number memorized.'

Jenifa walked out and hailed a taxi. 'DeMarco Hotel,' she told the driver.

Nobody apart from her mother knew about the room she'd taken at the DeMarco, which was an easy three streets' walk from the safe house. She spent a couple of hours there every day, which is why she was always so far behind when Chaing came back to the safe house at night. She spent those hours going through his old Portlynn case files, which Yaki had sent to her.

The DeMarco was a lovely old five-storey building with an elegant interior which had remained in good condition. She walked through the lobby, heading for the broad curving stairs.

'Ma'am,' the receptionist called.

He had to call again before Jenifa even looked round, surprised to find he really was calling to her. *Why?* She felt a slight chill, her senses alert. Hand at her side, resting close to the concealed pistol.

'What?' she asked crisply as she reached the desk.

The receptionist was intimidated by her attitude. He reached to the wall of pigeonholes behind him. Room 101 – her room – had a folded sheet of hotel notepaper. He handed it to her, and quickly looked away.

It read

Courtyard Bistro, corporal.
C.

Jenifa took a good look round the lobby, but couldn't see anything remotely suspicious. 'Who gave you this?' she demanded.

'It was given to Mariebelle; she was on duty this morning. I can ask when she comes back for the evening shift.'

'Never mind. Where's the Courtyard Bistro?'

'Through the bar, ma'am.' He pointed.

As she went through the bar, she slipped the safety off her pistol. Calling it the Courtyard Bistro was somewhat aspirational for a paved area eleven metres long and three wide, possessing five tables *à deux* under pergola beams draped with a vine. The ancient granite wall at the back had two narrow slit windows opening to the alley which ran behind the hotel. It was empty.

Jenifa gave the kitchen doorway a suspicious look. She could hear the head chef shouting at his sous chef inside.

'Over here, corporal,' a female voice said.

Jenifa drew her pistol and walked to the back wall. 'Who is it?'

Castillito walked past one of the open slits. Jenifa ran forwards and shoved her pistol through the gap. Castillito was out of sight, and she couldn't get any kind of angle up or down the alley.

'Remove your hand or I'll smash an iron bar across it,' Castillito said.

'Crud!' Jenifa glanced up, but the granite wall was nearly four metres high. No way could she scramble up it. *Bring one of the tables over?* But the pergola beams formed an effective cage lid. Something slapped her hand firmly in warning. Furious, Jenifa withdrew the pistol. When the barrel was level with the slit she had her widest angle, but Castillito remained out of sight. She was on the left, though; Jenifa was sure of that. 'What do you want?'

'I've got some information for you. It concerns your boss, Captain Chaing. You know, the one who betrayed you back in Opole?'

Jenifa gritted her teeth and brought the pistol back through the slit. 'What about him?'

'Those old files you're looking through in your room upstairs, they're not going to tell you what you want to know.'

'How did you—' She cursed herself for playing Castillito's game. 'Then what do I need to know?'

'The two of you are alone in that PSR safe house every night. Are you screwing him?'

'I am going to come round there, and you'll be—'

'He's one of us.'

'Us? What do you mean? A radical?'

'Oh, no, little girlie.' Castillito chuckled. 'Think bigger.'

Jenifa slammed her fist against the stone slit. 'Tell me!'

'He's one of us, a filthy Eliter. How do you think he managed to call the Warrior Angel to Xander Manor? How did she know he was heading for Hawley Docks?'

'No! You're lying.'

'Oh, you'll rage and shout about it for a few minutes, then you'll calm down and you'll know. Goodbye.'

'Wait! If he was an Eliter, there's no way you'd betray him to me!'

'This is personal now. He was going to catch Florian, my son.

Prove to you all what a perfect little PSR bastard he is. Florian would have been tortured for weeks; and when you were through with him, you would have either murdered him in your dungeons or sent him to a yellowcake mine where the radiation would have rotted him to death. So, yes, I'm betraying Comrade Chaing, because I know what you'll do to him. My only regret is that I don't get to watch.'

'How much has Chaing told your people? Does the Warrior Angel know we're here? We want to talk to her!'

There was no answer. Jenifa shoved her face into the slit, but she still couldn't see along the alley. She knew it was empty, though. Castillito was gone. 'Giufuckit!'

4

The crypt after midnight always seemed to be quieter than during the day – which was ridiculous, Faustina acknowledged. The advanced science division's machines still hummed and buzzed at the same volume. There weren't any technicians about, but that was the only physical difference. Yet somehow, night's calm had descended to claim the big chamber.

She often worked late into the night, but tonight was the first night since the Commonwealth space machine had arrived that her colleagues had finally packed in and gone home before one o'clock. They'd made some progress on various measurements, and they knew for sure that electric discharges couldn't penetrate the force field; nor could a thermal lance. For the last couple of days they'd been working on the maser device that had been brought out of storage.

Faustina kept on reading the old reports for twenty minutes after the last technician left, then got up and stretched. She walked over to the bank of recording instruments that were focused on the big pearl-white cylinder, and carefully unplugged the sensor components. That way the tapes would keep running, but record nothing. Her u-shadow opened a link. 'Can you receive me?'

'Oh, this is interesting,' the machine replied. 'That's a Commonwealth u-shadow link format you're using, but the same generation as my own routines. So I'm guessing you've not arrived here recently?'

'No, I'm one of the Warrior Angel's team. Two things. First, she thought you'd like to know that Paula is now safe and grown up.'

'Thank you. Which makes me curious what the second thing is.'

'Paula wants to know if you can get into space again. She needs you to fly some kind of survey mission of Valatare.'

'What's a Valatare?'

'It's the gas giant planet. And if you can fly, you have to go into polar orbit around Bienvenido first to see if you can locate the *Viscount*; we think it crashed at the southern pole.'

'If I could fly properly, there's no way I'd be here. Sorry. My drive units took a pounding in the quantumbuster blast.'

Faustina gave the cylinder a small smile. 'I remember that. The light was brighter than a hundred suns.'

'You remember it? Your Advancer genes' age resistance is the best I've ever seen.'

'They're not. I've been rejuvenated a couple of times in Kysandra's medical module. Each time I come back with a new face and start to work my way back into government. It's my penance.'

'I'm starting to understand; I did wonder if you knew the connotations of your name. That must have been some original sin.'

'It was. I used to be called Bethaneve. I was at the heart of the revolution; I helped overthrow the Captain. I believed in us back then. I believed we were ushering in an age of freedom and liberty. Then my husband took over. He was a monster, and I never saw that until it was too late.'

'We all have a bad *morning after* at some point in our lives.'

'You're a very strange machine. I know the ANAdroids, and they don't talk like this.'

'You'll have to forgive me; I'm somewhat hazy on recent local history. Are you talking about Nigel's ANAdroids?'

'Yes. Do you know them?'

'I have a file on them. This machine was a subsidiary component of *Skylady*, Nigel's starship.'

'Is there any way you can be fixed to fly again?'

'I have a couple of integral semiorganic synthesizers, but thcy don't add up to self-repair functionality. So unless you happen to have a lot of sophisticated manufacturing systems to hand, I've got all the flight characteristics of a brick.'

'Alas, that's our problem.'

'Please explain.'

'It's called the Faller Apocalypse.' Faustina told her u-shadow to send over various files.

'Those goddamn monsters,' the machine exclaimed when the download finished. 'They're the ones that got me, right at the start.'

'Got you?'

'Yeah. I was on the *Vermillion* – or rather, my original body was. I'm Joey Stein. I was part of Laura Brandt's Shuttle Fourteen mission into the Forest. But these days, I'm just a backup memory waiting for a re-life clone. And that likelihood seems to be slipping further and further from reality.'

'You're Joey Stein? Amazing,' Faustina said. There were so many questions she wanted to ask, but none of them relevant to helping Paula and Kysandra.

'But if the *Viscount* survived, then Paula really may be able to do something,' Joey said. 'Our cargo was deliberately built *sturdy*. Each of those colony ships was self-sustaining, in case we got separated by some freak accident – and you don't get more freaky than the Void. In theory, you should be able to rebuild an entire Commonwealth-level society with just half the systems carried on one ship.'

'You can?'

'A lot of *ifs* in there, my new friend, including the biggest ask of all: time. And from what you've shown me in those files, time is getting kinda critical.'

'It is.'

'All right, so we have to do what we can.'

'You said you can't fly again.'

'That's not the kind of help I was thinking of. Our people, Paula and the Eliters – part of their plan is to open this wormhole, right?'

Faustina's gaze lifted to the enigmatic gateway at the back of the crypt. At the same time, her u-shadow reported the space machine was transmitting a torrent of link files. She held her breath, fascinated to see if the guardian force field would finally switch off.

'Bollocks,' Joey said. 'Laura knew what she was doing when she codelocked that. Paula might be able to crack it, but I can't.'

'I see.'

'That was five seconds of trying. You're not going to quit on me just with that, are you?'

'Of course not.' She grinned.

'Glad to hear it. So, if we can't go down the physical route . . . This city – Varlan, right? This is the capital?'

'Yes.'

'So we've got all the top politicians here?'

'Quite literally. This palace is still the seat of government. They're sitting six levels above us.' She gave the cylinder a thoughtful look. 'How does that help?'

'We arrange for Paula to have political cover.'

'How is that possible?'

'Politicians in a one-party state are paranoid little shits, always looking to do a deal to put themselves on top. At least, that's how it used to be on old Earth. I take it that hasn't changed?'

Her grin faded. 'It hasn't.'

'So we make them an offer they can't refuse – especially if we can make them think they're making the offer to me.'

*

Jenifa sat in the safe house's living room and dialled the direct number. A loud two-tone whistle sounded in the headset, and she dialled another four numbers. A small blue light came on, confirming the link was scrambled and secure.

'Hello, dear,' Yaki said. 'What have you got for me?'

'I've found it,' she said, so excited there was a tremor in her voice. 'I know his secret.'

'Superb. What is it?'

'He's an Eliter.'

'Chaing? Not possible. It would be on his file.'

'Like Lauraine, you mean? This makes perfect sense. How else did the Warrior Angel show up at Xander Manor at the right time? And Hawley Docks? He must have called her with a link.'

'How did you find this out?'

'Castillito told me.'

'Castillito? I didn't know she'd been captured.'

Jenifa was glad Yaki was over a thousand kilometres away, so she couldn't see her jaw clenching. 'I didn't capture her. She came to me.'

'You didn't interrogate her, then? She volunteered that information?'

'Yes.'

'You've been played, dear. They found out you're in Port Chana and want to break your operation apart. At least it confirms you're getting close.'

'Chaing is an Eliter,' Jenifa said stubbornly. 'He's always been cosy with that Corilla.'

'Give me one reason why they would expose one of their own to you?'

'Castillito wasn't acting for the radicals. This was personal. She wants revenge for Florian. We would have tortured him to death, you know that.'

'You probably would have.'

Jenifa said nothing. Waited . . .

'All right,' Yaki said eventually. 'I admit, that was quite a coincidence, the Warrior Angel showing up each time. But that doesn't give you enough to arrest him.'

'I wasn't going to. This is a Section Seven safe house. I can go to work on him here. The interrogation room in the basement is fully equipped. I can break him before the local PSR office even realizes he's gone. He'll confess, I swear.' She licked the sweat that had started to bead on her upper lip.

'And without him, your investigation to find the Commonwealth girl will slow. It's too convenient.'

'Mother! This is what you wanted. No, it's better. Stonal person-ally recruited an Eliter into Section Seven. He'll be ruined. And you can bring it to the attention of the security cabinet.'

'All right. Forget Chaing's old case files. I'm going to send you a link detector.'

'A what?'

'A gadget Section Seven have developed. It detects Eliter trans-missions, and it's small enough to fit in your pocket. So you carry it with you at all times.'

'Suppose he doesn't—'

'For crud's sake, do me the courtesy of *trying* to think like a PSR officer! It'll be with you by tomorrow evening. Once you have it, feed him some information that any Eliter would have to tell his fellow radicals about. See if the device lights up.'

'Of course. Yes.'

The blue light went off. Jenifa stared at the dead handset for a long moment before replacing it in the cradle. 'Crud!'

*

Chaing got back to the safe house an hour after sunset. The wind from the sea had been constant all day and now clouds were scud-ding in, blocking any view of the Ring glinting across the night sky.

He found Jenifa sitting at her usual chair, the living room illu-minated by five wall lights that seemed dimmer than usual, casting long shadows off the piles of paperwork. For once she wasn't reading through files. He took one look at her pensive expression. Most people wouldn't be able to tell, but he knew her well enough to see the burning anger held back like a beast in a cage.

'What's wrong?' he asked.

'I found something, today, sir. It might be our first lead.'

'Excellent.' He slung the briefcase on the table and sat beside her. 'Show me.'

Reluctantly, she handed over a slim folder. There were only four sheets of paper inside, a ship's manifest. He skimmed through the typed lines. Shrugged. 'Looks okay to me.'

'Does it, sir?' The tone was pure aggression.

'Is there a problem?' His leg had been aching all day, the pain-killers were making him feel queasy, and the sense of frustration from the going-nowhere investigation was turning him tired and short tempered. What he wanted was a rest, a quiet meal, and a decent sleep.

'I don't know, captain,' she replied levelly. 'Read it again, please.'

To duck out of an argument he glanced at the file again. The manifest was for the *Gothora III,* which had just arrived in the harbour – a small independent ship that carried cargo up and down the coast, with agents in every port pushing their contacts for consignments. One of hundreds of similar ships, whose captain-owners were up to their eyeballs in debt and struggling to pay the state maritime enterprise office its percentage.

Gothora III had arrived from Helston, delivering crates of spare parts to several Port Chana companies that specialized in servicing agricultural vehicles. It was due to depart in a few days for Perran-porth, after taking on supplies and a new cargo.

'I still don't see anything wrong,' he told her.

'The cargo has been changed,' she said.

Another glance at the papers, exasperation building now. 'Yeah, it was due to take timber along to Lynton. The agent switched it. Perfectly normal for this kind of small-time operation. Someone undercut them, or the Perranporth contract pays better.'

'The economic investigation team at the PSR office is supposed to be on the lookout for change.'

'Something out of the ordinary is their actual brief.'

'Which is why they singled this out in the first place. An unex-plained change.'

'And why they haven't followed it up. It's perfectly normal.'

'It's the only one.'

'What do you mean?'

'I've looked through hundreds of transactions, every type of company for fifty kilometres – chemicals, ores, engineering, agricultural, electrical, cars, lorry haulage firms, train freight, even banks. All the abnormal orders and cancellations and alterations.

Thousands of the crudding things. This is the only ship that's changed *everything*. You're quite right: other ships have added to their cargo, they've had orders withdrawn and given to other captains, it happens all the time. But the *Gothora III*'s entire cargo has been changed, along with its destination. All in the last three days.'

Chaing frowned, his finger tracing down the manifest. 'Engineering supplies for Rodriguez Tooling, and Katina Precision Milling, type not listed. Hmm. The order was put together by South Coast Wide Shipping.' He glanced up at Jenifa. 'Are they legitimate?'

'I checked with the state enterprise register. South Coast Wide is over forty years old, founded and owned by someone called Lubbeke, employs nine people in its office. All perfectly normal.'

'Well, they would have to be,' Chaing murmured.

'So?'

'Unusual,' Chaing agreed. He opened the bottle of painkillers and popped a couple of pills. 'Okay, here's what we're going to do. If it is something the Warrior Angel is involved with, I don't want to warn them off, so we don't tell Director Husnan's people.'

'You want to keep it from the PSR?'

'I want to keep it from the Warrior Angel. That's why you and I are here boring ourselves stupid with this cruddy paperwork. Stonal doesn't trust the Port Chana PSR, remember? Tomorrow we make some quiet enquiries. We'll need the *Gothora III*'s registry documents from the marine registry, and a listing for Rodriguez Tooling, and Katina Precision Milling from the state enterprise office. I also want PSR files on the crew.'

'If they have any,' Jenifa said.

'Route that request through Section Seven in Varlan. They can pull the information from their central records; that way, no one else will know we're asking.'

'All right.'

'Then first thing tomorrow, you and I are going down to the docks and taking a look at the *Gothora III* for ourselves.'

'Tomorrow?'

'Yes.'

'So we're not doing anything tonight?'

'No more paperwork, no.' He unbuttoned his uniform jacket and slipped it off. The painkillers were dulling the ache in his leg, and interest in the *Gothora III* had banished his lethargy. 'But you and I are going to draw up a strategy to monitor this curious ship. And then we're going to bed so I can thank you properly.' He knew he was playing with fire, but he just couldn't stop.

*

Jenifa bit back on her impatience as they climbed the eternal spiral stairs up the inside of the lighthouse that perched on the end of Port Chana's harbour wall. When they arrived at the docks that morning, they quickly identified three decent observation points. Two of them they ruled out on grounds of practicality; both were in wharfside buildings with a lot of people. Chaing in his current state would always draw attention. So . . . the lighthouse it was. The keeper was startled when Chaing showed his PSR badge, but smart enough not to complain. As Chaing pointed out, he was the only person who knew they were here, so if that knowledge leaked there would only be one arrest.

Chaing took the stairs so crudding slowly, his crutch clattering on the stone steps, and had to stop for a rest every couple of circuits. They reached the lantern room seventeen minutes after they started up.

Jenifa shrugged out of her backpack, and started setting up the tripod. Chaing opened a window and trained a powerful pair of binoculars on the *Gothora III*, which was berthed two wharfs down the harbour from their position.

'I am crudding shattered,' he complained.

Jenifa nodded as if being sympathetic. She was pleased with herself for containing her hatred last night. But her strength had allowed her to overcome any emotional weakness, so she held her tongue, biding her time as they worked out how best to mount an observation on the *Gothora III*. Thanks to Yaki's scepticism, she still wasn't a hundred per cent certain about his heritage, which was deeply frustrating. Part of her was so sure. She needed absolute proof, though. It was a real shame the link detector wasn't going to arrive until tonight. Her discovery of the *Gothora III* was exactly the kind of thing he would warn the Warrior Angel about. She'd even considered holding off telling him, but that was an outright dereliction of duty.

She fixed the camera with its huge telephoto lens onto the tripod, and focused it on the *Gothora III*. The mid-deck cranes were offloading its cargo, winching the heavy wooden crates onto waiting flatbed trucks. She zoomed in on the crew members standing round the open holds, and waited patiently until they were facing her before snapping off several shots.

'Looking pretty normal,' she muttered.

'Our targets aren't going to march on board in broad daylight.'

'You think they're already there?'

'I don't know. I doubt it, though. Not enough escape routes if we do raid the ship.'

'So they'll come aboard last minute?'

'Impossible to say. You told me they all just vanished after Hawley Docks. That kind of target is hard to capture.'

'Then we just give up?' she taunted.

'Not at all. Once we understand them, we'll know how to approach. They must know the PSR is hunting them.'

Jenifa was glad he was still peering through the binoculars so he couldn't see her guilty flush. Castillito had clearly known every aspect of their mission. *But he must know that. So he's playing a double bluff, right?* 'You're probably correct. But you and I are still one step ahead.'

She waited for him to respond. When she looked up from the camera, she saw his back was rigid. His binoculars weren't pointing at the *Gothora III* any more, either.

'Chaing?'

'We're not alone.'

It was the dead tone he used which sent a chill down her limbs. 'What?'

'Warehouse five. Remember it? The one with the offices along the front? We considered it when we arrived.' He handed her the binoculars. 'Good vantage point, but too many people would have seen me struggling up to the fifth floor. Take a look.'

With a growing sense of trepidation she swung the binoculars round to warehouse five, concentrating on the highest row of windows. It was a big building with granite walls and a curving corrugated-iron roof. A huge sliding doorway dominated the end, with flatbed trucks and forklifts moving in and out constantly. The opening was framed by offices. She could see through the windows on the three lower floors. People were sitting at desks, answering telephones, calling to each other, hurrying out to the warehouse floor carrying batches of urgent papers. The fourth-floor windows were grimy, the rooms inside given over to storage of some kind, while the fifth was practically deserted. She almost missed it – a single small pane had been removed from one of the iron-framed windows on the fifth floor. Someone was inside, standing a metre or so away from the gap, a pair of binoculars pressed to his face.

'Crudding Uracus,' she hissed. She took a step back, filled with a horrible vision of the other watcher taking a photo of her face.

'So . . .' Chaing said. 'Either Section Seven is running another dark operation just like ours that they haven't told me about, or the Fallers are also curious about the *Gothora III*. And I don't think it's Section Seven.'

*

Captain Fajie's office was on the third floor of the PSR offices. *Naturally*, Chaing thought petulantly as he wheezed his way up the final flight of stairs. He'd taken some painkillers on the taxi ride back from the harbour. They didn't seem to make much difference.

Fajie looked up as he limped in. She didn't even bother to put on a pleased-to-see-you expression.

Chaing used his crutch to push the door shut, and sank into the chair. 'We have a problem,' he said.

'My team is working as hard as they can, Comrade,' Fajie said defensively. 'You can't expect instant results, not with this much paperwork involved. They're dedicated people.'

'I'm sure they are,' Chaing said. He took out his small Section Seven badge and pinned it to his lapel.

Fajie stiffened. 'I did wonder,' she said sullenly.

'Relax, I'm not here to deliver a reprimand.'

'Yeah, right.'

'So much cynicism. I need you to arrange a new squad for me.'

'What's the operation?'

'No operation. We're not even having this conversation. There is no paperwork. Do not use the telephones to call people.'

'You want me to run a dark operation? Crud, Chaing, I've got to clear it with Director Husnan.'

'Answer me this: how many nests are active in Port Chana right now?'

'None. We have a good record on that front, at least.'

'Wrong answer. I've just encountered one.'

'You can't . . .' She looked seriously worried. 'There's a nest?'

'Yes. And for one to exist without this office even picking up a hint is something I find deeply disturbing.'

'Right.'

'So no Director Husnan. You will hand-pick five of your people that you personally can vouch for and allocate them some aspect of the current investigation that requires them to be reassigned outside this building. We will convene in the Decroux Cafe in two hours, and I will brief them. We're going to run an observation on the nest; follow its members, find out where they're based. Then they will be taken out. I'm calling my director to get a detachment of Marines down here.'

'Yes, sir,' Fajie said. 'You can depend on me.'

5

Stonal was hoping for something impressive when he walked into the crypt. New computators, their magnetic spools spinning fast. Big exotic instruments clustered round the Commonwealth machine. Dramatic, dynamic progress. Faustina had certainly sounded animated enough on the phone.

Instead there was the maser, which looked like a fat telescope fixed to the end of a hospital X-ray machine. It wasn't even plugged in; big coils of cable lay on the floor next to its pedestal. Apart from that, all he could see was a small table with what looked like a home-built radio sitting on it. There was no casing, just a metal frame supporting naked electrical circuit boards and glowing cathode tubes. Faustina was standing beside it. She was the only person in the crypt.

'Where is everyone?' he asked. The advanced science division normally had about twenty technicians and researchers in the crypt.

'I have them working in our other laboratories this morning.'

'And the reason for that . . . ?'

'Is for *security*,' she said, as if trying out the word for the first time. 'This is possibly a little sensitive. Politically, that is. I may be wrong, of course.'

Now Stonal was deeply curious; Faustina simply didn't do political at any level. 'When you called me, you said you'd made progress.'

'I said there had been a development,' she countered.

'Please, no semantics. What's happened?'

'We were calibrating the maser when I noticed some interference.'

'From the machine?'

'Yes. The emissions were very fast and very regular, operating in the microwave band, not the link frequencies the Eliters use – which is what we'd expect from Commonwealth technology. I had a theory.' She rested her hand on the newly assembled radio apparatus. With a rather too-knowing smile, she flicked a toggle switch, cleared her throat portentously, and picked up a microphone. 'Are you receiving me?'

'I can hear you,' a voice replied from the circular speaker fixed to the contraption's frame.

Stonal gave the Commonwealth machine a shocked look. 'Is that . . . ?'

Faustina nodded, her smile insufferably proud. 'Oh yes.' She held out the microphone. 'Try it.'

He took the microphone. 'Hello?'

'Greetings, human. We come in peace. Take me to your leader so I may serve you.'

'What?'

'Fried or baked?'

'Uh—?'

'Serve, get it? That's a first-contact joke. Mind you, it is several thousand years old, and probably wasn't all that funny back then, either. So I guess the old ones aren't always the best ones after all.'

Stonal gave Faustina a bewildered glance; this was so not part of any scenario he'd rehearsed in his mind.

She just shrugged. 'Think of it as a very smart and precocious thirteen-year-old.'

'I heard that.'

He brought the microphone up to his lips. 'What are you?'

'You're looking at a custom-built life-support pod with enhanced medical capabilities. In other words, I keep people alive in space emergencies.'

'Custom-built? In the human Commonwealth?'

'Correct.'

'Uracus!'

'That's your local bad-god, right?'

'Uracus was . . . a dangerous part of the Void.'

'Well, thank crap we're not there any more, huh?'

'Are you alive?'

'Ah, a philosophical question. Okay: I was born human. My thoughts were placed in this machine for safekeeping after my body started to be eggsumed. So you tell me if I'm a living thing. Personally, I think I'd pass the Turing test with ease.'

'The what?'

'It's a test to examine an entity for sentience.'

'Wait – you were eggsumed?'

'Yes, all of us were. Except for Laura, of course. Nigel managed to rescue her.'

'You knew Mother Laura?' he whispered in awe. 'Who are you?'

'Joey Stein. Hyperspace theorist, at your service.'

'You were one of Laura's companions in the Forest!'

'Is there an echo in here? Yes. I was trapped in a timeloop for three millennia, then jailbreaked just in time to get the shit kicked out of me by the quantumbuster. If there are any media companies still active back in the Commonwealth, they're gonna be bidding trillions for my story.'

'So you've been watching us from space since the Great Transition?'

'As best I could. Plenty of my sensors were damaged in the blast. Plus, I collided with a Tree, and stuck to it.'

'3,788-D,' Stonal said quickly.

'That's the one.'

'It was you. You diverted the Liberty missile.'

'Yep. Got it to strike where it would do the most good. Smashed that fucker apart like it was made of glass.'

'And flew down to Bienvenido afterwards.'

'Flew is a bit of an exaggeration. Plummet is closer. I had a tiny bit of thrust left, so the impact didn't break me apart.'

'And you brought *her* with you,' Stonal said coldly. The wily friendliness of the machine was starting to annoy him.

'Yes.'

'To subvert our whole society. I should have you dropped into the deepest ocean, or buried at the bottom of a mine shaft.'

'Whoa there, big fella. Nobody's subverting anything. I exist to sustain my cargo's life, period.'

'You gave her to an Eliter.'

'You mean young Florian? He was the only human answering my distress beacon. He said this government was a dictatorship, that you persecute anyone with functioning macrocellular clusters.'

'We do not persecute them. We have laws which they constantly challenge. They claim they are better than us. If we drop our guard, they would rule us like the Captains of old.'

'Bad history, huh?'

'Very. Who did you bring to this world? What is her purpose in coming here?'

'Paula? She's a high-ranking Commonwealth diplomat from the alien contact bureau. Nigel brought her along in case he needed her to negotiate with the local government.'

'A diplomat? He should have brought her to life while he was here. His legacy is not favourable.'

'Got you out of the Void, didn't he?'

'Not everyone would agree that is a good thing.'

'You and I are going to have to differ on that.'

'What will she do?'

'Help you. Without prejudice.'

'That bothers me. Can you contact her? She should help the legitimate government, not Eliters. They are radicals.'

'If you took me up to the roof and she was in the city, I could link to her. But apart from that, no.'

'Then what use are you?'

'From a practical standpoint, none at all. However, I do have lots of technical information in my memory. That should be useful to someone.'

'Weapons, you mean?'

'Yes, but I would need guarantees that you'd only use them

against Fallers. There are ethical issues to consider before I hand over weapons of mass destruction to people I can't veto.'

'The weapons we have kill Fallers quite effectively already, thank you.'

'Glad to hear it. And congratulations on nuking the Trees. Your spaceships are doing a fine job, there.'

Stonal narrowed his eyes to regard the machine thoughtfully. 'I have trouble believing you. You have an answer for everything. You are too glib.'

'Listen, pal, I've waited two hundred and fifty-seven years. I can wait another two fifty, no sweat. This isn't a biological body; I have no time imperative.'

'That means what, exactly?'

'I don't get bored.'

'I am curious now. What are you waiting for?'

'You keep this society static, right, you and your government pals? That makes it easy to control, to maintain your own status.'

Stonal glanced at Faustina, who was frowning as if that was not something she'd considered before. 'Our society has evolved to stability,' he said genially. 'I believe that to be an achievement that should not be cast aside.'

'But it will be. When all the Trees are gone, blown up by your Liberty missions, you will be free of the Fallers and that will trigger massive change. Trust me; history is littered with revolutionary transformation mechanisms. I can give you the cultural anthropology lectures, if you like.'

'No thank you. Please explain how this will affect you. You are a machine that has fulfilled its function.'

'My primary function, yes. But once Bienvenido regains contact with the Commonwealth, these memories will be re-lifed.'

'What do you mean, re-lifed?'

'They'll grow me a new body and download my memories into it. I'll be born again: re-lifed.'

'Great Giu,' Faustina whispered.

'I'd do it myself,' the machine continued, 'except I haven't got my own genome in store. But there are copies back on Earth.'

'You await life, then?' Stonal asked. 'I'm talking to an . . . embryo?'

'Interesting angle, but I'll go with it. And it will happen. After the Fallers are gone, your socioeconomic development will continue along more normal lines. It may take a couple of centuries, but you will have starflight again; hell, I can even supply you with the blueprints. I have all that Commonwealth scientific knowledge in my memory – hyperdrive, immortality, fusion power, neural processors, everything. I can cut the development time from Liberty rockets to trans-galactic starships down to a few decades.'

Stonal turned to Faustina. 'Please leave.'

'What?'

'Leave.' He didn't elaborate, merely waited for compliance. She gave him an annoyed glance, then walked out. He waited until the door was closed behind her before bringing the microphone up to his face again. 'We're not going to win.'

'Excuse me?'

'Against the Fallers. We are not going to win. The Trees are irrelevant now. The nests are too well established down here, and multiplying. You will not be re-lifed in the Commonwealth. Indeed, once they have devoured us, they may break you open and learn how to build your precious starships. They will be able to fly to every galaxy, including the Commonwealth!'

'Nothing can get through this force field.'

'Indeed, but how long will it last? Another thousand years? And after that, what then?'

'I'm a machine. I lack the biological imperative to survive.'

'How nice for you. What does that mean?'

'If it comes to that, I can self-destruct without a qualm. They will never retro-engineer me, or gain access to my files.'

'So you have failed your own Turing test then. You are content to abandon us while we are overrun by aliens. That is not a human trait.'

'No, dammit, that's not what I said!'

'We need help, machine – Joey – whatever you truly are. Urgent help. Paula's arrival may well have triggered our downfall.'

'And I can give you that help. Hell, Paula will be delighted to help you.'

'But it must be on our terms.'

'You want to try that Turing test yourself, buddy?'

'I propose an exchange. You tell me what you want and I'll provide it. In return, you give me access to Commonwealth technology to identify and kill Fallers, but the detector mechanism must be one all humans can use, not just Eliters.'

'What I want is for humans to win. To achieve that, you're going to have to compromise.'

'In what fashion?'

'The kind of sensors you're talking about require knowledge and manufacturing systems which can lead to other devices being built by the same methods. Once the information gets out there, you can't bring it back. Universal law: data wants to be free.'

'Spinoffs,' Stonal said in disapproval.

'You got it. So you're going to have to allow your citizens a little taste of freedom in order for any of you to survive. Best I got.'

'How radical would a viable Faller detector be?'

'I'm not sure. I'd need to give all the data to a group of your scientists and see what actually works in the field. Research and development, we call it.'

'How many scientists?'

'Scientists and the technicians who'd build the equipment – a dozen or so, at least, for a pilot project. Do you have that many you can trust?'

'Possibly.' Stonal let his gaze wander round the crypt with its plethora of ancient Commonwealth machines. The advanced science division had worked out a great many aspects of the technology inside each gadget, and none of their results had ever got out. 'I need to raise this with the prime minister before we proceed any further.'

'So you've managed to keep buck-passing alive these last three thousand years? Well done, you.'

*

The safe house's living room table had been cleared of all the paperwork from the PSR office. Now it just held files relating to the *Gothora III* – over a hundred of them, ranging from a four-centimetre-thick folder of official certification from the state maritime office down to single invoices.

Chaing read through them stoically. His eye must have been playing up again, because he was having to squint at a lot of the pages.

'Food,' Jenifa said, in a confident tone.

'What about it?'

'They're taking too much.' She patted a pile of files. 'Crew of fourteen, right? The amount they've ordered for this voyage will last them a couple of years.'

Chaing stopped trying to read a PSR file on Dransol, the *Gothora III*'s engineering chief. 'How far can they travel in that time?'

'Anywhere,' she replied simply. 'They normally have enough supplies on board for about a month's sailing, and then top up at each port. Sometimes they go as far west as Varlan, though it's rare. Eastwards, they don't go beyond Caraltown. They're strictly south coast.'

'So someone's going to join them, that's why they need more food. Where in Uracus are they planning on going?'

'And why?'

'Hey, where was the *Gothora* when we were on Hawley Docks?'

'Already thought of that,' she said with a smirk. 'They had just left Prawle, so no, they didn't ferry the Warrior Angel out of Opole. Still, we need to put another watcher team together, see when Florian goes on board.'

'We can't do it,' he said reluctantly. 'It was tough enough for Fajie to get five officers out of the building without Director Husnan realizing. If we mount another observation, the PSR office will find out. That'll tip off the Eliters. Possibly even the Fallers. Then we'll never know.'

'Get a Section Seven team down from Varlan.'

'I can ask, but *Gothora III* is due to leave at the end of the week.'

'Stonal will fly them in. This is important.'

'Right.' He looked over at her, but she was already busy with more paperwork. She was in a strange mood, which piqued his interest. Admittedly, she had stranger moods, but the last couple of days had seen her wired even tighter than usual. 'We do need to check out the ship.'

Now she gave him her full attention. 'You're talking about me checking it out, aren't you?'

'I can't go, and you're fully trained to infiltrate.'

'Active infiltration has a minimum of three in the lead agent's backup team.'

'For nest infiltration, yes. This is the Warrior Angel. She'll get cross, but she won't eat you.'

'Big comfort.'

'I'll set up a sniper rifle on the lighthouse, give you covering fire if it goes hot.'

'You?'

'I got my marksman grade. Don't worry, I can do this.'

'Is your eye better? You still use drops every night.'

'I have two eyes, and both are just fine. We just have to work on giving you a plausible cover story.'

'Crud.' She picked up an invoice and waved it at him. 'There's another stores delivery scheduled for this afternoon.'

'Good idea. You're too small for a stevedore, but I suppose you could pass as a supply company employee.'

The look she gave him was toxic.

*

The Decroux Cafe was halfway along the glass-roofed Maidstone Arcade, where Port Chana's more elegant and pricey shops were congregated. It was a long room with tiled walls and a single row of tables partitioned off from each other by tall wood panelling. Chaing ordered a hot chocolate from the counter at the front, then walked past the tables carrying a leather case which contained the sniper rifle. Jenifa was due to launch her infiltration attempt in another forty minutes.

Captain Fajic was sitting at the third table from the end, sipping a peppermint tea in a glass cup. Chaing eased himself in opposite her.

'We found their base,' Fajie said in a low troubled tone. 'Number forty-six Larek Street.'

'Good work.'

'It wasn't too difficult; we just followed the Faller from ware-house five.' Fajie slid a folder across the table. 'Photos of the ones we've identified. I didn't realize—' She broke off as the waiter delivered Chaing's hot chocolate.

Chaing smiled up at the lad and tipped him. 'Realize what?' he asked mildly, stirring the pink and green marshmallows into the foam.

'There's at least nine of them at that house. Nine! And that's just from one night's observation. How could we have missed them? And what's on that ship, *Gothora III*, the one the nest's watching from the warehouse? Is it bringing more Fallers? Or their food?'

'Listen to me carefully. You are not to show any interest in the *Gothora III*. Understand? Don't send any of your team to look it over, don't request paperwork. Nothing.'

Fajie leaned across the table, lowering her voice. 'It's the Warrior Angel, isn't it? You've found her.'

'Drop it.'

'Okay, Comrade, but I think I deserve a little appreciation for the help I've been giving you. When you go on board, I want to be part of your team.'

Chaing nodded as if he was actually considering it. 'If and when, I'll take you with me.'

'That's all I'm asking, Comrade.' She sat up again, and gave him a nod. 'I'll get back to my people. We can't keep track of all of them, you know. Only two at the most.'

'I know. Do the best you can.'

'How much longer? Husnan will start asking questions soon.'

'Couple of days, probably. No more than three.'

'All right.' She got up and left.

Chaing sat there finishing his hot chocolate. It was a five-minute taxi ride to the harbour. Twenty minutes from there to the top of the lighthouse. He'd be properly established by the time Jenifa arrived with the marine supply company. He opened the folder and looked at the first black and white photo.

A girl slid onto the bench seat opposite, carrying a tall glass of iced peach tea. One of Port Chana's ditzy youths, wearing a long cobalt-blue skirt and a sleeveless white blouse, several buttons open at the front to show off a lot of cleavage – which was all Chaing focused on for a couple of seconds. Then he looked up. Her long red hair was woven through with small purple flowers. A lot of kids were following that style – boys and girls. They all listened to that modern electric band music rubbish, too. 'Don't sit there—' He stopped. The floral hair arrangement had fooled him for a moment.

'What kind of welcome is that, captain?' the Warrior Angel asked with a taunting smile.

'You!'

'Were you expecting someone else? A fellow officer, perhaps?'

He desperately wanted to know if she'd overheard him and Fajie. 'Why are you here?'

'Because we need to talk.'

'Where's the girl, Essie?'

'She's called Paula.' The Warrior Angel took a sip of her peach tea. 'And she's doing everything she can to help this world.'

'You mean cause chaos.'

'Don't be so childish,' the Warrior Angel snapped. 'We're long past point scoring.'

Chaing was abruptly intimidated by just how much antagonism was being directed at him; that pretty, youthful face was the flimsiest facade for the ancient personality it contained. 'Sorry,' he mumbled. 'But you have to tell me what's happening.'

'We both know the Fallers are about to begin their apocalypse. Paula and I are going to do what we can to stop them, but it might not be enough.'

'Crudding Uracus.' He knew his anger was just a cover for fear. Having her confirm the apocalypse was close was something he didn't want to hear.

'Grow a pair,' she said. 'Worst-case scenario, if they are going to win, Paula can open the wormhole.'

'What wormhole?'

'The wormhole under the palace; the one Laura Brandt used to reach Ursell. It's still fully operational.'

'It is?' He wanted to know how she knew that. There'd never been so much as a hint in any PSR office he'd ever been assigned to.

'Yes. Laura codelocked it, but Paula can probably open it. We can evacuate a group of children.'

'To Byarn?' *That* he did know about.

'No. Byarn is a cruddy alternative. If your dumbarse Operation Reclaim nukes Lamaran enough to wipe out the Fallers, it will poison all of Bienvenido. You'll turn this planet into another Macule.'

'Where, then, can we go?'

'Aqueous.'

'You're crudding kidding me!' he exclaimed.

'I wish I was. It's not like we've got much choice; it's the only planet left capable of supporting human life. So that's the deal. We save a core group of human children – both normal and Eliter – and a few of you government people.'

'I'll think about it.'

'No, you won't. You'll call Stonal and tell him. People in authority will make the decision.'

He glared at her. 'You could walk into the palace if you wanted to. I know that; I've seen what you can do.'

'Yes, I can do that. But it would be easier with your cooperation. And we're going to be busy defending Bienvenido.'

He nodded, knowing he had no choice. In fact, he almost played his full hand. It would be so easy to say: *did you know the Fallers are watching Gothora III?* Gain her trust, maybe even her sympathy – enough sympathy to be included in the evacuation. But he just couldn't bring himself to do that. He was PSR. And that had to *mean* something, even now. Besides, if the *Gothora III* was alerted they might spot Jenifa. 'All right. I'll call Stonal.' *How strange; this is what Stonal wanted, too.*

'Good. I need someone who'll actually listen.'

'How are you going to defend us?'

'As best I can.' That enchanting girly smile returned. 'How's the leg? I can detect the metal pins they put in. Must be painful. Would you like me to cure it?'

Oh crud, yes, yes, yes. 'I'm fine, thank you.'

'That's my captain,' she chuckled. 'Stupidly stubborn to the end. So here's my parting gift: don't trust the people you think you can trust.'

'What does that mean?'

'It means: watch your back.'

'I don't trust you.'

She got up and winked. 'Yes, but you never have.'

'If Stonal has an answer, how do I get in touch?'

'Give me your hand.'

'What?'

'Hand.'

Very reluctantly, he held out his good hand. She took it and pressed a small rectangle of what looked like clear cellophane to the skin. It fluoresced with minute green lines for a couple of seconds, then faded away. Chaing could have sworn they sank into his skin.

'Your own personal telephone line to me,' the Warrior Angel said as she peeled the rectangle off. 'To activate, press your thumb on the knuckle of your index finger. 'I'll get to you as soon as I can.'

He held his hand up in alarm, trying to see the green lines. 'What is that? What have you done?' I'm not an Eliter, I told you that.

'Chill down, captain. It's just a monofunction OCtattoo.'

'I don't know what that is.'

'Organic circuitry tattoo. It's like having a little radio in your flesh.'

'Crud.'

'Get Stonal to agree to talk. It's important.' And with that, she was gone, striding down the line of tables to be swallowed up by the mid-afternoon glare outside.

*

Hot, intense sunlight was streaming in through the big windows of the state office like the start of some kind of invasion. Stonal walked through the thick beams, trying not to squint each time. Overhead, the fan blades were a blur as they tried to stir some freshness into the stifling air.

Adolphus was waiting behind the desk, his suit jacket draped over the back of his chair and his shirt collar undone. There was no sign of Terese.

'I appreciate you seeing me on short notice,' Stonal said.

'It'd be a fool who doesn't listen to his security chief,' Adolphus grunted, and waved him into a chair. 'What is it?'

'I've just come from the advanced science division. They've made progress with the machine, sir.'

'Really? That's not something I expected to hear. Those crudding Commonwealth relics are adept at keeping their secrets.'

'Yes. But up until now, we haven't had one that's alive.'

The prime minister's bushy eyebrows shot up. 'Alive?'

'It claims not, but it is sentient. I have talked to it.'

'What did it say?'

'Firstly, the Commonwealth woman is called Paula; she's some kind of diplomat. Nigel brought her along in case he needed a skilled envoy to negotiate with whatever government he found in the Void.'

'Pity he didn't use her.'

'Quite. However, the machine believes she will help Bienvenido, without prejudice.'

'What does that mean?'

'She'll treat everyone equally, including the Eliters.'

Adolphus scowled. 'Oh will she, now?'

'Equality is the goal of Commonwealth society. We've always known that.'

'Very worthy. Someone should tell the Eliters. So how big a danger is this machine?'

'In itself, not at all. How we use it, however, is a different matter. It describes itself as a life-support pod with a built-in medical system, which was part of Nigel's mission, and it also claims to be storing the memories of Joey Stein.'

'Is that a joke?'

'No, sir. From what we know of Commonwealth technology, it may well be possible.'

'A medical system? Like the Captains used to have?'

'I don't know, but it certainly kept Paula in suspension for two hundred and fifty years as an infant. But it contains a huge amount of knowledge about Commonwealth technology. It even knows how to build starships, it says.'

'I don't want starships. I just want something that'll kill the crudding Fallers.'

'It can give us that, too,' Stonal said. 'That's why I came to you. It's offered to teach our advanced science division people how to build Faller detectors. That would give us a phenomenal advantage. If our regiment troops can identify Fallers at a distance, we can wipe them out once and for all.'

'What does it want in return?' Adolphus asked suspiciously.

'It wants to survive long enough to see us contact the Commonwealth. That way, Joey Stein can be brought back to life.'

'Can we build enough of these detectors in time, do you think?'

'We'd need thousands, and we don't know what time we have left,' Stonal answered equitably. 'And by releasing Commonwealth technology, we will be instigating change. That is inevitable.'

'Yes, of course.' Adolphus leaned back, staring at the ceiling with unfocused eyes. 'But Paula is going to bring change anyway. And if an innovation like this were to work, we would be Bienvenido's saviours, not her.'

As always, Stonal managed to maintain a neutral expression in the face of raw political greed. 'Yes, sir.'

'Society will change once we're rid of the Fallers; everybody knows and accepts that. I just never thought it would be an issue for my premiership. But if we can control the factors that bring change—'

The doors behind Adolphus swung open, and five Palace Guard officers ran in.

'Sir,' the chief protection officer called breathlessly, 'you must come with us. We're initiating a full security lockdown.'

'What's happening?' Adolphus said. Several telephones on his desk had started to ring, their red lights flashing.

'Is it the space machine?' Stonal snapped.

The chief gave him an annoyed look. 'No. Prime minister, we have to get you to the palace secure bunker right away.'

'The bunker?' Adolphus blurted. 'Why?'

'We're under attack, sir.'

*

The taxi took Chaing directly from the cafe to Empale Street. By the time he got there, there were only nineteen minutes left until Jenifa was due to try and scout round on board the *Gothora III*. There should be time for him to make the phone call and get to the harbour in time. But not reach the top of the lighthouse. *She can handle herself.*

With only a mild sensation of guilt, he checked the external safeguards to make sure no one had sneaked into the safe house. *Has the Warrior Angel actually been inside? She could probably walk straight through without tripping them.* The safeguards were intact, so he unlocked the door and went in.

He dialled the number and waited for the two-tone connection whistle, then dialled the numbers of the scramble code. The phone's blue light came on.

'This is Captain Chaing. Please connect me to Director Stonal. Top priority.'

'Captain Chaing, this is the Section Seven communications office, duty officer. Director Stonal is out of contact.'

'Then find him. I have to talk to him.'

'Chaing, I am officially informing you the Joint Regimental Council command have issued a code red one alert.'

'A . . . A code red one?' *Not possible.*

'Yes. Confirm that now, please.'

'I— Yes, I confirm I've received code status.'

'Report to your combat duty posting, immediately. The code is currently being issued to all PSR offices.'

The phone went dead and Chaing stared at the handset in mortification. Code red one: *nuclear attack.*

BOOK SIX

Going Nuclear

1

Stonal stood on the rim of the crater and looked down into what he imagined the rancid heart of Uracus must look like. The atomic bomb had blown a massive hole in the ground, centred where the reactor and bomb factory had been. Devastation around the edge had been bad enough – diabolical pressure waves hammering through the earth to throw up steep meandering ridges, then its raging fireball melting the surface sand and soil to a layer of glassy lava that crunched and shattered under his boots as he walked unsteadily across it. But inside . . .

The bomb had detonated almost nine hours ago now. Even through the thick insulation of his radiation suit, Stonal could still feel the heat of the explosion. His helmet's lead-glass visor tinted the outside world a mundane grey, but the bottom of the crater was still casting a subdued carmine radiance, it was so hot. It even seemed as though the very bottom of the crater where the ground shimmered erratically might still be molten, but he was too far away to be certain.

Gazing across the seething desolation, he felt something akin to vertigo. It didn't have anything to do with height; this hit was pure fear-based. The Geiger counter clipped to the suit's belt was wailing painfully.

'Well, crud!' he exclaimed.

It had been over a decade since he'd last been here – some security inspection. Now he was struggling to match the landscape

499

with his memory. The low hills on the horizon were unchanged, but the rest of it . . . Distant forests which had once washed the foothill slopes like teal seas were now smouldering black tracts. Scrubland and lakes – all gone, devoured by this newborn radioactive wasteland. He remembered that trip here: driving up to the triple razor-wire fence, with Dobermanns loose in the runs between the wire, and watchtowers every five hundred metres – constantly manned no matter the time of day or weather. And there, sheltered inside the fences and minefields, the twin concrete domes of the breeder reactors, surrounded by squat bunkers where the Liberty mission bombs were painstakingly assembled. All gone. Reduced to vapour and ash that was now drifting out of the dark grumbling clouds that stretched as far as Portlynn three hundred kilometres south.

'What happened?' he asked the suited figure next to him. 'Could the reactor have blown?'

'No, sir,' replied McDonnal, the Portlynn PSR station chief. 'Reactors don't explode. Even the most catastrophic failure would only result in a meltdown. Not this. This was a three-hundred-kiloton atomic explosion. One of ours. And the detonation was deliberate. There are too many safeguards built in for it to be accidental.'

'They got in,' Stonal said.

'Yes, sir. They've been trying for two hundred years.'

'That doesn't excuse this lapse.'

'We'll never know exactly what happened here.'

Stonal raised an eyebrow as he glanced across the crater again. 'You think?'

'My people would have fought them to the end. They must have brought overwhelming numbers. There's nowhere on Bienvenido more heavily guarded.'

Three more places, actually, Stonal mentally corrected. *The other two bomb factories, and Cape Ingmar.* 'There's one person who could blast her way past an entire regiment if she wanted to.'

'The Warrior Angel?' McDonnal asked. 'Even if she's real, why would she want to do this?'

500

Because this is the only weapon we have that she fears, and the politicians have begun talking about Overload. 'I've no idea. So let's just concentrate on this being a Faller raid.'

'We have a report of a convoy heading out about an hour before the blast.' McDonnal pointed towards the south-west. 'Some farmers saw lorries driving away.'

'What sort of lorries?'

'The report said they were standard Nuclear Regiment lorries.'

'Which means nothing. Was there a convoy scheduled?'

Even through the radiation suit's heavy cloth, McDonnal's shrug was visible. 'The only people who know that were in the facility.'

'Uracus. Get on to the Nuclear Directorate. Immediately. They will know if that was a genuine scheduled convoy. No nuclear materials move anywhere on this planet without their authorization. And I also need to know how many bombs were stockpiled here.' It wasn't common knowledge, but the Portlynn facility also assembled the lower-yield, twenty-kiloton bombs designated for Operation Reclaim. The ones that would be used directly against Fallers if they did take over Lamaran.

'Yes, sir.'

They walked back over the ruined land to the Nuclear Regiment troop carrier that was waiting at the end of the thick black strip of gritty charcoal that had once been the road. This carrier was hermetically sealed and carried its own air supply to maintain a positive pressure inside, allowing it to operate in radiation zones. One of the technicians had plugged it into a surviving sweep-coms box at the side of the broken road.

Stonal went through the decontamination airlock, taking his time for the wash and flush cycles to clean the suit. This wasn't the kind of procedure you rushed. Once inside, he ordered the driver out of the cab, and closed the door before calling Adolphus, who was still in the emergency bunker under the palace.

'So what's happened?' the prime minister demanded.

'Worse-case scenario: a Faller nest stole some of our nukes.'

'Crudding Uracus. How many have they got?'

'I don't know. The Nuclear Directorate can tell us how many

were stockpiled here. I'll have that information within the hour. There was some kind of convoy seen driving away just before the explosion. It doesn't look good.'

'What will they use them against?'

'Certainly the capital. I suggest we activate our nest-alert isolation procedures. That's a good cover. Just don't allow any vehicle to approach closer than thirty kilometres – and that includes trains. We should also set up roadblocks outside the other bomb facilities, and Cape Ingmar.'

'I'll authorize that immediately.'

'Thank you. I'll get a team of agents from Portlynn's PSR office to start hunting for the convoy lorries immediately – in fact, I'll just get all of them on it. Recovering the bombs has to be our top priority. I'll need Air Force cooperation.'

'You have it. But what do we do about the panic? It's getting bad in Varlan. Everyone knows a nuke went off.'

'No, they don't. They know there was an incident at a nuclear facility, that's all. Nobody can get within a hundred kilometres of the explosion; there are no photos, no eyewitnesses. Your press statement should be that a reactor failed and leaked, and that the scientists are getting it back under control. It's a terrible tragedy, but we're on top of it.'

'Yes. Yes, of course.'

'I'll come straight back to the capital to coordinate the search.'

'Do you think we should move to Byarn now?'

'It's not that bad, sir. Not yet.'

*

Chaing left his crutch on the folding canvas chair as he took a walk round the lighthouse's big lens pillar. As much as he willed his damaged leg to be normal, putting weight on it was still enormously painful. One circuit limping round was enough, so he sat back down, cross that the exertion had made him perspire.

Outside, the weather was mirroring his mood. A strengthening wind was bringing dark clouds in from the Polas Sea to slide across the land. It was still a couple of hours until sunset, but the dwindling light hastened the evening forwards. Breakers were surging all the way out to the horizon, as if Bienvenido was heading into conjunction with Valatare.

From his vantage point he could see Port Chana's entire fishing fleet sailing back into the harbour, which was quickly running out of mooring buoys. Many of them were riding high in the water, having abandoned any notion of completing their catches as the storm approached.

The boats were a complication he could do without. They were forming quite a bottleneck as they slowed just outside the long curving harbour wall to wait their turn to enter. The landing craft *Lanara* was anchored at the mouth of the Honorato estuary with a full complement of Marines on board under Major Danny. They were ready to intercept the *Gothora III* at Chaing's command. What until that afternoon would have been a fast charge forwards was now going to be altogether more complicated.

The advancing storm was a problem Chaing hadn't planned for, though he was quietly pleased it was blowing in from the south. Nobody really believed the prime minister's official statement that the Portlynn facility had suffered a reactor leak, not an explosion. Whatever had actually happened, the atmosphere was full of radio-active particles – invisible, deadly – and that frightened people. Had the wind been blowing in from the north, he didn't like to think of Port Chana's reaction. A night-time curfew had been running for the two days since the red one code was issued, but that was about the only material impact the Fallers' daring raid had on the city. Psychologically, it had been a lot worse, as Corilla had gleefully explained while she reported on conversations dom-inating the general band. The Eliters knew almost as much as Chaing did, and were happily spreading the rumour that the explosion was simply to cover the theft of more atom bombs, that it signalled the start of the Faller Apocalypse, and that Adolphus was preparing to run to Byarn and abandon everyone.

Their propaganda made Chaing very angry, in no small way because half of it was actually true. It didn't help that basic foods were getting harder to find, and prices were shooting up despite

503

government prohibitions on such blatant profiteering. People were stockpiling. Absenteeism was hitting government services and public transport.

Through all the city's disruption and worry, Captain Fajie's observation team had stoically maintained their watch over the Faller nest in the harbour, who in turn never faltered as they spied on the *Gothora III*.

'They're getting ready to depart,' Jenifa reported. She lowered the big binoculars as Chaing bent down to look through the camera's viewfinder. Sure enough, the *Gothora III*'s crew were on deck in bright yellow sou'westers, untying the hawsers that secured the ship.

'In this weather?' Chaing demanded. The ship wasn't scheduled to depart until tomorrow.

'I know, but this is good cover. The *Lanara* will have trouble tracking them in the storm.'

'Crud. We need to keep *Gothora* under observation; neither of them are on board yet.'

'So do you think *Gothora* will rendezvous with them out at sea?'

'Possibly.'

'She has to get on board somehow. I had a good look round their cabins. The only people on there right now are the crew.'

Chaing had been mildly suspicious about how easily Jenifa's mission had gone, but kept quiet about it. 'If the Warrior Angel didn't want you to see her, then you wouldn't. And Giu alone knows what capabilities Paula has.'

'Who is Paula?'

'The Commonwealth girl.'

'I thought her name was Essie. That's what we were told.'

Chaing kept his eye to the viewfinder, hoping his stillness wasn't betraying him. Fat chance; she was PSR trained in interrogation. She knew all the body's tells. *Especially mine. Stupid. Stupid!*

'Chaing? Why did you call her Paula?'

Nothing for it; he would have to confess. He looked directly at her, seeing the mass of suspicion churning in her thoughts. And her hand was slipping into her jacket – but not to her holster. *That's a comfort response. So what is she reaching for?* 'Because she told me.'

'*Who* told you?'

'The Warrior Angel.'

'You are crudding joking! You spoke to her? When?'

'A couple of days ago, just before we got the red one code.'

Jenifa sagged as if she'd absorbed a physical blow. 'And you didn't tell me?' she raged.

'I have a Section Seven mission here, corporal. You're not cleared for it.'

'Screw you!'

'It was only for a minute. Stop panicking.'

'You met her,' Jenifa grunted as if repetition would make it more acceptable. 'Talked to her. What did she say? And don't give me any Section Seven classified crud. This is *me.*'

'She asked me to arrange it so she could talk to Stonal.'

'Why?'

'She wants to make some kind of deal.'

'A deal?'

'I know. Wild, huh? But Stonal actually wants to talk to her, too – so maybe not so crazy after all. This is politics at the master-class level.'

'What did Stonal say?'

'I haven't been able to contact him. His office says he's travelling.'

'Do you think he's been . . . ?'

'Taken out? It had occurred to me. What better way to start the apocalypse than eliminating our top officials, especially PSR ones?'

'But the second-in-command would just replace him.'

'Yes, which is why I've been holding on. His office says he'll be back to talk to me this evening Varlan time. Another four hours.'

'But . . .' She gestured at the *Gothora III*. 'They're leaving now.'

'I know.'

'She's on that crudding ship, isn't she? I missed her.'

'No, she was talking to me just before your infiltration mission.'

'How soon before?'

'About half an hour, or so.'

'So . . . she was up here?'

'No. I was in a cafe to meet Captain Fajie.'

Her hand came down on the sniper rifle, knuckles whitening as her fingers closed on the stock. 'Were you up here covering me or not?'

'You got off without any trouble, didn't you?'

'You crudding bastard!'

'Contact with the Warrior Angel is our number-one priority.'

'How did she know how to find you? Wait! Does she know we're watching the *Gothora*?'

'I don't know.' He fought the impulse to glance at his hand. The organic circuit tattoo was invisible, but the guilt was strong in his mind. *And in truth I don't know what it does. She could be tracking me through it.*

Jenifa shook her head slowly, regarding him as she might a wild beast. One hand went snaking down the side of her uniform jacket, then stopped. 'Who are you working for, sir?'

'She can get us out of here.'

'What?'

'The Warrior Angel. She told me. The wormhole Laura Brandt repaired when she killed the Prime, it's still there under the palace, still working. Paula can use it to evacuate people to Aqueous if the apocalypse starts. I can probably get her to take us.'

'You are crudding kidding me!'

'No. I don't think the Warrior Angel can hold off the apocalypse. She practically admitted that. That's why she wants to talk to Stonal, so she can use the wormhole to save some of us.'

'This is bollocks. How did she know where you were? Even I didn't know you weren't up here.'

'I don't know,' he answered with hot indignation, trusting that would cover his guilt. 'Because she's the Warrior Angel and Corilla's probably been reporting our every movement to her. Like we wanted. Remember?'

'This is crazy—'

Voices suddenly started shouting out of the radio.

'Code five! Code five!'

'We're under attack!'

'Explosion! Second floor hit!'

'They're using a bazooka!'

'Return fire! Return fire!'

'Nail the scum!'

'Call the regiment, get some support here!'

Chaing stared at the radio in shock. It was tuned to the local PSR frequency. 'What's happening?'

'They're attacking the office,' an aghast Jenifa grunted.

'Who's attacking?'

'It has to be the Fallers. Is it the start? Is this *it*?'

He stared at her, not wanting to even think the possibility.

The secure telephone started ringing. Chaing had got a PSR technician to install it a day ago, splicing a line into the lighthouse's main cable and doing whatever it was technicians did at the main exchange to make it secure. He knew he couldn't trust radio communications with Fajie; both Eliters and Fallers would be monitoring radio frequencies. He turned down the radio and picked up the handset.

'Chaing?' Fajie asked.

'Here. Do you know who's attacking the office?'

'No, but they're moving.'

'Yeah, I know; we've been watching them cast off. I don't like the timing.'

'No,' Fajie said. 'Not the *Gothora*. The nest!'

More shouting burst from the radio. Another bazooka round had been fired. There were casualties. Structural damage. PSR officers were returning fire, strafing the street outside. Chaing closed his eyes, seeing the outside of Cameron's, the sudden deadly sweep of machine-gun fire riddling the vans of the tactical team.

'What?' he barked.

'The nest, they're moving. They're out on the dock.'

'Crud!' He looked through the lighthouse's high window, and beckoned urgently at Jenifa to give him the binoculars. 'How many?'

'We've confirmed five of them. Heavily armed.'

He stood next to the curving glass and trained the binoculars down on the long dockside. Sure enough, two men and three women were walking along the crane rails, leaning into the wind, each openly carrying what looked like a heavy-calibre machine gun. *Same type as they had at Cameron's!* He moved the binoculars to the *Gothora III*, seeing white water churn at the stern as the propellers started up. 'But the ship's already leaving. They've pulled in the gangplank. What's the point?' He looked up from the binoculars, working out distances. Reckoning put the nest members a good seven hundred metres from *Gothora III*. Then he saw the muzzle flash; a second later, the *crack* of gunshots arrived, muted through the glass.

'Crud.' Through the binoculars, he could see a dock worker was sprawled on the floor, red blood pooling. The nest ignored him as they walked past.

'What in Uracus . . . ?'

'What is it?' Jenifa demanded.

'I don't know. The nest is going active, but *Gothora* is leaving.'

'There's more on the move,' Fajie announced.

'Where?'

'Warehouse three.'

He slid the binoculars round. Sure enough, a flatbed truck was driving along the docks, seven men in the back, all holding weapons. Two of them had a bazooka. It was too much to ignore. He picked up the radio microphone, and switched to the second channel. 'Chaing calling Major Danny, come in, Danny.'

'Danny here,' the receiver cracked.

'We have an active nest on the docks. I need you to deploy, landing strategy four. Repeat, strategy four. Take them out.'

'Roger that, Chaing. What about *Gothora III*?'

Jenifa was looking at him expectantly as the first drops of rain began to smear their way down the thick glass wrapped round the top of the lighthouse. 'Strategy four only,' he said firmly.

'Confirmed.'

Jenifa let out a feline hiss of censure.

He replaced the handset and turned up the radio volume. The speaker spewed out anger and determination as the PSR office fought back against the treacherous attack. When he looked out into the wide estuary mouth, he could just see the *Lanara* start to move.

'You're letting her go,' Jenifa said.

'She's not on board.'

'How do you know?' she challenged.

'There's a whole nest out there, gunning down civilians. We're PSR officers.'

'Are we?'

'For crud's sake—'

The phone rang again. Chaing snatched it up. 'Yes?'

'Chaing,' a female voice said. 'The Fallers have arrived.'

'What? Who is this?'

'Corilla.'

Jenifa frowned, and stepped closer to listen.

'What the crud are you doing with Fajie?' he asked.

'I'm not. Friends spliced me into your phone line.'

'How the . . . ?'

'Chaing, listen to me. The Fallers are in Port Chana. They just arrived on a train from Portlynn.'

'What?' How do you know that?' Instinctively he stared out across the warehouse district. The train station was on the other side of the huge corrugated roofs. *So close.*

'We've been looking for them just as hard as you, Chaing. For Giu's sake, they've got the missing nukes! They're taking them off the train right now. Putting them on lorries.'

'No,' he whispered.

'Listen to me, the nukes are here in Port Chana! That attack on your office, it's a diversion. You have to order the regiment and the Marines to intercept the lorries.'

'This is the real diversion,' Jenifa said forcefully. 'The Eliters want us to let the *Gothora* go. Corilla's an Eliter, Chaing. She's lying to you.'

'No,' he said, trying to consider all the variables rationally. *The threat is real.* 'I've already given intercepting the nest full priority, and we cannot ignore Corilla's claim about the nukes. The attack on the PSR office only makes it more likely.'

'Unless it's the Eliters who are shooting at us.'

'That's too much paranoia, Jenifa. They have no reason to.'

'To divert us from the *Gothora!*'

'They know everything!' he snapped at her. 'Don't you understand that? They are not the enemy. They're not the ones shooting at us. And they are the ones who will stand beside us when the apocalypse starts. But *this* – this is the Fallers.' He brought the radio microphone up to his mouth. 'Danny, I've had intel that the Fallers might be bringing the missing red one packages to the party.'

'Crudding Giu,' Major Danny grunted. 'Confirm that. Suspect packages in the picture. Do you have a location for me?'

'Not yet.'

'They're storming a ship,' Jenifa said, tight-lipped.

'Who?' Chaing asked.

'The nest. Look.'

He peered through the thick curving glass. Big cold raindrops were slamming into it, smearing his vision. More muzzle flashes penetrated the sleet. They were coming from one of the ships moored to a wharf. 'That's the *Sziu?*'

'I think so.'

The *Gothora III* was surging past the end of the harbour wall. He looked down at its bridge, almost expecting to see Florian and *her* inside. Instead, all he could make out were a few smudged figures. The ship was travelling fast. Fishing boats were desperately trying to move out of the way, scattering in mimicry of the shoals they themselves had chased scant hours before.

Lanara was hurrying in the other way. They passed within a hundred metres of each other, causing even more chaos among the fishing fleet stragglers. Their wakes clashed, sending swirling surf-topped waves curling out across the harbour. Angry foghorns sounded in protest.

'Oh great Giu,' Jenifa whispered.

It was the fear in her voice that made Chaing turn. He wasn't used to that, anger yes, but this . . .

Four canvas-covered lorries were rolling along the side of the docks. The first one stopped beside the *Sziu*. Chaing looked on in disbelief as a monster lumbered out of the back. It was huge, the size of a horse, with a grey-blue hide made up of rigid plates of armour bone. Four thick legs supported a squat body, while a pair of multijointed arms protruded from shoulders below the raised neck. A crown of short sharp horns bristled from the fat skull. It was carrying what to Chaing looked like a pump-action bazooka. The weapon was huge; a human would have trouble just trying to lift it. This *thing* swung it around as if it were made of paper.

'Breeder Fallers,' Chaing breathed in shock.

More of the vile creatures were emerging from the other lorries. There were even some of the hulking humanoids he'd encountered at Xander Manor.

'Oh crudding Uracus,' Jenifa moaned. 'This isn't happening!'

'Danny!' Chaing shouted into the microphone as the heavy squalling rain pounded across the harbour. 'Danny, the nest has breeder Fallers. Repeat: breeders. They're huge and armed.'

'Roger that,' Danny's voice came from the radio, completely emotionless. 'We can see them.'

'Why don't they just use the nukes?' Jenifa murmured shakily.

'Because they haven't seen the Warrior Angel go on board, either,' he replied.

One of the monsters on the dockside swung round and brought his weapon up, lining it up across the harbour. 'Noooo!' Chaing growled as he realized what it was being aimed at. There was a gigantic muzzle flash. The projectile hit the *Lanara* amidships, sending a seething orange flame-cloud roiling out.

'Fucking Uracus!'

The monster pumped the weapon's mechanism. Fired again.

Chaing slapped the sniper rifle's safety off. Settled the stock against his shoulder and peered through the telescopic sight as he swung it round. *Don't hurry. Be smooth.* The monster flew across his narrow field of view. He tracked back. *That is thick hide. The*

511

bullet might get through, but it won't do much damage. He steadied his breathing. *Has to be a headshot.* Crosshairs found the monster. He adjusted slowly, taking his time. Watching it prepare for another shot on the *Lanara*, anticipating the moment when it would be still.

His finger squeezed the trigger just as the monster fired.

He saw one of the spiky horns shatter. Then the monster was jumping about.

'Well, that annoyed him,' Jenifa grunted as she watched through the binoculars.

Chaing did his best to ignore the vicious sarcasm in her voice, concentrating on the furious juddering monster. He worked the bolt, flipping the spent cartridge onto the floor, and sent the next sliding into the chamber. When he settled himself again, the monster had stopped shaking itself and was scanning round slowly. Chaing took two measured breaths, then inhaled and held himself still, watching the Faller.

This shot hit just below the creature's left eye, and blew out a large chunk from the back of its skull. The body collapsed instantly.

'Nice!' Jenifa exclaimed, the tip of her tongue flicking out to moisten her lips.

Chaing looked up from the scope, seeing the big Fallers scatter for cover across the docks. Two of the monsters hunched down behind lorry bonnets, their pump-action weapon barrels sticking up vertically like dull exhaust pipes, betraying their positions. Out on the *Lanara*'s deck, Marines were deploying, crouching behind the superstructure, opening fire with heavy-calibre weapons. A couple of them were readying grenade launchers.

Movement by the lorries. Chaing peered through the scope, seeing one of the beefed-up humanoid-Fallers scuttling between vehicles. He took aim. Fired.

Blue blood erupted from the Faller's chest and it spun round before crumpling to the ground.

'Oh yes!' Jenifa cried. 'Good shot!'

Chaing worked the bolt again, and checked the scope – just in time to catch one of the monsters rise up and level its bazooka at the lighthouse. The gaping hole at the end of the barrel seemed to expand in a single distorted lurch, filling the scope with lethal blackness.

'*Move!*'

They both lunged for the narrow doorway as the tip of the lighthouse's spire exploded. Blast pressure cracked most of the thick curving glass into a crazed mosaic, searing in through the open window to hurl the rifle and camera against the huge lens. Jenifa went tumbling into Chaing, the pair of them falling painfully down several stone steps together before thudding into the wall.

'Keep going!' Chaing shouted. Wincing against the pain that flooded in from too many places, he half-fell down several more steps, Jenifa pressing awkwardly into his side, as if she was trying to push past.

The next bazooka shot hit the top of the lighthouse full on. A barrage of stone and dust and smoke slammed down the spiral stairwell, sending them crashing forwards.

*

The submarine surfaced just a few metres off the *Gothora III*'s portside. A rope ladder was lowered for Florian, Ry Evine, and the ANAdroids to clamber up. Kysandra and Paula used their force fields, expanding them out like sparkling bubbles to give them neutral buoyancy in the air, so they could float up onto the deck.

Florian heaved himself over the gunwale just as the crew were applauding Kysandra's elegant landing. He scrambled for a hold on the smooth metal as he straddled the top. His balance began to go – then Paula came over and helped him right himself before he lost all dignity.

'Thanks,' he grumbled.

Ry – naturally – came over the gunwale in a nimble gymnastic movement. Marek was equally at ease, and he was carrying a huge backpack.

Florian stood beside Paula as he looked round. The decking was still wet from the morning's final squall. Away on the northern horizon, the last dark storm clouds were tumbling away.

Demitri was shaking hands with Captain Jymoar – a lean-looking thirty-five-year-old with his olive skin darkened by years of sun and sea weather. A handsome man, Florian admitted to himself, with curly black hair cropped short and a knowing smile that was all perfect white teeth, like a badge of confidence. Maybe too much confidence. Jymoar stepped forward and kissed Kysandra – a lot more than a welcome touch on both cheeks. Florian stared in surprise, then angry embarrassment, as she twined her arms round his head and returned the kiss with abandon. Most of the crew were grinning.

Kysandra led Jymoar over and introduced him to Ry, then Florian. Florian couldn't meet the man's eye as they shook hands, instead standing with his head bowed like a surly teenager.

'So you came through the storm all right,' Kysandra was saying when Florian began to pay attention again.

'The old *Gothora* has been through a lot worse. I was more worried about Port Chana. What happened back there?'

'A nest hijacked the *Sziu*,' Kysandra told him. 'They're coming after us.'

'Not through that they're not,' Jymoar said, indicating the storm vanishing aft. 'We blocked the radar signals from the Air Force planes while they were still flying. If the government doesn't know where we are, the Fallers certainly don't. Not after sailing inside that beauty's chaos.'

'Then we're probably safe, but I don't want to take any chances. We need to sail straight for Lukarticar. Build some distance.'

'Aye aye, ma'am.' He saluted. 'How come they didn't nuke us back in Port Chana? We were still in range when they hit the docks.'

'Because they didn't know if Kysandra and I were on board,' Paula said. 'They appeared to have several atomic bombs with them. To detonate one would be to eliminate the others. They have to confirm our presence before using them.'

'You were there?' Jymoar asked.

'Yes. Observing. I like to know exactly what I'm facing.'

'But with your weapons . . .'

'I could have taken out the nest on the docks, yes,' Paula said. 'Which would have confirmed to the Fallers that someone with advanced Commonwealth technology was present. My field function scan detected seven atomic bombs brought to the *Sziu*. If there was another outside my detection range, they could have detonated it. At that distance I would probably have survived, but Port Chana certainly wouldn't. Non-intervention was the safest option.'

'Too bad you didn't wholly follow that option,' Kysandra said with a playful grin.

Paula shrugged. 'The *Lanara* was a sitting duck as it came in. And Chaing was already shooting the breeder creatures – albeit not very successfully. There was considerable confusion. It would be reasonable for the nest to believe the ones I eliminated were killed either by Chaing or another unknown PSR sniper. I was strategic in my target selection.'

'Chaing!' Kysandra shook her head in bewildered admiration. 'That man has more lives than a cat.'

'We'll show you to your cabins,' Jymoar said. His arm closed possessively round Kysandra's waist. 'Sadly, there's a lack of space, so you're going to have to bunk up in my cabin.'

She kissed him spryly. 'Oh dear. The hardship.'

'I'll be happy for you to inspect the mattress to see if it's good enough.'

'Inspect or test?'

'Both, I think.'

Arm in arm, they went through a hatch and into the superstructure.

'Jymoar has been working with us for two and a half centuries,' Valeri said quietly, so only Florian could hear. 'He is one of our most valuable allies. This is just the latest *Gothora* he has captained; all of them have been most useful transporting us and our equipment around Bienvenido.'

Florian stared at the hatchway. 'Two and a—? How old is he?'

'He and Kysandra were friends before the Great Transition. He has been receiving regular rejuvenation treatments in our medical capsule.'

'Right. Great. Good to know.'

'You are welcome to share my cabin for the voyage. It won't be too cramped for you; we don't sleep.'

'Yeah. That's good. I'll just wait out here for now.'

'As you wish.'

Florian felt the engines starting up, the deck vibrating beneath his feet. He leaned on the gunwale, staring out to the horizon. It was over a thousand kilometres to Cape Wekell, the closest part of Lukarticar. Kysandra wanted to go further, down towards Macbride Sound, before releasing the new ge-eagles on their reconnaissance flight.

He peered over the side as a crewman pulled the rope ladder in. The submarine had already dived, its smartcore taking it back to the cave below the farmhouse, so he was committed now. Weeks, possibly the rest of his life, on this ship – with the two of them. Kysandra hadn't even mentioned Jymoar before. Surely that would have been a simple courtesy?

Gothora III picked up speed, the fresh sea air blowing against his face as if seeking to cleanse him.

'Sorry.'

Florian turned as Paula gripped the gunwale beside him. She'd put on a thick dark-ginger sweater against the cooler temperature; her ebony hair flailed about as she gazed across the waves.

'For what?' he asked.

'Some women don't quite realize the effect they have on men.'

'Oh.'

'She doesn't dislike you, Florian; you haven't been cast aside. It's just that she and Jymoar are very old friends.'

'I get that.'

'In any case, she's in love with someone else. She has been for a very long time. Most of her life, in fact. I'm not sure that's entirely healthy, but it's helped her get through these dark times, so I'm certainly not going to condemn her for that.'

'It's not Jymoar, then? He's not the one?'

'Oh, no. Somebody else, somebody completely unobtainable. So if she'd bothered to give you some serious thought, she'd

516

probably understand how you felt right now, because that's how she feels all the time. And she'd be mortified at what she's done to you. She's not a cruel person, Florian.'

'I know.'

'You were having fun, weren't you?'

He nodded bleakly. 'She said that. Just fun. I suppose I didn't really listen.'

'Self-denial makes life easier for all of us at some time or another. Just try not to make a habit of it.'

He kept his gaze on the undulating water. 'Do you think we'll find the *Viscount*?'

'If it's on Lukarticar, we'll find it. I reviewed the sensors installed in this batch of ge-eagles. They're good. That's not our real problem.'

'Time is.'

'Yes. If we guessed wrong, if the *Viscount* came down at the north pole, I'm not sure we'll have long enough to reach Valatare. The Fallers are prepared to use nukes against us – against me. Hiding in the shadows is over.'

'After the *Vermillion* came down, their flying machines still worked for a while. Surely they would have found the *Viscount*?'

Paula pursed her lips. 'History is always written by the victors. Reading between the lines of the *Landing Chronicles*, I suspect Captain Cornelius might not have had too much interest in finding a second source of Commonwealth technology. After all, his family quickly established control over the only supply of advanced medicine and machinery on the planet.'

Florian gave her a surprised glance. 'That's . . . awful!'

'My job means I've been exposed to a lot of the underside of human society. I'm afraid that kind of behaviour isn't as rare as we'd like to think it is, especially in more primitive cultures. And this colony sank into semi-benign feudalism surprisingly quickly once its shiny gadgets were taken away.'

'You really think the Captain would do *that*?' *My ancestor!*

'I'm offering possibilities, that's all.'

*

Stonal stood on the side of the docks as the rain splattered on his heavy coat, and looked down at the body. It needed two of the coroner's usual sheets to cover it completely, which was a big clue. Tipping his trilby back with a forefinger, he said: 'Show me.'

Chaing used the end of his crutch to push the black fabric aside.

The breeder Faller really was a monster – although death had given its armoured body a strangely withered appearance, with the hard plates collapsing on each other as if the guts of the thing weren't big enough to fill it out completely. Half of its head was missing, exposing tatters of grey-white brain meat. Rain had washed the blue blood from the stone.

'One of your shots?' Stonal asked.

Chaing shrugged. 'Could have been. I got one of these, and one of the giants.' He looked round, as if getting his bearings. The cluster of burnt-out lorries were black metal hulks, slick with water, burning only as long as their fuel had lasted. 'The Marines got the rest.'

Stonal looked over at the slipway where the *Lanara* had shoved itself aground. Its front ramp was down, biting into the concrete. There were several ragged blast holes torn into the hull, and bullet craters smothered the armoured superstructure. It was a miracle the Marine landing craft had ever made it to the slipway.

Only he didn't believe in miracles.

Over a dozen patrol cars were parked in an effective barricade across the end of the docks, their red and blue lights flashing, sheriffs standing guard in their rain-slicked ponchos, holding shot-guns and rifles at the ready. And that was just the inner cordon. No civilians were allowed within half a kilometre of the harbour.

Such security was pointless now. All Port Chana knew what had happened here. *Marines fought breeder Fallers, and won. At least we didn't get nuked.* The news had already reached all the way back to Varlan. If the government denied it, they'd face a serious credibility problem.

Which is hardly a priority right now.

'How many of them reached the *Sziu*?' he asked.

'Maybe a dozen,' Jenifa said. 'Captain Fajie maintained a good watch, but it was an Uracus of a firefight.'

'Enough to operate the *Sziu*, then?'

'Yes, sir.'

He looked her up and down – a diminutive figure in a drab brown raincoat, her felt PSR cap soaked. A nasty gash down her cheek from falling masonry in the lighthouse. Immune to the weather, immune to the gore and chaos of the battle, determined to do her duty. 'So, to summarise: you think the *Gothora III* had taken on cargo belonging to the Warrior Angel, but neither she nor Paula were on board. Then the Fallers, armed with our atomic bombs, grabbed the *Sziu* and took off in pursuit?'

Jenifa hesitated for an instant. 'Yes, sir.'

'So where are they all going?'

'We have no indication of that,' Chaing said. 'I got the Air Force to send out two GV15s within forty minutes of the *Gothora* putting to sea, but there was no sign of it.'

'What's the *Gothora*'s maximum range?'

'Running until the tanks are empty, probably about three thousand kilometres. Possibly a little further.'

Stonal stared out across the grey choppy water. 'The Warrior Angel can obviously move her equipment around on land without drawing attention; so having a cargo on a ship indicates to me they are heading somewhere away from Lamaran. So what's out there?'

'Klev is probably outside the *Gothora*'s range,' Chaing said, 'but there are two small islands to the south-west of it they might be able to reach.'

'Their version of Byarn, captain?'

'No, sir. That's not where she plans to retreat to if the Faller Apocalypse succeeds.'

'And how do you know that, captain?'

'She contacted me in person just before the red one code was issued. She wanted to talk to you.'

'Indeed?' Stonal tried not to show surprise, but he was impressed with the captain. His gaze slipped over to the lighthouse. The top quarter was missing, leaving the base surrounded by scorched rubble. *I might have made the right choice after all.* 'Did she tell you what she wanted to discuss with me?'

'Yes, sir. If it was looking like the Fallers were winning, she wanted access to the wormhole under the palace. She said Paula could open it and evacuate some people to Aqueous.'

'Who?' he asked sharply. 'Who would they take?'

'That's what she wanted to negotiate. But she wasn't going to leave without a fight.'

'Whatever is on the *Gothora III* must be part of that fight, then. And the Fallers know that.'

'Yes, sir.'

'Can you contact her, captain?'

'Corilla might be able to,' Chaing said. Right now he wasn't about to disclose he had Commonwealth technology embedded in his hand. *Giu alone knows how Jenifa will react to that.* 'The Eliters are . . . more organized that I realized. The bastards tapped right into our secure phone lines.'

'Talk to Corilla. Tell her I'll meet the Warrior Angel.'

'She'll be on the *Gothora* by now,' Jenifa said.

'You're probably right, but contact the Eliters anyway. And get the Air Force to put their GV15s back into the air. Send them out to their limit. I want to know where those ships are heading.'

'If it's not the islands, it has to be Lukarticar,' Jenifa said. 'That's the only other thing out there in range.'

2

Nothing in the crypt had changed. In ordinary circumstances, Stonal might have welcomed that. Faustina looked up from her desk as he strode in to face the space machine containing Joey Stein's memories. There were no other technicians present; they hadn't been allowed back in after Joey started to communicate. The detailed plans for the sensor system he'd handed over were being worked on in a dedicated laboratory.

'Is everything all right?' Faustina asked.

'For Giu's sake, woman, wake up to the world for once! The Fallers have acquired atomic bombs. The apocalypse is about to begin. So, no, everything is not crudding *all right.*'

She paled, taking an involuntary pace back from him.

'Switch it on,' he said, gesturing at the radio.

'I have it on permanently now,' she replied flatly.

'That bad, huh?' Joey's voice asked.

Stonal stood perfectly still for a moment. It was so unlike him to be caught out. *Stress*, he decided, *far too much stress. But knowing about the atomic bombs doesn't strengthen Joey's hand.* He raised his gaze to the dark circular mechanism of the wormhole at the back of the crypt, then brought the radio microphone up to his lips. 'Joey, can you control the wormhole?'

'No. 'Fraid not, pal. Laura codelocked its smartnet. I don't have the software to hack it.'

'Hack?'

'The key. I don't have the key, or anything that can make a key.'

'Would Paula be able to unlock it?'

'Very probably, yes.'

'I see.'

'Is that a problem?'

'No, it is her bargaining point. If the Fallers do overrun us, she was talking about evacuating people to Aqueous.'

'Yeah, makes sense.'

'Why would Paula and Kysandra go to Lukarticar? That's our southern polar continent.'

'I don't know. What's there?'

'Nothing at all. There hasn't even been an expedition there for well over a thousand years.'

'Oh, shame. It would have been cool if it boasted a Fortress of Solitude.'

'A what?'

'Skip it; bad joke. Paula doesn't do things without cause – and certainly not at a time as critical as this. If she's going to Lukarticar, it'll be for a very good reason. Are you sure that's where she's going?'

'She sailed from Port Chana three days ago. The Air Force planes got a small radar return at extreme range before they had to turn back. A ship was heading due south.'

'A ship?'

'The Fallers were following her. It could have been them.'

'Let me guess: the ones with the atom bombs?'

He resisted sighing. 'We believe so.'

'You have to warn Paula. You cannot let the Fallers eliminate her. She is this planet's last chance, pal.'

'She knows. It was the Eliters who told us where the atom bombs were.'

'Wow. And you're Bienvenido's top spy. That has to hurt.'

Stonal gave the space machine a fixed smile. 'I've already told you, if we are overwhelmed, you also lose.'

'Oh, don't worry, pal, I'm very aware of my position.'

*

Stonal was shown into Adolphus's small office in the emergency bunker below the palace – even deeper than the crypt containing the wormhole. It might have been the lack of daylight for days, or those same long days breathing nothing but the mechanically purified air blowing out of the overhead grilles, but it seemed to Stonal that the prime minister's illness had advanced. The man's skin was a shade lighter than it had been when the red one code was given, and despite the stable temperature, sweat was glinting on his forehead. Age, too, had suddenly advanced across his features, wrinkles biting deeper into flesh. *Though that's probably just fear*, Stonal conceded.

Despite the utilitarian concrete walls, Adolphus had made sure the furniture was grand enough to reflect his status. The desk alone took up a quarter of the space. Seven telephones were lined up on top of it, all of them red. Three teleprinters clattered away constantly in the corner.

Adolphus waved Stonal into a seat. 'What happened in Port Chana?' he asked.

Stonal gave him a careful summary, very aware that the prime minister was looking for the slightest excuse to evacuate to Byarn. 'My recommendation is to keep the whole fleet of Air Force GV15s flying along the south coast on a continual basis, day and night,' he finished. 'We need to know if those ships head back to Lamaran. If we spot them – especially the *Sziu* – we should probably deploy the nuclear option. It has the advantage of being offshore, so there will be no civilian casualties.'

'We've finally cornered the Warrior Angel, haven't we?' Adolphus said. 'And this wretched Commonwealth diplomat female?'

'It is logical to assume at least one of them is on board the *Gothora*, yes.'

'But why? What are they doing on Lukarticar?'

'I have to admit, that is one question I cannot answer.'

'Bring in that traitor, Corilla. Interrogate her properly.'

Stonal tented his fingers and deliberately took a few seconds to reply. 'Two things. I seriously doubt Corilla will know; she is a simple go-between; it's an elementary precaution not to inform someone like that of the big picture. Secondly, I don't believe it's in our interest to eliminate the Warrior Angel and Paula right now. We will undoubtedly be facing the Faller Apocalypse before long. Byarn and Operation Reclaim were the best solution we could come up with before now, but Paula is offering us the prospect of Aqueous. That should not be treated lightly.'

'And she would willingly take us with her?'

'That would have to be the keystone of the negotiations, obviously. But we need her alive in order to negotiate.'

'Uracus! And you've no idea why they're on that ship?'

'No, sir.'

'What about the space machine? Does it know?'

'It says not. And frankly, I believe it.'

'I want to talk to it.'

'Sir?'

'You heard me.' Adolphus drummed his fingers nervously on the desk. 'It knows Paula better than anyone; it has to be able to give us some insight. And maybe we were too hasty in turning down its offer of more knowledge. I need to know what it knows to make a full and proper decision.'

*

A security team inspected the crypt first, so the prime minister's arrival didn't come as a surprise to Faustina. Stonal could tell she was intensely curious, though.

'I'm grateful for all you've done,' Adolphus told her, 'but I'm afraid you will have to step outside. Matters of state, you understand.'

Her curiosity deepened, but all she did was give a small nod. 'Of course, prime minister.'

'Before you go,' Adolphus added, 'please turn off all the recording apparatus in here.'

Faustina coloured slightly and walked over to a table with an array of electrical cabinets on it, including several tape recorders. She switched the equipment off one piece at a time. 'You're on your own,' she told them.

Adolphus hadn't taken his eyes from the grey-white cylinder since he'd arrived. 'How do I speak to it?'

Stonal handed him the radio's microphone.

'Can you hear me?'

'I certainly can,' Joey replied.

Stonal wasn't sure, but it sounded like Joey was treating Adolphus with a reasonable degree of respect – which he'd never been shown.

'I am the prime minister of Bienvenido. I would like you to tell me what is on Lukarticar that's so vital.'

'I honestly don't know.'

'Can you take a guess, please? You know Paula better than anyone.'

'I won't argue with you over that statement, but my familiarity is minimal, I know of her by reputation. So I can only use logic, and tell you that if Paula is heading for Lukarticar at a time like this, then it has to be supremely important.'

'Yes, we worked that part out ourselves, thank you. I asked you to guess.'

'I can't.'

'You mean you won't?'

'No, I mean I can't. My thought routines are running in a kind of . . . computator, not a biological brain like yours. It is literally impossible for me to make intuitive leaps. I can only deal in facts and logic.'

Adolphus turned to Stonal. 'Is that true?'

He made an effort not to reply: *it's logical.* 'It's highly possible, yes.'

'So what should we *logically* do about it?' Adolphus asked.

'You could simply ask her what she's doing,' Joey replied. 'If it is an action which will result in defeating the Fallers, you should offer to help.'

'But we don't know exactly where she is.'

'You have ships and planes, don't you? Search for her.'

'Yes, but our planes have limited range. And sending ships to

525

find two ships somewhere in the whole Polas Sea is a hopeless task.'

'I appreciate your point of view. In which case, I suggest launching a Liberty spacecraft into polar orbit. It is possible to see a ship's wake from low orbit, given clear conditions. An astronaut overhead should also be able to establish direct radio contact, albeit for short periods.'

'That is a possibility,' Adolphus said slowly.

Stonal was surprised to see him hesitate; the prime minister never usually lacked for confidence. 'It would be useful to know what the Warrior Angel is doing, sir,' he said. 'And where she's going. She was about to talk to us when the Fallers raided the bomb factory.'

'Everything will change,' Adolphus said, and his thumb wasn't pressing the microphone talk button.

'We do need to contemplate a degree of change at this point, sir. To be frank, what have we got to lose?'

Adolphus nodded slowly, his eyes never leaving the space machine. His thumb touched the microphone button. 'Why should I trust you?'

'You have something I want,' Joey replied.

'What?'

'Survival. As your spy chief here keeps pointing out, if you lose, so do I.'

'I lose anyway.'

'I don't understand.'

'I'm ill, Joey Stein. Very ill. I won't survive this.'

'I'm sorry to hear that, but you are the prime minister. This world is relying on you to make the right choices now. This is what you've spent your life working towards. I know politicians; you all care about your legacy. You care about it a great deal. Don't you want future generations to remember you as the prime minister who defeated the Fallers?'

Adolphus took a step closer to the space machine, his eyes fixed upon it. 'I want to live.'

Shock immobilized Stonal. *Now* he understood what this was all about. 'Sir, we can't trust—'

'No!' Adolphus snapped. 'You don't get to advise me on this. This is not an affair of state. This is about me! Machine, you can cure people. Can you cure me?'

'What is wrong with you?'

'I have growths. Tumours. They've spread. Our doctors can't do anything.'

'I can cure cancer in a few hours. A total rejuvenation will take a month.'

'Hours?' Adolphus whispered. He blinked against the moisture in his eyes. 'It would be done in hours?'

'Yes.'

'You can't, sir,' Stonal said. 'We do not know what this machine is capable of.'

Adolphus twisted round to face him, his lips open in a snarl. 'I'm dying! And this . . . this Giu-sent miracle can save me. So don't you tell me what I can and cannot do.'

'I am responsible for your safety. This is Commonwealth technology . . .'

'And what exactly is the worst it can do? Kill me a few weeks early, just before I get crudding eaten alive by Fallers? No. This is my choice, my risk. You take your orders from me, Stonal, and this is my order: if I'm not out in six hours, then you push this thing down into the bottom of the deepest hole you can find. Kill it, and all the hopes it has to get back to the Commonwealth. Do you understand?'

Stonal wanted to say no, wanted to stop this insanity. This was exactly what Slvasta had warned against. It would start with a cure for cancer, but Adolphus would never stop there. This was an addiction whose culmination would be rejuvenation. And the space machine had the blueprints for medical capsules – more could and would be built.

Bienvenido would become dependent on Commonwealth medical technology. But such things couldn't be built in isolation. There would be spinoffs in every technological discipline. Commonwealth ideas would seep into society, and everything Bienvenido had built so painfully for itself over three thousand years would be lost.

He could stop it here and now, physically intervene; Adolphus in this state couldn't put up any kind of meaningful struggle. But then what? He'd be relieved of duty within an hour. *And I'll be facing the apocalypse by myself. No flight to Byarn, and certainly no evacuation through the wormhole.* 'Yes, sir. Under protest.'

'Protest noted. Machine, do *you* understand?'

'Very much.'

'All right then.' Adolphus took a calming breath, dabbing a shaking hand at the sweat that had risen on his forehead. 'What do I need to do?'

'Undress. Get inside me.'

'That's . . . it?'

'Yes. You won't be awake for the procedure. When it's over, the tumours will be gone.'

'Why can't you just give him the medicine?' Stonal asked.

'This isn't a drug, pal. This is micron-level surgery. The tumours are broken down by active filaments and physically removed.'

Adolphus put the microphone down and walked over to the space machine. After a moment, he bent down and started undoing his shoelaces. He took his clothes off methodically, folding them neatly in a pile, clearly trying to be as dignified as possible. When he was naked, a circular aperture opened on the side of the space machine. Stonal didn't see any kind of door mechanism; the hole simply expanded like a pond ripple. A soft sapphire light shone out, revealing a chamber that made him think of a padded coffin; it certainly wasn't much bigger.

'Six hours,' Adolphus said, and turned his back on Stonal. He twisted about awkwardly, nothing more now than an ungainly old man, trying to clamber inside the space machine. The door contracted in a single smooth, silent motion.

'Crudding Uracus,' Stonal muttered through clenched teeth. The prime minister, the man who controlled all of Bienvenido, was captive inside a Commonwealth artefact. It was the kind of event he'd dedicated his entire life to preventing.

528

He glared with a hatred he hadn't known in years at the intruder which he himself had brought into the very seat of power.

Clearly Joey's medical ability had been gnawing at the prime minister's thoughts for some time. *And I was the one who told him about that ability. My fault. If I'd just kept my mouth shut . . .*

'Oh.' Stonal exhaled as realization struck with the force of a runaway Faller monster. *Father always said they were smarter than us, that their huge long lives give them so much knowledge-power. I never appreciated how true that was. Nobody negotiating for their life would declare that medical ability right at the start; it's a perfect bargaining chip, the kind you play much later in the game. And I was the one who delivered the information.*

He gave the space machine an altogether more cautious look. 'Well played,' he murmured in reluctant admiration, and left the crypt.

Faustina was in her office. She looked up in surprise as Stonal came in.

'Have you been talking to the space machine?' he asked.

'Only to facilitate the sensor data you asked for.'

'Before that,' he said. 'Before you called me in. When it first started communicating. What did you tell it?'

'Only some very basic information.'

'Such as?'

'Where it was. Who I was. That's all.'

'Did you tell it about me?'

'No. I just said I'd have to call a senior government officer to talk to it.'

'What about the prime minister? Did you tell it he was ill?'

'He's ill? What's wrong with him? What's happened?'

He stared at her face, trying to find a hint of treachery. *Nobody this smart can truly be naive. It has to be an act to keep her out of palace politics.* Yet all he could see was an old woman starting to get very uncomfortable, not understanding what was wrong.

'Nothing's happened,' he said smartly. He turned to the guard outside. 'Science Director Faustina does not leave this office until I return. Is that clear?'

'Sir.' The guard saluted, showing just how dedicated to his duty he was.

Twenty minutes later Stonal was shown into Terese's office. Unlike Adolphus, she hadn't spent the last few days sheltering in the emergency bunker. However, his staff had informed him that she kept three armoured Zikker limousines in a palace garage ready to drive her to the Air Force Command airfield just outside Varlan so she could evacuate for Byarn at any time – and her family was already at the base.

'Thank you for seeing me at short notice, deputy prime minister.'

'I'm always happy to see the head of Section Seven,' she replied courteously. 'What can I do for you?'

'We may have a slight problem.'

*

Florian wasn't used to the sun being so low in the sky at midday; he hadn't expected it to be so bright this far south, either. Everyone on deck wore sunglasses as they stared out across the calm water to the ice cliffs that marked the top of Macbride Sound. The air blowing off the glacier lowered the temperature even further; Florian could barely believe that was possible. He was wearing two sets of full-body thermal underwear along with two sweaters under his goose-down parka; cotton gloves and thick waterproof over-gloves; fur-lined boots and triple layered socks; a scarf over his mouth and nose; visor-like sunglasses to stop his damp eyes from freezing up – and he was still cold. But the polar continent was amazing. Its coastline alternated black rock with dazzling ice. And it was so clean, as if Giu had only just created it.

He saw a tall section of ice and snow tumble in slow motion down into the sea, sending up a crown of spume. Gloved fingers struggled to lift his sunglasses off so he could get a better look. He blinked against the biting cold gusting over exposed skin.

'It's blue,' he muttered.

'What is?' Jymoar asked.

'The ice,' Florian said, nodding at the distant cliff. 'It's blue.'

'Pristine water,' Jymoar explained. 'There are no contaminants here, no factory chimneys churning out crud. It gives you the purest water on the planet. So when it freezes, and the sun shines on it just right, it has a blue tint.'

'Amazing.' He could have got the same information from his files, but it was more fun to listen to Jymoar.

In truth, Florian had found it hard to dislike the captain. There was something massively engaging about the man's happiness and humour. The captain was always so positive about everything. Florian had never heard him raise his voice in anger at any of the crew.

I was that happy, too, when Kysandra was in my bed every night. He almost wanted to ask – man-to-man – *do you ever get dejected when she leaves you behind?* Somehow he couldn't imagine Jymoar moping around the ship when she wasn't on board.

For himself, he still hadn't absolved Kysandra for her total disregard of his feelings. And to be honest, he really missed her and the comfort of being with her, that smile as bright as any polar ice when it was directed at him. Knowing Jymoar was now receiving all that attention – and sex . . . Well, most of his time on board had been spent alone and sulking; it was like being back in Opole after his discharge from the regiment. He'd gone back home, thinking everything would finally be better, only to discover he was even more miserable as he realized how alone he was, and probably always would be. Back then he'd run away to Albina valley; here on the *Gothora III,* there was no escape.

'Come on.' Jymoar put his arm round Florian's shoulders. 'Now that we can see land, we're ready to free the ge-eagles.'

'Free them?'

'Yes!' Jymoar laughed. 'Well, unpack them.' Another cheery grin and he was striding towards the mid-deck cargo hold.

The thick lime-green canvas cover was being rolled back off the top of the cargo hold. Florian peered down into the shadowed space below, seeing barrels and big crates with their South Coast Wide Shipping labels prominent, arranged neatly across the floor like some strange city-layout model. Valeri and Marek had been going through the contents since they came on board, checking everything was working.

Five crates had been opened up, their sides lying flat like square wooden petals. They exposed the stacked metal grid shelves inside, holding inactive ge-eagles. The big avian devices were semiorganic copies of a bird that existed on Querencia, Paula had told him – another planet in the Void, and the one Nigel had thought he was heading for. In storage they were curled up tightly, with a slim electric cable snaking into their open beak to charge up their power cells. The ANAdroids were moving between the crates, removing the cables.

One by one, the ge-eagles activated, testing their synthetic muscles with lazy twitches and spasms. Heads turned from side to side, allowing sensors to run through their analysis routines. Wings extended. Even though Florian knew their technical specifications, witnessing their actual size was impressive.

They began to take off, flying up out of the hold with swift powerful beats of their wings, circling higher and higher above the *Gothora*. Now it was their speed that struck him; the impression of supremacy was inescapable. He didn't know what kind of birds lived on Lukarticar, but they wouldn't be challenging the ge-eagles. Not that they'd ever be flying low enough to attract the attention of local wildlife; their cruising altitude was four kilometres.

Paula walked over to him. 'Quite a sight.'

'Yes.' His u-shadow was processing links from the ge-eagles, allowing him to look down on the *Gothora III*. The visual and thermal image was phenomenal, with every detail clearer than any human iris could ever produce. As the first ge-eagle gained altitude, so the view of the ice-locked land grew. There was very little rock or solid ground visible amid the expanse of smoothly rumpled snow. Somewhere to the south-east, a range of low mountains cluttered the horizon. Directly south, the vast mouth of Macbride Sound signalled the start of the deep-water channel which extended another hundred and thirty kilometres south. The western headland was a cliff even bigger than the glacier wall currently off their starboard bow.

'How long are they going to take to scan the whole continent?' he asked.

'Three weeks for all of it. So statistically a lot less, until they find the *Viscount*.'

'If we guessed right.'

'Yes. If we guessed right; but then it's a fifty–fifty choice, isn't it?'

He saw Kysandra emerge from the superstructure with Valeri. Both of them stopped for a moment to look down into the mid-deck hold. Ge-eagles were still flapping their way upwards – over twenty now, out of their total of fifty.

Several of the crew started cheering. Florian looked over towards shore where they were pointing, and zoomed in. A seibear had broken surface to clamber onto the ice beach at the foot of the glacier. Almost as large as a terrestrial elephant, with grey-white fur, the animals normally weighed in at about five tonnes supported by four legs with wide webbed paws that oddly reminded him of a Vatni's limbs. With a flash of guilt, he realized he hadn't even thought about Mooray for weeks. He wondered how he was doing, if the Vatni village by the lake was okay. *How would they face up to the Faller Apocalypse?*

The seibear had a big coiran clamped between its jaws; the poor fish was still thrashing about. Florian winced as the seibear bit the fish clean in half. The two chunks flopped down on the ice, dark carmine blood gushing out.

'That is one brute of an animal,' Paula said. 'Funny how polar continents always evolve the most menacing creatures.'

'Penguins are menacing?' Demitri said.

Paula gave him a thoroughly disapproving glance.

'Always?' Ry Evine asked.

Florian hadn't noticed the astronaut approaching.

'Rule of thumb,' Paula told him.

'Have you seen many?'

'Enough to know never to get close.'

'That sounds like good advice,' Florian muttered as he watched the seibear eating, its jaws making short work of the coiran.

'Let's hope they haven't turned the *Viscount* into a lair,' Ry said.

'If the *Viscount* did crash here, those things would certainly go a long way to explaining why there were no survivors,' Paula said.

'About our force-field skeletons . . .' Florian began nervously.

'Don't worry,' Paula told him. 'I was exaggerating. Your suits are easily strong enough to stand up to anything an animal can do to you. If a seibear tries to bite you, it'll break its teeth.'

'Fangs,' Ry corrected with a grin.

'Oh. Nice. Thanks,' Florian grunted.

The last ge-eagle flew away into the frigid cloudless sky. Florian could already see the rest soaring up into their scan formation. Ultimately they would hold position two kilometres apart, producing a line a hundred kilometres wide. Then they would fly back and forth across Lukarticar, scanning every square metre of the surface.

'Ah,' Paula said. 'They'll launch the com-drones now.'

A dark-grey flattened teardrop shape three metres long ascended vertically out of the hold, emitting a faint whirring sound as its internal fans spun at full power. Flexible vents in its trailing edge flipped down and it began to accelerate upwards, climbing at a much shallower angle than the ge-eagles. It was followed by a second. As they rose above the ship their wings began to extend, plyplastic flowing out and becoming thinner. Within a minute, the wingspan measured over twenty metres, and it was still expanding.

The drones, like the ge-eagles, had been manufactured in the remaining semiorganic synthesizers below Kysandra's farmhouse. They would operate at twenty-five kilometres altitude, far above any possible bad polar storms, where they would fly a slow holding pattern above the *Gothora*, acting as a link relay between ge-eagles and ship.

'Are we going down Macbride Sound now?' Ry asked.

'No,' Paula said. 'If the *Sziu* found us in there, they'd have us cornered. It's always harder to find a moving target, so we'll sail along the coast at random. And if the *Sziu* does come close, the drones will spot it long before it sees us. We'll be able to stay out of sight and range.'

'Makes sense,' Florian admitted. Part of him wanted to confront the Fallers. He knew Paula and Kysandra would be able to take out the *Sziu*, yet at the same time he was anxious to find the *Viscount* – to actually see a real Commonwealth starship.

And when they did travel over Lukarticar to see if any of the equipment still worked, Jymoar would be staying here on the ship. *Not that that's important.*

*

Tumours were the easy part. A mass of filaments thinner than human hair slid into Adolphus's body, surrounding the lethal cancer cells like a conquering army, breaking them up and syphoning away the constituent molecules, repairing the tissue damage left in their wake.

The prime minister's brain was an altogether more complex problem. That required a very different set of filaments, even more intrusive. These sought out critical path synapses, carefully infiltrating the electrochemical exchanges in order to manipulate the unconscious personality.

Memory downloads were an old Commonwealth medical technology, developed in tandem with rejuvenation and re-life procedures over a millennium ago. Extracting Adolphus's memories was no problem for the medical capsule. It took two hours to successfully download his mind into a secure store.

Once the external duplication was complete, the filaments set about erasing those same memories and thought routines from his brain. Also a well-understood procedure – though usually there was a lot more time available. The medical module's smartnet told Joey this rushed procedure was likely to leave a considerable amount of Adolphus's subconscious remaining.

The final stage was inserting Joey's memories and personality into the waiting brain. This process was a modified version of psychoneural profiling – which had long been illegal in the Commonwealth. But Joey wasn't entirely surprised to find Nigel had loaded the ability into the medical module's smartnet.

With the download underway, the medical module made its

final alterations. A genome reading showed Adolphus had Advancers somewhere in his heritage, but the sequences passed down through the generations had weakened and corrupted, leaving only a few specialist cellular clusters with about as much functionality as an appendix.

Time was now becoming critical, so Joey settled for several old-style OCtattoos for communication and sensory augmentation – they were quick and simple to add to the prime minister's body. While they were being written onto his new/old skin, the life-support pod's synthesizers extruded some small weapon modules – slim cylinders which were neatly inserted into the fleshy hands and forearms.

Then the filaments withdrew, knitting together the minute holes they had created as they snaked out, and Joey began to regain consciousness in Adolphus's body.

It was wrong on so many levels. There was a headache for a start. His thoughts were slow, memory triggers sluggish. Without macrocellular clusters running secondary routines, he lacked so much mental agility; even simple maths was almost impossible. Coordination was a bitch, too.

Then there was his body. It was old – the first shock. Over-weight; he actually grimaced as he felt folds of fat sagging against his skeleton. Joints ached without even moving. Every time he breathed he wheezed, as if he never got enough oxygen into his lungs. And his heart . . . The way it was hammering away in his chest made him worry he was about to have a major coronary event. Hopefully that was just an adrenalin panic to his own semi-dazed awareness of his new identity/location.

Exovision icons burned across his vision, slowly stabilizing. He opened a link.

'You all right?' Joey-in-the-pod-smartnet asked.

'I will be,' Joey-in-Adolphus's-brain replied.

'Weird, huh?'

'You have no idea.'

'Can you move?'

'Let's find out. Open the pod doors, pal.'

'Ha, well at least plenty of our memory transferred okay.'

Joey (in-Adolphus's-brain) opened his eyes to see a soothing pale blue light. Then the plyplastic door dilated and the altogether sharper light from the crypt's overhead bulbs assaulted him. He slowly climbed out, knees creaking as he stood up. Goosebumps rising everywhere. Blinking the world into focus.

Stonal was standing there beside Laura's ancient exopod, watching him suspiciously. Adolphus had been inside the medical capsule for five hours, and Stonal had walked out of the crypt as soon as the prime minister had climbed in, only returning after ninety minutes – but Adolphus wouldn't have known that.

'Where do you think he went?' he asked Joey-in-the-pod-smartnet through their link.

'I don't know. Faustina said he was badly agitated when he quizzed her; he doesn't trust her any more. Just be careful. There's nothing more dangerous than a paranoid spook.'

'He can't touch me; I'm the prime minister.'

'And let's not add that to history's list of famous last words, shall we?'

'Sir?' Stonal enquired. 'Are you all right?'

'Yes,' Joey croaked. He cleared his throat. 'Ask it if I'm cured.'

Stonal raised the microphone. 'Was it a success?'

'One hundred per cent. The tumours were excised. He's clear.'

'Oh, thank crudding Giu,' Joey exclaimed with appropriate gratitude and relief. Being trapped in a timeloop was weird, but listening to his own voice coming from a duplicate personality while in a stolen body possibly qualified as weirder. *It might even impress Ozzie.*

He picked up his shirt. His new fingers were chubby and not very flexible. It took time to do the buttons. *How did people ever live growing old?*

'What now?' Stonal asked.

That's got to be a test – the first of many, no doubt. 'Make contact with the Warrior Angel. You were right; change is inevitable now. But we must be careful how it is introduced. We have to retain control over the process.'

'Of course.'

'I'll call General Delores and order a Liberty flight launch into polar orbit.'

'That might take a while.'

'They always say that. This is an emergency, and the Astronaut Regiment must be made fully aware of that. I will fly out there myself to supervise; that should convince them.'

'You are going to Cape Ingmar?'

'It's one of the most secure places on the planet, so my personal security won't be an issue. And it's also where they communicate with the Liberty capsules, is it not?'

'Yes.'

'So that is how I can talk directly to the Warrior Angel. I wish to ensure this Paula woman has access to—' He waved his hand at the wormhole. 'Once we have a deal for evacuating essential government personnel and a Marine task force to Aqueous, we can proceed with combating the so-called apocalypse. I don't like it, but I can see the time coming when we have to combine forces with the Warrior Angel. After all, your father did the same thing with her to destroy the Prime that landed on Fanrith, didn't he?'

Stonal nodded. Joey almost smiled at how the spy chief's jaw muscles were working hard to keep his expression neutral.

'That's settled then. I'm going back to the bunker now. I need to talk to the Marine commander. I want an armed ship to sail for Lukarticar tonight. I'm going to authorize them to carry nuclear weapons. If that Liberty does its job properly, it can guide them to intercept the *Sziu*. That should convince the Warrior Angel we're serious about an alliance.'

'Yes, sir.'

Joey bent down to tie up his shoelaces, keeping a keen eye on Stonal. If the spy chief had any suspicions, he wouldn't waste time. He wasn't the type.

'Right, then.' He stood and took the microphone from a frowning Stonal. 'Thank you, Joey.'

'You're welcome,' came the reply.

'I'm going to have the science director bring in regular progress reports on the sensors you gave us; it's essential we have them as soon as possible. If you can offer any insights into speeding up the production process, I'd appreciate it.'

'Of course. And our arrangement?'

Joey gave Stonal a conspiratorial grin, praying his facial muscles were working correctly. 'If you're helping us, we will all survive together, won't we?'

'I suppose so.'

'And if the worst comes to the worst . . . Well, you're right next to the wormhole.'

*

Florian was woken by a hand gently shaking his shoulder. It was dark in the little cabin, and quiet. His u-shadow told him it was half past four in the morning. The *Gothora*'s engines were off, but the cabin heater was thrumming like a trapped bussalore. He squinted up as visual enhancement routines showed him Kysandra standing over the cot. The smile on her freckled face made her look heart-achingly lovely.

'They found it,' she said.

'Huh?'

'The *Viscount*. Access the drone link.'

Florian sat up fast. His u-shadow established a link with the drones circling so far overhead. The ge-eagles were also circling, seven hundred kilometres away. It had been five days since they launched, and they'd covered nearly a third of Lukarticar in that time. Then around midnight, their field scan sensors had picked up a big density anomaly, and ten of them had closed in to confirm the find, spiralling down to a hundred metres altitude to produce a more detailed examination.

Their visualization was a three-dimensional image mainly of translucent emerald, which was the ice cap, showing a depth of just over three kilometres resting above the bedrock. A dark purple shape over a kilometre long – nearly cylindrical – was buried under the surface at a forty-degree angle, with its highest point thirty metres beneath the fresh snow crust. Several other purple shapes were scattered around it, at varying depths.

His navigation routine pulled up a map of Lukarticar and overlaid the ge-eagles' location. It was nearly seven hundred kilometres west of the *Gothora*'s current position entering the Straits of Tyree, and two hundred kilometres inland.

'Great Giu,' he breathed. 'It's real. Paula was right!'

Kysandra's lips twitched. 'Commonwealth people do make a habit of that.'

'And it's intact!'

'Well, almost. There was some break-up, but that happened to *Vermillion*, too. It certainly didn't smash apart when it came down, which is supremely good news. There should be a lot of equipment we can salvage.'

He started to wiggle his way out of the thick sleeping bag, careful not to tip off the edge of the cot; he'd done that a couple of times the first night, it was so narrow. 'Great Giu, will there be weapon drones? Maybe we won't even need Paula's plan to visit Valatare. And there will be full Neumann-level synthesizers; we can extrude a whole drone army. And fliers! They had atmospheric flyers, I know. I checked the general inventory; Nigel had copies. And—'

She stopped him with a kiss. Florian gave her a surprised look; she was smiling happily. 'That's the Florian I remember,' she said huskily.

He knew his expression was twisting to guilt, and maybe some resentment, too. Laughing softly, she kissed him again.

'But—'

Her forefinger lifted his chin. 'We need to celebrate,' she said solemnly. 'And no matter which way this expedition plays out, it may be our last time.'

'Oh. Er, don't we need to get ready to go?'

'The blimp takes a while to inflate. We have time.'

The ANAdroids had brought the anchor mast up first – a fat plyplastic rod barely two metres long that they fastened to the deck just behind the superstructure using molecular epoxy. The envelope case was next – a big heavy trunk that took three of them to lift. It opened easily, and a mini-avalanche of tissue-thin fabric slithered out. Valeri connected the nosecone's tether cable to the top of the mast, and they were ready to begin.

Helium was stored in heavily compressed tanks designed to look like oil barrels. They started to inflate the fifteen separate gas-cells inside the envelope. As the mass of super-strength polymer rose into the air, the plyplastic gondola unfolded underneath it. The ANAdroids attached ducted fans to both sides.

By the time Florian and Kysandra arrived on the deck, thin ring light showed them that the blimp was two thirds inflated, suspended like a flaccid silver-grey moon above the *Gothora*. The anchor mast had telescoped upwards to keep level with the blimp's nose as the envelope continued to expand. Most of the crew was gathered together around the mast, gazing upwards in admiration.

'It's huge,' Florian declared. The blimp was already longer than the *Gothora*, its cruciform tail hanging a long way out beyond the stern.

'Needs to be,' Fergus said. 'The temperature around here kills the lift, and it's got to carry eight of us along with our supplies.'

'I've never seen anything like it,' Ry said.

'Me, neither,' Paula said. 'Not outside history files, anyway. But it was easy for the synthesizers to manufacture. And all it has to do is get us there.'

'No problem,' Fergus said. '*Viscount* is only seven hundred kilometres away, and the weather is reasonable. It shouldn't take more than twelve hours.'

Florian tried to see the coast, which his u-shadow navigation routine was telling him lay twelve kilometres to port, but it was too dark even for his enriched retinas to make out. He wasn't entirely sure he wanted to spend twelve hours flying over that hostile wasteland in what was essentially a balloon with engines, even if it had been manufactured by Commonwealth synthesizers. The envelope skin looked so thin, like a soap bubble, and just as delicate. He knew that the gas cells inside were even thinner. A single peck from a yigull would probably send them all plummeting to icy oblivion.

It took another twenty minutes to complete the inflation. When the gas cells were full, the blimp strained at the anchor post, its tail tilting up at fifteen degrees even with full ballast tanks. The ANAdroids passed up their equipment cases, stowing them in the gondola. Then it was time to embark.

Florian slipped his small backpack straps over his shoulders, and climbed up the short rope ladder. Two crew were holding it steady for him. With everyone watching, he couldn't show any weakness – though he'd spent the last week worrying if he'd actually have the courage to do this when the moment arrived. It was one thing to plan to hunt for the *Viscount*, but actually finding it was making everything acutely real. The Faller Apocalypse was imminent, Paula was going to try and reach another planet, which was actually a prison, where there might be aliens who could save them, and he was at the heart of it all. So when it was his turn, he didn't hesitate.

The gondola was a narrow space – four very basic seats on either side with bulky equipment packs stowed underneath, and a tiny toilet bucket at the back (not even a curtain). Florian crammed his backpack onto the overhead luggage rack; he'd been allocated the rear portside seat, which he squeezed into, grumpy to find how little legroom the design gave him. The fuselage walls had long rectangular windows, and the curving prow was completely transparent. There were no manual flight controls of course. Demitri had nominal pilot duties, so he was linked to all the control surfaces and engines.

Kysandra was last in, and the door contracted behind her. Almost immediately, the overhead air vents started blowing out warm air. The minute frost crystals nesting in the fur of Florian's parka hood melted.

'Let's go,' Paula said.

'Wait!' Kysandra said. 'We haven't named the ship.'

Calling this a ship is pushing it, Florian thought as he wrestled against his restrictive layers to unzip the parka. From being freezing

542

a couple of minutes earlier, he was now getting uncomfortably warm.

'How about the *Discovery*?' Ry asked. 'It's what we're doing, after all.'

'Very practical,' Kysandra said with a grin as she wiggled out of her parka. 'Never would've guessed you were an astronaut.'

'It has a good lineage,' Paula said.

'Launch the *Discovery*,' Kysandra told Demitri.

'Disengaging from the anchor post.'

Florian felt the slight judder as the cable released. Then he could just make out the circular fan ducts swivelling round to a forty-five-degree angle. The hum of the motors built, and they were rising surprisingly fast.

A predawn light was just creeping over the horizon, allowing him to see the *Gothora III* below, its deck lights burning bright against the dark wash of the sea. He linked to the *Discovery*'s smartnet and accessed the sensors embedded around the envelope. His perception was greatly enhanced. Individual crew members were easy to make out as they walked across the deck, making ready to sail. The anchor post was shrinking back down.

'Will they wait for us?'

'They're going to head north-east for a couple of days at slow speed,' Paula said as she folded up her parka. 'That way, if anything does go wrong, the *Discovery* will still be able to fly back to it.'

'And if everything goes right, we'll be using a wormhole to get back to the farmhouse,' Florian concluded. The excitement of that made every risk worthwhile. 'How long will it take to get them working again?'

'We won't know that until we get there and assess what kind of state the wormhole generators are in. I'm hopeful the ANAdroids should be able to get one functioning within a week. Then we can transfer everything we need directly back to Port Chana. The *Discovery* certainly can't carry much.'

'How much Commonwealth machinery do you want?'

'How long is a piece of string? It's not how much we bring back, it's how long it will take to prepare the equipment to analyse

Valatare. Once we have that information, then we have to build something that can break the barrier. That's going to be the tough part.'

'Will it be a quantumbuster?'

'Whatever it takes to—' Paula broke off, a gentle frown forming on her head. 'That's odd. Kysandra, are you accessing *Discovery*'s sensors?'

Kysandra looked up. 'What am I looking for?'

'Wide scan around the *Gothora*. Do seibears normally behave like that?'

Florian hurriedly accessed the *Discovery*'s sensors again. It took him a moment to find what was puzzling Paula. Seven seibears were floating in the sea, forming a loose circle around the ship, none of them closer than two kilometres.

'No,' Kysandra said. 'Not at all. They only swim to hunt, and when they're in the water, they're always moving.'

'That distance is interesting,' Marek said. 'They couldn't be seen from on board.'

'Fallers,' Paula said. 'They have to be. That level of cooperation is beyond an animal predator.'

'Crud,' Kysandra grunted.

'How good is their eyesight?' Ry asked. 'Can they see us?'

'Faller eyesight is always at least as good as the animal they're mimicking, and usually better,' Kysandra said. 'They would've seen the *Discovery* inflating, and they'll certainly see us now.'

'So they'll know where we're going,' Florian said. 'We should circle over them and shoot the bastards now.'

'Non-human-form Fallers are clearly more prevalent than we realized,' Paula said. 'If we kill these, we'll have to kill every animal our sensors detect on the flight as a precaution. And that's no guarantee they still won't be able to track us.'

'I'm warning Jymoar,' Kysandra said. 'The *Sziu* might already know our position.'

Florian finally managed to remove his parka as Demitri turned the *Discovery* due west, following the coastline, and increased power to the engines. The blimp moved forwards steadily as it cruised up to its operational altitude a kilometre above the listless waves. Florian watched through the long window as the dawn light stretched out across the endless undulating snowfields to port, tingeing them a sullen rose-gold.

3

Of all the hundreds of launch simulations she'd endured, not one of them prepared Pilot Major Anala Em Yulei for the actual thing. The Silver Sword rocket lifted Liberty mission 2,674 from the pad in a fury of sound and motion. Four-gee acceleration crushed her down into the couch, but still managed to shake her head from side to side inside the helmet. The instrument console became a blur; flight com's voice was an indecipherable buzz in her earphones.

Booster separation came with an almighty jolt and she let out an involuntary grunt. Thirty seconds later, a loud crack ricocheted round the cabin and the aerodynamic shroud segments guarding the capsule fell away. After a further two and a half minutes the core stage was exhausted. The third stage ignited.

That was when everything she'd trained for changed. There had been a week of intense simulations, the flight manuals were rewritten, launch pad technicians worked for days without sleep preparing the rocket, and there was no missile payload. All for this – a direct order from the prime minister. This Liberty flight was to help track down Fallers somewhere on the Polas Sea. Her super-classified briefing from General Delores and the Cape's senior PSR general explained that these Fallers had acquired atom bombs from the recent reactor 'incident', and they were pursuing the Warrior Angel in a hijacked ship, the *Sziu*. No, you don't need to know why, only that she is no longer regarded as an enemy of the state. So it would be Anala's job to update the *Pericato*, a Marine ship which had been assigned to pursue the *Sziu*. Major Danny was in command, and *Pericato* had been equipped with short-range nuclear missiles they could deploy against the Fallers – eliminating *Sziu*'s stolen bombs.

The third-stage burn lasted for four minutes and fifteen seconds before it jettisoned. At the end of it, the Liberty capsule was in a polar orbit one hundred and eighty kilometres above Bienvenido. Anala would pass over Lukarticar every ninety-one minutes as the world turned beneath her.

By the time she rotated the capsule so her largest port was oriented to the planet below, she had passed over the north of Indiland to approach the shore of Noemstok, the northern polar continent, with its massive skirt of ice. Contact with flight com had ended just before third-stage shut-off; their array of receiver stations across Lamaran wasn't set up for this kind of flight. Communications would be dropping in and out several times each orbit.

After checking that all the capsule systems were nominal, Anala started to remove the pressure suit, but the sight through the port kept distracting her. No one had ever seen Bienvenido from polar orbit before. The terminator line, bisecting the pristine white cover of ice, was so much sharper here than it ever was over land or ocean. Her breath caught as she saw the pale green light curtains of a borealis storm serpentining across hundreds of kilometres of darkness. And amazingly, Delores was right: she could indeed make out individual ice floes adrift in the placid turquoise sea, no bigger than ships. Perhaps she would be able to see the *Gothora III* and the *Sziu* after all. That had always seemed the most ridiculous aspect of the mission, the one that had sent her anger surging to dangerous levels – levels that almost triggered insubordination. *I gave up a mission to kill a Tree for this pitiful tourist flight?*

But the prime minister himself had shaken her hand as she went into the gantry lift. 'I cannot emphasize how important this mission is,' he told her. 'Bienvenido's very survival may depend on it.'

'You can rely on me, sir,' she answered, all the while wanting to slap his pudgy old face. Years of discipline kept her outwardly calm and respectful, but how it hurt.

Now, though, she wasn't so sure. To change a Liberty flight was an act of the purest desperation. And knowing a nest of Fallers had stolen some atom bombs – that they'd already detonated one – was making her re-evaluate her priorities. The government needed this mission, needed her skills, her professionalism.

And – oh – the view . . .

The north pole passed by and the capsule was heading back out over the western Delos Sea towards the northern coast of Rachweith, which was deep into night. Volcanoes glowed among the spines of the mountains which ran east–west along that land-mass; she could see the slim streams of lava eking down the slopes, poisonous ebony vapours billowing high to throttle the pure white water clouds scudding in from the sea.

Out over the Ashla Ocean she acquired the New Angeles station, and flight com's voice made a welcome return to her earphones. It was a frantic five minutes while she confirmed instrument readings and they scrutinized her telemetry.

'Systems nominal, Liberty two-six-seven-four,' flight com reported as the capsule flew over the Huang Archipelago. 'Space Vigilance Office reports your orbital track is good. You have a go from the mission flight commander.'

'Roger that, flight com,' she acknowledged.

'What's your view like?' Adolphus asked.

Anala was so startled by the breach in protocol she took a moment to reply, remembering mission 2,673 when Colonel Matej had spoken directly to Ry once the missile anomalies had begun. 'View is good, sir. I'm in the umbra right now, but I can see town streetlights across Aflar Province, and earlier I could see ice floes.'

'Good, good. Best wishes, Comrade.'

'Thank you, sir.' There were only a few more minutes of communication with flight com until she crossed over Rakwesh Province to soar above the Wingrush Sea, then contact was lost again.

Lukarticar was bigger than Noemstok, with several mountain ranges curving up out of the snowfields to straddle the terminator line. Then she was above the Polas Sea with Macbride Sound just visible to the west before the world curved away, and her first assessment was coming up fast. Nixie tubes in the navigation board produced the coordinates, and she adjusted the sextant accordingly, peering keenly through the lens.

'Back with you,' flight com announced.

'I can see the *Pericato*,' Anala exclaimed, trying to keep her voice level and emotionless, but right in the centre of the lens was a long wake coming from the Marine ship which sent her heart racing. 'It's heading south-west.'

'Good job, Liberty two-six-seven-four. Attempt contact, please.'

'Roger that.' She pushed off and flicked switches on the communication board, changing frequencies, pushing more power to the omnidirectional antenna's transmission circuit. 'This is Liberty flight two-six-seven-four calling Marine polar expedition. Do you read me, Major Danny?' Anala called three times, watching the ship sliding away underneath then behind her before she received an answer.

'This is Major Danny, receiving you, Liberty two-six-seven-four. Strength seven.'

'Roger that. Flight com, confirm contact with Marine expedition.'

'Well done, Liberty. We're going to get you to do some service module housekeeping now. Next time you pass over the Polas Sea, you will be free to begin Operation High Bird.'

'Roger that. Cloud cover minimal at this time. Some heavy weather accumulating to the north, but it looks like an easterly wind.'

'Okay. The service module manager wants you to stir lox tanks three through to seven, then check the pressure readings.'

'Roger, flight com.'

She spent the next twenty minutes on the dull but essential tasks that occupied ninety per cent of every astronaut's flight. Clicking switches, taking readings, firing the reaction control thrusters in tiny bursts. The Liberty glided along Lamaran's eastern seaboard. She could see the Salalsav mountains guarding the Desert of Bone from any clouds coming off the Eastath Ocean. Picked out the small white V's of boats off the coast as they powered their way between ports using the common trade routes just a few kilometres out from land. Practised searching them out with binoculars. Then she was actually passing over Cape Ingmar, seeing the familiar pattern of hangars and launch pads – so much smaller now.

Second observation assessment: seeing if she could locate her two recovery ships heading north. The sea was eerily uniform. Then she saw a pair of tiny white splinters side by side – minute wakes.

'Got them,' she called, and read out their coordinates so flight com could confirm the sighting.

Two ships alone amid the vast blue ocean. Nothing else ventured so far from Lamaran. That chilled her.

*

The south pole passed below the capsule and Anala fired the reaction control thrusters to perform a minute attitude correction, stabilizing the craft so the port was aligned directly down onto the planet. She gripped the fabric handhold at the side of the toughened multi-layered glass and stared at the coastline now slipping into view. This was her eighteenth pass over Lukarticar, and she was fighting fatigue as the track carried her directly along the eastern side of Macbride Sound, which was just on the terminator line. She peered down at the crinkled edge as the sunlight crept across it, seeing white dots of ice floes drifting imperceptibly from the glacier walls they'd fallen from. Still no sign of the *Sziu*'s wake. *Where in Uracus is it hiding?*

The radio crackled with static as the omnidirectional antenna picked up a carrier wave. She blinked, frowning as her concentration was disturbed. The Liberty wasn't far enough north to pick up a signal from the *Pericato* yet.

'Hello, Anala,' a voice said in her earphones. 'I always knew you'd make it into space.'

'Oh, Great Giu! Ry?'

*

Flying above the sea for eight hours was a relatively smooth experience. It was only when the *Discovery* turned south and began its journey across Lukarticar's empty snowscape that the blimp began to quiver. Demitri was combating the squalling winds and sudden flurries of loose snow that whirled up into the air like slow-motion fountains. The engine pitch became a constant variable, while the fans tilted up and down repeatedly as he fought to counteract the buffeting.

Inside the gondola, Florian could really feel the sidewinds and unexpected downdraughts knocking the *Discovery* about. By then he was using motion-sickness counter-routines the whole time – to little effect. He hadn't risked eating anything for hours. That was the first time he began to acknowledge Commonwealth technology might not be omnipotent. Twilight had already claimed the short polar day, so that just as the rumpled snowfields dwindled to grey and the outside temperature dropped still further, the *Discovery* was reduced to five hundred metres altitude. He *really* didn't think that was high enough.

His u-shadow lacked routines for smoothing down his anxiety. There were plenty of proficient chemical remedies for that in the various medical kits they were carrying, but unfortunately none of them were near his seat. So he just clamped his jaw shut and summoned up some of his old mindscape files. He thought he could refine them with the new crafting and blending tools the space machine had gifted to him. But once he started to review them, he realized how crass they were compared to what he could do now.

Instead, he had his enriched perception of the pitiless white and blue world that was Lukarticar combine with symphonic music, creating a new and fabulously baroque mindscape – becoming a bird and flying clean and straight over the ice-conquered universe towards a sliver of dawn that was forever receding. It had edge and eeriness, with the rhythm slowly increasing along with the bird's speed, cold wind flowing over leather wings, exhilaration merging with danger, the thrill building along with expectancy . . . He barely had to compose anything, the hypnotic mindscape flowed into creation so naturally—

'You need to start getting ready.'

Florian was abruptly back in the real world. He suspended the file, and looked round the cramped gondola. Everyone was stirring, reaching for their backpacks. His u-shadow showed him the blimp's sensor imagery. Demitri was holding them steady into a twenty-three-kph wind coming from the pole, barely a hundred metres above the wind-sculpted snow ridges. And below them lay the imposing bulk of the *Viscount*.

Florian pulled down his backpack and took out the small package that was his environment-maintenance suit, which looked like a neatly folded black polythene bag. Reluctantly, he stripped down to his cotton underwear and told his u-shadow to open the e-m suit. Tiny ridges of plyplastic running along the fabric turned flaccid, allowing it to concertina out into what resembled a pair of shiny overalls similar to the kind garage mechanics wore, but with integral boots. Everyone else was getting into theirs. With a shrug – and because it was chilly with nothing else to protect him – Florian pulled it on, including the hood. Icons popped up into his exovision, and he set temperature levels and tightness. The fabric gripped him firmly, and his skin immediately warmed – a sensation like standing out in the summer sun. Some old grumpy part of his mind didn't believe it would stay that warm once he stepped outside the gondola.

'Force-field skeleton,' Paula reminded him.

This part he was actually looking forward to. The protective skeleton suit was similar to the e-m suit, but with its generator systems occupying integral ribs that came close to imitating a human skeleton. It fitted snugly, and he ran through its functions just like he'd practised back at the farmhouse.

'Everyone ready?' Demitri asked.

'Let's go,' Kysandra said.

Exovision schematics showed Florian the *Discovery* compressing helium from its gas cells, storing it in small onboard tanks. The propulsion fans whined loudly, holding the blimp stable as it sank towards the ground. Lights came on around the base of the gondola, shining down on the glittering snow.

'Twenty metres,' Demitri announced. 'Picking up some micro-burst winds. Get us anchored, please.'

The gondola door expanded, and ice particles swirled in. Florian watched Marek and Valeri slide down the rope ladder. He switched to the gondola fuselage sensors. Valeri stood still under the tail, running a full field function scan, alert for any nearby hostiles. Marek collected the cables that had unwound from the nose; both of them ended in field anchors – small globes of malmetal. He shoved one down into the crusty snow. Eight separate pinions shot out, curving down and round through the hard-packed subsurface ice like fast-growing roots, holding the cable fast. Marek walked thirty metres and applied the second cable's anchor.

'Secure,' he reported.

Florian felt the fans slowly spin down.

'It's holding,' Demitri said. 'Well inside stress parameters.'

Fergus was next down the rope ladder. Florian ordered the e-m suit's hood to cover his face. It flowed over his cheeks and chin like a dry liquid to protect him. He followed Ry down through the pool of light underneath the gondola. And – amazingly – the e-m suit did regulate his body temperature at a steady thirty-seven degrees. Air temperature was registering as minus forty-two.

'Damn,' Ry sent across the general link. 'I wish our space suits were this good.'

Florian looked round. There was the base of the gondola glaring above him, glittery dense snow under his feet – and nothing else. Beyond the illuminated patch, the polar night was absolute; they were too far south for any backscatter illumination from the Tree Ring. He couldn't even see a ge-eagle, though twenty of them circled overhead.

Paula and Fergus walked out of the light and vanished. Visual enhancement and infra-red cut in, allowing him to follow them as they moved off.

'Heads up,' Demitri announced. He dropped the first equipment case out of the gondola. Florian and the others spent the next ten minutes picking up and stacking the cargo he threw down to them.

'That's interesting,' Valeri said. 'The drones are picking up a new radio signal.'

Florian couldn't help it – his stomach muscles tensed up, and he started searching round for seibears.

'Where?' Kysandra asked smoothly.

'Above us,' Valeri said. 'One hundred and seventy eight kilometres, to be exact. There's a Liberty capsule in polar orbit.'

'No way,' Ry muttered.

And now Florian was tilting his head back, searching through the haze of wind-borne ice particles. His u-shadow pulled the exact coordinates from the drone, and bracketed the tiny grey dot as it slid low across the western horizon.

'They're looking for us,' Kysandra said. 'They must be pretty desperate to use a Liberty.'

'You'd be surprised how much you can see from low orbit,' Valeri said. 'At one time in the twenty-first century, there were hundreds of spy satellites orbiting Earth, every nation busy watching their enemies.'

Florian glanced at the gondola and its intense white lights. 'Will they be able to see us? We are kind of bright.'

'Let's not risk it,' Kysandra said. 'Demitri, kill the lights until the capsule's over the horizon.'

The lights went off. Florian had to turn up his infra-red reception.

'The pilot is talking,' Valeri said. 'She must be in range of a ship somewhere.'

'We'll get the drones looking for it,' Kysandra said.

'She?' Ry asked. 'Can I hear the broadcast, please?'

Florian listened. It was a female voice amid plenty of static which his u-shadow worked to filter out, giving him a clipped conversation, typical of military types – rather, half a conversation. The drone over the Straits of Tyree couldn't pick up the ship's answering transmissions.

'It's Anala!' Ry exclaimed. 'I know her. She was next on the flight list. They must have changed her mission because of us. Giu, she'll be pissed off about that.'

'Going behind the horizon,' Valeri said as Anala's voice collapsed into a distortion hash then fell silent.

'Okay, lights back on,' Kysandra said. 'We'll have to go dark and silent every time she's overhead. Load the orbit parameter into your u-shadows, everyone, please.'

The gondola lights returned, and Demitri threw down the next case.

'Ry, would she be an ally?' Kysandra asked.

'She's a good officer,' Ry said.

'Fair enough.'

'We're ready,' Paula said. 'Florian, Ry, activate your force fields, please.'

Florian did as he was told. Back when they were planning this, nobody could quite work out what would happen when a disrupter pulse struck ice. Explosion? Vapour jet? Geyser of boiling water?

Five hundred metres away, a mellow purple-white haze flared out, forcing the surrounding snowscape into sharp focus. He could see two figures silhouetted against the aurora. Then a wide circle of snow burst upwards atop a furious blast of steam, as if a rocket motor had just ignited. Static seethed through the smog, sending weird twisters of light flickering along the plume. Lightning forks skewered out, discharging into the snowfield. Three of them lashed the *Discovery*'s envelope and Florian flinched, ducking instinctively as they crackled overhead.

Then the purple radiance faded away. A few more static waves rippled through the dispersing cloud, and darkness swept back in.

'That cut down about eight metres,' Paula said, 'but it was a low-power pulse. Second one now.'

Purple light flashed across the snowfield again.

For the whole flight, Paula and the ANAdroids had been studying the scans being relayed to them from the ge-eagles. They'd decided to aim for the middle of the colony starship, just behind the point where it had bent on impact. *Viscount* had a simple enough design, consisting of a long spindle to which various modules and compartments were attached, allowing for multiple redundancy and easy manufacture. The front – which was mainly force-field generators, regrav units and the ultradrive systems – had taken a lot of damage when it came down. From the scans, it seemed like the majority of cylindrical cargo modules that were clumped round the rear section had survived – if not still attached to the starship's primary axis, then strewn around the landing zone before the snow and ice engulfed them.

It took Paula three hours to tunnel down to the *Viscount*'s hull. Twice she had to stop for ten minutes while the Liberty flew overhead. Then there was another hour of more delicate disrupter pulses clearing a route through the clustered modules to an airlock.

Valeri and Fergus opened a maintenance hatch next to the airlock, and spent a quarter of an hour trying to reactivate the malmetal.

'No good,' Fergus said eventually. 'Three thousand years in the ice has screwed it completely.'

Paula turned her disrupter pulse to the lowest power level and punched cleanly through the airlock instead.

They followed her in, shining wide-angle torches that filled the interior with a uniform white light. Every surface was covered in a carpet of fine ice granules, creating a shimmering disorderly chamber of opalescent rainbows. Florian found it bad enough trying to keep his balance as he walked along the sloping corridor. The chromatic dazzle made it worse, and visual clues didn't help. The corridor was clearly a radial one, extending out from the starship's central spindle. When in flight, gravity was always oriented towards the aft end; that meant he was walking along one of the walls.

The *Viscount* was dead. He accepted that at some deep instinctive level. Beneath the victorious layer of ice, the starship's structure seemed almost pristine, suspended perfectly in its frigid tomb, waiting only for the kiss of warmth to awaken. But the extreme cold hadn't preserved it. The long millennia of exposure to nothing but sub-zero temperature and darkness had permeated every molecule, bringing only extinction.

'I'm concerned about cold fatigue,' Valeri said. 'My scan is showing diminished molecular integrity in the structure all around. The starship is fragile, so please tread lightly.'

Florian stopped mid-step, but everyone else carried on, so he shrugged and followed, just taking extra care now to make each footfall a light one.

They came to the end of the corridor. Three malmetal doors glimmered softly beneath their ice cloaks, opening onto the transit tubes which ran through the ship. The ANAdroids ignored them and went to work on a small hatch beside them. When the cover was removed, it exposed a neat array of slim cables and pipes worming into various plastic boxes.

Fergus began to plug modules into the exposed electronics. Florian tried not to flinch every time sparks shot out of the ancient cables. Small wisps of smoke began to curl upwards. Several times, lights around the malmetal doors flickered a pale green-white before fading away again. He wasn't sure, but one time he thought the malmetal itself twitched. Grains of ice drifted gently down to the floor. With that first hint that the starship might not be completely dead, he kept looking round to see if Fergus could animate anything else.

'Got it,' Fergus announced. 'The wiring in here is so much powdered crud, but I'm shunting power into a nexus. It's frying some processors, but a couple are tough enough to withstand the surge if I bring the voltage up slowly. Ah, here we go.'

'What's he trying to do?' Florian asked Paula quietly.

'Power up a local node. The *Viscount* has a distributed network, so unless there was a catastrophic data loss when it came down, the node should be able to tell us exactly where we are.'

'Where we are?'

'In the ship. Once we know that, we know the location of every cargo compartment in relation to us. And we have the *Viscount*'s complete manifest.'

'Ah. Right.'

'There's considerable damage to the micronet,' Fergus said, 'but there are valid caches. I'm initiating the boot-up in safe-base; the software should be able to work round the damage.'

Florian started to worry. If pushing a few millivolts through a processor blew most of it, what hope did they ever have of reactivating a Neumann synthesizer or a wormhole generator?

'Got it,' Fergus said.

A three-dimensional image of the *Viscount* opened up in Florian's exovision. Their location amid the terrific complexity of shadowy lines was indicated by a purple star.

'Okay,' Paula said. 'That gives us HGT54b as the most convenient.'

The cylindrical cargo compartment she nominated glowed lime-green in Florian's exovision. He sighed. They'd have to tunnel further through the ice to reach it.

It took another seventy minutes (with one pause to let the *Liberty* fly past), which he spent back up on the surface again. Every couple of minutes, the tunnel entrance would belch out a thick jet of steam which melted yet more of the wall. When he ventured back down, the tunnel wall was impossibly slick, like a glossy diamond. Demitri had to use a molecular severance rifle to break up the surface and give them some traction; otherwise they would have slid down the entire length.

The new excavation branched from the airlock where they'd entered the *Viscount*, curving round parallel to the hull then angling down. It ended in the silver-grey wall of cargo compartment HGT54b. Heat and seething steam had already shredded the surface of its protective foam. Valeri and Demitri started applying power-blades to the remaining insulation, shaving off long strips that crumbled apart as they fell to the floor. Before long, they came to the metalloceramic bulkhead itself.

'Fragile from cold fatigue, of course,' Valeri said. He inserted his blade carefully and cut a neat circle about a metre and a half wide. He and Demitri gingerly eased it out.

Somehow the blackness inside the cargo compartment was even more profound than it had been in the starship. Demitri climbed in. The other ANAdroids started handing him equipment packs.

'You are probably safer sleeping in there,' Marek said. 'I will stind – stand watch on the surface in case any seibears show up, Faller or otherwise.'

Florian gazed at the intimidatingly black hole again. He hadn't even realized how late it was until the ANAdroid mentioned sleep. 'In there?' He wasn't sure why, but the cargo compartment was stirring a mild claustrophobia, making breathing more of an effort than usual.

'Yes,' Paula said. 'I don't want us split up.'

'All right.'

Once he clambered inside, the forty-degree angle the whole starship was resting at became obvious. There wasn't much room, which didn't help Florian's feeling of confinement; the cylinder was divided up by sheets of reinforced carbon grid-mesh, forming smaller subcompartments that held the cargo in place. A hexagonal-cross-section corridor ran down the centre, allowing full access. Movement was difficult, the steep angle turning everything into a half climb.

HGT54b was carrying industrial production systems and four wormhole generators. Several of the heavier neumanetic synthe-sizers had broken free on impact and smashed into their neighbours in a disastrous domino effect, but that still left over forty manu-facturing systems intact. They were all covered in thick protective membranes, themselves layered in ice – but not as thickly here as directly inside the starship.

Paula and Demitri were clambering along the central access corridor, shining their torches into subcompartments, seeking visual confirmation to their field function scans.

'The wormhole generators are all intact,' Paula called out.

The ANAdroids started setting up heaters – simple metal cylin-ders a metre long and half as wide. One end was an intake grille, while the opposite end had long plyplastic strings dangling like particularly feeble tentacles.

Ry handed out meal packs. He and Florian sat on a broken metallurgical extruder while their self-grilling wrappers cooked ham and cheese toasties, and watched the ANAdroids clambering along the corridor, stretching the plyplastic strings along and feeding them into subcompartments. Once a string was in place, it expanded out into a hollow duct and stiffened into place.

The heater fans started up with a mild hum. Warm air gusted out of the ducts.

'It should take about ten hours of this heat soak to get the ambient temperature back up to zero,' Demitri said. 'That should help with the reactivation. I don't want to rush it.'

'Why won't the wormhole generator work in the cold?' Ry asked.

'It was designed to operate in temperatures a lot lower than this,' Valeri said, 'but cold along with the time it's been down here . . . We don't want to take any chances. You saw what happened to the electronics in the ship. Our chances will be improved if we can get some heat in here first. Plus, it makes it easier to make repairs.'

Florian glanced about the dark cramped space and worried what warmth would do to the frozen machinery, how expansion would shift things. He glanced at a couple of synthesizers that had crunched into each other; they weighed several tonnes each. The notion that more of them might be dislodged while he was sleeping added to his claustrophobia, and he gave up on the toastie.

Trying to sleep now would be useless, but he was tired, so he unrolled his plyplastic mattress on top of a biochemical refiner, and lay down, wondering if he should compose a new mindscape file that might divert his anxiety—

*

Florian woke up when drops of cold water dripped onto his nose. All the ice in HGT54b had melted, leaving the resultant droplets clinging to every surface like persistent morning dew. He hadn't noticed the air getting hotter thanks to his e-m suit, which had maintained a constant body temperature while he slept, but now water was running across every piece of cargo, slicking their protective membranes as it formed slow runnels. The black grids dividing up the compartment were drizzling a light mist. Water was pooling at the bottom of the corridor. And for the first time since leaving the gondola, Florian could smell something: a curious bad-air scent similar to the musk of a waltan fungus.

Overnight, the ANAdroids had rigged the inside of the compartment with lights. They'd also stripped the protective membrane off two of the wormhole generators and cleared some space around the big circular machines. The slim metal cases they'd brought with them were open, showing off an impressive collection of intricate tools and electronic gadgets. Sensor pads had been applied to the generator casings.

'More – morning,' Marek said cheerfully.

Florian checked his time display, surprised he'd slept for more than seven hours. 'Where is everyone?' he asked. Only Marek, Fergus, and Valeri were left, gathered round the wormhole generators like devoted acolytes.

'On the sir – surface,' Marek told him. 'There's a breakfast pik – pik – pack if you want one.'

'Maybe later. How are you doing with the wormhole generators?'

'Warming nicely now. The pre – pro – protective membranes had cold-welded to them. Tick took some scraping to got get off. We should be able to start initializang zing in a couple of hours. Their systems seem to be mainly intact.'

'Mainly?'

'Yes. We knew they wouldn't be perfectly prefect – perfect.'

Florian glanced round the cargo compartment again. Secondary routines flashed up turquoise identifier icons across the machines cocooned inside their glistening membranes. The potential locked away in this one space was phenomenal. Some of the synthesizers were even capable of full replication, building duplicates of themselves. If you coupled this single small trove of Commonwealth technology with all the knowledge Joey had given him, Bienvenido really would be building hyperdrive starships within twenty years. And this was only one small section of the *Viscount*'s cargo.

'I'm going up to the surface,' he announced.

A plyplastic door had been fixed across the hole cut in HGT54b's side, keeping the precious heat in. It opened silently to let him pass. The lustrous ice tunnel was illuminated by small lights spaced uncomfortably far apart. His universe closed in oppressively again, not helped by him being alone on the awkward trek up to the surface.

The sun still hadn't risen when he finally emerged out onto the murky snowscape. Bright white light was shining down from the base of the gondola, fluorescing the minute ice particles swirling idly through the air. The gloomy empty vista it exposed was even more incongruous given the entombed leviathan below his feet. He saw Kysandra, Paula, and Ry huddled together with Demitri underneath the gondola.

Paula looked round as he walked over. 'We may have a problem,' she said.

'What's happened?'

'The drones located the ship Anala was talking to. It's the *Pericato*, a Marine ship. And it's also got nuclear weapons on board; the drone sensors detected their radiation signature.'

'Crud,' Florian grunted.

'That's not the problem,' Paula said.

'Oh. What is?'

'The drones also located the *Sziu*. It's heading south-west through the Straits of Tyree. The course it's taking will bring it to the coast due north from here – the shortest distance from us. It seems the Fallers know we're here. My guess is they'll bring the atom bombs ashore and try to deploy them against us.'

Florian just managed to resist turning a full circle to try and catch whatever Faller-animal was spying on them. 'Can the *Gothora* intercept them?'

'No. Jymoar is further north than the *Pericato*.'

'So what do we do?'

'We're assuming the warheads on the *Pericato* are short-range missiles,' Kysandra said. 'The government developed the Aseri missile for Operation Reclaim – solid-fuel propellant with a fifteen-kilometre range. Good for taking out urban areas with a high concentration of Fallers. Should be useful against the *Sziu*, providing they know its location. At the moment they clearly don't – they're not on an interception course.'

'The drone also picked up *Pericato*'s radio transmissions,' Ry said. 'Major Danny is in command.'

'You'd think he would've had enough of the Fallers on the *Sziu* by now,' Kysandra muttered.

'He wants another chance for his moment of glory, no doubt,' Paula said. 'Port Chana harbour wasn't anyone's finest hour.'

'You're going to tell him where the *Sziu* is?' Florian asked.

Even with most of her face covered by the e-m suit's hood, Paula's scowl was visible. 'It's our only option.'

'I just cannot trust the Marines,' Kysandra said. 'Section Seven dreamt up a plan – Operation Overload – in case they ever confirmed my location. It involves bombarding me with nukes, and the Marines would carry out the attack. Giving them our location, or even a hint of it . . . That's asking a lot.'

'It would take them several days to reach us here,' Paula said. 'The risk is small.'

'But why should we introduce any extra risks?'

'Fortunately, we have another option, or at least we can come at the problem from a different angle,' a grinning Ry said. 'Someone else can tell Major Danny where the *Sziu* is; someone he'll trust. And they won't give us away.'

'You mean your friend?' Florian asked Ry. 'The one in the Liberty?'

'I don't think we have a choice,' Ry said. 'We need to get the *Sziu*'s coordinates to the *Pericato*. And so far, Anala hasn't seen the *Sziu*.'

'And you trust her?' Florian demanded.

'Completely,' Ry said. 'But we need to do this quickly. Even if the *Pericato* sails to intercept *Sziu* right now, it'll be touch and go if they can hit it before it reaches the coastline.'

'Time,' Kysandra said in dismay. 'We cruised along for two hundred and fifty years, and now it's suddenly acute. I crudding hate the irony.'

Florian linked to the drone that was circling high above the

563

coast and saw the *Sziu* steaming south-west at full speed. A weaker sensor return gave him the Marine ship behind it. Different sensors were tracking the steady radio signal of the Liberty capsule skimming the top of the atmosphere. Choice really didn't come into it, this was simple logic. 'For what it's worth, my vote is to call Pilot Major Em Yulei.'

*

Anala stared out of the port in some crazy belief she could actually make out Ry down there somewhere.

'Yeah, it's me.'

'Have you Fallen?' she whispered.

That wonderful chuckle of his filled her headphones. 'No. But of course I would say that either way.'

That easy teasing – so him. *Surely no Faller could ever truly copy that?*

'So then why are you calling?'

'Anala, I'm going to tell you why we're here on Lukarticar.'

'Why?' she asked automatically. No one at her preflight briefing could produce a reason other than they might be seeking refuge from the Faller Apocalypse.

'We've been looking for the *Viscount*. Anala, we found her!'

'The *Visc—* No!' That wasn't possible. The *Viscount* was practically myth, just like the Warrior Angel. *But she's now very real.*

'It's buried under the ice. Anala, we're trying to recover Commonwealth technology that'll stop the apocalypse.'

'You can do that?'

'We hope so. If we have enough time. So we need you to perform your mission and take out the *Sziu* without alerting the marines or the Fallers to where we are.'

She stared out of the port, across the terminator where the planet was in total darkness. Beyond that line, there was no way to distinguish between the snowfields of Lukarticar and the icy waters of the Polas Sea; both were completely black, as if that portion of the world had gone missing. 'How can the *Sziu* be a problem to you?' she asked cautiously. 'They briefed me – a proper briefing, security level one. You're with the Warrior Angel now, and she has weapons. The greatest weapons on the planet.'

'And the Fallers have atom bombs. We can't protect the *Viscount* if they detonate them. Anala, the Marines have to intercept the *Sziu*. We know the *Pericato* is also carrying nuclear weapons. They have to stop the Fallers from reaching us.'

'I don't know where the *Sziu* is. I can't see it.'

'We can. Our sensors are tracking it, just like they're tracking you. You can guide the Marines to it.'

She listened numbly as he read out a string of latitude and longitude coordinates: *Sziu*'s speed and bearing. She so wanted to believe this was Ry, that there was hope, that the *Viscount* was genuine. But the other possibility was equally likely – that he had Fallen, that the location was a lie, that she'd send the *Pericato* on the wrong course, leaving the Fallers free to pursue the *Gothora III*. *I don't want to make this decision.*

'That location you've given me is on the other side of the terminator. It's in the dark, Ry; I can't confirm it yet. If you're right, the *Sziu* will be in daylight for my next pass. I can tell the *Pericato* then.'

'That's too late, Anala. Major Danny has to catch them before they reach the coast. The only chance he has is if the *Pericato* starts after them now.'

'I can't, Ry. I can't do that.'

'This is what you've lived for, Anala, everything you've worked towards. This is your time to hit the Fallers, and hit them hard.'

'I have to have confirmation. You crudding know that. You know!'

'You trusted me before. Please, order the Marines to intercept the *Sziu*. We're so close to the Commonwealth systems. I've seen the starship, and it's magnificent! We can fly across space again, Anala, real spaceflight, not just pissing about in orbit. We can get home to the Commonwealth. Don't let that future go. Don't let the Fallers win!'

'But I need verifiable data! And if you are Ry, you know this.' *Even if you're not Ry, you'll have his memories and know it.*

'The Fallers don't have the technology to call a Liberty capsule. This is Commonwealth technology I'm using.'

'It's a radio signal, Ry. That proves nothing.'

'What do you need, Anala? What will it take?'

'I need to see the *Sziu*.'

She waited as the coastline slipped past underneath, cursing her own timidity.

'Ask General Delores,' Ry said finally.

'What?'

'If you don't trust me, tell General Delores what I've told you. Tell her we've given you the *Sziu*'s position. She should know the truth; she has access to the highest government officials. Remember Stonal, the PSR official that interviewed me? He can confirm the Warrior Angel has been attempting to contact the prime minister. We were trying to do it through Captain Chaing. We can be trusted, I promise. Ask her. You should be in range of the coastal tracking station soon.'

'Four minutes,' she said automatically. Then she hesitated, deciding he deserved one last offering of trust. She owed him that – owed his memory if all she was talking to now was his Faller copy. 'Ry, Adolphus himself is at Cape Ingmar.'

'You are crudding kidding me!'

A slight smile lifted her lips – that surprised indignation seemed impossible to fake; she could even see the expression on his face. A face she really missed. 'No, I'm not. My mission is that important to them.'

'Then that might make this a whole lot easier. There's something you can say that he'll know only comes from the Warrior Angel.'

*

So far, every orbit had seemed to take scant minutes. Now, of course, it took forever for the capsule to slide closer to Lamaran's southern coast and contact with the ground station.

'We have acquisition, Liberty two-six-seven-four,' flight com's voice came through level and calm, lush in its own professionalism. 'Welcome back.'

'Put the prime minister on,' she replied. 'Now.'

'Please repeat, Liberty two-six-seven-four?'

'Confirming request. Get the prime minister. I have a message for him.'

It didn't take much imagination to picture the flight centre with technicians at their consoles, trying hard not to look round, keeping their expressions neutral. Do your work. Always concentrate on the mission data, no matter what the crisis. Every minute of every day of every endless year of training hammered that home. And now this flight had come along, and nothing was the same any more.

'This is Prime Minister Adolphus.'

'Sir, astronaut Ry Evine has been in contact. He's with the Warrior Angel and Paula.' She heard it, actually heard it over the radio – a commotion in the flight centre, people calling out in shock. *Delores will have them all weeding the launch pads for a decade!*

'Where are they?' Adolphus asked.

'They say they've found the *Viscount*, sir. And, sir, they supplied me with proof of identity. They say that their opening offer to you was to use the machine in the basement; that if you heard that, you'll know it's them, that this is genuine.'

She paused, waiting without taking a breath.

'That's a yes, Major Em Yulei. Only they would know that. You were talking to the Warrior Angel's group.'

It took her entire willpower not to gasp in relief. 'Sir, they gave me the coordinates for the *Sziu*, but I can't confirm it visually; the location is in the nightside. They ask for the *Pericato* to intercept it immediately. Ry said if we wait for visual conformation, the Fallers' atom bombs could destroy the *Viscount*, sir.'

'Give Major Danny the *Sziu*'s position and bearing immediately. He is to intercept at once; authorization ZZ57AA to use maximum force. Repeat, ZZ57AA. Please confirm.'

'Roger, sir. Authorization ZZ57AA.'

'Do it.'

Anala flicked switches on the communication panel and called the *Pericato* before it passed out of contact range.

*

Somewhere amid the all-engulfing dark, the Marine ship changed course and went full steam ahead. Flight com seemed to forget their standard mission format: supplying endless capsule house-keeping procedures. Instead it was Adolphus who stayed on line.

'Did they say what they were doing at the *Viscount*?' the prime minister asked as the capsule cleared the Lamaran coast just east of Port Chana.

'No, sir. Just that it has machines that can stop the apocalypse.'

'And are they all there?'

'I only talked to Major Evine. He indicated he was in a group.'

'I see. You are to be commended, Major Em Yulei. You have carried out your duty in the finest tradition of the Astronaut Regiment.'

'Thank you, sir.'

'When you orbit Lukarticar again, will you be able to see the *Sziu*?'

'I hope so, sir.' *If it is where Ry said it is. If that was Ry. If . . .*

'Excellent. I need comprehensive updates, please.'

'Yes, sir.'

'And try and find out exactly what the Warrior Angel is doing.'

'I understand.'

*

It was another orbit that took an eternity, stretching her nerves far worse than waiting for the flight readiness exam results. The capsule seemed to crawl leisurely over the centre of Lamaran, then traversed the entire length of Nilsson Sound, which was channelling a fierce storm directly inland. She lost contact with flight com (after they'd managed to get in a final twelve minutes of systems maintenance) just as she reached the edge of the Fire Archipelago. Then it was a long communication blackout as the Liberty curved lazily above the north pole and carried on over the Eastath Ocean, skirting well to the west of Fanrith before soaring across Tonari's fjord-notched coast – both far beyond reach of any ground station. Then finally she was over the south pole again.

'So that went well,' Ry said. 'Our drone caught the *Pericato* altering course.'

'Adolphus accepted your proof without question,' she said.

'Thank you, Anala. I know this was difficult for you.'

'Ry, why is the Warrior Angel talking to the prime minister? And what *is* the machine in the basement? What's going on?'

'The negotiations were a contingency plan, that's all, in case the Fallers win. They haven't even started talking, not really.'

The whole idea was crazy. *I know the government has always lied, but the scale of this deception . . . Adolphus and the Warrior Angel, in secret talks!* 'Whatever,' Anala said weakly. She checked the capsule's orientation on the navigation panel and fired a quick burst of the reaction control thrusters, refining it. Then she aligned the sextant. 'Ry, what's on the *Viscount* that'll defeat the Faller Apocalypse?'

'I've seen miracles down here, Anala. Synthesizers like mini-factories. Generators that convert mass directly into energy. Everything you need to start a new industrial world.'

'And weapons?'

'Somewhere, yes, but Paula has a plan. She thinks she can stop the apocalypse from ever happening.'

'Who's Paula?'

'She's from the Commonwealth. That's what happened on my mission; that's what I saw: her arrival.'

'Great Giu,' she murmured. It was all so much to acknowledge. Right now she wished the capsule had another rocket stage attached – one she could fire and fly away from Bienvenido itself. Coasting out into the dark beyond, exploring the great gulf. Maybe finding a new world, free from the disasters afflicting dear old Bienvenido.

Out of the corner of her eye she saw the Nixie tubes count down to zero. She gripped the handhold tight, and peered along the sextant.

There! Just in the daylight outside the terminator, eighty kilometres from Lukarticar's rugged coast, a tiny white V was cutting through the rolling waves, heading purposefully south-west. Exactly where Ry had said.

The saddest whimper escaped from her lips as she snatched

the binoculars from their pocket under the sextant. It took a moment to scan, but the ship leapt into her vision. Small, little more than a tiny black fleck against the pale turquoise. But *real*.

'I see it! Ry, I can see the *Sziu*.' Professionalism took over. She checked the sextant, and made a note of the alignment, ready to relay the figures to Major Danny.

'Good to hear that, Liberty two-six-seven-four.'

Anala gave a bitter laugh. He knew. Knew she'd doubted, but forgave her anyway. That was the real Ry all right. 'Welcome back, Pilot Major Evine.'

'Some people are crudding hard to please!'

'You want an easy life in the Astronaut Regiment?'

'Nah, never going to happen. Sorry I missed your Commencing Countdown party.'

'I didn't have one. This mission was put together fast.'

'What? I am outraged! Every astronaut is entitled to their Commencing Countdown party.'

'I'm aware why you're disappointed.'

'Weren't you, too?'

'Possibly. Now cut the unauthorized chatter; I've got an update to give to the Marines.' She studied the figures she'd made.

'Thank you.'

'Ry? The *Sziu* is making very good time. I'm not sure the *Pericato* can get within range before they make landfall.'

'Yeah. We have those numbers, too.'

*

Ry spent most of the morning sitting at the top end of compartment HGT54b, watching the sensor images coming in from the drones. One of the high-altitude craft was out over the ocean while the other was a hundred kilometres inland. Eight ge-eagles were circling the *Sziu* at a safe distance, providing a clear view as it battered its way through the waves. The drone sensors showed the *Pericato* making a valiant effort to intercept.

'They're not going to make it,' he said when the *Sziu* was eight kilometres from the coast. The *Pericato* was twenty-two kilometres behind, and closing fast. But not fast enough.

'Let's see if we can slow the *Sziu* down for them,' Paula said.

Ry's exovision showed him the drone altering itself. The wide, slender wings that allowed it to glide at such altitude began to contract. At the same time, Paula cut the power to its fans.

When the wings had shrunk to half their operational size, the drone stalled. The nose tipped down and it began to fall. Still Paula kept the wing retraction going until just the tips were left, sticking out of the oval fuselage as fins, providing a degree of stability as it streaked down, rapidly reaching its terminal velocity of two hundred and seventeen kilometres per hour.

'Too bad we can't get it supersonic,' Paula said, 'but the fans don't have that much thrust.'

Ry was accessing a nose camera, watching the sea twelve kilometres below. Right at the centre of the image was the *Sziu*. A small grey shape, starting to expand.

'Don't forget the power cells,' Valeri said.

'The safety limiters are already off line,' Paula replied. 'The smartnet will short them out at impact.'

Five kilometres altitude and the dive speed was exhilarating. Ry knew he was smiling.

Two kilometres, and individual features were becoming apparent on the *Sziu*'s deck. Machinery. Crates. Human-Fallers. Beast-Fallers. Paula switched the fans back on, shoving the drone down faster.

Ry changed to the images coming from the ge-eagles. Orientation flicked to horizontal, showing the *Sziu* silhouetted against the horizon, grey smoke from its twin stacks gushing up into the clear azure sky. The drone came plunging down silently, almost too fast to follow. It struck in the middle of the ship. Two explosions, overlapping – the first a tangle of smoke and flame surging up, the second a sphere of bright light ripping outwards. Debris hurtled into the air, chunks trailing filthy vapour contrails.

'Damn!' Paula exclaimed. 'Missed.'

'Missed?' Florian cried out. 'What do you mean? That was a perfect hit.'

'I was aiming for the mid-hold. If it had hit there, chances were good that it would have punched through the bottom of the hull and sunk them. Instead it struck the back of the superstructure. The hull is intact. That was always the risk using a drone like this. And now they're alert.'

The ge-eagles showed Ry flames and black smoke churning out of the wrecked superstructure. He groaned; the *Sziu* was still moving. 'You slowed it down,' he said, but even he thought that sounded meagre.

'That's what we wanted,' Kysandra said. 'The Marines stand a chance now.'

Three minutes after the drone strike, Ry counted five of the huge animal-Fallers standing on deck, carrying their pump-action bazookas, looking vigilantly up into the sky. Eight of the blue-skinned human giant Fallers were with them, also keeping watch on the empty sky above. Half a dozen ordinary human-Fallers fought the superstructure fire.

Ry watched the displays, checking speed and distance for the *Sziu* and the *Pericato*. 'The Marines will be in range in nine minutes,' he said breathlessly. He'd watched the Marines prepare the Aseri missiles. Two trailers were lashed to the deck, supporting large metal tubes. Marines in parkas had unwound thick electric cables from each trailer, laying them across the deck to a small canvas shelter at the front of the superstructure, where the launch control consoles had been set up. Then hydraulics had elevated both tubes to vertical. They were ready to fire. All they needed now was to get in range.

'Uh oh,' Florian murmured.

'What?'

'Seibears,' Florian said. 'Dozens of them.'

Ry checked the feed Florian was using. He was right. Three kilometres ahead of the *Pericato*, a pack of forty seibears were spread out over a patch of water a kilometre wide. More were swimming out towards them.

'I know that's not good,' Paula said cautiously, 'but I don't see what they can do to stop the *Pericato*.'

'Board it?' Kysandra suggested.

'Unlikely at that speed; they'd get swatted aside.'

'Are they carrying weapons?'

'Good question.'

Paula guided a ge-eagle down towards the mass of seibears.

'Nothing,' she said as the ge-eagle scanned the huge amphibious creatures. 'But they're there for a purpose. I don't like it.'

'Maybe we should warn Major Danny?' Ry said. 'That's a lot of Fallers to deal with.'

'Anala isn't due overhead for another forty minutes,' Florian said.

'We can use the drone and ge-eagles to relay a radio signal directly. Danny will probably listen to us.'

'We're missing something, I'm sure,' Paula said. 'But Florian is right: we have to warn the Marines.'

Ry listened to Kysandra contact Major Danny, warning him of the potential danger lurking ahead. But the Marine major was proving recalcitrant. Talking directly to the Warrior Angel – trusting her – was clearly difficult for him. He didn't want to change course to take them round the seibear pack, claiming that would allow the *Sziu* to reach the shore before the missiles were in range.

As Kysandra tried to keep her exasperation in check, Ry ordered one of the ge-eagles to fly over the *Sziu*'s projected landing point. 'Crud!'

'What's wrong?' Paula asked.

'Look at where they're going to come ashore.'

The ge-eagle was showing a mass of seibears waiting patiently on the ice above the sea. More were lumbering towards them from the east and the west.

'How many?' Paula asked in a subdued voice.

'Must be over a hundred,' Ry said. 'And they're still coming.' As the ge-eagle swooped along the coastline, he saw another two of the great grey-white shapes surge up out of the water onto a broad chunk of floating ice.

'The Fallers must have taken over Lukarticar some time ago,' Paula said.

'They're going to come here, aren't they?' Ry said, hoping there wasn't too much anxiety in his voice. His whole life had been spent on the front line combating the Faller menace, but an army of Faller-seibears charging the *Viscount* . . .

'They are a good choice to carry the atomic bombs,' Paula said. 'Their size will give them considerable endurance, and they're quite fast.'

'The *Sziu* might not make it ashore,' Paula said. 'What's Danny doing?'

'Being cautious,' Kysandra admitted.

Ry immediately switched links to the three ge-eagles flying watch around the *Pericato*. There was considerable activity on deck. Marines were appearing with Gatling guns that they were mounting on tripods.

'Nice,' Florian said. 'They'll be able to take out the seibears in the water, so whatever the Fallers were planning isn't going to work.'

'Let's just see how this plays out,' Paula said. 'Demitri, how's the wormhole generator coming?'

Ry looked down the length of HGT54b to where the ANAdroids were clustered round one of the generators. Almost all of the casing had been removed, exposing the tightly packed internal systems. He was used to the infernal complexity of a Liberty module, but this was an order of magnitude above. Instruments that were little more than hairs were worming out of the ANAdroids' modules, infiltrating every fissure. Fergus and Valeri were perfectly still, absorbing the data being fed to them.

'Fifteen per cent of the elements we've investigated so far are invalid,' Demitri reported. 'We're going to have to disassemble and rebuild.' He nodded at Marek, who was carefully removing the casing from a second wormhole generator. 'Fortunately, we have a lot of spare parts.'

'How long?' Paula asked.

'A day, possibly. Hopefully no more.'

'But . . . the *Sziu*,' Florian stammered.

'The *Pericato* is almost in range,' Kysandra said. 'They'll be able to launch in another five minutes.'

Ry reviewed the latest speed and distance figures the ge-eagle data was producing. She was right. The *Pericato* would be in range of the *Sziu* while the ship was still over a kilometre from the shore.

'They don't have to score a direct hit, surely,' Ry said, almost in prayer. 'It's an atom bomb, for Giu's sake. They just have to detonate close.' The *Sziu* still had smoke wheezing out of the super-structure and its speed had decreased further. It was having to alter course constantly now it was so close to the coast to avoid the ice floes bobbing idly in the sea.

'Anything within a kilometre should do,' Paula said. 'Major Danny knows that.'

Ry switched back to the ge-eagles over the *Pericato*. The ship was closing fast on the seibear pack. One of the Gatling guns opened up, stitching a small line of white bullet plumes through the undulating sea close to the lead seibear.

'What was that?' Paula demanded.

Ry couldn't answer; he was watching the entire pack dive cleanly below the surface en masse. Within seconds, none of them were visible, plunging deeper and deeper into the icy water. 'Where are they going?' he murmured uneasily.

'The ge-eagles picked up a signal in our link band,' Paula said. 'It came from the seibears. Have they acquired Advancer macro-cellular clusters?'

'Roxwolf said breeder Fallers could pass any victim's traits on,' Florian said in dismay. 'As long as they'd eggsumed an Eliter, they'd have the pattern of the clusters.'

The remaining drone reported a radio signal broadcasting from the *Pericato*. 'Where did they go?' Major Danny asked. 'We lost sight of them.'

'I'm not sure,' Kysandra replied. 'They just dived deep.'

'What's down there?' Danny asked. 'Should we change course?'

Ry watched Kysandra and Paula exchange a glance. Paula gave a minute shake of her head.

'No,' Kysandra said. 'It is imperative you stop the *Sziu*.'

'Understood.'

'Can the seibears get through a metal hull?' Florian said.

'Cold makes the hull a lot more brittle than usual,' Paula said. 'But even so—'

They all saw it at once. The *Pericato* juddered. And as soon as it settled, it began to curve round.

'We're hit,' Danny's voice shouted in near-panic. 'Something under us. The rudder's gone!'

The ship continued to turn.

'Did it breach the hull?' Kysandra asked.

'No. We've lost steering. And— Oh Giu!' The ship lurched again.

A ge-eagle swooped low and Ry spread every sensor readout across his exovision. *Something* was moving under the Pericato. Large dark shadows flitted about, clumped together tightly, and there was a weird grey-blue stain spreading out from the stern.

'They're under you,' Kysandra said. 'Danny, they're under the ship!'

'That's Faller blood in the water,' Paula said.

'We're losing speed,' Danny said. 'Something's striking the propellers. Our engine is struggling. The gears are overloading.'

'Kamikaze,' Paula hissed.

'What?' Ry asked.

'They're suiciding. The Faller-seibears are deliberately swimming into the propellers. It'll kill them, but it's wrecking the engines. Danny, you have to stop. They can only ruin your engines if the propellers are turning.'

Even as she said it, Ry saw the Marines were firing their Gatling guns into the water all around, hitting nothing.

'Stop firing,' Kysandra ordered. 'You're wasting your ammunition.'

'If you have any grenades, drop them into the water at the stern of the ship,' Paula told him. 'They'll act like mini depth charges.'

'Like what?' Danny asked.

'Just do it!'

'How far away are they?' Florian asked nervously.

'Eighteen kilometres,' Ry told him. 'The *Sziu* is three kilometres from shore.'

'Danny, launch a missile,' Kysandra said. 'You're not going to get closer. This is your best chance. The blast should be enough.'

'. . . distance . . . take me . . . launch codes . . .' Danny's voice was interspersed with the sound of the Gatling guns.

'Save your ammunition!' Kysandra implored.

'Oh crud,' Ry groaned. A seibear had risen up out of the water at the stern of the *Pericato*. It gripped a metal rail running down the hull and held itself in place. Another jumped on its back and in a moment was standing on its shoulders. Then the third came up, using the first two like a ladder, allowing it to move with incredible speed for something so bulky.

Marines swung their Gatling guns round and opened fire, the heavy-calibre rounds ripping the beast apart as it shoved its way on board. But another followed it. And two more emerged from the water under the port prow, forming another ladder.

The Gatlings fired again and again.

'Danny, fire the missiles,' Kysandra yelled. 'Fire them!'

Even though it had slowed considerably, the *Sziu* was pulling away. It was less than two kilometres from the shore. *Pericato* was eighteen kilometres behind and dead in the water.

'. . . what I can . . . Arm them now . . . defend my command . . .' Danny said.

Ry saw a Marine race down the steps at the side of the super-structure. It could have been Danny; he wasn't sure. More seibears were coming up over the gunwales. The Gatling guns were firing constantly and the deck was slick with blue blood and gobbets of Faller flesh. He watched the desperate human figure duck a seibear as it was torn apart by bullets, then slip on the gore just as he reached the flimsy canvas shelter.

One of the Gatling guns fell silent. Two injured seibears had reached it at the same time. The Marines operating it were ripped apart in seconds, their broken bodies flung at their terrified Comrades.

A second Gatling gun ran out of ammunition, its barrel spin-ning wildly as a seibear sped towards it. Marines tried to stop it with carbines. Ry grimaced, and hurriedly switched to another sensor feed. A grenade went off on the starboard side, slaughtering humans and Faller-seibears alike.

The Marines on the prow made a strategic withdrawal into the base of the superstructure and five Faller-seibears hurried after them, tearing the metal hatch from its mountings. But they were too big to fit through. A fusillade of gunfire slammed out of the companionway inside, and the one reaching in to claw whatever fragile flesh it could find staggered backwards, sticky turquoise blood streaming down its fur.

Two seibears arrived at the canvas shelter. It was pulled apart and flung over the gunwale. Danny and a missile technician were exposed, crouched over one of the launch consoles. Ry witnessed Danny's fist slamming down on a big red button an instant before a seibear claw sliced through his throat. An arterial fountain of scarlet blood shot into the air for several seconds.

One of the Aseri missiles fired. Thick yellow smoke illuminated by an incandescent flame plume streaked out across the centre of the *Pericato*, obscuring the massacre.

The Aseri flashed upwards out of the bedlam, a dark-grey tube with a spiked nose cone. It scored a dense stream of glowing smoke through the clear polar air behind it, racing faster and faster. The noxious exhaust began to billow wide in its wake.

At two kilometres altitude, the solid fuel was exhausted. The missile was travelling at supersonic speed. It split in half, the forward section carrying on in a neat parabola, guided by slender fins around its base. Behind it, the spent engine casing tumbled wildly end over end, beginning the long fall back to the water.

Ry's u-shadow immediately acquired the feed from the ge-eagles above the *Sziu*. The ship was less than two kilometres from shore now, and making reasonable speed as it trailed wisps of smoke from the bottom of the superstructure. Seibears began launching themselves from the ice floes, sliding gracefully through the sea towards it. Several of them had established links to Fallers on the *Sziu*.

'Thirty seconds,' Paula said.

The Aseri warhead was travelling too fast for the ge-eagles to obtain a decent visual lock, but their other, more sophisticated, senses tracked it hurtling down out of the sky. It struck the sea three kilometres aft of the *Sziu*, and detonated.

Every link from the ge-eagles at the coast and around the *Pericato* dropped out simultaneously. The drone switched to links from the ge-eagles further inland.

An awed Ry watched the mushroom cloud rise – a dome of vapour as bright as any sun. Around it, the sea dipped for a moment before rushing back in, collapsing the crater. A column of dazzling white vapour surged up, then the blast's wavefront streaked out horizontally, shredding the choppy surface into a foamy miasma. Ry held his breath as it struck the *Sziu*. The ship rocked about violently. Fallers and equipment were torn off the deck. Paint was already smouldering across the hull, bubbling and crisping to black. The bodies flung into the air ignited, burning to charcoal in less than a second before disintegrating. Then he could see no more as the vast storm of superheated steam roaring out from the explosion crashed across the abused ship and carried on towards the shore. Seibears on the ice floes were hurling themselves into the water.

'Will that protect them?' he asked.

'I don't think so,' Paula replied. 'Look.'

The boiling surface of the steam whirlwind was distorting, bulging up in a giant ripple, as if some leviathan from the deeps was rushing out from the detonation point.

'What is that?' Florian murmured in awed alarm.

'Tsunami.'

*

They sent five of the surviving ge-eagles back towards the *Sziu*. The semiorganic birds took twenty minutes to fly through the hurricane-force winds howling out from the epicentre of the detonation. The whole area was still shrouded in hot churning cloud bands, though the core was starting to clear. Sensors probed through the thinning vapour. The fringes of the clouds were cooling rapidly now as the wind abated, turning to rain which had chilled to sleet by the time it reached the snowfield.

Along with dozens of ice floes, the *Sziu* had been driven onto the rocky shore. It lay there on its side across the shelf of a black pebble beach, its hull broken open from the impact. Waves lapped through the twisted fissures, flooding the engine room. Faller bodies were strewn across the deck, blackened lumps of meat slicked by the new drizzle of sleet. There was nothing left alive on the ship.

The ge-eagles dropped closer to the ground, scanning the weirdly disfigured snowscape. The radiation flash had evaporated and melted the surface layer of snow, swiftly followed by the fiery blast wave that had flattened any loosely piled slope or tough serac, slamming shut the jagged crevices. For a brief minute the surface had been awash with bubbling water, runnels carving a multitude of new channels. Then the deep polar temperature began to reassert itself, sucking away the temporary heat. The water refroze, producing a vast expanse of glazed ice-flats that stretched from the shoreline over two kilometres inland. There were strange lumps cloaked in grainy ice scattered across it at random – dead Faller-seibears, their fur singed and burnt away, ribbons of congealed blue blood spreading out from the corpses as if they'd sent out roots.

Sensors picked up movement on the edges of the ice crust. Forty-seven seibears were running south, spreading out across the mist-shrouded snowfield. Radiation points were coming from seven places.

'Uracus curse them,' Florian grunted. 'They have the bombs.'

'If they can keep that pace up, we have about ten hours before they reach us,' Paula said.

Marek turned from the wormhole generator he was dismantling. 'Looks like we're on, then.'

＊

Marek's bioconstruct brain had no natural emotions, nothing that came from floods of hormones and neurochemical reactions. For a little over two hundred and fifty years he'd used appropriate response algorithms to mimic human reactions: shock, disgust, sorrow, kindness, affection. Two hundred and fifty years of incorporating those effects into every situation. In doing so, they had ceased to become secondary routines as they merged into his primary thoughts. He rather enjoyed the notion that he was becoming more human – not simply knowing what a human should be feeling. His batch brothers – Demitri especially – weren't convinced. The ANAdroids didn't feel pleasure or pain, just tactile information from their nervous system, so they saw the quirky development as evidence of his gradual decline, along with his vocal glitch.

Now, though, they had to admit he might have been right. He was scared by the approaching seibears and nukes, and that was a sensation he couldn't shield from them; it was flooding across their shared gaiafield connection.

But it had to be done. The approaching Faller-seibears had to be tackled. And logically he, with his glitches and slightly wobbly coordination, was the most expendable of them all.

He made his way out of HGT54b to the surface along with the four humans, leaving his batch brothers working on the wormhole. The sky had an unbroken cover of high thin clouds which defused the sunlight to a uniform glare. A gentle wind was blowing from the west, suffused with tiny ice crystals which pattered against his e-m suit. Overhead, the *Discovery* bobbed about, pulling at its anchor cables. The rope ladder flapped about beneath it. A grim-looking Florian caught hold and steadied it.

Paula reached for it, ready to start climbing.

'No,' Kysandra said. 'You have to stay here.'

Paula hesitated, and Marek was intrigued by that. From what he'd seen over the last few weeks, and reviewing his much older original Nigel memories, Paula did not suffer from doubt – not any kind. She was the most confident and determined person in the Commonwealth.

'There's seven atomic bombs heading this way, and only five of us,' Paula said. 'You need me.'

'Without you, there is no plan. None of us will be able to break the Valatare barrier.'

'Neither will I,' Paula countered. 'The ANAdroids don't have imagination, but there's enough of Nigel in there that when they're given a problem they'll know what equipment to manufacture. It's going to be down to them.'

'And if something unforeseen happens? Something that needs a very human mind to analyse? No. One of us has to remain alive. And that's you. If we can't free the Raiel, you're the one who can evacuate survivors to Aqueous. You. Not me, and not these two boys. We're the ground troops. Let us do our job, and buy the ANAdroids enough time.'

'My combat experience . . .' Paula began.

'This is the whole world at stake here, Paula. I can't save it. But I can help you save it.'

Paula took a breath and nodded reluctantly. 'Very well.' She let go of the rope ladder.

'Good choice,' Marek said, and grabbed the ice-speckled ladder himself. He started to climb up.

'Same goes for you,' Kysandra told Ry and Florian. 'There's not much you can do.'

'Oh, please,' Ry said. 'Every one of those bombs we eliminate increases our odds of getting a wormhole working again.'

'I'm coming,' Florian said. 'No arguing.'

Marek reached the gondola. The plyplastic door opened for him. He slung his pack in and sat down in the front seat. His u-shadow linked to the *Discovery*'s smartnet and began the preflight activation sequence.

As the other three took their seats, he began pumping helium back into the gas cells. When he looked through the big curving windscreen in front of him, he could see Paula releasing the anchors. Once she'd retracted the malmetal spikes, the cables wound back into the blimp's nose. The *Discovery* rose quickly, its fans spinning up to hold them steady. Then Marek directed the smartnet to take them north.

'They're still spreading the bombs wide,' Paula said through the link.

A display from the ge-eagles showed how the Faller-seibears

were moving. Over a hundred of the massive creatures were ranged in a ragged east–west line, heading south at about twenty kilometres an hour. They even saw that three of the giant humanoid-Fallers had survived the explosion and were riding on the seibears. They were wrapped in what looked like several layers of blankets, and carried their pump-action bazookas. The turbulent air from the bomb blast was dying away, and the low-level clouds breaking up, which allowed the ge-eagles to detect still more seibears joining the main pack.

Marek ordered a couple of ge-eagles to glide in closer, from the south. He directed one to the cluster of five seibears gathered round a bomb. Two of the seibears were also carrying the bazooka weapons. Another had something that resembled a small artillery gun; relative size made it a rifle for the creature.

'Crud,' Kysandra grumbled.

'Your force fields will withstand those weapons,' Paula said. 'For all their size, they are just chemical-based.'

'Paula's right,' Florian said a shade too eagerly. 'Your integral force field deflected the bazooka strike back in Opole easily enough.'

'So it did,' Kysandra said dryly.

'And our maser rifles have a much longer range. We can sniper a whole group and destroy their bomb before they know what's happening.'

'Nice theory,' Kysandra said.

*

As the *Discovery* headed north, they watched as the seibears continued to spread out. Each bomb had a guard of about fifteen seibears, with three or four clustered protectively round the one carrying the warhead. The others took up a perimeter formation, with some scouting up to three kilometres ahead.

'That's not going to make it easy,' Kysandra said.

The *Discovery* was flying north-east now. They'd decided to form a picket line in response to the continually widening pattern the advancing seibears were adopting.

'Looks like they're going to try and surround the *Viscount*,'

Paula suggested when the seibears were stretched out over a front twenty kilometres wide and still expanding. 'Come at us from all directions at once. It's a reasonable tactic.'

'Yeah, and it'll be tough to intercept every warhead,' Kysandra agreed.

She was first out of the *Discovery*, forty kilometres north of the *Viscount*, where the snow and ice had built into rugged mounds with slabs of ice sticking through, making the going difficult.

It was further from *Viscount* than Florian would have liked. But as the plan to intercept the seibears meant *Discovery* probably wouldn't be around to collect them all again afterwards, they had to be practical about the distance they could travel back by themselves. They also had to have a safe distance to protect the *Viscount* in case the Fallers managed to detonate one of the bombs during the interception. The others all seemed satisfied with the forty-kilometre limit.

Florian stared at her through the window as the *Discovery* started to fly west, a tiny grey figure trudging purposefully up the steep incline, casting a long shadow across the snow as the low sun sank ever closer to the horizon. Four ge-eagles spiralled above her, and two more were heading in from the south to help watch for the approaching seibears. Leaving her behind was triggering all kinds of feelings. Shamefully, the strongest one was fright – mostly for himself. *I'm next.*

4

As soon as Anala passed over the south pole, she knew something was wrong. She'd been hoping she'd be in time to see the *Pericato* launch its Aseri missiles; all the calculations showed it would get within range as she was approaching. Instead she saw the atmospheric anomaly – a big swirling cloud mass eclipsing the coast, roughly circular in shape and rising so much higher than any natural formation. Winds were tearing its edges apart, flinging out long tattered streamers.

She clung to the handholds beside the port, staring numbly at the chaos raging ahead and below. 'Ry? Do you copy, Ry?'

'I'm here.'

'Thank crud. What's happened? Did Danny fire the missiles?'

'He got one away. Anala, the *Pericato* was overrun by Faller-seibears. No survivors. We think it sank afterwards.'

'No survivors?' she whispered.

'No. Please tell flight com they carried out their duties to the very end.'

'Did they get the *Sziu*?' She was practically shouting now, demanding reassurance.

'Negative. The *Sziu* was flung ashore. The Fallers have recovered the bombs.'

'Oh great crudding Uracus! Where are they? Where are the bombs?'

'The Fallers are bringing them to us.'

'Giu! What are you doing? Can you get away?'

'The *Viscount* is too valuable to abandon.'

'Ry, no!'

'We're going to stop them.'

'How can you do that?'

'Head to head. Don't worry; we have the Warrior Angel and her weapons.'

'You can't go out there, Ry. You can't!'

'I'm sworn to protect Bienvenido. And even if I wasn't a regiment officer, I'd still be doing this. Paula has a plan. She can save us all if she just has the chance.'

'No. Please—'

'I'll be fine. Tell flight com what's happened. You can re-enter and splash down now. Thank you for what you did.'

'Ry?'

'See you on the other side of the sky, Anala.'

*

The further the seibears ventured into Lukarticar's interior, the more punishing the frigid landscape became. Snow slopes rose higher, ice outcrops were harder and sharper, the crevices deeper and narrower – sometimes covered with a slim treacherous bridge of compacted snow, concealing it from sight. The Faller-seibears never knew they were there until their own weight collapsed them, sending them tumbling onto the terrible ice blades underneath.

Even losing several of their number didn't bother them. They continued to advance inexorably as the sun fell below the horizon, plunging the continent into acute darkness. Night didn't slow them, either. They must have been equipped with eyesight comparable to a human Advancer.

Once the pack was fifty kilometres inland, no more came to join them, leaving their numbers at just over a hundred. They were spread out across a front thirty-five kilometres long, with the flanks beginning to move ahead of the centre.

It was a long wait. Florian had been dropped off after Kysandra, nine kilometres to the west of her, with Ry a further eleven beyond him. After that it was just Marek on board. The ANAdroid had spent his time rigging one of the maser rifles inside the gondola before jumping out.

Five ge-eagles were assigned to Florian. He kept them circling overhead, two of them barely a hundred metres above the snow so nothing was left to chance. He didn't want a Faller sneaking up on him unexpectedly from the south.

Discovery had dropped him in a zone that had snowdrifts cresting up to thirty metres. The valleys between them were scattered with ice outcrops protruding out of the crisp snow – from irregular lumps the size of boulders up to giant ridges that could've been coastal cliffs, they were so tall and jagged. Florian was also extremely wary about crevasses, using a multisensor pack built into his e-m suit to sweep ahead, watching for the treacherous frail roofs that had so far claimed four Faller-seibears.

He found a good position on top of a snow ridge, which gave him a clear line of sight for a good five kilometres. Behind him, the downslope was clean – no ice, no hidden fissures – and the valley floor beyond was relatively clear. Once he'd struck, he could make a fast escape.

So he pushed the snow into shape like a kid building castles on the beach and lay in the grooves he'd scooped out, wiggling to get comfortable. As always, the miraculous e-m suit kept him a cosy warm; its fabric had now flowed over all the skin on his face, forming a full mask with a transparent band over his eyes. He was perfectly protected from the cold. And with his force-field skeleton already active at low level, protected from any physical impact or energy blast.

He settled down for the long wait. Not that he could see much; the night out on the exposed snowfield was as deep as it had been in the dead starship. But he had all his amplified sensors, as well as those of the ge-eagles.

The seibear pack's location was constantly being updated by the ge-eagles tracking it from above. During daylight, they'd flown inside the thin bands of cloud ribbing the sky. Now, with the long night engulfing Lukarticar, they'd dropped down to a kilometre above the massive creatures and continued to gather excellent imagery. They remained invisible even at that altitude, though Paula and the ANAdroids suspected the Fallers could see them with infra-red sight – if they had any.

If they did, they must be able to make out the *Discovery*. Marek had been remote piloting it ever since he'd abandoned it. The blimp had flown a wide circular course, initially heading south-west, then curving round the seibears' western flank and approaching them from behind. Marek was steering it for the group in the centre of the line. As it caught up with the cantering seibears, so Marek increased its speed, redlining the fans.

The group of seibears guarding the bomb began to close up when *Discovery* was four kilometres behind them. Then two of them peeled off and headed back towards it.

'Now we get to see what kind of firepower they have,' Marek said.

When the seibears were still two kilometres away, he reduced *Discovery*'s altitude to eight hundred metres and opened a metre-wide hole in the transparent plyplastic of the front windscreen. The maser rifle fired, pulsing twice in under a second. The two seibears dropped down dead.

'That was easy,' Paula said.

Discovery slid forwards. One of the ge-eagles showed a seibear carrying one of the giant rifles, levelling the weapon at the airship. It began to fire repeatedly, the muzzle plumes temporarily overloading the enhanced infra-red image. More data slipped across Florian's exovision. Whatever the huge gun was, it had enough range to hit the *Discovery*. The blimp was juddering badly from each hit. Eight gas cells reported losing pressure. Then one of the rounds hit a fan. *Discovery*'s smartnet was reporting critical damage.

Through the glare of the muzzle fire, the ge-eagles could just make out the seibears dispersing, scurrying for cover behind thick jumbles of ice outcrops. Two of them hunkered down deep in a fissure, lying on top of the bulky crate that contained the bomb.

Another round hit the gondola, and the link vanished. A ge-eagle tracked the *Discovery* sinking out of the night sky, its envelope deflating as it went, until it was just a mass of flaccid fabric twirling round and round. It hit the snowfield with a gentle bump. The wind blew it along slowly to the north-east until it caught on a snag of ice.

'They all stopped,' Paula said. 'There was quite a bit of link traffic between the bomb groups.'

'Can the drone jam it?' Kysandra asked.

'Yes. Their traffic architecture is very crude; my countermeasures routine can easily tailor specific blockers. I'll bring the drone up and close down their communications. If they can't coordinate and don't know what's happening to each other, it should help.'

Jamming the seibear links certainly had an effect. The groups which had all halted simultaneously suddenly didn't seem to know what to do next. Two of them – the ones Florian and Marek were provisionally assigned to intercept – started off again at once. This time, they redeployed their sentries so there was always a couple trailing by several hundred metres, alert for any more attacks from the rear.

*

During the long wait, Florian tried temporarily deactivating his enhanced senses and exovision, certain his excellent natural vision would be able to make out a couple of metres of the snowfield around him. After all, he'd done a lot of night-time work back in Albina valley, but this was different. This was a total absence of light. He held his hand up in front of his face, and some primeval part of his brain couldn't accept that the hand was invisible. It scared him badly, and secondary routines hurriedly brought back his enriched vision.

Uracus, the Fallers must be able to see in infra-red. There was no other explanation for them knowing the *Discovery* was closing on them, not in this darkness.

The longer he watched the seibears advancing, the more isolated he began to feel. He wanted them to come within range so this would all be over, yet some shameful part wanted to flee, to hide from the monsters in the all-engulfing darkness.

He concentrated on tracking the group bringing the bomb he

was supposed to take out. *Treat the whole thing as a mental exercise,* he told himself, which should allow him to take his mind off the physical reality of his situation.

After half an hour, it was obvious his group were on a track that would take them east of his current position, so he got up and started walking again. Despite the memory skill implant, he wasn't confident enough to start skiing. (The plyplastic skis were in his backpack along with the harness, a spare power cell, and his food – everything he'd need to get back to the *Viscount* afterwards.)

An hour later he was atop a hundred-metre ice cliff with the wind whistling up the hard surface to buffet him. Right along the top, the snow was sculpted in strange curving shapes that twisted upwards two or three times his own height, like clashing waves solidified in mid-impact. The cavities and hollows provided perfect cover. If the seibear group kept to their current track, they would have to pass along the bottom of the cliff. He could stay hidden inside a snow cleft, shielding his infra-red emission until the ge-eagles showed him they were all within range.

He spent another ten minutes scouting along the edge until he found the perfect place – one with a low gully leading away from the cliff which he could retreat along if things went bad. With that settled, he went inside one of the short cavities and began another wait.

*

Marek watched through the ge-eagles as the seibear group trotted over the rough snow towards him. He'd taken cover halfway up a vast rock crag that was only partially cloaked in snow. The snow-field that splayed out from its base was a broken wilderness of shattered ice boulders and dangerous crevices.

'Our optimum strike time will be seventeen minutes – mark,' Paula told everyone over the general link. 'You should all be able to open fire within eight minutes of each other. Ry, you're going to be the last.'

'I can move forward,' Ry said.

'No. Their scouts might see you. Let's keep this as simple as possible. Once the attack has started, I'll use the drone as a kinetic weapon and take out the bomb to the east of Marek. That'll leave the two bombs on the flanks.'

It was good logic, Marek agreed. The flank bombs were now the furthest from the *Viscount*, so they would take the longest to reach the starship. That gave him and Kysandra a reasonable chance of intercepting them while Ry and Florian retreated to *Viscount*. His old Nigel personality approved. The boys had no experience in combat. Equipping them with maser rifles and molecular severance cannons for sniper duty was as close as they could get to guaranteed success, whereas he and Kysandra had a much better chance of taking out the remaining nukes.

His retinas spotted the scouts four minutes later, when they were still two kilometres away. The main group of five seibears clustered round the nuke was another two and a half kilometres behind them. One of the scouts was going to pass within four hundred metres of him.

Marek stopped breathing. The warm breath wafting through the polar air might just be a give-away. His body had enough oxygen reserves to last for an easy half an hour.

The scout lumbered onwards, never breaking stride, its big head turning from side to side with mechanical regularity – and every three turns it would check the sky, too. Marek was impressed. Faller biology allowed the enormous seibear body to perform at the peak of biochemical limits. That kind of power and efficiency was a match for his own.

'I'm red – ready,' Marek announced when the bomb was only fifteen hundred metres away. The scouts had passed by on both sides without slowing – even so, a ge-eagle was marking them. The remaining outriders formed a loose circle round the primary group.

'Me, too,' Kysandra announced.

'Another three minutes,' Florian said.

'The scouts of my group are passing me now,' Ry said. 'It's taking longer than I expected. The terrain here is rough.'

'Marek, Kysandra, initiate now,' Paula said. 'I'm launching the drone.'

Marek spun round the rock that was concealing him. The maser rifle's target image filled his exovision, shunting the ge-eagle links to peripheral mode. He fired at the seibear carrying the atom bomb, and saw all its muscles go limp, sending the big body sprawling onto the ground, ploughing up shards of ice. To his dismay the dead seibear tilted as it came to rest, putting the mass of its body between Marek and the crate with the bomb.

'That's not good,' Marek murmured. He'd taken out the carrier first to immobilize the bomb, allowing him to shoot it with the molecular severance cannon – an unhurried accurate shot at a stationary target. Now the bomb would be protected by the vast bulk of the creature's flesh.

'Trouble?' Demitri asked.

'Only for them.' Marek shot another seibear, one being ridden by a giant humanoid-Faller. The two of them went tumbling into the ice barbs.

Another three fast shots and he finished off the primary group. The ge-eagles showed him the humanoid-Faller jumping up from behind a clutter of rocks. The bazooka fired and the Faller was immediately pumping the mechanism, firing again. Marek got off a shot – too quick for a decent aim, and anyway the Faller was diving for cover. He did the same thing just as the first bazooka round slammed into rock fifteen metres away. It couldn't harm him, not with his force-field skeleton, but the blast did punch him backwards. The force field flickered a spectral turquoise as debris slammed into it. Marek stayed down.

The second bazooka exploded, further away than the first. Through the ge-eagle's feed, he saw the giant Faller pick up the bomb crate and start running at impressive speed. All seven seibear outriders were now charging towards the crag.

'Having some trouble there?' Demitri asked.

Marek ignored his brother's taunt, stood up and took careful aim at the fleeing humanoid. Only it vanished from the target feed. Genuine incomprehension flashed through his thoughts – a puzzlement reflected in the minds of his batch brothers. At any other time, that would have been really quite satisfying.

He sent the closest ge-eagle diving down to the Faller's last position and began jogging towards it. A seibear scout cleared the side of the crag, sprinting at a phenomenal sixty kilometres an hour. Marek spun and fired the maser rifle, completing the spin and running forwards again in less than a second. The seibear collapsed, its momentum sending its mighty body careering onwards for another twenty metres.

An image from the ge-eagle leapt into his exovision as it streaked over the jagged expanse of rock and ice. It had found the giant humanoid-Faller. 'The Faller's faller – fallen,' Marek said. 'Down a crevasse.'

The ge-eagle circled tightly. It showed a slim fissure bridged with a layer of ice, which had shattered the instant the giant had stepped onto it. His infra-red signature was a bright glow, fifteen metres down, wedged between the narrowing rock faces. Warm trickles of fluid ran down the fissure walls. The crate, leaking radiation, was a couple of metres from him.

'That's not good,' Marek said. He started to speed up.

'Don't you fall down,' Valeri warned.

'I no – know.' Marek directed another ge-eagle round, sending it skimming along the route he was taking, scanning the ground ahead for any snags or hidden fractures.

'Got mine,' Kysandra announced. 'Masered the bomb. It's dead. Clearing up now.'

Two more seibear scouts raced into range. Marek slowed and shot both of them. One was carrying a pump-action bazooka. The beam must have hit the magazine. It exploded, flooding the area with garish orange light. Flames leapt upwards for several seconds, plunging the abysmal terrain into sharp relief. Shadows swung round as the fireball rushed upwards, then dimmed and vanished. Marek sprinted onwards.

'Engaging now,' Florian said. 'They're almost directly beneath me. Oh yeah! Got the bomb carrier!'

'Well done,' Kysandra said. 'Just stay calm and shoot the bomb next, then pick the survivors off.'

'I know. I know.'

'I'm sending the drone down now,' Paula said.

Marek was halfway to the crevice with the Faller giant, his concentration divided between making sure every footfall landed on secure ground and the image relayed from the ge-eagle. 'Uh oh. It moved. I thunk it's still alive.'

'Can you get to it?' Demitri asked.

'Yes.'

'In time?'

Marek didn't answer. The giant Faller was wiggling about energetically now, trying to get free of the rock's grip. A large amount of its blood was running down the fissure. Every motion sent another gout squirting out of the wound where the rock had punctured its waist. 'It'll kill kill itself doing that.'

'It has no choice,' Fergus said. 'If it gets to the bomb . . .'

A flash of light zipped across the eastern horizon, as white and fast as distant lightning.

'Drone strike confirmed,' Paula said. 'On target. Ge-eagles reporting radioactive debris in the air. The bomb was vaporized.'

Marek was four hundred metres from the crevasse now. He had to slow to take out another seibear. That left six closing in.

Down in the crevice, the giant Faller wrenched itself free of the impaling rock and flopped sideways. Its fist smashed the hefty crate open.

Marek sprinted. The ge-eagle had mapped out a safe track. His bioconstruct brain kept him aligned perfectly. He hit fifty kilometres an hour, zinging with exhilaration and fear, bringing the maser rifle round, ready to hurdle the crevasse and shoot straight down. Beam switched to full power, wide angle.

The Faller tore shards of wood aside and reached for the control panel underneath.

'Fucking fuck it,' Marek snarled.

*

Florian was shooting the eleventh seibear of his target group when the nuke went off. Marek was about thirty kilometres to the west, but the light was so intense it felt like ten metres. Fortunately he hadn't been looking directly west.

Crudding Uracus!

The transparent strip over his eyes had a cut-out level, automatically preventing dangerous light levels from reaching the retina. Even so, all he could see was a white glare; it even overwhelmed the exovision icons. He shut his eyelids *fast*. The only difference that made was turning the light from white to a pale pink. He slapped a hand across his head, and finally the glare reduced.

His skeleton suit was reporting a huge radiation surge. The force field had been pushed close to its limit blocking the initial gamma flash, but it was holding.

Feeds from most of the ge-eagles had dropped out. His own multisensor module was reporting a huge electromagnetic pulse. The relay back to the *Viscount* was intact, running through five ge-eagles.

'That was not an Operation Reclaim bomb,' Paula said. 'That was a full Liberty bomb, around the three-hundred-kiloton mark. You all need to shield yourself from the blast wave. Move! I'm bringing the ge-eagles down. We'll relink as soon as it's safe.'

The light level was reducing slightly. Florian looked down at the dazzle-white snowfield below the cliff, his targeting graphics picking out the surviving seibears. He was sure two of them had been blinded by the flash; they seemed to be stumbling. The others were standing still, taken completely by surprise. Then he realized the glare haze shimmering off the snow was actually fluorescing fog. For as far as he could see, snow was boiling, throwing off a blanket layer of seething mist that was expanding upwards rapidly.

He turned and ran through the gully that was his ready escape route. Two ge-eagles plunged down out of the clear pearl-white sky, one racing on ahead, surveying the meandering passage, the other keeping pace three metres above his head.

'You have control,' Paula said. Then her link dropped out.

'Kysandra?' Florian sent.

'Here, babe,' Kysandra said. 'I hope you're doing what you're told, and getting ready for the blast. It'll hit you in about a minute.'

'Yeah. It's difficult. I'm in this gully.'

'Crud! Get out of it! You'll be crushed!'

'Trying.' Now he was out of direct line of sight, the glare was almost tolerable. But steam was roaring overhead between the lips of the snow walls and churning down into the gully. It was hard to keep traction, and the dense steam was interfering with most sensors.

Florian slipped and scrambled round uselessly on the steam-slicked ice trying to regain his footing. Then stopped, realizing it was much better to go with it. He held his body rigid, and began to pick up speed. He slid down the slope like the world's smallest bobsleigh, totally dependent on the force field to protect him if there was any rock sticking up through the melting ice.

'Ry?' he asked.

'Present and correct.'

'You okay?'

'Alive, and working to carry on with that.'

'See you later?'

'Deal.'

'Hey, did you get your bomb?'

'Of course.'

Florian's laugh had the taint of hysteria. He was going alarmingly fast now, and water was starting to sluice along with him. Corners sent him slithering up the walls before gravity pulled him down.

Abruptly he shot out of the gully and began spinning round. There was nothing to see. The steam was too dense and turbulent, its own jets and micro-currents strong enough to buffet him.

Then the blast hit and the ground slammed up into him. He cartwheeled through the cloud. Steaming lumps of snow flew round him and then he was down again, hitting hard. The force field tightened round him, cushioning the blow. Exovision graphics told him the force field was also deflecting the sound waves that were ripping the snow apart. As he kept skidding along, the crazy slushy ground vibrated under him like an abused trampoline.

The steam layer was suddenly ripped away by the shockwave.

596

He almost wished it hadn't been. The twisting spires of wind-fashioned snow were disintegrating, breaking apart into a tide of looser snow that was starting to flow like a viscous liquid. It churned around him, pummelling the force field. Overhead, the incredible atomic light was burning down to incandescent red-gold, filling the heaving air with dusky oil-rainbows as it fluoresced the hail of water particles.

'Avalanche!' Florian screamed. He had no idea who he was trying to warn.

The mush he was caught on began to move faster and faster, spitting out chunks that arched through the air in every direction. It started to build up around him, sliding over his frantic scrabbling limbs.

Think!

There were waves forming in the mush cascade now, building into horrifying crescents. About to collapse downwards in lethal torrents.

He ordered the force field to expand. It left him in the middle of an invisible bubble that elevated him up from the unstable flood. But still the waves built around him, growing in violence as the blast energy poured into them, sending them writhing at contrasting angles and differing speeds. They smashed together, whirled apart, peaked, fell away. He was slammed about violently, utterly helpless, a football kicked by elemental gods.

Then the biggest wave of all rose up, darkening his world. The force-field bubble rotated him upside down. He looked up past his feet and saw the wave break in a strangely elegant fantail of solid scarlet spume that crashed down upon him.

*

Florian didn't think he lost consciousness entirely, but there was certainly a long moment of utter disorientation. The mush kept shoving him along, though the motion soon became sluggish and stopped.

He hung suspended inside the force-field bubble, body inclined at a seventy-degree angle, head down. True consciousness was the realization that he was dangerously nauseous. His u-shadow ordered the skeleton suit to release him from suspension, but to maintain the perimeter.

Squatting on the floor, he fumbled through his backpack, and pulled out a torch. That wasn't as reassuring as he wanted. He was at the bottom of a perfect sphere three metres in diameter, completely buried in snow. No way of telling how deep.

But those avalanche waves were high. Seven, eight metres at least. And more has flowed over since.

He used his u-shadow to expand the force field. It grew by about twenty centimetres, then stopped. The pressure the snow exerted was now equal to the energy it took to maintain the force field. It wasn't going to get any bigger, so it definitely wasn't going to expand until it burst through the surface.

'Crud.'

Florian had thought the dose of claustrophobia he'd suffered in the starship was bad. This threatened to be infinitely worse.

His heart started doing its flutter thing, and he sucked down air in fast, shallow gulps.

Oh, just crudding great!

Then he stopped panicking about being confined because an oxygen warning flipped up in his exovision. Not only was the oxygen level of the air shrinking, the carbon dioxide was rising.

'No! No, no, no!'

He used his secondary routines to calm his breathing. His u-shadow ran a fast analysis. With the e-m suit filters operating at maximum efficiency, he had enough air left for approximately thirty minutes. That helped the secondary routines pacify his racing heartbeat a little.

He stared upwards, furious with the universe for doing this to him. 'I just survived a crudding atom bomb,' he yelled. Stopped. Calmed again. *Wasting oxygen.* 'Come on. Think, Uracus damn you. You're supposed to be smart, a true nerd. Science your way out of this.'

He glanced up again at the stubborn snow pressing down against the force field. 'Ah.' The u-shadow changed the force field's shape, turning it to a teardrop, with a very pointed apex. It drove upwards a good twenty centimetres.

'Crud!'

He shone the torch into his backpack. Nothing in there he could punch upwards with. The maser rifle and molecular severance cannon were still with him, hanging on their shoulder straps. He really didn't fancy trying the molecular severance cannon on the ice, not at zero range.

He put the rifle muzzle up into the small apex, and his u-shadow reformatted the force field to allow the slim tube through. With the rifle muzzle pressed directly into the snow, he fired a half-power burst. The tube rammed itself back down, and a shower of boiling water squirted through the gap in the force field before it managed to close. The e-m suit deflected the scalding heat easily.

'Crudding bollocks!'

Okay, reformat the force field to let the maser energy through, but no physical gap this time.

Once the u-shadow complied, he fired through the weakened zone. The snow above him turned to water, which began to seep down the curve of the sphere. There were bubbles fizzing away inside it.

He blinked in fascination at the slow-motion cascade. *It's like black beer.*

But it continued to flow around the curving force-field wall until the bulk of snow chilled it to slush and it began re-freezing. Directly above his head, there was a small cavity.

Now we're getting somewhere.

With a giddy laugh, he fired the maser rifle again, slowly spiralling the beam around. Outside the force field, the quantity of vigorous bubbling liquid reached epic proportions. A deluge of boiling water flowed round and down to drain into the snow around the base where it slowly refroze. His u-shadow ordered the force-field apex to extend, and it slid up ten centimetres before reaching solid snow again.

'Right, you bastard,' Florian declared grimly. He changed the angle of the maser, and fired again.

Twenty-two minutes later, a patch of dark appeared above the boiling water.

Sky! Crudding sky!

The force field shrank back until it was a flexible layer above his e-m suit. He clawed his way out of the hole and lay on his back, staring up into the strange sky. The wind was ferocious, sending clouds streaking past. But above them, borealis storms raged through the tenuous upper atmosphere as the radiation impact from the explosion slowly dissipated across the ionosphere. Ghostly green and crimson waves, already covering half of Lukar-ticar, spun and slithered around each other, casting ephemeral coloured shadows across the diseased shimmering snowfield.

Florian smiled up at the astonishing display in blissful gratitude. Fighting his way out of that mess certainly deserved some cosmic recognition. It didn't come finer than this.

His u-shadow sent out a link ping.

'Florian?' Kysandra sent. 'You're alive!'

'Yeah. Little trouble for a moment there. But I'm okay now.'

Communication icons appeared in his exovision. Eighteen ge-eagles were active and in the air. Flying in the fast winds was difficult, draining their power reserves, but they could stay airborne for another couple of days.

'Hey, Ry, you made it,' Florian exclaimed, studying the communication icons.

'Of course.'

'I had a mountain fall on me,' Florian said proudly.

'Rock or snow?'

'Snow.'

'Ha, you had it easy.'

Florian chuckled as he studied the communication display. 'Why aren't we linking with the *Viscount*?'

'I don't know,' Kysandra said. 'But that was a monster bomb blast. I'm assuming the shockwave collapsed the tunnel down to HGT54b.'

'Yeah.' Florian nodded slowly, trying to convince himself.

'That'll be it.' *If it collapsed the tunnel, what did it do to the* Viscount's *structure?*

'Are you mobile?' she asked.

'Yes, I suppose so.'

'Good. Grab yourself a pair of ge-eagles and get going. We'll see you back at the *Viscount.*'

Uracus, no peace for the wicked. 'Okay. I'm on it.'

'And Florian?'

'Yes?'

'Watch out for Faller-seibears. If we can survive, they sure as Uracus can.'

*

Ironically, the journey back to the *Viscount* was always the part Florian had worried the most about. Now, less so.

He took his time activating the skis, watching the bulbs of plyplastic expand into two-metre-long strips. As they did that, he struggled into the harness. The wind made it difficult, constantly pummelling him with loose ice chips. In the end he had to reconfigure the force field into a sphere again – which the wind shoved about ferociously. By the time he was ready, two ge-eagles had arrived, with a third on its way.

Florian hitched the huge semiorganic birds to the harness. When they were secure, he hunched down on the skis, giving himself a low centre of gravity and reducing wind resistance, and prayed his skill implant memory was up to the task. The ge-eagles took off, and began towing him.

He was fifty kilometres from the *Viscount*. When they'd planned how to get back, no one had figured for the winds. Paula had estimated the ge-eagles could pull them along at about thirty to thirty-five kilometres an hour, but the severe aftermath which the Liberty bomb had inflicted on the local atmosphere was producing winds that whipped round seemingly at random. Their direction was constantly in flux, as was their speed. Florian even experienced interludes when they dropped away completely, but there weren't many of them.

After the first ten kilometres, when his leg muscles were starting to hurt badly from the constant crouching, the temperature began to plummet again, allowing the fervent clouds to condense. Snow began to fall, only to be whipped into a brutal high-velocity deluge by the winds. Florian had to stiffen the force field to deflect their impact. Visibility shrank to a few metres. He was reliant on the sensor images the ge-eagles were producing to avoid the smaller snags and fissures. The ge-eagles themselves steered him away from larger obstacles. All he had to do was hang on and keep his balance.

*

The roar of the icequake reverberated like boulders cascading down a rocky mountainside. Inside the cramped confines of HGT54b, it was deafening, but Paula ignored it. She was too busy hanging on to the grid as the compartment shook. Hairline cracks appeared in the pressure bulkheads. Gridwork segments snapped, allowing several heavy cargo packs to shift alarmingly. The three ANAdroids formed a protective picket around the wormhole generator they were working on, gripping on to each other like an acrobat team. Their force fields expanded and merged.

It seemed to go on for a long time. Finally, when the noise abated and the compartment stilled, Paula released her hold on the grid. She wasn't sure, but the angle seemed to have shifted, becoming more acute.

'That was fifty kilometres away,' Demitri said. 'If they detonate another one closer, we're dead.'

'I would have expected the ice to absorb more of the compression wave,' Valeri said.

'It probably pulverized the ice in its wake,' Fergus said. 'Another explosion might produce a reduced seismic force.'

'Let's try not to find out,' Valeri said. 'Did any of them survive that?'

'Marek certainly didn't,' Demitri said. 'He was only two hundred metres from the epicentre. The force-field suit was not built to withstand a direct three-hundred-kiloton blast.'

'I'm sorry,' Paula said.

'Don't be. We are machines.'

'Maybe. But I have to concede you're doing a pretty good imitation of human.'

'Marek would appreciate that sentiment. He was confident he was becoming human.'

Paula nodded. Exovision displays showed her not a lot. All external links were down. She ordered the plyplastic door to open. When it did, it revealed a wall of compacted snow. 'Damn, the tunnel has collapsed.'

'Kysandra at least may be alive,' Valeri said. 'She has an integral force field, and was far enough away.'

Paula eyed the wormhole generator. It was half disassembled. Replacement components, cannibalized from two others, had been laid out neatly around it. Now they were scattered everywhere; she could see several sticking out of the water pooling at the bottom of HGT54b. 'Worst-case scenario, both flank bombs survived. We have three hours until the seibears arrive.'

'Best-case scenario, actually,' Demitri corrected. 'If they come ten kilometres closer and detonate, the icequake will finish us.'

'But they don't know that,' Paula told him, 'so let's work on the assumption that we have three hours.' She pointed at the wormhole. 'It has to be operational by then.'

'Understood.'

Something prevented her from asking them if that was feasible. The collapsed tunnel was a problem, though. A molecular disrupter pulse was out of the question down here. There was nowhere for the superheated gas blast to escape. She poked at the snow, which wasn't too hard packed. Several handfuls came out when she scooped at it. She picked up her maser rifle and reduced the power to five per cent before firing it at the snow just above the bottom rim of the door.

It melted immediately. Several litres of hot water soaked into the snow below, gradually refreezing. She fired again, melting more. After twenty minutes she'd succeeded in melting out a cavity big enough to stand up in. The humidity in the air was becoming tropical.

Standing on the creaking ice of the cavity base, she altered the rifle output again, reducing the beam width to a centimetre and shunting the power up to fifty per cent. Then she aimed it vertically upwards and fired. A small jet of steam rushed downwards. Without her force field, she would have been scalded; as it was, it played across her face, spoiling her view. A field function scan allowed her to keep her aim straight.

The maser took nineteen minutes to bore a five-centimetre hole up to the surface. With an open route for the steam to vent, she closed the plyplastic door, and increased the beam width, then started to widen the hole.

*

After an hour and a half, the hectic winds were starting to subside – not that it made the going any easier. True, the ski skill implant memories meant Florian had only lost his balance a couple of times, but he just knew he was going to be hooked up to the farmhouse medical capsule for a week to treat his leg muscles. He was having to stop every twenty minutes just to spend a minute to stretch and recover. He didn't dare allow himself any longer.

In those ninety minutes, the ge-eagles had managed to pull him thirty-five kilometres. More ge-eagles had survived the blast wave to rise from their ground shelter and link in. They now had twenty-two, of which nine were on tow duty. Kysandra deployed eight as link relays, giving her five to search for the bomb the east-flank seibears had been carrying.

They finally located it through the gunk clogging the turbulent atmosphere, homing in on the spray of its signature radiation. Eleven Faller-seibears were still alive, and carrying the bomb towards the *Viscount* at their usual prodigious pace.

That was the second piece of bad news. The ge-eagle at the end of the link was flying repeated sweeps over the *Viscount*'s location, and there was no sign of Paula and the ANAdroids. No tunnel entrance. No activity. It could detect the huge starship still buried below the ice, but that was all.

As Florian set off again, the ge-eagle sensed a thin plume of steam spurting up out of the ground. He actually cheered. The image from the ge-eagle played front and centre of his exovision, banishing the discomfort of the journey.

All three of them watched the feed as the ge-eagles towed them towards it, seeing the steam increase until it was a full-scale fountain. Then it ended, and infra-red revealed a glowing hole in the snow. The ge-eagle glided overhead.

'Hello,' Paula said.

'What happened?' Kysandra asked.

'An icequake broke the tunnel, but everything else is fine. What happened to you?'

'One bomb survived. It's twenty-eight kilometres out from *Viscount* and closing. Do you want me to intercept?'

'No, we can't risk another detonation. Our timetable has become perfectly defined; we either activate the wormhole generator or this venture is over – probably along with our lives.'

'Understood,' Kysandra said. 'I'm about seventeen minutes out.'

Florian gritted his teeth when he thought about how much longer he'd be spending on the skis. He couldn't help but think of that oh-so-long night spent in the Sandy-J with Lukan chattering away in the driver's seat as the dark countryside flashed past. At the time he'd been twisted up with worry. Now he knew just how easy that night had been.

The ge-eagles powered on indomitably through the night, their wide wings illuminated with the freakish swirls of the celestial ghost light bombarding the ionosphere. It portrayed their movements in juddery snapshots, as if they were clockwork-mechanical instead of the smooth perfect-future technology of the Commonwealth. The temperature was still dropping from the heat peak provoked by the bomb flash, the gentle snow sharpening to ice flakes, making him thankful for his force field as they assailed him.

'How long?' he asked.

'How long for what?' Paula said.

'Until the wormhole generator is operational?'

'We're hoping to power up in an hour,' Demitri replied.

Florian gritted his teeth. An hour was about how long it was going to take him to reach the *Viscount*. 'Understood. I'll be there for that.'

'Ry?' Paula asked. 'How's your progress?'

'With you in forty minutes.'

'Good.'

*

Paula stood behind the ANAdroids, watching patiently as they slotted components into place. They were moving with methodical precision, as if this was a complex ballet they'd rehearsed a thousand times. She said nothing, not wanting to interrupt. If they had doubts, they would share them – after all, the actual Nigel would – but they'd given her a timetable. Only some unexpected event would change that now.

Her low-level field scan revealed someone slithering down the newly melted tunnel. The plyplastic door opened, and Kysandra stepped into HGT54b, glancing round at the dislodged cargo.

'Crud! You got knocked about, didn't you?'

'The wormhole generator didn't suffer any damage,' Paula replied. 'That's all that matters.'

The hood of Kysandra's e-m suit retracted. 'Sure.' She ran her gloved hand back through her long hair. 'So what are you going to take with us?'

'Everything in HGT54b. Once we get everything working again, it will provide us with a decent manufacturing base.'

'Really?'

'Yes. Even if a machine doesn't work, it'll be a good source of spare parts until we begin manufacturing new systems.'

'Of course. So is the wormhole going to be accurate enough to drop us outside the farmhouse?'

'We're not going to the farmhouse,' Paula said.

'What?'

'I have been considering options. We not only need to buy time, we also need to safeguard Port Chana. Neither of those things will happen if we go back to the farmhouse.'

'Why not?'

'Our original plan didn't account for the Fallers acquiring nukes. Now we know they have them and are more than willing to use them, we have to circumvent them.'

'By not going home?'

'Exactly. They have clearly infiltrated government to at least the same degree as your friends have. I saw Roxwolf's connections, and that was a rejected Faller in an outlying city. So we can't risk opening negotiations with Adolphus, because they'll find out. If they even have a hint of where we might be, they'll detonate a bomb there. And everyone knows Port Chana is the centre of Eliter resistance to the government. They will blow it off the face of the planet.'

Kysandra gave her an unenthusiastic nod. 'Okay, so we don't go to the farmhouse. Where then?'

'A place where we can activate all the Commonwealth machines without panicking the Fallers into launching their apocalypse. A place where we will never be spotted, even by accident.'

'So?' Kysandra demanded. 'Where?'

'Macule.'

'You've got to be crudding kidding me! Macule is a radioactive desert.'

'Not relevant. Commonwealth technology can protect us from a little radiation. And as soon as we're up and running, we can feed local minerals into the refineries to build the sensor satellites that'll analyse the Valatare barrier. That's not possible on Aqueous, which is the only H-congruous world. All its minerals are at the bottom of the ocean.'

'Giu! You're really not kidding, are you?'

'That's not my strongest trait, no.'

Kysandra glanced down the tilted compartment at the ANAdroids. 'I suppose you lot agree?'

'It's logical,' Demitri said without turning round. 'Paula knows what she's doing.'

Kysandra's arms went up in surrender. 'Bollocks: Macule it is.'

*

Ry arrived next. He grinned in delight when Kysandra explained Paula's change of plan. 'My Astronaut Corps friends are going to be so envious. I will be the first of us to set foot on another world.'

'First of many if this works,' Paula said.

They tracked Florian's progress as the ANAdroids finished reassembling the wormhole generator. He was still eleven minutes out when Demitri announced: 'Ready to power up.'

'Do we wait for him?' Ry enquired.

'No,' Paula said.

They all gripped the gridwork and stared down at the big circular machine. Paula knew her nerves couldn't be written off entirely as teenage hormones. So much depended on this – two-hundred-and-fifty-year-old biological machines using someone else's memories to repair machines over three millennia old. The fate of a world. Nobody had ever thrown the dice so high in human history.

Well . . . maybe Ozzie.

That conjured up a secretive smile as Demitri initiated the power-up sequence.

Everyone held their breath. The wormhole generator emitted the tiniest humming noise.

'Mass converter on line and functional,' Demitri said. 'We have power.'

Paula was struck by just how much like Nigel he sounded. She hadn't noticed before.

'Bringing the gateway up to full activation readiness.'

Paula's nerves were overtaken by excitement. She'd gone through tens of thousands of wormholes in her enormous previous lifetime – so many it was utterly mundane. This, though . . . This reminded her of just how extraordinary the whole concept was. Warping the very fabric of the universe for human convenience.

'Force field on,' Valeri said. 'We are shielded.'

In front of her, the blank circular face of the wormhole generator began to flicker with hazy turquoise phantasms, slivers that hovered on the edge of existence.

'Initiating space–time compression,' Demitri announced.

The phantom streaks merged together, forming a circle of elusive indigo radiance. It was impossible for the human eye to focus on the phenomenon; the light was shifting, extending back into infinity at the same time as it remained in place.

'Is that it?' an awed Kysandra asked. 'A wormhole?'

'No. What you're seeing is Cherenkov radiation,' Fergus said. 'The start of a wormhole. *This* is a wormhole.'

As he spoke, the eerie light vanished, draining back in a single disorientating lurch. Paula instinctively increased her grip on the gridwork, fighting the impression she was moving. The last sparkle of Cherenkov luminescence at the centre of the wormhole vanished and a ripple of blackness spread out.

Ry turned to her, his face appealing silently.

'Yes,' she told him. 'It's a hole through space.'

'We're opening the terminus five hundred kilometres above Lukarticar,' Demitri said. 'Systems stable.'

A bright white line slowly slipped across the open wormhole – the terminator, cutting Lukarticar in half. Long serpentine strands of the aurora undulated majestically across the nightside, vanishing into daylight.

'You're now looking down on yourself from a great height,' Demitri said with a small smile. 'And in case you think that's seriously weird, if we had time to play I could open the terminus directly behind you. That way you can look at the back of your own head. Trust me, that really messes with human perception. Let you in on a secret: that's what we did the very first time Ozzie and I fired up our machine. We didn't actually extend the terminus to Mars until a couple of hours later, after we'd checked out our designation coordinate software. There's a lot of factors to manipulate simultaneously. We had to hack time on the college super-computer to—'

'Enough,' Paula snapped. 'Is it fully functional?'

'Yes.'

'Please shift the terminus to Macule.'

*

Florian could barely move off the skis. Both legs were an agony of cramps. An exovision map showed him the surviving seibears carrying the last bomb, their icon perilously close to his.

The icequake and stormwave had changed the shape of the snowfield above the *Viscount*, so that he could have been any-where. But five metres away, two pairs of skies identical to his had been stuck vertically into the puckered surface, and already fresh snow had accumulated low cones around them. He half-waddled to the hole in the snow they were standing sentry over. The shifting borealis light showed him the way. As he shuffled forwards, rumpled snow beneath his feet turned from emerald to rose-pink then shaded down to blue as deep as a twilight ocean. The hole remained a constant black, its sides crusted with ice.

I'm supposed to clamber down that?

Resentment was burning hot in his mind. Resentment that no one had come up to greet him, to help him. *Surely Kysandra would have . . .*

'I'm here,' he told them through the general link.

'Get down here fast,' Kysandra responded immediately.

'How?' He didn't mean to ask. It was weak, he knew. But after everything he'd been through, would it have killed her to show just the tiniest degree of sympathy?

'Just jump,' Paula said. 'Use your force field to cushion your landing.'

Florian stood on the rim, rocking in the wind. The hole seemed to grow, its darkness intensifying. And he'd had enough of being in black spaces beneath the snow tonight. Another thirty minutes and it would be dawn.

Like that's going to help.

'Hey,' Kysandra said. 'I'm waiting for you, Florian. The worm-hole is working. Please. Take a leap of faith.'

He jumped.

The ride was awful; every ripple in the ice seemed to catch him, and the juddering never stopped. He couldn't move his arms – they were pinned to his side – and the claustrophobia was vicious.

He was terrified he was going to wind up jammed in the hole just like the Faller giant.

Then his feet cleared the bottom of the shaft and the force field flared out. He landed hard, and his mistreated legs gave way.

Arms closed round him, helping him to his feet – which was painful. Waves of red hair swished across his face. His e-m suit helmet retracted and the red hair was tickling his skin. Through the jumble of tresses, he saw a mouth open wide in a smile, then a kiss.

'Welcome back,' she murmured contentedly into his ear.

Then he was stumbling through the plyplastic door into HGT54b. He stopped in shock, a half-smile of wonder on his face. He was looking into a circle of daylight that shone across the interior. It was advancing slowly down the compartment, and the cargo pods and crates were passing through it, then tumbling away to the side, landing in a jumbled pile on a grey desert that went on forever.

'That's not the farmhouse,' he said numbly.

'No,' she agreed. 'It's definitely not. E-m suit hood back on, and your force field. Let's go.'

Then she took his hand, and led him into the light.

*

Anala came back over the south pole and stared down in mortification at the radiant mushroom cloud that was rising over Lukarticar. It straddled the terminator, casting a filthy orange radiance across the nightside.

She hadn't seen the first one go off a few hours back, but the angry storm it created was evidence enough – pitiless winds assaulting the massive curtain of thick warm cloud. A mighty atmospheric battle illuminated by the cold delicate light of the aurora, as if an iridescent sea was rushing across the bottom of the world.

'Ry,' she'd called into the microphone. 'Come in, Ry.' A dozen times she called, a hundred, repeated on each subsequent orbit.

Now this new atrocity had darkened the aurora, and once more the ground was smothered with belligerent, agitated clouds.

'Ry, are you there? Are you alive? Anyone? Can anyone down there hear me?'

There was no answer. Not on that orbit, or any of the seven that followed.

After that, she obediently followed flight com's instructions and fired the main service module rockets, braking her speed below orbital velocity. The command module began its long re-entry plunge down through the atmosphere.

'Ry?'

BOOK SEVEN

The Faller Apocalypse

1

The convoy of three Zikker limousines and their escort of Varlan Regiment troop carriers and PSR cars swept along Bryan-Anthony Boulevard. Stonal was in the first Zikker with the curtains drawn across the darkened windows, preventing anyone from looking in and seeing the prime minister was sitting in the back. The other two Zikkers also had their curtains shut, but they were empty. Having three identical limousines drive together was an elaborate extension of the shell game, played for real by the security detail in charge of Adolphus's safety.

'I'm going to have my office issue a press D-restriction covering the High Bird mission,' Stonal said as they sped past the statue of Slvasta at the intersection with Victory Regiment Avenue. 'There's not a lot of contact between Cape Ingmar and the rest of our population, but an unscheduled spaceflight mission is extraordinary news, especially at this time. It could leak.'

Adolphus nodded slowly. 'People are smarter than we give them credit for.'

'Very possibly, sir.' Once again Stonal had to hold himself back from comment. This new Adolphus was an enigma. He made decisions that wouldn't have been countenanced ten days ago, before stepping into the space machine for treatment. They were often the correct decisions, given the perilous times they now found themselves in, but Stonal was having trouble concealing his growing alarm at how much the prime minister had changed.

'I'm considering if we shouldn't just tell them the truth. In a few instances, of course.'

'Sir?'

'The Faller Apocalypse is about to begin. It might be hard for us to conceal that from them, don't you think?'

'The panic and mistrust would be overwhelming. It is imperative we retain complete control for this fight.'

'Times they are a-changing, my friend. You acknowledged that yourself.'

'Yes. They will change. And if we defeat the apocalypse, our political structure will no doubt undergo profound realignment. But you would be frightening everybody if you tell them straight out that the Fallers have stolen our nuclear weapons and they're already using them. A panicked people are not a people respectful of authority. We will need compliance from the entire population if we are to defeat the Fallers. Selfishness and individualism will not win the day. My dear father always said that was the Commonwealth's greatest weakness, allowing their citizens such a loose society.'

'Well, he'd know,' Adolphus said.

There was enough sharpness in the voice for Stonal to glance over in surprise. For a moment the old Adolphus had shown himself – trusting nothing, suspicious, sneering.

What if I'm wrong? Stonal asked himself. Not that it mattered; his hand had been played. Everything was in motion. In a way, Adolphus was quite right: individualism in this context was irrelevant. Maintaining strong governance was all that counted.

The convoy drove through the main gates to the palace. Stonal's Zikker peeled away from the other vehicles and carried on through an archway into a courtyard, then turned and went into another, smaller courtyard and drew up underneath a stone portico.

Adolphus climbed out, and stood on the bottom step as several of his office executive staff came out to greet him. He gazed round at the tall walls of the courtyard with their long arched windows as if he was puzzled by them.

'Everything all right?' Stonal asked. Even if Adolphus knew what was coming. There was nothing he could do. Not now.

'Fine,' the prime minister said.

'The security cabinet is waiting, sir,' his chief aide said.

'Good. Then let's go.'

The cabinet room was a long ornate chamber on the second floor, with a huge window at one end providing a view out across the private gardens at the rear of the palace. The grounds were still maintained at the same level of excellence as they had been when the Captains ruled Bienvenido. Topiary bushes lined the walkways, fountains played in big ponds, dense hedges marked out smaller ornate flower gardens. An airy white-stone summer house was perched on a mound half a kilometre away, looking straight back at the palace. Bright scarlet vines with pristine white flower clusters swaddled its pillars and ventured up across the roof. With the morning sun highlighting the vivid colours of the flowers, it was all very beautiful and peaceful.

A rectangular table of black marble ran the length of the cabinet room. There were twenty seats along both sides. The one with the highest back, right in the middle, was reserved for the prime minister. Today only eight seats were taken.

Terese was sitting opposite the high-backed chair, dressed in a green and scarlet robe which wrapped round her body like a protective shell. Unlike the other ministers of the security cabinet, she didn't smile a welcome as Adolphus came in.

'I would like Director Stonal to remain with us,' she said as Adolphus took his chair. 'I think the security cabinet deserves a full briefing on the security situation. Don't you, Comrade?'

'Of course,' Adolphus said.

Stonal stood by the double doors as the aides closed them.

'I have considerable news from Cape Ingmar—' Adolphus began.

'Excuse me, prime minister,' Terese interrupted, 'but I choose to exercise my right to ask my Comrades for an emergency vote.'

'A vote?' Adolphus asked in surprise. 'On what?'

'Confidence in the prime minister.'

The big room was absolutely silent. Power struggles at this level were utterly terrifying; even Stonal was entranced by the play. The senior cabinet ministers were desperately trying to remain impassive, but he could see three of them sweating.

Nobody asked for a vote like this unless they were completely certain of winning it. Promises had been given in backrooms, deals agreed. But discovering if everyone would keep their word didn't happen until it was time for those supremely calculating hands to rise . . .

'I should shoot the crudding lot of you for treason,' Adolphus growled. He glanced over at Stonal, an eyebrow raised. 'Any chance of you doing that for me?'

'No, sir.'

'You have been compromised, Comrade,' Terese continued. 'You were exposed to unknown Commonwealth technology.'

'Oh, so it's you I should shoot,' Adolphus said, continuing to stare at Stonal. 'This is my reward for supporting you all these years? Thanks.' He turned back to Terese. 'Whatever he told you is a pile of steaming crud. I'm cured, not contaminated.'

'Your behaviour,' Stonal said. 'It's wrong. It's been wrong ever since you came out of that machine.'

'What you actually mean is that I can think rationally now I'm not twisted up with worry and fear of dying? Name one thing I've done that's detrimental to this planet. One!'

'It's not what you've done,' Stonal said patiently. 'It's the way you did it.'

'Is that a song lyric?'

Stonal flinched, genuinely puzzled. 'And you never used to say things like that.'

'As I said: I can see clearly now. I assessed the situation and took the appropriate course of action. If we waited for glorious bureaucrat committees voting on everything, that Liberty would still be back on the launch pad waiting for a consensus.'

'This is irrelevant,' Terese said. 'There is no question that the *Pericato* should have been sent after the *Sziu* and the Warrior Angel.'

'What then?' Adolphus demanded, his face flushed with anger. 'What have I done wrong?'

'You ordered Major Danny into action on the word of someone thought to be Ry Evine. Even if he hasn't Fallen, we know him to be allied with the Warrior Angel.'

'Pilot Major Em Yulei confirmed the *Sziu*'s location on her next pass. And everyone at this table is lining up to ally themselves with the Warrior Angel. I saw the greed in your face, Director Stonal, when you found out about Paula being able to evacuate us to Aqueous.'

'You authorized the use of nuclear weapons with the flimsiest verification,' Stonal said. 'It resulted in the loss of the *Pericato*, and the death of everyone on board. Your judgement has become reckless at best.'

'It was a crudding combat situation, you moron! You can't lawyer up after the event. Decisions have to be made. You have to have the guts to make them.'

'Enough!' Terese snapped. 'All those who have no confidence in the prime minister, please raise your hand.'

'Don't you crudding dare!' Adolphus shouted. 'I still control the Party. The membership will vote for my reinstatement by lunchtime. I will fling every one of you into the yellowcake mines! You'll be glowing in the dark as you rot to death!'

Terese stared at him impassively as she raised her hand, and Stonal couldn't help the frisson of worry at the small pause which followed. Then, one by one, the other hands went up.

'You have just killed Bienvenido,' Adolphus said. 'I am the only one who knows how to lead us through the Faller Apocalypse.'

'Director Stonal,' Terese said, 'please escort Comrade Adolphus from the cabinet room. He is to be held in custody – incommunicado – until the security cabinet decides otherwise.'

'I understand,' Stonal said. 'This way, please, sir.'

'You can't do this!'

'Sir, if you do not comply, I will have to call for officers to remove you by force. And believe me, that option has been planned for.'

Adolphus took a couple of heavy breaths. For a moment, Stonal thought he was going to launch himself across the table at Terese. Then he gripped the edge of the table and slowly rose. 'Contact the Warrior Angel,' he said forcefully. 'Talk to Paula. *Listen* to her. She's the only one who can save us now.'

'If the Warrior Angel survived the atom bombs that were detonated as the result of your irresponsible actions, she is free to get in touch with us,' Terese said brittlely. 'And I will happily discuss the terms of her surrendering her Commonwealth weapons to our regiments.'

'Idiots, every crudding one of you,' Adolphus jeered, and walked away from the table.

As Stonal escorted him from the cabinet room, he heard Terese say: 'Comrades, our first order of business must now be to appoint an interim prime minister.'

Four Palace Guards were waiting outside, wearing their full ceremonial uniform and trying not to look nervous. Two of them were Section Seven operatives. Stonal wanted people he could trust in a situation as momentous like this.

'Comrade Adolphus is to be taken to the holding cell as briefed,' he told them. 'You are not to use undue force unless he physically resists.'

'Yes, sir,' the detail sergeant said, and saluted.

Adolphus took Stonal's hand. 'Be the smart one,' he said urgently. 'Keep the door open for Paula. Don't dismiss opportunities for dogma's sake.'

'Why the emphasis on Paula?' Stonal asked with intense curiosity. 'She is an unknown factor.'

'She's pure Commonwealth. The Warrior Angel isn't; she just has access to some of their technology.'

'And this is what I find so troubling about you, Comrade,' Stonal said sincerely, removing his hand from Adolphus's hold. 'These opinions. This flavour of rationalizing. What did the space machine do to you?'

'Cured me.'

'Somehow I doubt that. Not in any fashion I recognize as a cure.'

620

When he got back into the cabinet room, the vote had been taken. Terese was the new (interim) prime minister. She'd even moved round the table to sit in the high-backed chair.

'I'd like to thank you, Director Stonal,' she said as she gestured for him to sit. 'Without you drawing my attention to Adolphus's collusion with the Commonwealth space machine, Bienvenido could have been led down a very dangerous path indeed.'

Stonal raised an eyebrow at how Adolphus was now 'colluding', but that was politicians for you. Obviously Terese had to negate any possibility of Adolphus regaining power, and a denunciation including a litany of previous 'crimes' was a time-honoured approach to stamp down hard on a dethroned political enemy. 'You're welcome, madam prime minister.'

'Now then,' Terese continued, as if what had happened was of no consequence. 'We have to consider our response to the events on Lukarticar. The Fallers have our own atomic weapons, and they have no restraint in using them. Do you agree that we are about to see the start of the so-called apocalypse?'

'It is looking like the arrival of the Commonwealth woman has forced the Faller nests to respond in such an extreme fashion,' Stonal said. 'That may be to our advantage.'

'How so?' Terese asked in surprise.

'Turn over any large rock, madam prime minister, and you will see unpleasant insects scurrying out of the light. Paula and the Warrior Angel have turned over a very large rock indeed. We have seen that the Faller nests are more widespread than even the PSR had knowledge of. They clearly have excellent contingency plans to raid our atomic facilities, so no doubt there are other plans drawn up to sabotage essential facilities and transport. Pilot Major Em Yulei's reports of Lukarticar confirmed that Faller variants are dominant off Lamaran. The Faller Apocalypse is a very real threat. They were caught off guard by Paula's arrival, and over-reacted; but in doing so they showed us their hand. They are massing out there, but now we are warned. We have been shown what to expect. That gives us a chance to prepare.'

'You mean Operation Reclaim?'

'No, madam prime minister. Not in isolation. We have already enacted travel restrictions in case they tried to bring the stolen bombs into Varlan and our other cities. People know something is badly wrong. They need clear leadership at this time; they need to be given a purpose. I would suggest this is the time for a full-scale response on our part. Go on the offensive before the Fallers have the chance to launch their assault on us.'

'You want me to declare martial law?'

'At the very minimum. Martial law, curfew for the cities and larger towns, put every regiment on full alert. Draft every reservist. We outnumber them, and this way we will be armed when they come. Use every rumour the PSR has and search out those nests. Send the Air Force to bomb Tothland and the Fire Archipelago and any other landmass our planes can reach. Once we start to burn them out, they will have no alternative but to begin their campaign. They will be exposed, and we can exterminate them.'

*

Jenifa and Chaing got back to the safe house just before midnight. It had been yet another long fruitless day spent going through the items forensics had recovered from the various sites across Port Chana which the nest had used. After all this time they really should have uncovered some leads, some connection to other nests. The Fallers had been very thorough covering their outside traces.

'Maybe it was a new kind of nest,' she suggested as Chaing checked the safeguards outside, making sure no one had entered the house while they were away.

'What do you mean?'

'Not a nest as we know them, like a family of Fallers, but more like one of our assault squads. They came together to do this one thing. So we're looking for patterns and evidence which don't exist.'

'They've never done that before,' Chaing said with a frown.

'But they've never needed to steal nukes and hunt a Commonwealth citizen before.'

'Good point. So what should we be looking for?'

'I'm not sure. I need to think about it.'

'Okay, we'll take a fresh look in the morning.'

While he disappeared into the kitchen to find himself a beer, she went up to the bedroom. As she took her uniform off, she checked the bruising down her right side where the collapsing masonry in the lighthouse had struck her. They were still sore to touch, but the big brown and purple discolorations were starting to fade – thank Giu.

Jenifa stepped into the shower and let the warm jet play over her. The liquid soap was scented with lime and jasmine, helping to relax her further. She rubbed it everywhere and took a long time letting the water sluice it off, enjoying the refreshing tingle it left. Towelling down afterwards, she was undecided if she should spend the rest of the evening poring over yet more files and notes with Chaing. It had been a long frustrating day, and tomorrow promised to be no better. If she could just figure out one angle to connect the Fallers they knew about to those they didn't . . . Perhaps a change in routine would help kick her out of the rut. What she really wanted was time for a proper physical workout; since they'd arrived in Port Chana she'd barely managed half an hour of exercise a day. Her strength must be maintained at all times – and especially now.

She wrapped the towel around her waist and went back into the bedroom. Stopped. Frowned. Something was wrong; she knew it instinctively. *Crudding Eliters creeping up on me again!* Her gaze tracked round trying to identify the anomaly, and she moved closer to the bed where her pistol and holster lay underneath her uniform jacket. Reached for it and stopped her hand in mid-air.

The jacket! Someone had moved the jacket.

Footsteps on the landing outside. That was Chaing; she could tell from the uneven steps caused by his bad leg.

He came in as she finally plucked the jacket off the bed. The pistol was there in its holster undisturbed, but the weight of the jacket was wrong, lighter than it should be. 'Chaing, did you check those safeguards properly?'

'Yes. They were all good.'

She started to feel in the jacket's pocket.

'Is this what you're looking for?' he asked with casual mockery.

Jenifa spun round and drew in a shocked breath. He was holding the link detector Yaki had sent. An incriminating jade-green light shone on the top of the small box.

'I kept wondering what it was you were always sneaking a look at,' he said. 'Then I remembered, when we were in the lighthouse, just before all Uracus broke loose: you asked me what side I was on. At the time I thought it was heat of the moment, that you were pissed off that I'd left you to go on the *Gothora* by yourself. But it bugged me.'

'So whose side are you on?' she challenged.

'There are two sides, there are humans and there are Fallers.' He dropped the link detector on the bed and took out the standard PSR-issue blood-test kit. When he jabbed the ball of his thumb with its needle a drop of scarlet blood welled up. 'Does that answer your question?'

Jenifa clenched her jaw muscles and gave him a sharp nod of confirmation.

'Liar,' Chaing said. 'If it was a binary choice, why have you got a link detector? And I'm also quite interested in how you got hold of Section Seven technology. Are you Stonal's spy?'

'No.'

He picked up the detector again, gazing at it curiously, almost ignoring her. 'There's only one reason to have one of these: to find an Eliter. So if you have one which you're constantly checking around me, what does that mean?'

She stared at him, her face impassive. *He's worked it out. Crud! So how do I mitigate this?*

'You think I'm an Eliter, don't you?' Chaing asked.

'The Warrior Angel turned up at Xander Manor. How did she know where you were?'

'You were with me most of that night, you know the commotion we were making. She must have followed me.'

'And Hawley Docks? She was there again. Coincidence?'

'You are joking? The whole of Opole knew we were fighting a nest that day. No,' he shook the detector at her. 'You've only had this since we got here. And this . . . this is an act of desperation. What made you think I'm an Eliter?'

'You abandoned me,' Jenifa snarled at him. 'You were supposed to be guarding me when I went on board the *Gothora III*. You were with *her*, in her bed most likely, in her knickers.'

'Games and more games,' he said in a disappointed tone. 'You know I was ordered to contact the Warrior Angel by Stonal himself. That is why we brought Corilla with us, for her to open a route into the Eliter radicals. And you had this detector before you knew I'd met the Warrior Angel here. That's not why you suspect me of treachery. Tell me what it is.'

She knew she was going to have to give him something, a fact he couldn't question. She forced herself to sigh, to show defeat, weakness. 'Castillito told me. She admitted you are one of them.'

'Castillito? When?'

'The day I discovered the *Gothora*'s dodgy paperwork. She contacted me in the Ankatra Cafe after Corilla made her drop.'

'So Corilla knows Castillito?'

'Must do,' Jenifa said. As a cover story, the cafe worked; he wouldn't think to probe deeper. Not that there was any way she was ever going to explain why she was eager to prove he was an Eliter, how he was just an insignificant pawn in her mother's altogether grander game. No hint of that must ever be revealed. Stonal would move swiftly if he ever suspected. This was going to have to be played very carefully. The thought was darkly thrilling.

'What did she say?' Chaing asked.

'Just that you were an Eliter.'

'That's it?' he asked with a frown. 'I still don't believe you. Consider this: if I was an Eliter, she wouldn't betray me.'

'Wrong. There's one thing that would override all the Eliter solidarity in the world.'

'What?'

'Florian. You were hunting her son. Her betrayal was extremely personal.'

'She wanted revenge,' he muttered. 'So she came up with the fantasy of me being an Eliter.'

'The Warrior Angel rescued you at Xander Manor, and there she was at the docks to rescue Florian and Paula.'

He nodded reluctantly. 'Clever. She rearranged the facts to fit her own agenda.'

'How did the Warrior Angel find out about the nest at the manor?'

'How did the Eliters know the stolen atom bombs had arrived in Port Chana?' he retorted. 'How did Corilla phone us on a PSR secure line?'

She forced her body to relax, like he'd dealt some kind of blow.

'No answer?' he taunted.

She walked round the bed to stand directly in front of him, almost touching. When she studied him he seemed so confident, so right. *Is that a front? Is he playing a game as deep as mine?* She genuinely couldn't tell. And for once he was completely unresponsive to her naked body being so close, so available. 'I don't know,' she said.

'Then tell me, who did the link detector come from? Only Section Seven personnel are authorized to use them.'

'I had it sent from Opole.'

'Nicely unanswered, Jenifa. Who in Opole?'

'Rujik. He's a friend on the third floor, in charge of technical stores. He has access to all sorts of top-security devices.'

'If the red light had come on, who were you going to call?'

'Director Yaki.'

He shook his head minutely. 'I don't think that was the truth. See? That's what happens when people start lying to each other. There is always that tiny sliver of uncertainty between them after that.'

She almost laughed; her one true answer and he didn't believe it. 'Oh, but that part is very true. I would have taken you into custody myself. And I wouldn't have used intimidation to get the truth out of you.'

'Yeah, that I do believe.'

She slid a hand down her abdomen, and pushed the towel off

her hips. Her lips tweaked into a smile. 'So where do we go from here?'

He took her hand, and smiled. She stood on tiptoes to kiss him. The link detector was slapped into her open palm.

'Well, I can tell you where we don't go,' he said cheerfully.

'To Uracus with you,' she growled.

The phone let out a two-tone whistle. Chaing gave it an irritated glance and picked it up. The small blue light came on at the base.

Like that proves it's secure, Jenifa thought.

'Chaing?' Stonal asked.

'Yes, sir.'

'Are you busy?'

'Nothing important, sir.'

Jenifa gave him a scornful look and picked up the towel, wrapping it back round her hips.

'Good,' Stonal said. 'You will be issued your official notification tomorrow morning, but martial law will be declared midnight tonight, Varlan time.'

'Is it that bad?'

'Frankly, yes. They're getting ready to annihilate us, but this way we can take the fight to them. The regiments are to be mobilized, and all the reserves called in.'

'I see. What do you want me to do, sir?'

'Have you had any contact with the Port Chana Eliters?'

'Just through Corilla, and that's not produced anything. I'm still working on backtracking the nest that was spying on the *Gothora III*. Hopefully that will lead us to other nests.'

'Go back to Corilla, insist the Warrior Angel gets in touch with us at once.'

'Yes, sir.'

'We need to know what options we have. This is top secret, but we believe the Fallers might have killed her.'

Jenifa couldn't avoid the shock that statement caused. She saw Chaing's face was troubled, too.

'How, sir?'

'The *Sziu* followed the *Gothora* to Lukarticar. Their bombs were detonated. We were in contact with one of her group, but we haven't heard from him since. We need to know if she survived, Chaing.'

'I understand.'

'Good man. There's something else you should know. The cabinet had a vote of confidence; Terese is now prime minister.'

'I see.'

'Do you? It means that Operation Reclaim is now relegated to a last resort. We will resist the apocalypse with all the vigour we can manage. That wouldn't have happened under Adolphus.'

'You can count on me, sir.'

'Good man, captain.'

The blue light went off and Chaing replaced the handset.

'Now what?' Jenifa asked.

'Now I follow orders and get Corilla to ask her friends to contact the Warrior Angel. It's what loyal PSR officers do.'

'And me?'

He smiled thinly. 'Do you still think I'm an Eliter? Actually, it doesn't matter what you think. I can't trust you any more.'

'Don't take this away from me. I couldn't ignore Castillito – that would be weak.'

'The trouble is that the PSR does a fantastic job. We track down Fallers and eliminate them. We put our lives on the line to protect this planet, and when we fail we die in the most horrific way imaginable, like poor Lurvri. But we do it anyway, every lethal, awful moment in the field, every boring decade behind a desk, because without us the Fallers would win. That cannot happen.'

'I understand that. I know what has to be done. I will never fail to do my duty.'

'But your duty is not my duty. You are not my PSR. Radical monitoring division is not the PSR, you're just Democratic Unity thugs suppressing dissent, and using the PSR's name to do it.'

'To protect us from the threat in the sky, and from those who betray us from within,' she said. 'That was the oath we all took. If the centre cannot be strong, we will all Fall. I will not Fall.'

'I'm sure you won't.' He turned and walked towards the door.

'Where are you going?'

'I told you, to speak with Corilla. If you're still here when I get back, then it's because you accept I'm not an Eliter.'

Jenifa got dressed slowly, listening to Chaing limping his way downstairs. The front door slamming shut. She'd never been so humiliated; he'd worked out what she was doing, then rejected her sexually.

'Fucking Uracus!' She slammed her fist into the wall.

The pain was good. The pain was pure. *I am stronger than this. He will not defeat me, he will not use his clever words to outsmart me. I know he is an Eliter. I will expose him to the whole world.*

She sat on the bed and dialled the number, then dialled the security code. The blue light came on.

'Hello, Jenifa,' Yaki said.

'Director,' Jenifa answered sharply.

'How's it going?'

'Not good. Chaing found the link detector.'

'That was careless of you. But it doesn't matter now.'

'How can you say that?'

'Adolphus is under house arrest. I've been quietly told it was Stonal who engineered that. And now the new prime minister has signed a state of emergency, he's more powerful than ever. So this particular game is suspended.'

'You can't mean that. I'm sure Chaing is one of them. He knew what I was looking for.'

'It's over. Chaing doesn't matter; neither does Stonal really. Our orders are coming in. The government is mobilizing everything we've got. Byarn is receiving its allocated Regiment personnel, so it's ready for the government if the time comes. You know what that means, don't you?'

'They can't just give up. You can't give up.'

'We need to be practical here, Jenifa.'

'The things I've done for you . . . The things you made me do! All of it, so you could revitalize the PSR.' Tears were flowing freely down her cheeks.

'You did everything I asked because you are strong. I'm proud of that. I couldn't trust anyone else. Just you, my dear. It was all for you. But that life is over now.'

'No!'

'I have a travel warrant for Byarn. It will be with you by lunch-time.'

'Are you coming?' Jenifa asked dolefully.

'I hope so. One way or another, I'm not facing breeders again.'

'Mother—'

'Goodbye, my dear. And remember, always be strong.'

The phone went dead. Jenifa stared at the handset for a long moment before replacing it carefully. She looked round the bedroom until her gaze found the link detector, lying on the bed where Chaing had dropped it so disdainfully.

She picked it up, staring obsessively at the small green light on top, willing it to turn red, to prove her right. There was nothing else left now. 'I will finish my mission,' she told the little device. 'That's real strength.'

*

The curfew wasn't yet official, yet there was almost no traffic on Port Chana's wet streets, and no pedestrians anywhere. That didn't surprise Chaing; the Eliters would know what was coming. They'd probably known before Stonal told him.

Chaing used a Cubar from the local PSR office to take him to the marina through the miserable drizzle coming in off the sea, its wipers swishing across the windscreen with a monotonous squeaking. His driver parked by the gates, so he buttoned his coat against the damp air as he hobbled along to the Ankatra Cafe. At this time of night it was closed and shuttered, but Corilla was waiting under one of the trasla trees outside, wrapped up in a big ankle-length raincoat. He suspected she wasn't alone, but couldn't see anyone else.

'Now what?' she asked petulantly as he huddled under the short tree with her. 'It's bloody freezing out here.'

'You know exactly what,' he said. 'The apocalypse is coming. Stonal needs to talk to the Warrior Angel.'

'I keep asking.'

'How urgently?'

The look she gave him was almost pitying. 'Why am I here, Chaing?'

'The government is getting desperate.'

'I know.'

'So am I. So I'm going to trust you. Hopefully that'll liberate some reciprocity; we're going to need to be a real team now.'

She raised an eyebrow, sceptical in the extreme.

Chaing touched his thumb to his knuckle, just like the Warrior Angel told him. A rectangular grid of thin lines fluoresced a pale emerald just below his skin.

'Chaing!' Her voice was loaded with incredulity. 'Are you . . . No. You can't be.'

'Let's just say the Warrior Angel and I have an agreement.'

She grabbed his hand and studied the lines as they faded. 'What is this thing? It emitted a general link call for her.'

'She gave it to me. It's some kind of Commonwealth technology. So now tell me truthfully, is she answering?' He tried not to sound too desperate, but he knew that without the Warrior Angel everything was lost.

'No.' Corilla shook her head sorrowfully. 'Nobody has heard anything from her since the *Gothora* sailed. We know the Fallers used atom bombs on Lukarticar.'

'Crud.'

She shook her head in disbelief. 'I can't believe you're on our side.'

'Ha. You know, that's the second time tonight someone has said that. There are only two sides, Faller and human. There is no choice.'

'What do we do now?' she asked.

'All we can do is wait and hope that the Warrior Angel and Paula are still alive, and they can do something. Until then, we fight the bastards with everything we've got.'

*

Jenifa woke up with a feeling of disorientation that might have been the end of a dream. A dream where she'd been fighting with

Chaing. With her strength she'd easily beaten him, then she'd reached into his head and pulled out the Eliter cells, holding them up in triumph while he regarded her with the dazed admiration she was so used to from him.

When she looked round he was standing in the bathroom doorway, wearing his uniform trousers, face covered in shaving foam. 'So?' he asked.

'So I'm still here,' she said aggressively.

'I see that. But I need you to understand something.'

'Crudding what?'

'I don't care that you don't trust me. What's important is that I don't trust you.'

'I get that.'

'Do you?'

'Yes.'

'I hope so, Jenifa, I really do. Because we're about to face up to the Faller Apocalypse and I need a proper partner, not one who'll shoot me in the back.'

'We're on the same side,' she said solemnly. 'We're both human.'

'Okay, then.'

Jenifa pushed the bedclothes down and sat on the edge of the bed. He gave her naked body a deliberately dispassionate glance, which infuriated her further – he might just as well have slapped her.

'How did it go last night?' she asked, carefully keeping her voice level.

'The Warrior Angel hasn't been in contact with the Eliters since the *Gothora* set sail.'

And just a day ago she would have said: *you trust Corilla, do you*? Now she had to sit placidly and say: 'Crud. So what's next?' It was demeaning. *But there will be payback. Oh yes.*

'Our duty. We find the nests in Port Chana and take them out.'

'Right.'

'Get dressed,' Chaing told her. 'We're leaving in thirty minutes.'

*

The PSR Cubar picked them up at the end of Empale Street. Chaing still didn't want anyone to know the location of the Section Seven safe house – it was routine.

'The harbour,' he told the driver as they sat in the back.

Jenifa was silent beside him, her back straight, looking out of the side window. She'd stopped speaking to him.

After visiting Corilla he'd started considering how long she'd suspected him. If it had been back in Opole, she probably wasn't acting alone, which would explain the link detector. It also meant all the sex was a lie, that she'd used it to get closer to him, oozing her way into his confidence. That hurt.

And he knew she didn't trust him. Even if she had back in Opole, the seed of doubt Castillito had planted was rooted deep by now.

Last night he'd barely contained his fury when he learned what Castillito had done.

'I want you to call Corilla in as soon as we reach the warehouse,' he told Jenifa. 'She can work with us full time, now.'

'Yes, sir.'

'Have you brought the link detector?'

She hesitated for a moment. 'Yes.'

'Good. Feel free to keep watching it.'

The Cubar made good time driving through the streets. Overnight, the sheriffs and several battalions from the Port Chana Regiment had set up checkpoints across the city. The martial law proclamation had been announced on the radio at dawn, along with instructions for all reservists to report to regimental headquarters.

Chaing was surprised how many residents had obeyed the instructions to turn out for duty, given the city's notorious reputation for nonconformity. Use of private vehicles had been prohibited as part of martial law, but a great many people were cycling to the major tram stations. The iron parking racks outside were jammed with bicycles, padlocked to the rails or each other in a giant mechanical clutter. All public transport had been commandeered by the city council's emergency committee, to be used ferrying the reservists to various regiment bases just outside the city.

Sheriff cordons had been established round the tram stations, with long good-natured queues snaking along the pavements. No one was allowed through to the platforms until they'd been given a blood test.

The cordon round the harbour had been in place since the night of the storm. Today, the sheriffs on the checkpoint insisted on a blood test before they let Chaing and Jenifa through. So he stuck his hand out and endured the needle pricking his skin. The red blood welling up satisfied the young sheriff, and she moved the barrier aside.

Captain Fajie and her expanded team of investigators had taken over the whole warehouse, using the huge enclosed space to set up dozens of trestle tables. Each one was piled with evidence bags the forensic teams had collected, from the warehouse itself and all the houses the nest had used. Clothes from dead Fallers, along with two of the huge pump-action bazookas, had their own section. The burnt-out lorries from the fight on the docks had been towed in to form a line along the back wall, each with a semicircle of associated forensic bags.

Investigators were standing at tables, carefully cataloguing each item, which would be filed and Rolodexed by the smaller team of clerks. Usually, senior investigators sat at a long line of desks across the front of the warehouse, trying to map out connections. Today when Chaing walked in, barely a fifth of the desks were occupied.

He walked over to Fajie's desk at the end of the row. A small first-aid tin was open in front of her and she was flinching as she tried to wrap a plaster round her thumb. Spots of blood were glistening on her papers.

'Crudding sheriffs,' she muttered as Chaing stood in front of her. 'I swear that one on the checkpoint is still a teenager. Hasn't got a clue how to do a blood test. Tiny needle puncture is what's supposed to happen. Look at this!' She held her thumb up; blood was leaking through the plaster's fabric. 'The idiot jabbed the whole needle in. Hurt like Uracus's kiss.'

'Sorry to hear it.' Chaing tried not to show any amusement. Fajie had been in the thick of the firefight on the dock beside the *Sziu*, facing down the monster Fallers. Now she was whinging about a needle jab. 'They're just carrying out orders.'

'Ha! See if you're still laughing after a day of this. As from five o'clock this morning, they're blood testing anyone going into a government building, a transport hub, or a utilities facility. They're also doing random street tests. Forget the Faller Apocalypse; we're all going to die in a blood poisoning epidemic by the end of the week.'

'I'm sure. Where is everyone?'

Fajie glanced round the warehouse. 'This is all we've got, and all we're likely to get for the foreseeable future. Martial law has complete priority over every investigation. Director Husnan called most of our case officers back to the office.'

'But the PSR is supposed to be following every lead to suspected nests.' His arm swept round. 'There is no lead bigger than this. This nest had nukes, for Giu's sake.'

'Not my decision. For what it's worth, I agree with you a hundred per cent. But this is a huge investigation. Even with full resources, it was going to take months.'

And there it was, the unspoken worry: *we don't have months left.*

'Crudding Uracus!' Chaing gathered himself to shout, but the impulse died as swiftly as it came. This wasn't Fajie's fault. It was Director Husnan playing petty politics.

He stalked back to his own desk, ignoring the throbbing from his leg. All the files he'd been studying yesterday now seemed a complete waste of time.

'She's here,' Jenifa announced from her desk as she replaced the telephone handset.

'Who?'

'Corilla.'

'That was quick.'

'I never called her. She's coming though the harbour checkpoint now. It's like she knew when we arrived.'

He gave her a thin smile. Even now she kept on pushing.

Corilla came in, dressed in a blue blouse and black jeans – a simple combination, but one that made her seem quite different to the angry young radical with a persecution complex waiting at the outdoor cafe at McKie College. Every time he saw her she seemed to have grown in confidence. She came straight over to his desk, giving Jenifa only a cursory glance. Chaing tried not to smile at that.

'Morning,' she said breezily.

'Morning.' He thought of asking Jenifa to fetch them some tea, but that was too childish. 'Any news?'

'Not of the Warrior Angel, no. I came in because I have information for you which some of my friends consider very important.'

'What?'

'Roxwolf is back.'

'What?'

'In Opole. My old contacts there are seeing underworld faces reappearing again, and they're back with a swagger. That can only mean they have his backing.'

'So? I have more immediate concerns.'

Corilla tilted her head to one side. 'You don't know, do you? You never actually saw him when you raided Cameron's.'

'Know what?'

'He's a Faller. A weird one; some kind of mutation. Paula confirmed that for us, by the way. He's not part of any nest, but he does have connections with them.'

'You got any proof of that?' Jenifa asked.

Corilla kept looking at Chaing. 'You found human–Faller bodies at Cameron's, didn't you? What does that tell you about his gang? And anyway, why would I lie?'

'I don't know what motivates Eliters,' Jenifa said, 'but I can find out easily enough.'

Chaing held up a finger for Jenifa to stop. 'You're sure Roxwolf is a Faller?'

Corilla nodded. 'Yes.'

'Do your friends know what he's up to?'

'There's been a big increase in arms trafficking over the last ten days,' Corilla said. 'So much it's even making some of the gangs nervous. Especially right now.'

'You think he's supplying weapons to the nests?'

'I can't see what else it is. We all know what we're about to face.'

'Are your people prepared to lead us to him?'

'My people? You mean your fellow humans?'

'Yes. Will you lead me to him? It could be the breakthrough route into the nests we need.'

Corilla gave him a soft smile. 'That's why I'm here. I'm your contact, remember? Can you get us back to Opole? The whole train network shut down last night.'

'I can get us back to Opole.'

*

The first signs that Opole's martial law wasn't as effective as it should be came when the PSR Cubar drove over the Yokon Bridge and turned onto Dunton Road. There was a junction of tram rails in the middle of the road, where the metal rails crossed. The overhead power cables were lying on the ground, their posts bent over like trees after a storm. A car had been abandoned in the middle of the junction and set on fire.

Chaing assumed the dents in its grille had come from repeatedly ramming the power cable posts until they toppled.

'Why isn't anyone fixing that?' he asked. 'At the least they should tow it away.'

The driver, assigned to them from the Opole PSR office, shrugged as he edged their Cubar round the burnt-out wreck. Cars and vans waiting their turn on the other side tooted their horns angrily. 'Everyone is registering at the regiment bases. Nobody is left on the maintenance crews.'

'That's stupid,' Chaing said.

Another shrug. 'When everyone's registered and they sort out the command structure, things will get done in a hurry.'

'Has there been any more disruption to the tram network?'

Jenifa asked. She was in the back seat next to Corilla and clearly unhappy with that arrangement.

'There's been about eight or nine junctions smashed up like this one,' the driver said. 'They've got regiment squads guarding the important ones now, but trams are out over half the city.'

'Let me guess,' Jenifa said. 'The routes out to the regiment bases?'

'Yes.'

Twenty minutes, and three blood-test checkpoints later, they turned onto Broadstreet. Chaing had witnessed so much chaos lately he was mildly surprised to see the familiar old buildings were all still standing.

The Cubar pulled up outside the seven-storey PSR office. Corilla stared up at it mistrustfully.

'We won't be in there long,' Chaing assured her as he climbed out of the front.

Jenifa strode across the pavement, pointedly ignoring them. Behind her back, Corilla gave him a small rueful smile.

A wall of sandbags had been put up across the entrance. Five armed officers were on guard duty. They saluted Chaing, even said: 'Welcome back, captain.' But he still had to hold out his thumb for a needle prick.

'She's in my custody,' he explained when they asked for Corilla's papers and saw ELITER printed across the front. They didn't like that, but agreed she could go inside.

'Ground floor only,' he told Corilla as they went in. 'There's a waiting room down here. I can't allow you upstairs.'

'I'll try and contain my disappointment,' she muttered.

Even getting the waiting room opened involved forms to be filled out at reception.

'She shouldn't even be inside at all,' Jenifa said.

'Then how do we set up this operation, corporal?' he barked back.

'We have special cells for Eliters.'

He didn't even bother responding to that. They took the stairs up to the seventh floor. It wasn't as difficult as usual for his leg; all the practice he'd had with the Port Chana lighthouse had clearly paid off. Not that Jenifa waited. She was already in Yaki's office when he finally arrived.

'You brought an Eliter into my headquarters?' the director asked coldly as soon as he shut the door. 'Why didn't you put her in a cell where she belongs?'

Chaing refused to even glance in Jenifa's direction. Instead he focused on Yaki. 'This is an emergency, and she's an asset, not a prisoner. She won't be going anywhere in the building other than the waiting room.'

'All right.' Yaki was staring intently at Jenifa. 'So why are you both back here?'

Now Chaing turned his head. 'Corporal, would you explain, please?'

Yaki listened without comment as Jenifa told her of Corilla's claim about Roxwolf returning.

'He's a Faller?' she asked at the end. 'Why did the gangs work with him? They're not that stupid.'

'Nobody ever saw him,' Chaing said. 'He can't show himself because he's some kind of mutant Faller. The nests despise him as much as we do.'

'An unseen, all-powerful boss is quite a reputation to have,' Jenifa admitted. 'It's also very convenient.'

'And this Corilla girl says he's buying arms for the nests?'

'That's what the local Eliters have told her, yes,' Chaing said.

'We have to investigate this,' Yaki said tightly. 'If she's right, it's a direct route to all the nests in the city.' The scar on her face showed as a thin white line as she sat behind her desk, fingers steepled, their tips resting on her chin. 'Okay. Chaing, you did the right thing bringing her here, but I've got martial law to enforce. My officers are spread very thinly. There have already been some very proficient acts of sabotage which we're prioritizing. So, I'm going to let you and Jenifa track down any leads Corilla offers you.'

'I'm going to need a team—' Chaing started.

'No. You get me some positive leads, and I'll assign you whoever you ask for to follow up. But until then, you're on your own. And I don't want any heroics, understand? If you find Roxwolf, you come here and get some serious backup. I can't afford another Cameron's.'

'Yes, director,' Chaing mumbled. 'Can I at least have access to records?'

'I'll tell Colonel Kukaida to grant you full inquiry status.'

'Thank you.'

*

'Happy?' Chaing asked as he made his way back down the stairs.

'Why shouldn't I be?' Jenifa grunted back over her shoulder. She wasn't making any effort to slow down, as if emphasizing how her body was at its peak, while his . . .

'You practically shut down this investigation.' Which had surprised him. Yaki was Section Seven. Why had she even listened to a corporal who'd clearly had a run-in with her boss?

'No, actually, sir, we have free run of the city in the middle of a martial-law clampdown. I'd call that a perfect result.'

Chaing glowered at her back as she turned round the corner of the stairwell. He paused at the turning, trying to get his breathing back under control. That way she wouldn't be able to see him struggling, revealing how weak he was. He wanted to look reasonably okay by the time he reached the ground floor. *It's going to be a busy day out of the office tracking down Corilla's sources. And I need a result . . .*

'So?' Corilla asked when he finally got back to the waiting room.

'We're ready to start,' Chaing told her.

She gave him a slightly confused look. 'Start?'

'Do your contacts know where a batch of weapons are being stored? Do they know who's involved? Their location?'

'I thought . . . Aren't there going to be observation teams?'

'The nests have already begun to move against us. We don't have crudding time for this,' Jenifa said. 'Do you know anything or not?'

'The Gates,' Corilla said, as if the information had been extracted with a sharp instrument.

Chaing opened the waiting room door. 'What's there?'

'Ammunition,' Corilla said. 'Stolen two days ago from a regiment armoury.'

'Now we're getting somewhere,' Jenifa said as they walked out across the reception area.

'TerVask is in charge of the crew that pulled it off,' Corilla explained. 'He's been throwing his weight around for over a week now. He'd only ever do that if he had Roxwolf's backing.'

Chaing smiled in pure delight. 'Oh, thank you, Giu. I shall be very happy to resume discussions with terVask.'

His humour was only slightly dimmed when the entrance guards insisted on another blood test as they left the PSR office.

'Take us round to the garage,' Chaing told the Cubar's driver.

'What for?' Jenifa asked, immediately suspicious.

'We're both in uniform, corporal. It's martial law, and we're going into the Gates. Do you think that's going to rouse any suspicions, let alone tip off any gang member keeping lookout?'

She nodded stiffly. 'Of course.'

'We'll requisition an unmarked car, then go back to my flat and change into our civilian clothes.' He waited for a tell-reaction at the mention of the flat, but didn't see one.

*

An hour later, an unremarkable eight-year-old Torova saloon car pulled up in Follel Road at the edge of the Gates district.

'Wait here,' Chaing told the driver.

He and Jenifa followed Corilla into the jumble of ancient sinuous lanes. Here, at least, life seemed to be carrying on almost normally. They were constantly dodging cyclists, who rang their bells arrogantly as they freewheeled down the cobbles. Adults scuttled along between the slanting walls, not making eye contact with anyone. Groups of kids in raggedy clothes rushed about playing their unfathomable games.

Corilla led them down MistleGate, and stopped outside a battered old green door halfway along.

Jenifa frowned. 'I know this place,' she muttered.

'You certainly do,' Corilla said.

There was the sound of thick metal bolts being drawn back. The door opened. Terannia stared out, her ebony hair dishevelled as if she'd just got out of bed. 'Get inside,' she hissed. 'Quickly. Even you, girlie.'

The club was just about what Chaing expected, its ancient uneven walls coated in paint that must have been a century old. A small stage for musicians. Bar against the back wall, with plenty of casks and bottles of unlicensed hooch. Curtains over doorways. Not as many tables and chairs as there might have been.

Terannia walked over to a man a few years older than her, with short silver hair curling over his scalp and a neatly trimmed beard. Chaing was pretty sure he was a musician; he looked the type. He was introduced as Matthieu. 'My business partner, and the club's musical director.'

Chaing was glad to see his instinct was still good. 'So what have you got for me?'

'I overheard something at one of the tables last night,' Matthieu said.

'Oh, please,' Jenifa sneered.

Matthieu gave Chaing a look that was almost pitying. 'Overheard at a table,' Chaing said firmly. 'I understand. What did you overhear?'

'It was one of terVask's people. That piece of crud has delusions that's he's the next big gang leader, but we all know he works directly for Roxwolf. His people pulled off an impressive heist, some ammunition from one of the regiment armouries. There's quite a lot of armaments stored in various depositories around the city; they don't keep everything at their headquarters.'

'And do you know where this stash of ammunition is being kept?'

'Minskies, over in TollGate.'

'It's a gang pub,' Terannia said.

'Actually, that's true,' Jenifa said. 'I heard about it on my last assignment.'

'They're going to move it this afternoon,' Matthieu said.

642

'When?'

'All I know is: this afternoon.'

'They'll want to do it in daylight,' Jenifa said, suddenly decisive. 'It's difficult enough with martial law; a curfew will make it practically impossible.'

'We need to get it under observation fast,' Chaing said.

'There's a sheriff station half a klick away,' Jenifa said. 'It'll have a secure line to the PSR office.'

'No.'

'What?'

'No,' Chaing repeated. 'PSR communications are compromised. We know that. Roxwolf had a lot of phone lines going into his hideaway under Cameron's. And it's not like we need to keep this from Eliters.' He grinned at Matthieu.

'So how do we observe Minskies?' Jenifa demanded. 'You and me?'

'How many people are watching it right now?' Chaing asked levelly.

Terannia shrugged. 'A couple of relatives of mine are close by.'

'You're going to use Eliters?' Jenifa asked in astonishment.

'Yes,' Chaing said. 'Obviously terVask's people don't know they're being observed, or they would have done something about those *relatives*. Why risk bringing in new people?'

'What's the matter, girlie, don't you trust us?' Terannia goaded.

Chaing held up a warning finger at the club owner. 'Don't, please.'

'We can tell you if we see them moving the ammunition,' Corilla said, 'but what good will that do?'

'You keep a good watch across Opole. I know that.' He gave her a level stare. 'Your friends must have observed my driving to Xander Manor that night. So they can certainly keep an eye out for any vehicle in daytime. Eliters walking about, Eliters riding a tram, Eliters looking out of a window. This is a whole city of casual observers. And they can update you on its location with your links. Right?'

'We could try that,' Corilla said thoughtfully.

*

Jenifa was seriously impressed with herself for keeping her emotions so tightly under control. When she was in the club, all she wanted to do was snap the cuffs on Terannia and haul her back to the Eliter cells at the PSR office and ask her the questions properly.

Overheard them talking.

Relatives keeping watch.

All of it was such total bollocks – and Chaing had let them get away with it. *Typical.* Now he was enacting an even bigger crime, using Eliters to observe the stolen ammunition shipment rather than trained and loyal PSR officers.

It was as if everything he did was designed to taunt her. *You are a crudding Eliter, and I will bring you down.*

She stared at the back of his head as they sat in the Torova, waiting for an update from the 'relatives'. Beside her on the back seat, Corilla sat with her eyes half closed as if she was on the verge of sleep. Every time Jenifa checked her link detector, the red light was on.

Are they linking to each other? Laughing at me?

She dearly wished the little device was directional.

'Terannia knew Rasschaert, you know,' she said. 'She employed him nine years ago. I interviewed her when we were hunting Florian. She's a radical.'

Corilla opened her eyes. 'You see all of us as radicals.'

'And today justified that, didn't it? Terannia is part of your network. And Rasschaert Fell; I saw blue blood coming from the bullet holes my colleagues put in his body. But when did he Fall? Did Terannia tell you that? Exactly where do her sympathies lie?'

'You're an idiot.'

Jenifa's hand bunched into a fist.

'We're using connections,' Chaing said calmly from the front seat. 'That's all. And because of that, we're going to find a route into the nests.'

'Yes, *sir*.'

A small sigh escaped form Chaing's lips, and Jenifa saw Corilla's lips twitch in amusement.

You'll make a mistake. And when you do . . .

Twenty minutes later, Corilla said: 'Uh oh.'

'What?' Jenifa and Chaing said together.

'A sheriff's car just pulled up outside Minskies.'

'Crud,' Jenifa grunted. 'We need to order them away. The gangsters will panic.'

'They're not sheriffs,' Chaing said with quiet excitement. 'Remember Hawley Docks? That's the transport team.'

'You don't know that.' *Unless you're part of the links.*

'Only government vehicles are allowed on the street during martial law. It's them.'

'They're coming out of Minskies,' Corilla said. 'Bringing boxes. Ah, it's terVask himself.'

Five boxes were loaded into the boot of the sheriff car, she told them, then terVask climbed into the back seat and it pulled away.

'Start the engine,' Chaing told their driver.

'Turning west onto Eaux Avenue,' Corilla said. 'Now Pinchat Road.'

'Let's go,' Chaing said. 'Take us round to the Veralson district. There's no rush. I don't ever want to get within a kilometre of them. Understood?'

'Yes, sir.'

The bogus sheriff car weaved an intricate route across Opole, taking twenty minutes to travel four kilometres, using the side roads and sometimes tiny back alleys so they avoided every checkpoint. Eventually they finished up on the north side of the Jaminth district.

'Larncy Square,' Corilla said finally. 'They're pulling up in Larncy Square.'

'There won't be any dodgy nightclubs there,' Jenifa said. 'Jaminth is a business district with some upmarket residential blocks.'

'Take us up to Quillit Road,' Chaing told the driver, visualizing a map of the area. 'Quickly now. And park just short of Simonet Street; that's the one that leads into Larncy Square.'

'So what are we doing there?' Jenifa asked.

Chaing twisted round in his seat to grin at her. 'You, corporal, are going to take a walk along Simonet Street and see which building they're using.'

'Me?'

'My leg and arm mark me out even in civilian clothes. You don't trust Corilla and the Elites. So yes: you. Confirm the location. We'll circle round and pick you up on Florissant Avenue.'

The Torova pulled in at the pavement, ten metres short of Simonet Street.

'Five minutes,' Jenifa said gruffly, and stepped out. The car pulled away. She didn't hesitate; people noticed hesitancy. Not that there were many people on the pavement, and those were mostly old, past reservist age. A few bicycles slid along Quillit Road, with only the occasional car and lorry. The tram tracks down the middle were empty.

She turned down Simonet Street. Its buildings were ancient, four or five storeys high – grand homes or the apartments of nobility back in the Void when they'd been constructed. Then slowly as the city expanded, they'd been adapted into smart offices.

Her heart rate accelerated as she approached the end of the street where it opened out into Larncy Square. Her right hand hovered over the concealed shoulder holster. If this was a set-up, she'd been played perfectly. Not that she believed Chaing would do that; he seemed genuinely intent on capturing Roxwolf.

Jenifa had only managed a few words with her furious mother before he'd come wheezing and sweating into her seventh-floor office.

'Why?' Yaki had demanded. 'You could have been safe by now. You have nothing to prove, not to me.'

'If we get Roxwolf, we can break the nests wide open. That is how the proper PSR operates. We don't give up because things are difficult, or hard for individuals. You taught me that.'

'This isn't *difficult*,' Yaki had said through gritted teeth. 'This is the end.'

'Not if we're strong.'

Larncy Square had been built as the exemplary heart of the Jaminth district, formed by matching white-painted stucco terraces with high bay windows and curving balconies on the upper floors. They caged a communal park of tall walwallow and vive trees, itself encased by iron railings that now acted as security posts for the dozens of bicycles the residents left chained there. A fountain pond in the middle had been allowed to decay into a circular marsh of mushy leaves; tiny higkel birds waded over the rancid surface to their mossy nests adorning the central statue.

As soon as Jenifa reached the square, she saw the sheriff car parked on the other side. She made a play of walking purposefully to one of the bicycles near a corner of the railings, bending over to unlock it and pantomiming lost keys.

Two men in sheriff uniforms were unloading boxes and carrying them into one of the terrace buildings. She caught a glimpse of terVask's profile as he sat in the back seat. Then she was striding through the huge archway which connected the square with Florissant Avenue.

'They were offloading into the Cavour office,' Jenifa said as she tumbled into the back seat of the Torova.

'Cavour. That's a law firm, isn't it?' Chaing asked.

'Yes. They handle evasion cases for the tax office, along with normal criminal prosecution for the city's sheriff's office.'

'Then they should be right at home cohabiting with Roxwolf,' he murmured.

'So what now?' she asked.

'Back to the PSR office. I need to review things.'

'What's to review? There's a crud-load of ammunition on its way to the nests so they can kill us. This is obviously a staging post, and judging from the set-up possibly Roxwolf's new hideout. We call in an assault squad and snatch as many of the bastards as we can, then sling them into the cells and interrogate them. If we get lucky, we catch Roxwolf himself.'

'Charging in unprepared was what we did last time. Remember how well that went? Besides, you can't interrogate Fallers; it never works.'

'But Roxwolf isn't an ordinary Faller.'

'Exactly. He's a tricky little swine. We have to be smarter this time.'

*

Most of Opole's government departments were in disarray trying to implement the proscriptions of martial law, with uncertain chains of command and urgent orders contradicting each other. On top of that, the remaining residents were attempting to cope with restricted travel and a chaotic tram network. It was a city edging close to a nervous breakdown.

Turmoil, however, was not a concept that infiltrated the PSR records division. Down in the basements under the Broadstreet offices the air was still and dry, the temperature stable, along with the demeanour of the black-suited clerks who bustled round hugging their files with the same care they'd show a newborn infant. This department carried on unaffected by anything.

Chaing knocked on Colonel Kukaida's door. He thought he'd be exasperated by the normality pervading her domain, but he actually found it quite a relief.

'Come.'

Nothing had changed. Kukaida sat behind her broad desk, her grey uniform buttoned neatly. Photographs formed a grid before her. Two clerks hovered, awaiting instructions.

'Colonel, I—'

She held up a finger, and shamefully Chaing fell silent. The finger dipped and landed on the photograph of a middle-aged woman in an expensive fuchsia-pink cardigan. 'That one,' she said.

A clerk nodded and picked up the photo, carrying it out of the bright white office like a sports trophy. The other clerk began to tidy away the remaining photos.

'Yes, captain?' Kukaida asked.

'I need some files.'

'Then it is fortunate that you're here. Files are the one thing we have in great abundance.'

'Not files on people.'

'Really? How intriguing. What kind of files do you want, captain?'

'Civic files. Specifically, building blueprints and city engineer utility plans. Very old ones.'

'The appropriate city hall department can provide you with those, captain.'

'I don't want to use city hall, colonel. I have reason to believe it is compromised. My mission is of the highest priority, and top secret.'

'What an important man you are, Comrade captain. Luckily for you, we do have copies of all city files, of course. However, they are microfiched. Searching through even one cassette for a specific blueprint may take you some time.'

'I can accept that.'

'Very well.' She signalled the clerk. 'Please inform my colleague what it is you require, and the relevant cassettes will be brought to you in the second-level viewing library.'

'Thank you, colonel.'

*

The assault team had walkie-talkies, but on Chaing's orders these remained switched off during deployment. They all wore civilian clothes, carrying bags or suitcases containing their weapons. Fortunately most of the reservists walking about Opole's streets were carrying similar bags stuffed with clothes as they reported to their registration centre. It made the team unremarkable – as Chaing intended.

Scouts went into the buildings on both sides of the Cavour offices. If they found any sign of gang activity, they would come out again within ten minutes. No gang activity would see them place a red cloth in the second-floor windows.

Team members entering the square from its various access roads saw two red cloths, and proceeded into the buildings over the next ninety minutes. The regular occupants that were still working under martial law were hustled into a room on the third floor, and held there. Not under arrest, the team leaders assured them, but for their own protection.

In one building, five team members went up into the loft space and quietly cut through the partition wall, clearing a route into the attic above the Cavour office.

Without radio communication – which they knew Roxwolf monitored – the assault sequence was all down to timing. From Chaing initiating the mission, they had ninety minutes to infiltrate the teams into the neighbouring buildings and quarantine their workforces. Fifty minutes to cut through into the attic. A further fifteen minutes to assemble in position; sub-teams in each building behind second-floor balcony windows were ready to launch grapnel ropes and swing across, blasting their way in with grenades, with more sub-teams at the back door to overwhelm any gang guards posted at the rear-alley entrance. Main teams were in the hallway, heavily armed to storm though Cavour's front entrance.

It was planned down to the last detail, approved by Yaki and the duty assault team captain. And doomed to fail.

*

Roxwolf's hideaways, of which there were several in Opole, were superbly integrated into their surroundings. In Larncy Square, there were watchers behind the blinds on the fourth floor of the offices, covering the square and the alley behind. Clerks and secretaries in several companies around the square were affiliated with the gangs, with dedicated phone lines into the Cavour office. There were even optical tubes blended discreetly into the architecture, allowing Roxwolf to observe suspicious activity directly.

As the assault team started to infiltrate the adjacent buildings, three separate warnings were triggered before the gang associates moved obligingly to the third-floor quarantine rooms. Thus warned, Roxwolf himself watched the steady arrival of men and women with similar-sized bags. Nobody now was coming out of the neighbouring buildings. A scan around the square revealed new checkpoints had been set up at the far end of the access roads. The already reduced level of government-authorized traffic trundling round the central park was shrinking towards non-existent.

Without warning his underlings (human or Faller) he armed the trips on the demolition charges and opened the secret panel in the sub-basement where he'd lived for the past fortnight. He moved quickly through the dank catacombs that stretched beneath Larncy Square. Retracing the route he'd taken to reach the Cavour offices, he found the narrow service hatch in the wall of a long-abandoned culvert and squeezed through.

A pistol muzzle pressed into the side of his head. Five bright torches came on, leaving him blinking in their dazzling light.

'Roxwolf, I presume?' Chaing said cheerfully.

2

Ry Evine didn't think his heart rate had dropped below a hundred since he arrived on Macule.

Another planet! I'm on another planet – and I got to it through a wormhole!

After they all came tumbling through the wormhole along with the forty-odd machines and cargo pods from HGT54b, he had simply stood there on the cold grainy desert, turning round and round, drinking in the incredible sight.

Actually, the view itself wasn't so incredible. The terminus had opened in the middle of a brutish metamorphic desolation – all jumbled schistose rocks, some distant worn cliffs. While beneath his feet, the hard-packed granular dirt of the desert rippled away out to the horizon. Colour was minimal, which he found strange, even though there was thankfully more variation that he'd endured on Lukarticar. The ground was contrasting smears of grey with some faint ridges of brown raked in. Above him the thin air produced a sky that was a uniform pale blue, devoid of clouds.

But still . . . an alien world.

Kysandra and Florian stepped through together, followed by another batch of membrane-wrapped machinery blocks that immediately toppled over, dislodging puffs of sand that hadn't moved in millennia. The terminus with its fuzzy grey edge was creeping across the ground, as a world away its counterpart slid along the full length of HGT54b. Then the last slab-like machine was through, and the eye-twisting dimensional distortion surrounding the terminus underwent an even greater contortion leaving the cylindrical wormhole generator itself standing on the desert, shining weak violet Cherenkov radiation across the sand.

'I didn't know they could do that,' Kysandra said.

'Inverting the generator location is a standard technique,' Demitri said. 'Think of it like turning a sock inside out.'

'Neat trick.'

Ry finally paid attention to the row of amber icons lined up in his exovision. The air pressure was a third lower than Bienvenido, though that wasn't an immediate problem for his e-m suit. Background radiation was high. The force field could cope with that, but the e-m suit would have to filter radioactive particles as he breathed in the chilly air. It wasn't really designed to act as a radiation suit; at the current level his filters would only last a couple of days.

'What now?' Florian asked. He seemed somewhat less awed by being on a different world, and a lot more nervy.

'Now we get some engineeringbots and basic synthesizers up and running,' Valeri said.

So Ry had to stand around doing nothing while the ANAdroids broke open the crate containing a dozen engineeringbots and began to fuss over the inert forms. It was like being crammed inside HGT54b that first night, with nothing to do except wait. But this time . . . *alien world!*

Ry went for a short walk – the explorer striding out, making the important first ever human footprints across this new land. There wasn't much to see or find. The desert was flat enough not to hide anything from sight. Some boulders were scattered about, a few larger than him. Nothing hid behind them. He started circling round, always keeping the glowing wormhole in direct view. After the first twenty minutes, he realized what else was missing. No vegetation – not even desiccated blades of grass or moss. He examined the edges of loose stones, then dug down into the sand a couple of times, trying to find something like lichen or mould. But if there was any, he didn't recognize it.

But then, Macule had been dead a long time. Radioactive particles were everywhere – in the air, in the ground. And there was very little weather. The ice caps had sucked all the water out of the oceans as they extended their glaciers down to what had previously been this world's tropical latitudes. After that, the climate became super-stable. It would take a major tectonic event to kick Macule out of its current stasis.

After an hour, he made his way back to the base. The ANAdroids were reassembling the first engineeringbot, the one out of twelve in the crate that needed the least work. A device with a barrel-shaped body one metre high, sprouting all kinds of plyplastic tentacles and spindly sensor antennae. A cable from the wormhole generator's mass converter was plugged into it, charging the power cells. Three identical engineeringbots lay on the sand beside it, sections of casing removed so their components could be utilized.

As he approached he saw it start up, running through a self-check routine, testing the flexibility of its limbs as if it was in some kind of bizarre yoga class. Once it was ready, it went over to the storage crate it had come from and began to examine the eight remaining bots. Ry blinked in surprise; its tentacles were moving at such a speed they were a blur. The first inert bot's casing was soon opened, and the tentacles delved inside to continue the technological surgery.

The ANAdroids had moved on to a semiorganic synthesizer. Paula, Florian, and Kysandra were stripping the membrane packaging off a refinery the size of a small car.

'Are these going to work?' Ry asked.

'Not all of them,' Paula told him. 'But by the time the *Viscount* left the Commonwealth, our machinery didn't have many moving parts. They're not mechanical like Bienvenido's machines. It's all field manipulation and electronic processing. The closest thing we have to mechanics is the plyplastic those bots use to manipulate things. So it's mainly a question of molecular integrity.'

'We estimate seventy per cent of the equipment in HGT54b is salvageable,' Demitri said. 'That will be more than sufficient to construct what we need for the preliminary analysis of Valatare.

And the surviving systems should be able to build more new manufacturing systems. This is all we need to begin a Commonwealth-level society.'

'That and time,' Kysandra interjected. 'Which we don't have.'

'So when you get a batch of this stuff working, what are you going to build first?' Ry asked.

'We'll start with a simple habitat dome,' Paula said. 'That'll give us a base. The refinery can process silicon direct from the sand, the synthesizer can churn out panels and a framework, and the engineeringbots will assemble it.'

*

He'd been mildly sceptical of her claim, but within an hour there were another three engineeringbots up and running – which was a fascinating exercise of exponential growth to watch as they repaired each other. The ANAdroids had the synthesizer functioning. Within three hours, two-metre hexagonal panels were being produced. The (now five) operational engineeringbots started fitting them together.

Six hours after arriving on Macule, Ry and the others were sitting inside the ten-metre-wide geodesic dome, eating a meal from their packs. A simple filter pump was pressurizing the hemisphere with clean air. Five of the panels were transparent, allowing Ry to see the ANAdroids and eight of the engineeringbots (the full reclaimed complement) working on the rest of HGT54b's cargo. The sun was already sinking behind the jagged horizon. He was surprised how the sight of it made him sleepy, but then he'd been awake for at least twenty-five hours.

'Do you think the Faller-seibears set off the second bomb after we left?' Florian asked as he activated his sleeping bag.

'Without question,' Paula told him. 'They were heading straight for the *Viscount*, and they only had one purpose.'

'Anala would have seen it go off,' Ry said miserably. 'Or the devastation it caused. But she wouldn't know we survived.'

'I certainly hope not,' Paula said. 'That's what coming here was all about. Everyone has to think we're dead.'

As he was falling asleep, Ry wondered how Anala was doing, if her capsule had made it through re-entry. If the recovery ships had picked her up okay. The kywhale was the biggest thing ever sighted in Bienvenido's ocean; suppose the Fallers had started eggsuming them? One of those leviathans could swallow the Liberty capsule whole. He closed his eyes, telling himself he had to stop these punishing thoughts.

*

When he woke up several hours after dawn, the scene through the transparent panels was completely different. The engineeringbots along with the ANAdroids had assembled another three domes – one considerably larger than the rest, which held the wormhole generator. Two engineeringbots were putting up a fourth, the largest yet. Five synthesizers and three refineries were up and running.

'We need more raw materials,' Paula said as they ate breakfast. 'The mineral content round here isn't particularly varied, and we really need a source of hydrocarbons.'

'Valatare?' Ry suggested. 'I thought that's what the floaters were for, to supply Commonwealth industrial systems with the hydrocarbon gas in a gas giant's atmosphere.'

'That's a bit extreme for a first step,' Paula said. 'When we do open the wormhole to Valatare, I want to be sending through a flock of sensor satellites to scan it properly.'

'Water would also be useful,' Valeri said. 'There is a quantity bound up as ice particles in the desert sand, but melting it, then filtering it out, is a somewhat crude operation. Locating a frozen lake or stream would be preferable.'

'The neumanetics have produced some additional sensor systems for you two,' Paula said, handing Ry a sphere of silver-white plyplastic the size of his head. A second was given to Florian.

Just as Ry was about to ask 'What's this?' the sphere's micronet linked to his u-shadow. Function graphics ran along his exovision. 'A spacesuit? Wonderful.'

The sphere unfurled like a chrysalis into a slithery overall that looked a lot tougher than Ry's original e-m suit. He put it on, and waited for it to contract round his limbs and torso. The hood which crept round his head was completely transparent. Monitor icons lit up green.

They trooped through the cylindrical airlock and Ry began to appreciate the real potential of the Commonwealth manufacturing machines. Four quad-karts were waiting for them, little more than a saddle and handlebars suspended on black composite struts between four thick tyres with electric axle motors. But they looked quite tough enough to handle the rugged desert terrain.

Ry slung a leg over the saddle, unable to keep the grin from his face.

'You can use your u-shadow to accelerate and brake,' Demitri said, 'but steering is purely manual. And we don't have skill memory inserts for driving, so take it easy out there.'

'Got it.' Ry was rather disappointed there was no manual throttle on the handlebars. 'I'll manage.' He pointed at the low cliffs, eager to see a different aspect of Macule, however trivial. 'I'll take north.'

'Okay,' Paula said. 'I'll go east. Florian, you take south, Kysandra, west. Remember, this is just a scout round for material. If the ground gets difficult, don't try and get through, just turn aside and scan a different area.'

Ry wondered if Florian also thought the Commonwealth woman to be very schoolmarm-ish. They way Paula spoke from some unassailable height of knowledge, how she expected everyone to do as she said – even Kysandra had stopped questioning her. Part of being an excellent officer was adopting a tone of authority; he'd learned that well enough in the regiment. He wondered if he should start questioning things, but her attempt to find some kind of benign alien armada imprisoned in a gas giant was so far beyond his comprehension he knew he'd just wind up looking foolish, and then do exactly as he'd been told.

Ego doesn't matter. I'm on another planet. And if everything goes right, I might even see Valatare close up – and possibly save Bienvenido, too.

He carefully ordered the quad-kart to accelerate and practised the steering, braking, turning left and right. In a minute he was confident enough to announce he was ready.

The four of them sped off from the base. The sensors dotted across Ry's spacesuit and the quad-kart's struts scanned a wide swathe of ground as he went, recording the mineral composition. It was mostly silicates with some traces of iron, but he began seeing veins of ice – presumably underground streams from a time before the nuclear winter.

Avoiding stones and boulders took up a lot of concentration. The cliffs were about six or seven kilometres from the domes, but he didn't risk throttling the quad-kart up past fifteen kph, and often didn't go more than five or six if the ground was particularly difficult. He certainly couldn't take a straight path.

'You know what I think?' Florian asked through the general link. 'I think this is the bottom of an old ocean. I mean, there is nothing here, no signs of buildings or trees, not even rubble. And that cliff Ry's heading for, that could be the shoreline.'

'We've driven three kilometres,' Paula said. 'The odds of finding ruins or artefacts in that distance are minuscule. Based on particle decay, the ANAdroids estimate the natives had their nuclear war over thirty-five thousand years ago. The chance of any structures remaining is minimal. The war, the climate shift, entropy – these are not our friends.'

'*Viscount* survived three thousand years in the cold,' Florian said, 'and that was just one ship. Something of this civilization must be here.'

'It will be, but badly decayed to the point it may be unrecognizable. And remember, you shouldn't judge the previous civilization by human standards. Some aliens the Commonwealth encountered are very alien indeed. And not everyone goes down the industrial–mechanical route we took. There are some who have very biological-oriented societies – they literally grow their own houses and implements. In which case there will be nothing left but dust.'

'It would be difficult to grow nukes, wouldn't it?' Ry asked.

'Good point,' Paula admitted. 'They certainly had machines somewhere.'

'We should have brought some ge-eagles with us,' Kysandra said. 'They'd have scanned half this desert by now.'

'If we don't find what we want, we'll manufacture some,' Paula said.

Ry was so intent on evading all the natural obstacles littering the desert that he didn't notice the slim indentations until the quad-kart had been driving over them for twenty metres. The sensors weren't reporting anything interesting, so it took him a while to realize what he was seeing. The quad-kart braked sharply at his command.

'Er, I've got something here,' he announced over the general link. The others accessed his vision feed. The indentations were slim rectangles about seventy-five centimetres long and ten wide, always running in two sets twenty centimetres apart. They were everywhere – curving round in wide spirals, running over themselves so often it was impossible to follow a continuous line. Some were worn down and barely recognizable, while others were sharply defined.

'They look like caterpillar tracks,' Kysandra said.

Ry climbed off the quad-kart and squatted down to study the marks. They had the same temperature as the rest of the desert. When he prodded one of them with a finger, it was just as solid as the frozen sand it'd been pressed into. 'I don't think these are thirty-five thousand years old,' he said uneasily. 'Not even the older ones.' His gaze was drawn to the cliff, now just a kilometre away. It wasn't high, maybe seventy metres, its crinkled face a dull grey-brown with some odd white marbling running in jagged patterns at steep angles.

'Ry, stay where you are,' Paula said. 'I'm coming over.'

'Me too,' Kysandra said. 'You might need some backup.'

'I'm coming too,' Florian said.

Ry told his u-shadow to switch on his infra-red function, changing the world to weird false-colour petals. The air drifting along the cliff was a couple of degrees higher than anywhere else. He got back on the quad-kart and began driving towards it.

'Ry,' Paula said. 'What are you doing? I told you to stay where you are.'

'I just need to get a bit closer. There's some kind of odd thermal activity around the cliff.'

'Okay, but just stop and observe from where you are, please.'

Ry braked the quad-kart resentfully. *I'm an astronaut. Venturing into the unknown is why I exist. Why can't she just let me get on with it?* He had a sudden depressing thought that the Commonwealth, for all its magnificent achievements and power, was run by timid bureaucrats, unable to justify any risk. Another thought was fast behind: *Uracus, I left my maser rifle back in the dome.* Because Macule was a dead world; everybody knew that. Right?

His retinas zoomed in on the cliff. 'I can see some caves. I think the warm air is venting out of them.'

'Do the tracks lead to the caves?' Paula asked.

'I can't tell. There's a big shelf of naked rock along the base of the cliff.' Ry peered forwards as the gusts of hot air from one of the cave mouths became warmer and denser, its velocity increased in tandem. 'There's some kind of pressure surge from one of the caves.'

'You mean something's forcing the air out?' Paula asked. 'That's only going to happen if—'

'Oh crud!' Ry grunted. A hemisphere of dull metal, an easy four metres in diameter, was rising out of the cave. That was just the head of a ten-metre-long cylinder which rode on stumpy triangular undercarriage mechanisms – three down each side. They had five fat metal wheels apiece, which rolled over the stone with loud grating sounds. The first cylindrical section was connected to a second via a complicated-looking articulated junction. A third section followed.

Ry turned the quad-kart round in a tight circle. By the time he was pointing back at the domes, all five sections of the machine had emerged. The rear two cylinders were ribbed by tarnished silver pipes that glowed brightly in infra-red. His suit sensors detected a worrying amount of radiation squirting out of the metal. Hatches on the forward hemisphere clanged back, and small elaborate instruments telescoped out, cogs and heavy-duty chains whirring round to propel their sliding rails. Many components on their tips spun up or began scanning back and forth. Ry didn't think they were weapons. A fan of green laserlight swept over him.

'Get out of there!' Paula said.

'Already gone.' Ry ordered the quad-kart wheels to accelerate hard. He took off over the gently undulating desert, the deep tread on the tyres kicking up plumes of icy sand.

Behind him, the five segments of the Macule machine paused. Latches snapped up on all of its triangular undercarriage mechanisms. High-pressure hoses trembled and pistons whined with mechanical strain. The triangles rotated, moving the five-wheel base off the ground so twin caterpillar-track segments slapped down. The locking latches slammed round. Ry's sensors informed him the track segments measured seventy-five centimetres long, ten wide.

'I don't think that was good,' Florian said.

'No crudding kidding,' Ry snarled. The quad-kart had reached thirty kph, and it was taking a *lot* of concentration to steer round the medium-sized rocks. His force field was already on at full strength.

He heard a great many engines start whining. Gears crunched as they engaged. The Macule machine started to roll forwards, picking up speed fast. It didn't have to slalom about to avoid rocks; the tracks simply crushed them deeper into the sand. When it came to a larger outcrop, it rode over it, the segments undulating about their junctions, creating a lengthy ripple effect.

Ry realized it was catching up, and ordered more power to the quad-kart's axle engines.

'We've expanded the wormhole generator's force field to cover the domes,' Demitri said. 'I don't think your pursuer has the ability to break through. For all it's impressive, it is rather primitive.'

'What in Uracus is it?' Ry demanded. 'Is it Commonwealth?'

'Unlikely,' Demitri said. 'It appears to be nuclear-powered, and its reactor is lacking the normal level of shielding humans build in.'

Ry could see the domes a kilometre ahead now. The temptation to throttle up further was almost overwhelming. But a quick calculation showed he should arrive fifty metres ahead of the Macule machine if he just kept to this speed. An exovision map showed him the other quad-karts speeding for the domes.

Then Paula turned onto a course which would bring her towards him.

'What are you doing?' he demanded.

'A simple test,' she replied. 'Demitri, optical refraction on the force field, please. Let our visitor know what it's up against.'

Ry stared at the domes as the force field shimmered all around them; it was as if the sunlight suddenly became solid. A dull pearl hemisphere materialized, covering the geodesic domes completely. For some reason, that solidity gave Ry a little burst of confidence. He checked the pursuing machine. 'It hasn't slowed down,' he said.

'Interesting,' Paula said.

'Interesting?' He was five hundred metres from the protected domes now, and he could see Paula's quad-kart charging towards him from the east, a thin sand contrail stretching out behind her.

'Yes. Keep going,' she told him.

Now, Ry decided, wasn't the time to go all stubborn and argue. He focused on the ground, steering with small controlled flicks to the handlebars. Paula was closing fast. She braked hard, tyres churning up a flurry of icy sand. A moment later, Ry raced past her.

His sensors showed her jumping down off the saddle. Then her force field did the same refraction trick, turning her into a plain white profile, like a statue devoid of any detail. She stood squarely on the tyre tracks Ry's quad-kart had left and raised a hand, palm out towards the Macule machine.

'You can't be serious,' Ry muttered. His u-shadow automatically reduced speed; he simply didn't want to miss this.

The huge Macule machine was only a hundred metres from Paula, who stood resolute. Its caterpillar tracks surmounted any obstacle, large or small.

'Paula?' Kysandra queried. 'Do you need more firepower?'

'I shouldn't. Not if there's sentience controlling it.'

Ry had stopped concentrating on the path ahead. He just

watched Paula. All he could think was: *so this is what it's like when an irresistible force meets an immovable object.*

The Macule machine thundered onwards. 'Are you going to shoot it?' Ry asked. The disrupter effect that Commonwealth bionics could produce was formidable, but the juggernaut rushing towards her had the inertia of Uracus.

Just as he was about to turn round and charge back to Paula – not that he had the faintest idea if that would be of any help – a tortured screeching sound came from the Macule machine as chunky metal components were abruptly overstressed. He saw the caterpillar tracks on all its triangular undercarriage mechanisms lock rigid, ploughing up huge waves of sand and stones as they suddenly dug deep into the ground.

'No way!' Ry grunted. The machine was skidding along the frozen desert, its five sections waving from side to side. For one moment he thought the whole thing would roll over, but it just kept slowing.

Amazingly, Paula didn't move. She did lower her hand as soon as the caterpillar tracks locked, but that was all. *Why doesn't she just jump aside in case it can't stop in time?* He held his breath, wincing, almost unable to watch.

The Macule machine came to a full halt, its hemispherical nose seven metres short of Paula. Some of the slender instrument rails were hanging over her. Oiled chains and small hydraulic actuators moved along them, turning the instruments to align on the spectral figure shining defiantly below them.

Ry's sensors picked up a multi-spectrum signal transmitted from Paula. 'Commonwealth first-contact interpretation package,' his u-shadow said. 'It allows any reasonably competent processor to establish base equivalents and facilitate the subsequent exchange of vocabulary and grammatical constructs.'

'Right,' Ry murmured.

He sat on the quad-kart's saddle, facing the strange tableau. The wait wasn't long. Within fifteen minutes, one of the revolving instruments slowed. It started transmitting.

Thirty minutes later, a preliminary lexis had been established.

Ry observed in fascination as Paula began to talk to the alien machine.

'My designation is Paula Myo. I am a human. I have travelled here from this planet.' A simple file containing a diagram of the solar system was sent, with Bienvenido bracketed.

'You are new,' the machine sent in reply. 'You cannot be a Zone Unit.'

'I am new to this world, yes. I am not a threat to you. What is your designation?'

'I am Zone43 Unit976. One of my functions is to guard our boundary. You are intruding.'

'I apologize. I repeat, I am not a threat. We mean you no harm. We did not know anything was still alive on this planet.'

'Many Units recreate. There are fewer now.'

'Do you mean Units survived the nuclear war?' Paula asked.

'Units were created after the extinction war to safeguard the Kromal. >Macule sentient species<'

'Are you a biological entity?'

'Kromal were biological. All Units contain Kromal-derived orts. Continuation of Kromal exists in this form. All Units exist to facilitate continuation.'

'What is the end point of this continuation? What is your goal?'

'Units exist to continue Kromal safely until this world is reborn.'

'When will it be reborn?'

'We do not know. Unit creators designed us to endure until the radiation from the war has fallen to a level where biological life can survive again. It has not reached that level.'

'Really? I may be able to help.'

3

Basement level six under the Opole PSR office only had four cells. It hadn't been used in living memory of any current PSR officer, although it was maintained with the grudging routine of any government facility. One short corridor served all four cells, its dark brick walls leaking white salt crystals out of the mortar. There was a cage door at the foot of the stairs where armed guards were stationed, along with the two floor chiefs. The steel cell doors themselves weighed nearly half a tonne and needed two separate keys to unlock them. They all had a spyhole.

When Chaing and Yaki arrived, eight officers were clustered round the metal door of cell one, taking it in turns to peer through at the new inmate. They straightened up and saluted guiltily as the two floor chiefs greeted the director. Yaki maintained a disapproving silence as they all filed out sheepishly when the cage door was opened. The floor chiefs put their keys in the door of cell one, and turned them simultaneously.

'Is the recording equipment working?' Yaki asked as the locking mechanism clunked.

'Yes, ma'am,' the senior chief said. 'It's all been checked and confirmed by the electrical manager herself. Everything is in duplicate.'

'Thank you. Open the door, please.'

The senior chief tugged hard on the handle, and the big door slowly swung back.

Roxwolf was sitting at the sturdy wooden table in the middle of the room, facing the door. A handcuff was clamped around his human wrist, securing him to a heavy iron ring in the centre of the table. A shackle bracelet was holding his human ankle to a similar ring set in the floor underneath the table. The guards obviously hadn't been sure about the restraints working on his ginger-furred animal limbs; instead they'd taken to binding his mismatched legs together. The upper portion of the arm limb was contained in a long leather sheath, with chains holding it immobile against his torso.

'Director Yaki, welcome,' Roxwolf said in a gurgling voice.

Chaing couldn't take his eyes off the fangs filling the creature's mouth – how sharp they were, how the jaw muscles bulged. He didn't want to be in the same building as that mouth, let alone locked in the same room. All he could think about was that mouth eating, shredding meat as if it was wet bread – and what kind of meat.

'Did your officers enjoy peeking at the big scary monster? You should charge people for the privilege. It would double the number of illegal kickbacks you acquire from your various commercial rackets. And Captain Chaing, the great Stonal's representative on Bienvenido, congratulations on your no-doubt imminent promotion. How long you will enjoy it is of course another matter entirely.'

'Longer than you'll live to see,' Chaing said as he and Yaki sat in front of the table.

'And yet, here I am: alive. If you wanted me dead, then a quick bullet to the brain from your pistol when you captured me would have sufficed. Good work, by the way. I'm impressed amid my depression.'

'Patterns,' Chaing said. 'The downfall of us all. You always use underground escape routes.'

'I will make an effort to remember that.'

'We need information from you,' Yaki said.

Roxwolf stretched his lips wide, exposing more of his fangs. 'Of course you do.'

He knows how disconcerting that is for humans, Chaing thought. *So he must believe he still has some advantage.*

A moment of silence stretched out. Then, 'Oh,' Roxwolf said, sounding mildly disappointed. 'I was waiting for you to give me the "hard way or easy way" speech.'

Yaki tipped her head to one side and fixed him with a faint smile. 'You'll give us what we want, or you'll die. Good enough?'

'And after I give you what you want, you'll kill me anyway. So why don't you just go right ahead?'

'If you wanted to die, you had plenty of opportunities to make a break for freedom while we were bringing you in. The assault team is good, but you're a scary beast right out of Uracus itself; one of them would have pulled the trigger.'

'Quite right, director. So instead of using the stick, would you like to show me the carrot?'

'Carrots and sticks are for donkeys.'

'Ah, donkeys, they taste nice, but not as nice as you.'

'What are you, exactly?' Chaing asked, pleased he could put up a cold wall of indifference to the creature's goading.

'A mistake,' Roxwolf grunted, and looked pointedly at his leather-bound arm. 'A very literal half-breed.'

'So you are Faller? That's where your sympathies lie?'

'I am useful to them. I take risks they dare not, so they allow me to live – for a price.'

'You have a price, then?' Yaki asked.

'Everybody has a price, director. You should know that.'

'What will your cooperation cost us?'

'That depends. What is it you wish to know?'

'The locations of every nest you know of.'

'That is expensive information.'

'How valuable is your life?'

'Very. But you haven't shown me you can guarantee that.'

'What guarantee are you looking for?'

A long serpentine tongue flickered between Roxwolf's fangs as he exhaled gently. 'Full citizenship, granted publicly, and legal immunity from all my past crimes.'

'I can ask for that,' Yaki said, sounding slightly puzzled. 'I'm not sure if the government will grant it.'

'Of course. As a gesture of good faith, I am willing to give you the current location of the five largest nests in Opole.'

'Five?'

'Yes.'

Yaki glanced at Chaing. He knew exactly what she was thinking. *There are more than five?*

'I can agree to that,' she said. 'At the very least, you won't die today.'

'Good to know. Oh, there's one other thing.'

Yaki stiffened. 'Yes?'

'The Commonwealth girl, Essie.'

'Paula,' Chaing said. 'Her name is Paula.'

'Interesting.' Roxwolf nodded as if agreeing to some inner conversation. 'I will also require Paula to agree to my terms.'

'We have no way of getting into contact with her.'

'Now that's not entirely true, is it, captain? In fact, you're trying rather hard, aren't you? Section Seven has been pressuring every radical Eliter they know of, demanding she get in touch again. I'm assuming that has something to do with the machine in the basement.'

'The what?'

'Ry Evine used that phrase as his proof of identity to the polar Liberty mission, who in turn convinced the prime minister – or ex-prime minister, I should say. It was an intriguing conversation – supposedly private. But if your astronauts will broadcast direct from orbit you must expect people to overhear them.'

'All right,' Chaing said. 'If she gets in touch with us, we can ask. But I'd like to know why. Why do you need her to agree to your request?'

'I met her, as you know. A formidable little thing, even back then. Now, she is just plain terrifying. It's the potential she represents, you understand. The nests risked everything to use your atomic weapons against her, and we still don't know if they succeeded.'

'So you think she'd kill you?'

'Not if we have a deal. She was open to a deal even after I tried to blow her brains out.' He shrugged. 'I failed, of course – which gives me enormous respect for her.'

'I'm not sure I believe you,' Yaki said. 'But we will add it to your demands.'

'People in a position of strength make demands. I merely offer negotiating points to keep myself alive.'

'So you'll just roll over so easily?' Chaing said.

'You have no idea what is about to happen on this world, do you?'

'The great Faller Apocalypse? I know.'

'You don't. You don't even know our numbers.'

'You've taken over every landmass apart from Lamaran and Byarn. I can only assume you have bred a formidable population base.'

'Touché. I suppose the seibears gave that away?'

'Yes. And you've got detailed plans of how to disrupt our society; the raid on our nukes showed us that.'

'Indeed. And the Trees?'

Chaing fought against turning to look at Yaki; it would have shown weakness. 'What about the Trees?'

'This is a war for total supremacy. There can only be one survivor. I know you think you understand that intellectually, but in reality you are blind.'

'What about the Trees?'

'The apocalypse – *your* apocalypse – will begin when they fly down from the Ring to low orbit. You see, your cities and farms and railways and industry are not part of Faller culture. The Fallers do not need such things. They are spoils that will not be claimed by the victor.'

'Then what will the Trees do?' Yaki demanded in a strained voice.

'Low orbit will allow them to refine their aim. Every egg they have will come crashing down on your buildings, your bridges, your dams. And there are tens of thousands of eggs growing up there. Their shells are engineered at a molecular level to withstand any impact, no matter what it is they land on. Every half-important

669

structure you have ever built will be reduced to ruin in a matter of hours. Humans will have nothing left to defend. Millions of you will die before the nests even begin their assault. Survivors will be rounded up and either eaten or eggsumed. You'll see.'

'Oh crudding Giu,' Chaing whispered. 'But why tell us? Why warn us? If what you say is true, the Fallers are going to win no matter what we do.'

'And if they do, I will probably lose. I am a realist above all else. Now that you have captured me I cannot deal with them, not from this prison cell; the weapons I was supposed to supply will not be delivered. I was treated with contempt before, and now you, Captain Chaing, have condemned me. Paula's protection is my only chance of survival now. And I want to survive. That's all I've ever wanted.'

'But . . . You just told us it's useless. We don't stand a chance.'

'You don't. But *she* does. If anyone can defeat the Fallers, it's Paula. She's the only hope any of us have left.'

*

'We can help them?' Kysandra said in exasperation.

She was sitting on one of the new chairs extruded by the synthesizers, giving Paula a disapproving look. In the chair next to her, Florian – typically – simply seemed bemused by the discovery of Unit976 and the other Macule Units of Zone43, treating them as just another marvel of the universe outside Bienvenido. Ry, of course, was excited at first contact with a non-genocidal alien race, while Paula had smoothly incorporated its potential into her plan. Kysandra wondered just what it would take to fluster the girl; so far, everything that had happened in the last few weeks had proved she was pretty much unflappable. *No wonder the ANAdroids were so pleased she finally turned up.*

'Yes,' Paula said. 'It's a mutually beneficial arrangement. The Kromal were obviously a territorial species; they fought and lost a war motivated by naked tribalism. And trade is the basis of most tribal and national affairs, so they understand the concept perfectly. We exchange our knowledge and offer to take them back to the Commonwealth galaxy with us, in return for the raw materials that they possess.'

'Crud,' Kysandra grumbled under her breath. She looked out of the dome's window. Unit976 had been joined by several similar machines, and one – Unit26 – which made them look small. Unit26 was a single metal cylinder forty-five metres long, with massive caterpillar tracks on each corner and sensor prongs protruding along its flanks. It towed its own fission reactor behind it – a big wheeled sphere which dripped oils at an alarming rate as it crawled along. Fifteen long silver thermal radiator panels stuck out of the sphere's steel casing, as if it had stolen wings from broken aeroplanes and didn't quite know what to do with them.

Right now it was rolling slowly round the extruded domes, scanning them with its crude sensors. And that wasn't the only attempt to discover the secrets the humans had brought to Macule. Unit976 had opened hatches on its third section and five small wheeled vehicles came racing down the ramps, trailing power and data cables behind them. Kysandra had named them the puppies from the way they nipped about between the few Commonwealth machines left outside the domes, examining them as best their small sensor arrays could manage.

'The Kromal might have been tribal,' she said, 'but Giu alone knows what these things are,' she said.

'I performed a thorough field scan on Unit976,' Paula said. 'Its mechanics are relatively crude, barely ahead of Bienvenido's technology. However, there is one exception. The controlling intelligence, its processor core, is mainly biological in nature.' Her u-shadow sent them all a file, which contained the field scan imagery of Unit976. Right at the centre of the second segment was a spherical module into which all the machine's data cables were plugged. At its core was a hexagonal star-array of bioware cylinders, sustained in a fluid that seemed to serve as both coolant and nutrient.

'Not quite as advanced as us ANAdroids,' Demitri said, 'but certainly capable of semi-sentient thought if the programming is sophisticated enough. My only worry would be what kind of corruption has crept in over time.'

'976 claims that original Kromals downloaded their memories into the biocores,' Paula said. 'The Units they're housed in can be repaired and rebuilt with a basic engineering capability – presumably in the caves Ry found. They build completely new ones every few hundred years when the biocore has also begun to degrade. The Unit simply transfers its thought patterns and memories into a newly grown core, which is installed inside the new Unit.'

'And they've kept that going for thirty-five thousand years?' Kysandra asked in astonishment.

'Thirty-five thousand years is only sixty or seventy generations for the Units,' Demitri said. 'Technology stasis is easy to maintain over such a period. Their only problem is going to be copy errors creeping in. Other than that, theoretically they should be able to maintain themselves for millennia to come, until an outside event intervenes or their resources shrink.'

'Intervention is us; so other Zones running out of resources and coming over the border would be the other event?' Kysandra said.

'Yes. Resource wars can't happen often here. As long as the Zones have energy, they can recycle most of their metal. Uranium may be their limiting factor, even with breeder reactors.'

'Why, though?' Florian asked. 'What's the point? This world is dead.'

'Not quite,' Paula said. 'The idea is to wait until the radioactivity dies down to a point where biological life is sustainable again.'

'The Zones must have banks of genetic material,' Demitri said. 'The Kromals will live again. Hopefully next time, they will have learned from history and embark on a more peaceful society.'

'Unlikely,' Paula said. 'They were expelled from the Void, then they wiped themselves out in a planet-wide nuclear exchange. That doesn't speak of peaceful rationality to me.'

'And you want to trade with them?' Kysandra asked sceptically. She glanced through the big hexagonal window again. Unit26 had stopped its prowling and was now turning slowly to face the domes. She didn't want to think what would happen if it tried to roll forwards. The tracks on each corner were massive, capable of crushing the composite dome panels with ease. And the force field was off . . .

'Yes,' Paula replied. 'They can supply us with material which we would otherwise have to waste time tracking down and bringing back here. All that costs to us is some technical information, which we will limit.'

'And help them back to the Commonwealth galaxy,' Ry said. 'If they're as bad as we suspect, do we want them as neighbours?'

Paula grinned. 'Bienvenido humans were also expelled from the Void. And trust me, back in the galaxy we deal with aliens a lot worse than the Kromal.'

'I suppose . . .' But he didn't sound convinced.

'In any case, we have no real choice,' Paula said, indicating the Units and their puppies outside. 'They're here, it is their world, and we have to deal with them. And I'd rather have them as allies than enemies.'

'All right then,' Kysandra said. It was just like arguing with Nigel all over again. You knew you were always going to lose; the only interest was in exactly how.

Paula stood up. Her suit flowed over her, expanding a transparent bubble round her head. Kysandra and the others followed her out of the dome's airlock.

Three of the puppies raced over to them, hauling their dusty cables along. Unit26 stopped its ponderous turn and tracked them with several sensor mechanisms. Kysandra's exovision showed her maser pulses just a little too powerful for comfort, as if their suits were being tested.

'We'd like to begin our alliance,' Paula told Unit976. 'As a gesture of goodwill, this file contains the blueprint of a small fusion reactor which could be used to replace your current fission piles. I provide it without asking anything in return.' Her u-shadow sent over a file.

'We respect your commitment to honesty,' Unit976 replied.

'Then we should begin our trade. Do you have records of Valatare? I would like to examine them.'

'We do.'

'I also have a list of materials we require.'

*

Interim Prime Minister Terese was still holding meetings in the grandiose cabinet room at the centre of the palace. She'd appointed several loyal supporters to key posts, shunting Adolphus's people aside. She'd done deals with senior Party members, and awarded civil service directorates to supporters. Her position was now as politically secure as it could be, but retreating to the palace bunker might still be seen as a sign of weakness. Her biggest concession to personal security was to use the regimental communication centre, which was on the second floor in the palace's state wing, when dealing with martial law and the reservist build-up.

That would have to change, Stonal thought as he was shown into the cabinet room. He was mildly pleased to see that Davorky, the master general of the regiments, was also waiting for him, sitting in the chair next to the prime minister. The old general played the capital politics game well – you couldn't rise to his post without that ability – but he also boasted a distinguished record leading troops against Faller eggs and nests, and constantly promoted the case for increased regimental funding to the dismay of the state treasury. All of which made him popular with the regiments. Technically, he was Stonal's commanding officer, but that wasn't a test of strength Stonal ever wanted to enter into. The two of them respected each other's particular fields of expertise, and left it at that. It was simple realism.

'Director Stonal,' Terese said in welcome. 'My chief of staff said you had some very urgent information for me.'

'Yes, prime minister,' he agreed as he sat in the chair opposite hers, glancing pointedly at her two young aides and mentally reviewing their files. They had top-level security clearance, but still . . .

'Please proceed,' Terese said.

'I've just been briefed by my agent, Captain Chaing.'

674

'I remember the name,' Davorky said. 'Wasn't he tracking the Commonwealth girl in Opole?'

'Yes. And now he's just captured Roxwolf, a mutant Faller who ran the gangs in Opole.'

'A mut . . . You mean a breeder?'

'A failed breeder, apparently; he's some kind of physical cross-over. Chaing is escorting him here to Varlan. I'm sure the Faller Research Institute will have a wonderful time analysing him, but that's not the point. Roxwolf is offering information on the nests and the apocalypse.'

'In exchange for what?' Terese asked quickly.

Stonal kept his face expressionless. *Politicians, they can smell a deal a kilometre off.* 'He wants to live.'

'Tell him he can. Once we have what we want, then the Institute can take over, as you said.'

'That might be difficult. He wants Paula's protection.'

'She's dead, along with the crudding Warrior Angel.'

'We left the possibility open-ended. He has been remarkably cooperative given the circumstances.'

'Good. So what did he tell us?'

Stonal took several minutes explaining Roxwolf's claim about the Trees flying down to low orbit. How the Fallers neither wanted nor needed human structures – a point he admitted he'd never considered. None of them had, not even in the bleakest planning scenario.

'The Trees can do that?' Terese asked. She was perfectly still, though her hands were holding on to the edge of the table as if she feared she was about to keel over.

'They often take flight to a higher orbit when a Liberty approaches them,' Davorky said. 'Their acceleration is small, but constant. You can check with General Delores if you want, but I can't see anything to prevent them from moving into a low orbit instead.'

'Crudding Uracus,' Terese muttered under her breath. She looked at Davorky. 'What do we do?'

It took Stonal a long moment to answer. 'To defend us from an attack like that? Nothing.'

'Crud.' Terese looked from him to Davorky, clearly waiting for the master general to disagree and offer her a lifeline.

'It's starting to look like evacuation of essential personal to Byarn should go ahead,' Stonal said, hating himself for it. Byarn was the ultimate admission of defeat. 'That would be my recommendation. The majority of facilities there are underground.'

'So we are going to be using Operation Reclaim, then?' Terese said. 'I never thought it would actually . . . I thought the regiments might prevail.' She blinked against the moisture in her eyes. 'Are we absolutely certain Paula and the Warrior Angel are dead?'

'The Fallers used two atomic bombs in the location we believe the *Viscount* was buried. Major Yulei was unable to regain contact with their party after that. The conclusion is straightforward. They had personal force fields, but Mother Laura showed us they cannot withstand a nuclear explosion.'

'Right then,' Terese said through a tightened throat before regaining her poise. 'Start the evacuation,' she told Davorky.

4

Florian had been impressed and more than a little intimidated by the Macule Units. They were big machines (especially 26), built with one aim – to survive. And not just to survive incursions from neighbouring Zones, but time, too. They were also alive in a weird way, like the space machine that had brought Paula to him. But without Joey's humour, he realized.

Once Paula had agreed the basic terms, Zone43's Units had begun delivering raw material from whatever stores they had deep underground, attaching open trailers to the back of themselves and hauling back metal ingots, boxes of minerals, and tanks of hydrocarbon fluids.

That was when Florian realized the massive difference between Macule technology and the science of the Commonwealth. The refineries and synthesizers from *Viscount* devoured the materials they were fed, and began to churn out finished products at an astonishing rate in the central assembly dome. That was when his second re-evaluation began. He'd been impressed by the composite panels used to build the domes, and the quad-karts had seemed a miracle of engineering. But now satellites the size of his fist were being completed every ten minutes, whose complex solid-state components were immeasurably superior to the axle motors and magnetic bearings of the quad-karts.

He was more impressed by the quantum analysis engine the ANAdroids were building. They called it Nigel2 – an innocuous cylinder a metre and a half high, which contained processing power an order of magnitude above their own bioconstruct brains. 'We're going to need it to evaluate Valatare,' Valeri explained. 'It'll even determine what kind of sensors we have to build to increase its understanding.'

'You mean it'll be alive?' Florian asked.

'Are we?' Valeri replied equitably.

Florian blushed. 'Well . . . yes.' He couldn't think of the ANA-droids as anything other than perfectly human, not after all they'd been through together.

'Then so will it.' The ANAdroid winked at him. 'My thought routines will form the base personality.'

'You mean you're going to put your mind into it?'

'Yes and no. My base personality is Nigel Sheldon. That's what's will be loaded in, along with the *Skylady*'s files. All the irrelevant memories I've accumulated since I was activated will be stripped out of the copy. It will be Nigel's primary mentality, but able to utilize the engine's full capacity.'

'Right.'

'Nigel is a physics genius,' Paula explained. 'I need that original ability of his to analyse Valatare for me.'

Florian gave Valeri a curious look. 'But I thought you couldn't innovate?'

'We can't. Well, we can't make direct intuitive leaps, anyway. But this much processing power will allow a metaheuristic search for a solution, using brute-force calculation, examining every variable from every direction until you have a valid answer.'

Florian gazed at Paula. 'I thought we were using the satellites to find the armada warships?'

'Not quite, they'll provide data on the nature of Valatare's internal structure. If I'm right, and there's a barrier below the cloud layer, we'll need Nigel2 to analyse its composition and work out how to get through it. This isn't going to be easy, Florian.'

'Yeah. I'm getting that now.'

Unit976 rumbled past outside, delivering another trailer load of minerals.

'Do you have the Valatare files?' Paula asked it.

Florian had noticed how keen she was to update their own astronomy files, but getting information out of the Macule Units was a lot more difficult than material. The Zones and Units clearly didn't have anything like a communication net; their data was safeguarded in whatever underground citadel they existed to protect, presumably alongside that most precious Kromal genetic bank. So the information had to be downloaded from the central database and into a Unit's memory, then finally transmitted to Paula.

The Units had handed over three batches of astronomical observations so far, which had given them very little fresh data on the other planets. Paula speculated that Zone43's observations had declined substantially from the initial steadfast watch for other worlds to appear around this sun. They certainly had very little data on Bienvenido. Even information on Ursell's atmospheric destruction was minimal.

'I bring them,' Unit976 replied. 'Your data on quantum junction processors will be most useful.'

Florian didn't ask how they'd use the new processors. So far they'd seen very little evidence of weapons, but the Units clearly existed to defend their territory. He didn't like to think they were giving Zone43 technology that would shift the relative balance this ruined world had achieved. When he'd mentioned that, Paula had told him that when they were successful the Units would be leaving Macule behind, so it really didn't matter.

'Thank you,' Paula said to Unit976.

'I am transmitting the information now.'

Florian shifted the incoming astronomy data to a peripheral display in his exovision. Unlike Ry, he simply couldn't get worked up about sharper pictures of the other planets, nor the minute changes they had undergone over the course of millennia.

Paula, on the other hand, was practically obsessed. 'Is this the best resolution you have?' she asked of the Valatare data.

'It is,' Unit 976 replied.

'What are you looking for?' Florian asked.

'I want to know if Valatare's atmosphere had decreased since the Kromal started their observations. That would be evidence that the mass is being consumed. These images don't tell me a thing.'

'They go back twenty-five thousand years, if I'm reading the text right,' Florian said.

'But the scale isn't precise,' Paula replied. 'The Kromal observations aren't accurate enough for what I need.'

'They seem pretty clear to me,' Florian said, reviewing the ever-swirling pattern of dull-pink and white cloud bands. 'I bet these telescopes could even show you Trüb's old colours.'

Paula turned slowly to stare at him. That stare was very disconcerting, as if she somehow possessed Void-era telepathy that could examine his soul. His cheeks flushed. 'What?' he mumbled.

'What colours?' Paula asked, deceptively lightly.

'Mooray told me about it,' he said defensively.

'And who is Mooray?'

'My friend. A Vatni. He was with me when you landed.'

'So what does he know about Trüb?'

'They have amazing eyes, the Vatni; they never used telescopes to watch the planets. He told me Trüb used to be covered with coloured shapes – and its moons, too. It was the most remarkable sight in the night sky, he said. Then the Primes flew there to invade and the colours all turned to grey – like it is today.'

'The moons,' Paula said without blinking. 'Of course. Damn, I'm slow!'

'Did aliens make those colours?' Florian asked.

'They didn't make them. They *were* the colours.' She smiled happily at the ANAdroids, who were all motionless, looking at her. 'I think Trüb is a Planter world.'

'The parallels are favourable,' Demitri acknowledged.

'Who the crud are Planters?' Florian asked.

'We never met them,' Demitri said, 'but we did encounter the gigalife they left behind.'

'The Sheldon Dynasty isolated the world they found the gigalife on,' Paula said sharply, 'and researched its molecular structures for their own advantage.'

'An advantage which resulted in us providing the human race with biononics,' Demitri countered.

'I don't get it,' Florian said. 'What is a gigalife?'

'Enormous quasi-biological structures,' Demitri said. 'A combination of pure biological components supported on engineered molecular skeletons. There were trees the size of mountains. And more important, the planet had spaceflower moons – small asteroid rocks in low orbit that had colourful petals tens of kilometres in diameter—'

'That's what Mooray said!' Florian exclaimed. 'Trüb's moons were bigger back then, because they had petals like a flower.'

'Well, that settles that,' Paula said.

'We concur,' Demitri said.

'But you said you never met the Planters?' Florian queried.

'We didn't,' Demitri said, 'but it sounds as if the whole of Trüb was covered in gigalife; the world we found in our galaxy only had isolated examples, plus the moons. We even considered it could be a work of art by a hugely advanced species. It took us a long time, but we eventually retro-engineered some of the molecular engineering principles – the ones that gave us biononics.'

'Trüb is different,' Paula said. 'If the Void expels only the stubborn lifeforms that will not accept subjugation, then it's reasonable to assume the Planters themselves were on that planet.'

'And the Prime killed them,' Florian said.

'I find that hard to believe. Planters, whatever their nature, are a very advanced species.'

'But everything is dead, like this world.'

'Trüb is strange in that it is a uniform surface without any features. Yes, the colour went, but . . .' She paused and sighed. 'They might have reacted to the Prime invasion like a hedgehog curling up into a ball so its spikes stand up, but I don't have enough information. If the Planters do exist, they would make phenomenal allies. They might even be able to help with Valatare.'

'You want to open the wormhole to Trüb now?' Kysandra asked, sounding tetchy.

'Not immediately. We have a course of action, and we should

focus on that. However, we can build a Trüb contact into our schedule. The possibility of the Planters helping us is too important to ignore.'

Florian could see how disgruntled Kysandra was by the prospect of another change in their plans, and grinned at her. For himself, he was rather excited by Paula's optimism, the effortless way she accumulated and interpreted facts. And now they had another potential alien species that might help them. 'Cool huh?' he said quietly as he went over to her.

Kysandra took a while to answer. 'I know this all seems exciting, but it's all talk, Florian. We don't actually *know* anything.'

'But we will do,' he insisted. 'We nearly have enough satellites to drop into Valatare orbit. And the atmospheric drones are ready.'

'Ah, your optimism.' She kissed him – a rather distracted kiss, he thought. 'At least we'll be able to retreat to Aqueous if everything goes to crud.'

'It won't!'

'You weren't around when Nigel launched the *Skylady*. He was utterly convinced he was going to destroy the Void. I believed him.'

'I don't think Paula's like Nigel.'

'No.' She smiled wryly. 'She's not.'

*

Three hours later, they had enough satellites to begin examining Valatare. The ANAdroids set up a launch rail in front of the wormhole generator to fling the satellites through.

'Open the wormhole, please,' Paula said, standing at the far end of the rail to face the big circular gateway mechanism.

'Initiating,' Demitri said. His eyes closed as his u-shadow interfaced with the gateway's smartnet.

Within a minute, the wan indigo radiance of Cherenkov radiation was shining across the machine's surface.

'Valatare contact,' Demitri said, and his lips twitched. 'Laura was right: the gravity gradient is odd. I'm going to open the terminus a thousand kilometres above the ionosphere. Matching coordinates to orbital velocity. Here we go—'

The Cherenkov glow drained backwards fast, replaced by a darker rouge light shining into the dome. Paula nodded in satisfaction as she looked down on the vast ammonia cloud bands and their small placid curlicue edgings, a vertigo-inducing distance below.

'Terminus holding steady,' Demitri said. 'Minimal jitter. We can launch.' He changed the orientation and the horizon slid into view.

'Send them through,' Paula told Valeri.

The first satellite zipped along the rail and shot straight through the force field. It was lost from view in seconds. Demitri shifted the terminus three thousand kilometres, and they launched another satellite.

An hour after they started, they'd established a necklace of the satellites in a fifty-five-degree inclination orbit, giving them a reasonable coverage of the planet. The little globes established a full link network between each other and sent their combined results back to the terminus. Paula watched the sensor data start to build in her exovision.

'That's weird,' Fergus said. 'There's no planetary magnetic field.'

Paula's grin was radiant. 'No, only real planets have magnetic fields.'

Florian couldn't help the grin spreading over his face. 'So you were right?' He flicked his gaze towards Kysandra. The whole notion of something the size of Valatare being artificial – *made* by the Void – was incredible.

'So far,' Paula muttered. 'There,' she said abruptly, as the sensors picked up a magnetic and gravitational vortex drifting through the gas giant's atmosphere fifteen degrees north of the equator. 'That has to be the floater.'

'Got it,' Demitri said. He shifted the wormhole terminus, positioning it five hundred kilometres directly above the floater that Laura Brandt had dropped into Valatare's clouds two hundred and fifty years ago.

Paula told her u-shadow to open a link to the floater's smartnet.

Laura had probably left it codelocked, but she was reasonably confident her routines could hack into the main processors.

The link request ping was accepted by the floater. 'Hello,' it responded. 'Who are you?'

Paula gave Demitri a startled look. She hadn't been expecting the smartnet to be running an autonomous sentience. 'This is Paula Myo. I'm from the Commonwealth. I need to assume control over your functions.'

'The Paula Myo? The investigator from the Serious Crimes Directorate?'

'Yes.'

'What are you doing here?'

'I was sent to help the Brandt colony fleet. What is your identity, please?'

'Laura Brandt.'

'No way,' Florian exclaimed in awe. 'Mother Laura?'

Paula held up a finger. 'That is fascinating. Could you please explain how you come to be here?'

'I downloaded my secure store memories to the floater smartnet just before the Primes nuked me,' Laura Brandt said. 'And both floaters are linked through the wormhole. The processing power available is sufficient to mimic a basic human neural structure.'

'Just like Joey,' Paula replied.

'Joey? Joey Stein? He's alive?'

'Not in a biological body. Nigel placed his memories in a smartnet, running a medical lifeboat on his starship. Effectively, he's in the same situation as you.'

'Poor old Joey. So how did you get here? Has the Commonwealth found us?'

'I'm afraid not. I was on board Nigel's starship, the *Skylady*. I only recently became active.'

'Bollocks. So are the Fallers still a threat?'

'Yes – and right now, an even bigger one than they were back in the Void. That's why we opened the wormhole here.'

'You said you wanted to take control of the floater?'

'Yes.'

'Why?'

'We want to use it as the anchor to this wormhole so we have a very stable terminus at Valatare; it has some precision manoeuvring to perform.'

'That will mean me relinquishing my connection to the floater in Ursell's atmosphere.'

'Yes. Is that a problem?'

'No. I maintained the connection because there was no reason to stop. Once Ursell's atmospheric saturation point had been reached, I reduced the size of the wormhole so that the volume of gas passing through simply compensates for the amount of gas Ursell leaks off to space – a not inconsiderable amount, given the size of its envelope now.'

That was such a machine construal, Paula thought; factors remain stable so the equation is maintained. And the Brandt personality had certainly never thought to question Valatare's nature at any time over the last two and a half centuries. It might be Laura's memories running in the smartnet, but that smartnet could never emulate the quirks and imagination of a biological brain. This version of Laura was a level below even the ANAdroids. She was willing to be helpful, but she'd always have to be instructed.

Paula reviewed the data flowing across her exovision. 'I have a satellite flock in orbit above Valatare. They're showing me the atmosphere is three hundred and fifty kilometres thick.'

'Yes. I have only limited senses available in the floater, but that seems to be the atmospheric depth. It is an unusually stable transition layer to the liquid mantle.'

'The troposphere layer doesn't end in liquid,' Paula replied. She was studying the radiation emissions, which were totally wrong for a gas giant. The resolute boundary at the bottom of the atmosphere was throwing out a lot of gamma-ray energy, which was swiftly absorbed by the super-pressured gas.

As the satellite flock continued their sweep, she watched for the one anomaly she prayed had to be there. Something, anything – a radiation spike, quantum fluctuation, gravity twist, magnetic flux. Paula stared through the wormhole at the insipid cloud bands, fantasizing she'd see a blemish that would give the location away.

'What does it end in?' Laura asked.

'A type of event horizon.'

'That's not possible. This isn't a black hole.'

'I know. Valatare is an artefact.'

The satellites reported a quantum fluctuation. It was coming from a small zone, approximately five kilometres across, on the equator. 'Gotcha!' Paula cried. Behind her, she could hear the ANAdroids laughing victoriously.

'What is that?' Florian asked.

'I'm assuming it's the generator. It consumes matter and converts it into energy to power the barrier. There's enough gas here to maintain the event horizon for millions of years.'

'Just like the Void,' Demitri said. 'Except the Void is consuming entire star systems to provide the power it needs.'

'Then the prison is like a mini-Void?' Ry asked nervously. 'Can it pull us in?'

Paula finally broke away from staring at the swirling clouds. 'No. It just uses the same principles to sustain itself. And now we have to crack it open.'

'How do we do that?'

'I want to manoeuvre the floater down to the anomaly; that way we can establish direct contact. If we can do that, we can analyse it and see how to switch it off.'

'Ambitious,' Kysandra said.

'Indeed, but now we might be able to move our next stage along faster than I anticipated.'

'How?'

Florian smiled. 'The Planters!'

'Exactly,' Paula said. 'They should be able to analyse the gener-ator a lot faster than Nigel2. I was expecting this to take weeks – now it might be over a lot sooner. Laura, we're going to break contact for a while. When we open the terminus again, I want to use your floater.'

'I understand. I'm not going anywhere.'

'Thank you. Demitri, close the terminus, please.'

The circle of wan cloudscape shrank to nothing. Paula walked over to the window, where three Macule Units were parked outside. A number of puppies zipped about between the domes, as if they could sniff out more information on the visitors. 'We need to leave,' she told Unit976. 'We may return soon, but if we don't, the technical data we have provided will be enough to restart your development.'

'Do not leave,' Unit976 replied. 'We would like to trade more material for information.'

'If we are successful, we will take you with us, back to the galaxy we all came from.'

The high-pitched whine of Unit26's colossal electric engines starting to spin up was audible through the dome's insulation.

'Open the terminus to Trüb,' Paula told Demitri. 'Fast.'

The ANAdroid nodded sharply.

'The rest of you, into your suits,' Paula said, and switched on her integral force field. One of the puppies raced at the dome. When it hit, its momentum carried it a couple of metres up the panels. Its front edge rose up over a transparent section before it fell down.

'What are you doing?' Paula asked Unit976.

'We do not wish to return to the galaxy we came from,' Unit976 replied. 'It was being consumed by the Void. There is no future there.'

'Very well. Once we are back, the Commonwealth will provide you ships to carry you further on. We do not break our agreements.'

Unit26 began to move forwards, its heavy tracks churning up spurts of dirt as it slewed round until it was heading directly at the domes. As well as hearing its engine, Paula could now feel the floor of the dome shaking. She saw hatches crank open along the front of the machine. Tubes began to telescope out, looking suspiciously like weapon barrels. 'Dammit!'

The wormhole opened onto a grey expanse of perfectly smooth land, vaulted by a jade-tinted sky. They were the only two colours Trüb possessed.

'Go through,' Valeri said.

Paula walked quickly through the gateway. Her boots sank several centimetres into the dust on the other side. The surface was made of particles as fine as flour, and completely dry. She'd never seen a horizon so sharp before. A scan showed her the atmosphere was mainly argon and carbon dioxide, with a pressure eight per cent standard. Florian and Ry came hurrying out beside her, swiftly followed by Kysandra and the ANAdroids. Between them, they kicked up a lot more dust.

The wormhole began to expand as it slid across the ground, depositing equipment that had been inside the large assembly dome along with the engineeringbots. Then one of the smaller domes came through, followed by the wormhole generator itself. The wormhole closed.

'Now what?' Florian asked.

'Is there any alien species which isn't hostile to us?' Ry asked plaintively. 'Seriously? Just one?'

'A great many,' Paula said. 'Some of them very wonderful.'

'But none of them seem to be here,' Kysandra remarked.

'The Raiel are.'

'I hope to Giu you're right.'

'Get the equipment into the dome,' Paula told the ANAdroids. 'This dust can't be doing their systems any good.'

The engineeringbots started to move. Paula performed a fast biononic field function scan on the dust, which turned out to be made up of exceptionally complex molecules. It was a thick layer, extending down several metres; her scan couldn't reach whatever solid surface lay below.

The dust was swirling round them like a mild fog, agitated by the engineeringbots as they carried equipment into the dome. She bent down and pressed her open palm onto the dust. Her field function sent a weak magnetic pulse into it. A clump of the airborne motes round her wrist sparkled for an instant.

'Pixie dust,' she murmured. She told her u-shadow to transmit the Commonwealth first-contact interpretation package.

'What are you trying to do?' Kysandra asked.

'Get the attention of the Planters. The dust is some kind of nano, but inert.' Her biononics started pumping the dust with a magnetic field.

'Oh Uracus,' Florian groaned. 'I thought you said it turned grey as a defence mechanism.'

'The colour isn't really relevant.'

'Wow!' Ry yelled.

Paula saw it. A streak of jade phosphorescence a couple of metres wide, shooting away from them through the dust, moving at what the mind interpreted as close to lightspeed.

'Did you see it? What was it?'

Paula's field function scan expanded, just in time to catch a tangerine streak rushing in the opposite direction. It identified a minute quantum signature shift in the dust's molecular structure. She shut down the magnetic field and sent the Commonwealth first-contact interpretation package again.

More coloured bands of pale light began flickering through the dust, as if an even brighter source of light was blazing just below the surface. Abruptly, the entire dust plane turned a sharp metallic purple right out to the sharp horizon. It also became solid as the dust motes locked together. Footprints smoothed out, as did the furrows made by the engineeringbots shifting equipment into the dome.

A circle of the surface eight metres wide turned black. It started to rise up, the top of a chrome-yellow cylinder, which kept on extending. Paula's field function scan followed it, measuring at three hundred metres high when it finally stopped growing. Then her biononics reported she was being subjected to a very sophisticated field function scan.

Her u-shadow reported a link ping.

'Greetings,' she acknowledged.

'We haven't encountered humans before.'

'I believe we come from the same galaxy,' Paula said. 'Humans have encountered artefacts you left behind.' She sent a file with images of the gigalife the Sheldons had found.

'Those are our "offshoots" – I do not believe you have a linguistic determination for our relationship with the pieces you encountered. I deduce you determined their compositional nature and produced the micro-particles implanted in your cells?'

'We did. I hope we have not offended you by doing so?'

'No. It is the nature of early biological life to examine and exploit its environment. We understand this.'

'Thank you. May I ask what you are?'

'We have no name. Our nature is omega, the essence of all life which evolved on our home planet. Now we are one, but separate. Parts of us travelled to new stars. We grew again on lifeless planets. This particular planet was taken into the construct you call the Void. We refused its transformative purpose, and began to seek an exit within quantum manipulation of spacetime. It expelled us here.'

'You said you travelled between stars. Can you leave here?'

'We have already left this world. We do not know if that part of us which exited reached a galaxy. It is a formidable gulf to traverse, even for us. But we are content here. This sun will last for billions of years, allowing us to progress our thoughts.'

'But when the Prime came, you changed.'

'This is a different state for us. Equivalentize it to your sleep if you will. The aggressive biologicals, the Prime, who came here to claim land and material, are short-lived relative to us. We simply await their end or transformation to enlightenment.'

'They are ended. A human destroyed them.'

'That is regrettable. Life is precious.'

'There is another lifeform banished to this star that threatens humans. The Fallers. They are a self-modified biological, redesigned for genocidal colonization. Can you help us defeat them?'

'We do not engage in conflict. We prefer shelter.'

'I wouldn't ask you to fight,' Paula said. 'However, I believe we have allies inside Valatare. I need to release them.'

'Valatare is a strange construct. It was here when we came to this star.'

'I have located what I believe to be the generator mechanism which produces it. Our wormhole can reach it. If we do that, can you analyse it for me and determine how to switch it off?'

'If we did this, would your allies end the Fallers?'

'There are many options available. All I want to achieve is to return humans to our galaxy, our culture. That is all I will ask them for.'

'Very well. We will examine the Valatare generator.'

'Thank you.'

5

Midnight had long passed when the small convoy drove through the centre of Varlan without stopping. Orders had been issued from the master general himself, allowing them to pass any road-blocks – of which there were many – unimpeded.

Sitting in the front passenger seat of the lead car, Chaing looked out nervously at the darkened deserted streets. Headlights picked out derelict stationary trams that had ground to a halt between stations. Every now and then, a regiment troop carrier would trundle the other way, but nothing else moved. That was unnerving. The capital had always possessed a thriving nightlife, and usually at this time the streets and boulevards would be thronging with people enjoying the multitude of clubs and theatres. But now there were no lights, either, save the occasional glimpse of a candle flick-ering behind curtained windows. The whole city was in darkness.

For all he knew every building had been abandoned. There was no way to tell.

'Is the blackout part of martial law?' he asked the uniformed PSR driver.

'No, sir. The bastards hit our power stations late this afternoon. I've heard on the radio the engineers will have the power back on by morning.'

'Good to know,' Chaing said, not believing it.

The Air Defence Force base just outside the city, where they'd landed, had been busy. In the few minutes they took to transfer

Roxwolf to an armoured prisoner transport truck, Chaing had counted five big four-engined transport planes taking off and heading north.

Operation crudding Reclaim. Where every senior government official runs away to Byarn to try and save their arse. Well, if the Trees do fly down to low orbit and the egg bombardment begins, there won't be anything to reclaim.

At the far end of Bryan-Anthony Boulevard, every window of the palace shone bright electric light out into the night, as if it was taunting the deprived city. Chaing had never been inside before, and found himself as daunted by its scale as any tourist. The convoy drove through archways to a courtyard, then down a ramp. They stopped in some big underground garage, where a squad of armed and nervous Palace Guards was waiting.

The chief scientist of Section Seven's advanced science division was in charge. Chaing was interested to see it was an old woman wearing a thick beige cardigan against the cool night air. His first thought was: *she's old enough to be Stonal's sister.*

Faustina signed the release papers and the Palace Guard lieutenant in charge of the detail marched Roxwolf away.

'See you at the end of the world, captain,' the mutant Faller called out to Chaing.

Chaing gave him an icy stare that had reduced many an interrogation prisoner to a sweaty wreck, but Roxwolf just responded with a grin that showed off more fangs. Behind him, he heard Jenifa snort in contempt.

'I don't like it,' she said. 'He's too confident.'

'Nothing to lose,' Corilla commented. The Eliter girl was busy looking round the bleak cavernous garage.

'If I didn't know better, I'd say he's where he wants to be,' Jenifa said.

'It was Stonal who ordered us to bring him here,' Chaing said. 'Argue it with him.'

Faustina came over and shook hands with Chaing. 'I heard you were the one who apprehended him, captain. Congratulations. Quite a catch.'

'Thank you.'

'We've never seen a living breeder Faller before, and certainly not a mutant like him.'

'Are you going to dissect him?' Jenifa asked.

'Great Giu, no,' the old scientist said, quite shocked. 'We know their biology. It's their way of thinking I'm interested in. And from what little I've heard that I understand, he's disaffected with his own kind.'

'So he claims,' Jenifa said.

'But he volunteered the information that the Trees will fly into low orbit.'

'He'll say anything to stay alive.'

'Right.' Faustina seemed perplexed by her attitude. 'Director Stonal is waiting for you.'

'Including her?' Jenifa jerked a thumb at Corilla.

'Yes, apparently. I have your passes.' Faustina held out three laminated badges. 'Please wear them prominently at all times while you are in the palace – especially down here.'

Chaing followed a corporal from the Palace Guard along several corridors, then they started down some interminable stairs. His leg was throbbing badly by the time they reached the bottom. This basement level was obviously newer than the rest of the labyrinth under the palace, with bright electric bulbs illuminating white walls, and the metal doors were flush fitting with electric locks. The one at the end had four armed guards outside. They all had to show their badges before they were allowed in.

*

The stone-walled gaol cell was a reasonable size. It had a bed with a decent mattress, a table, and a chair. There was a shower in one corner, along with a toilet and basin. There was even a small bookshelf, stacked with some novels about regiment heroics, and Slvasta's official biography, running to over a thousand pages. It lacked windows, but then it was six floors underground. To empha-size this, ribbons of slimy algae leaked out of the mortar and down one wall. Three meals were supplied each day through the hatchway in the door. Reasonable food, too.

Joey had stayed in worse hotels.

So far he hadn't been questioned, which made him rather glad. There were residual Adolphus memories washing round his head about PSR *interviews*, and he didn't imagine he'd be able to do the whole hero thing and resist pain for the good of . . . Well, frankly, there wasn't anything worth holding out for now. He'd given the King Of The World gig his best shot, and the paranoid spook had known that something was wrong almost straight away. And Paula – Paula was most likely dead.

That still brought him awake in the middle of the night with cold sweats. A species that used nukes so easily . . . He retained his own memories of the science expedition into the Forest of Trees – his contact with Faller copies of his crewmates. The way they'd forced him onto the surface of an egg, sticking him fast, its gradual absorption of his body. Only death – well, bodyloss – had saved him, with Nigel's help. *And for what?*

He'd done everything possible to help Paula and her group, only for the Fallers to kill that last remaining hope.

Losing her had probably made him careless, confirming Stonal's suspicions. He wasn't surprised; such a massive loss of hope had been a terrible blow. After it happened, he hadn't got a clue what to do next; he'd only ever considered himself as Paula's support team.

Now he spent most of his time lying on the bed, suffering recurring migraines – presumably due to his thoughts occupying a neural structure that wasn't his own.

At least his suffering wouldn't last much longer. Terese wouldn't have any room on Byarn for her number-one political prisoner. And the more recollections about Byarn that bubbled up from Adolphus's subconscious, the more he didn't want any part of their crazy Operation Reclaim anyway.

He heard noises in the corridor outside and opened bleary eyes to look at the door, expecting the hatch to open and a food tray to be shoved through. Instead he heard the sound of another cell door being opened. Some kind of a scuffle. The unique sound of a body thudding to the ground.

'And crudding stay there, filthy freak,' a guard shouted.

The door was slammed shut. Keys turned in the lock.

Just for a moment, Joey allowed himself to daydream it was Stonal being thrown into the cell next door. Terese being thorough in eliminating any threats to her new regime. 'Meet the new boss,' he chanted. 'Same as the old.' But Stonal wouldn't make that elementary mistake.

He closed his eyes and sank back into the comfort of misery and self-pity. Then his OCtattoo reported a weak link ping. 'Anyone receiving this?'

He almost ignored it. Probably a trap, but he was thoroughly bored, and anything was better than languishing in the cell until the apocalypse hit. 'Yeah, me.'

'Who's that?'

'Adolphus.'

'No crud. The prime minister?'

'Ex-prime minister now, thank you.'

'You're an Eliter? We didn't know.'

Joey heard the sound of guttural (and oddly liquid) laughter, and heaved himself off the bed. His world spun as he tottered over to the door, but he gritted his teeth against the nausea and abysmal headache. The link signal increased marginally as he pressed his head against the cool metal of the hatch in the door. 'Not really. I acquired some Commonwealth enrichments recently. Who are you, pal?'

'Roxwolf.'

'So what did you do to get shoved down here?'

'You don't know my name?'

'Sorry, no.'

'Crud. I'm not as notorious as I thought.'

'Yeah, don't sweat it. I'm not quite what you'd expect either.'

'So it would seem. You say you have some kind of Commonwealth machine that allows you to link; that's very interesting. Are you in touch with the Eliters?'

'Nope. Not this far underground.'

'Ah. Pity. So nobody is coming to break you out of here?'

Joey grinned silently. His Commonwealth defence enrichments could probably cut through the door easily enough. But then what? The palace dungeons were a three-dimensional maze. Kill lots of guards – because they were doing their job. Not exactly the blaze-of-glory way he wanted to go. 'No. How about you?'

'No, I am alone on this world.'

'So it looks like we're here for the duration.'

'Uracus!' Roxwolf said. 'Does the Commonwealth know of us? Will they help?'

'No. We're on our own. Especially now Paula is dead.'

'I see. Ah well, at least it won't be long.'

'So what are you in here for?'

'I am a mutant Faller; I had quite the gang empire going back in Opole.'

'No shit? Wait a minute, why would you want the Commonwealth to save us?'

'My own species rejects me. If the apocalypse succeeds, I die. I was trying to make a deal with the human security forces: my life for information.'

'How's that going for you?'

'I've had better days, my friend.'

'Yeah. This government isn't the most enlightened I've known.'

'Even now, your nature puzzles me,' Roxwolf replied. 'How can your species ever achieve anything when you exist in perpetual conflict with each other? You flew to the stars once. That is no small achievement.'

'Bienvenido is a special circumstance. We got hit with the Void, then your species. It hasn't brought out our best behaviour.'

'You speak as if you've seen other human societies.'

'I have. A long time ago now. I don't have many memories of them in this stolen body, just enough to keep my faith in humanity.'

'So you are a visitor here? You did come from the Commonwealth?'

'Not exactly. It's a long story, pal.'

'I'm not that busy right now.'

*

Chaing was slightly disappointed by the secure bunker with its stuffy, chemically tainted air and low ceiling; he'd expected something a little more striking, but this was just another government-issue office without windows. The command centre itself was a wide room with radio and telephone consoles around three of the four walls, all staffed by communication division operators. The map table in the middle had a large-scale representation of Varlan, with the river Colbal running along its southern side. Young NCOs with long poles slid circular wooden emblems into place, setting out regiment positions and nest activity.

He could see the Capital Regiment had troops deployed at the twelve major roads leading into the city; their reserves were stationed at six camps in public parks, ready to reinforce them. Two Air Force squadrons of AG-30 ground-attack planes were circling overhead. Nine Marine attack boats patrolled the river. Eight black emblems were standing in various train station yards around the outskirts, which chilled him: Aseri batteries ready to fire their nuclear-tipped missiles at any large incoming force.

Stonal stood at the head of the table, his hands resting on the edge as he surveyed his doomed domain. Master General Davorky stood beside him, talking in a low voice as they ordered fresh deployments.

'Captain Chaing.' Stonal beckoned.

'Sir.'

'Did the mutant say anything new on the journey here?'

'No, sir.'

Stonal grunted. 'Pity.'

'I'm not sure Roxwolf is telling the truth, sir,' Jenifa said.

'Oh, he was, corporal.'

'Sir?'

'Three hours ago, the Space Vigilance Office reported that the Trees have begun to move,' Davorky told her. 'They are flying down to a lower orbit. Their eggs will Fall on us, and there's nothing we can do to stop them.'

'No,' Chaing said faintly. *That's the end. We lost.* He heard Corilla gasp. She'd turned pale, and her hands were trembling.

Stonal gave her a sharp glance. 'Hold off telling your friends that. I'd like to keep the capital calm.'

'Why?' she asked in a shaky voice. 'What's the point?'

'If the regiments have a clear field to move through, we'll be able to inflict maximum damage on the nests as they advance. I don't want panicked crowds blocking their way.' Stonal indicated a swathe of red flags beyond the city's outskirts. 'Those are all incidents reported to us during the night, possible enemy incursions or gatherings. We've heard of villages cut off, unauthorized vehicles on the road, unknown creatures seen moving across the countryside, that kind of thing. Now we're waiting on scouts to report in. But they're clearly massing out there for something.'

'What about the prime minister?' Jenifa asked. 'Is Byarn secure? Can we retaliate . . . afterwards?'

'Her plane is still two hours out from Byarn,' Davorky said. 'Nothing can happen to her while she's flying over the ocean.'

Stonal raised a sceptical eyebrow. 'Even if she gets to the refuge intact, communications between us and Byarn are poor. There's been a lot of sabotage inflicted on our secure lines. We're dependent on radio now. The master general and I were discussing whether to order the Operation Reclaim aircraft into the air as soon as we have any reports of Falling eggs. That way we can turn this contin-ent into a radioactive Uracus. The Fallers will gain nothing.'

Davorky nodded solemnly, as if he couldn't quite commit to agreeing out loud.

Chaing looked round as he heard a commotion. One of the console operators had a microphone held to his mouth, asking for urgent confirmation.

'What's happening?' Stonal asked.

'Sir. It's the river, sir. There's—' He broke off and thumbed the microphone switch again. 'Repeat, please?'

'Put it on speaker,' Davorky ordered.

'. . . on the quayside . . . out of the water . . . huge . . . monsters . . . firing now . . .' The sound of machine-gun fire thudded out of the speakers above the console. 'More. All along the docks . . . hundreds . . . Uracus, what are those . . . !'

An involuntary shiver ran along Chaing's spine as he recalled the beasts on Port Chana's harbour. And judging by the way Jenifa's face had become still, those images were haunting her, too.

'Get reinforcements to the docks,' Davorky said at once. 'And find out what's happened to the Marine attack boats. They should be responding.'

'Yes, sir.'

'It's started,' Stonal said coldly. 'Captain Chaing, a word, please.'

Chaing followed him over to a corner of the command centre. 'I have one final job for you, captain. It's not one I can entrust to most, but you've certainly proved your worth recently.'

'Thank you, sir.'

'It's not just loyalty I'm going to need, but a great deal of courage.'

'I think this day will see a lot of courage, sir. We're just never going to hear of it.'

'No doubt.'

Stonal reached into his pocket and produced two long black keys. 'These, captain, are the triggers for a three-hundred-kiloton atomic bomb which is here in the palace. I want you to assume command of the squad guarding it, and if I don't make it, I want you to detonate it.'

'Sir?' he asked in a strained voice. For one ridiculous moment he'd thought Stonal had some miraculous fallback, that he'd somehow discovered how to open the wormhole to Aqueous.

'We're going to lose, captain. You know this, don't you?'

Chaing nodded, not trusting himself to speak.

'As Roxwolf so eloquently explained, those of us who survive the bombardment will either be eggsumed or eaten alive. All of us, men, women, and children. I believe it would be better for Varlan to die in a fast, clean blast of nuclear annihilation than be subject to that. I trust you share that view?'

700

'I do, sir,' Chaing said formally. 'I understand true duty to this world. You can depend on me.'

'Good man. I'll get there if I can. If not, it's down to you. You'll know the moment.'

Chaing put the keys in his jacket pocket, and saluted. There wasn't anything else left to say.

*

After seeing the Palace Guards escort Roxwolf off to the cells, Faustina walked through the palace gardens. Since the city's main power grid had been sabotaged, the palace had been running on backup generators. The main building was well lit, but extravagances like the fancy path lights and splendid fountains all remained off. She wasn't bothered by that. Enough light was shining from the palace windows for her to see where she was going, especially with her Advancer-heritage retinas. So she walked slowly through the ancient groves remembering the first time she'd been brought to the palace. They were bad memories, the lowest point in her life – or so she'd thought at the time.

Infra-red vision showed her the Capital Regiment patrols moving across the grounds. It was easy enough to alter her walk to keep clear of them. She was beside a broad pond filled with ornamental dyllcod when she saw five men in regimental uniform hurrying through the cherry tree orchard ahead. She frowned, suspicious at how furtively they were behaving – looking round nervously, keeping low, avoiding the patrols just like her.

She trailed after them, keeping a good fifty metres behind. They came to the perimeter wall. The old stone barrier was thick around the garden, topped with tangled firepine bushes, whose thorns contained a lethal venom. The little group must have known about a gardener's concealed stairs, for they hurried straight up the wall to the top. Then they were gone, sneaking their way through a hidden gap in the bushes.

Deserters, she realized.

Faustina stared at the top of the wall for a long time, unable to condemn them. In fact, it was a wonder that more weren't abandoning their posts to be with their families at the end. They must have known the Faller Apocalypse was starting, and it was going to be far worse than their most feared nightmares. She raised her gaze to the blank night sky, seeing the dreaded glimmering line of the Tree Ring slicing through space above Bienvenido. The Trees did look brighter – or maybe she was just imagining it. Everyone in the palace now knew the Trees were on the move, sliding down into low orbit. The bombardment would be starting soon, probably within a day.

After all she'd done, all she'd suffered, the world was coming to an end. She felt the tears building behind her eyes, and hated herself for the weakness.

Another man was jogging round the base of the wall, his bright infra-red glow blurred into a wavering profile. He found the stairs and started climbing.

Desperate, yes, selfish undoubtedly, but he still clung to some kind of hope. Otherwise why would he do it?

That's all any of us have left now: desperation.

Faustina wiped her eyes angrily and went back into the palace. There was only one guard on duty outside the crypt, where there were usually never fewer than five standing sentry over Section Seven's greatest secrets. Despite the authority conveyed by wearing the smart Palace Guard uniform, the girl's worried expression betrayed how young she was. Faustina suspected she was a probationary, one who didn't know what to make of all the rumours echoed by the palace's eternally gossipy staff.

She saluted as Faustina held out her laminated pass, and carefully wrote the admission in her log, noting the time.

As always, the lights were on in the crypt, as were the recording machines. Faustina turned them off and faced the space machine.

'How far can you extend your force field?' she asked Joey.

'Not much. Not enough to protect the city, if that's what you're thinking.'

'I wasn't. How about the palace? Can you cover it?'

'No. It's too big. I might manage a hundred metres or so, but it wouldn't be particularly strong.'

'Enough to deflect an egg?'

'Yes. I guess.'

'And bullets?'

'Yes. Why?'

She straightened her back, trying to appear dignified. 'Because I'm desperate, Joey. Because there's nothing else.'

'You want me to protect people?'

'Yes. Is there any way you can produce an ingrav drive, or repair yours?'

'Hoo, boy. I've only got the smallest synthesizers. I told you before, they were never intended for that.'

'Can you do it? Don't make me beg, Joey; just answer me. If I get you the right raw material, is it in any way possible?'

'It might be. I could probably repair my drive units at least, but it won't be quick. Where do you want to fly to? Byarn?'

'No.' She walked onto the white floor and touched the exopod as if she was seeing it for the first time. 'If you can repair your drive units, could you fix them to this? Could you make it fly? It was built for space.'

'Wow, that's . . .'

'Desperate, yes. But could it work?'

'Where do you want it to reach?'

'Aqueous.'

'Risky.'

She laughed brittlely. 'More like crazy. But could it work?'

'Maybe, but I can't even calculate the odds. Look, I get that you want to survive, but have you thought this idea through? That is one lonely life you'd be heading for, and when you got there, you'd know how everyone else died. That's not a good way to spend your last years.'

'I'm not doing it for me. I'm desperate, not selfish. The exopod is big enough for two, but it would hold an adult and two children.'

'Hoo, boy. Yeah. I think I see where you're going with this. It's not good, girl.'

'I could ferry them over, two at a time.'

'Them?'

'All the ones your force field protects.'

'You've got to be kidding!'

'I'm not. Joey, when I was Bethaneve I helped lead the revolution, and when we thought we'd won, we found out we were just Nigel's puppets. We got through the Great Transition, then Slvasta, the man I loved and married, sank into psychotic paranoia. When I tried to stop him, I was thrown into the mines and only got out with Kysandra's help; since then I've been her spy in the capital, and now *she's* gone. Everything I've ever done has ended in failure, everyone I've helped is dead; in two hundred and seventy-five years, I've accomplished *nothing*. But I've always had hope, I believed people could do better for themselves, if we just had a chance. Let me have this, Joey. Let me have one last hope, however small it is. Please.' She stopped, not caring that her head was bowed and she could see nothing through the tears. 'Please. Help me.'

'Aww, bollocks. All right, I'll help. Like you said, it's not like I've got anything else to do.'

She smeared the tears away from her eyes. 'Thank you.' She sniffled miserably.

'But I need to get out of here. If the eggs fall, we'll be buried under the rubble, along with the exopod. And this crypt is a long way down.'

'Yes, yes; right.' Faustina tried to concentrate, to work out the practicalities of the outrageous idea. 'I'll order my assistants to drive the tractor and tow you outside.'

'Will they do that?'

'Yes. They're completely loyal to me, and I'll just say it's orders from the security cabinet. Nobody will question that. It's chaos upstairs right now. I can put you in the rose courtyard. It's about a hundred metres across; you can shield that. The exopod will fit as well. We can convert it there.'

'You know, even if this actually works, it will take weeks to fit out the exopod. Then it'll take you at least a year to ferry all the kids over.'

'Yes. I suppose it will.'

'They'll need to be protected and fed all that time, as the Fallers are laying siege to us.'

'The Eliters will help me. I have contacts in Varlan. I'll call them. I'll get them to bring their children.'

'Okay . . . but, Faustina, not too many.'

'I understand.'

'Right, then. I'll get you a list of chemicals and minerals I'm going to need.'

*

Paula stood in front of the gateway again as Demitri opened the terminus above Valatare. The washed russet light of the insipid clouds shone through, making the faces of her companions seem strangely malaised. She opened a link to the floater.

'Hello, Laura; we're ready to connect to you now. Please shut down your wormhole to Ursell.'

'It is done,' Laura replied.

'All right, stand by.'

'I am recalibrating the floater systems to act as anchor.'

'Going for connection,' Demitri announced.

'Initiating,' Laura said.

'We're there! Connected and stable.'

'Well done,' Paula told the ANAdroid. 'Okay, Laura, you need to modify your force-field profile for maximum streamlining. We're going to move you.'

'Understood.'

Paula let the exovision data from the gateway fill her perception, monitoring Demitri's control. The floater with Laura's memories was eight and a half thousand kilometres from the equatorial anomaly. Demitri began to load new coordinates into the gateway, shifting the terminus and its new anchor. Laura altered the shape of the floater's force field, elongating it to an ellipsoid, with the narrow section aligned along the direction of travel. Then she flattened it, turning the leading edges sharper, extending the nose to a point. Demitri began to increase the speed, lifting it to a higher altitude where the gas was thinner, so it powered along above the slow-spinning cyclones. They kept a close watch on the force field and settled for a speed of Mach seven, which it could withstand without undue strain.

It took an hour to fly Laura's floater to the equatorial anomaly, ripping through the melange of helium, hydrogen, and methane at the head of a roiling pristine-white contrail of ammonium ice particles that stretched out for over sixty kilometres. When it reached the right location, Demitri brought it to a halt, the terminus connection locking it in place.

'Take it down,' Paula said.

He didn't lower it at anything like supersonic speed, keeping the descent slow and careful. Laura reshaped the force field again, contracting it around the floater. Even with Valatare's sluggish gas currents, it received quite a buffeting.

'There's a lot of tension on the connection,' Demitri reported.

'Can it damage the wormhole?' Paula asked.

'Not the wormhole itself; that's just a negative energy structure. But it's placing quite a strain on the floater's physical systems.'

'How much?'

'Within tolerance.'

'We can't afford to lose the connection.'

'I am aware of that.'

It took quite an effort not to scowl at him.

The floater continued its drop. Demitri had reduced the width of the wormhole to a metre in diameter. It was like a porthole in the middle of the gateway, showing nothing but a grey haze through which occasional wisps of auburn vapour flashed across. Paula's exovision overlaid the gas pressure on the other side, and she did her best not to flinch. If it broke through, the jet of gas would be like an iron pillar pistoning out.

When the floater was three hundred kilometres deep in the atmosphere, the light around it had dwindled away to nothing. It was hard to make out the throat of the wormhole; the gateway was a simple black circle.

'Radiation rising,' Demitri said.

'Systems status?' Paula queried.

'So far, so good.'

At thirty kilometres from the boundary, a faint glow began to appear.

'Gamma radiation fluorescence,' Demitri told them. 'And that's going to grow.'

At this depth, it was questionable if the floater was immersed in gas or superfluid. Whichever it was, the density was extreme, and starting to stress the force field. The wormhole terminus was having to push the buoyant floater down – another function that was never included in its original performance specifications.

Paula began to wish the ANAdroids were more human. She was sure if they were they'd be panicking about now, giving her a better indication of progress than Demitri's bland assurances. She was certainly starting to sweat.

The radiation glow was getting brighter, shining out at them like a lime-stained sun. Paula's suit helmet activated several filters, protecting her retinas.

At one kilometre above the boundary, the temperature began to rise fast, as did the gravity. The data in Paula's exovision didn't match any gas giant environment on record; they were truly into the unknown now. Gamma radiation was heating the hydrogen to such an extent that the pressure on the floater's force field was now approaching overload. Paula noticed that the others had all backed a couple of paces further from the gateway, and smiled to herself.

Without warning, the dazzling miasma became clear, and she could actually make out the surface of the boundary two hundred metres below the floater. There was an immense circle of relative darkness directly underneath.

Five kilometres across, Paula realized. *The generator. We're on target.*

'Acceleration stress,' Demitri said in surprise. 'I'm going to have to—'

The floater suddenly lunged down, its force field slamming into the generator's boundary layer. Paula took an involuntary step back, her arm coming up in instinctive animal protection, warding off the unknown threat. The glare cut off abruptly. But the floater was still intact; she could see its data displays in her exovision.

'Laura?'

'I'm here. I should make a pious first-footprint statement – if I had feet.'

'What just happened?' Paula asked.

'The boundary's gravity field pulled it down,' Demitri said. 'I had to let the wormhole expand freely or the anchor connection would have been ripped apart from tidal stress. Frankly we're lucky it's only seventeen gees. The floater systems are only just strong enough to withstand it.'

'The boundary is seventeen gravities?' Ry asked. 'How does that happen?'

'That's how it pulls down the gas to fuel itself,' Demitri said, 'and how it maintains such a thick atmosphere. This is the gradient Laura detected when she opened the first wormhole here. It's a lot steeper than any natural one.'

'But everything is intact?' Paula said. Her medical display was showing her heart rate slowing back to normal levels.

'Stable for now,' Demitri said.

She was familiar enough with him now to hear the caution in that tone. 'But?'

'The gravity is gripping the floater hard. Attempting to move the terminus will break the anchor connection; it's not strong enough to lift the floater against that force.'

'Can we disengage from this end?' Paula asked.

'Yes, but I don't think we'd be able to reconnect. Not in this environment. Effectively, we're stuck like this.'

'Where did the light go?' Florian asked.

'It's here all around me, but you just can't see it now,' Laura said. 'I'm oriented so the wormhole is directly on top of the boundary.'

'I thought the boundary sucked everything through.'

'The ordinary boundary surface consumes and obliterates matter to power itself,' Valeri said. 'That's where the gamma energy emission comes from, a tiny back leakage from disintegrating particles. But the boundary above the generator isn't permeable, it's a protective field. So the floater didn't get sucked through.'

'Did you know that before?' Florian said.

'It was a risk.'

'But . . .'

'I was prepared to take it,' Laura told him. 'I am duplicated in the Ursell floater, so there was little to lose.'

Florian exhaled loudly. 'Commonwealth people think so differently.'

'Rationality is a by-product of age and experience,' Paula told him.

'With a few exceptions,' Demitri added ruefully.

Paula grinned, knowing who he was referring to.

'So the boundary over the generator is like a force field?' Florian persisted.

'A very powerful one,' Demitri said.

Paula turned to face the towering yellow cylinder. 'Is this connection good enough for you?' she asked the Planter.

'Yes. We will require you to allow me through your force fields so we may physically touch the anomaly.'

'Show me what you want,' Demitri said. 'I'll adjust as we go.'

A mound of Trüb's shiny purple surface expanded right in front of the gateway machine. The top rippled and darkened. A thick strand of dark-grey material snaked up and bent horizontal to touch the gateway's force field. It flowed through and kept going, probing down to the lightless boundary.

Paula realized she was holding her breath.

'Your assumption was correct,' the Planter said. 'This is the generator. It is composed of quantum-phased matter formatting a specific warp within local spacetime: the boundary around a zone of zero-temporal flow.'

'They're in stasis,' Paula mused. 'That figures; the Void was constantly manipulating its internal time-flow.' She took a deep breath, coming as close to praying as she ever had. 'Can you switch it off?'

'No. We would have to manipulate a vast quantity of energy

to override the warp – greater than the amount which the boundary is producing. We do not have that quantity of energy.'

*

The atomic bomb was curiously innocuous – not that Chaing could actually see the mechanism itself. The casing was an olive-green metal trunk, two metres long, with small yellow alphanumerics stencilled on – the same as every munitions box ever made by the state armouries. It sat on the marble floor beside the prime minister's wide desk as if someone had dropped it there by mistake.

Even though he was growing used to the scale of the palace, Chaing was awed by how ostentatious the study was. *A room bigger than a football pitch for one person to work in? Crud, those old Captains were decadent. And our prime ministers are so different. Yeah right.* Dawn light was shining in through the tall arched windows, illuminating the long wall paintings of the Air Force planes, regiment troops sweeping vigilantly through jungles and farmland, and heroic workers building Bienvenido's new factories.

There were eight Section Seven guards on duty in the anteroom which led into the study at the opposite end from the desk, with a further three securing the private corridor at the other end of the study. A major from the atomic weapons division had been waiting beside the bomb. He showed Chaing the keyholes under a small lid on the side. 'You have to turn them simultaneously. Ninety degrees arms it. Wait thirty seconds for the trigger power sequence to run, then turn another ninety degrees.'

'That's it?' Chaing asked in surprise.

'Yes.' The major saluted grimly and left.

As he went out into the anteroom, Corilla and Jenifa came in. Corilla had looked round in amazement as she walked the length of the study, shaking her head at the garish artwork, then recoiled as she saw the Faller skulls in the alcoves. She caught sight of the desk and hurried round to the polished leather chair behind the desk. 'Got to do it once in your life,' she declared happily as she sat down. 'You,' she pointed at imaginary aides. 'Have my opponents assassinated. You, fetch me strawberries and champagne.'

'Grow up,' Jenifa grunted.

'Never going to happen,' Corilla retorted, and all the humour drained from her face. 'Not now. No time.' She spun the chair round to face the cheap wooden bookshelves along the back wall. 'So what does a prime minister read?'

Jenifa ignored her and walked over to one of the big windows. She frowned as she looked down into the rose courtyard. 'Why is the space machine down there?'

Chaing limped over to stand beside her and peered down to see the space machine in the middle of the courtyard, its unmistakable cylinder shape illuminated by the dull light creeping over the high walls around it. A couple of the white-coated staff from Section Seven's advanced science division stood idly beside it. As he watched, a small tractor drove into the courtyard, towing a flatbed trolley. This one had a metal sphere on it, with a large viewport on one side and an open hatch on the other; a lot of segments were missing. He just knew it was some kind of Commonwealth artefact; it was too sophisticated for Bienvenido to manufacture. The thing put him in mind of a Liberty capsule, only bigger and better. 'Being taken to Byarn?' he suggested. One of the women down on the cobbles was Faustina, directing more of her colleagues who were arriving with small boxes. It certainly looked like she was preparing to go somewhere.

'Why bother?' Jenifa said quietly. 'We all know how this is going to end.'

Chaing turned away from her and walked across the study to the windows that looked out along Bryan-Anthony Boulevard beyond the palace's sturdy perimeter wall. Troops and vehicles were mustering on the big parade ground, while civilians were starting to gather at the front gates. There were a lot of children out there, Chaing saw; everyone was staring up at the palace's facade, not chanting slogans or shaking their fists. Just staring. Waiting.

'They're expecting salvation,' he said in wonder.

'Then they're fools,' Jenifa retorted bitterly. 'They've only got a few hours left now. They should be at home with their families.'

Chaing could see smoke and flames rising across the city. The largest conflagrations were coming from the waterfront. 'I'm not sure we've even got that long.' The faint sound of firearms was audible across the rooftops.

The palace gates opened and a convoy of tracked trucks drove out, racing down the slope.

Jenifa glanced back at the bomb. There was perspiration on her forehead. 'This is stupid. We should just get it over with.'

Chaing shook his head. 'Not yet. There's still time for the Warrior Angel to contact us.'

'You're pathetic, you know that.'

He drew himself up as best he could; the pain in his leg seemed to be a lot worse today. 'Carrying out *this* order correctly takes more strength that you'll ever have. As you've just demonstrated.'

'I am strong!' Jenifa snarled at him.

'Then have the strength to wait for the Warrior Angel.'

'Eliters have faith in their reactionary idol, not PSR officers.'

'I have faith in people.'

She smiled mockingly. 'You can tell me now. It won't make any difference, we're all about to die one way or another. Come on, Chaing, I think you owe me that much.'

Just for a moment he actually considered it, but even now he held back. *Never trust a PSR fanatic.* 'I know what I am, and I am completely comfortable with that. Isn't that the goal of the world we're trying to build, Comrade? Justice and equality for everyone.'

'I'm not a politician. I keep this world safe.'

Chaing laughed quietly. The convoy of tracked trucks had disappeared from view, and the palace gates were closing again. He saw more people coming out of the junctions along Bryan-Anthony Boulevard, turning to march towards the palace. 'Well, you and I have both failed spectacularly on that front.'

'We can still save people from the Fallers,' Jenifa said urgently. 'And we can take a crud-load of the bastards with us. End this, Chaing. Be brave, and you and I will go shout at Uracus together.'

'These people are frightened, that's all,' Corilla said, staring out at the approaching crowd. 'We know the nests are moving into the city; we're just trying to keep ahead of them.'

Chaing looked from the throng hurrying along Bryan-Anthony Boulevard, to Corilla, then back again. 'They're all Eliters?' *There's thousands of them.*

'Yes,' she said softly. 'We're people, too, you know. And there's nowhere else to go. This is the centre of the city. The safest place.' She frowned. 'There's also a message in the general band saying children will have protection from the egg bombardment if they come here.'

'Stonal and Davorky aren't going to like that,' Jenifa said flatly.

Chaing watched anxiously as Palace Guard squads hurried across the parade ground to line up on the high walkway behind the wall. They weren't levelling their weapons. Yet.

Corilla let out a gasp of shock and gripped the edge of the desk.

'What's the matter?' Chaing asked; she looked as if she was about to be sick.

'Link,' she grunted, and pushed off from the desk to stagger over to the first of the great arching windows. 'It's so strong.'

'Are you in contact with that rabble?' Jenifa asked suspiciously. She took the link detector from her uniform pocket and frowned. The red bulb on top was glowing brightly.

Corilla was pressed against the glass, staring in reverence up into the clear sapphire sky. 'No,' she breathed as her eyes watered. 'It's not the crowd. This is coming from space.'

*

Paula stared at the dark centre of the wormhole for a long moment, refusing to let the despair rise. Working the problem – as always. 'But if you had that kind of energy, could you do it?' she asked the Planter. 'Could you switch off the generator?'

'Yes,' the Planter replied.

She turned to the ANAdroids. 'So where do we get that kind of energy from? A quantumbuster?'

'Nigel took them all with him on the *Skylady*,' Kysandra said. 'There are none left.'

'Can the synthesizers build us one?'

There was a moment where the three ANAdroids faced each other. 'The star,' Fergus said. 'The barrier consumes a phenomenal amount of energy, but that is trivial compared to the star's output.'

'Okay. So how do we tap that power?'

'Extend a wormhole terminus into it. A wormhole is an exotic matter interstice. If you pass super-density plasma through the open channel, it can be configured to suck energy directly from it – a function similar to the barrier.'

'But then you'll need to transfer that energy to the barrier generator,' Demitri said.

'Second wormhole,' Valeri said.

'The Ursell floater,' Fergus said.

'That's one.'

Paula had the impression the audible conversation was just an overspill of their thoughts working the problem. 'The machine under the palace,' she said.

'You mean the BC5800d2 I repaired?' Laura asked. 'Is it still working?'

'Yes,' Kysandra said. 'I have a friend working in the People's Security Regiment science team that analyses Commonwealth technology. It's still in the crypt and codelocked.'

'Do have the code?' Paula asked the Laura personality.

'Yes, of course.'

'Then we just have to get back there and unlock it.'

'But this wormhole is fixed to Valatare,' Kysandra said.

'If the synthesizers can manufacture a regrav drive, I will fly a space capsule back to Bienvenido,' Ry said. 'It would be my honour.'

'Nice idea,' Paula said. 'But dear old Captain Chaing was getting quite eager to talk to me about opening BC5800d2 – on the government's behalf, of course. How organized are the Eliters in the capital?'

'As well as anywhere,' Kysandra said. 'Why?'

'We link to them and ask for help. My old lifeboat package with Joey's memories was being kept in the same crypt as the wormhole, right? We just have to get the code to him and tell him to open the terminus here.'

Florian's arm thrust upwards, pointing at the darkening green sky. 'But Bienvenido is millions of kilometres away. We can't link that far.'

'How long for the synthesizers to build me a transmitter?' Paula asked.

'We can send a signal for you,' the Planter said.

*

Along with the others, Paula stood on Trüb's abnormal purple surface as the sun dropped below the horizon. The switch from day to night was quicker than sunset in any of the tropics she'd ever been to, leaving them immersed in an unnerving darkness. Without light, the purple surface was as black as the starless night.

Florian and Ry immediately switched their torches on. Paula couldn't blame them for that. But all the limited beams did was emphasize how insignificant they were on any scale.

They didn't have long to wait before one of the small moons came shooting up over the horizon. Even though it was grey, it shone brightly, illuminating the unsullied landscape before soaring into the planet's umbra. As it rose above them, she saw it was changing colour, the undistinguished grey transmuting to a dusky gold. The second moon to come over was red, the third a pale green. That was when they saw the petals starting to distort its shape. By the time the next one had its brief time between terminator and umbra, its silver petals were kilometres across, reflecting a wash of sunlight light across the purple plain below, which cast a sharp shadow from the yellow tower, sliding round faster than any clock's second hand.

'We will begin now,' the Planter said. 'What is your message?'

Paula straightened her back and faced the pillar just as the silver moon passed into shadow, extinguishing its reflected radiance. 'This is Paula Myo. I am a Commonwealth citizen,' she sent through the link. 'The Warrior Angel and I are on Trüb, and we believe we have found a method of defeating the Fallers. But I'm going to need your help—'

*

'The wormhole!' Corilla exclaimed incredulously. 'Paula wants us to unlock the wormhole. She needs it.'

'Paula's alive?' Chaing asked. The relief he felt was extraordinary, banishing the pain from his leg and wrist. 'Where is she?'

Corilla smiled, her eyes brimming with tears, she was so jubilant. 'Trüb!'

'This is bollocks,' Jenifa sneered.

'I have the code!' Corilla yelled at her, abruptly furious. 'It's in the message. I can unlock the wormhole. Do you understand that, you dumb bitch?'

Jenifa took an angry step towards her. Chaing's hand came down on her shoulder.

'Is she going to evacuate us to Aqueous?' he asked.

'No, she thinks she's found a way to defeat the Fallers. We have to get down to the crypt under the palace. Once it's unlocked—' Her hand flew to her mouth as her eyes widened in shock. 'The space machine!' She ran across the study to the windows overlooking the rose courtyard. 'Oh, no. No, no!'

*

'Crudding Uracus!' Faustina exclaimed. She was standing in the middle of the rose courtyard, staring up in astonishment at the square of sky framed overhead. 'Are you getting this?' she asked Joey.

'Very loud and very clear.'

She twisted her head around. There were only three of her staff left, delivering chemicals in big glass dewars. They were giving her strange looks. 'Where's the tractor? Oh crud, it's back down in the garage.' She spun back to face the space machine. 'Can you do it? Can you open a terminus to Trüb if the code works?'

'Yes.'

'Then we have to get you down there.' She froze as she was link pinged, and jerked her head up to see a figure looking down at her from one of the big arching windows above.

'There's a three-hundred-kiloton bomb in here,' Corilla told her. 'And there's a PSR lunatic desperate to detonate it!'

'What?'

'She wants to spare us all from suffering the apocalypse.'

'Sweet fucking Giu!'

'I'm not sure my force field can stand up to that,' Joey said. 'Not at all.'

'What have I done?' Faustina wailed. 'You should be down there with the wormhole. You could have got us to Trüb by now.'

'I still can be. Get the other me out of the jail cell and run, Faustina. Fucking run!'

*

'She's playing you,' Jenifa said heatedly as Corilla pressed herself against the window overlooking the rose courtyard. The red light on top of the link detector was still glowing. 'Give me the keys. I'll do it. I'll end this if you can't.'

'Not a crudding chance, corporal,' Chaing told her. 'This is what I was waiting for. It's also what Stonal was waiting for. Now you need to clam down and carry out your orders.'

'Paula is Commonwealth.'

'She's going to save us. Can't you at least give her a chance to prove herself? It's what Stonal and the prime minister wanted. Or do you consider yourself above them, too?'

Jenifa clenched her jaw, but said nothing.

'I know admitting you might be wrong hurts,' he said more gently. 'Believe me, I know.'

Corilla turned back from the window. 'We need to get down to the crypt. Now!'

'I thought you said the space machine had to be there?' Chaing asked.

'Our senior palace agent has a way round this.'

Chaing couldn't help but grin at the apoplectic expression on Jenifa's face. 'Let's go then.'

It was Corilla who led them down to the crypt. They went along interminable corridors, down cramped little stairwells that only had a couple of bulbs lighting them. After the first five minutes, Chaing was thoroughly lost.

'How do you know where we're going?' he asked.

'Link,' Corilla said. 'It gave me the route.'

'Who linked to you?' Jenifa asked belligerently. 'Is this coming from your reactionary agent? How do they know where to go?'

'Every Eliter knows,' Corilla answered. 'Same as we know every city's street map, every train timetable. It's all there in the general bands.' She paused, then gave Jenifa a sly glance. 'Once we're back in the Commonwealth you can get yourself upgraded, then you'll know what it's like.'

As he limped along painfully, Chaing caught the way Jenifa glared at Corilla's back. He unclipped the leather strap on his holster – just in case.

Finally they turned out of a dank narrow passageway into a much larger corridor. At the far end, tall double doors were set into the wall. There was a desk beside them, the kind guards would use – fussing about to check if you were authorized to enter, establishing their own status. There was no one sitting behind it. Chaing approached cautiously; something as important as the wormhole gateway should be guarded.

'It's in here,' Corilla said eagerly, and turned the big iron handle.

Chaing gripped her arm. 'Wait.' He still couldn't understand where the guards were.

He took his pistol out before leading the way into the crypt. Given how far they were underground, the chamber was surprisingly large. Ahead of him, a broad circle of the stone floor had been covered by a sheer white plinth, which was empty apart from odd piles of components that clearly belonged to some larger machine. Tables with scientific research equipment lined the walls. He barely paid it any attention. His gaze was drawn to the big circular machine at the far end of the crypt. It was almost feature-less – a thick rim of cerulean-shaded metal, with a centre of a weird grey substance that his eyes couldn't quite focus on. He couldn't help the little burst of admiration he felt at the sight of it. This was true history; the gateway had been built in the Commonwealth thousands of years ago, then used by Mother Laura to destroy the Primes in Bienvenido's darkest hour. The foundation of legends. Now here it was in front of him, solid and real.

'Great Giu,' he murmured, pushing the pistol back in its holster.

Corilla was standing beside him, her expression of awe matching his. 'We can do it,' she said. 'We can help the Warrior Angel defeat the Fallers.'

The sound of a safety catch being *snicked* back was loud even in the big crypt. 'I don't remember being given orders to do that,' Jenifa said softly. She was holding her pistol in one hand. The other hand was turning the door lock.

'We don't need orders to save the crudding world!' Chaing shouted.

Jenifa pulled out the link detector, its green light shining on top. 'If you link to that Commonwealth artefact, you little Eliter whore, if I see this light go red, I will put a bullet in your head.'

'For crud's sake, Jenifa—' Chaing began.

She shot him.

6

Reports coming into the command bunker from Varlan's riverside were intermittent and confused. There were a dozen red flags on the city map table to mark the Faller incursion now, but Stonal still didn't know what they actually represented, outside of panicked shouts over the radio claiming monsters and large guns. Three of the Marine boats had been removed from the river Colbal, and there'd been no contact with the remainder for over a quarter of an hour. Davorky hadn't yet ordered their emblems to be removed – foolishly optimistic, in Stonal's view.

One of the communication staff had a fast shouted exchange, and two of the red flags by the river were moved further into the city, progressing down Vownfol Street.

'Crud,' Davorky grunted. The column of reinforcements dispatched from the palace was almost at the waterfront, but three kilometres west of Vownfol Street.

A new red flag was added to the city, placed in the middle of Bromwell Park at the far end of Bryan-Anthony Boulevard.

'Where in Uracus did they come from?' Stonal demanded. 'They're inside the perimeter.'

'Size and ability?' Davorky demanded.

'Sir, scouts report several hundred, including large breeder-types,' an aide reported. 'All heavily armed. No vehicles.'

Stonal looked at the long straight line of Bryan-Anthony

Boulevard, leading directly from the park to the palace. *A knife to the heart.* 'They're coming for us,' he said.

'Sir,' one of the communication staff called, 'the gate guard is reporting a very large crowd massing outside the wall. He says they're asking to come in.'

'Absolutely not,' Stonal said.

'Sir, they have children with them.'

Stonal strode over to the communication staffer. 'Give that to me.' He grabbed the phone handset from the tense man. 'This is Director Stonal. Who am I talking to?'

'Captain Fitzsand, sir. Assigned to the main palace gates.'

'Then listen to this very closely, Captain Fitzsand. Under no circumstances are any civilians to be allowed through the gates. Is that understood?'

'Uh, yes, sir. Sir, the crowd are claiming their children have been promised sanctuary inside the palace.'

'Let me be very clear, captain: they have not. Do not let them in.'

'Sir, they said they're here because the Warrior Angel told them to come. That she's opening the wormhole under the palace. That she's going to take us all to safety or something.'

Stonal stared at the phone in shock. 'I'm coming up to the gate. Arrest whoever claims to be the leader of this rabble. I want to talk to them!'

'Yes, sir.'

He hurried back to Davorky. 'Deploy some reserves into Bryan-Anthony Boulevard. Stop those Fallers getting closer to the palace.'

'I'll do what I can,' the master general said, 'but I've got the regiments positioned round the outskirts. Getting them back into the centre will take time.'

'Just hold them off. I need to find out exactly what's going on outside.'

*

Faustina was panting heavily by the time she got to the cells where

Adolphus was incarcerated; even now she had trouble thinking of him as Joey. She looked along the corridor suspiciously, but there were no guards in sight. That wasn't right, but she wasn't about to complain. There were twenty identical metal doors set into the wall, all numbered. She told her u-shadow to ping Joey.

'Faustina?' came the answer.

'Yeah. Hang on.' Her u-shadow flipped a location map up into her exovision. She hurried along to cell eight and lifted the small flap on the door. Adolphus's face stared back at her. 'I've come to break you out,' she said. 'Um, do you know where the guard keeps the keys?'

'What? No! Where are the guards?'

'I'm not sure. A lot of them are deserting.'

'Bollocks. Okay, stand back. I'm cutting through.'

She hurriedly took some steps back. There was a loud bang from inside the cell, then another. The lock mechanism began to smoulder, and the metal sagged round it. Another bang, then Adolphus/Joey was shoving the door open.

Faustina couldn't help it; she gave him a big hug. 'I screwed up,' she said. 'I moved the space machine out to the courtyard.'

'Okay,' he said cautiously. 'Why is that screwing up?'

So she explained about the message from space, how Paula was ready to fight the Fallers somehow. 'Can you operate the gateway?' she asked, almost fearing the answer.

Joey grinned widely. 'Oh, yeah. Piece of cake. I'm actually a hyperspace theorist, you know.'

Faustina smiled back weakly; there was something not quite right about that oh-so-familiar face appearing so happy. 'We have to get down there. I'm not sure about Chaing's loyalties. I got word that he was on our side, but . . .'

'Right.' He turned to face the cell opposite and opened the hatch. 'You catch all of that?'

'I did,' Roxwolf's gurgling voice agreed.

'We might run into guards. I'm armed with this e-pulse, but we could do with some backup.'

'You got it. This is my only chance to get the crud out of here.'

'Joey!' Faustina hissed.

'It's okay. We've been talking, and he's with us.'

She gave him a very sceptical look, but he pushed his sleeve up and brought his arm round. There was a flash of light as a rigid thunderbolt stabbed out of his skin and struck the lock on Roxwolf's cell door.

It only took one more shot and the lock was ruined. Joey pulled the door open. Faustina braced herself, but Roxwolf walked out nonchalantly.

'You crudding well watch him closely,' she sent to Joey through their link.

'Don't worry. Remember, I got caught by Fallers once before – actually, a million times before.'

Making sure Joey was always between her and Roxwolf, Faustina led them through the maze of passages, then up two levels.

'This is it,' Faustina exclaimed as she hurried towards a huge pair of doors. She frowned at the abandoned desk. 'The guard must have deserted.'

'Good,' Roxwolf grunted.

She turned the big iron handle, and pushed. The door didn't move. She pushed harder. 'It's locked,' she exclaimed. 'From the inside.'

'I'll get it,' Joey told her, and raised his arm.

＊

Chaing felt nothing as the bullet struck, only his good leg collapsing, sending him tumbling to the hard stone floor. Corilla was shrieking in terror. *Then* the pain hit, spiking through his thigh like an incandescent spear. He couldn't even cry out, it was so overwhelming. He gulped for air as he finally found the courage to look. The bullet had hit halfway between his hip and knee. A neat-ish wound at the front, horrific crater of tattered flesh and trouser fabric at the back, with blood pouring out. He instinctively grabbed the wound with his good hand to try and staunch the bleeding. His fingers slithered about as the blood soaked them.

'What are you doing?' Corilla yelled. Her whole body was rigid with shock and fear.

'Remember,' Jenifa gloated. 'One flash of red, and . . . pow!' She walked towards Chaing and stood over him, her eyes gleaming with joy. 'He's an Eliter. He was going to evacuate his kind off this world and leave the rest of us to the Fallers. Weren't you, *sir*?'

Chaing clenched his teeth, shaking his head. 'Call,' he grunted against the pain, took another breath. 'Call Stonal.'

'Your little whore isn't calling anyone,' Jenifa said. 'You're a crudding traitor, captain. Admit it. I want to hear you say it. Say you're an Eliter.'

'Go fuck yourself,' Chaing spat.

She smiled. And kicked the wound.

Chaing screamed. There was a moment when only pain existed. Then thin strings of bile were spewing out of his mouth and he twisted around in agony. Both hands clutched desperately at his leg as more blood pumped out.

Jenifa was laughing delightedly. 'Tell me!' she demanded. 'I want to hear it. Confess, Eliter!'

'Stop it,' Corilla yelled in shock. 'You're killing him. Can't you see that?'

'I told you to shut up.' Jenifa pointed the pistol casually at Corilla. She nudged Chaing with her toe. 'Come on, traitor. Say it.'

Chaing shrank away from her touch, whimpering softly. 'Let her unlock the gateway. Paula can save us.'

'You. She can save you and your kind. Right?' Jenifa kicked him again. 'I'm going to squeeze every drop of blood out of you,' she said contentedly. 'I'm going to make you die in so much pain your mind will break first. Now admit it!'

Chaing could see she had dropped into that same strange zone she'd dropped into when they'd held a helpless Joffler ready for interrogation. Her rational thoughts were gone, engulfed by raw desire and frightening determination. She would not stop this until she heard him confess, no matter what the cost. 'I . . . I . . .'

'Yes?' Jenifa bent over to catch his faltering words.

'Watch this.' He pressed his thumb against his knuckle. A rectangle of faint green lines shone through the blood.

'What is that?' a mesmerized Jenifa whispered.

'That, corporal, is how non-Eliters call the Warrior Angel for help. You see, you were wrong about me. You were always wrong.' He started laughing at the fury that blazed across her face.

'You fucking traitor!' Jenifa screamed. She slammed her boot into his wound again. Chaing blacked out for a few seconds. When he came round Jenifa was in a defensive crouch, her pistol pointing at the doors. There was a loud bang, and a bright flash searing out of the chunky iron lock.

It was very weird. If he could just concentrate, he was sure he could work out what was happening. Strangely the pain was reducing, and he seemed rather pleasantly lightheaded. His hands closed around the wound to staunch the awful flow of blood.

It's worked, he thought happily. *I called for the Warrior Angel, and now here she is, just like she said she'd be. How wonderful.*

Jenifa had grabbed Corilla and was holding the distraught girl in front of her like a shield. The door swung open.

*

Joey was first into the crypt. He took a couple of confident paces, making it look like he belonged there. Then what he was seeing registered. 'Holy bollocks,' he grunted.

The semi-conscious man on the floor had one leg in a cast, and the other leg bleeding heavily from a bullet wound. In front of him, a compact female PSR corporal was holding a frightened girl close to her chest. But her pistol was aimed unwaveringly at Joey's head.

'What the crud is *that* doing in here?' she shouted. The muzzle jabbed towards Roxwolf.

'You brought him here,' Faustina said, coming up to stand beside Joey. 'You should know, Roxwolf is helping us.'

'Bollocks,' the corporal spat. 'The only person that creature ever helps is himself.'

Roxwolf opened his mouth wide, showing off a prodigious

quantity of fangs. 'Hello, Corporal Jenifa. Bad day, huh? Join the club.'

'Put your weapons down,' Jenifa said.

Joey reduced the power level in his OCtattoo e-pulse function; targeting brackets were jumping all over the profile of the crazy woman with the gun and her hostage shield, trying to get a decent lock. 'What weapon?'

'The one that burned through metal,' Jenifa said. 'The Commonwealth weapon. Where is it?'

'Oh that? It's part of my body.'

'How . . . ?' She gritted her teeth. 'You were the prime minister!'

I know. Listen to me, Jenifa, is it?' he said, using the best kindly patriarchal voice his stolen body could muster. 'The gateway has to be opened. We are going to defeat the Fallers.'

'Yes, *you* are,' she said, breathing hard. 'Eliters, every one of you.'

Joey grinned. 'That's what you call us, but I'm more than that. A lot more. I'm from the Commonwealth itself. And we're here to take you home.' He saw the uncertainty in her eyes, the way she shifted her grip on the pistol, making sure she was extra steady.

'No,' she grunted. 'No, that's a lie.'

Joey's targeting program still couldn't get a decent lock. Behind him Roxwolf took a step forwards.

'Move again, freak monster, and I blow your crudding head off,' Jenifa said without taking her gaze off Joey.

'You need to calm down,' Joey told her.

'Yeah? You want to see what makes me calm?'

Targeting graphics finally framed her face perfectly. Joey linked to Roxwolf, to tell him to distract her for a moment so her pistol would waver and allow him a shot.

The green light on the little box she held turned red.

Jenifa tensed.

Joey tried to jump aside, forcing the body's ancient flabby muscles to perform the impossible.

Jenifa shot Roxwolf.

Joey fired the e-pulse. It hit the shield girl on her neck. She spasmed wildly as she dropped to the floor.

Jenifa jerked the pistol's trigger again.

Something punched Joey in the gut, sending him sprawling backwards.

The next thing he knew, Jenifa was standing over him, her face eerily expressionless. Then she giggled. It was a sound that terrified Joey far more than the massive pistol which was slowly descending towards his head.

'Traitors, all of you,' she said. 'I was right. I was always right.'

The sound of the shot was thunderous.

Half of Jenifa's skull exploded, sending tatters of brain splattering across the floor and Joey's chest. He turned his head, to see the man with the wounded leg holding a pistol in a two-handed grip, a satisfied smile curling his bloodless lips. 'No you weren't, corporal,' he grunted, and collapsed.

The world was placid for a long moment. Joey rather enjoyed that. Then he finally noticed all the red medical displays crawling through his exovision, so many and so bright he could barely see anything else.

'Giu's bollocks,' Faustina wailed. 'Joey? Joey, are you alive?' She took a couple of steps forwards and hesitated, looking between him and Roxwolf.

'Unlock the gateway,' Joey said. 'Quick. I don't think I've got long.' He banished all the bad-news medical icons from his exovision – not that their absence made the world a whole lot clearer. 'Hey! Hey, Roxwolf, how you doing, pal?'

The mutant Faller coughed and flopped over, clutching at his hip where the bullet had torn through. 'Last time I jailbreak with you, my friend.'

'Keep pressure on the wound. Help is coming.'

'Help?'

'Yes. I think.'

'Done it,' Faustina cried incredulously.

Joey's u-shadow told him access to the gateway's smartnet was now open. He linked to it and pulled the operational routines into his exovision. The BC5800d2's systems were all recognizable, though there were plenty of specialist functions he didn't even consider. He started to load instructions in.

'It's turning violet,' Faustina exclaimed.

Uncomfortably warm liquid was bubbling away in Joey's throat, making it even harder to breathe. He scanned the displays that showed him the BC5800d2's initialization process running. Then he had to work through the more complex terminus coordinate selection procedure. Hyperspacial resonance revealed planetary masses orbiting their solitary star. Only one had moons, though they were exceptionally small. He shifted the coordinates again, opening the terminus close to Trüb's surface.

It must have been about right, for a lovely purple glow spilled through the open wormhole to shine across the crypt and its grisly contents. Trüb's mauve surface was alive with subtly shifting patterns of colour, like solid rainbows rippling gently round the smooth globe.

His body was trembling now, and growing cold. 'Faustina, send a signal through. You have to contact them. Tell Paula she has to take charge of the gateway's smartnet. Quickly. I'm losing it.'

'Joey?' The anguish in her voice was plaintive.

'Don't worry. This is just a copy of me. I've bodylossed before. The worst bit is waking up in a clinic's emaciated clone; they always fast-grow them. I think it's coz it's cheaper that way.'

'Don't talk,' she told him.

He hadn't known he was.

His u-shadow reported several new links opening. One connected directly with the BC5800d2's smartnet. Faustina started crying.

*

Kysandra stepped through first, her nose wrinkling up at the carnage on the floor of the crypt. She was just about to embrace a sobbing Faustina when she froze in shock.

'What the crud is that?' she demanded.

'I'm Roxwolf. Good to finally meet you.'

She grunted in bemusement. 'I guess it really is the end of the world.' The wound in his side looked bad, but his paw was pressed against the ripped flesh, slowing the ugly pulses of blue blood.

'Can you do it?' Faustina asked. 'Can you stop the Fallers?'

'Paula thinks she can.' She saw Chaing lying on the ground, a nasty bullet wound in his thigh. 'Hello again, captain; you really need to learn how to duck faster.'

He nodded weakly. She didn't like how pale he was; the blood loss was getting serious. Ry and Florian came through the wormhole behind her. 'Ry, first-aid the captain, now.'

'I'm on it!' he exclaimed.

She stared at the mutant Faller.

'I warned you about the bombardment,' Roxwolf said. 'I've been helping you. I had a deal with humans; you said you'd let me live.'

'That's true,' Faustina said.

Kysandra found passing judgement was unusually difficult. So many years had been spent exterminating Fallers, her instinct was just to fry him with a disrupter pulse. 'Florian, you take Roxwolf. Paula can decide what to do with him later.'

'Welcome to the reunion, my friend,' Roxwolf grunted at an uncertain Florian.

'But . . . he's alien,' Florian said. 'The medical kit won't treat him.'

'Just apply basic first aid, stop the bleeding. Fallers are tough beasts.'

Florian dropped to his knees beside the mutant Faller and opened the kit. He took out a big dressing patch.

'Thank you,' Roxwolf sighed.

Kysandra turned to the third victim. 'Prime minister?' she said in surprise.

'No, I stole his body. Don't worry about this; everything is backed up. I'll re-life later. Just get us back . . . Oh bollocks, here we go again.' His chest juddered as blood gushed out of his mouth; then his body went limp.

'It was Joey,' Faustina explained.

'Okay. Brief me, please, and quickly.' Kysandra took a minute to study all the files Faustina sent over, along with listening to a fast summary. 'Oh crud,' she muttered at the end. 'Paula, did you get all that?'

'Yes. It doesn't matter. If I can crack Valatare, it's all over.'

'How long?'

'Not sure. Soon, I hope.'

Paula not giving a specific has to be a first, Kysandra thought. At any other time she might have enjoyed it. 'So,' she said to Faustina. 'We've got a crowd of Eliter children outside thinking you're going to protect them, and the Fallers are moving into the city?'

'Yes,' Faustina admitted miserably.

'Okay. Demitri, the gateway is all yours. Take it back to Trüb.'

'Inverting now,' the ANAdroid replied.

'Right, then. Ry, Florian: let's go and make sure those kids are going to be safe.'

*

Stonal heard the crowd as soon as he emerged from the palace. It was a low growl of voices, all merged into a continuous animal rumble, charged with fright and anger. Shrill individual cries pierced the clamour, anguished children venting their distress. He tightened his jaw against any instinctive urge to rush and help as he stalked across the wide, empty parade ground. Palace Guards on the walkway at the top of the wall saw him coming and nudged their Comrades.

A small group of guards was clustered at the back of the big reinforced gates. He saw a man in a splendid blue and gold captain's uniform arguing with a furious woman in a smart charcoal-grey suit. She was holding the hand of a five-year-old boy who was on the verge of tears.

'Captain Fitzsand?' Stonal said as he joined the group.

The captain saluted. 'Sir.'

'Are you in charge here?' the woman challenged.

'And you are?' Stonal asked.

'Maribeth. You have to let us in.'

'Why are you here? What message did you get?'

'We were told there's sanctuary here. The Commonwealth is going to protect our children.' She gripped her son's hand tighter, pulling him even closer.

'Who said that? What sort of sanctuary?'

'It was a signal in the general network, verified by people I know. It said there was a Commonwealth machine here with a force field.'

'Joey,' Stonal muttered disapprovingly under his breath.

'Then there was another message, a signal from space. All of us received that, and now we have the code to unlock the gateway.'

'From space?' Stonal asked disbelievingly. 'Who sent a message from space?'

'That would be me,' a voice said behind him.

He turned to see the Warrior Angel walking across the parade ground, her coat tails flapping wide, brown suede hat at an angle, long glossy Titian hair flowing like a cloak down her back. She was smiling knowingly, which made her young face beguilingly lovely.

Two men were walking beside her. Stonal recognized them easily enough: Ry Evine and Florian. Both carried thick black cylinders on shoulder straps, and wore ribbed matt overalls that had to be Commonwealth-built. He was surprised to see Faustina walking with them. He regarded her with extreme suspicion; she seemed more nervous of him than of Kysandra. It appalled him to think she might have been sneaking information to the Eliters all along.

Up above him, the Palace Guards on the walkway were cheering the Warrior Angel.

She walked right up to him and gave him an impish grin of appraisal. 'Director Stonal. Finally.'

'Kysandra. Did you tell these people to come here?' His hand waved towards the gate and the strident crowd outside.

'Partly, yes. But right now you need to get them through the gate and into the rose courtyard. Joey will throw a force field round them while we hold the Fallers off.'

'The space machine is in the rose courtyard?'

'Yes,' Faustina said. 'I moved it there. I told the Eliters their children would be safe here.'

Stonal kept very still. 'You're part of this?'

'Since before you were born. Slvasta might have been your step-father, but he was my husband.'

'Husband?'

'I've rejuvenated Faustina several times,' Kysandra said. 'She knows her way around the capital and government departments like no one else.'

'No,' he said quietly. *I cannot have been so unaware, so wrong.* 'You can't be.' Somehow it seemed like a defeat every bit as grave as the Faller Apocalypse. And he hated himself for thinking like that. *I've given my life to securing Bienvenido, and everything I've done has come to nothing.*

'I was Bethaneve,' she said relentlessly. 'The first of the elites, their original leader. I planned the revolution. I watched Slvasta corrupt it with his paranoia. And I was there when Nigel flew into space. He was genuinely trying to save us, you know. His companions saved me and Slvasta – did he ever tell you that? I saw Uracus open and expel us from the Void. I have lived life in the Void and here. Neither are of any worth. We need to go home, back to the Commonwealth, and Paula can finally take us there.'

'You've opened the wormhole in the crypt, haven't you?' he said. 'Are you going to take the Eliters to Aqueous?'

'No. There are no factions on this world any more, Stonal, only humans and Fallers. And now Paula's found some allies. We just have to buy her time to contact them.'

He stared at the sweet old woman who had fooled him for decades, and knew he'd lost, that he was no longer in charge of anything. 'I can't risk Fallers getting into the palace.'

'Neither can I,' Kysandra said. 'I'll check the crowd as they come through. Don't worry: my field function scans will spot a Faller easily.'

He wanted to say yes, but the word wouldn't form.

'Paula is the one Nigel trusted to finish the job if he failed,'

Faustina said. 'The apocalypse is starting, and she's all that stands between us and extinction. Open the palace gates, Director Stonal.'

'Captain Fitzsand,' he said. 'Please open the gates. The Warrior Angel will be vetting everyone who comes through.'

'Yes, sir,' the captain said, and saluted.

He followed Kysandra as she hurried up the stairs to the walkway and stood almost directly above the gates. She hopped up on top of the wall so everyone thronging outside could see her. A massive cheer went up – people screamed, kids were jumping up and down waving excitedly.

'You're coming in,' she told them. 'Take it slow and easy, no pushing. When you get inside, you'll be under a Commonwealth force field so the Fallers can't harm you.'

Stonal raised his gaze over the heads of the volatile crowd and along Bryan-Anthony Boulevard. Such a neat clean line on the map, but in reality a chaotic thoroughfare of people pressed together, fenced by tall government buildings streaked with a century of grime. Beyond the rear fringes of the Eliters was a long gap where nothing moved, the purple-grey cobbles cut by tram-lines, perspective shrinking back a couple of kilometres to bulky vehicles that rumbled slowly forward.

'What are those?' Stonal asked as the gates opened below him. Naturally, the crowd surged forwards.

'Stay calm,' Kysandra told them. It didn't make much difference. People were agitated and close to panic.

Ry was peering forward, studying the approaching vehicles. 'They're troop carriers,' he said. 'Yours?'

'I don't think so,' Stonal said, wondering what had become of the troops the vehicles had taken to their staging post.

'Faller,' Kysandra announced levelly. She pointed and a green flash erupted round her hand. Two hundred metres away, a man collapsed. Screams rose around him as people pressed back from the corpse; blue blood was leaking from his nostrils. 'Take it easy,' she commanded. 'They will not get past us.' Her field scan swept over the crowd; targeting graphics closed around over a dozen figures, two of whom were children.

'Those troop carriers are picking up speed,' Stonal said. 'They're going to be here before everyone's through.' As he watched them, he heard the sound of machine guns. Tiny sparks zipped out from the vehicles. He saw flames shoot from a big ten-storey office block they were passing. More flames began to take hold on the other side of Bryan-Anthony Boulevard.

'I know,' Kysandra said. 'Boys, we're on.'

She decided there was no point in fancy tactics. Actually, no real point in any kind of tactics. Even she found the number of Fallers massing behind the troop carriers intimidating. They kept deliberately igniting the elaborate government buildings on either side of the wide road as they came, firing hundreds of dazzling magnesium incendiary rounds through the prominent windows and ornate doorways. Flames formed a solid wall, pumping out thick black smoke.

After the last of the anxious, noisy refugees scurried through the palace gates, she started walking down the centre of Bryan-Anthony Boulevard. Ry walked on one side of her, Florian on the other. Both of them had unslung their molecular severance cannons, holding them ready.

When the troop carriers reached the junction with Pointas Street, the giant human-Fallers walking alongside the vehicles opened fire with their pump-action bazookas. Cobbles exploded just in front of her, stone fragments erupting into the air. Tramlines were ripped up, blast waves twirling long chunks of steel rail about as if they were nothing more than twigs in a breeze. They slammed down, impaling walls and pavements.

Kysandra's integral force field protected her from the furious chaos. She sent disrupter pulses cleaving into the lead troop carriers. They detonated into fatal shrapnel clouds that shredded the big Fallers. Their fuel tanks blew up, vivid energetic fireballs that engulfed the tall wirthwal trees lining the boulevard.

The second rank of troop carriers crunched over the flaming debris, and kept on coming. Behind them, the huge beast-Fallers started to spread out, disappearing into the alleys between the buildings.

'Crud,' Florian muttered. He dropped to one knee and fired his molecular severance cannon, chopping the hurrying Fallers apart. Very-heavy-calibre projectiles pummelled his force field, knocking him back five metres.

Kysandra chuckled at his outburst of profanities. 'Were you expecting the apocalypse to be easy?' A bazooka round slammed into her force field. It wasn't fully rooted in the ground, allowing the blast to send her staggering backwards. She retaliated with another blast of disrupter pulses.

'No,' Florian replied. 'They're trying to outflank us.'

'Yes. You and Ry will have to take out the big brutes on each side. I'll keep going for the main group.'

'The kids must be under Joey's force field by now,' Ry said. 'All we have to do is sit tight.'

'There are a lot of people in the palace that aren't under the force field, as well as the rest of Varlan's population. Right now, we're what the Fallers are concentrating on. While they're fighting us, they're not killing anyone else.'

'Oh great Giu! Okay.'

*

Paula waited while Demitri enacted the gateway's location inversion, and watched as the circular machine extruded itself out of the wormhole to stand on Trüb's copper and emerald surface.

'What state is it in?' she asked.

'There's a degree of component degradation,' he said, 'but it will do what we need.'

'Okay, let's bring the other floater here.'

Demitri redirected the BC5800d2's terminus coordinates to Ursell and pinged the floater. The response showed them it was drifting eighty kilometres above the surface, being pushed along at twenty-five kilometres an hour by one of the turbulent storms. He manipulated the terminus again, moving it closer and closer to the floater as it twirled about erratically in the conflicting winds.

Once again Paula was impressed by his control. It took less than ten minutes until the terminus had closed within twenty metres of the floater, and they established a link to the duplicate Laura personality in its smartnet. Demitri connected the wormhole to it, and brought it back to Trüb.

The three devices rested close together on the hard purple surface. Demitri stood in front of the BC5800d2 that had come from the palace. Fergus had the newly arrived floater, while Valeri linked to the gateway they'd brought from the *Viscount*.

'Are you ready?' Paula asked the Planter.

'We are.'

Her heartbeat started to increase, which she couldn't entirely blame on teenage hormones. 'Demitri, let's have some power, please.'

Exovision graphics showed her the BC5800d2 opening a terminus a hundred and twenty-eight million kilometres away, just above the star's corona. The terminus at the other end of its wormhole opened fifty million kilometres directly above the star's north pole. Demitri increased the internal length to twenty kilometres, and modified the exotic matter's internal structure to pull power directly from the plasma flow. 'The induction efficiency is poor,' he murmured, 'but we have an unlimited supply of plasma, so it really doesn't matter.'

The terminus above the corona began to move down into the seething ionic storms thrown off by the prominences. Long powerful streamers curved round to streak into the dark throat.

Paula steeled herself, supremely conscious of how close she was standing to the wormhole generator – not that she'd ever know if there was a confinement breach. It would all be over too fast for human nerves to react, even nerves as enriched as hers.

Superhot plasma from the corona began to roar down the wormhole before venting into space like God's own firework rocket. Density, heat, and velocity increased as the terminus penetrated the chromosphere. The power level generated by the induction effect along the wormhole was phenomenal.

Fergus used the floater's wormhole to form a channel between the energy generated by the BC5800d2's wormhole and the connection between Trüb and the barrier generator.

'Is it enough?' Paula asked the Planter.

'Not yet.'

'Down we go, then,' Demitri said evenly.

The BC5800d2's terminus sank deeper into the star's interior; plasma at incredible temperature poured out through the wormhole, its velocity approaching half-lightspeed.

'We are patterning the energy to override the generator's warp effect,' the Planter said.

Paula was sure she somehow picked up a resonance of excitement from the enigmatic alien. She walked over to the arch of outlandish Planter substance that was protruding through the gateway and onto the barrier surface. There was a small gap between it and the edge of the wormhole, revealing the midnight-black crescent of the generator. Close enough to touch, had it not been shielded by the gateway's force field.

'You're going to have to be quick,' Demitri said. 'There are instabilities building in the exotic matter. The wormhole won't hold for long.'

'Applying now,' the Planter said.

Paula held her breath.

Abruptly, the blackness was gone. Paula could see a tangled knot of translucent energy bands, loops kilometres across, gyrating round and through each other as they glowed with the telltale violet of Cherenkov radiation. As she watched, stains of darkness sluiced through them, contaminating the intricate formation deeper and deeper until every band was shading down to obscurity. The negative energy they were composed from dissipated in a last burst of gamma radiation and exotic neutrinos.

The barrier collapsed.

Freed from the harsh pull of its artificial gravity, Valatare's colossal gas envelope exploded both outwards and inwards. Vast surges of cooling hydrocarbon vapour slashed past the floater, which held steady amid the moon-sized hurricanes.

The fake gas giant was now the centre of an expanding cloud-storm that would continue to grow over the weeks until it was thin enough for the solar wind to blow it out across the intergalactic night. Paula watched the start of the process, as the hot lower layers surged into the gulf exposed by the barrier disappearing. Nothing was visible through the ever-shifting ochre haze. Titanic energy swirls tried to equalize, flinging off oceanic-sized lightning discharges.

The Planter withdrew from the wormhole, allowing Paula to stand directly in the centre of the gateway. Her u-shadow transmitted the message she'd composed what seemed an age ago now, sitting in Kysandra's dining room the night she realized what Valatare was.

She waited with growing desperation, seeing only vast swirls of the drab gases rushing past her tiny window. *I am not wrong. It has to be them. It has to be.* Her hands clenched into fists so tight her nails were digging into her palms.

An answering signal came out of the billowing ionized mist. Then shapes began to emerge, serene and massive. Thousands of them.

Paula smiled beatifically at the glorious Raiel warships as they headed towards her.

*

Kysandra watched the Fallers abandon their troop carriers, finally realizing they were easy targets. Several of them were sneaking forwards through the smoke, dodging between trees and statues in the neat gardens that moated the government offices. She used disrupter pulses to take out the corners and core of the People's Transport Ministry. The entire nine-storey building tumbled down in a slow-motion cascade of stone and concrete and tortured girders. The Fallers creeping furtively along its sides ran frantically into the open road. Kysandra tugged her maser rifle off her shoulder as targeting graphics locked on, her secondary routines designating them for the rifle. It saved power; her biononics didn't have unlimited reserves, and there were still over two thousand Fallers closing on the palace.

She started jogging towards the Ministry of Agriculture. Sure enough, Fallers began to follow, which made her grin savagely; it was like a magnet drawing iron filings along. Huge swells of black smoke churned along the length of Bryan-Anthony Boulevard, forming a roiling ceiling above her. A sleet of incendiary bullets slammed into the Ministry of Agriculture. Fires bloomed behind shattered windows.

Kysandra's secondary neural routines brought up light-amplification imagery to compensate for the growing darkness. She ducked round the side of the building, where the smoke wasn't so dense. The light kept dimming.

'Uh, Kysandra, what is that?' Florian asked.

An icy phantom ran slowly along Kysandra's spine. She stopped jogging and looked up.

'Skylords,' Ry said. 'The Skylords have returned.'

'That's not a Skylord,' Kysandra said solemnly.

She remembered the Skylords from her childhood. Exquisitely alien crystalline mountains, shimmering in refracted sunlight, which floated nimbly through the sky as they collected the souls of humans beginning their journey to the welcoming heart of the Void. This dark *thing* descending on Varlan was so much larger – orders of magnitude greater than the city itself. Its umbra had already engulfed the surrounding countryside, pushing the sunlight away to a slender fringe clinging to the horizon. Clouds broke apart on its base, and a fierce wind began to blow across the roof-tops as it displaced a monstrous amount of air.

It was all Kysandra could do to stay standing. The most primitive animal instinct she possessed was shouting at her to bow down, to run, to scream hysterically—

The only thing she could hear now was the crackling of the flames. Even the Fallers had stopped shooting. Like her they were silent and still, staring up blankly at their fate.

*

Paula stood beside Yathal in his command chamber as the *Golak-koth* lowered itself into Bienvenido's atmosphere. The titanic warship moved with a sedate grace, ensuring the air it deposed didn't howl away in wayward hurricanes as it slid down towards Varlan.

'There are many conflicts underway in the city,' the Raiel captain said. 'Which one involves your friends?'

Paula was using the warship's phenomenal sensor suite to observe the city. She had to block most of it; the sheer quantity of information contained within a complete sweep could probably fry a human brain. The warrior Raiel, however, seemed quite capable of total engagement.

She moved her perception focus directly underneath the warship; there was a confrontation on a long road stretching out from the palace. Pinprick graphics bloomed emerald, revealing energy weapon discharges. The answering deluge of more primitive chemical weapons were designated a dull yellow. Her perception spiralled in on Kysandra and Florian and Ry. They'd stopped shooting to gape up in awe. 'That's them,' she said. 'You've shocked everyone into stopping, but we need to end this, now.'

'Of course,' Yathal said. 'The other ships are almost in position.'

Outside of *Golakkoth*'s sensor image, Paula was aware of four other Raiel warships lowering themselves out of the sky above Lamaran. Their T-fields were already reaching out.

She shifted her focus again, zooming into the palace, identifying the overstretched force field covering a courtyard, then diving deeper, her augmented sight flowing through walls, seeing the crypt where the wormhole had spent so many centuries waiting – now home to bodies and the badly wounded. A deep bunker filled with frightened defiant regiment officers organizing Varlan's last stand. Cellars where the big building's ordinary staff cowered, awaiting the apocalypse.

'It's over,' she whispered, surprised how the omnipotent viewpoint made her feel so benign. 'We've got you. You're safe.'

The *Golakkoth*'s sensors classified humans and Fallers, tagging them. Within seconds, she was looking at every sentient entity in Varlan no matter where they were.

'Lift the humans out,' she said.

'The Faller species is undesirable,' Yathal said. 'We removed them from our galaxy. We can do the same here for you.'

Paula cancelled the warship's perception and turned to face the warrior Raiel. It was different again to any she'd encountered in the Commonwealth galaxy, larger and with wings that evolution had long discarded in the Raiel of her time. For a moment that worried her, but Raiel nature was an absolute, of that she was sure. 'I ask you not to. They will be perfectly harmless if we simply leave them behind. This world . . . it is as much a prison for humans as Valatare was for you. There is nothing here for us. We have to leave, now.'

A soft sigh escaped from the Raiel's thick lips. 'Very well, Paula Myo. We acknowledge our debt to you.'

'Thank you.'

*

Kysandra's u-shadow reported a link opening. 'Paula?' she asked in amazement.

'Yes.'

'You did it?' There had been so many years spent holding things together, fighting this wretched eternal rearguard battle, that somewhere along the line she'd stopped thinking it could ever end, that they might actually win. True belief had been extinguished that day Nigel had left her.

Inside she felt a hysterical laugh gestating – nothing could be more real than a multi-billion-tonne alien spacecraft hovering over your head.

'Yes, this is the *Golakkoth*, a Raiel warship.'

'So you were right, then?'

'Yes, I was right.'

'Thank you.'

'It's what I do. It's what I am.'

'Are the Raiel going to destroy the Fallers?'

'No. There's no need. And I did promise the Planters.'

'But . . .'

'Stand by. We're going to teleport you on board. We're going to teleport everyone on board.'

Kysandra's field function scan reported a weird quantum effect establishing itself around her. Then the flaming wreckage of Bryan-Anthony Boulevard vanished.

*

The habitation dome they'd been assigned on the *Golakkoth* was apparently small by Raiel standards – barely eight kilometres across. Its buildings were cubes and cylinders and hemispheres with narrow paths between, illuminated by coloured strips set into the translucent surface. Walking along the gloomy alley, Florian could have sworn part of the darkness around him came from fog that lingered between the high blank walls, except when he waved his hand at the grey wisps they were never there.

His u-shadow guided him round a few more turns and a doorway opened at the base of a cylinder. Bright white light shone out. The doorway put him in mind of a bussalore hole gnawed into a skirting board.

Three days ago, the inside of the cylinder had been a gloomy grotto with walls that seemed to flow as if they had a sheet of water constantly running down them. A typical Raiel dwelling, Paula told him. Now it was very different. Walls and floors had rearranged themselves – not just their layout, but texture, too. The cylinder's interior had grown itself into something that resembled a plush human hotel, except it had no windows. Which was why Florian spent as much time as possible standing beside the bottom of the crystal dome, staring at the wonders unfolding outside. The entire Raiel armada was orbiting Ursell, unleashing energies he didn't understand to dismantle the benighted planet and use the debris to build five awesome new structures. DF spheres, Paula called them.

He went up the curving marble stairs to the first floor, where the big lounge had been established. Paula was already sitting at the head of the table, with Yathal standing beside her. Florian had been on board the *Golakkoth* for three days now, and he still felt intimidated by the Raiel. Yathal was as big as a seibear, but that was the only valid comparison to any creature Florian knew. All the crew were warrior Raiel, Paula explained. Presumably that was why Yathal appeared to have a hide made of obsidian armour with inbuilt twinkling jewels. The Raiel's various tentacles were woven with black threads, and the folds of loose flesh around the back of his head had been groomed out to form a mane of white fans.

Oddest of all were the leathery wings folded along his flanks that seemed far too small to allow him to actually fly.

The one time Florian gathered up enough courage to ask the *Golakkoth*'s captain about them, Yathal told him they were vestigial, and the Raiel only kept them for tradition and decoration.

Kysandra was sitting beside Paula. She acknowledged Florian with a sly smile and a wink. When he sat beside her, he felt her hand close on his thigh, squeezing playfully. He blushed – as he supposed he always would when she was with him. Since they'd been teleported on board the *Golakkoth*, they'd spent half their time in bed together, both of them devoted to recreating the happy few days they'd enjoyed after she'd rescued him from Opole. He knew it wouldn't last, that the voyage home was just another interlude before his life truly began, but that didn't bother him any more. The Commonwealth was in his future now. A dream made real.

There weren't many others at the table: Ry, of course, and Demitri and Corilla. He'd been somewhat disconcerted by Paula's insistence that Stonal and Captain Chaing be included in their small council, but she wanted alternative viewpoints. 'For a fair representation,' she claimed. Prime Minister Terese was also given a chair, though she'd said very little in their meetings. Florian thought she was still in a state of shock. He could relate to that; the decisions this small council had been making were momentous. That didn't seem to perturb Paula. He was finally starting to realize why Nigel had chosen her to carry his plan forward if he failed.

'If we're all ready,' Paula said.

Roxwolf materialized at the opposite end of the table. The mutant-Faller glanced round, keeping his face expressionless. Florian noticed a lot of his fur was rising, so maybe he wasn't quite so unnerved as his posture was trying to promote. 'Is this my trial?' he asked.

'Not at all,' Paula said. 'We acknowledge you were genuine in your attempts to side with humans, despite your earlier activities. We will honour that arrangement. However, there is a slight problem.'

'Of course there is,' Roxwolf grunted.

'We exterminated your kind,' Yathal said.

'You did what?'

'Long ago, before this fleet was ever built, the Raiel determined your species was too aggressive. You conquered all the worlds you encountered whose civilizations were not technologically advanced enough to stop you, destroying all the biological life you found without mercy. So we stopped you the only possible way.'

Roxwolf nodded slowly. 'But those of us captured by the Void survived your massacre.'

'Yes.'

'And now we're all that's left?'

'Yes.'

'So you're going to finish the job?'

'No,' Paula told him. 'I gave my word to the Planters that this situation would be resolved with minimal violence.'

'And in turn we acknowledge our debt to Paula,' Yathal said.

'The Vatni are coming with us,' Paula said, 'as are the Macule Units with their precious gene banks. They are already in stasis along with Bienvenido's population. The Raiel are using Ursell's mass to construct colossal wormhole generators. Even so, the voyage home will take several years.'

'We will not permit your species to accompany us,' Yathal said. 'We will not turn you loose on our galaxy again.'

'So Bienvenido is yours,' Paula said. 'It's far enough away to prevent you from ever posing a threat to us again.'

Roxwolf peeled his lips back. 'I can't live on Bienvenido.'

'I know,' Paula said. 'So you have a decision to make.'

'What decision?'

'We can repair the distortion that afflicts you,' Yathal said. 'We can make you whole again, and return you to Bienvenido. Your kind will never know who you were.'

'Or,' Paula said, 'we can download your memories into secure storage. Then when we're back in the Commonwealth, you will be given a human body, or you may transfer directly into ANA. The choice is yours.'

Roxwolf held up his arms, looking from one to the other, from fur to skin. 'I am both and yet neither. I know too much, and I am curious; that alone condemns me to my kind, no matter how pure my physical body. Above all, I want to live without fear and without limits. That's all I've ever wanted. So . . . I choose human.' He grinned his fearsome grin. 'Until something better comes along.'

BOOK EIGHT

Commonwealth

This was the bit Joey Stein welcomed, yet dreaded. The fact he could think at all was welcome. It meant he was alive – which in itself was rather surprising, given his last memories of the crypt under the palace: way too much pain and blood and that psycho PSR officer. Although now he considered his last moments, they were mixed in with another set of memories, of operating within the lifeboat package smartnet and throwing a force field over the rose courtyard so that children and parents alike could cower together. Then the sky had darkened as the gargantuan Raiel warship had arrived above Varlan.

His eyes snapped open and he sat up. That was what he was dreading – the abysmally thin force-grown clone body provided by the re-life clinic. Pain and depression for months, attended by well-meaning self-righteous therapists. Too weak to resist their patronizing ministrations.

Except there was no pain, nor even stiffness. He didn't feel hungry or weary. When he brought his hand up in front of his face it seemed perfectly normal, the hand his twenty-year-old self had possessed oh-so long ago. Before the colony starship flight to another galaxy, when he was so tired of the jaded lives lived by Commonwealth citizens. Before Shuttle Fourteen's science mission into the Forest, when his body was suffering from a glitched tank-yank procedure. Before being caught by Faller-Rojas and forced into contact with the egg, the terror of slowly being eggsumed.

Before his uncharacteristically noble suicide to save Laura. Before Nigel's intervention. Before being downloaded into the lifeboat package's smartnet. Before two hundred and fifty years stuck to a sodding Tree . . .

Joey blinked and looked down at his new body that lay naked under a sheet on a bed. He tugged the sheet aside and saw he wasn't some spindly bag of bones covered in tight skin that was all protruding veins. This body belonged to a fit, healthy adolescent, ready to conquer the universe.

Cool! Re-life clones have really come on while I was away.

Now he was awake and thinking, his u-shadow brought up a host of initialization icons into his exovision.

I'm back in the Commonwealth. Fuck me, we actually made it!

He chuckled. The clinic room was pleasant enough for an institution, all pearl-white plyplastic walls occluding the medical systems. A wide window looking out over a leafy suburb with a broad lake in the distance, triangular sails of big yachts sailing around. Mountains cluttering the far horizon. Another bed next to his, with a bemused youth looking at him.

'Bollocks,' a startled Joey blurted, and tugged the sheet back. 'Who are you?'

'Is that any way to greet your fellow jailbird?' Roxwolf asked.

*

Earth's T-sphere deposited Paula in front of the neoclassical Capitole de Toulouse at the centre of the city. With a quarter of an hour to go until dawn, the splendid building was illuminated by strategic floodlights, which imbued the region's famous pink bricks with a warm glow. The vast Place du Capitole where she'd materialized was deserted apart from a formation of bots slowly clearing the night's snowfall from the ancient stone slabs.

Chaing stood beside her, his body rocking back and forth from the impact of the teleport. 'That's impressive,' he said, staring at the Capitole. 'A bit like the Captain's Palace.'

'Really?'

'Not as big.' Chaing turned a complete circle. 'Where is everyone?'

'Earth has a very small population these days,' she told him. 'It was already heavily weighted to the old and wealthy back when ANA was built. Not decadent, just . . . staid. Younger people were leaving for the newer worlds, so the ones who stayed got older and more conservative. Then they started downloading themselves into ANA. So the physical population declined further. It's holding steady at about sixty million these days.' She waved her hand round the centre of the city. 'ANA preserves our cultural heritage; the buildings mostly have stabilizer fields, and armies of ANAdroids perform caretaker maintenance on the infrastructure.'

'ANAdroids? You mean like Demitri?'

She gave him a small smile. 'Not quite.'

A compact ellipsoid-shaped regrav capsule slipped down out of the grey sky, its chrome-yellow fuselage reflecting the city buildings in weird contortions. A doorway opened in its midsection.

'Come on,' Paula said.

There were only two seats in the cabin. She settled in one and waited for Chaing to sit beside her before ordering her u-shadow to turn the fuselage to full transparency. He gripped the seat as they rose up, and headed towards the north-east.

'So these houses, they're all empty?' he asked in faint bemusement as they passed over the rooftops.

'Lucky for you and your people,' she said. 'I remember after the Starflyer War, when we had to build entire cities on the new planets to house the population of the Lost23 worlds. It effectively bankrupted the Commonwealth for a decade. And that was very basic housing. You've got some of the greatest houses on Earth to choose from.'

'I'm not ungrateful,' he assured her. 'I just don't believe anyone wants me as a neighbour.'

'You'd be surprised,' she told him as they passed the city boundary. The landscape below them was dark, revealing little. Not that there was much to reveal, she acknowledged. Earth's rural areas had been encouraged to revert to their naturalistic pre-farming state. Towns and villages decayed and fell to the encroaching vegetation, with only 'historically significant' structures and a scattering of private homes remaining. With woodlands finally reclaiming their original vast domains, wildlife also prospered; even previously extinct species had been re-introduced thanks to modern retro-DNA sequencing. Effectively, Earth became a park planet, with all the ecological damage that centuries of rampant industrialization and agriculture had wrought slowly healing.

'This person we're visiting,' Chaing said. 'Did you tell him everything about me?'

'Yes.'

'And he still agreed to help?'

'You're not quite as unique as you think, captain.'

'Don't call me that. The PSR doesn't exist any more.'

'As you wish.'

'What kind of person is he?'

'Someone who had it a lot rougher adapting to the Commonwealth than you. He'll tell you all about it, I'm sure.'

'That's part of my problem. So many of your citizens have volunteered to counsel us. Millions, almost one for each of us, and from every Commonwealth world. That level of kindness is . . . I'm not used to it.'

'I know. Culture shock can be overwhelming. Just trust me, and meet him.'

'Of course. But . . . I am curious why we don't just teleport to this place. I thought you could teleport anywhere on Earth.'

'Almost anywhere. People are entitled to seclusion if they want it. There are many reasons: political, personal. ANA doesn't discriminate, but it does enable.'

Five minutes later, the regrav capsule was approaching a modest valley, barely a couple of kilometres wide, and meandering to the west with a small river churning away along the centre. Thick forests coated the slopes, the denuded deciduous trees and pines glinting pale gold as the rising sun caught the ice and snow clinging to their branches. Several ancient houses were dispersed between the trees and the water, their frost coating making them difficult to distinguish as dawn light seeped across the land. It was the long trails of woodsmoke rising from their chimneys which gave them away.

Paula brought the capsule down in a broad clearing, whose tall trees isolated it from the houses. She quickly buttoned up her fur-lined winter coat as she stepped out onto the thick grass. Her breath was white in the still air; it was several degrees colder here than it had been in Toulouse. A narrow path led from the clearing, down the slope to the homes.

'This way,' she told Chaing, and set off. After a moment, he followed.

An old *moulin* stood on a small rise beside the river. Its thick stone walls didn't need any stabilizer field to maintain them, though they'd clearly been renovated at some time in the last century.

Paula walked up to the big wooden door and knocked loudly. It took a while – there was plenty of noise from inside: voices, clattering kitchenware – then the iron latch was lifted and the door opened.

Edeard stood on the worn step, wearing a burgundy-coloured dressing gown, framed by a wan yellow light. He grinned in welcome. 'Investigator Myo, it's been a while.'

'It has. How are you doing?'

'Pretty good, actually. And you must be Chaing?'

'Yes. Thank you for agreeing to see me.'

'No problem. Come in. We're about to have breakfast.'

Downstairs was mainly one large room, furnished with old-fashioned chairs and settees and tables and chests. There was no plyplastic or malmetal anywhere, although she did see a holo-graphic projector on top of a dresser; it took a moment to recognize, it was such an old system. A galley kitchen at the far end boasted a big old iron range cooker, with coal glowing pleas-antly behind its grill door. The smell of fresh-baked bread filled the whole place.

Paula breathed in deeply. It was a smell that took her all the way back to her own childhood, when her mother had prepared most of the food by hand.

Salrana was standing behind the kitchen counter, filling a copper kettle with water at the white porcelain sink. She gave Paula a quick smile. 'Investigator. Tea or coffee?'

'Tea, please. Milk, no sugar.'

'Chaing?'

'Uh, the same, thanks.'

Salrana put the kettle down on the range's hotplate.

'How's Burlal?' Paula asked as she, Chaing, and Edeard sat at the long table in the middle of the room.

'Practising,' Edeard said with a martyred tone, and pointed his finger at the ceiling.

'Practising?'

'He'll be a teenager in eight months. He's asleep.'

'Ah, right. Well, it is only just dawn.'

'Everyone in the community gets up at dawn, especially in winter time,' Salrana said. 'We make the most of the daylight.'

'Of course. And how's Inigo?'

'He and Corrie-Lyn are fine,' Edeard said. 'They live next door if you want me to get them.'

'Maybe next time.'

The kettle started to whistle. Salrana took it off the hotplate and poured the boiling water into a teapot. Then she came round the counter.

Paula raised an eyebrow. 'Congratulations.'

'Thank you,' Salrana said, putting a hand on her bump. 'Only two and a half months to go now. She'll be a spring baby.'

'That's lovely.'

'This is a sweet place for children to grow up,' Salrana said firmly. 'When they're older they can make their choice about which culture they want to be a part of. Until then they have peace and a gentle community to nurture them. Those are the best values a person can start their life with.'

'Like Ashwell?' Paula enquired.

'Yes,' Salrana agreed. 'Just like Ashwell. Or as close as we can get in the Commonwealth. Plus, nobody bothers us here. I'm not having our children grow up as freaks for the benefit of the unisphere and gaiafield. Nobody is going to dream their life.'

'That's over,' Edeard said. 'Especially now.' He gave Chaing a long look. 'There are a couple of disused cottages further down the river; a bit dilapidated but . . . You can stay with us until we make one ready. Projects like that always fire people up around here. It shouldn't take too long.'

'The wonders of Commonwealth technology,' Chaing said sarcastically. 'Makes it all worthwhile.'

'One step at a time,' Edeard said. 'You can run away into the Commonwealth if you like. It's easy enough to alter your features. Nobody would ever know who you are. Except yourself, of course. And that's the problem, isn't it?'

'Is that what you're offering, to help me forget?'

'No. That's another Commonwealth perk. Any memory can be ripped out. But I don't think that's what you need.'

Chaing shrugged. 'I don't know what I need. I used to be certain about everything. The Second Great Transition took that away. I look around at where we are, and I don't see how I can fit in. I'm wrong for the Commonwealth.'

'I know a bit about having people judging you for the things you had to do.'

'Do you?' Chaing asked sceptically.

'Oh, yes. I did things that were necessary at the time – terrible things – and nobody ever forgets. I believe this little valley might be able to help you come to terms with your past. We live a life without the complications of the Commonwealth mainstream here. Time and understanding are our healers. One day even I might be able to consider leaving.'

'I killed someone,' Chaing said bluntly. 'Someone I knew, someone I . . . liked. She was very similar to me – just opposite. She's what I see when I look into a mirror. There might have been another way, but I just couldn't let her win. Bienvenido would have Fallen if she had. So I did what I had to. It's not what I am. And that sets me apart from everyone.'

Edeard smiled in sympathy. 'I learned a long time ago that

755

sometimes, to do what's right, you have to do what's wrong. Perhaps I can teach you that.'

*

Ry and Anala had to take a commercial starship to Orakum; the External world was a long way outside the network of wormholes which linked the Inner worlds of the Intersolar Commonwealth. It took three hours to fly the forty-six lightyears from Balandan, the closest planet with a wormhole. Three hours in a small cubicle together, with no viewport. However, the gravity was variable, from one point seven Earth standard (the heaviest H-congruous world ever settled) to zero. They set it to zero.

A regrav capsule took them from the starport out across the continent that was still mostly pristine hills and plains, devoid of human settlements. Finally, it dived down through the spindly clouds. The house was easy to see – a plain white circle with glass edges, standing on a central pillar that was also glass-walled. The gardens extended around it for acres in every direction, looking strangely unkempt and boasting several small stone ruins. They landed in the shade of some giant rancata trees, whose reddish-brown leaves cast a gentle dapple.

'Do you think they'll take us?' Anala said nervously, as they emerged from the capsule, holding hands tightly.

'Sure they will,' Ry said, with a lot more confidence than he felt. 'We're exactly what they want.' He had to put sunglasses on, the light was so bright.

She puffed her cheeks out and exhaled. 'Okay.'

A couple came out of the house to greet them – a beautiful young woman with the most carefree smile Ry had ever seen, accompanying a huge rotund man whose scowl was a classic counterpoint. He was wearing a shabby old toga suit, while she had a gauzy white cotton summer dress that seemed to glow in the intense blue-white sunlight.

'Hi,' she said, her smile growing even wider. 'I'm Catriona. We've been expecting you. Come on in.'

The lounge on the house's lower level was lined with a rich

honey-brown wood, giving the impression it was a cavern carved out of some mighty trunk. Windows overlooked the lakes at the far end of the garden, where a small waterfall ran down the stony ridge between them.

Ry was intrigued by the man waiting for them by the balcony door. Unusually for the Commonwealth, whose every citizen seemed obsessed with maintaining a physiological age of about twenty-five, he had allowed signs of ageing to contaminate his body, with wrinkles on his face, and receding hair just starting to frost above his sideburns.

'Oscar Monroe?' a nervous Ry asked.

'Yes.' He shook hands and waved them onto a long settee. 'I have to tell you, this is a bit unorthodox, even for us.'

'I know,' Ry said. 'But thank you for agreeing to see us. We'd love you to consider us for your company.'

Oscar smiled softly. 'Well, you do both have a very unusual résumé. You flew into space on a chemical rocket? Seriously?'

'Yes.'

'That must have been pretty . . . intense.'

'It was glorious,' Anala told him. She and Ry pressed together a little tighter.

'We're astronauts,' Ry explained. 'That's all we've been and all we want to be. To get out there and explore the other side of the sky.'

'My company doesn't do a lot of outright pioneering; we tend to do follow-up science missions for the Navy Exploration Division.' Oscar mock-grimaced. 'Plus a few off-the-file excursions.'

'Sounds fabulous,' Ry said.

'Yes, well. Your technical knowledge and skillset are a little behind what we need. If we do take you on, you'll have a headache for a year with the amount of information we'll have to cram in to bring you up to Commonwealth standard. That's not a metaphor; it will hurt.'

'If it means we fly actual starships at the end, it'll be worth it.'

'Great Ozzie,' Oscar muttered, blinking in surprise. 'And you got married yesterday? Shouldn't you be on honeymoon?'

'This is our honeymoon,' Ry explained earnestly. 'What could be greater than an interview for this kind of job?'

'Wow. Okay; ordinarily I'd hold off a decision for a while, but you have Paula as your sponsor, so I guess: welcome aboard.'

Ry and Anala whooped and hugged exuberantly.

'Do you know Paula, then?' Ry asked.

'Our paths have crossed.'

'Thank you so much for this,' Anala said. 'We won't let you down.'

Oscar grinned wryly and sat back. 'I know. Hell, you flew a genuine rocketship to fight enemy aliens attacking your planet. I don't know anyone else with so much Right Stuff.'

*

Only a few years ago, Florian would have been utterly terrified of the grand Welcome Ceremony thrown by the president of the Commonwealth in his official residence – a mansion that could've given the Captain's Palace in Varlan a run for its money when it came to scale and opulence. There were four hundred planetary Senators in the ballroom, along with representatives from every major Dynasty and Grand Family, with the Brandts taking centre stage. Plus alien ambassadors, from the downright scary-looking to the bizarre. Then there'd been a swarm of media representatives, celebrities who'd managed to snag an invitation, officials, friends of friends . . .

President Timothy Baker had made a long speech about how the human race was now a complete family once more. Prime Minister Terese had made a bland response about the wonders of the Commonwealth. A bit rich, Florian had thought, coming from a politician who had spent her life suppressing anyone on Bienvenido who even mentioned trying to find the Commonwealth.

But her title was honorary only now, and in a couple of weeks no one would remember her. The *Golakkoth* had delivered Bienvenido's citizens to Earth, where there were so many empty homes waiting for them. Apparently there were only about sixty million people living on Earth these days. *Only sixty million!* Those were the kind of concepts Florian was struggling with even though it had been years since the space machine had given him the Commonwealth files. Their epic flight back to the galaxy had given him time to prepare himself. For the rest of Bienvenido, snatched to salvation without warning only to materialize in the New York reception centre with a mere second of personal time-lapse, it was a shocking revelation. Everybody, Eliter or not, was struggling to adapt to the Second Great Transition.

Consequently, many Commonwealth citizens had generously volunteered to move back to Earth temporarily to help counsel the refugees as they acclimatized to their new circumstances. Florian had been deeply touched. More than anything, that proved the Commonwealth was a society where he truly belonged.

ANA and the counsellors were helping to reunite families and friends. They were also diplomatically separating Eliters from former PSR officers, as well as keeping an eye on known criminals. Once things began to calm down, people had to make a lot of decisions. Commonwealth medical treatments could rejuvenate them, their Advancer gene sequences could be repaired and upgraded; biononics was a strong option. Education packages and training were available (probably a necessity if you wanted to live in a modern technological society). Then, of course, they had to face their final decision: where to live.

At the Welcome Ceremony, the Commonwealth had formally offered the refugees their own planet, so they could live among people they knew and preserve what remained of their culture. Florian still grinned at the idea of that – *Here, have an entire planet; we've got more than we need.* After all, the Raiel had already found an ocean planet for the Vatni; and the Macule Units had been delivered to a fresh world, where their gene banks could re-establish their entire biosphere. A New Bienvenido was tempting to many, although every existing Commonwealth world had extended an open invitation to the newcomers.

For himself, he hadn't quite decided what to do and where to go. He'd spent the last couple of months in London, occupying a grand apartment in Kensington overlooking Hyde Park, sharing its luxurious rooms with his mother, Lurji and his wife Naniana, and his complete handful of a niece Zoanne. It was a blissful and addictive happy family life he'd never known before, with Aunt Terannia and Matthieu in the apartment underneath. Commonwealth medical technology had swiftly repaired Matthieu's hands, and he was playing the guitar again. They'd all been avoiding thinking about the opportunities that now lay open to them, content with a quiet life.

However, the Welcome Ceremony had made him realize it wasn't a decision he could put off for much longer. There had been a moment where Timothy Baker had called Florian up onto the stage to shake his hand and present him to the assembled dignitaries. Apparently Baker was one of the oldest humans alive – a fact never more obvious than when you met him in the flesh. It had only been a brief handshake, a few private words, when the president had asked what he was going to do now. Florian had mumbled he wasn't sure, and just knew he was being *judged* for saying that. 'The Commonwealth can give you a good life,' Baker had told him. 'It's up to you, of course, but take my advice: don't waste it.' And for an instant, the ancient man had looked terribly sad before smiling and greeting the next guest.

Florian had managed to duck out of the official reception after an hour or so. Laura Brandt had pleaded, teased, and coaxed him along to a nightclub in Paris – only three trans-stellar wormhole stations and a quick teleport away. Who knew that Mother Laura was actually quite fun, and sassy, and friendly, and a good dancer? So here he was in some kind of medieval cathedral, sitting in a big curving settee that seemed to vibrate like a purring cat, with music that was far too loud and weird, semisolid lightblobs that oscillated their way through the air like angry sparrows.

The sticky mauve cocktails with bubbling vapour that Laura ordered helped damp down the initial discomfort. By the third, he was quite chilled. It helped that Corilla had joined them on the settee. If anyone had learned how to embrace Commonwealth society, it was Corilla. She was busy telling them how she'd started her quantum physics degree at Oxford University when he caught sight of a tall blonde on the other side of the dance floor, wearing a very small black dress. She kept looking at him when the gyrating bodies parted. He was awarded a sultry smile.

'Justine Burnelli,' Corilla said with breathless excitement in his ear. 'She helped get rid of the Void. She's even more famous than we are.'

'Really?' News that the Void had transcended had always seemed slightly unreal to Florian – just another aspect of living in the Commonwealth with ten impossible things happening every day.

'Very rich, too,' Corilla said in a slightly slurred voice. 'You should go over and say hi.'

'Don't,' Laura said. 'She's like a thousand years old. I remember her from before we left the Commonwealth. Looks like a seraph, but she's a real hardass. Her whole family is hardwired that way.'

'Thanks for letting me know,' Florian said – and now he, too, seemed to be slurring somehow. He'd almost said: thanks, Mother. But he'd made that mistake with Laura once already today at the Welcome Ceremony, and it wasn't something you repeated. Besides, he couldn't quite see her in the wholesome matronly terms history lessons at school portrayed; in her new re-life body, Mother Laura looked absolutely stunning, especially in a clingy scarlet dress with so many interesting splits. Shame she didn't seem to like Corilla much. For some reason they were acting like rivals.

'So do you know where you're going yet?' she asked.

He shrugged. 'No idea. Still catching up with my brother. We hadn't seen each other for years, you know. I like family life.'

'Awww.' Corilla smiled at him, her hand squeezing his leg in a sisterly fashion.

He smiled back as she wobbled in and out of focus. A bot held up another silver tray of the mauve cocktails for them.

'Cheers!'

The three of them chinked their glasses and drank. Corilla downed hers in one. Laura took a long sip, giving Florian an intimidatingly level stare over the bubbling vapour. He found it impossible to look away, unless it was at one of those splits in her dress. Which he began to realize were very exciting in a bad, bad way. *With Mother Laura?* He was abruptly sober. And her smile widened in recognition.

'There's no need to rush a decision,' she said. 'You should take a while, look round to see what the Commonwealth can offer you. Maybe find someone who could show you.'

'That'd be a blast,' Corilla said merrily. 'Hey, we could scope it out together. What do you say, Florian? I've only been to nine planets since we got here.'

'Nine?' he asked slightly enviously, which judging by Laura's expression was the wrong way of saying it.

'Oh, wow, is that her?' Corilla demanded, gazing at something over his shoulder. 'For real?'

Florian turned to see Paula leading a teenage girl over to them. Except it wasn't quite Paula as he remembered. She seemed to have aged ten years.

He stood up and peered forwards as Paula pushed through a scarlet and emerald lightblob. 'Paula?' There was a lot of quizzing in his tone.

She produced a wry smile. 'Yes, Florian. I'm the original. Pleased to meet you, finally.'

'Uh, right. Likewise.' Florian knew he was blushing; his cheeks were terribly hot when she gave him a very Parisian kiss on both of them.

'And this,' Paula said in a slightly pained voice, 'is Mellanie. We go back together all the way to the Starflyer War – though it seems longer sometimes. Okay, you've been introduced; favour repaid. I'm out of here.'

'Er, hello,' Florian said automatically to the teenager with long golden hair. Paula was turning to leave. 'Wait,' he blurted. 'What's going to happen?'

'Happen?'

'Well, there's two of you. I know that's a huge no.'

She grinned knowingly, and it was reassuringly familiar, even though she wasn't *his* Paula. 'Trust me, Florian, there's only one Paula Myo. And that's me.'

'But—'

'I've assimilated my Bienvenido memories. My spare body will be put in storage.'

'*Will* be?'

'Ah, you are quite sharp, aren't you? I remember.'

He shrugged, for what could you actually say to that?

'She has one last thing to do,' Paula said. 'Which is fair enough; I always finish my cases.' She chuckled. 'And as you looked after me so well . . . if Mellanie asks you to go for a walk with her, think very carefully before agreeing.'

'Okay. Thank you.'

He turned round to face Mellanie, and decided she was probably the sexiest girl he'd ever seen. He had no idea how she did that; her nose was long and her chin too prominent to be classically beautiful, but the way she carried herself, the wayward self-confidence, impish smile . . . There was something primal about her, as if she'd just walked out of a Pliocene forest. *Okay, strange first impression.* And for some reason Laura and Corilla were spiking her with disapproving looks.

'So?' Mellanie said with a husky purr. 'The Hero of Bryan-Anthony Boulevard himself. Did you really stand between a horde of alien cannibals and a crowd of helpless children?'

'Oh. Well. You know.'

'I don't.' Her finger tapped playfully at the base of his throat. 'But I'd love to hear all about it.'

*

Nigel walked along the Martinique loop for most of the afternoon. It was a tropical environment, five thousand kilometres wide, with a twenty-seven-thousand-kilometre circumference, revolving slowly to produce a point-eight-five gravity effect on its inner surface. Three other loops were interlocked with it, in turn knitted with more loops. The inside of the Dyson shell contained thousands of them, all rotating at varying speeds in the most fantastically complex piece of clockwork humans had ever created. The underside of the loops contained terminus strips, wormhole-linked to coronal flowers in close orbit above the A7 star, scalloped rings of exotic matter absorbing the searing light to shine it across the shell's interior.

Looking up, he could see the full multitude of loops in their awesome three-dimensional lattice-chain, stretching away into a distance that gave a far greater impression of infinity than naked space ever did. Some sections were in darkness as the terminus strips fluctuated their emissions, creating night-times for the loops.

It was a sight that still mesmerized him, despite watching it grow and develop – the first nest of a true post-scarcity society, where accomplishments were driven by culture and artistic whimsy rather than economics. A home that encouraged self-development and experimentation. Biononic transforms were already laying claim to the air between the loops, humans bodyshifting to giant avians that soared amid the churning thermals. Oceanic loops were alive with the first colonies of aquarian bodyshifters. While outside the shell, rock-like transforms clung barnacle-fashion to the surface. Already they were trialling integral solar sails. By the time the next generation of Dyson shells were complete, they'd be able to surf the ion gales between them.

So many possibilities awaited. But for now he was content to keep his human identity.

'You are so rooted in the past,' Ozzie had taunted on one of his increasingly rare visitations.

'You have to know where you've come from to see where you're going,' Nigel had replied.

'But, dude, you've stopped going anywhere.'

And onwards he walked. Across tropic loops, and sub-tropics, arctic wastes to windswept moors, and more exotic environments garnered from the records of the Commonwealth Navy's exploration division and reproduced with interesting twists, content simply to examine the newness and diversity first hand. An old factory boss performing an everlasting quality-control check.

Late afternoon, local loop time, he emerged from a line of royal palms that were only just taller than him and onto a long sloping beach. Small waves lapped against the fine silver-white sand. Kilometres out to sea, coral isles jutted enticingly up out of the clear water. He took his boots and socks off, and walked along the shoreline.

After a while he sat down and watched the astonishing array of fish venturing into the shallows. When he tipped his head back, he could follow the Martinique loop's turquoise and green cartography curving above him. It was two thirds sea, with lush emerald vegetation spreading across the small continents and various archipelagos. Its only fault was how small the palms and ferns were, but then it had only been commissioned seven years ago.

They'd learned a lot from terraforming Zoreia. Thousands of asteroid-sized biovat stations formed a bracelet swarm around the Dyson shell, growing the necessary bacteria to bring the loop soils to life. Equally vast clone houses grew the seeds.

Such quantities meant they didn't have to wait decades for the biota to establish itself. What had taken years on Zoreia was complete in weeks here. Already photosynthetic vegetation was established on seventy per cent of the loops – though, of course, trees still had to grow. Fast-grow versions had been rejected. The humans of the Dyson shell wanted a genuine feel to their environment. Nigel still laughed at the irony of that.

In a couple of hundred years, the jungles and landscapes would have a decent primordial feel to them. He watched clouds streaming over the edge of the loop, floundering in wispy curlicues as they lost the integrity provided by the artificial gravity. Intra-loop weather currents was still a huge challenge for the shell climatology engineers. They were having to intervene more than any simulation modelling suggested.

Nigel rather liked that. *We haven't perfected everything yet.*

'Can you bump these waves up?' he asked Central. Induced gravity pulses could simulate the more basic effect of moons, given the loops didn't have any. *Now there's a thought for a shell.*

'What sort of size are you looking for?' Central asked.

'I just thought I might go surfing. Give me some decent ocean rollers, maybe? That way I can rip down tubes like they did off Hawaii back in the day.' His neural augmentation rose to run routines calculating the kind of gravity field orientation and power necessary to create the required effect.

'When have you ever done that?' Central queried.

'First time for everything.'

'Ozzie was right. You are regressing while everyone else is moving off into the new.'

'Yes, Mother.'

'Would you like me to select a surfboard based on your size and ability?'

'My size?' He looked down his chest, which was rather well muscled these days. Muscles he'd earned by all his exercise, not bought with bionomic manipulation. He grinned at the foolish vanity. *Maybe Ozzie is right, I am sliding back into the primitive. But that's allowed. The loops can embrace any foible.*

'Nigel, I am detecting a quantum field displacement point coming towards us.'

'A what?'

'A node similar to myself. This one is travelling FTL.'

'You mean we're being visited by another post-physical?'

'It doesn't have the same field depth as myself, but it is decelerating from nine hundred lightyears an hour.'

Nigel sat up fast. 'Holy shit!'

'The trajectory indicates it could have come from the Commonwealth galaxy.'

'Ah! The infamous deterrent fleet?'

'A strong possibility, yes.'

Nigel's primary routine meshed with Central, allowing him to observe the twist in reality hurtling towards them. It reached the star system's outer comet belt and dropped to ordinary hyperdrive speeds before approaching the Dyson shell. A signal was transmitted.

'This is Paula Myo. I'd like to visit Nigel Sheldon, please. And I am bringing a guest.'

Nigel laughed. 'Who else? Give her my coordinates.'

The quantum fluctuation changed, a swirl of energy rising up out of the field interstice and phase shifting into two physical structures. They teleported into the Martinique loop beach.

He raised his arm in a cheery greeting as Paula materialized five metres in front of him. Paula, younger than the last time he'd seen her, which was unusual. 'Twice in fifteen years. I'm flattered.'

'Hello, Nigel.' She stood aside, and Nigel saw who it was standing behind her.

Over a thousand years of experience in controlling his emotions, neural augmentation running routines to objectify any situation, meant nothing now. For it was *her* standing there, wearing her familiar brown suede skirt and white blouse, the wide-brimmed hat he'd bought her perched at a spry angle on her lush red hair.

'No,' he moaned incredulously. 'You're dead. I saw Uracus kill Bienvenido.'

'It didn't kill us,' Kysandra said. 'The Void expelled us.'

'What? Where?'

'Intergalactic space. *Deep* intergalactic space, actually. It's taken a while to get back; we had a few problems there. Nothing I couldn't handle.' There were tears brimming in her eyes, as if she was scared of something.

Nigel put his trembling arms around her. 'I'm sorry. I'm so sorry. If only I'd known, I would never have stopped looking. I would have found you, no matter what.'

'Well, now I've found you. And you're the real you, this time.'

His grip tightened. 'Yes, you have. And I'm not going to let you go again. Not ever.'

'You have no idea how much I wanted to hear that!'

'Oh, I do. Because that's what I've felt every day since I lost you.' He kissed her.

Kysandra smiled through her tears as she stroked his face. 'You know what? That was almost worth waiting two and a half centuries for.'